Praise for *The Sagas of Icelanders*

"What better way to begin a new century than with a generous collection—the first such in English—of some of the greatest stories ever told . . . Irresistible tales that are, as surely as the masterpieces of Homer and Cervantes, the forerunners of the modern European novel." —*Kirkus Reviews*

"The Sagas are the literature not only of the island where they were written, but of the whole Western world of their day—undoubtedly one of the greatest contributions made by Nordic culture to world literature. Even today, they provide the modern reader with fascinating insights; they are stories which reveal an immense variety of human conduct and condition."
—Jostein Gaarder

"Wonderful . . . this splendid edition will inaugurate the discovery of these great works by adventuresome readers of English for years to come." —*The San Diego Tribune*

"Excellent . . . It would be hard to imagine a finer introduction to this extraordinary body of work . . . the best thing is the selection itself, which reflects the great variety of saga narrative, from complex family chronicles to brief, witty tales. We are taken from the male-dominated world of feuding and killing to the remarkable depiction of powerful, clever women in *The Saga of the People of Laxardal*; from the farmsteads in Iceland to the North America of the Vinland sagas . . . full of vivid and haunting scenes."
—*The Sunday Daily Telegraph* (London)

"The English is wonderfully accessible to this modern reader. Only now can I fully appreciate my own deep debt as a storyteller to Icelandic writers of long ago." —Kurt Vonnegut, Jr.

WORLD OF THE SAGAS

THE SAGAS OF
ICELANDERS

A Selection

Preface by JANE SMILEY
Introduction by ROBERT KELLOGG

PENGUIN BOOKS

PENGUIN BOOKS
Published by the Penguin Group
Penguin Group (USA) Inc., 375 Hudson Street, New York, New York 10014, U.S.A.
Penguin Group (Canada), 90 Eglinton Avenue East, Suite 700, Toronto,
Ontario, Canada M4P 2Y3 (a division of Pearson Penguin Canada Inc.)
Penguin Books Ltd, 80 Strand, London WC2R 0RL, England
Penguin Ireland, 25 St Stephen's Green, Dublin 2, Ireland (a division of Penguin Books Ltd)
Penguin Group (Australia), 250 Camberwell Road, Camberwell, Victoria 3124, Australia
(a division of Pearson Australia Group Pty Ltd)
Penguin Books India Pvt Ltd, 11 Community Centre, Panchsheel Park,
New Delhi – 110 017, India
Penguin Group (NZ), 67 Apollo Drive, Rosedale, North Shore 0632, New Zealand
(a division of Pearson New Zealand Ltd)
Penguin Books (South Africa) (Pty) Ltd, 24 Sturdee Avenue, Rosebank,
Johannesburg 2196, South Africa

Penguin Books Ltd, Registered Offices: 80 Strand, London WC2R 0RL, England

First: published in the United States of America by Viking Penguin,
a division of Penguin Putnam Inc. 2000
Published in Penguin Books 2001

35 36 37 38 39 40

Copyright © Leifur Eiríksson Publishing Ltd, 1997
Preface copyright © Jane Smiley, 2000
All rights reserved

Translations first published in *The Complete Sagas of Icelanders* Volume I-V
(forty-nine tales), Leifur Eiríksson Publishing Ltd, Iceland 1997
Leifur Eiríksson Publishing Ltd gratefully acknowledges the support of the Nordic
Cultural Fund, Ariane Programme of the European Union, UNESCO, and others.

THE LIBRARY OF CONGRESS HAS CATALOGED THE HARDCOVER EDITION AS FOLLOWS:
The sagas of Icelanders: a selection / preface by Jane Smiley;
introduction by Robert Kellogg.
p.   cm.—(World of the sagas)
"The sagas and tales in this book are reprinted from the Complete sagas
of Icelanders I-V, published 1997 by Leifur Eiríksson Publishing, Iceland,
with minor alterations"—P.[viii].
Includes bibliographical references (p.   ).
ISBN 0-670-88990-3 (hc.)
ISBN 978-0-14-100003-9 (pbk.)
1. Sagas—Translations into English.   2. Old Norse Literature—
Translations into English.   I. Series
PT7262.E5 S34 2000
839'.63008—dc21   99-044111

Printed in the United States of America
Set in Monotype Janson

Table of Contents

TALES

REFERENCE SECTION

Illustrations and Tables

MAPS

Preface

JANE SMILEY

The prose literature of medieval Iceland is a great world treasure – elaborate, various, strange, profound, and as eternally current as any of the other great literary treasures – the Homeric epics, Dante's *Divine Comedy*, the works of William Shakespeare or of any modern writer you could name. Mysteries surround these stories – how were they composed and by whom? what were the motives of the authors? why were they written in prose when the currency of medieval literature was poetry? how did their contemporaries understand them – did they even read them, or did they hear them read aloud? But the questions fall away as we read the sagas and tales themselves. They are written with such immediacy and forthrightness and they concern such basic human dilemmas that for the most part they are readily accessible and seductive. Reading one creates the appetite for another and another. In the present volume, Penguin has drawn upon the newly translated and edited *Complete Sagas of Icelanders* to offer the English-speaking reader a rich selection of Icelandic prose. Long and short, complex and simple, fantastic and realistic – there is a taste of everything here, an abundant introduction to a world a thousand years separated from ours, both intensely familiar and intensely strange.

The Icelandic sagas, in form and apparent purpose, were anomalous for their time, the thirteenth, fourteenth and fifteenth centuries, that is, the time of Chaucer, the *Romance of the Rose* and Dante. If English, French and Italian readers had had access to them in their own day, they might have found them stranger than we do. We have been trained by the form of the novel, which arose in England in the eighteenth century, to accept the significance of a prose narrative that concerns itself with the doings and opinions and fates of what we would call ordinary citizens, that is, men and women who live in communities of people who are more or less their equals, whose personal qualities determine the outcome of their intentions and whose stories constitute models of social and psychological behaviour. Much of the medieval literature we know of had an aristocratic, leisured audience. Icelanders wrote for each other, that is, a relatively small population of related and isolated (in the world-geographical sense) families who were all aware of who their ancestors were and how their ancestors had settled and developed the world that saga writers and readers lived in. Medieval Iceland shared with the modern world a considerable degree of social mobility and a considerable ambiguousness about how men (and women) of exceptional qualities (strength, talent, beauty, passion) could be fitted into the fabric of society. Such concerns arose in mainland Europe in times of social and economic disruption, for example during the Black Death, but less so than they did at times of social and economic stability; they were at the very heart of how Icelandic society created itself and sustained itself. Just as the settlement of Iceland in the ninth century prefigured the westward expansion of Europe into America five and six centuries later, the literature of Iceland written in the high Middle Ages prefigured the literature of the modern world.

And yet, these stories are so clearly medieval.

And yet, they are not.

This is their fascinating paradox.

A powerful man, Hrafnkel, makes an unbreakable vow that his horse is dedicated to his favourite god, and that he will kill anyone who rides the horse without his permission. He announces this vow to every one of his workers. One day some sheep are lost, and, of course, the only horse who will allow itself to be caught is the forbidden animal. When the man who attempts to ride the horse in secret finally dismounts, the horse gallops straight to his master and presents himself, dirty and done-in. Hrafnkel fulfils his vow, then attempts to soften the blow by offering to take care of the victim's family, but they are so incensed by his attitude that they turn down his offer.

Another powerful man, Thorstein, has a dream that his daughter will be so beautiful as to cause the death of two men. He attempts to evade this fate by having the child exposed, just as Laertes attempted to evade his death at the hands of Oedipus by having Oedipus exposed. Thorstein is as unsuccessful in his evasion as Laertes is.

A beautiful and well-meaning woman, Gudrun, falls in love with a suitor she cannot have. Her frustration leads her into other, unsuitable marriages.

Several couples live together in close quarters. Jealousies and tempers flare, and two men are killed. Conflicting loyalties and readiness for revenge interfere with the early resolution of the argument, and a man, Gisli, who might otherwise have lived a peaceful and prosperous farming life with his well-loved wife, is forced to live by his wits in exile and outlawry.

These stories are familiar – not because we have read them before (though in some cases we have), but because they sound just like things that happen all the time. People are always making rash commitments and foolish choices, speaking unwisely, taking stubborn positions, ignoring the wise counsel of others, hoping to get something more on a gamble than what they are already assured of, refusing to submit or lose face. Like Hrafnkel's horse, animals often seem to act with perverse intelligence. In some quarters of the world and in some periods these mistakes lead to unhappiness. In other quarters and other periods they lead to death and social devastation. These Icelandic stories are unique because their understanding of the consequences of foolishness and folly, especially in its relationship to character, is uniquely plain, unvarnished and direct.

Typical saga style bespeaks an agricultural world where leisure was at a premium. The sagas and tales are full of work. The action takes place in a context of sheep-herding, horse-breeding, weaving, cooking, washing, building, clearing land and expanding holdings, trading by ship with mainland Europe and the British Isles. Disputes often begin humbly – in *The Saga of Ref the Sly*, for example, a man kills his neighbour's shepherd so that his sheep can have access to his neighbour's grazing. His motives go without analysis – greed needs no analysis. What is interesting to both writer and audience is what happens next and what the other characters say about it. Likewise, that a man like Egil Skallagrimsson should be a great poet as well as hot-headed, stiff-necked and dangerous also needs no analysis. Much more is to be learned from what happens to Egil than from investigation of the whys and wherefores of his character. Thus Icelandic sagas and tales seem far removed from modern literary subjectivity, and yet, the gossip and the comments of other characters supply a practical and readily understandable psychological context. Characters speak up. They say what they want and what their intentions are. Other characters disagree with them and judge them. The saga writer sometimes remarks upon public opinion concerning these events. The result is that the sagas are psychologically complex and yet economical in their analysis. Nothing like the courtly manners of the rest of Europe gets in the way of plain-speaking, and we seem to be hearing the true words of true everyday people.

This, of course, is an illusion, especially in the context of the translation from Icelandic to English. The plainness of saga style is also highly ritualized. Similar incidents occur in similar ways throughout the body of the literature. The entire body of sagas and tales is a country unto itself, and no less idiosyncratic than any other literary country – it is only that the country has different expectations and customs, and they go in a different direction from that of other medieval literatures.

There is no single saga that stands with other single works as an unalloyed example of greatness and universality, like *The Divine Comedy, King Lear* or the Homeric epics. A saga not included in this volume, *Njal's Saga,* and two sagas included here, *The Saga of the People of Laxardal* and *Egil's Saga,* make the strongest claims for greatness, but one of the unique characteristics of saga literature is its cohesiveness as a group of stories in which, although they are by different authors, their similarities are greater and more obvious than their differences. They are like an extended family of individuals who all look rather alike and all share basic values. Our enjoyment of Shakespeare's or Dickens's or Mozart's works is not significantly enhanced by reading or understanding the works of their contemporaries – the context is interesting but not essential to the average reader or listener. The reader of *Njal's Saga,* though, can hardly understand or appreciate this great work out of the context of the other sagas. They surround it the way a landscape of fields surrounds the best, most fertile one – they are an essential part of its eco-system, its plant pattern, its water pattern, its weather pattern. Its goodness is set off by their differing characteristics of sandiness, steepness, weediness. Medieval Icelandic literature is different from almost every other world literature – it is a literature in which individual authors seem to disappear, while the voice of an entire way of life seems to speak distinctly. In that sense, this anthology is a single work, a map of a world whose inhabitants knew it well and were quite self-conscious – Iceland was Iceland before France was France or England was England or Italy was Italy. In Iceland, everyone was employed in more or less the same enterprise. In Iceland, people customarily travelled about the countryside and were familiar with each other's homes and regions. It is thus a literature of unity rather than diversity, where the inability of an individual to fit in is noticed, remarked upon, analysed and perhaps admired, but always dealt with in the end.

*

I came to Icelandic literature from Old English, and read it along with Old and Middle English works like *Beowulf* and *Sir Gawain and the Green Knight* and *The Canterbury Tales*, as well as certain Old Irish works, like the exploits of Cuchulain. While I was interested enough in the other medieval works to read and study them, nothing drew me in like the Icelandic sagas. Their simultaneous strangeness and familiarity was a potent and never-ending source of pleasure to me, and further, it was clear that the saga writers knew perfectly well how to tell a good story, and that their techniques for setting the scene, describing character, following out a conflict and finding meaning in apparently meaningless action were highly sophisticated. There was, in fact, plenty for an aspiring novelist to learn from the saga writers. However scholars answer the questions of who they are and what they meant, a novelist can recognize a fellow artist at once, and in fact, the stripped-down narrative style and the focus on the individual and social consequences of conflict is a good beginner's manual in techniques of plotting and characterization. In Icelandic sagas, characters have looks and habits. They also act and speak, sometimes about themselves, and others speak about them. In the end, that's all you need to distinguish one character from another, even when all the names look and sound alike.

The incidents that propel the action and reveal character are often mundane, but always quite specific. In *The Saga of Hrafnkel Frey's Godi*, for example, Hrafnkel is lying in bed one morning after he has lost his original farm and established a new one, and one of his servant-women sees the brother of his old antagonist pass by with some other men. She rushes into the house and berates Hrafnkel for being a coward and a fool, and goads him into seeking revenge. Although he speaks little, his humiliation and anger are readily understandable, because her words are clear and relentless, and show him that he is held in contempt by at least some portion of his associates. In *Gisli Sursson's Saga*, men set up a horse-fight, which leads to angry words and blows. In every saga, the fates of men turn on small moments and misjudgements, very distinctly rendered. That is a lesson for every novelist.

Some sagas gain cohesion from being about one man, like Grettir the Strong or Gisli. A natural interest collects around the exceptional qualities of that man. Grettir, for example, twice swims a fjord in the winter that is so cold that he comes out covered with ice. These sagas have the coherence of biography, but give up social context. Other sagas, like *The Saga of the People of Laxardal*, attempt to follow out the consequences of rashness and folly as they extrapolate through a whole region. In these, a certain amount of dramatic force is dissipated as characters come and go. A novelist of any era finds that such choices are always with him or her – the temptation to take the simple route falsifies experience in one way, the temptation to take the complex route falsifies experience in another way. Prose narrative is prose narrative is prose narrative. Stripped of the most obvious idiosyncrasies of the authors' individualities, Icelandic prose narrative takes on a kind of paradigmatic quality.

That the Icelandic saga writers were using prose narrative to consider their history and their present situation also seemed obvious, and uncannily modern, to me. The saga writers lived in an unsettled age. One of the few known authors, Snorri Sturluson, possibly himself the author of *Egil's Saga*, was assassinated. This, too, seemed instructive. The apparently disinterested contemplation of historical events could and would shed light upon contemporary events – whole conflicts, from beginning to end, were examined. Human nature was revealed. A fault in the political structure (the lack of an executive arm of government) was diagnosed. The effects of spiritual and religious commitment were set into a context of unbridled violence and social turbulence. In 1262, the Icelanders came up with an answer – they placed themselves under the Norwegian king. To me as a citizen and a novelist, the worth of serious art as a form of social discourse seems evident in the enterprise of Icelandic prose literature.

When I was studying Icelandic literature, translations were piecemeal and highly variable. Some were published in mass editions, others in expensive university press editions. There was no co-ordination, and so some translations were very literal and almost clotted, while others were so loose and fluent as to be easy to read but suspect. These problems have been solved by the editors of *The Complete Sagas of Icelanders*, from which this selection was taken. These translations are uniformly accurate and readable. More importantly, they are gathered together in one informative volume. The reader may enter the literary world of medieval Iceland with ease and pleasure, and the literary works of the nameless saga writers may take their rightful place beside those of Homer, Shakespeare, Socrates, and those few others who live at the very heart of human literary endeavour.

Introduction

ROBERT KELLOGG

I. THE AGE OF THE VIKINGS

The later Middle Ages in Europe were a time of striking innovation in literature. In the second half of the twelfth century, the French poet Chrétien de Troyes gave a rich and permanent poetic shape to the old Celtic narratives of King Arthur and his court. With Dante's *Commedia* and Chaucer's *Canterbury Tales* in the thirteenth and fourteenth centuries, the national literatures of Europe began to declare their independence of medieval Latin. The local dialects of central France, of Florence and of London established themselves as the rivals of the languages of antiquity. Similar movements occurred in the other countries of Europe, especially in Germany with the brilliant poetic narratives of Wolfram, Hartmann and Gottfried. Nowhere, however, was this literary activity more remarkable or in certain paradoxical respects more ahead of its time than in medieval Iceland, where nearly all the books that have survived in the language of the 'Norsemen' were written.

The mention of medieval Norsemen summons images of pagan Vikings, in beautiful, far-sailing ships, who for two hundred years terrified the peaceful coasts of France and the British Isles. As far as it goes, this is an appropriate association. The Norsemen were not merely Viking marauders, however. A people of great organizational genius and maritime skill, they were traders, explorers, settlers, landowners and, on an increasingly large scale, able political leaders. The settlement of Iceland, which began about 870, was part of a larger movement of Norse expansion. While most of the first settlers came to Iceland from the west coast of Norway, a significant number came from Norse communities in Ireland and Great Britain, bringing people of Celtic origin with them. The city of Dublin had been founded and governed by Norsemen. York in England was a centre of Norse power. In France, King Charles III was forced to turn over the territory since known as

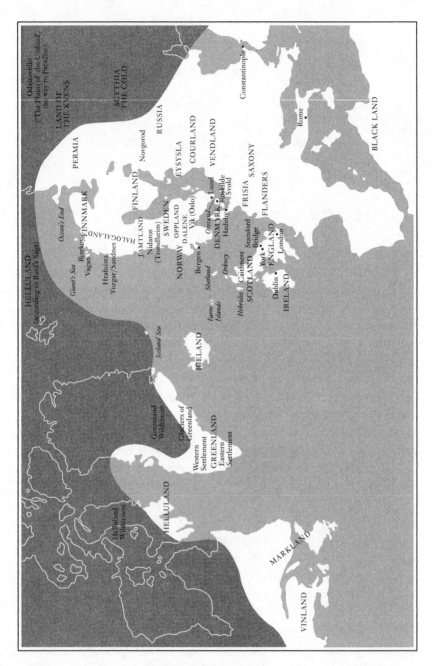

The World of the Sagas

Normandy to a Norwegian Viking named Hrolf (also called Rolf and Rollo), the great-great-great-grandfather of William the Conqueror. The Icelanders in their turn began settling in Greenland in the tenth century, and from there they went on to explore the coast of North America.

The restless and expansive age of the Vikings lasted for about two hundred years. Their first notable attack on England came, according to the *Anglo-Saxon Chronicle*, in 793, when the church on the island of Lindisfarne was plundered and some people were slain. But by 1000 a new cultural phase was under way, with the conversion of many Norsemen to Christianity, which made their raids on churches and centres of learning more difficult to justify. The introduction of ecclesiastical institutions into Norse culture – monasticism, literacy and the internationalist perspective of the church hierarchy – laid the foundation for a post-Viking educational system that was based on the reading of books.

The growth of centralized religion and education was accompanied by the growth of larger, more centralized governments. The small regional kingships of early Viking society were being replaced in the eleventh century by powerful national monarchies, whose interests were not served by freebooting Viking raiders. Literacy made possible the conversion of rich ancient Viking oral traditions of myth and legend into written literature, as was also happening in Celtic Britain. It provided the means for recording recent events in the history of Scandinavia, especially the deeds of Norway's charismatic king and saint, Olaf Haraldsson (reigned 1014–30), and his Viking Christian precursor, King Olaf Tryggvason (995–1000).* By the beginning of the twelfth century, writing in Iceland and elsewhere in Scandinavia was being extended from Latin to the vernacular language. And the circumstances were right for the production of a large, varied and innovative body of literature.

---

* The names of these two kings illustrate the common practice in medieval Scandinavia of naming people. Family names did not exist (as in general they still do not in modern Iceland). Both men and women were called by their given names (e.g. Olaf, as here), to which was added their father's name (e.g. Harald or Tryggvi) or in some cases their mother's (e.g. the sons of Hildirid in *Egil's Saga*). Two of Iceland's most important writers were Ari, the son of Thorgil (i.e. Ari Thorgilsson) and Snorri, the son of Sturla (Snorri Sturluson). The central character of *Eirik the Red's Saga* is a woman, Gudrid, the daughter of Thorbjorn (Gudrid Thorbjarnardottir). In some cases Icelanders had titles and epithets attached to their names, such as Ari Thorgilsson the Learned or Leif Eiriksson the Lucky.

II. FORMS OF ICELANDIC NARRATIVE

In Iceland, the age of the Vikings is also called the Saga Age. About forty interesting and original works of medieval Icelandic literature are fictionalized accounts of events that took place in Iceland during the time of the Vikings: from shortly before the settlement of Iceland about 870 to somewhat after the conversion to Christianity in the year 1000. They were written mainly in the thirteenth and fourteenth centuries, but they concern characters and events in Iceland, and to some extent the larger Norse world, from three hundred years earlier. All of the sagas in this collection are historical fictions of this type, a form known in Icelandic as *Íslendinga sögur* (sagas of Icelanders) and often in English as 'family sagas'. These works are the crowning achievement of medieval narrative art in Scandinavia, and when people speak of 'the Icelandic sagas' they usually mean the *Íslendinga sögur*.

In spirit the *Íslendinga sögur* are much like epics. While women are more prominent and interesting characters in the sagas than in Homeric epic or *Beowulf* or the *Song of Roland*, the world of the sagas is still a man's world. Such heroic virtues as honour, fortitude and manly courage count for a great deal, and the definition of heroes in a variety of situations is one of the main points. The sagas differ from epics in two important ways: formally, by being in straightforward, clear prose rather than verse, and culturally, by not being about kings and princes and semi-divine heroes but about wealthy and powerful farmers.

Saga heroes occupy a social space on the edges of society. The heroes of three of the sagas, *The Saga of Grettir the Strong*, *Gisli Sursson's Saga* and *The Saga of Hord and the People of Holm*, are in fact outlaws. Gunnar Hamundarson of Hlidarendi in *Njal's Saga* is also technically a criminal when he is killed. Most of the saga heroes are just barely on one side or the other of the law, but it also seems to be true that the law itself is being tested along with the finest men. Epic and saga are enough alike to make a comparison interesting and instructive, especially in the degree to which both genres synthesize history, myth, ethical values and descriptions of actual life. Sagas differ from romance, the other great medieval narrative mode, by focusing attention on actual social types of people in a historically and geographically precise context, with little apparent interest in fantasy and the spiritual and psychological experience of what is sometimes called 'courtly love'. There are

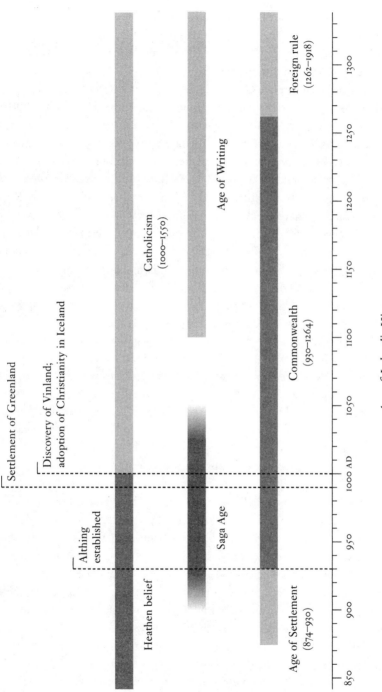

Ages of Icelandic History

lovers in the sagas, but far less frequently do they end happily ever after than do their counterparts in romance. Generically, the sagas stand not so much between epic and romance as between epic and that other great European narrative form, the novel.

The word *saga* is related to the English word *say*. Its various meanings in Icelandic can be roughly understood as denoting something said, a narrative in prose. English has no precise equivalent, so *saga* often appears in the titles of Icelandic books untranslated, although 'story', 'tale' or 'history' would come close, with some combination of the three even closer. Literary scholars now distinguish several kinds of sagas, depending on subject matter or historical setting. In addition to the *Íslendinga sögur*, with which we are concerned here, there are chivalric romances (*riddarasögur*); legendary sagas of pre-Icelandic Germanic heroes (*fornaldarsögur*); lives of the kings of Norway (in the great collection called *Heimskringla* and other individual *konungasögur*); saints' lives (*heilagra manna sögur*); and histories of 'contemporary' events (*samtíðarsögur*) that took place in Iceland after the Saga Age, many of which are preserved in the huge collection known as *Sturlunga saga* and others in the lives of Icelandic bishops (*biskupasögur*).

Closely related to the *Íslendinga sögur* is a genre of short tales called *Íslendinga þættir* (tales of Icelanders), six of which have been selected for inclusion in this collection. *Þáttur* (plural *þættir*) means, among other things, 'part' or 'chapter', and the *Íslendinga þættir* do, whether they occur separately or as part of a larger work, give the appearance of being anecdotes that can perform a variety of functions within a larger work, such as illustrating a king's character or providing an authenticating historical or learned detail. They occur mostly in large manuscript collections of kings' sagas and often concern some kind of comic encounter between a humble Icelander and a king of Norway, frequently Harald Sigurdarson the Stern, in which an initial conflict is resolved.

The characters in many of the *þættir* are familiar to us from the roles they play in the sagas, and take on a special interest for this reason, as though they exist in a network of story that is larger than that encompassed by any single text or group of texts. The texts we have are, from this perspective, but a selection from the events of this larger saga world, in which ultimately every *Íslendinga saga* is connected to all the others.

Whether a short narrative is titled a 'saga' or a 'tale' sometimes seems quite arbitrary, and while the categories of saga narrative are useful and the various kinds of sagas can be distinguished fairly easily, they do overlap.

Individual works have their own character and are often somewhat 'mixed' in style. An example of a short and entertaining saga with many of the features of a 'tale' is *The Saga of Ref the Sly*. The hero's name, Ref, means 'fox' in Icelandic, and he can be thought of as 'the sly fox', which King Harald the Stern had in mind when he gave him 'the sly' as a nickname. Like many of the tales of Icelanders, *The Saga of Ref the Sly* does not involve trolls or berserks or the supernatural for its entertainment, but Ref's extraordinary skill and ingenuity in highly naturalistic settings in Iceland, Greenland, Norway and Denmark. *Ref the Sly* is unique among all the sagas in allowing itself the anachronism of a reference to writing (Ch. 6). Ref is asked by his uncle as he is leaving Iceland to have his adventures written down in case he does not come back. The rationalism and ingenuity of the story, the identification of the hero as a fox and the reference to writing as a way of preserving the hero's exploits, all point towards the likelihood that the widespread literary tradition of *Reynard the Fox* is here given Icelandic attire.

The *Íslendinga sögur* are, however, in some cases quite hospitable to elements found abundantly in the legendary *fornaldarsögur*, such as trolls, ghosts, berserks and magical enchantments. On the other hand, the seriousness of their intellectual purpose gives the *Íslendinga sögur* much in common with the sagas of contemporary Icelanders and the kings' sagas. The freshest approaches to saga narrative in Icelandic scholarship today concern the fringes and overlappings of saga genres. The sagas are being seen as stylistically more self-conscious than we have realized, raising new questions of controlled parodies, in which stylistic effects may have been designed to produce humour and subtle, at times touching or nostalgic, reminders of a time and a sensibility from which the reader is for better or for worse now cut off.

Prose as good as that which evolved into the classic saga style was rare in medieval European literature. It tended to appear later, in the sixteenth and seventeenth centuries. Exceptions do exist, such as the *Decameron* of Boccaccio and (much closer in spirit to the sagas) the French Vulgate cycle of Arthurian romances. Still, the development of a prose fiction in medieval Iceland that was fluent, nuanced and seriously occupied with the legal, moral and political life of a whole society of ordinary people was an achievement unparalleled elsewhere in Europe.

The most famous manuscript to survive in Iceland from the Middle Ages is not a saga. It is a collection of poems about Odin and the other gods and about the major characters in the heroic story of the Volsungs. Like several other old Icelandic books, the physical object is named *Codex Regius* (The King's Book). The manuscript itself was written about 1270, but is based on somewhat older written texts. The anthology of poems it contains has traditionally been known in English as the *Poetic Edda*. We do not know who compiled the *Codex Regius* of the *Poetic Edda* nor very much about the history of the texts that it contains. The poems are arranged according to a plan and interjected prose passages provide narrative contexts for many of them. The metre and diction of these poems link them to a much earlier Germanic poetics, as illustrated in Anglo-Saxon, Old Saxon and Old High German poetry. Despite the antiquity of its roots everything points to the compilation of *Codex Regius* as being, like many of the sagas, an achievement of the thirteenth century.

Another thirteenth-century work, as precious as the *Poetic Edda*, also concerns myth and poetry. It is believed to have been written by Snorri Sturluson (1179–1241) and is called *Snorra-Edda* in Icelandic. In English it is usually known as the *Prose Edda*. Intended no doubt as a kind of textbook, it begins with a retelling of the myths and legends found in the *Poetic Edda*, often amplifying and clarifying them. But then it develops in the second section, called *The Poetics* (*Skáldskaparmál*), into a truly remarkable treatise on poetry, with examples of complex poetic metaphors that were based on the myths, as well as examples of poetic forms. Nothing like *Snorra-Edda* exists anywhere else in medieval European literature. These two separate works, one entitled *Edda* by its author, the other acquiring the name in modern times by association with Snorri's book, illustrate the extent to which Icelanders of the thirteenth century felt an impulse to collect and preserve what they could of the culture of pagan antiquity. As were the *Íslendinga sögur*, the two books called *Edda* were antiquarian efforts to preserve a distant past through the perspective of a liberal and inquisitive impulse in thirteenth-century Christian scholarship. They illustrate likewise the balanced attention that was directed by thirteenth-century literary culture to prose and poetry. It was a golden age, in which many kinds of stories and literary forms were familiar to readers of the *Íslendinga sögur*.

The genres of thirteenth-century Icelandic literature were not restricted to the sagas and eddas. The kinds of knowledge that formed the basis for a conventional medieval education in religion and the liberal arts were also set down in books. *The Icelandic Homily Book* (composed around 1200) mentions a number of learned medieval authors from whom ideas have been received:

Pope Gregory the Great, St Augustine, the Venerable Bede, Alcuin, Fulgentius. There were Icelandic translations of *Elucidarius* by Honorius Augustodunensis and a *Physiologus*, as well as the works of other important authors. These translations appear in various collections, such as the fourteenth-century *Hauksbók*. In addition to these more commonplace elements of medieval intellectual life, some particularly Icelandic matters, close in spirit to the sagas, were also written early, and the Icelandic laws were among the first, in the early twelfth century. Since the adoption of a national constitution in 930, the laws of the Icelandic Commonwealth (*þjóðveldi*) had been recited by the Lawspeaker (*lögsögumaður*), one-third each year for three years, at the national assembly, the Althing (*Alþingi*), which met on the plains of the Althing, Thingvellir, every June. The circumstances of their writing are described in a small book called *Íslendingabók* (The Book of Icelanders), written about 1130 by the priest Ari Thorgilsson (1068–1148), known as 'the Learned': in 1117 the innovation was decided upon at the Althing of having sections of the law written in a book during the following winter. Accordingly, at the home of Haflidi Masson, the laws were dictated by the Lawspeaker, Bergthor Hrafnsson, and written down under his supervision and that of other wise men. They were read the following summer to the unanimous approval of the Althing.

Ari Thorgilsson was born shortly after the Saga Age and was therefore separated by only two or three generations from some of its most famous people. His great-grandmother was Gudrun Osvifsdottir, the heroine of *The Saga of the People of Laxardal*. His book is a concise history of Iceland from its settlement in the late ninth century (*c.* 870) to 1118, and it contains the main features of Iceland's foundation story and subsequent history as it is told in a large number of the *Íslendinga sögur*. Ari, unlike their anonymous narrators, is very much an author in the modern sense. He cites in detail the oral sources of the information that he has written down, including such remarkable things as a list of the names and periods of tenure of the Lawspeakers, from Hrafn Haengsson in 930 to Bergthor Hrafnsson.

As the founder of Icelandic historical writing, Ari was cited as an authority by other writers who in all likelihood derived little from him directly, aside possibly from his account of the conversion of Iceland to Christianity. One manuscript of *The Saga of Gunnlaug Serpent-tongue*, for example, is bold enough to advertise itself as 'the saga of Hrafn and of Gunnlaug Serpent-tongue, as told by the priest Ari Thorgilsson the Learned, who was the most knowledgeable of stories of the settlement and other ancient lore of anyone who has lived in Iceland'. Some version of this saga of the poet Gunnlaug probably did exist in oral tradition in Ari's time and he might well have told it. But there is no possibility that the version as we now have it was told by him in a text composed at least a hundred years after his death. As a rhetorical device, however, the citation of Ari adds to its interest and authority.

After Ari's *Íslendingabók*, a second important work of historical scholarship is the vast undertaking called *Landnámabók* (The Book of Settlements) which describes the settlement of Iceland and the establishment of the original families, region by region around the country. It mentions about 3,500 people by name (more than 430 of whom were original settlers) and the names of 1,500 farms. *Landnámabók* has existed in a number of versions, some of which are now lost. Some of its stories and the genealogies of Icelanders that are traced back to Norwegian royalty suggest the folk imagination at work. An early version of *Landnámabók* may have been begun at about the same time as *Íslendingabók*, in the twelfth century, but the earliest version still extant is credited to Sturla Thordarson (1214–84), the nephew of Snorri Sturluson, 150 years later. It reflects in both form and substance the influence of the *Íslendinga sögur*, with which it is contemporary, and draws on the same combination of oral and written materials.

None of the *Íslendinga sögur* can be attributed to an author. Even when a thirteenth-century writer such as Snorri Sturluson or Sturla Thordarson is associated with a particular text, he largely functions as a collector or reteller rather than as an inventor of the story. In fact, there is no medieval source naming Snorri Sturluson as the author of *Heimskringla*, the great collection of kings' sagas, although modern scholars follow the convention of attributing it to him. Even when we think we know an author's name, his writing persona is that of the historian, who works in a style that is essentially indistinguishable from the anonymous norm. He derives his authorial authority not from the originality of his style or story but from his fidelity to the events, or to others' accounts of them and their judgements on those who were involved – in other words, to what has been *said*. The sense of authorship, in so far as it exists in Icelandic prose, is far different from that of the great medieval poets. The works of Chrétien, Dante and Chaucer were new and exciting partly because of the way the poets inserted some version of themselves into the telling of their stories. This never happens in Icelandic narrative, which remains focused on the autonomous world of its people, ideas and events and not at all on the particular personality through which these have been shaped for presentation to the reader. Therefore a large field of potential irony is not there to be exploited in the sagas. Without a named and identified narrator, as in many novels and other narrative forms, there is no actual or potential gap in knowledge or sympathy between the narrator and the implied author, as for example between the pilgrim Chaucer and the author of *The Canterbury Tales*. The sagas, especially the *Íslendinga sögur*, leave us with the impression that the source of their art is a tradition that stretches back for generations. The anonymity of their authors has become a feature of their style.

III. THE RHETORIC OF HISTORY

There is rarely a disjunction in the art of the *Íslendinga sögur* between our sense of the events they describe and the method of their telling, as if their language were a clear window on to the world of the saga. Sagas never follow the example of Homer by opening 'in the middle of things'. They attempt, as much as possible, to tell events in the normal chronological order of their occurrence. Occasionally a flashback will be necessary if the plot has divided into separate strands and two or more groups of characters need to be imagined acting simultaneously. This produces an inconspicuous narrative intrusion such as 'Now we will go back to where the story was left earlier when . . .' An exception to prove the rule is *The Saga of the People of Ljosavatn*, (not in this collection). Its structure is more experimental than most. In addition to incorporating three closely related *þættir*, without fitting them precisely into the chronology of the narrative, it also uses a subtly managed short flashback to describe an episode in the childhood of the two brothers, Gudmund the Powerful and Einar from Thvera:

It is told of the brothers that when they were young, Gudmund had a bald foster-father whom he loved greatly. One day when he was sleeping outside in the sun, mosquitoes kept settling on his bald spot. Gudmund drove them away with his hand, thinking that his foster-father would be bitten.

'Use your axe on his bald spot, brother,' Einar said.

He did so, aiming the axe so that it nicked the bald spot and made it bleed, but the mosquito flew off.

The old man woke up and said, 'It's a hard thing when you take weapons to me, Gudmund.'

'Now I realize for the first time that Einar's advice to me isn't well intended,' he replied, 'and this probably won't be the last time.'

This incident kindled a long-standing resentment between the brothers. (Ch. 16)

Like the English word *story*, *saga* can refer either to a literary text or to the events themselves that are recounted in it. We can say that a story 'takes place' at a certain time and in a certain place, in which case we are referring to the events, whether actual or imagined. Or we can say that a story moves us or holds us in suspense, in which case we are referring to the way it is told, that is to a literary text. This ambiguity is something we live with quite comfortably, resolving it almost unconsciously according to context. The *Íslendinga sögur*, however, blur this distinction between saga as event and saga as story more readily than most other forms of narrative do. It often happens, for example, that a character is said to be 'out of the saga', meaning both that he has no further relationship with the events being reported and that he will therefore not be mentioned again.

The rhetoric of the *Íslendinga sögur* is designed to give the impression that they relate events exactly as they happened, or at least as people have said they happened. Contributing to this effect is the minimal sense of a narrative voice that is in any way distinct from the anonymous author's. Neither the existence of a reader nor the presence of an analysable meaning beneath the surface of the story is acknowledged by the saga author. All is made to appear unified in the perfect fit of language, event and meaning. The saga authors were adept at creating humour, wit and subtle ironies in their characters and situations. None was more accomplished in this than the author of *Njal's Saga*, the great masterpiece of saga art. A somewhat macabre sarcasm is one of his favourite rhetorical devices, and Skarphedin is a master of the form. He observes, after a series of household killings which had been carried out by the servants of his mother and Gunnar's wife Hallgerd, that 'Slaves are a lot more active than they used to be' (Ch. 37), and that 'Hallgerd does not let our servants die of old age' (Ch. 38). But his irony can also assume a gentler, more tragic tone when he says of Njal, as he composes himself to die in the burning of his house, 'Our father has gone to bed early, which is to be expected – he's an old man' (Ch. 129). The ironic double vision, which in the novel is located in the disjunction between narrative voice and author (and hence between narrator and reader) – producing richly moving and comic effects but nevertheless weakening our allegiance to the truth and stated values of the story – in the sagas infuses instead the language and actions of the characters.

Saga composers were aware, however, that the events they narrated happened long ago; by drawing attention to this they did open a space between themselves and their story, explicitly acknowledging the temporal distance between the 'then' of the story and the 'now' of its telling. The motivation for doing so was sometimes to authenticate a story by pointing to the continued existence of some physical object mentioned. This device is used in *The Saga of the People of Eyri*, to add plausibility to one of the few references in the sagas to human sacrifice in Iceland: 'It is still possible to see the judgement circle in which men were sentenced to be sacrificed. Within the ring stands Thor's stone, across which men's backs were broken when they were sacrificed and the stain of blood can still be seen on the stone' (Ch. 10). Such a device can also enhance the apparent antiquarian precision of the saga by indicating that customs and cultures have changed between then and now. To explain how an Icelander in London could understand what Englishmen were saying, *The Saga of Gunnlaug Serpent-tongue* informs us: 'In those days, the language in England was the same as that spoken in Norway and Denmark, but there was a change of language when William the Bastard conquered England. Since William was of French descent, the French language was used in England from then on' (Ch. 7). The remarkable thing about this bit of authenticating detail is not so much the idea that Englishmen stopped speaking English after the Norman Conquest, but that the topic should have occurred to the composer in the first place. While the manuscript's attribution of the saga to Ari Thorgilsson is far-fetched, the saga composer here and elsewhere in the work shows an ability to sketch a believable historical context.

A charming and surprising feature of saga style that probably began as an authenticating device is the inclusion in almost all of the sagas of poetic verses. In addition to the cultural and linguistic variety that poetry introduces, it is also a source of multiple difficulties, not least for the translator. In contrast to the poetic forms used in the *Poetic Edda*, which resemble traditional heroic poetry in the other early Germanic literatures, the poetry in sagas is notoriously difficult and is a poetic form that is confined to Scandinavia, particularly to Norway and Iceland. It was probably a challenge to people even in the thirteenth century, which is why Snorri Sturluson wrote the *Prose Edda* to explain and illustrate it. Poetry of the kind found in the sagas is known in English as 'court poetry' or 'skaldic poetry', from the Icelandic word *skáld* (poet). It has many metrical forms and schemes of internal rhyme and alliteration, the most common of which is called *dróttkvætt* measure. A reasonable explanation for the convention of putting poetry into the *Íslendinga sögur* is to see it as a carry-over from the practice of the somewhat earlier kings' sagas, in which poetry and poets played a large part. In the Prologue to *Heimskringla*, his collection of kings' sagas, Snorri Sturluson had this to say about poetry as a source of historical information:

When Harald Fair-hair was king of Norway, Iceland was settled. At the court of King Harald there were poets, and people still remember their poems and the poems about all the kings who have since been in Norway; and we have taken the greatest amount of information from what is said in poems that were recited before the great men themselves or their sons. We consider everything as true that is found in those poems about their exploits and battles. It is the habit of poets to praise him most in whose presence they are; but no one would have dared to recite to him deeds which everyone who listened, as well as he himself, knew to be fantasy and falsehood. That would have been mockery and not praise.

Poetry for Snorri was the best single source of information about the great events of the past. The inclusion of poetry in a king's saga was the equivalent of the modern scholarly footnote, laying out the authority for specific details of the story. It was for this reason that an ability to understand skaldic poetry was important to the historian.

In the *Íslendinga sögur* individual stanzas or small groups of them are composed by many of the characters as a comment on particular occasions or as an expression of personal feeling. These occasional verses (*lausavísur*) are the form that poetry most often takes in the *Íslendinga sögur*. But *dróttkvætt* stanzas can also be linked together in longer compositions: the more formal is the drapa (*drápa*), a poem that is divided into sections by one or more refrains; and the other is simply a sequence of stanzas, called a flokk (*flokkur*, i.e. group). In both the kings' sagas and the *Íslendinga sögur*, these longer compositions are usually presented to kings, in the manner suggested by Snorri. The greatest Icelandic poet was Egil Skallagrimsson, a saga of whose life and adventures is included in this collection. *Egil's Saga* ingeniously attempts to integrate his poetry (including three long poems) into the hero's exciting Viking life.

Many of the *Íslendinga saga* heroes were poets, in the sense that their sagas include poems said to have been composed by them. Language is often a field of conflict and competition, with poems and speeches serving as missiles that are intended to harm and humiliate. Some of the greatest fighters (Egil, Gisli, Grettir, Viglund) were poets. But four of the *Íslendinga sögur* are about men whose main claim to fame is as love poets: *Kormak's Saga, The Saga of Hallfred the Troublesome Poet, The Saga of Bjorn, Champion of the Hitardal People* and *The Saga of Gunnlaug Serpent-tongue*. Both love poetry and heroic poetry are important themes in a fifth 'poet's saga', *The Saga of the Sworn Brothers*. If this group deserves to be distinguished from the sagas of other poets it is on account of their focusing on the notion of language as a field of combat, with two rival poets contending for the hand of the same woman.

There may be good reason for believing that the earliest of the *Íslendinga sögur*, including some of these poets' sagas, used poetic verses in the spirit of the kings' sagas, that is as sources of information and historical authority. But as the genre evolved, the verses lost their antique flavour, which suggests that they were probably composed as a means of characterization as well. The saga style does not permit either interior monologue or a narrator's paraphrase of a character's thoughts, and the verses occasionally serve as the only available window into a character's mind.

Ari the Learned was not the only scholar whose authority was cited as a source or as a commentator on the significance of the saga's events. There are several examples in the *Íslendinga sögur*. Here is a rich combination of authenticating devices in *The Saga of Grettir the Strong*, a saga of an outlaw and poet (which is to appear in Penguin Classics):

The spear that Grettir had lost was not found for a long time, until the days that people still alive today can remember. It was found towards the end of Sturla Thordarson the Lawspeaker's life, in the marshland where Thorbjorn was killed, which is now known as Spjotsmyri (Spear-Mire). This is taken as proof that Thorbjorn was killed there, although some accounts say that he was killed in Midfitjar. (Ch. 49)

Such an apparently painstaking effort at recording variant accounts, citing the evidence of a place-name and tracing the relationship between a distant historical past and the 'present time' is a characteristic feature of saga style, an aspect of a narrative art which aspires to counterfeit reality. But the question also arises of the extent to which this style reflects an intellectual feature of the saga's method as history, as it does in Snorri's kings' sagas. The question itself may be seeking a distinction where none existed when the sagas were being written. The *Íslendinga sögur* create fictional worlds

An occasional verse (*lausavísa*) from Chapter 58 of *Egil's Saga*

The technical features of the typical *dróttkvætt* stanza are illustrated in this verse, which is by Egil Skallagrimsson. It has eight lines (*vísuorð*), each with six syllables. The lines are rhymed in three ways: alliteration, half-rhyme and full-rhyme.

The sounds represented with bold letters are in alliteration (*stuðlun*). There are two alliterating sounds (*stuðlar*) in the odd lines and one (the 'head letter' or *höfuðstafur*) that comes at the start of the even lines: st**ó**rt, st**á**li and st**a**fnkvígs (the höfuðstafur) in lines 1–2. The sounds represented with italics are internal rhyme. They are either half-rhyme (*skothending*) as in þ*él* and st*ál*i or full rhyme (*aðalhending*) as in st*afn*kvígs and j*afn*an.

Þ*él* höggr st**ó**rt fyr st**á**li
st*afn*kvígs á veg j*afn*an
út með éla m*eit*li
*andæ*r jötunn v*and*ar
en sv*al*búinn s*el*ju
sverfr *eir*ar vanr þ*eir*i
G**e**stils álft með g**u**st*um*
g**a**ndr of stál fyr br*and*i.

With its chisel of snow, the headwind,
scourge of the mast, mightily
hones its file by the prow
on the path that my sea-bull treads.
In gusts of wind, that chillful
destroyer of timber planes down
the planks before the head
of my sea-king's swan.

The greatest difficulty in understanding dróttkvæði, at least for the beginner, may be its departure from conventional prose word order. For example, the logical order of the words in this verse would be this: *Andærr jötunn vandar höggr stórt þél fyr stáli með éla meitli út á jafnan veg stafnkvígs, en svalbúinn selju gandr sverfr eirar vanr of stál þeiri Gestils álft með gustum fyr brandi.* To convey some idea of the challenge faced by the translator of such verse, here is a very literal and somewhat nonsensical rendering of the rearranged words:

'The opposite-rowing giant of the mast strikes hard, a file before the prow, with a chisel of sudden hail out on the smooth road of the young prow bull, and a cold wolf of wood files mercilessly with it about the prow of Gestil's swan with gusts before the decorated prow board.'

What makes this verse far from nonsensical in the original language is its use of a form of metaphor called *kenning*. Kennings consist of two parts: one which calls a thing by the name of something that it is not and then a second part which modifies the first in such a way as to make it poetically appropriate. Here 'giant' (or 'enemy') is one half of a kenning for 'wind', a thing that a giant is not. But when 'of the mast' is added to 'enemy', 'enemy of the mast' becomes a good metaphor for 'wind'. Going through the rearranged phrases of this verse we might paraphrase it:

jötunn vandar = giant (enemy) of the mast = wind; *andærr* = rowing in opposition: wind rowing in opposition = headwind

þél höggur stórt = a file strikes hard

fyr stáli = before the bow stem

með meitli = with a chisel; *éla* = of sudden hail: a chisel of sudden hail = a storm

út á jafnan veg = out on the smooth road

stafnkvígs = prow + young bull's; young prow bull's = ship's: ship's smooth road = the sea

en svalbúinn = and a coldly dressed

gandr = wolf (enemy); *selju* = wood (of which the ship is made): enemy of wood = wind

sverfr eirar vanr = files without mercy

of stál þeiri = around the prow with it (i.e. *þél*, the file)

Gestils álft = Gestil's (a sea king's) swan = ship

með gustum fyr brandi = with gusts of wind before the decorated prow board

which are largely consistent with those of *Íslendingabók* and *Landnámabók*, including the settlement of Iceland, the establishment of a national government, the testing of its laws and constitution, the discovery of Greenland and North America and the conversion to Christianity. Many of those great events can be confirmed by archaeology and the testimony of historical writing in other languages. By and large they must have happened more or less as they are said to happen in the fictional worlds of the sagas. They constitute a story, a national myth, within which the more local and detailed stories of the individual *Íslendinga sögur* take shape.

IV. THE AMERICAN ADVENTURE

For readers interested in North America, few historical events in the sagas arouse greater curiosity than do the Icelandic settlement of Greenland and the discovery of America. The settlements in Greenland lasted for about 500 years, beginning with Eirik the Red's arrival from Iceland in 985–6. They perished by gradual stages in the fifteenth century, apparently on account of increasingly cold weather and the difficulties of sailing in ice-filled waters to and from Iceland and Norway. Archaeologists have excavated the remains and even the earliest of them are as impressive as Icelandic sites of the same period. A movement is now under way to reconstruct some of the

Viking Age buildings in Greenland, as has been done in Newfoundland and, of course, Iceland. In the Saga Age, Greenland was an independent country with a population at the height of its prosperity of about 4,000. It had an annual national assembly like Iceland's at a place called Gardar. An extremely interesting and well-told episode in *The Saga of the Sworn Brothers* takes place at the assembly at Gardar. Six other *Íslendinga sögur* have episodes set in Greenland.

The story of the discovery and exploration of America is told in two works, *Eirik the Red's Saga* and the shorter *Saga of the Greenlanders*. These differ from each other in a number of details, *Eirik the Red's Saga* agreeing more frequently with other written sources, such as *Heimskringla*. Neither work is among the best sagas, and yet in their blending of myth and historical tradition they are typical of the genre. Modern archaeology, especially the work of Helge and Anne Stine Ingstad in the 1960s at L'Anse aux Meadows in northern Newfoundland, has confirmed that explorers from Greenland and Iceland spent time in North America and constructed buildings of the sort found in Iceland. *The Saga of the Greenlanders* attributes the first sighting of America to a merchant named Bjarni Herjolfsson, who in about 985 went off course on his way to Greenland, whereas *Eirik the Red's Saga* gives the credit to Eirik the Red's son Leif, who made the discovery through a similar accident about 1000. Altogether, *The Saga of the Greenlanders* describes six trips to America, including Bjarni's sighting and an extensive expedition by Leif. *Eirik the Red's Saga* mentions only three, the most thorough of which was made by Thorfinn Karlsefni, a very able Icelandic merchant who also figures importantly in *The Saga of the Greenlanders*.

The sagas describe three different landscapes from north to south along the American coast, *Helluland* (Stone slab land, probably southern Baffin Island or northern Labrador), *Markland* (Forest land, southern Labrador) and *Vínland* (Vine land, possibly the St Lawrence Valley, but more likely the coast of New England). Written evidence indicates that the Greenlanders maintained a connection with *Markland* as a source of timber until at least the fourteenth century. With *Vínland*, however, contact seems to have been lost after the explorations of Leif and Karlsefni in the early eleventh century. About the country we know very little with precision, although we do know that it was not an invention of the two sagas. Well before they were written *Vínland* was mentioned by Ari in *Íslendingabók* and even earlier by Adam of Bremen in his *History of the Archbishops of Hamburg-Bremen* of about 1075. Both *The Saga of the Greenlanders* and *Eirik the Red's Saga* describe a land that has wine grapes, maples and self-sown grain (probably wild rice). They report that the weather in *Vínland* was warm enough for cattle to graze outside all winter, pointing to both a southerly location in New England or Long Island and a milder overall temperature than exists today. (There is much other evidence, including the demise of the settlements in Greenland, that the northern hemisphere experienced a radical cooling off in the fourteenth century.) The accounts of *Vínland* include descriptions of a fierce native population, whom the sagas call *Skraelingjar* (the origin of this word is obscure: it may be related to words meaning 'wrinkle' or 'shrink', possibly referring to the treatment of animal skins; it is translated in this edition as 'natives'). The same word is used of the natives of Greenland, who must have been a quite different people.

The Saga of the Greenlanders and *Eirik the Red's Saga* blend to an equal extent the navigational and geographical accuracy for which they are famous with stories of magic and the supernatural. Both employ all of the standard authenticating techniques of the *Íslendinga sögur*, together with other features of saga style. Both are associated with King Olaf Tryggvason and the conversion of Greenland to Christianity. Leif Eiriksson, in fact, had reluctantly accepted from the king the difficult duty of converting Greenland when he took the voyage that resulted in his lucky discovery of *Vínland*. His father Eirik was a hard-bitten old Viking, who was banished from Iceland and who resented Christianity. He had several children, the most memorable of whom – aside from Leif – was an illegitimate daughter named Freydis. She is the epitome of evil in *The Saga of the Greenlanders*, being responsible for killing a number of her fellow explorers and for personally taking an axe to five women whom her men had refused to kill. Somewhat more benignly but no less mythically, in *Eirik the Red's Saga* she frightens off an attacking band of natives by running after them, even though she is pregnant, and then, when surrounded by them, picking up a sword from a dead Greenlander, pulling one of her breasts out of her clothing and slapping it with the naked sword. The natives were terrified at the sight and ran to their boats and rowed away. Almost as good a woman as Freydis was evil, Gudrid Thorbjarnardottir was the wife of Thorfinn Karlsefni and the mother of Snorri, the first person of European ancestry to be born in America. She has been described as the true central character of these sagas. After a pilgrimage to Rome, she lived out her life as an anchoress in Iceland, and from her were descended several of the early bishops of Iceland. What precisely these extreme examples of good and evil in the Vinland sagas, as well as other instances of magic and the paranormal, might have to do with the coming of Christianity to the north, the saga composer (as usual) does not tell us.

V. A FICTION OF SOCIAL REALISM

How the traditional poetry and the sagas came to be written down in the late twelfth or early thirteenth century is something of a mystery. We do not have an account of the circumstances and method, such as Ari gives for the writing of the laws. We do not know, for example, what division of labour might have existed between the people who gave a final shape to the texts and the scribes who wrote them down on vellum, made of calf-skin. None of the *Íslendinga sögur* has been preserved in an original draft or a saga author's holograph. Most of the surviving texts were written in the fourteenth and fifteenth centuries from originals or copies of them now lost, which were not necessarily a great deal older. Some are even later paper manuscripts, again based on lost vellum originals. Quite a few have come down to us in more than one distinct version, providing their editors with considerable worry and leading to learned debate. The single largest and most valuable collection of *Íslendinga sögur* is a mid-fourteenth-century manuscript known as *Möðruvallabók*, which consists of 200 vellum leaves and contains eleven sagas.

However the earliest manuscripts came about, it is apparent that some of them contain material that had existed in oral tradition for a long time. The *Poetic Edda* and the *fornaldarsögur* (some of which also contain eddic poems), include legendary characters and motifs based on historical figures from the fifth century. They appear in the oldest survivals of English and continental epic. Although it is scarcely possible to reconstruct much about ancient religious belief or ritual from the stories of the gods in the two eddas, they do preserve ancient imagery and motifs, as we know from their appearance in old stone inscriptions. For stories and poems to be transmitted through centuries of oral tradition, they have to make sense to their audiences from generation to generation, and to do this they must conform to the values, tastes and perceptions of successive new audiences. It is unlikely that fixed and unchanging texts, of the sort we are accustomed to in an age of printing, would survive this process from one performance to another, much less through centuries of cultural change. The oral sagas and poems of the Viking Age, to which reference is made in the sagas, were not exactly the same texts as those that were written down three hundred years later, although much about their art and content may have been similar.

The style of the *Íslendinga sögur* reflects their life in oral tradition. Their unadorned language and sentence structure are suited to the voice of a reader or storyteller, around whom an audience listens – in Iceland today it would be a radio audience. The sagas are formulaic in language and structure and yet full of suspenseful and exciting moments, great and small. The genre itself is different from anything else in medieval literature, and yet from saga to saga it follows the sort of tightly controlled rules that are associated with oral forms. Conventions govern the nature of plot, theme, characterization and narrative style, and yet those constraints somehow permit enough variation to make the greatest sagas distinct and distinctly memorable.

One convention by which the sagas develop a dense and plausible historical context is to introduce their major characters into an explicitly defined historical setting. Often this is accomplished with a rich background of genealogical information – more sometimes than the non-specialist reader can appreciate. The memory and transmission of these genealogies was apparently one of the cultural functions of the *Íslendinga sögur*. The genealogies were an important element of the network of story out of which the individual sagas came: they were a directory or map of Icelandic society. Their presence illustrates the obligation of these works to instruct as well as to entertain. Here is the opening chapter of *The Saga of Gunnlaug Serpent-tongue*, from a slightly different manuscript from the one that was used for the translation in this collection:

There was a man named Thorstein. He was the son of Egil Skallagrimsson. Skallagrim was the son of Kveldulf, a hersir from Norway. Thorstein's mother was named Asgerd, the daughter of Bjorn.

Thorstein lived at Borg in Borgarfjord. He was wealthy, a great chieftain, wise and gentle, and a moderate man in every way. He was not outstanding for size and strength as was his father Egil, but he was very powerful and well liked by everyone. Thorstein was a handsome man, with light-coloured hair and extremely fine eyes. He was married to Jofrid, the daughter of Gunnar Hlifarson. She had been married before to Thorodd Tungu-Oddsson and their daughter was Hungerd, who grew up at Borg with Thorstein. Jofrid was a woman of strong character.

She and Thorstein had many children, although few of them come into this saga. Skuli was their eldest son, the second was Kollsvein and Egil the third.

(Ch. 1) (my translation)

This genealogy tells us among other things that, socially and historically, Thorstein Egilsson will be the most important person in the saga. Although he is not the hero, it is appropriate to begin with him. His farm at Borg is mentioned in many sagas because it was the political and social centre of the district; from the time of the settlement until the time of writing the saga it was one of the most important farms in the nation. Some of the great men associated with the family at Borg are named explicitly in the manuscript used in this volume; for many Icelanders, those associations were well enough known from other sagas that they hardly needed stating. In this case, the noted ancestor was Egil Skallagrimsson, the poet/Viking hero of *Egil's Saga*, where many of the characters of *The Saga of Gunnlaug Serpent-tongue* are also mentioned, but that does not necessarily mean that one of the sagas is the 'source' of the other. We can readily imagine that such cross-references were an authenticating device of saga rhetoric in oral tradition, an element of the 'saga network' against which any particular saga or tale was composed and understood by its audience. For example, *Njal's Saga*, *Eirik the Red's Saga*, *The Saga of the People of Laxardal* and *The Saga of the People of Eyri* all trace some of their characters back to Olaf (Oleif) the White and his wife Unn (Aud) the Deep-minded, who founded one of the greatest dynasties of the Saga Age.

The abruptness and plainness of the saga opening is also typical. Thorstein is introduced in the absolutely standard saga way: 'There was a man named Thorstein.' The use of patronymics in the introduction of saga characters, especially the prominent and powerful ones, sometimes sets up a genealogical chain, as here, identifying fathers' fathers and so on several generations back. Stylistically, these chains are easy and natural in Icelandic but seem a little awkward in English translation, where a few extra words are sometimes necessary.

The description of Thorstein's character and appearance is also a narrative convention, although it derives an added significance here from the contrast of the son with his father. He is not so big and powerful as Egil and yet much easier to get along with; he has inherited the good looks and pleasant disposition of the two Thorolfs, Egil's brother and uncle. And for those who know the story of the men of Borg, this genealogy, taken together with the personal description, serves as a form of characterization. Thorstein's wife Jofrid is characterized with a single Icelandic word: *skörungur*, translated here as 'a woman of strong character'. That one word, however, raises suspense. Many of the women in the sagas, like the women in Greek tragedy and in the nineteenth-century novel, play large and interesting roles. 'A woman of strong character' is bound to be an intelligent, independent and courageous person, although we do not know, from the word *skörungur* itself, how she will be outstanding, or even whether she will be a force for good or for evil.

The precision with which historical context is established at the opening of an *Íslendinga saga* is a requirement of the genre. This can be accomplished by referring to one of the original settlers or the king of Norway, usually, but not invariably, the semi-legendary King Harald Fair-hair (*c.* 860–930), the first national king of Norway, who is the central figure in the foundation myth of Iceland. We have already noticed Snorri's allusion to this myth in the Prologue to *Heimskringla* and it is a story repeated often in the sagas, as in this example from *The Saga of Hord and the People of Holm* (not in this volume):

Most of Iceland was settled in the days of Harald Fair-hair. People would not endure his oppression and tyranny, especially those who belonged to aristocratic families and who had ambition and good prospects. They would rather leave their property in Norway than suffer aggression and injustice – whether from a king or from anyone else. Bjorn Gold-bearer was one of these. He travelled from Orkadal to Iceland and settled South Reykjadal, which was between the rivers Grimsa and Flokadalsa, and lived at Gullberastadir.

Other sagas that open with Harald Fair-hair and the story of families leaving Norway to settle in Iceland include *Gisli Sursson's Saga*, *The Saga of Hrafnkel Frey's Godi*, *Kormak's Saga*, *The Saga of the People of Svarfadardal* and *Viglund's Saga*. In *The Saga of Grettir the Strong*, *The Saga of the People of Eyri* and *The Saga of the People of Laxardal*, the reference to Harald comes just a few sentences into the saga. The most interesting and extensive story of Harald and the founding of Iceland is told in the first twenty-seven chapters of *Egil's Saga*, when Egil's father and grandfather resist the king and depart for Iceland. It is with Harald Fair-hair, in fact, that Ari Thorgilsson had begun *Íslendingabók*:

Iceland was first settled from Norway in the days of Harald Fair-hair, the son of Halfdan the Black, at the time ... that Ivar, the son of Ragnar Shaggy-breeches, killed St Edmund, the king of England, which was 870 years after the birth of Christ, according to what is written in his life.

The Saga of the People of Floi begins in an unusual and instructive way, with a genealogy of Harald. It demonstrates what a liminal figure he was in Icelandic story, standing at the juncture of two great eras, and consequently of two different fictional worlds. Because he was in effect the initiating force of the Saga Age, his family tree reaches back into another world, that of the eddas and the legendary *fornaldarsögur*. According to the genealogy in *The Saga of the People of Floi*, his great-great-grandparents were Brynhild and Sigurd the Volsung, who slew the dragon Fafnir. They are central characters in *The Saga of the Volsungs* and in many of the eddic poems. Five generations back from Sigurd, according to the saga, was Odin, who ruled Asgard.

The historical precision of the *Íslendinga sögur* is matched by the detail and accuracy of their geographical reference. The sagas tell of people and events that are primarily located in a specified district of Iceland. Although it extends over nearly all of Iceland and is something of an exception to this rule, the main actions of *Njal's Saga* occur primarily in the south. *Egil's Saga* and *The Saga of Gunnlaug Serpent-tongue* are, as we have noted, located primarily at the farm Borg in Borgarfjord in the west, although the scene does shift, as it does from time to time in most other sagas, to adventures in Britain and Scandinavia. *The Saga of the People of Laxardal* reflects its geographical setting in its title, as do a dozen other *Íslendinga sögur*.

The sagas tell stories that fall into a rather simply schematized general pattern. After an introduction of the main characters in their geographical and historical settings, the saga tells of a conflict that arises out of what are usually the events of everyday life in Iceland. Conflicts grow out of marriages, divorces, inheritances, sporting events, horse-fights, robberies, the destruction of property, thoughtless words, frustrated loves and jealousy, taunting and goading, disputed fishing rights, even rights to beached whales. The conflict may begin with the action of a rash or overbearing person, but then it grows until it reaches a climax, sometimes quite terrible and bloody, and producing a countering act of vengeance. Saga plots are often tragic, involving men of goodwill pitted against each other, sometimes even members of the same family. In the end there is a reconciliation. Longer sagas manage several of these feud plots, either interlaced with each other or concatenated.

All classes and stations of Saga Age society become involved. It is, however, a relatively homogeneous society by medieval standards. There is no royalty or courtly culture, no clerical hierarchy, no urban trade and commerce, no armies. It is a conservative rural society composed of some powerful leading men (*höfðingjar*, sing. *höfðingi*) at the top; freemen farmers (*bændur*, sing. *bóndi*), in various ways dependent upon the *höfðingjar*, hired labourers, both transient and permanently attached to one farm; and slaves. (These designations cannot be translated with complete satisfaction. 'Chieftain', which is the usual translation of *höfðingi*, does not seem entirely appropriate in such a highly evolved society as medieval Iceland; and the title 'farmer' does not do justice to the fact that some of the farms over which the *bændur* ruled in the Saga Age, and for some centuries afterwards, were as large as whole villages. The 'farmer' may have had as many as fifty or sixty men working for him and a household of over a hundred persons.)

The society described in the *Íslendinga sögur* comes about as close as medieval society ever did to the middle-class society of eighteenth-century Europe, in which the novel arose as an important narrative form. The society imagined by the *Íslendinga sögur* is as precisely observed as those of Daniel Defoe and Jane Austen. The quality that underlies the social realism in these two similar fictional worlds is the ability to view the lives of normal human beings as serious and problematic. Even weddings and business partnerships could involve them in behaviour for which they were morally and socially accountable and from which, without ever being lectured to, the reader has things to learn.

The intense focus of the sagas on the incidents of everyday life is the reason that some of the most acute observation on their plots and settings has come in recent years either directly from social scientists or from literary scholars who have been influenced by their methods and insights. Whether the actual society of tenth-century Iceland was in fact as uniform, coherent and conventional as the one presented in the *Íslendinga sögur* may be doubted. Still, modern methods of ethnography, political science and legal and social history are usefully applied to rationalizing and generalizing the represen-tation of society in the sagas. In particular, such an approach enables us to understand the behaviour of the characters as going either with or against the cultural norms in such matters as compensation for an injury, conflict resolution, gift-giving, gender roles, hospitality, family loyalty and personal honour. From the sagas we learn not only the history and geography of Saga Age Iceland in minute detail, but also precise details of prices, money, ships and boats, the layout of houses and outbuildings, weapons, clothing, sports, agricultural practices and domestic manufacturing.

Honour (*sæmd*) is to the conception of character in the sagas as feud is to the plot. Honour does not consist merely of avoiding shame or disgrace. It is the more powerful desire for approbation, good reputation, distinction. Its social function is to forge and maintain bonds of kinship, marriage, friendship and political alliance. Its narrative function is to keep the saga moving forward, in accordance with ethical rules that give the feud plot a sense of heroic inevitability. Men are drawn into the plots through the operation of social laws over which they have little individual control. As the sagas' emphasis on genealogy attests, the extended family (*ætt*) was a more important social and historical institution in medieval Iceland than it is in most modern Western societies. The branches of blood-relationship that govern the inheritance of property also govern the degree of obligation a man has to seek compensation for injury done to a kinsman. A man's closest relationship according to the laws is (1) his father, then (2) his son, (3) his brother, (4) his father's father, (5) his son's son and so on all the way to (14) the son of his mother's sister. Viewed in this way, the Icelandic extended family is 'ego-centred', with a man's relationship to it changing as other members come into the family or leave. This is indicated by the 'I' at the centre of the chart.

A person's more immediate family or household often included relationships outside the *ætt*, with important implications for honour. Many saga characters have 'foster' relationships, in which an adult (usually a male, as the head of a family) will assume responsibility for raising another person's child. The foster-father is regarded as the social inferior of the child's actual father, although on some occasions the 'inferiority' is more theoretical than actual. These relationships with foster parents and their families are often profound and loving and play a conspicuous role in many sagas. A somewhat similar kind of voluntary relationship can be formed between two young men in 'sworn brotherhood', a sort of foster relationship with each other.

Honour is an aristocratic and chivalric concept appropriate to a warrior class. In many societies it is manifested outwardly, in such things as rank, title and dress. In the *Íslendinga sögur*, however, a lively sense of honour is maintained by a society of farmers that functions largely without such institutional distinctions. Honour is a social construct. It is bestowed by the community as a reward for moderate and generous behaviour as much as for warlike derring-do, although strength and courage in fighting are greatly admired. The pursuit of honour is also internalized in individual characters in ways not easy for us to comprehend. While a desire to earn or to preserve honour in a social conflict is a saga hero's most notable trait, a character's conception of what his (or her) honour demands will sometimes strike us as idiosyncratic, exaggerated and humorous. One of the most profoundly complex instances of this is the character Egil Skallagrimsson: his particular

The Duty of Revenge and the Right to Inheritance

The duty of revenge was inherited in the Saga Age, in exactly the same way as claims to inheritance and property, according to a clear pattern of succession. This simplified chart is based on *Grágás* (Grey goose), the law book of the Commonwealth, and Preben Meulengracht Sørensen's *Saga and Society* (1993).

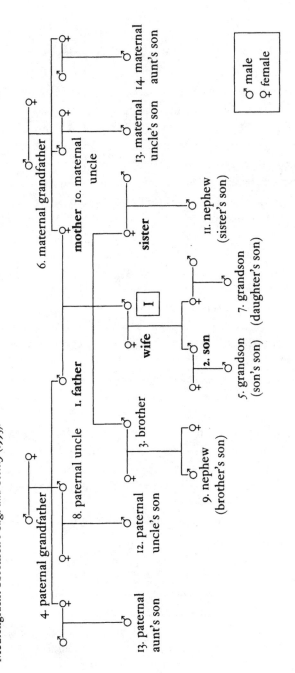

blend of Viking ferocity, greed and sensitivity to the requirements of his honour is closely associated in *Egil's Saga* with his poetic genius.

VI. MYTHIC TRACES

But neither an exaggerated sense of Viking honour nor any other social consideration is sufficient to account for his character or that of any other complex saga hero. Egil's verbal gifts extended, for example, to the composition and interpretation of magic inscriptions. With poetry he could perform magical curses as well as cures, even though usually doing so in a socially defined context, such as avenging some real or imagined slight. The patron of all poets was Odin, who was sometimes known as the one-eyed god. According to *Völuspá* (The Sibyl's Prophecy) in the *Poetic Edda*, in a stanza that is also quoted in *Snorra-Edda*, Odin gave away his eye in order to drink from the underworld well of the wise god Mimir and thus to acquire wisdom. Egil is not only the beneficiary of Odin's gifts of poetry and magic, but also to some small degree an embodiment of the god. Odin's temperament is too vast and his powers too enormous to be accommodated fully in human form of course, nor does the saga suggest the identification of the god with his worshipper, but that mythic presence is a component of Egil's nature which shapes and qualifies its more purely social dimensions.

In Chapter 55 of *Egil's Saga*, the hero illustrates something of this mythic nature as he mourns the death in battle of his brother Thorolf, who was fighting for King Athelstan of England. As Egil sits in King Athelstan's hall he seems to sink into a terrible grief. 'He wrinkled one eyebrow right down on to his cheek and raised the other up to the roots of his hair. Egil had dark eyes and was swarthy. He refused to drink even when served, but just raised and lowered his eyebrows in turn.' When the king begins to understand that Egil is depressed because he has no compensation for his brother, he gives him a large arm ring. 'When Egil sat down, he drew the ring on to his arm, and his brow went back to normal. He put down his sword and helmet and took the drinking-horn that was served to him, and finished it. Then he spoke a verse.'

The mythic component of saga characterization is not easily distinguished from its more rationalized elements, such as the inheritance of family traits, conformity to recognized social and personality types, or even a plausible individual eccentricity. Also the slightly mad, touchy poet may have been a literary type, judging from the protagonists of the other poets' sagas. The mythic element does not usually involve, as it does with Egil, conformity to aspects of a particular mythic being. Freydis, for example, in *The Saga of the Greenlanders* is a character larger than life and more evil: she brings some of her nature with her from a world of myth and legend rather than from her social or psychological situation. And yet it would be difficult to identify a specific literary prototype illustrated in her character as Odin is for Egil. Perhaps because the important male saga characters are located in significant social and ethical contexts, the mythic component of their characterization is less apparent than is the case with some of the most powerful and memorable women. A fuller and more interesting characterization than Freydis is that of the beautiful, headstrong and wicked Hallgerd, the wife of Gunnar of Hlidarendi in *Njal's Saga*. Like Freydis, however, Hallgerd comes into the saga with qualities suggestive of an uncanny nature. In the opening scene Hallgerd is playing with some other girls on the floor of the hall, where her father Hoskuld is holding a feast. His half-brother Hrut is there, sitting next to him.

Hoskuld called to her, 'Come over here.'

She came at once, and he took her by the chin and kissed her. Then she went back.

Then Hoskuld said to Hrut, 'How do you like this girl? Don't you find her beautiful?'

Hrut was silent. Hoskuld asked again.

Then Hrut answered, 'The girl is very beautiful, and many will pay for that. But what I don't know is how thief's eyes have come into our family.'

Hoskuld was angry at this, and for a while there was coolness between the brothers. (Ch. 1)

The hint of mythic characterization provides a device for building suspense with a prophecy of future events. It illustrates, too, the extreme importance of dialogue in the narrative art of the sagas, which permits the narrator himself very little leeway in commenting on characters or plot. The characters are not often quoted at length, but their remarks do much of the interpretative and thematic work of the saga.

Another brilliantly conceived female character comes into her story with a prophecy. That is Gudrun Osvifsdottir in *The Saga of the People of Laxardal*:

They had a daughter named Gudrun. She was the most beautiful woman ever to have grown up in Iceland, and no less clever than she was good-looking. She took great care with her appearance, so much so that the adornments of other women were considered to be mere child's play in comparison. She was the shrewdest of women, highly articulate, and generous as well.   (Ch. 32)

When she enters the saga this extraordinary woman has had four dreams during the previous winter. They are accurately interpreted for her by a kinsman of hers, the great chieftain Gest Oddleifsson, who has some ability to see into the future, and they foretell the nature of her four marriages. Conceiving of character as to some extent informed by a pattern of events foreordained affects our response to the plot as it unfolds. The outlines have been foretold, so what remains is to see in detail how that anticipated effect comes about. Gudrun's force of personality and her complex response to her frustrated love for Kjartan Olafsson, whom she does not marry, lead her into a bloody-mindedness that is reminiscent of another Gudrun, the mythological Gudrun Gjukadottir, the heroine of *The Saga of the Volsungs* and of half a dozen poems in the *Poetic Edda*. From the same myth, however, an even more likely precursor is the Valkyrie Brynhild, who alone of the characters is by nature the equal of the hero Sigurd and yet who is by circum-stances deceived into marrying the second-best man Gunnar. In her misery at having been betrayed by the hero she trusted she orders her husband to have Sigurd killed. Brynhild is not the Gudrun of *The Saga of the People of Laxardal*, of course, but a precursor in the world of myth to which the historical figure can be understood as conforming in certain ways. Most saga characters have traits that cannot be explained naturalistically and that remind us of events in the Eddas and the *fornaldarsögur*, although in most large ways this mythic dimension has been displaced by a conception of human behaviour that is entirely plausible in its social context.

Like any great fictional character Gudrun Osvifsdottir is defined and determined by the whole work of which she is one part. *The Saga of the People of Laxardal* has many strong women characters besides Gudrun, including Unn the Deep-minded, the founder of the dynasty in Iceland; Melkorka, the Irish princess and slave, whose illegitimate son Olaf Peacock becomes one of the most illustrious men in Iceland; Olaf's wife Thorgerd, the daughter of Egil Skallagrimsson; her daughter Thurid; and Olaf Tryggvason's sister Ingibjorg. In some ways these women are all more effective and reliable than their illustrious, charismatic and inconsiderate husbands and lovers.

This too is a pattern one might find in the myth of the Volsungs. The most loving relationships in the saga are between men and women of different generations: mothers and sons, fathers and daughters. And the moral force behind many of the killings also originates with the women.

VII. A STURLUNG AGE ANATOMY OF POWER

The one social rank that plays a large role in the sagas is that of the godi (see *Glossary*). In heathen times the godi had a duty to build and maintain a temple for worshipping one or more of the gods and to provide ritual feasts. The *Íslendinga sögur* describe Icelandic paganism, although we cannot help but wonder how much their authors knew about the subject. Several of the godis in the sagas are represented as being pious in their ritual duties. A remarkable saga is *The Saga of the People of Eyri*, which includes information about Icelandic antiquities that are described more fully than elsewhere. A pagan temple is said to have been built by an original settler, Thorolf Moster-beard who:

... established settlements for his crew and set up a large farm by the cove Hofsvog which he called Hofstadir. There he had a temple built, and it was a sizeable building, with a door on the side-wall near the gable. The high-seat pillars were placed inside the door, and nails, that were called holy nails, were driven into them. Beyond that point, the temple was a sanctuary. At the inner end there was a structure similar to the choir in churches nowadays and there was a raised platform in the middle of the floor like an altar, where a ring weighing twenty ounces and fashioned without a join was placed, and all oaths had to be sworn on this ring. It also had to be worn by the temple priest at all public gatherings. A sacrificial bowl was placed on the platform and in it a sacrificial twig – like a priest's aspergillum – which was used to sprinkle blood from the bowl. This blood, which was called sacrificial blood, was the blood of live animals offered to the gods. The gods were placed around the platform in the choir-like structure within the temple. All farmers had to pay a toll to the temple and they were obliged to support the temple godi in all his campaigns, just as thingmen are now obliged to do for their chieftain. The temple godi was responsible for the upkeep of the temple and ensuring it was maintained properly, as well as for holding sacrificial feasts in it. (Ch. 4)

The most striking and memorable example of a godi as pagan priest is Hrafnkel in *The Saga of Hrafnkel Frey's Godi*, who dedicated a horse to the exclusive use of the god Frey and himself and swore a sacred oath that no one else was permitted to ride it. When a good-hearted young man rides the horse to search for Hrafnkel's lost sheep, the godi feels a compelling religious duty to kill him, providing the occasion for the conflict on which the plot is built. The outcome of the saga suggests that the author felt both a respectful curiosity about paganism and an obligation not to seem to approve of it. Two men in *The Saga of Hord and the People of Holm*, one a godi, the other an ordinary farmer, are described in their temples exchanging words with the gods; both die soon afterwards.

It is with the function of the godis as secular leaders that the *Íslendinga sögur* is most concerned. For a feud or legal case to be conducted with any hope of success a godi's help and leadership were necessary. The office of godi, called the godord (*goðorð*), could be inherited, traded, bought and sold, or divided among one or more men, although only one individual at a time could officially perform its functions. The country was divided into four quarters (*fjórðungar*) and the number of godis was fixed at thirty-nine: twelve in the northern quarter and nine each in the eastern, southern and western quarters. At the annual Althing these thirty-nine 'full and original' godis, along with nine others, three each from the east, south and west, served as the forty-eight voting members of the Law Council (*Lögrétta*), a legislative assembly. They reviewed the laws which the Lawspeaker recited, made new laws, set fines and punishments and were informed of sentences of outlawry and banishment that were passed by the courts in local spring assemblies. Four local assembly districts existed in the northern quarter, and three in each of the other quarters. Each year a Spring Assembly (*vorþing*) was convened by the three 'full' godis who lived in each local assembly district (*samþingsgoðar*). After a constitutional reform around 965 the four quarters also had courts (*fjórðungsdómar*) that met at the Althing, and the godis appointed judges for these courts from the farmers in their districts. Neither imprisonment nor officially administered execution was used as a punishment by the powers-that-be, although men declared outlaws were killed when they were captured. By comparison with other European societies in the Middle Ages, Iceland was unique in its reliance on legislative and judicial institutions, without an executive branch of government.

In local matters, the godis are represented in the sagas as performing countless informal acts of leadership and assistance to the farmers in their districts. But their effectiveness derives more from personal power and position than from constitutional authority. An isolated community with essentially no foreign affairs to conduct or foreign armies to repel, Iceland of the Saga Age could function, even prosper (according to the sagas), on the ideology with which the first emigrants left Norway: freedom from central authority, especially in the form of a king. The operation of Icelandic society was perceived as being coextensive with Icelandic law. Local systems of welfare, for example such things as caring for orphans, compensating people for losses, assisting farmers in collecting damages awarded to them by the national Law Council, were carried out according to the law, with the assistance and guidance of the godis, but without the notion of a government being in charge: '... with law,' Njal said, in what is now a proverb, 'our land will rise, but it will perish with lawlessness' (*Njal's Saga*, Ch. 70).

The *Íslendinga sögur* began being written in a brilliant and tormented period of Icelandic history known as the Age of the Sturlungs (*Sturlungaöld*). The history of this critical time, from about 1220 to 1264, is told in the huge collection of contemporary sagas called *Sturlunga saga* (The Saga of the Sturlung Family). The Sturlungs were one of five great families locked in a struggle for power that led finally to the collapse of the old Icelandic Commonwealth. They derived their family name from the fact that they were the sons and grandsons of Sturla Thordarson, a chieftain who lived at a farm called Hvamm in the middle decades of the twelfth century. One of Hvamm-Sturla's sons was Snorri Sturluson and a grandson was the great historian, his namesake Sturla Thordarson. The five feuding families became extremely powerful, capable of assembling armies of 1400 men and of amassing to themselves most of the godords. In the Age of the Sturlungs, learned people were assembling and writing down a priceless heritage of history and historical fiction, myth, legend and poetry. And yet at just this time the nation was witnessing unprecedented instances of violence, atrocity, abuse of power, meanness of spirit, arrogant violations of decency, not to mention of honour. One of many victims was Snorri, killed in his home on 22 September 1241, by a war party which included two of his former sons-in-law.

In the Sturlung Age, the Icelandic foundation myth, with a king at its centre and a stubborn refusal by independent and ambitious farmers to serve him, was a pattern for thinking about the relationship of Icelandic chieftains to the Norwegian crown four hundred years later. There are many such stories of Icelanders and the Norwegian kings in the kings' sagas, in the

Íslendinga sögur and in the closely related genre of *þættir*. In addition to the dire effect of their feuds and power struggles, the great families of the Age of the Sturlungs also began accepting honours and official duties from the king of Norway. Finally in 1262–4, as an alternative to social dissolution and anarchy, the Icelanders formally agreed to become his subjects. The literary activity of the Sturlung Age, especially the *Íslendinga sögur*, must be connected with the military and moral adventures that were threatening to destroy the laws and values inherited from the noble and independent farmers of the Saga Age.

In general the kings of Norway were fascinating to the Icelanders, but the kings about whom most was written were Olaf Tryggvason and St Olaf Haraldsson, both of whom were descendants of Harald Fair-hair, with long and highly interesting sagas of their own, versions of which are included in *Heimskringla*. The Icelanders credited Olaf Tryggvason with having converted their nation to Christianity. He was also important as the forerunner of his namesake the saint, in the way John the Baptist had been the precursor of Christ. Energetic warriors and enthusiastic missionaries, both kings were killed in battle. They are frequently mentioned in the *Íslendinga sögur*, to some degree as markers by which to date events historically, but more because of their association with the entry of Christianity into the history of Iceland and of the Christian chieftain into the ethical world of the sagas. The conversion had added a complicating element, not only to Icelandic law but to the structure of society, with the bishops and other clergy increasingly under the discipline of a foreign church governance. This became a form of foreign influence, like that from the royal court of Norway, that produced much of the complexity and strain of the Age of the Sturlungs. The Christianity of the *Íslendinga sögur* is not this kind of large, complex and politicized institution; instead it is something simpler. It is more like a new view of human nature, which produces in some instances a subtle qualification of the traditional demands of honour, and in others a magical possibility of the divine will's manifesting itself through miracle. A Christian perspective is one of the components of the ethical nature of idealized Icelandic leaders as they are presented in the *Íslendinga sögur*. Like their ambiguous relationships with the kings, and their search for a workable balance between the integrity of the individual and the preservation of law, the moral natures of the old saga heroes were a mirror in which people of the Sturlung Age could aspire, at least in imagination, to see themselves.

VIII. THE WORLD OF THE SAGAS

In selecting the sagas and tales of Icelanders to be included in this volume, the editors wanted to illustrate different characteristics of their art, and to suggest the varieties of experience that made up 'the world of the sagas'. Iceland was the newest and most remote nation in Europe when the stories recorded in these sagas took place. It was first inhabited in the expansion of the Norse hegemony westward, and like other frontier societies it was a good place for people unhappy or in trouble at home to get a new start. The sagas describe, in the first few generations of what we think of as the Icelandic nation, a restless class of able and ambitious young men, on the move back and forth, largely concerned with making fortunes and earning reputations on a larger stage than Iceland offered. A hundred years later, the coming and going, within Iceland but more especially abroad, was associated with Christianity and the missionary activities of pious Icelanders and clergy from abroad. Iceland was by no means imagined as the centre of the world. An element of movement – travel, discovery and exploration – was an aspect of the earliest narrative literature in Icelandic, even before the *Sagas of Icelanders* were put into writing. It has seemed appropriate, therefore, to conceive of the selection in this volume as itself a journey into a saga world that can be characterized (not altogether metaphorically) in terms of the various spaces and locales these stories tell us about.

The first stage describes the emigration of important families from Norway to Iceland, often with a temporary stop in Britain. It is the single most enduring element of the foundation story of Iceland, and is mentioned in most of the sagas in this collection, nowhere more fully than in *Egil's Saga*, where we see that even the patterns of movement as they become established in Icelandic society are an inheritance from a former life in Norway. The more or less constant movement over long distances by the younger men of an aristocratic family is contrasted to a deep and defining relationship with the particular place that is the inherited family seat. *Egil's Saga* offers in greater detail the conventional story of a family's inability or unwillingness to adapt to a form of government headed by a single national king.

A second convention of the emigration story is the symbolic token that determines the particular site where the new home or family estate is to be built in Iceland. In *Egil's Saga* it is the place where Kveldulf's coffin comes ashore after his burial at sea. As famous as this place, Borg, becomes, it is matched in historical importance by Hvamm in *The Saga of the People of Laxardal*, which was built where Unn's high-seat pillars had come ashore. Typically, leaving the old home in Norway is described in constitutional and political terms, whereas finding a home in Iceland is guided by a more magical agency that sanctions the foundation of new houses and the communities that surround them. *The Saga of the People of Vatnsdal* is unique in telling an emigration story that is determined entirely by this magic. Ingimund, the founder, is a loyal and valued friend of King Harald Fair-hair, but as the result of a Lapp woman's magic he considers himself destined to abandon his property in Norway and head for Iceland, where she has hidden an amulet sacred to Frey, in a place from which only he can retrieve it. It is several years after his arrival before Ingimund finally finds his predestined homeland, the beautiful valley of Vatnsdal, where he builds a large temple and in the process discovers his amulet. He calls his farm Hof (Temple) in acknowledgement of the auspiciousness of this place.

The first generations of settlers had the task of adjusting the laws and traditions they brought with them to their new situation where, to an extent far greater than in Norway, they were lords of their own domain. They found suitable areas in which to live and divided them into workable farms among the people who had followed the founding chieftain to Iceland. This meant giving names to the mountains, valleys, fjords and headlands – as we see Ingimund do on his way to Vatnsdal, Aud on her way to Laxardal and Skallagrim when he explores Borgarfjord. In these sagas little stories explain the origin of place-names, and a close connection develops between features of the land and historical memory; in an oral culture these names serve as a 'memory theatre', reminding those who walk over it of the great stories associated with the places.

In the realistic novels and stories of the nineteenth century, there was a convention of beginning the way Nikolai Gogol does in *Dead Souls*: 'Through the gates of the inn in the provincial town of N. drove a rather handsome, smallish spring britzka, of the sort driven around in by . . .' An Icelandic saga could never begin this way. Particular, identifying places are too important to its art and thought, so in this respect the realism of saga style is closer to that of the twentieth century than the nineteenth. 'The town of N.' is both a coy way of suggesting that the author wants to protect the identity of his characters, who are real people, and, at the same time, of implying that it is really the typical rather than the actual in which universal human truths are to be found. The saga authors assume, however, that life manifests itself through the particular and that universality derives, paradoxically, if at all, from reconstructing particular men and places: 'Herjolf was the son of Bard Herjolfsson and a kinsman of Ingolf, the settler of Iceland. Ingolf gave to Herjolf the land between Vog and Reykjanes' (*The Saga of the Greenlanders*).

Another reason that 'the town of N.' would not be found in a saga about Iceland is that until the eighteenth century Iceland had no towns. The cosmopolitan blending of nationalities, the accumulation of wealth, together with the openness to commercial and artistic innovation and subtleties of class and manners – all of the things we associate with medieval towns elsewhere in Europe – had no place in Iceland. It is to the tales of the Icelanders, which characteristically take place abroad, or to separate episodes in longer sagas, that we must turn for anything like an urban experience – in Norway, Denmark or England, and often the scene is the court rather than the strictly urban neighbourhood. There is a wonderful market in *The Saga of the People of Laxardal*, where Hoskuld buys his concubine Melkorka, and a good street scene where Kjartan irritates the followers of King Olaf Tryggvason. Audun in *The Tale of Audun from the West Fjords* travels from Greenland to an unnamed town in Norway where he rents a room before going to see the king, and in another unnamed town in Denmark, he wanders the streets begging for food for himself and his bear. These urban scenes are a kind of moral holiday from the more problematic life within the constraints of Icelandic society. *The Saga of Gunnlaug Serpent-tongue* largely takes place abroad, in kings' courts and in more urban settings than would be possible in Iceland. It has, as a result, a sense of distance and romance. Gunnlaug, like Gisli and Egil, is a poet, but his verses are less directly related than theirs are to particular social situations, and suggest a freer, more purely emotional expression.

Because Iceland was exclusively rural, it was a conservative society, closed to the newly rich or the landless, one in which the 'best farmers' managed every aspect of labour, production and property, as well, of course, as defining and propagating appropriate social custom. The social, political and geographical centre of Iceland in the Saga Age and later was at Thingvellir during the Althing, which like so much of life in the sagas went on out of doors. An oral culture had no use for government archives and the files they contain. There were no contracts or records, deeds or proceedings that had any existence other than in the memory of witnesses. To see Icelandic society at work on the national level the scene moves from individual farms to the outdoor assemblies in the local districts and then, later in the summer, to Thingvellir.

In the settlement stage, effective leaders were cultivated who could attempt to settle disputes over territory and local authority and to tame a sort of 'wild western' high-handedness that was a feature of life in the new land. The finest saga of settlement is *The Saga of the People of Laxardal*, although it is much more than that, defining over several generations ideals of chieftaincy and heroic character. It is worth noticing, too, how large a role women play in it, and more complex and problematic ones in some respects than those of the men. We are not allowed to forget in this saga, or in *The Saga of the People of Vatnsdal*, that it was families who moved, not merely aspiring or desperate Vikings. Where the saga does its hardest intellectual work is in telling the stories of how the succeeding generations in these founding families tested each other and the laws of Iceland in their competition for power. The saga never tells us what it 'means', but its thought resides instead in the narration of events and in the particularities of character and event. We are not told that such-and-such a thing will always happen, or even that it will ever happen again, but rather that this is a case in which serious and responsible people of goodwill landed in a conflict that tested their characters and abilities, as well as the social structure of the nation. And it usually sounds true enough to what we know about people that we believe it and remember it.

Two of the sagas in this collection, *The Saga of the Confederates* and *The Saga of Hrafnkel Frey's Godi*, are tightly focused on a single theme: the limits of individual wealth and authority of a chieftain. They are very different in tone, but both are less broadly conceived than are the regional sagas, and it is interesting to note that women play essentially no role in them. Although it is so limited in scope and setting, Hrafnkel's saga is one of the masterpieces of saga art. Since both Hrafnkel and Odd, the protagonist of the comic *Saga of the Confederates*, are 'taught a lesson', some commentators have been tempted to assign a didactic purpose to these two sagas, as though we readers should somehow learn the same lesson: don't let your conduct be guided by allegiance to a pagan god; or just because you are three times wealthier than the next wealthiest man in the land, don't consider yourself the equal of the 'best farmers'. The sagas are about the intrinsic superiority of chieftains, despite their excesses and follies. Each, through the special lens of its art, sounds true, without recourse to allegory.

*

There are places in Iceland that are neither fertile valleys and upland pastures nor the sanctified sites of assemblies. They are the uninhabited places, often in the interior, where outlaws take refuge, sometimes in the company of spirits only partly human. It did not take long for this demarcation of social space to develop, as Iceland evolved into a reasonably stable and conservative rural society. People who found the constraints of normal social life impossible to accept, whether for reasons of honour or of excessive animal spirits, were often condemned to exile. They sometimes chose, as did the hero of *Gisli Sursson's Saga*, to attempt survival in the uninhabited places in Iceland. Like *The Saga of Hrafnkel Frey's Godi*, this saga is another little masterpiece of characterization. Gisli is a great hero, a good and patient man, but one of too little good fortune.

The classical hero as a social and psychological type was under increasingly sceptical scrutiny as time went on in Iceland. A response to the military excesses of the Age of the Sturlungs may account for it. Even though many different literary conventions contribute to the characterization of saga heroes, so that there is considerable variety among them, they all occupy a liminal space that is barely on one side or the other of what normal Icelandic society can tolerate. Typically they acquire their skill at arms and their martial reputations in the larger world of action abroad, either (as in the case of Gisli) before they settle in Iceland, or as a conscious element in the education of the aspiring hero, or in the course of temporary exile.

Ref the Sly and Gunnlaug Serpent-tongue in different ways illustrate the Icelandic hero's dependence on the wider scope of foreign society. As a poet, Gunnlaug relies on the larger Norse cultural scene to earn his reputation: even so, his competitive nature and outspokenness are barely contained within the fine line of royal tolerance. Emblematic of the neccessity for a foreign setting is the fact that Gunnlaug's passionate ambition for superiority in love, in poetry and in feats of arms culminates in a duel that must take place outside Iceland, where it has been prohibited by law. It is because of these lively heroes that we read and enjoy the sagas so much. But we also learn what a dangerous game they play if they attempt to carry out a heroic career in Iceland itself, a place that is devoted to social tranquillity and to a virtual experience of the heroic through literature rather than to an actual one. When Ref the Sly is forced to leave Iceland, as mentioned above, his uncle encourages him to have a story written about his achievements, which serves to make the point that Icelanders will enjoy reading his adventures as long as they don't have to experience them in reality.

At the end of *Gisli Sursson's Saga*, when the characters are all accounted for, we are told that Gisli's wife's nephew, also drawn into Gisli's outlawry, was able to go beyond the reach of Icelandic authority, and is on a ship bound for Greenland. Greenland was the new frontier of the Saga Age – rough, tough, but a lively and human place, where a man could make some money. *Eirik the Red's Saga* illustrates the progress to Iceland, as a refuge from Norwegian law, and then to Greenland as a refuge from Icelandic law. As saga places, Greenland and the interior of Iceland were somewhat analogous to Finnmark in Norway, which figures in the early chapters of *Egil's Saga*. Such places outside conventional Icelandic society help to define what is meant by civilization, and also for us to distinguish between the forms of behaviour that can be tolerated in society and those, even at times heroic and noble, which are 'beyond the pale'. Greenland is less magical and better suited to a fresh start in life than either the interior of Iceland or most other places of refuge abroad. The action of half a dozen sagas includes episodes in Greenland, and they all illustrate the vitality and renewal associated with the place. America as a saga place is so complex and special that it cannot be spoken of briefly. It is a world beyond Greenland, Finnmark or the interior of Iceland, a brave new world, within the reach of Norse seamanship, but beyond the grasp of its civilization.

Further Reading

Listed below are some of the more recent books in English about the *Íslendinga sögur* and their historical and cultural backgrounds. Much authoritative work on the sagas exists only in the Icelandic language or in journal articles and is not included. References to this more specialized literature may be found by consulting Pulsiano and Wolf, *Medieval Scandinavia: An Encyclopedia* and Clover and Lindow, *Old Norse-Icelandic Literature: A Critical Guide* (see below).

Andersson, Theodore M. *The Problem of Icelandic Saga Origins: A Historical Survey*. New Haven, Conn. 1964.

—. *The Icelandic Family Saga: An Analytic Reading*. Cambridge, Mass. 1967.

Andersson, Theodore M. and Miller, William Ian. *Law and Literature in Medieval Iceland: Ljósvetninga saga and Valla-Ljóts saga*. Stanford 1989.

The Book of Settlements (Landnámabók). Trans. Hermann Pálsson and Paul Edwards. Winnipeg 1972.

Brøgger, A. W. and Shetelig, H. *The Viking Ships*. Oslo 1951.

Byock, Jesse L. *Feud in the Icelandic Saga*. Berkeley 1982.

—. *Medieval Iceland: Society, Sagas, and Power*. Berkeley 1988.

Clover, Carol J. *The Medieval Saga*. Ithaca, NY 1982.

— and Lindow, John (ed.). *Old Norse-Icelandic Literature: A Critical Guide*. *Islandica* XLV. Ithaca, NY 1985.

Clunies Ross, Margaret. *Prolonged Echoes: Old Norse Myths in Medieval Northern Society*. Vol. I: *The Myths*. Vol. II: *The Reception of Norse Myths in Medieval Iceland*. Odense, Denmark 1994, 1998.

Ellis Davidson, H. R. *Gods and Myths of Northern Europe*. Harmondsworth 1964.

Foote, Peter and Wilson, D. M. *The Viking Achievement*. Revised edn. London 1980.

Frank, Roberta. *The Old Norse Court Poetry Dróttkvætt Stanza. Islandica* XLII. Ithaca, NY 1978.

Gade, Kari Ellen. *The Structure of Old Norse Dróttkvætt Poetry. Islandica* IL. Ithaca, NY 1995.

Graham Campbell, James. *The Viking World.* London 1980.

Hallberg, Peter. *The Icelandic Saga.* Trans. Paul Schach. Lincoln, Neb. 1962.

Hastrup, Kirsten. *Culture and History in Medieval Iceland.* Oxford 1985.

Ingstad, Helge. *Westward to Vinland: The Discovery of Pre-Columbian Norse House-sites in North America.* Trans. Erik J. Friis. New York 1969.

Íslendingabók (The Book of the Icelanders). Trans. Halldór Hermannson. Ithaca, NY 1930.

Jesch, Judith. *Women in the Viking Age,* Rochester, NY 1991; Woodbridge, England 1992.

Jochens, Jenny. *Women in Old Norse Society.* Ithaca, NY 1995.

—. *Old Norse Images of Women.* Philadelphia 1996.

Jones, Gwyn. *A History of the Vikings.* 2nd edn. Oxford 1984.

Ker, W. P. *Epic and Romance: Essays on Medieval Literature.* 2nd edn. London 1908; rpt. New York 1957.

Kristjánsson, Jónas. *Eddas and Sagas: Iceland's Medieval Literature.* Trans. Peter Foote. Reykjavík 1992.

Kunz, Keneva. *Retellers of Tales: An Evaluation of English Translations of Laxdæla Saga.* Reykjavík 1994.

The Laws of Early Iceland: Grágás, The Codex Regius of Grágás with Material from Other Manuscripts, I. Trans. Andrew Dennis, Peter Foote and Richard Perkins. Winnipeg 1980.

Lönnroth, Lars. *Njáls Saga: A Critical Introduction.* Berkeley 1976.

Madelung, Margaret A. *The Laxdæla Saga: Its Structural Patterns.* Chapel Hill, NC 1972.

Meulengracht Sørensen, Preben. *Saga and Society: An Introduction to Old Norse Literature.* Trans. John Tucker. Odense, Denmark 1993.

—. *The Unmanly Man: Concepts of Sexual Defamation in Early Northern Society.* Trans. Joan Turville-Petre. Odense 1983.

Miller, William Ian. *Bloodtaking and Peacemaking: Feud, Law, and Society in Saga Iceland.* Chicago 1990.

Nordal, Sigurður. *Icelandic Culture.* Trans. Vilhjálmur T. Bjarnar. Ithaca, NY 1990.

Ólason, Vésteinn. *Dialogues with the Viking Age: Narration and Representation in the Sagas of Icelanders.* Trans. Andrew Wawn. Reykjavík 1997.

Pálsson, Hermann. *Art and Ethics in Hrafnkel's Saga*. Copenhagen 1971.

The Poetic Edda. Trans. Carolyne Larrington. Oxford 1996.

Pulsiano, Phillip and Wolf, Kirsten, *et al.* (eds.). *Medieval Scandinavia: An Encyclopedia*. New York 1993.

Sawyer, Birgit and Peter. *Medieval Scandinavia: From Conversion to Reformation, circa 800–1500*. Minneapolis 1993.

Schach, Paul. *Icelandic Sagas*. Boston 1984.

Sigurðsson, Gísli. *The Gaelic Influence in Iceland: Historical and Literary Contacts*. Reykjavík 1988.

Steblin-Kamenskij, M. I. *The Saga Mind*. Trans. Kenneth H. Ober. Odense 1973.

Strayer, Joseph R. (editor-in-chief). *Dictionary of the Middle Ages*. New York 1982–8.

Sturluson, Snorri. *Edda*. Trans. Anthony Faulkes. London 1987.

—. *Heimskringla*. Trans. Samuel Laing, revised Jacqueline Simpson and Peter Foote. 3 vols. London 1961–4.

—. *Heimskringla*. Trans. Lee M. Hollander. Austin, Tex. 1964.

Sveinsson, Einar Ólafur. *The Age of the Sturlungs: Icelandic Civilization in the Thirteenth Century*. Trans. Jóhann S. Hannesson. *Islandica* XXXVI. Ithaca, NY 1953.

—. *Njáls Saga: A Literary Masterpiece*. Ed. and trans. Paul Schach. Lincoln, Neb. 1971.

Tucker, John (ed.). *Sagas of the Icelanders*. New York 1989.

Turville-Petre, E. O. G. *Origins of Icelandic Literature*. Oxford 1953.

—. *Myth and Religion of the North*. London 1964.

—. *Scaldic Poetry*. Oxford 1976.

A Note on the Texts

The sagas and tales in this book are reprinted from *The Complete Sagas of Icelanders I–V*, published 1997 by Leifur Eiríksson Publishing, Iceland, with minor alterations. This was the first complete edition of the forty sagas of Icelanders in English, and included forty-nine tales. All the material was translated specifically for the edition, with the exception of three sagas that were adapted to the general editorial policy. Robert Kellogg's introduction has been expanded to reflect more closely the thematic framework of the present volume.

Örnólfur Thorsson chose the sagas and tales and supervised this volume, provided material for prefaces to individual sagas and compiled the explanatory material accompanying each. Gísli Sigurðsson wrote the preface to the *Vinland Sagas* and produced material for the Vinland maps. Bernard Scudder contributed to the prefaces and reworked all the explanatory material into the final English versions. Robert Kellogg and Robert Cook also read all the prefaces and made invaluable suggestions. Jean-Pierre Biard designed the maps. Örnólfur Thorsson and Viðar Hreinsson produced the Index of Characters.

The Reference section comes from Vol. V of *The Complete Sagas of Icelanders*, but in a slightly altered form here.

THEMES AND CLASSIFICATION — A REPRESENTATIVE SELECTION

All the *Sagas of Icelanders*, also known as the *Family Sagas*, share certain characteristics of form and content, but they can be classified into several closer groupings. Three sets of criteria are generally used to classify them: time of writing and textual considerations; historical and geographical setting;

and literary considerations (in particular theme and point of view). The present selection includes texts from most periods in the 'Age of Writing', but its chief aim is to show the diversity of good literature within the family saga canon, and it contains representatives of all main literary types, set in virtually all the known Viking world.

Many sagas in this selection begin with a prelude in Norway and trace the arrival of a particular family as settlers in a particular part of Iceland. Sometimes Norway supplies more than distant noble roots for the main characters – in *Gisli Sursson's Saga*, for example, Gisli displays the blind obedience to the revenge ethic which will send him into exile in Iceland too, and in *Egil's Saga* the first third of the action takes place in Norway, launching the running feud with the royal family there. The main focus of most sagas, however, is the third and fourth generation after the settlement. Although the *Sagas of Icelanders* as a whole span virtually all the Viking Age from the second half of the ninth century to the middle of the eleventh, most deal in the greatest detail with 975 to 1025. By this time the political and legal structure of the Commonwealth was firmly in place, so that the dominant theme of the conflict between individual and society has a clear frame of reference. Perhaps even more significantly, the fulcrum of these fifty years is the adoption of Christianity in 1000, when a new system of values and ethics replaced the ancient Viking code of personal honour, and also when the seeds of a new, centralized power structure were sown. The maturing society of farmers would become increasingly intolerant of the heroic individualism on whose vision and ideals it was originally founded. The friction between public law without executive power and men of action driven by personal motivation is crucial to the plots of most sagas.

A basic distinction can be established according to whether the point of view of the saga is the individual or society.

Biographical sagas concentrate on an individual and his conflicts and relation-ships either with other individuals (seen in the *sagas of poets and warriors* such as Egil or Gunnlaug Serpent-tongue) or with society as a whole (in the *sagas of outlaws* such as Gisli Sursson). Since outlaws live on the fringes of society, we often see in them elements of a supernatural world which contrasts with the typical saga realism, although it is generally described with the same objective nonchalance. Significantly, we also see elements of fantasy on the fringes of the known geographical world in Greenland, both in the otherwise realistic *Vinland Sagas* and in the fantastical *Saga of*

Biographies

SAGAS FROM GREENLAND AND VINLAND

Eirik the Red's Saga
The Saga of the Greenlanders
The Tale of the Greenlanders

Sagas of Feud

POETS AND WARRIORS

Egil's Saga
Kormak's Saga
The Saga of Hallfred the Troublesome Poet
The Saga of Bjorn, Champion of the Hitardal People
The Saga of Gunnlaug Serpent-tongue
The Saga of the Sworn Brothers
Killer-Glum's Saga
Viglund's Saga

OUTLAWS

Gisli Sursson's Saga
The Saga of Grettir the Strong
The Saga of Hord and the People of Holm

CHAMPIONS

Bard's Saga
The Saga of Finnbogi the Mighty
The Saga of the People of Kjalarnes
The Saga of Thord Menace
The Saga of the People of Floi
The Saga of Ref the Sly
Gold-Thorir's Saga
The Saga of Gunnar, the Fool of Keldugnup

REGIONAL FEUDS

SOUTH ICELAND: Njal's Saga
WEST ICELAND: **The Saga of the People of Laxardal**
The Saga of the Slayings on the Heath
NORTH ICELAND: The Saga of the People of Ljosavatn
Valla-Ljot's Saga
The Saga of the People of Svarfadardal
The Saga of the People of Reykjadal and of Killer-Skuta
The Saga of the People of Vatnsdal
EAST ICELAND: The Saga of the People of Vopnafjord
The Saga of Droplaug's Sons
The Saga of the People of Fljotsdal
The Saga of Thorstein the White
Thorstein Sidu-Hallsson's Saga

WEALTH AND POWER

The Saga of the People of Eyri
Hen-Thorir's Saga
The Saga of the Confederates
Olkofri's Saga
The Saga of Hrafnkel Frey's Godi
The Saga of Havard of Isafjord

Individual

Society

Types of Sagas

Ref the Sly. Ref is an example of a champion, a strong individual who defends the weak or undertakes ordeals. This branch of saga writing often has a picaresque or roguish element to it and is sometimes closer to folk legend than to history. Certain episodes in *Gisli Sursson's Saga* and *Egil's Saga* are in this vein too; interestingly, even champions have to perform their noble deeds either outside Iceland or outside human society in outlawry.

Opposing the biographical sagas are the *sagas of feuds*, typically located in a relatively small district which in a sense assumes the central role in the action. An example is *The Saga of the People of Vatnsdal*, which is a family saga describing five generations of chieftains who live in a district with which they clearly have strong emotional bonds. The concept of the man of authority, the godi, is essential to this saga, but even more to two others spanning a much shorter time, *The Saga of Hrafnkel Frey's Godi* and *The Saga of the Confederates*. These two sagas are succinct but thorough examinations of local power and authority: the emergence of a leader of men, his duties as well as his rights, his response to subversion of his authority. It could be said that the leader figure is the antithesis of the outlaw figure at odds with society, and of the inwardly motivated poet at odds with himself.

In the longer sagas of feud a vast gallery of characters is introduced, but inevitably a few strong personalities dominate the stage – for example Ingimund the Old and his son Jokul in Vatnsdal, and the triangle Bolli, Kjartan and Gudrun in Laxardal. *The Saga of the People of Laxardal*, like *Njal's Saga*, is usually regarded as superior to the majority of the regional feud sagas, a masterpiece of epic narrative with tragic dimensions. The saga charts the dissent and dissolution within a single family as sharply etched characters struggle nobly through a series of fated events over which they have no control. Feuds escalate from trivial local squabbles into unstoppable vendettas. The male protagonists are splendid figures who die heroic deaths, while the women are strong characters who engineer much of the action.

Somewhere between the two main saga classifications are the two *Vinland Sagas* and one tale, which describe the western outposts of the Viking world: Eirik the Red's discovery of Greenland and settlement there as leader of a large community, and the first European voyages to North America by his son Leif and later by Gudrid Thorbjarnardottir and Thorfinn Karlsefni.

From a historical perspective, the sagas in this selection map the Viking world and extend across the entire Viking Age: the movement from Norway, the flowering of national culture and localized settlements in Iceland, and the exploration and experience of new worlds. Characters and events recur

The Saga of

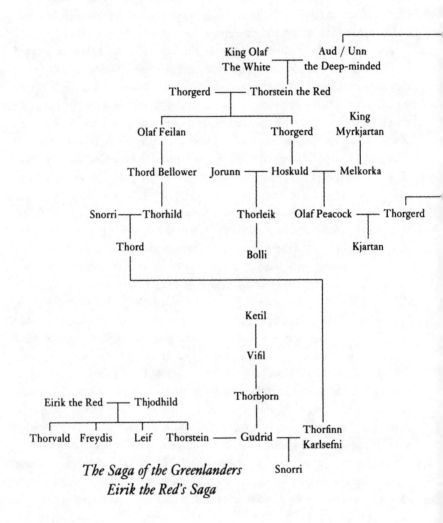

The Saga of the Greenlanders
Eirik the Red's Saga

Family Ties between Six Sagas

the People of Laxardal

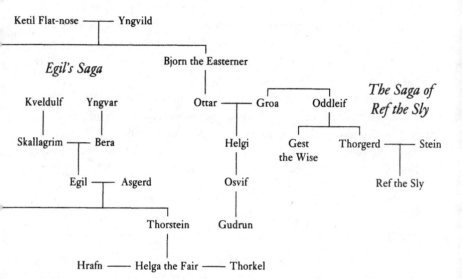

*The Saga of Gunnlaug
Serpent-tongue*

from one saga to the next, seen from different perspectives but nonetheless with striking resemblances, somehow inviting us to believe that the saga world is a large, unified tapestry of which we only see parts at a time. The settlement by Unn (Aud) the Deep-minded features in both *The Saga of the People of Laxardal* and *Eirik the Red's Saga*; Gest Oddleifsson is the wise counsellor in both the Laxardal saga and *The Saga of Ref the Sly*; in *The Saga of Gunnlaug Serpent-tongue*, poets clash for the love of Helga the Fair, who is the granddaughter of the hero of *Egil's Saga*, and so forth.

The recurrence of dramatis personae and action means that the sagas overlap thematically as well, so that no classification can be absolute. Classification by theme is nothing more than a way of highlighting certain salient features and guiding the reader towards a deeper appreciation of each saga's artistry and the rich dynamism of the saga world.

THE TRANSLATIONS

The editorial aims of *The Complete Sagas of Icelanders* were: (1) to produce accurate and readable modern English versions of the original texts, and (2) to reflect the homogeneity of the saga world, by means of a co-ordinated translation of key vocabulary, concepts and phrases, but at the same time to capture the individuality of the separate sagas. As Robert Kellogg states in the Introduction, the world of the sagas is a unified whole in several senses: the geographical setting, time frame, social background and to some extent the characters of the sagas are identical, and in addition the narrative technique defines these works as belonging to a conscious genre. The thirty translators, all native speakers of English, were supplied by the Editorial Team with directions and suggestions which would ensure the desired consistency. Each translation was read over by an Icelandic scholar, and later by a native English-speaker.

The Reference section explains a number of recurrent key terms and concepts: legal terms (such as outlawry and compensation), legislative structures (e.g. Spring Assembly, Autumn Meeting and Lawspeaker), social ranks (godi, earl and slave), games (ball game, horse-fight, board-game), customs and rituals (arch of raised turf and foster-), supernatural elements (berserk, shape-shifter, scorn-pole, troll and giant), the ancient calendar and important days of the year (Moving Days and Winter Nights), weights and measures (hand, ounce and hundred), and certain physical details, such as those relating to the layout of houses (main room, high seat and bed closet) and farms (hayfield wall and shieling). Where practicable, some distinctions between types of ships (e.g. longship, knorr) and weapons (halberd) have also been established by co-ordinating the vocabulary. Some additional entries of a general nature have been included in the Glossary.

SPELLING CONVENTIONS AND PROPER NOUNS

English equivalents have been used for Icelandic letters in personal and place names: Þ/TH, Ð/D, Á/A, É/E, Í/I, Ó/O, Ú/U, Ý/Y, Æ/AE, Ö/O. For example, *Þaralátursfjörður* becomes Tharalatursfjord, after the nominative ending has been dropped as well. Icelandic is an inflected language, in which the endings of words change according to grammatical context. A main rule in the treatment of personal and place-names for this edition has been to drop the nominative singular endings and use the stems instead. Thus, the name *Egil·l* becomes Egil; and the modern Icelandic *Auður* (old Icelandic *Auð·r*) becomes Aud. For the sake of consistency in the appearance of the English, the *·ur/·r* ending has also been dropped even when strictly speaking it belongs to the stem: thus *Ósvíf·ur/·r*, for example, becomes Osvif. Plural endings are common in place-names and this distinction has been retained: for example *Breiðabólstaður* (singular) becomes Breidabolstad, but *Hrafnkelsstaðir* (plural) is written Hrafnkelsstadir.

Nicknames are a common feature of Old Icelandic texts, and these are translated when the meaning is clear and makes sense. In some cases, however, depending on the context, they are left untranslated in the text but suggested translations are given in parentheses the first time they occur. All nicknames which occur in more than one saga have been standardized. Some nicknames assume the full status of proper names, as for instance when Thorfinn Karlsefni is referred to as Karlsefni.

For easier recognition, the modern form of mainland Scandi..avian place-names has been used when it is known, with a few exceptions. In place-names outside Scandinavia, the common English equivalent is used when known; otherwise the Icelandic form has been transliterated. The meaning of place-names in Icelandic is often self-evident and the last part of a place-name usually refers to a topographical feature. The modern Icelandic form of place-names is preferred, but readers should bear in mind that a few are now lost and do not appear on modern maps. In some cases place-names are translated in parentheses, for example when there is a direct association with a character or when the story hinges on an understanding of the name. In place-names that include topographical features (e.g. Hvita = lit. White river), the feature is translated in the first appearance of the name in each saga (e.g. 'the Hvita river' first, and then usually 'Hvita'). The last element of the longest types of place-names is often translated, as in words ending in *heiði* (e.g. Arnarvatnsheiði = Arnarvatn heath). Variant forms of the same place-name have been standardized, generally on the basis of modern Icelandic spelling or usage.

SAGAS

EGIL'S SAGA

Egils saga Skallagrímssonar

Time of action: 850–1000
Time of writing: 1220–40

Egil's Saga is acknowledged as one of the masterpieces of the genre, a magnificently wrought portrait of poet, warrior and farmer Egil Skallagrimsson, loosely contained within the framework of the family saga, but with an unusual twist – the feud that Egil and his forebears wage is with the kings of Norway.

Spanning some 150 years, much of the action takes place outside Iceland and repeatedly returns to Norway, where the saga starts and where its main themes are laid out against the background of King Harald Fair-hair's merciless unification of the realm. Egil's grandfather Kveldulf and father Skallagrim refuse allegiance to the king, while Kveldulf's other son Thorolf enters his service but dies at the king's own hands, the victim of malicious slanders. Beyond the closely mapped sites in Norway, the setting extends into vaguer territory elsewhere in Scandinavia, deep into the Baltic and East Europe, far north to Finnmark, and to England – much of the known Viking world at that time. Often the adventures and heroics are larger than life, but are outrageous and delightfully gross rather than implausible or fantastic. Egil's enemies are motivated by treachery, self-interest and malice, and he confronts them as his forebears did, with the family traits of obstinacy, ruthlessness, animal strength and an instinctive inability to accept authority. To his friend and advocate Arinbjorn in Norway, however, and to others whose favour he wins, Egil shows loyalty and unswerving devotion, and he heroically adheres to a brutal but not entirely unappealing sense of justice.

The action in Iceland falls into several phases. Skallagrim settles at Borg and is an ideal of pioneer and craftsman, but the social order which he builds is threatened by the unruly and rebellious Egil. When Egil many years later

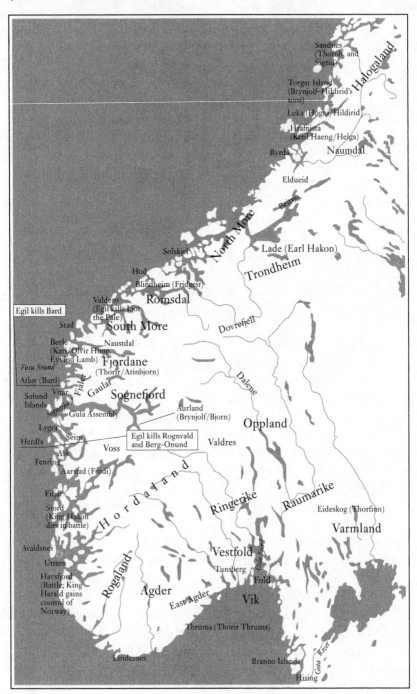

Sandnes
(Thorolf and
Sigrid)

Torgar Island
(Brynjolf–Hildirid's
sons)

Leka (Hogni/Hildirid)

Hrafnista
(Ketil Haeng/Helga)

Byrda

Naumdal

Eldueid

Halogaland

Beitsio

North More

Lade (Earl Hakon)

Solskjel

Trondheim

Hod
Blindheim (Fridgeir)

Valdero
(Egil kills Ljot
the Pale)

Romsdal

Egil kills Bard

Stad

South More

Dovrefjell

Berle
(Kari/Olvir Hump,
Eyvind Lamb)

Naustdal

Furu Sound

Fjordane
(Thorir/Arinbjorn)

Atloy (Bard)

Solund
Islands

Vitar

Fialir

Gaular

Sognefjord

Dalene

Sognefjord

Gula Assembly

Aurland
(Brynjolf/Bjorn)

Oppland

Lygra

Seim

Egil kills Rognvald
and Berg-Onund

Herdla

Ask

Voss

Valdres

Fenring

Aarstad (Frodi)

H o r d a l a n d

Ringerike

Raumarike

Fitjar

Eideskog (Thorfinn)

Stord
(King Hakon
dies in battle)

Varmland

Avaldsnes

Utsten

Vestfold

Ula Fjord

Havsfjord
(Battle; King
Harald gains
control of
Norway)

Rogaland

Agder

Tunsberg

Fold

East Agder

Vik

Lindesnes

Thruma (Thorir Thruma)

Branno Islands

Gota River

Hising

Norway

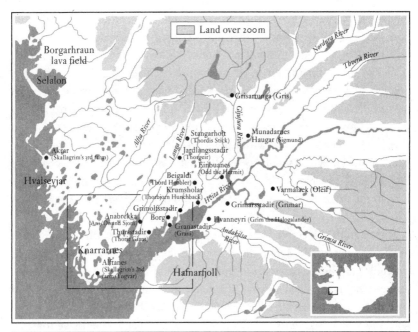

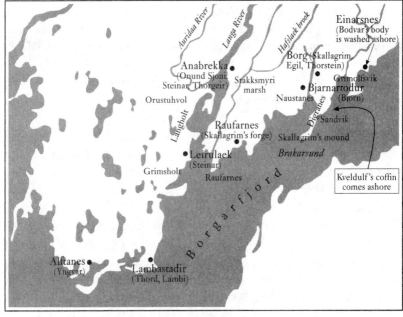

Borgarfjord

inherits his farm, he becomes a respected figure of authority himself, and does not engage in feuds in Iceland; his main involvement in a dispute occurs when he rules in his son Thorstein's favour, acting as a figure of authority rather than of force. However, the trick he plans to humiliate the greedy thingmen in his eighties shows that his relish for provocation has never been entirely lost. At intervals he had been drawn away from Borg to pursue his feud with the Norwegian royal family, which escalates into a sheer battle of personalities with King Eirik Blood-axe and Queen Gunnhild. After their deaths he seems to realize that Norway is gradually changing into a world in which he can never be accepted, and Iceland becomes for him, as for so many other saga heroes, a kind of retirement home for ageing Vikings.

Although the objective style of the sagas does not allow direct revelation of the characters' thoughts, the portrayal of Egil is exceptionally rich in psychology. His gestures are dramatic, almost ritualistic, as he sulks or broods, suffers personal sorrow in silence, flies into a rage or succumbs to childlike joy on receiving a noble gift. And while the saga is clearly a man's world in which Egil fears no adversary, he is timid and submissive towards women, as shown by his almost blushing love for his brother's widow Asgerd, who later becomes his wife, and by the way he allows his daughter Thorgerd to trick him out of his sympathy-seeking act of pining away after the death of his sons.

Scholars have pointed out the psychological tension between the ugly Egil and his 'exemplary' brother Thorolf, the jealousy which sometimes manifests itself in irresponsible pranks and then turns into self-reproach after Thorolf's death in battle. Egil seems to have inherited this jealousy from his father, who was always overshadowed by his own brother, also named Thorolf, in the first part of the saga. Macabre tension between father and son is another psychological theme: Skallagrim even comes close to killing the young Egil once in a savage, shape-shifter's fury.

Another window into Egil's psyche is his poetry, which ranks with the most personal as well as the most accomplished in the sagas. We see Egil glorifying his own ugliness as if it were an archetypal landscape, depicting the living forces of nature and mythology in brisk, dramatic strokes, and exalting the values he cherishes most. The scene where Egil saves his life in York by reciting his 'Head Ransom' to King Eirik abounds in irony, since the poem has an empty, tongue-in-cheek ring to it compared to his other verse and seems, so to speak, to go over the king's head anyway. By contrast, the eulogy for Arinbjorn is heartfelt, engaged, stacked with monumental metaphor and tinged with nostalgia for the lost Viking lifestyle. In 'The Loss of My Sons' Egil lays his soul bare, delves into thwarted ambition for his family and unrealized affection in the bonds that have been lost, and breaks with the god Odin who has given him gifts in both poetry and war, but deprived him of personal fortune.

Egil's Saga is preserved in a number of vellum manuscripts and fragments dating from the second half of the thirteenth century onwards, although the most important is *Möðruvallabók* (AM 132 fol., dated 1330–70). Composed in the second quarter of the thirteenth century, the saga is generally attributed on stylistic and other grounds to Iceland's greatest medieval historian, Snorri Sturluson (1179–1241), who was a descendant of Egil. If the attribution is correct, *Egil's Saga* is the only one whose author is known. It is translated here by Bernard Scudder from the version printed in *Íslendinga sögur*, vol. 1 (Reykjavík 1987), and incorporates a number of emendations based on Bjarni Einarsson's new reading of *Möðruvallabók* and paper manuscripts deriving from it.

I There was a man named Ulf, the son of Bjalfi and of Hallbera, the daughter of Ulf the Fearless. She was the sister of Hallbjorn Half-troll from Hrafnista, the father of Ketil Haeng. Ulf was so big and strong that no man was a match for him; and he was still only a youth when he became a Viking and went raiding. His companion was Kari from Berle, a man of high birth who had the strength and courage to perform great deeds. Kari was a berserk. He and Ulf shared all they owned and were close friends.

When they gave up plundering, Kari returned to his farm on Berle, a very wealthy man. Kari had three children, two sons called Eyvind Lamb and Olvir Hump, and a daughter named Salbjorg. She was a beautiful woman of firm character. Ulf married her, then he too returned to his farm. He was rich in both lands and possessions. He became a landholder like his ancestors and was a powerful figure.

Ulf is said to have been a very clever farmer. He made a habit of getting up early to inspect what his farmhands or craftsmen were doing and to keep an eye on his cattle and cornfields. Sometimes he would talk to people who were in need of his advice, for he was shrewd and always ready to make useful suggestions. But every day towards evening he would grow so bad-tempered that few people dared even address him. He always went to sleep early in the evening and woke up early in the morning. People claimed he was a shape-shifter and they called him Kveldulf (Night Wolf).

Kveldulf and his wife had two sons. The elder one was named Thorolf and the younger one Grim, and they both grew up to be big, strong men like their father. Thorolf was an attractive and highly accomplished man. He took after his mother's side of the family, a cheerful, generous man, energetic and very eager to prove his worth. He was popular with everyone. Grim was swarthy and ugly, resembling his father in both appearance and character. He turned out to be an active man; he was gifted at working in wood and iron, and grew to be a great craftsman. In winter he would often set off on a fishing boat to lay nets for herring, taking many farmhands with him.

When Thorolf was twenty, he made ready to go raiding, and Kveldulf gave him a longship. Kari's sons Eyvind and Olvir joined him, with a large band of men and another longship. In the summer they went raiding and took plenty of booty which they shared out among themselves. They went raiding for several summers, spending the winters at home with their fathers. Thorolf brought many precious things back to give to his parents, for in those days it was easy to win both wealth and renown. Kveldulf was very old by then, and his sons had reached full manhood.

2 Audbjorn was king of Fjordane at this time. One of his earls was Hroald, who had a son named Thorir.

Atli the Slender, another earl, lived at Gaular and had three sons, Hallstein, Holmstein and Herstein, and a daughter called Solveig the Fair.

One autumn when there was a great gathering at Gaular for the autumn feast, Olvir Hump saw Solveig and began courting her. Later he asked for her hand, but the earl, not considering him worthy enough, would not marry her to him. Afterwards, Olvir composed many love poems and grew so obsessed with her that he gave up raiding, leaving Thorolf and Eyvind to go by themselves.

3 King Harald inherited the titles of his father Halfdan the Black and swore an oath not to cut or comb his hair until he had become sole king of Norway. He was called Harald Tangle-hair.* He did battle with the neighbouring kings and defeated them, as is told in long accounts. Afterwards he took over Oppland, and proceeded northwards to Trondheim where he fought many battles before gaining full control of all Trondheim district.

After that he intended to go north to Naumdal and take on the brothers Herlaug and Hrollaug, who were kings there, but when they heard that he was on his way, Herlaug and eleven of his men went into the mound they had spent the past three years building, and had it closed upon them. Hrollaug tumbled from power and took the title of earl instead, then submitted to Harald and handed over his kingdom. King Harald thereby took over Naumdal province and Halogaland and appointed men to govern there in his name.

Leaving Trondheim with his fleet of ships, he went south to More where

* Harald became known as Fair-hair after unifying Norway.

he won a battle against King Hunthjof, who was killed there. Then Harald took over North More and Romsdal.

Meanwhile, Hunthjof's son Solvi Chopper, who had escaped, went to King Arnvid in South More and asked for his help.

'Although this misfortune has befallen us now,' he said, 'it will not be very long before the same happens to you, because I think Harald will be here soon, once he has brought slavery and suffering to everyone he chooses in North More and Romsdal. You will face the same choice we had: either to defend your property and freedom by staking all the men you can hope to muster – and I will provide my forces too against such aggression and injustice – or to follow the course taken by the people of Naumdal who voluntarily entered servitude and became Harald's slaves. My father felt it an honour to die nobly as king of his own realm rather than become subservient to another king in his old age. I think you will feel the same, and so will any other stalwarts who want to prove their worth.'

Persuaded by such words, the king resolved to muster forces and defend his land. He and Solvi swore an alliance and sent word to King Audbjorn, who ruled Fjordane province, to join forces with them. When the messengers delivered this message to King Audbjorn he discussed it with his friends, all of whom advised him to gather forces and join the people of More as he had been asked. King Audbjorn sent around an arrow of war as a signal to call men to arms throughout his kingdom and dispatched messengers to powerful men asking them to meet him.

But when the messengers told Kveldulf that the king wanted him to bring all the men on his farm to join him, he replied, 'The king would consider it my duty to go with him if he had to defend his land and battles had to be fought in Fjordane province. But I don't think it's any duty of mine to go up north to More and fight there to defend other people's land. Tell your king straight out when you meet him, that while he rushes off to battle Kveldulf will be staying at home, and will not muster any forces or set off to fight Harald Tangle-hair. I have a feeling Harald has plenty of good fortune in store for him, but our king doesn't have enough to fill the palm of his hand.'

The messengers went back to the king and told him how their errand had turned out, and Kveldulf stayed at home on his farm.

4   King Audbjorn took the band of men he had gathered and went north to More, where he met King Arnvid and Solvi Chopper, and together they amassed great forces. By then, King Harald had arrived from the north

with his forces, and the two sides clashed on the fjord near Solskjel Island. A fierce battle ensued, with heavy losses on both sides. On Harald's side, the two earls Asgaut and Asbjorn were killed, along with two of Earl Hakon of Lade's sons, Grjotgard and Herlaug, and many other great men, while King Arnvid and King Audbjorn were killed on the side from More. Solvi Chopper escaped by fleeing and became a great Viking, and often raided in Harald's kingdom, which was how he earned his nickname. Afterwards, King Harald conquered South More.

King Audbjorn's brother Vemund kept control of Fjordane province and became its king. This happened late in autumn, and King Harald's men advised him not to head south past Stad at that time, so Harald appointed Earl Rognvald to rule North and South More and Romsdal, and returned to Trondheim, keeping a large band of men with him.

The same autumn, Earl Atli's sons attacked Olvir Hump's farm, intending to kill him. They had far too many men for Olvir to fend off, so he fled. He went to More, met King Harald and became one of his men, then went north to Trondheim with the king that autumn and became close friends with him. He stayed with the king for a long time and became his poet.

That winter, Earl Rognvald travelled inland across lake Eidesjo and south to Fjordane, and received word about King Vemund's movements. Rognvald turned up one night at a place called Naustdal where Vemund was at a feast. He stormed the house and burned the king and ninety men inside. Kari from Berle joined Earl Rognvald with a fully manned longship and they went to More together. Rognvald took the ship that King Vemund had owned, and all the possessions he could manage. Then Kari travelled north to Trondheim to meet King Harald, and entered his service.

The following spring King Harald sailed southwards along the coast with his fleet, conquering the Fjordane and Fjaler provinces and appointing his own men to rule them. He put Earl Hroald in charge of Fjordane province.

Once King Harald had taken over the kingdoms he had recently won, he kept a close watch on the landholders and powerful farmers and everyone else he suspected would be likely to rebel, and gave them the options of entering his service or leaving the country, or a third choice of suffering hardship or paying with their lives; some had their arms and legs maimed. In each province King Harald took over all the estates and all the land, habited or uninhabited, and even the sea and lakes. All the farmers were made his tenants, and everyone who worked the forests and dried salt, or hunted on land or at sea, was made to pay tribute to him.

Many people fled the country to escape this tyranny and settled various uninhabited parts of many places, to the east in Jamtland and Halsingland, and to the west in the Hebrides, the shire of Dublin, Ireland, Normandy in France, Caithness in Scotland, the Orkney Isles and Shetland Isles, and the Faroe Islands. And at this time, Iceland was discovered.

5   King Harald stayed with his army in Fjordane, and sent out messengers through the countryside to meet the people that he felt he had reason to contact but who had not joined him.

The king's messengers went to Kveldulf's and received a warm welcome.

They told him their business, saying that the king wanted Kveldulf to go to see him: 'He has heard that you are a man of high birth and standing,' they said. 'You have the chance to receive great honour from the king, because he is eager to be joined by people who are renowned for their strength of body and heart.'

Kveldulf replied that he was too old for going on fighting ships: 'So I will stay at home now and give up serving kings.'

'Then let your son go to see the king,' the messenger said. 'He's a big and brave man. The king will make you a landholder if you serve him.'

'I don't want to be a landholder while my father is still alive,' Grim said, 'because he is my superior for as long as he lives.'

The messengers departed, and when they reached the king they told him everything Kveldulf had said to them. The king grew surly, remarking that these must be arrogant people, and he could not tell what their motivation was.

Olvir Hump was present then and asked the king not to be angry.

'I will go and see Kveldulf,' he said, 'and he will want to meet you when he knows how important it is to you.'

So Olvir went to see Kveldulf and, after describing the king's rage, told him he had no choice but to go to the king or send his son in his place, and that they would be shown great honour if they obeyed. He spoke at length, and rightly so, about how well the king repaid his men with both wealth and status.

Kveldulf said he had an intuition that 'this king will not bring my family much good fortune. I won't go to meet him, but if Thorolf comes home this summer it will be easy to persuade him to go and become one of the king's men. So tell the king that I will be friendly towards him and encourage every-one who sets store by my words to do the same. As far as acting on his behalf goes, I will maintain the same arrangement I had under the previous king, if that is what he wants, and then see how the two of us get along together'.

Olvir returned to the king and told him that Kveldulf would send him one of his sons, but that the more suitable one was not at home at that time. The king let the matter rest there. In the summer he crossed Sognefjord, and when autumn came he prepared to go north to Trondheim.

6   Kveldulf's son Thorolf and Eyvind Lamb returned from their Viking expedition that autumn, and Thorolf went to stay with his father.

When they were talking together, Thorolf asked about the business of Harald's messengers. Kveldulf told him that the king had sent word ordering him or one of his sons to join him.

'What did you tell them?' asked Thorolf.

'I said what I was thinking, that I would never join King Harald, nor would you or your brother, if I had any say in the matter. I think we will end up losing our lives because of that king.'

'That is quite different from what I foresee,' said Thorolf, 'because I feel I will earn great honour from him. I'm determined to go and see the king and join him, for I know for a fact that there are nothing but men of valour among his followers. Joining their ranks sounds a very attractive proposition, if they will take me. They live a much better life than anyone else in this country. And I'm told that the king is very generous to his men and no less liberal in granting advancement and power to people he thinks worthy of it. I've also heard about all the people who turn their backs on him and spurn his friendship, and they never become great men – some of them are forced to flee the country, and others are made his tenants. It strikes me as odd for such a wise and ambitious man as you, Father, not to be grateful to accept the honour that the king offered you. But if you claim to have an intuition that this king will cause us misfortune and want to become our enemy, why didn't you join the one you had sworn allegiance to, and do battle against him? Being neither his friend nor his enemy seems to me the most dishonourable course of all.'

'My foreboding that no one would triumph in battle against Harald Tangle-hair in More came true,' replied Kveldulf. 'And likewise it is true that Harald will do great harm to my kinsmen. But you decide what you want to do for yourself, Thorolf. I have no worries about your not being accepted as their equal if you join King Harald's men, or being a match for the best of them in the face of any danger. Just avoid aiming too high or contending with stronger men than yourself, but never give way to them either.'

When Thorolf was making ready to leave, Kveldulf accompanied him down to his ship, embraced him and wished him farewell, saying they should meet in good health again. Then Thorolf went north to meet the king.

7   There was a man named Bjorgolf who lived on Torgar Island in Halogaland, a powerful and wealthy landholder who was descended from a mountain giant, as his strength and size bore witness. His son, Brynjolf, resembled him closely. In his old age, when his wife had died, Bjorgolf handed over all control of his affairs to his son and found him a wife. Brynjolf married Helga, daughter of Ketil Haeng from Hrafnista. Their son Bard turned out to be tall and handsome at an early age and became a man of great accomplishments.

One autumn Bjorgolf and his son invited a lot of people to a feast, and they were the most noble of all those present. According to custom they cast lots every evening to decide which pairs would sit together and share the drinking horns. One of the guests was a man named Hogni who had a farm at Leka. He was wealthy, outstandingly handsome and wise, but came from an ordinary family and had achieved his position through his own efforts alone. He had an attractive daughter named Hildirid, who was allotted a seat next to Bjorgolf. They talked together at length that evening and he thought the girl was beautiful. A short while later the feast ended.

The same autumn old Bjorgolf set off from home on a boat that he owned, with a crew of thirty men. When they reached Leka, twenty of them went up to the farm, leaving the other ten behind to guard the boat. Hogni came out to meet him at the farmhouse and greeted him warmly, inviting him and his men to stay there. Bjorgolf accepted the offer and they went into the main room. After they had changed their sailing clothes for tunics, Hogni had vats of ale brought in and his daughter served the guests.

Bjorgolf called Hogni over and said, 'The reason I have come here is to take your daughter home with me and I will celebrate our wedding here now.'

Hogni saw he had no other choice than to let Bjorgolf have his way. Bjorgolf paid an ounce of gold for Hildirid and he shared a bed with her afterwards. She went home with him to Torgar, but his son Brynjolf disapproved of the whole business.

Bjorgolf and Hildirid had two sons, Harek and Hraerek.

Then Bjorgolf died, and when he had been buried, Brynjolf made Hildirid and her two sons leave Torgar, and she returned to her father's farm at Leka where she brought them up. They grew up to be handsome men, small but clever, like their mother's side of the family. Everyone called them Hildirid's sons. Brynjolf held them in low regard and did not let them have any of their inheritance. Hildirid was Hogni's heir, and she and her sons inherited the farm at Leka where they lived in plenty. Brynjolf's son Bard and Hildirid's sons were about the same age.

For a long time, Brynjolf and his father Bjorgolf had travelled to Finnmark collecting tribute.

In the north, in Halogaland, there is a large, fine island in Vefsna fjord called Alost, with a farm on it called Sandnes. A wise landholder named Sigurd lived there, the richest man in that part of the north. His daughter Sigrid was considered the finest match in Halogaland; as his only child, she was his heir.

Brynjolf's son Bard set off from home on a boat with a crew of thirty men, and sailed north to Alost where he visited Sigurd at Sandnes. Bard announced that his business was to ask for Sigrid's hand in marriage. His proposal was answered favourably and Bard was promised her for his bride. The wedding was set for the following summer, when Bard was to go back north to fetch his bride.

8   That summer King Harald sent word to the powerful men in Halogaland and summoned all those who had not yet been to meet him. Brynjolf decided to go and took his son Bard with him, and in the autumn they went south to Trondheim and met the king. He welcomed them and made Brynjolf a landholder, granting him revenues in addition to those he already had, as well as the right to collect tribute and trade in Finnmark and collect taxes in the mountain regions. Afterwards Brynjolf returned to his land, leaving Bard behind with the king's men.

Of all his followers, the king held his poets in highest regard, and let them sit on the bench opposite his high seat. Farthest inside sat Audun the Uninspired, who was the oldest and had been poet to King Harald's father, Halfdan the Black. Next to him sat Thorbjorn Raven, and then Olvir Hump. Bard was given the seat next to him and was nicknamed Bard the White or Bard the Strong. He was popular with everyone and become a close companion of Olvir's.

The same autumn, Kveldulf's son Thorolf and Eyvind Lamb, son of Kari from Berle, came to the king and were well received by him. They arrived with a good crew on a twenty-seater swift warship that they had used on Viking raids, and were given a place to stay in the guests' quarters with their men.

After staying for what they thought was a suitable length of time, they decided to go to see the king. Kari and Olvir Hump accompanied them and they greeted the king.

Olvir told the king that Kveldulf's son was there: 'I told you in the summer that Kveldulf would send him to you. He will stand by all his promises to you, and you may now see as a clear token of his desire for full friendship with you that he has sent his son to serve you, a fine figure of a man as you can see for yourself. Kveldulf and all of us implore you to receive Thorolf with the honour he is due and allow him to become a great man in your service.'

The king answered his request favourably and said he would do so, 'if Thorolf proves to be as accomplished as his brave looks promise'.

Then Thorolf swore allegiance to the king and joined his followers, while Kari and his son Eyvind Lamb went back south on the ship that Thorolf had arrived on. Kari went back to his land, and Eyvind too.

Thorolf stayed with the king, who gave him a seat between Olvir Hump and Bard, and they all became close companions.

Everyone agreed that Thorolf and Bard were equals in terms of looks, physique, strength and all accomplishments. Thorolf stayed there with the king, who was very well disposed to him and also to Bard.

When winter passed and summer came round, Bard asked the king's leave to go to fetch the bride to whom he had been betrothed the previous summer. Once the king became aware of Bard's obligation, he gave him leave to return home. When his leave had been granted, Bard asked Thorolf to go north with him, rightly pointing out that Thorolf might meet many kinsmen of high rank there whom he had never seen or heard of before. Thorolf thought this was a good idea, so they both got leave from the king, prepared a fine ship and crew for the journey, and set off when they were ready. When they reached Torgar island they sent men to tell Sigurd that Bard had arrived to claim the marriage they had arranged the previous summer. Sigurd replied he would keep every part of the bargain they had made, and they set the date for the wedding, which Bard and his men would go to Sandnes to attend. When the time came round, Brynjolf and Bard set off, taking a great number of important people with them, their relatives by birth and marriage. As Bard had said, Thorolf met many of his kinsmen there that he had never seen before. They went on their way until they reached Sandnes where a splendid feast was held. At the end of it Bard took his wife home and stayed there for the summer, and Thorolf was with him. In the autumn they went south to stay with the king and spent another winter with him.

That winter Brynjolf died. When Bard heard he had come into an inheritance, he asked for leave to go home, which the king granted him. Before they parted, Bard was made a landholder, as his father had been, and the king granted him all the revenues his father had held. Bard went home to his land and soon became an important figure, while Hildirid's sons received no inheritance, no more than they had before. Bard and his wife had a son named Grim. Thorolf stayed with the king in great honour.

9   King Harald mounted a massive expedition, assembling a fleet of warships and gathering troops from all over the country, then left Trondheim and headed south. He had heard that a great army had been gathered in Agder and Rogaland and Hordaland, mustered far and wide from the inland regions and Vik, with which many men of rank intended to defend their land against him.

The king moved his forces down from the north, sailing in his own ship. Thorolf, son of Kveldulf, Bard the White, and Olvir Hump and Eyvind Lamb, the sons of Kari from Berle, were at the prow, while the king's twelve berserks manned the gunwales. They clashed in Havsfjord in Rogaland, in the greatest battle King Harald ever fought, and there were heavy losses on both sides. The king kept his ship to the fore in the thick of battle. Eventually, King Harald won the battle. Thorir Long-chin, king of Agder, was killed there, and Kjotvi the Wealthy fled with all the men he had left who had not already surrendered. After the battle, when King Harald's troops were checked, many of them had been killed and others seriously wounded. Thorolf was badly injured, and Bard even worse, and none of the men from the fore of the ship came through unscathed apart from the berserks, whom iron could not bite. The king had his men's wounds treated, thanked them for the courage they had shown and presented them with gifts, singling out for praise the men whom he felt deserved it and promising them greater honour. He mentioned the skippers of the ships, and then the men in the prows and others who had been aforeships.

This was the last battle King Harald fought in Norway, for he met no resistance afterwards and gained control of the whole country. Those of his men who had a chance of living had their wounds treated, while the dead were prepared for burial according to the custom of that time.

Thorolf and Bard were laid up with their wounds. Thorolf's wounds gradually healed, but Bard's proved fatal.

He had the king called in and told him, 'If I should die of these wounds, I ask your leave to allow me to dispose of my bequest myself.'

Once the king had agreed, he continued: 'I want my kinsman and companion Thorolf to inherit everything, my lands and my goods, and I also want to place my wife and son in his care, for I trust him best of all men for that task.'

With the king's permission he sealed this arrangement as the law prescribed. After that he died and was prepared for burial, and was greatly mourned. Thorolf recovered from his wounds and accompanied the king that summer, and earned great renown.

When the king went north to Trondheim in the autumn, Thorolf asked his leave to go to Halogaland to take charge of the bequest which he had received in the summer from his kinsman Bard. The king granted him leave, giving him a message stating that Thorolf should take over everything Bard had left to him, with the king's consent and will, and gave his tokens as proof. Then the king made Thorolf a landholder and granted him all the revenues that Bard had previously held, and the right to collect tribute from the Lapps on the same terms. He gave Thorolf a fine, fully rigged longship and sent him on his journey as well equipped as he could be. Then Thorolf set off on his journey and he and the king parted in great friendship.

Thorolf was given a warm welcome when he reached Torgar Island. He told the people there how Bard had died and bequeathed his lands and goods and wife to him, stated the king's message and offered his tokens as proof.

Sigrid heard the news and took her husband's death as a great loss, but since she was already well acquainted with Thorolf and knew him to be a man of distinction and a good match for her, and since the king had ordered it, she and her friends decided that she should marry Thorolf if her father did not oppose the idea. After that, Thorolf took over all the duties there, including the king's tax-collecting.

Thorolf prepared to leave and had a longship with a crew of almost sixty men. When he was ready to sail he set off along the coast to the north, arriving at Alost on Sandnes one evening. They put into harbour, and when they had put up the awnings and got themselves ready, Thorolf went up to the farm with a band of twenty men. Sigurd greeted him warmly and invited him to stay, because they had been close acquaintances ever since Bard had married into his family. Thorolf and his men went into the main room of the farm and stayed there.

Sigurd sat down to talk with Thorolf and asked him if there was any news. Thorolf told him about the battle that had been fought in the south of Norway that summer and that many people Sigurd knew had been killed. He also told him how his son-in-law Bard had died from the wounds he had received in battle, and they agreed it was an enormous loss. Then Thorolf told Sigurd about the arrangement Bard had made with him before he died, repeating the king's message of consent and producing his tokens to prove it. Then Thorolf asked Sigurd for his daughter's hand in marriage. Sigurd took his proposal well, saying there were many points in its favour: it was the king's will, and also what Bard had requested, besides which he knew Thorolf well and considered him a fine match for his daughter. Sigurd consented readily, the couple were betrothed and the wedding was set to take place on Torgar Island that autumn.

Then Thorolf went back to his farm with his men and arranged a great feast there, and invited many people, including many of his high-ranking kinsmen. Sigurd arrived from the north, bringing a large longship and plenty of leading men with him. It was a huge gathering.

It soon became obvious what a generous and great man Thorolf was. He kept a large band of men which soon proved costly to maintain and was difficult to provide for, but the farming was good and it was easy to obtain everything that was needed.

That winter Sigurd from Sandnes died and Thorolf inherited everything from him, a large fortune.

Hildirid's sons went to see Thorolf and told him of their claim to their father Bjorgolf's inheritance.

'I knew Brynjolf well, and Bard even better,' Thorolf answered. 'They were men of such integrity that they would have given you the share of Bjorgolf's inheritance that they knew was yours by rights. I heard you make this same claim with Bard, and he did not sound as if he thought there was any justification for it. He said you were bastards.'

Harek said they could produce witnesses that their father had paid a bride-price for their mother: 'It's true that we did not approach our brother Brynjolf about the matter first, because that was still in the family. We expected nothing but honourable treatment from Bard, but our dealings with him did not last long. But now that the inheritance has passed on to people outside our family, we cannot completely ignore what we have lost. Our low standing might prove a handicap yet again, and prevent us from winning justice against you too, if you refuse to hear the witnesses we can produce to testify to our noble birth.'

'I don't even consider that you have any birthright,' Thorolf replied, testily, 'because I am told that your mother was taken by force and carried off to your father's house.'

At this point, they broke off the discussion.

IO That winter Thorolf went up to the mountains and took a large band of men with him, no fewer than ninety in number. Previously the king's agents used to take thirty men with them, or sometimes fewer. He also took a great quantity of goods to sell, soon arranged a meeting with the Lapps, collected their taxes and traded with them. All their dealings were cordial and friendly, partly because the Lapps feared them.

Thorolf travelled at large through the forests, and when he reached the mountains farther east he heard that the Kylfing people had been trading with the Lapps there, and plundering too. He posted some Lapps to spy on the Kylfings' movements, then went off to seek them out. In one place he found thirty and killed them all without anyone escaping, then found a group of fifteen or twenty more. In all they killed almost one hundred men and took enormous amounts of booty before returning in the spring. Thorolf went back to his farm at Sandnes and stayed there for some time. That spring he also had a great longship built with a dragon head on the prow, equipped it lavishly and sailed it from the north.

Thorolf harvested large amounts of provisions for himself in Halogaland, sending his men to catch herring and cod. There were also good seal hunting and plenty of eggs to be gathered, all of which he had brought to him. Thorolf never had less than one hundred free-born men at his farm. He was generous and lavish with gifts and made friends with all the local men of rank. He grew very powerful and set special store by equipping himself with the finest ships and weapons.

II King Harald went to Halogaland that summer and was welcomed with feasts that were held both on his own lands and by landholders and important farmers.

Thorolf threw a feast to welcome the king and spared no expense. Once the date of the king's arrival had been decided, Thorolf invited a large number of guests, including all the leading men. The king arrived for the feast with a party of almost three hundred men, and Thorolf had five hundred. There was a large barn that Thorolf had fitted out with benches so that the drink could be served there, because he did not have a room large enough to accommodate that number of people. Shields were mounted all around the building.

The king sat in the high seat, and when the upper and lower benches were both filled he looked around, very red in the face. He did not speak a word, but it seemed obvious he was angry. Although it was a splendid feast with all the finest provisions available, the king remained sullen. He stayed there for three days, as had been planned.

On the day the king was due to leave, Thorolf approached him and asked him to come down to the shore. The king agreed. Offshore lay the dragon-prowed ship that Thorolf had had made, with its awnings up and fully rigged. Thorolf gave the ship to the king, asking him to respect his intention in having so many men at the feast simply as a gesture of honour towards him, not as a challenge. The king took this well and grew friendly and cheerful. Many people rightly added words of praise for the splendid feast and noble gift that the king was given on departing, and the great strength that he enjoyed in such men. They parted in friendship.

The king went to Halogaland as he had planned, then back to the south as the summer progressed. He attended other feasts that were held for him.

12 Hildirid's sons went to see the king and invited him to a feast lasting three nights. The king accepted the invitation and named the date, and when it came around he arrived with his men. There were not many other people there, but the feast went very well and the king was in high spirits. Harek started talking to him and brought the subject round to his travels that summer. The king answered his questions, describing how well he had been welcomed by people everywhere as their means allowed.

'The feast at Torgar must have been in a class of its own,' Harek said, 'with more people there than anywhere else.'

The king said this was right.

'That was only to be expected,' Harek went on, 'because more was lavished on that feast than anywhere else too. But you were very fortunate that it turned out that you did not find your life in danger. Of course, someone as outstandingly wise and fortunate as you was likely to suspect a plot when you saw the great crowd that was gathered there. I'm told you either had all your men fully armed or that you kept a safe watch both day and night.'

The king looked at him and said, 'What are you suggesting, Harek? What can you tell me about it?'

'May I have your leave to talk as I please, King?' Harek asked.

'Speak on,' said the king.

'I cannot imagine that you would be pleased to hear everybody, when they are free to speak their minds at home, accusing you of imposing tyranny on them,' Harek said. 'But to tell the truth, the only thing that prevents the common people from rising up against you is lack of courage and leadership. And it is not surprising that people like Thorolf regard themselves as superior. He has strength and elegance in plenty, and keeps followers about him like a king. He would be enormously wealthy anyway, even if he made do with what is his own without disposing of other people's belongings as if they were his own too. And he was set to repay you badly for the large revenues you have granted him. To tell the truth, when people here heard that you had gone north to Halogaland with no more than three hundred men, they decided to gather forces and kill you, King, and all your men. Thorolf was the architect of that plan, because he had been offered the kingship of the provinces of Halogaland and Naumdal. He travelled back and forth through every fjord and visited all the islands gathering all the men and weapons he could, and made no secret of his plan to send the army into battle against King Harald. But it is also true that even though you would have had a smaller force when your armies met, those farmers were terrified when they saw you sailing up. They decided on another plan, to welcome you and invite you to a feast. The plan then was that if you all got drunk and fell asleep, they would attack you with fire and arms. To prove it, you were all housed in a barn, if I've been told the truth, and that was because Thorolf did not want to burn down his own fine new house. As further proof, every room was full of weapons and armour. But when all their trickery failed to work on you, they opted for the best alternative, which was to hush up the whole scheme. I imagine they will all keep the plot hidden, because I don't think many of them can honestly claim their innocence if the truth gets out. My advice to you now, King, is to take Thorolf into your company, make him your standard-bearer and station him in the prow of your ship; that's a task he is eminently suited for. But if you want him to be a landholder, then you should grant him revenues from lands down south in Fjordane, where his family comes from, so that you will be able to see to it that he does not grow too powerful. Then you can entrust your agencies here in Halogaland to less extravagant people who will serve you loyally, people whose families come from here and whose kinsmen have performed these tasks before. My brother and I are prepared and willing to do anything you wish to use us for. Our father was the king's tax-collector here for a long time and discharged his duties well. You need to take care in appointing people to manage your affairs here, King, since you visit here so rarely. This is not an important enough place for you to station an army here, but you should not visit with a small force because there are many untrustworthy people here.'

The king was furious at hearing these words, but spoke calmly as he always did when hearing important news. He asked whether Thorolf was at home on Torgar Island.

Harek said that was unlikely – 'Thorolf is clever enough to know he should avoid meeting your forces, King, because he cannot expect everyone to guard the secret so closely that you would never find out about it. He went to Alost when he heard that you were moving north.'

The king scarcely mentioned the matter to other people but it was obvious that he firmly believed what he had been told. When he proceeded on his way, Hildirid's sons sent him off respectfully, with gifts, and he promised them his friendship. The brothers found a pretext for visiting Naumdal and made detours so that they kept meeting the king, who was always friendly to them when they greeted him.

13 There was a man called Thorgils Boomer whom Thorolf regarded most highly among all the members of his household. He had been on Viking raids with Thorolf as his standard-bearer and sat in the prow of his boat. At the battle of Havsfjord he fought on King Harald's side, steering the ship Thorolf had used on his Viking raids. He was a man of great might and courage, and after the battle the king presented him with gifts and promised him his friendship. Thorgils looked after Thorolf's farm at Torgar in his absence and handled his affairs.

Before Thorolf went away, he had handed over to Thorgils all the tribute he had collected for the king on his voyages in the mountain regions, and told him to give it to the king if he did not return before the king travelled down from the north. Thorgils fitted out a great and fine cargo vessel belonging to Thorolf, loaded the tribute into it and took a crew of almost twenty men with him. He sailed south and met the king in Naumdal.

When Thorgils went to see the king he passed on a greeting from Thorolf and told him this was the tribute he had sent him.

The king noticed him there but said nothing, and it was obvious he was angry.

Thorgils went away, intending to choose a more suitable time to talk to the king. He went to see Olvir Hump, told him everything that had happened and asked if he had any explanation.

'I don't know,' Olvir said, 'but I have noticed that the king falls silent every time Thorolf is mentioned, ever since we were at Leka together, which makes me suspect that people have been slandering him. I know Hildirid's sons talk at great length with the king in private, and it's obvious from the things they say that they are Thorolf's enemies. I will find out from the king himself.'

Olvir went to see the king and said, 'Your friend Thorgils Boomer has arrived with the tribute due to you from Finnmark, much more than ever before and much better quality goods as well. He is eager to carry out his task properly, so please go and take a look, because such fine skins have never been seen before.'

Without saying anything, the king went to where the ship was moored. Thorgils immediately took out the goods and showed them to the king. When the king saw it was true that the tribute was much greater and better than before, his brow lifted somewhat and Thorgils was able to talk to him. Thorgils gave the king several beaver skins that Thorolf had sent along, and other precious things he had acquired in the mountains. The king grew happier and asked what had happened on their voyage, and Thorgils gave him a thorough account of everything.

Then the king said, 'Such a shame that Thorolf seems to be disloyal and to want to kill me.'

Many people who were present answered this comment, and were unanimous. They said that whatever the king had been told was slander put around by evil men, and Thorolf was innocent of such accusations. Eventually the king said he was inclined to believe them. He was cheerful when he spoke with Thorgils after that, and they parted on good terms.

When Thorgils met Thorolf, he told him everything that had happened between him and the king.

14   That winter Thorolf went to Finnmark again, taking almost a hundred men with him. Once again he traded with the Lapps and travelled widely through Finnmark.

As he advanced farther east and word about his travels got around, the Kven people came and told him that they had been sent to him by their king, Faravid. They told Thorolf how the Karelians had been raiding their land and gave him a message from the king to come there and give him support. Thorolf was offered an equal share of the spoils with the king, and each of his men got the same as three Kven.

It was a law among the Kven people that their king received a third of his men's plunder, but reserved all the beaver skins, sables and martens for himself.

Thorolf put the proposition to his men and gave them the option of going or not. Most of them chose to take the challenge because of the large amount of wealth at stake, so they decided to set off eastwards with the messengers.

Finnmark is a vast territory, bordered by the sea to the west and the north, and all the way to the east with great fjords, while Norway lies to the south of it. It extends as far south along the mountains as Halogaland does down the coast. East of Naumdal lies Jamtland, then Halsingland, Kvenland, Finland and Karelia. Finnmark lies beyond all these countries, and there are mountain settlements in many parts, some in valleys and others by the lakes. In Finnmark there are incredibly large lakes with great forests all around, while a high mountain range named Kjolen extends from one end of the territory to the other.

When Thorolf reached Kvenland he met King Faravid, and they prepared to set off, with three hundred Kven and a hundred Norwegians. They took the highland route through Finnmark and reached the part of the mountain where the Karelians were who had been raiding the Kven. When they realized an attack was pending, the Karelians joined ranks and advanced towards them, expecting another victory. But when the battle started, the Norwegians attacked fiercely, having stronger shields than the Kven. This time it was the turn of the Karelians to suffer casualties; many were killed, and others fled. King Faravid and Thorolf won a huge amount of booty and returned to Kvenland. Thorolf continued on to Finnmark with his men, parting with the king in great friendship.

Thorolf descended the mountain at Vefsna and called at his farm at Sandnes, spending some time there before travelling south to Torgar Island in the spring. When he arrived there, he was told that Hildirid's sons had spent the winter in Trondheim with King Harald and did not miss any opportunity to slander him to the king. Thorolf heard many accounts of the slanders they had put around against him.

'The king will not believe such lies even if he is told them, because I have no reason to want to betray him,' said Thorolf. 'He has treated me grandly in plenty of ways, and never badly. It is nonsense to claim that I would ever do him harm, even if I had the chance. I would rather be his landholder than have the title of king in the same country as another man who could make me his slave whenever he wanted.'

15   Hildirid's sons had spent the winter with King Harald, taking the men from their farm and their neighbours with them. There were twelve men there in all. The brothers spoke a lot to the king, always presenting Thorolf in the same light.

'Were you pleased with the tribute from the Lapps that Thorolf sent you?' Harek asked the king.

'Very pleased,' replied the king.

'You would have been even more impressed if you had received everything due to you,' Harek said, 'but it turned out quite differently. Thorolf kept a much larger share for himself. He sent you a gift of three beaver skins, but I know for certain that he kept thirty for himself that were rightfully yours, and I think the same happened with other items. It's quite true that my brother and I would bring you much more wealth if you entrust collection of the tribute to us.'

Their companions corroborated everything they said about Thorolf, and in the end, the king was furious with him.

16   In the summer Thorolf went to Trondheim to see King Harald, taking all the tribute with him and much more wealth besides, along with a band of ninety men, all well equipped. When he reached the king, they were shown into the guests' quarters and lavishly provided for.

Later that day Olvir Hump went to talk with his kinsman Thorolf. Olvir told Thorolf that heavy slanders had been put around against him, and that the king had listened to these accusations.

Thorolf asked Olvir to speak to the king on his behalf, 'because I will not be granted a very long audience with the king if he prefers to believe the slanders of evil men instead of the truth and honesty which he will hear from me'.

The next day Olvir met Thorolf and told him he had discussed his affairs with the king.

'I am hardly the wiser now about what sort of a mood he is in,' he said.

'Then I will go to him myself,' Thorolf said.

He did so; he went to see the king when he was at the dinner table and greeted him when he entered. The king returned his greeting and ordered someone to fetch Thorolf something to drink.

Thorolf told the king that he had brought him his tribute from Finnmark, 'and I have brought you even more things to honour you. I know that whatever I do in gratitude towards you is always in my best interest.'

The king said that he expected nothing but good from Thorolf, 'because I deserve no less. But there are conflicting stories about how careful you are about pleasing me.'

'If anyone says I have shown you disloyalty, then I have been wronged,' said Thorolf. 'I think people who make such claims to you are less your friends than I am. It is obvious that they aim to be my greatest enemies. But they can also expect to pay dearly for it if we clash.'

Then Thorolf went away again, and the next day he handed over the tribute in the king's presence. When it had all been made over, Thorolf produced several beaver skins and sables, saying that he wanted to give them to the king.

Many of the people there said this was a noble gesture, well deserving to be repaid with friendship. The king said that Thorolf had already taken his reward for himself.

Thorolf answered that he had loyally done everything he could to please the king: 'There is nothing I can do about it if he is still not satisfied. The king knew the way I treated him when I was staying with him as one of his men, and it strikes me as strange if he considers me a different character now from the one I proved to be then.'

'You dispatched yourself well when you were with me, Thorolf,' said the king. 'I think the best course is for you to join my men. Serve as my standard-bearer and defend yourself against the other men of mine, and no one will slander you if I can see for myself, day and night, the way you conduct yourself.'

Thorolf looked to either side where his own men were standing.

'I am reluctant to relinquish this band of men,' he said. 'You will decide my title and the privileges you grant me, King, but I will not hand over my band of men for as long as I can provide for them, even if I have to live by my own resources alone. I want you, I implore you, to visit me and hear the testimony given about me by people whom you trust, and then do what you feel is appropriate.'

The king replied that he would never again accept Thorolf's hospitality. Thorolf went away and prepared to travel home.

When he had left, the king granted Hildirid's sons the agencies in Halogaland that Thorolf had previously held, and collection of tribute from the Lapps. The king seized possession of the farm on Torgar Island and all Brynjolf's former property, and entrusted it all to Hildirid's sons.

The king sent messengers to Thorolf with his tokens, to inform him about the arrangements he had made. Thorolf took the ships that he owned and filled them with all the possessions he could, and took all his men, slaves and freed slaves alike, and went north to his farm in Sandnes, where he lived just as lavishly with just as large a household as before.

17   Hildirid's sons took charge of the king's tax-collection in Halogaland.
For fear of the king's power, no one spoke out against the changeover, although many of Thorolf's kinsmen and friends disapproved strongly. In the winter the brothers went up into the mountains, taking thirty men with them. The Lapps were far less impressed by these agents of the king's than they had been by Thorolf, and the tribute they were supposed to pay proved much more difficult to collect.

The same winter, Thorolf went to the mountains with a hundred men, and straight to Kvenland to meet King Faravid. They made their plans and decided to go up into the mountains as they had the previous winter, with four hundred men, and they came down in Karelia, where they attacked settlements that they felt they had sufficient numbers to handle. After raiding there and winning much booty, they returned to Finnmark as winter progressed.

Thorolf went home to his farm in the spring, sending men to Vagan to fish cod and others to catch herring, and he stocked up with all manner of provisions.

Thorolf owned a big ocean-going ship, which was lavishly equipped, richly painted above the plumbline and fitted with a black-and-red striped sail. All the riggings were well designed. Thorolf had the ship made ready to sail and sent his men to look after it, loading it with stockfish, hides and ermine, and a great quantity of squirrel skins and other furs from his expedition to the mountains, a very valuable cargo. He told Thorgils Boomer to take the ship to England to buy cloth and other goods that he needed. They skirted the coast to the south, then put out to sea and landed in England, where they did plenty of trading. After that they loaded the ship with wheat, honey, wine and cloth, and set off for Norway again in the autumn. They had favourable winds and landed at Hordaland.

The same autumn Hildirid's sons went with the tribute to hand it over to the king. He watched as they did so.

'Have you handed over all the tribute you took in Finnmark, then?' he asked.

'That's right,' they said.

'This tribute is both much less and much poorer than Thorolf used to collect. And you told me that he managed it badly.'

'It's a good thing you have considered how much tribute usually comes from Finnmark, King,' said Harek, 'because then you have a clear idea how much you will lose if Thorolf ruins it for you entirely. There were thirty of us in Finnmark last winter, as has been the custom among tribute collectors. Then Thorolf arrived with a hundred men. We heard he had said he was planning to kill my brother and me and all the men with us, on the grounds that you, the king, had granted to us the office he wanted for himself. We saw no option but to avoid a confrontation with him and leave, which is why we only went up into the mountains a short way from the settlements, while Thorolf travelled over the whole territory with his band of men. He took all the trade there and the Finns paid him tribute, and he gave them a guarantee that your collectors wouldn't enter the territory. He intends to proclaim himself king of the northern territories, both Finnmark and Halogaland, and it is astonishing that you let him get away with everything he does. As outright proof of the riches Thorolf has taken away from the mountain regions: the largest knorr in Halogaland was loaded at Sandnes this spring and Thorolf was said to be sole owner of all the cargo on board. I think it was more or less full of skins and there were more beaver and sable skins there than Thorolf let you have. Thorgils Boomer took the ship and I would guess he sailed it to England. If you want to find out the truth, you should spy on Thorgils' movements when he comes back, because I can't imagine that so rich a cargo has ever been loaded on any trading ship in our day. I think, if the truth is told, every penny on board was yours.'

Harek's companions corroborated that every word he had said was true, and there was no one there to speak out against him.

18   There were two brothers called Sigtrygg Travel-quick and Hallvard Travel-hard, who came from Vik and were among King Harald's men. Their mother's family came from Vestfold and they were related to the king. Their father had relatives on both sides of the river Gota. He had been a wealthy farmer in Hising, and they had inherited from him. In all there were four brothers, and the younger two, Thord and Thorgeir, stayed at home and looked after the farm. Sigtrygg and Hallvard handled all the king's

missions, both in Norway and outside it, and had made many dangerous voyages, both to execute people and confiscate property from people whose homes the king had ordered to be attacked. They took a large band of men with them everywhere and were not popular among the common people, but the king respected them highly. They were outstanding runners and skiers, capable of outsailing other men, and strong and shrewd in most respects.

They were with the king when all this happened. In the autumn he went to some feasts in Hordaland.

One day he had the brothers Hallvard and Sigtrygg called in, and when they came he told them to take their band of men and spy on the ship that Thorgils Boomer was sailing: 'He took the ship over to England in the summer. Bring it and everything on board to me, except the crew. Let them go in peace if they do not try to defend their ship.'

The brothers readily agreed and took a longship each, then went to look for Thorgils and his men. They heard that he had returned from England and had sailed northwards along the coast. The brothers set off north in pursuit of Thorgils and his men, and came across them in Fura Sound. Recognizing the ship, they attacked its seaward side, while some of their men went ashore and boarded it from the gangways. Thorgils and his men were not expecting trouble and had not mounted a guard. Before they knew it, there were fully armed men all over their ship, and they were all captured there and taken ashore, where they were left with no weapons and only the clothes they were wearing. Hallvard and his men threw the gangways off the ship, undid the moorings and towed it out to sea, then veered south until they reached the king. They presented him with the ship and everything on it.

When the cargo was unloaded, the king saw that it was very valuable, and that Harek had not been lying.

Thorgils and his companions found transport for themselves and went to see Kveldulf and Grim, whom they told of their ordeal. They were given a warm welcome all the same.

Kveldulf said everything was turning out as he had predicted: Thorolf would not enjoy the good fortune of the king's friendship indefinitely.

'And I would not bother much about the loss that Thorolf has just sustained, if there were not more to follow,' he said. 'I suspect once again that Thorolf will fail to realize his limitations in the face of the overwhelming force he has to deal with.'

He asked Thorgils to tell Thorolf that 'my only advice is to leave the country, because he may be able to do better for himself serving the king of England or Denmark or Sweden'.

Then he gave Thorgils a fully rigged boat, and tents and provisions and everything they needed for their journey. They set off without stopping until they reached Thorolf in the north and told him what had happened.

Thorolf took his loss well, saying that he would not go short of money: 'It's good to have a king to share your money with.'

Then Thorolf bought some meal and malt and other provisions he needed to keep his men, and said his farmhands would not be dressed as smartly as he had planned for a while.

Thorolf sold some of his lands and mortgaged others, but maintained the same style of living as before. He had no fewer men with him than the previous winters – rather more, in fact – and he was more extravagant in feasts and invitations to his friends. He spent all the winter at home.

19 Once spring arrived and the snow and ice melted, Thorolf had a great longship that he owned brought out, and had it prepared to sail and manned with more than one hundred of his men in all, an impressive and well-armed band.

When the wind was favourable, Thorolf sailed the ship south hugging the shore, then when he reached Byrda they headed out to sea beyond all the islands, sometimes so far that they could only see the top half of the mountains. They continued south and did not hear any news of anybody until they arrived in Vik. There they were told that the king was in Vik and would be going to Oppland in the summer. No one on land knew of Thorolf's whereabouts. With a favourable wind in his sails, he headed for Denmark, and from there into the Baltic, where he plundered during the summer without gaining much booty.

In the autumn he headed back to Denmark, around the time that the big Norwegian fleet pulled out from Oyr, after being stationed there as usual during the summer. Thorolf let them all sail past without being noticed, then sailed to Mostrarsund one evening. A large knorr had called there on its way from Oyr, skippered by Thorir Thruma, one of King Harald's agents. He was in charge of the king's land at Thruma, a large estate where the king spent much time when he was in Vik. Since a lot of provisions were needed for that estate, Thorir had gone to Oyr to buy cargo, malt and flour and honey, and spent a great amount of the king's money on it.

Thorolf and his men attacked the ship and gave Thorir's crew the option of defending it, but lacking the manpower to keep such a large force at bay, Thorir surrendered. Thorolf seized the ship and all its cargo, and put Thorir ashore, then sailed both ships north along the coast.

On reaching the river Gota they anchored and waited for nightfall. When it was dark they rowed the longship up the river and attacked the farm which Hallvard and Sigtrygg owned there. They arrived before daybreak, surrounded the farmhouse and shouted a war-cry. The people inside woke up and snatched up their weapons. Thorgeir fled out of the sleeping quarters, ran to the wooden fence surrounding the farm, grabbed one of the posts and vaulted over it. Thorgils Boomer, standing nearby, swung his sword at Thorgeir and chopped off the hand that was holding on to the post. Thorgeir ran off into the woods, while his brother Thord was killed and more than twenty men with him. Afterwards, the raiders took all the valuables and burned the farmhouse, then went back down the river to the sea, where they sailed on to Vik with a favourable wind. Once again they encountered a large ship owned by people from Vik, loaded with malt and meal. Thorolf and his band attacked the ship, and the crew surrendered, feeling that they had no chance of warding off the assault. They went ashore with nothing, while Thorolf and his men took the ship and its cargo and continued on their way. So Thorolf had three ships when he sailed into Fold from the east. He and his men followed the main sailing route to Lindesnes, travelling as quickly as possible but coming ashore at the headlands to plunder where they could. On the route north from Lindesnes they kept farther out to sea, but plundered where they went ashore.

North of Fjordane, Thorolf headed for land and went to see his father Kveldulf, who welcomed him. Thorolf told his father what happened on his travels in the summer. He spent a short time there, and his father and brother accompanied him back to his ship.

Before they parted, Thorolf and his father spoke together.

Kveldulf said, 'What I told you when you went to join King Harald's men was not wide of the mark: that the way things would turn out for you would not bring good fortune to any of us. Now you have taken the course that I cautioned you against most of all, by challenging King Harald. For all your prowess and accomplishments, you lack the good fortune to prove a match for King Harald. No one else has managed that in this country, whatever their power and force of numbers. I have an intuition that this will be our last meeting. Considering our ages, you should be destined to live longer, but I feel it will not turn out that way.'

Then Thorolf boarded his ship and continued on his way. Nothing eventful is said to have happened on his voyage until he arrived home at Sandnes, had all the booty he had taken carried up to his farmhouse and laid up the ships. He had no lack of provisions to keep his men through that winter. Thorolf remained at home all the time and kept no fewer men than the previous winters.

20   There was a powerful and wealthy man named Yngvar, who had been a landholder under the earlier kings. When Harald came to power, Yngvar stayed at home and did not serve him. Yngvar was married and had a daughter named Bera. He lived in Fjordane. Bera was his only child and heir.

Grim, Kveldulf's son, asked for Bera's hand in marriage, and a match was made. Grim and Bera were married the winter after he and Thorolf parted. He was twenty-five years old, but already bald, so he was nicknamed Skallagrim (Bald Grim). He was in charge of running the entire farm where he lived with his father, and looked after all the provisions, although Kveldulf was still fit and healthy. They had many freed slaves with them, and many people in their household who had grown up there and were of a similar age to Skallagrim. Many of them were men of great strength, because Kveldulf and his sons chose very strong men to join them and matched them to their own temperament.

Skallagrim took after his father in terms of physique and strength, and also in complexion and character.

21   King Harald had been in Vik when Thorolf went raiding, then went to Oppland in the autumn, and north from there to Trondheim, where he spent the winter with a large party of men.

Sigtrygg and Hallvard, who were with the king, heard how Thorolf had treated their quarters in Hising, and about the casualties and damage he had inflicted there. They continually reminded the king of this episode, and also that Thorolf had robbed him and his subjects, too and raided in his country. The brothers asked the king's permission to set off to attack Thorolf with the band of men they customarily had with them.

'You may think there are grounds for taking Thorolf's life, but I feel you badly lack the good fortune to perform that deed,' the king answered them.

'Thorolf is more than a match for you, even though you consider yourselves men of strength and accomplishment.'

The brothers said that this would soon be put to the test, if the king would grant them leave, adding that they had often taken heavy risks against people they had less reason to take vengeance upon, and had generally come off the better.

When spring arrived and everybody prepared to leave, Hallvard and his brother broached the subject with the king once again.

This time he gave them his permission to kill Thorolf, 'and I know that you will bring me back his head, with many valuables. But some people claim,' the king added, 'that if you sail north, you'll need to use your oars and sails as well on the way back.'

They prepared for their journey immediately, taking two ships and a hundred and fifty men. When they were ready, they sailed out of the fjord into a north-easterly wind, which was against them as they headed northwards along the coast.

22   King Harald stayed at Lade until Hallvard and his brother left, then as soon as they had gone he prepared to leave as well. He and his men boarded his ships and rowed towards land on the Skarnssund Sound, then across Beitsjo to the spit at Eldueid. Leaving his ships there, he headed across the spit to Naumdal, where he took a longship owned by the local farmers and put his men on it. He had his own men and almost three hundred men with him besides, and five or six ships, all of them large. They ran into a strong headwind and rowed night and day, as hard as they could; it was bright enough to travel by night then.

Reaching Sandnes at night after sunset, they saw a great longship floating off the farm with its awnings down, which they recognized as belonging to Thorolf. He had equipped it to sail abroad, and was drinking a toast to his journey. The king ordered all his men to leave their ships, and had his standard raised. It was a short walk to the farm where Thorolf's guards were sitting inside drinking. There was no guard, no one was outside and everyone was sitting indoors drinking.

The king had his men surround the house, then they sounded a war-cry, and trumpets sounded the call to battle. When Thorolf and his men heard that, they ran for their weapons that each kept above his bed. One of the king's men called out to the house and ordered the women, children, old people, slaves and bondsmen to leave.

Sigrid, Thorolf's wife, went out with the women who had been inside and the others who had been allowed to go out. She asked if the sons of Kari from Berle were there and they stepped forward to ask what she wanted of them.

'Take me to the king,' she said.

They did so, and she went up to the king and asked, 'Is it any use to seek a reconciliation between you and Thorolf, my lord?'

'If Thorolf is prepared to surrender and put himself at my power and mercy,' the king answered, 'then his life and limbs will be spared, but his men will be punished as they deserve.'

Olvir Hump went into the farmhouse and called Thorolf to talk to him, to tell him the option the king had given.

Thorolf replied, 'I will not accept any settlement that the king tries to force on me. Ask him to allow us to leave, and we will let fate take its own course.'

Olvir went back to the king and informed him of Thorolf's request.

'Set fire to the house,' the king ordered. 'I do not want to do battle with them and lose my men. I know that Thorolf will inflict heavy casualties upon us if we attack him outside. It will be tough enough to defeat him when he is inside, even though he has fewer men than we do.'

Then the house was set on fire and the flames rapidly engulfed it, because the timber was dry and had been tarred, and the beams were covered with bark. Thorolf ordered his men to break down the wall between the main room of the house and the entrance, which was easily done. When they had removed the beam from it, as many of them as could get a grip took hold of it and drove the end against one corner of the room so hard that the joints split on the outside and the walls came apart, giving them an easy way out. Thorolf went out first, followed by Thorgils Boomer, then the rest one by one.

Battle ensued then, and for a while the farm shielded Thorolf and his men from behind, but when it started to burn, the fire closed in on them, and many of them were killed. Thorolf ran forward, hewing to both sides, towards the king's standard. Then Thorgils Boomer was killed. When Thorolf reached the wall of shields around the king, he thrust his sword through the standard-bearer.

Thorolf said, 'I took three steps too few here.'

He was attacked with both swords and spears, and the king himself delivered the mortal blow, and Thorolf fell at his feet. The king called out, ordering his men not to kill any more, and they stopped fighting.

Then he ordered his men down to the ship. He said to Olvir and his brother, 'Take your kinsman Thorolf and prepare him for a fitting burial, along with the other dead; then bury them. Tend to the wounded who have a chance of living. There will be no plundering here, because all this wealth belongs to me anyway.'

After that the king went down to his ships with most of his men, and on board they began tending to their wounds.

The king walked around the ship, inspecting the men's wounds, and saw one man bandaging a skin wound he had received.

The king said Thorolf had not dealt that wound, 'for his weapons bit in a completely different way. I do not think many people will be bandaging the wounds he delivered. Such men leave a great loss behind them.'

In the morning the king ordered the sails to be hoisted, and they sailed straight south. In the course of the day the king and his men noticed many rowboats in every sound between the islands. Their crews were on their way to see Thorolf, because he had planted spies all the way to Naumdal and in many islands, and they had noticed Hallvard and his brother heading north with a large army to attack him. The brothers had met a steady headwind and been forced to stay in various harbours. Word had got around higher up on land and reached Thorolf's spies, which was the reason they were sailing in convoy to join him.

The king had favourable winds until he reached Naumdal, where he left his ships and crossed to Trondheim overland. There he rejoined the ships he had left behind, and the party set off for Lade. News of the battle soon spread. Hallvard and his brother heard about it where they had moored, and returned to join the king after what was thought to be a rather humiliating expedition.

Olvir Hump and his brother Eyvind Lamb remained at Sandnes for a while and administered to the battle-dead. Thorolf's body was prepared according to the prevailing custom for men of high birth, and they raised a burial stone in his memory. They had the injured nursed back to health, and helped Sigrid to put the farm back in order. All the property remained intact; most of the furniture, tableware and clothing had burned inside.

When Olvir and his brother were ready they set off from the north and went to see King Harald when he was in Trondheim. They stayed with him, kept a low profile and spoke little to other people.

One day the brothers called on the king, and Olvir said, 'My brother and I would like to ask your leave to return to our farms, because after these recent events we are not in the mood to sit and drink with the assailants of our kinsman Thorolf.'

The king looked at him and answered somewhat curtly, 'That I will not grant to you; stay here with me.'

The brothers left and returned to their seats.

The next day, the king had Olvir and his brother called in to him in his chamber.

'Now you will know the answer to the matter you raised when you asked my leave to go home,' the king said. 'You have been here with me for some while and conducted yourselves in a civilized fashion. You have consistently served me well, and I have thought well of you in all ways. Now I want you, Eyvind, to go north to Halogaland and marry Sigrid from Sandnes, Thorolf's widow. I will give you all the wealth that belonged to Thorolf, and you will have my friendship too, if you know how to look after such things. Olvir will stay with me; I do not want to let him go, on account of his skills in poetry.'

The brothers thanked the king for the honour he had shown them, saying they would readily accept it. Eyvind prepared to leave and procured a good, suitable ship. The king gave him tokens to prove his mission. Eyvind had a smooth journey and arrived in Alost at Sandnes, where Sigrid gave him and his men a warm welcome. Then Eyvind produced the king's tokens and message to Sigrid, and he proposed to her, saying the king had ordered that he should be granted this match. Given what had happened, Sigrid felt she had no choice but to accept the king's will. The marriage was arranged and Eyvind took Sigrid as his wife. He took charge of the farm at Sandnes and all the property that had belonged to Thorolf. Eyvind was a man of high birth. His children with Sigrid were Finn the Squinter, who was the father of Eyvind the Plagiarist, and Geirlaug, whose husband was Sighvat the Red. Finn the Squinter married Gunnhild. Her father was Earl Halfdan and her mother was Ingibjorg, the daughter of King Harald Fair-hair.

Eyvind Lamb and the king remained friends for the rest of their lives.

23   There was a man called Ketil Haeng, whose parents were Earl Thorkel of Naumdal and Hrafnhild, daughter of Ketil Haeng from Hrafnista. Haeng was a man of good reputation and noble birth; he had been a great friend of Thorolf Kveldulfsson, who was his kinsman. He had taken part in the call to arms when forces were mustered in Halogaland to support Thorolf, as was written above. When King Harald left the north and it

became known that Thorolf had been killed, the forces disbanded. Haeng turned back with sixty men and went to Torgar, where they encountered Hildirid's sons, who had only a small force with them. On reaching the farm, Haeng attacked them. Hildirid's sons were killed there, along with most of the others, and Haeng and his men seized all the booty they could take.

Afterwards Haeng took the two largest knorrs he was able to find and loaded them with all the belongings he could manage to take with him. He put on board his wife and children and all the men who had taken part in his deeds. Baug, Haeng's foster-brother, a wealthy man of good family, was at the helm of one of the knorrs. When they were ready to sail and the wind was favourable, they put out to sea.

A few years previously Ingolf and Hjorleif* had gone to settle in Iceland. Their voyage was much talked about and people said there was plenty of good land available.

Haeng sailed westwards in search of Iceland, and he and his men sighted land when they were off the south coast. But because of the stormy weather and heavy waves breaking on the shores and the poor harbours, they sailed westwards along the Icelandic coast, past the sands. When the storm began to lull and the seas calmed, they came to a large estuary into which they sailed their ships and moored off the eastern shore. This river is now called Thjorsa and was much narrower and deeper then. They unloaded their ships and set off to explore the land east of the river, moving their livestock there afterwards. Haeng wintered on the west side of the Outer Ranga river, and when spring came he explored the land to the east, claiming the territory between the Thjorsa and Markarfljot rivers, from mountain to shore, and built a farmstead at Hof by East Ranga.

In the spring of their first year in Iceland, Ketil Haeng's wife Ingunn gave birth to a boy they called Hrafn, and after they took down the buildings there the place became known as Hrafntoftir (Hrafn's Toft).

Haeng gave Baug the land in Fljotshlid from the Merkia river down to the river west of Breidabolstad. Baug lived at Hlidarendi and the large family in that district is descended from him. Haeng gave land to some of his ship's crew and sold land for a low price to others, and they are also considered among the original settlers.

* Ingolf Arnarson, the first settler of Iceland (who made his home in Reykjavik), and his sworn brother Hjorleif Hrodmundarson.

One of Haeng's sons, Storolf, owned the land at Hvol and Storolfshvol; he was the father of Orm the Strong. Another of his sons, Herjolf, owned the land in Fljotshlid bordering on Baug's, out to the brook at Hvolslaek. He lived at the foot of the slopes at Brekkur, and was the father of Sumarlidi, whose son was Veturlidi the Poet. Haeng had a third son, Helgi, who lived at Vellir and owned the land there as far as the boundary of his brothers' farms by the East Ranga river. Vestar, Haeng's fourth son, owned the land east of Ranga, between that river and Thvera, and the lower part of Storolfshvol. His wife was Moeid, the daughter of Hildir from Hildisey, and they had a daughter called Asny, who married Ofeig Grettir. Vestar lived at Moeidarhvol. Hrafn, Haeng's fifth son, became the first Lawspeaker in Iceland. He lived at Hof after his father died. Thorlaug, Hrafn's daughter, married Jorund the Godi, and their son was Valgard from Hof. Hrafn was the most prominent of Haeng's sons.

24 When Kveldulf heard about the death of his son Thorolf, he was so saddened by the news that he took to his bed, overcome by grief and old age.

Skallagrim went to see him regularly and tried to talk him round. He told him to take heart, saying that nothing was less becoming to him than to be bedridden.

'A more suitable course would be for us to take vengeance for Thorolf,' he said. 'There is a chance that we will come within reach of some of the men who were responsible for Thorolf's death. If not, there are men we can take that would not be to the king's liking.'

Then Kveldulf spoke a verse:

1. The spinner of fate is grim to me:
    I hear that Thorolf has met his end
    on a northern isle; too early
    the Thunderer chose the swinger of swords.   *Thunderer*: Thund, a
    The hag of old age who once wrestled with Thor   name of Odin; *chose*:
    has left me unprepared to join   i.e. for Valhalla, by
    the Valkyries' clash of steel. Urge as my spirit   letting him be killed
    may, my revenge will not be swift.

That summer King Harald went to Oppland, and in the autumn he headed westwards to Valdres all the way to Voss. Olvir was with the king and often suggested to him that he should consider making compensation for Thorolf, by offering Kveldulf and Skallagrim money or some honour they would accept. The king did not rule out the possibility entirely, if Kveldulf and his son would come to see him.

Then Olvir set off northwards for Fjordane, not stopping until he reached Kveldulf and his son one evening. They were grateful to him for his visit, and he spent some time there.

Kveldulf asked Olvir about the entire incident at Sandnes when Thorolf was killed, about the worthy deeds he had done in battle before his death, and who had struck him down, where his worst wounds were and how he had died. Olvir told him everything he asked, mentioning that King Harald had dealt him a blow that by itself would have sufficed to kill a man, and that Thorolf had dropped face down at the king's feet.

Kveldulf said, 'You have spoken well, because old men have said that a man's death would be avenged if he dropped face down, and vengeance taken on the man at whose feet he fell; but it is unlikely that we will enjoy the good fortune to do so.'

Olvir told Kveldulf and his son that he expected the king to show them great honour if they would go to see him and seek recompense. Speaking at great length, he asked them to take the risk.

Kveldulf said that he would not go anywhere on account of his old age.

'I will stay at home,' he said.

'Do you want to go, Grim?' asked Olvir.

'I do not feel I have any reason to,' said Grim. 'The king will not be impressed by my eloquence, and I do not think I would spend much time asking him for recompense.'

Olvir said he would not need to anyway – 'We will say everything on your behalf, as well as we can.'

Olvir was so insistent that Grim eventually promised to go when he felt ready. When the two of them had settled the time Grim was to meet the king, Olvir left and went back to him.

25   Skallagrim prepared for this journey and chose the strongest and boldest of his men and neighbours to go with him. There was a man named Ani, a wealthy farmer; another called Grani, and Grimolf and his brother Grim, who lived on Skallagrim's farm, and the brothers Thorbjorn Hunchback and Thord Hobbler. They were known as Thorarna's sons – she lived near Skallagrim and was a sorceress. Hobbler was a coal-

biter.* Other men in the band were Thorir the Giant and his brother Thorgeir Earth-long, a hermit called Odd and a freedman named Gris.

In all there were twelve in the party, all outstandingly powerful men, and many of them were shape-shifters.

Taking an oared ferry that Skallagrim owned, they followed the shore southwards and put down anchor in Osterfjord, then went overland to Voss, to the lake that had to be crossed on the route they had chosen. They procured a suitable oared ship there and rowed across the lake to a place not far from where the king was attending a feast. Grim and his men arrived when the king was sitting at table. They met some people in the yard, spoke to them and asked if there was any news. When they had been told what was going on, Grim asked someone to call out Olvir to speak to him.

The man went into the room to where Olvir was sitting and told him, 'A party of twelve men has turned up, if men is the right word. But they are more like giants than human beings in size and appearance.'

Olvir stood up immediately and went outside, guessing who it was who had arrived. He welcomed his kinsman Grim and invited him to join him in the room.

Grim said to his companions, 'It is said to be the custom here to meet the king unarmed. Six of us will go inside, and the other six stay outside and look after our weapons.'

Then they went inside. Olvir went up to the king and Skallagrim was standing behind him.

'Grim, Kveldulf's son, is here now,' Olvir announced. 'We would be grateful if you make his journey here worthwhile, as we are sure you will. Many people receive great honour from you who are less worthy of it than he is, and nowhere near as accomplished in most of his skills. You could do what matters more than any other thing to me, King, if you feel it is important.'

Olvir spoke at length and cleverly, because he was an eloquent man. Many friends of Olvir's approached the king and put the matter to him as well.

The king looked around, and saw a man standing behind Olvir, a whole head taller than all the others, and bald.

'Is that great man Skallagrim?' he asked. Grim said the king had recognized him.

---

* A layabout in his youth but he later proved his worth.

'If you are seeking compensation for Thorolf,' said the king, 'I want you to become one of my men, join their company and enter my service. I may be pleased enough with your service to give you compensation for your brother Thorolf or no less honour than I showed him. But you should be sure to act more carefully than he did, if I make you a man of his stature.'

Skallagrim answered, 'Everyone knows that Thorolf was much more able than I am in all respects, but he lacked the good fortune to serve you properly. I will not take that course. I will not serve you, because I know I lack the good fortune to serve you the way I would like and that you deserve. I imagine I would lack many of Thorolf's qualities.'

The king fell silent and his face turned blood-red. Olvir turned away immediately and asked Grim and his men to leave. They did so, left and took their weapons, and Olvir told them to get away as quickly as they could. Olvir accompanied them to the lake, with a large band of men.

Before he parted company with Skallagrim, Olvir said to him, 'Your visit to the king turned out differently from what I would have wished, kinsman. I urged you to come here, but now I must ask you to go home as quickly as you can, and also not to go to see King Harald unless you two are on better terms than you seem to be now. Keep on your guard against the king and his men.'

Then Grim and his men crossed the lake, while Olvir's men went to where the ships were beached and hacked away at them until they were unseaworthy, because they had seen a large band of men leaving the king's quarters, heavily armed and moving at great speed. King Harald had sent them after Grim, to kill him.

Shortly after Grim and his men had left, the king had begun to speak: 'I can see that huge bald man is as vicious as a wolf and will do harm to men over whose loss I would grieve, if he gets hold of them. That bald character cannot be expected to spare any of you, the people he claims have done him wrong, if he has the chance. Go after him now and kill him.'

Then they left and went to the lake but could not find any seaworthy ships. They returned to tell the king what had happened, saying that Grim and his men would have made it across the lake by then.

Skallagrim proceeded on his way with his companions until he reached home, and he told Kveldulf about the outcome of their journey. Kveldulf was pleased that Grim had not gone to the king in order to enter his service and repeated that they would receive nothing but harm from the king, and no reparation.

Kveldulf and Skallagrim discussed over and again what to do and were in complete agreement that they could not stay in the country, any more than other people who were engaged in disputes with the king. Their only alternative was to leave Norway, and they were attracted by the idea of going to Iceland, where they had heard of the fine land that was available. Their friends and acquaintances, Ingolf Arnarson and his companions, had already gone to Iceland to claim land and settle there, and had found land for the taking and were free to choose wherever they wanted to live. The outcome of their deliberations was to abandon their farm and leave the country.

Thorir Hroaldsson had been brought up as Kveldulf's foster-son when he was very young, and was the same age as Skallagrim. They were close friends as well as foster-brothers. Thorir was one of the king's landholders at the time this all happened, but he and Skallagrim remained constant friends.

Early in the spring, Kveldulf and his men prepared their ships. They had many fine ships and manned two large knorrs with thirty able men on each, not counting women and children. They took all the possessions they could, but no one dared to buy their land from them, for fear of the king's power.

When they were ready, they set sail and headed for the Solund Islands, where there are so many big islands with bays and coves that few people are said to know of all the harbours there.

26 There was a man named Guttorm, who was King Harald's maternal uncle, the son of Sigurd Hart. He had been Harald's foster-father and had acted as regent because the king was still a child when he came to the throne. Guttorm was in charge of Harald's armies when he conquered the territories in Norway and had taken part in all the king's battles during his campaign to win control of the country. When Harald had become sole ruler of Norway and ceased his warfare, he gave his uncle the territories of Vestfold and East Agder and Ringerike and all the land that his father Halfdan the Black had owned. Guttorm had two sons, Sigurd and Ragnar, and two daughters, Ragnhild and Aslaug.

Guttorm fell ill, and when his death was drawing near, he sent messengers to ask King Harald to take care of his children and lands. Shortly afterwards he died.

When the king heard news of his death, he called Hallvard Travel-hard and his brother to meet him, and told them they should undertake a mission on his behalf to Vik. The king was in Trondheim then.

The brothers equipped themselves lavishly for the expedition, choosing troops and taking the best ship they could procure. They took the ship that had belonged to Thorolf, Kveldulf's son, and had been seized from Thorgils Boomer. When they were ready to leave, the king ordered them to go east to Tunsberg. There was a town there, where Guttorm had lived.

'Bring Guttorm's sons to me,' said the king, 'but leave his daughters to grow up there until I give them away in marriage. I will appoint people to safeguard his realm and foster the girls.'

Once the brothers were ready they set off, and had a favourable wind. They reached Vik in the spring and headed to Tunsberg and stated their business, and Hallvard and his brother took Guttorm's sons and a large amount of money. Having done so, they set off to go back, but made much slower progress because of the winds. Nothing eventful happened on their journey until they sailed north into Sognefjord, on a good wind and in fine weather, and they were in high spirits.

27   Kveldulf, Skallagrim and their men kept a constant watch over the main sailing route during the summer. Skallagrim, who was extremely sharp-sighted, saw Hallvard's party sailing up and recognized the ship, because he had once seen Thorgils in command of it. Skallagrim kept watch on their movements and noted where they moored for the night, then returned to his men and told Kveldulf what he had seen. He told him he recognized the ship that had belonged to Thorolf and that Hallvard had seized from Thorgils, and that a number of men who would make a fine catch must be on board.

Then they prepared and equipped their boats, with twenty men on each. Kveldulf commanded one, and Skallagrim the other. They rowed off in search of the ship, and when they reached the place where it was moored, they put in to shore.

Hallvard and his men had covered the ship with awnings and gone to sleep, but when Kveldulf and his men reached them, the watchmen who had been sitting by the gangway at the prow leapt up and called out to the ship, telling the crew to get up because they were about to be attacked. Hallvard and his men rushed for their weapons.

When Kveldulf and his men came to the gangway, they went up it to the stern of the ship, while Skallagrim headed for the prow. Kveldulf had a gigantic double-bladed axe in his hand. Once he was on board, he told his men to go along the gunwale and cut the awnings from the pegs, while he stormed off back to the afterguard, where he is said to have become frenzied like a wild animal. Some other men of his went into a frenzy too, killing everyone they came across, and so did Skallagrim when he ran around the ship. Kveldulf and his son did not stop until the ship had been completely cleared. When Kveldulf went back to the afterguard, he wielded his axe and struck Hallvard right through his helmet and head, sinking the weapon in right up to the shaft. Then he tugged it back with such force that he swung Hallvard up into the air and slung him over the side. Skallagrim swept the prow clean and killed Sigtrygg. Many of the crew threw themselves into the water, but Skallagrim's men took the boat they had come on and rowed over to them, killing everyone in the water.

More than fifty of Hallvard's men were killed there, and Skallagrim took the ship which had sailed there and all the riches on it.

They captured two or three of the most paltry men, spared their lives and asked them who had been on the ship and what their mission had been. When they found out the truth, they examined the carnage on the ship and had the impression that more of the crew had jumped over the side and lost their lives there than had died on board. Guttorm's sons had jumped overboard and perished; one of them was twelve years old then and the other ten, both very promising lads.

Then Skallagrim released the men whose lives he had spared, telling them to go to King Harald and give him a detailed account of what had happened and who had been at work.

'You will also recite this verse to the king,' he added:

2. The warrior's revenge
    is repaid to the king,
    wolf and eagle stalk
    over the king's sons;
    Hallvard's corpse flew
    in pieces into the sea,
    the grey eagle tears
    at Travel-quick's wounds.

Skallagrim and Kveldulf sailed the ship and its cargo out to their own ships. They changed ships, loaded up the one they had taken and cleared their own, which was smaller, then filled it with rocks, knocked holes in it and sank it. Then they headed out to the ocean when a favourable wind got up.

It is said that people who could take on the character of animals, or went berserk, became so strong in this state that no one was a match for them, but also that just after it wore off they were left weaker than usual. Kveldulf was the same, so that when his frenzy wore off he felt exhausted by the effort he had made, and was rendered completely powerless and had to lie down and rest.

A favourable wind carried them out to the open sea, and Kveldulf commanded the ship they had taken from Hallvard and Sigtrygg. They had an easy passage and kept their ships together so that each knew of the other's whereabouts for most of the time. But as they moved farther out to sea, Kveldulf succumbed to an illness. When it had brought him close to death, he called his men and told them he thought he would probably soon be parting ways with them.

'I have not been prone to illness,' he said, 'but if it happens, as I think it probably will, that I die, make a coffin for me and put me overboard. Things will not turn out as I imagined, if I do not reach Iceland and settle there. Give my greetings to my son Grim, when you see him, and tell him too that if he reaches Iceland and, unlikely as it seems, I am there already, to make himself a home as close as possible to the place where I have come ashore.'

Shortly afterwards Kveldulf died. The crew did as he had told them, put him in a coffin and cast it overboard.

There was a man called Grim, a wealthy man of great family; his father was Thorir, the son of Ketil Keel-farer. Grim was one of Kveldulf's crew. He was an old friend of Kveldulf and his son, and had voyaged with them and Thorolf, incurring the king's anger. He took charge of the ship when Kveldulf died.

When they approached Iceland, they sailed towards land from the south, then along the coast to the west, where they had heard that Ingolf had settled. When they rounded Reykjanes and saw the fjord open up, they sailed both the ships into it. A storm got up, with heavy rain and fog, and the ships lost sight of each other. Grim the Halogalander's crew sailed along Borgarfjord beyond the skerries, then cast anchor until the storm died down and the weather brightened up. There they waited for the tide to come in, and floated their ship into the estuary of the river called Gufua (Steam river). After pulling the ship as far upstream as they could, they unloaded their cargo and spent their first winter there.

They explored the land along the coast, both up the mountains and towards the sea, and after travelling a short distance they found a bay where Kveldulf's coffin had been washed ashore. They carried the coffin out to the headland, laid it down and piled rocks over it.

28   Skallagrim reached land where a huge peninsula juts out into the sea, with a narrow spit below it. He and his men unloaded their cargo there and called the site Knarrarnes (Knorr ness).

Then Skallagrim explored the land, which stretched a long way from the shore to the mountains and had a great marshland and wide woods, and plenty of seals to hunt and good fishing. When he and his men explored the shore to the south they came to a great fjord, and they skirted it without stopping until they found their companions, Grim the Halogalander and his companions. It was a joyful reunion. They told Skallagrim about his father's death and that Kveldulf's body had come ashore and they had buried it, then accompanied him to the place, which Skallagrim felt was not far from a good site to build a farm.

Grim went back to his men, and each group wintered where it had reached land.

Skallagrim took the land from mountain to shore, all of the Myrar marshland out to Selalon (Seal lagoon) and the land up to the Borgarhraun lava field, and south to the Hafnarfjoll mountains, and all the land crossed by the rivers down to the sea. The following spring he brought his ship south into the bay closest to where Kveldulf had been washed ashore, built a farmstead there and called it Borg. He called the fjord Borgarfjord, and they named the entire district after it.

To Grim the Halogalander he gave a plot of land south of Borgarfjord, called Hvanneyri (Angelica spit). Nearby is a small bay jutting into the land, and because they found many ducks there, they named it Andakil (Ducks' inlet), and called the river that entered the sea there Andakilsa. Grim owned the land between that river and inland to another river known as Grimsa.

In the spring, when Skallagrim was driving his livestock from out along the shore, they came upon a little promontory where they caught some swans, and called it Alftanes (Swans' ness).

Skallagrim gave land to the members of his crew. Ani was given the land between the Langa and Hafslaek rivers, and lived at Anabrekka; his son was Onund Sjoni (Keen-sighted). Grimolf first lived at Grimolfsstadir; both Grimsolfsfit and Grimolfslaek are named after him. His son Grim lived to the south of the fjord, the father of Grimar, who lived at Grimarsstadir and was the subject of the quarrel between Thorstein and Tungu-Odd. Grani settled at Granastadir on Digranes. Thorbjorn Hunchback and Thord Hobbler were given the uplands beyond Gufua. Hunchback lived at Krumsholar (Hunchback's hills), and Thord at Beigaldi (Hobbler). Thorir the Giant and his brothers were given the land above Einkunnir and towards the sea along the bank of the river Langa. Thorir Giant lived at Thursstadir (Giant-Stead). His daughter was Thordis Stick, who later lived at Stangarholt (Stick-Holt). Thorgeir settled at Jardlangsstadir.

Skallagrim explored the uplands of the district, travelling along Borg-arfjord until he reached the head of the fjord, then following the western bank of the river which he named Hvita (White river), because he and his companions had never seen water from a glacier before and thought it had a peculiar colour. They went up Hvita until they reached the river that flows from the mountains from the north. They named it Nordura (North river) and followed it until they reached yet another river with little water in it. Crossing that, they continued to trace Nordura and soon saw that the small river fell through a chasm, so they called it Gljufura (Chasm river). Then they crossed Nordura and returned to Hvita, and followed that upstream. Once again they soon came across another river that intersected their path and entered Hvita, and they named it Thvera (Cross river). They noticed that every river was full of fish; and then they returned to Borg.

29 Skallagrim was an industrious man. He always kept many men with him and gathered all the resources that were available for subsistence, since at first they had little in the way of livestock to support such a large number of people. Such livestock as there was grazed free in the woodland all year round. Skallagrim was a great shipbuilder and there was no lack of driftwood west of Myrar. He had a farmstead built on Alftanes and ran another farm there, and rowed out from it to catch fish and cull seals and gather eggs, all of which were there in great abundance. There was plenty of driftwood to take back to his farm. Whales beached, too, in great numbers, and there was wildlife for the taking at this hunting post; the animals were not used to men and would never flee. He owned a third farm by the sea on the western part of Myrar. This was an even better place to gather driftwood, and he planted crops there and named it Akrar (Fields). The islands offshore were called Hvalseyjar (Whale islands), because whales congregated there. Skallagrim also sent his men upriver to catch salmon. He sent Odd the Hermit by Gljufura to take care of the salmon fishery

there; Odd lived at the foot of Einbuabrekkur (Hermit's slopes), and the promontory Einbuanes is named after him. There was a man called Sigmund who was sent by Skallagrim to Nordura and lived at Sigmundarstadir, now known as Haugar. Sigmundarnes is named after him. He later moved his home to Munadarnes, a better place for catching salmon.

When Skallagrim's livestock grew in number, they were allowed to roam mountain pastures for the whole summer. Noticing how much better and fatter the animals were that ranged on the heath, and also that the sheep which could not be brought down for the winter survived in the mountain valleys, he had a farmstead built up on the mountain, and ran a farm there where his sheep were kept. The farm was run by Gris, after whom the tongue of land called Grisartunga is named. In this way, Skallagrim put his livelihood on many footings.

Shortly after Skallagrim arrived in Iceland, a ship made land in Borgarfjord. It was owned by Oleif Hjalti, who had brought his wife, children and relatives with the aim of finding a place to live in Iceland. He was a rich, wise man of good family. Skallagrim invited Oleif and all his people to stay with him. Oleif accepted the offer and spent his first winter in Iceland there.

The following summer Skallagrim offered him land south of the river Hvita, between the rivers Grimsa and Flokadalsa. Oleif accepted it and moved there, building a farmstead at the brook called Varmalaek. He was a man of high birth. His sons were Ragi from Laugardal, and Thorarin, who succeeded Hrafn Haengsson as Lawspeaker. Thorarin lived at Varmalaek and married Thordis, who was the daughter of Olaf Feilan and sister of Thord Bellower.

30 King Harald Fair-hair confiscated all the lands left behind in Norway by Kveldulf and Skallagrim, and any other possessions of theirs he could come by. He also searched for everyone who had been in league with Skallagrim and his men, or had even been implicated with them or had helped them in all the deeds they did before Skallagrim left the country. The king's animosity towards Kveldulf and his son grew so fierce that he hated all their relatives or others close to them, or anyone he knew had been fairly close friends. He dealt out punishment to some of them, and many fled to seek sanctuary elsewhere, in Norway or left the country completely.

Yngvar, Skallagrim's father-in-law, was one of these people. He opted to sell all the belongings he could, procure an ocean-going vessel, man it and sail to Iceland, where he had heard that Skallagrim had settled and had plenty of land available. When his crew were ready to sail and a favourable wind got up, he sailed out to the open sea and had a smooth crossing. He approached Iceland from the south and sailed into Borgarfjord and entered the river Langa, all the way to the waterfall, where they unloaded the ship.

Hearing of Yngvar's arrival, Skallagrim went straight to meet him and invited him to stay with him, along with as many of his party as he desired. Yngvar accepted the offer, beached his ship and went to Borg with his men to spend the winter with Skallagrim. In the spring, Skallagrim offered him land, giving him the farm he owned at Alftanes and the land as far inland as the brook at Leirulaek and along the coast to Straumfjord. Yngvar went to that outlying farm and took it over, and turned out to be a highly capable man, and grew wealthy. Then Skallagrim set up a farm in Knarrarnes which he ran for a long time afterwards.

Skallagrim was a great blacksmith and worked large amounts of bog-iron during the winter. He had a forge built by the sea a long way off from Borg, at the place called Raufarnes, where he did not think the woods were too far away. But since he could not find any stone suitably hard or smooth to forge iron against – because there was nothing but pebbles there, and small sands along the shore – Skallagrim put out to sea one evening in one of his eight-oared boats, when everyone else had gone to bed, and rowed out to the Midfjord islands. There he cast his stone anchor off the prow of his boat, stepped overboard, dived and brought up a rock which he put into his boat. Then he climbed into the boat, rowed ashore, carried the rock to his forge, put it down by the door and always forged his iron on it. That rock is still there with a pile of slag beside it, and its top is marked from being hammered upon. It has been worn by waves and is different from the other rocks there; four men today could not lift it.

Skallagrim worked zealously in his forge, but his farmhands complained about having to get up so early. It was then that Skallagrim made this verse:

3.   The wielder of iron must rise
      early to earn wealth from his bellows,
      from that sack that sucks in
      the sea's brother, the wind.
      I let my hammer ring down
      on precious metal of fire,
      the hot iron, while the bag
      wheezes greedy for wind.

31   Skallagrim and Bera had many children, but the first ones all died. Then they had a son who was sprinkled with water and given the name Thorolf. He was big and handsome from an early age, and everyone said he closely resembled Kveldulf's son Thorolf, after whom he had been named. Thorolf far excelled boys of his age in strength, and when he grew up he became accomplished in most of the skills that it was customary for gifted men to practise. He was a cheerful character and so powerful in his youth that he was considered just as able-bodied as any grown man. He was popular with everyone, and his father and mother were very fond of him.

Skallagrim and Bera had two daughters, Saeunn and Thorunn, who were also promising children.

Skallagrim and his wife had another son who was sprinkled with water and named Egil. As he grew up, it soon became clear he would turn out very ugly and resemble his father, with black hair. When he was three years old, he was as big and strong as a boy of six or seven. He became talkative at an early age and had a gift for words, but tended to be difficult to deal with in his games with other children.

That spring Yngvar visited Borg to invite Skallagrim out to a feast at his farm, saying that his daughter Bera and her son Thorolf should join them as well, together with anyone else that she and Skallagrim wanted to bring along. Once Skallagrim had promised to go, Yngvar returned home to prepare the feast and brew the ale.

When the time came for Skallagrim and Bera to go to the feast, Thorolf and the farmhands got ready as well; there were fifteen in the party in all.

Egil told his father that he wanted to go with them.

'They're just as much my relatives as Thorolf's,' he said.

'You're not going,' said Skallagrim, 'because you don't know how to behave where there's heavy drinking. You're enough trouble when you're sober.'

So Skallagrim mounted his horse and rode away, leaving Egil behind disgruntled. Egil went out of the farmyard and found one of Skallagrim's pack-horses, mounted it and rode after them. He had trouble negotiating the marshland because he was unfamiliar with the way, but he could often see where Skallagrim and the others were riding when the view was not obscured by knolls or trees. His journey ended late in the evening when he arrived at Alftanes. Everyone was sitting around drinking when he entered the room. When Yngvar saw Egil he welcomed him and asked why he had come so late. Egil told him about his conversation with his father. Yngvar seated Egil beside him, facing Skallagrim and Thorolf. All the men were entertaining themselves by making up verses while they were drinking the ale. Then Egil spoke this verse:

4.   I have come in fine fettle to the hearth
     of Yngvar, who gives men gold from the glowing
     curled serpent's bed of heather;   *serpent's bed of heather*: i.e. the
     I was eager to meet him.   hoard of treasure it guards
     Shedder of gold rings bright and twisted
     from the serpent's realm, you'll never
     find a better craftsman of poems
     three winters old than me.

Yngvar repeated the verse and thanked Egil for it. The next day Yngvar rewarded Egil for his verse by giving him three shells and a duck's egg. While they were drinking that day, Egil recited another verse, about the reward for his poem:

5.   The skilful hardener of weapons   *hardener*: wielder or maker
     that peck wounds gave eloquent
     Egil in reward three shells
     that rear up ever-silent in the surf.
     That upright horseman of the field   *field where ships race*: sea; its
     where ships race knew how to please Egil; *horseman*: sailor
     he gave him a fourth gift,
     the brook-warbler's favourite bed.   *brook-warbler*: duck; its *bed*: egg

Egil's poetry was widely acclaimed. Nothing else of note happened during that journey, and Egil went home with Skallagrim.

32   There was a powerful hersir in Sognefjord called Bjorn, who lived at Aurland; his son Brynjolf inherited everything from him. Brynjolf had two sons, Bjorn and Thord, who were quite young when this episode took place. Bjorn was a great traveller and a most accomplished man, sometimes going on Viking raids and sometimes trading.

One summer, Bjorn happened to be in Fjordane at a well-attended feast, when he saw a beautiful girl whom he felt very attracted to. He asked about her family background, and was told she was the sister of Thorir Hroaldsson the Hersir, and was called Thora of the Embroidered Hand. Bjorn asked for

Thora's hand in marriage, but Thorir refused him, and they parted company.

That same autumn, Bjorn gathered a large enough band of men to fill a boat, set off north to Fjordane and arrived at Thorir's farm when he was not at home. Bjorn took Thora away and carried her back home to Aurland. They were there for the winter, and Bjorn wanted to hold a wedding ceremony. His father Brynjolf disapproved of what Bjorn had done and regarded it as a disgrace to his long friendship with Thorir.

'Rather than your marrying Thora here in my house without the permission of her brother Thorir,' Brynjolf said to Bjorn, 'she will be treated exactly as if she were my own daughter, and your sister.'

And what Brynjolf ordered in his own home had to be obeyed, whether Bjorn liked it or not.

Brynjolf sent messengers to Thorir to offer him reconciliation and compensation for the journey Bjorn had made. Thorir asked Brynjolf to send Thora home, saying that otherwise there would be no reconciliation. But Bjorn absolutely refused to return her, however much Brynjolf asked; and the winter passed in this way.

One day when spring was drawing near, Brynjolf and Bjorn discussed their plans. Brynjolf asked him what he intended to do.

Bjorn said it was most likely that he would go abroad.

'Most of all,' he said, 'I would like you to let me have a longship and crew so that I can go raiding.'

'You cannot expect me to let you have a warship and big crew of men,' said Brynjolf, 'because for all I know you might turn up where I would least prefer you to. You have caused enough trouble as it is. I will let you have a trading ship and cargo. Go to Dublin, which is the most illustrious journey anyone can make at present. I will arrange a good crew to go with you.'

Bjorn said that he would have to accept what Brynjolf wanted. He had a good trading ship made ready and manned it. Then Bjorn prepared for the journey, taking plenty of time about it.

When Bjorn had completed his preparations and a favourable wind got up, he boarded a boat with twelve other men and rowed to Aurland. They went up to the farm, to his mother's room. She was sitting in there with a lot of other women. Thora was one of them. Bjorn said that Thora should go with him. They led her away, while Bjorn's mother asked the women not to be so rash as to let the people know in the other part of the farmhouse, because Brynjolf would react badly if he found out and serious trouble would develop between the father and son. Thora's clothing and belongings were all laid out ready for her, and Bjorn and his men took these with them. Then they went off to their ship at night, hoisted sail and sailed out through Sognefjord and to the open sea.

The sailing weather was unfavourable, with a strong headwind, and they were tossed about at sea for a long time, because they were determined to keep as far away from Norway as possible. One day as they sailed from the east towards Shetland in a gale, they damaged their ship when making land at Mousa. They unloaded the cargo and went to the fort there, taking all their goods with them, then beached their ship and repaired the damage.

33   Just before winter, a ship arrived in Shetland from the Orkneys. The crew reported that a longship had landed in the isles that autumn, manned by emissaries of King Harald who had been sent to inform Earl Sigurd that the king wanted Bjorn Brynjolfsson killed wherever he might be caught. Similar messages were delivered in the Hebrides and all the way to Dublin. As soon as Bjorn arrived in the Shetlands he married Thora, and they spent the winter in the fort of Mousa.

In the spring, when the seas became calmer, Bjorn launched his ship and prepared it for sailing in great haste. When he was ready to set out and a favourable wind got up, he sailed out to the open sea. Driven by a powerful gale, they were only at sea for a short while before they neared the south of Iceland. The wind was blowing from the land and carried them west of Iceland and back out to sea. When a favourable wind got up again they sailed towards land. None of the men on board had ever been to Iceland before.

They sailed into an incredibly large fjord and were carried towards its western shore. Nothing could be seen in the direction of land but reefs and harbourless coast. Then they followed the land on a due east tack until they reached another fjord, which they entered and sailed right up until there were no more skerries and surf. They lay to at a promontory which was separated by a deep channel from an island offshore, and moored their ship there. There was a bay on the western side of the promontory, with a huge cliff towering above it.

Bjorn set off in a boat with some men. He told his companions to be careful not to say anything about their voyage which could cause them trouble. Bjorn and his men rowed to the farmstead and spoke to some people there. The first thing they asked was where they had made land. They were told that it was called Borgarfjord, the farm there was Borg and the farmer's name was Skallagrim. Bjorn realized at once who he was and went to see him, and they talked together. Skallagrim asked who these people were. Bjorn told him his name and his father's; Skallagrim was well acquainted with Brynjolf and offered to provide Bjorn with all the assistance he needed. Bjorn took the offer readily. Then Skallagrim asked who else of importance was on board, and Bjorn said that Thora was, the daughter of Hroald and sister of Thorir the Hersir, and that she was his wife. Skallagrim was pleased to hear this and said it was his duty and privilege to grant the sister of his foster-brother Thorir with such assistance as she needed or he had the means to provide, and he invited her and Bjorn to stay with him, along with all the crew. Bjorn accepted the offer. Then the cargo was unloaded from the ship and carried into the hayfield at Borg. They set up camp there and the ship was hauled up the stream that flows past the farm. The place where Bjorn made camp is called Bjarnartodur (Bjorn's Fields).

Bjorn and all his crew went to stay with Skallagrim. He never had fewer than sixty armed men with him.

34 That autumn when ships arrived in Iceland from Norway, a rumour began to spread that Bjorn had run away with Thora, without her kinsmen's consent. For this offence, the king had outlawed him from Norway.

When this news reached Skallagrim, he called Bjorn in and asked about his marriage, whether it had been made with her kinsmen's consent.

'I did not expect that Brynjolf's son would not tell me the truth,' he said.

Bjorn replied, 'I have only told you the truth, Grim; you should not criticize me for not telling you more than you asked. But I admit that it is true what you have heard, this match was not made with her brother Thorir's approval.'

Then Skallagrim said, very angrily, 'Why did you have the audacity to come to me? Didn't you know how close my friendship with Thorir was?'

Bjorn replied, 'I knew that you were foster-brothers and dear friends. But the reason I visited you was that my ship was brought ashore here and I knew there was no point in trying to avoid you. My lot is now in your hands, but I expect fair treatment as a guest in your home.'

Then Thorolf, Skallagrim's son, came forward and made a long speech imploring his father not to hold this against Bjorn, after welcoming him to his home. Many other people put in a word for him.

In the end Skallagrim calmed down and said that it was up to Thorolf to decide – 'You can take care of Bjorn, if you wish, treat him as well as you please.'

35   Thora gave birth to a daughter that summer. The girl was sprinkled with water and given the name Asgerd. Bera assigned a woman to look after her.

Bjorn and all his crew spent the winter with Skallagrim. Thorolf sought Bjorn's friendship and followed him around everywhere.

One day early in spring, Thorolf spoke to his father and asked him what he planned to do for his winter guest Bjorn, and what help he would provide for him. Skallagrim asked Thorolf what he had in mind.

'I think Bjorn would want to go to Norway above all else,' said Thorolf, 'if he could be at peace there. The best course of action would seem to be if you sent messengers to Norway and offered a settlement on Bjorn's behalf. Thorir will hold your words in great respect.'

Thorolf was so persuasive that Skallagrim gave in and found men to go abroad that summer. They brought messages and tokens to Thorir Hroalds-son and sought a settlement between him and Bjorn. When Brynjolf heard the message they had brought, he set his mind on offering compensation for his son Bjorn. The matter ended with Thorir accepting a settlement for Bjorn, because he realized that Bjorn had nothing to fear from him under the circumstances. Brynjolf accepted the settlement on Bjorn's behalf, and Skallagrim's messengers stayed for the winter with Thorir, while Bjorn spent the winter with Skallagrim.

The following summer, Skallagrim's messengers set off back to Iceland. When they returned in the autumn, they reported that a reconciliation had been made for Bjorn in Norway. Bjorn stayed a third winter with Skallagrim, and the following spring he prepared to leave, along with the band of men who had been with him.

When Bjorn was ready to set off, Bera said that she wanted her foster-daughter Asgerd to remain behind. Bjorn and his wife agreed, and the girl stayed there and was brought up with Skallagrim's family.

Thorolf joined Bjorn on the voyage, and Skallagrim equipped him for the journey. He left with Bjorn that summer. They had a smooth passage and left the open sea at Sognefjord. Bjorn sailed into Sognefjord and went to visit his father. Thorolf went with him, and Brynjolf received them warmly.

Then word was sent to Thorir. He and Brynjolf arranged a meeting, which Bjorn attended too, and they clinched their settlement. Thorir paid the money he had been keeping for Thora, and he and Bjorn became friends as well as kinsmen-in-law. Bjorn stayed at Aurland with Brynjolf, and Thorolf stayed with them too and was well treated.

36 For the most part, King Harald had his residence at Hordaland or Rogaland, on the estates he owned there at Utsten, Avaldsnes, Fitjar, Aarstad, Lygra or Seim. That particular winter, however, the king was in the north. After spending the winter and spring in Norway, Bjorn and Thorolf prepared their ship, mustered a crew and set off for the summer on Viking raids in the Baltic, coming back in the autumn with great wealth. On their return they heard that King Harald was at Rogaland and would be wintering there. King Harald was growing very old by this time, and many of his sons were fully grown men.

Eirik, Harald's son, who was nicknamed Blood-axe, was still young then. He was being fostered by Thorir the Hersir. The king loved Eirik the most of all his sons, and Thorir was on the best of terms with the king.

Bjorn, Thorolf and their men went to Aurland first after returning to Norway, then set off north to visit Thorir the Hersir in Fjordane. They had a warship which they had acquired while raiding that summer, rowed by twelve or thirteen oarsmen on each side, with almost thirty men on board. It was richly painted above the plumbline, and exceptionally beautiful. When they arrived, Thorir gave them a good welcome and they spent some time there, leaving their ship at anchor with its awnings up, near the farm.

One day Thorolf and Bjorn went down from the farm to the ship. They could see Eirik, the king's son, repeatedly boarding the ship, and then going back to land to admire it from there.

Then Bjorn said to Thorolf, 'The king's son seems fascinated by the ship. Ask him to accept it as a gift from you, because I know it will be a great boon to us if Eirik is our spokesman. I have heard that the king is ill-disposed towards you on account of your father.'

Thorolf said this was a good plan.

Then they went down to the ship and Thorolf said, 'You're looking at the ship very closely, Prince. What do you think of it?'

'I like it,' he replied. 'It is a very beautiful ship.'

'Then I would like to give you the ship,' said Thorolf, 'if you will accept it.'

'I will accept it,' said Eirik. 'You will not think the pledge of my friendship much of a reward for it, but that is likely to be worth more, the longer I live.'

Thorolf said that he thought such a reward much more valuable than the ship. They parted, and afterwards the prince was very warm towards them.

Bjorn and Thorolf approached Thorir about whether he thought it was true that the king was ill-disposed towards Thorolf. Thorir did not conceal the fact that he had heard such a thing.

'Then I would like you to go and see the king,' said Bjorn, 'and put Thorolf's case to him, because Thorolf and I will always meet the same fate. That is the way he treated me when I was in Iceland.'

In the end Thorir promised to visit the king and asked them to try to persuade Eirik to go with him. When Bjorn and Thorolf discussed the matter with Eirik, he promised his assistance in dealing with his father.

Then Thorolf and Bjorn went on their way to Sognefjord, while Thorir and Prince Eirik manned the warship he had recently been given, and went south to meet the king in Hordaland. He welcomed them warmly. They stayed there for some while, waiting for an opportunity to approach the king when he was in a good mood.

Then they broached the subject with him, and told him that a man had arrived by the name of Thorolf, Skallagrim's son: 'We wanted to ask the king to remember all the good that his kinsmen have rendered to you, but not to make him suffer for what his father did in avenging his brother.'

Although Thorir spoke diplomatically, the king was somewhat curt in his replies, saying that Kveldulf and his sons posed a great threat to them and he expected this Thorolf to have a similar temperament to his kinsmen.

'All of them are so overbearing they never know when to stop,' he said, 'and they pay no heed to whom it is they are dealing with.'

Then Eirik spoke up and told him how Thorolf had made friends with him and given him a fine present, the ship that they had brought with them: 'I have promised him my absolute friendship. Few people will make friends with me if this counts for nothing. Surely you would not let this happen, father, to the first man who has given me something precious.'

In the end the king promised to leave Thorolf in peace.

'But I do not want him to come to see me,' he said. 'You may hold him as dear to you as you wish, Eirik, or any of his kinsmen, but either they will treat you more gently than they have me, or you will regret this favour you ask of me, especially if you allow them to remain with you for any length of time.'

Then Eirik Blood-axe and Thorir and his men went back to Fjordane, and sent a message to Thorolf about the outcome of their meeting with the king.

Thorolf and Bjorn spent the winter with Brynjolf. They spent many summers on Viking raids, staying with Brynjolf for some winters and with Thorir for the others.

37 Eirik Blood-axe came to power and ruled Hordaland and Fjordane. He took men into his service and kept them with him.

One spring Eirik Blood-axe made preparations for a journey to Permia and chose his men carefully for the expedition. Thorolf joined Eirik and served as his standard-bearer at the prow of his ship. Just like his father had been, Thorolf was outstandingly large and strong.

Many things of note took place on that journey. Eirik fought a great battle by the river Dvina in Permia and emerged the victor, as the poems about him relate; and on the same journey he married Gunnhild, daughter of Ozur Snout, and brought her back home with him. Gunnhild was outstandingly attractive and wise, and well versed in the magic arts. Thorolf and Gunnhild struck up a close friendship. Thorolf would spend the winters with Eirik, and go on Viking raids in the summer.

The next thing that happened was that Bjorn's wife, Thora, fell ill and died. A short time later Bjorn took another wife, Olof, daughter of Erling the Wealthy from Ostero. Bjorn and Olof had a daughter called Gunnhild.

There was a man called Thorgeir Thorn-foot who lived at Fenring in Hordaland, at the place called Ask. He had three sons; one was named Hadd, another Berg-Onund, and the third Atli the Short. Berg-Onund was uncommonly strong, pushy and troublesome. Atli was short, squarely built and powerful. Thorgeir was very wealthy, made many sacrifices to the gods and was well versed in the magic arts. Hadd went on Viking raids and was rarely at home.

38 One summer, Thorolf Skallagrimsson made ready to go trading. He planned to go to Iceland and see his father, and did so. He had been away for a long time, and took a great amount of wealth and many precious things with him.

When he was ready to leave, he went to see King Eirik. At their parting,

Eirik presented Thorolf with an axe, saying he wanted Skallagrim to have it. The axe was crescent-shaped, large and inlaid with gold, and its hilt was plated with silver, a splendid piece of work.

Thorolf set off when his ship was ready, and he had a smooth journey, arriving in Borgarfjord where he went straight to his father's house. It was a joyful reunion. Skallagrim went with Thorolf to the ship and had it brought ashore, then Thorolf and eleven of his men went to Borg.

When he was in Skallagrim's house he passed on King Eirik's greeting and presented him with the axe that the king had sent. Skallagrim took the axe, held it up and inspected it for a while without speaking, then hung it up above his bed.

At Borg one day in the autumn, Skallagrim had a large number of oxen driven to his farm to be slaughtered. He had two of them tethered up against the wall, with their heads together, and took a large slab of rock and placed it under their necks. Then he went up to them with his axe King's Gift and struck one blow at both oxen. It chopped off their heads, but it went right through and struck the stone, and the mount broke completely and the blade shattered. Skallagrim inspected the edge without saying a word, then went into the fire-room, climbed up on a bench and put the axe on the rafters above the door, where it was left that winter.

In the spring, Thorolf announced that he planned to go abroad that summer.

Skallagrim tried to discourage him, reminding him that '"it is better to ride a whole wagon home". Certainly you have made an illustrious journey,' he said, 'but there's a saying, "the more journeys you make, the more directions they take". You can have as much wealth from here as you think you need to show your stature.'

Thorolf replied that he still wanted to make a journey, 'and I have some pressing reasons for going. When I come to Iceland for a second time, I will settle down here. Asgerd, your foster-daughter, will go with me to meet her father. He asked me to arrange this when I was leaving Norway.'

Skallagrim said it was up to him to decide, 'but I have an intuition that if we part now we will never meet again'.

Then Thorolf went to his ship and made it ready. When he was fully prepared, they moved the ship out to Digranes and lay there waiting for a favourable wind. Asgerd went on the ship with him.

Before Thorolf left Borg, Skallagrim went up and took down the axe, the gift from the king, from the rafters above the door. The handle was black with soot and the axe had gone rusty. Skallagrim inspected the edge, then handed it to Thorolf, speaking this verse:

6. Many flaws lie in the edge
    of the fearsome wound-biter,   *wound-biter*: axe
    I own a feeble tree-feller,
    there is vile treachery in this axe.
    Hand this blunt crescent back
    with its sooty shaft;
    I had no use for it,
    such was the gift from the king.

39 One summer while Thorolf was abroad and Skallagrim lived at Borg, a trading ship arrived in Borgarfjord from Norway. Trading ships would be given shore-berths then in many places: in rivers or the mouths of streams, or in channels. There was a man named Ketil, whose nickname was Ketil Blund (Snooze), who owned the ship. He was a Norwegian, of a great family and wealthy. His son, Geir, had come of age by then and was on the ship with him. Ketil intended to settle in Iceland; he arrived late in the summer. Skallagrim knew all about his background, and invited Ketil to stay with him, together with all his travelling companions. Ketil accepted the offer, and spent the winter with Skallagrim.

That winter, Ketil's son Geir asked for the hand of Thorunn, Skallagrim's daughter, and the match was settled; he married her. The following spring Skallagrim offered Ketil some land to settle on up from where Oleif had settled, along the river Hvita between the Flokadal and Reykjadal estuaries and all the tongue of land between them as far as Raudsgil, and all the head of Flokadal valley. Ketil lived at Thrandarholt, while Geir lived at Geirshlid and had another farm at Upper Reykir; he was called Geir the Wealthy. His sons were named Blund-Ketil, Thorgeir Blund and Thorodd Hrisablund, who lived at Hrisar.

40 Skallagrim took a great delight in trials of strength and games, and liked talking about them. Ball games were common in those days, and there were plenty of strong men in the district at this time. None of them could match Skallagrim in strength, even though he was fairly advanced in age by then.

Thord, Grani's son from Granastadir, was a promising young man, and was very fond of Egil Skallagrimsson. Egil was a keen wrestler; he was impetuous and quick-tempered, and everyone was aware that they had to teach their sons to give in to him.

A ball game was arranged early in winter on the plains by the river Hvita, and crowds of people came to it from all over the district. Many of Skallagrim's men attended, and Thord Granason was their leader. Egil asked Thord if he could go to the game with him; he was in his seventh year then. Thord let him, and seated Egil behind him when he rode there.

When they reached the games meeting, the players were divided up into teams. A lot of small boys were there as well, and they formed teams to play their own games.

Egil was paired against a boy called Grim, the son of Hegg from Heggs-stadir. Grim was ten or eleven years old, and strong for his age. When they started playing the game, Egil proved to be weaker than Grim, who showed off his strength as much as he could. Egil lost his temper, wielded the bat and struck Grim, who seized him and dashed him to the ground roughly, warning him that he would suffer for it if he did not learn how to behave. When Egil got back on his feet he left the game, and the boys jeered at him.

Egil went to see Thord Granason and told him what had happened.

Thord said, 'I'll go with you and we'll take our revenge.'

Thord handed Egil an axe he had been holding, a common type of weapon in those days. They walked over to where the boys were playing their game. Grim had caught the ball and was running with the other boys chasing him. Egil ran up to Grim and drove the axe into his head, right through to the brain. Then Egil and Thord walked away to their people. The people from Myrar seized their weapons, and so did the others. Oleif Hjalti rushed to join the people from Borg with his men. Theirs was a much larger group, and at that the two sides parted.

As a result, a quarrel developed between Oleif and Hegg. They fought a battle at Laxfit by the river Grimsa, where seven men were killed. Hegg received a fatal wound and his brother Kvig died in the battle.

When Egil returned home, Skallagrim seemed indifferent to what had happened, but Bera said he had the makings of a true Viking when he was old enough to be put in command of warships. Then Egil spoke this verse:

7. My mother said
    I would be bought
    a boat with fine oars,
    set off with Vikings,
    stand up on the prow,
    command the precious craft,
    then enter port,
    kill a man and another.

When Egil was twelve, he was so big that few grown men were big and strong enough that he could not beat them at games. In the year that he was twelve, he spent a lot of time taking part in games. Thord Granason was in his twentieth year then, and strong too. That winter Egil and Thord often took sides together in games against Skallagrim.

Once during the winter there was a ball game at Borg, in Sandvik to the south. Egil and Thord played against Skallagrim, who grew tired and they came off better. But that evening after sunset, Egil and Thord began losing. Skallagrim was filled with such strength that he seized Thord and dashed him to the ground so fiercely that he was crushed by the blow and died on the spot. Then he seized Egil.

Skallagrim had a servant woman named Thorgerd Brak, who had fostered Egil when he was a child. She was an imposing woman, as strong as a man and well versed in the magic arts.

Brak said, 'You're attacking your own son like a mad beast, Skallagrim.'

Skallagrim let Egil go, but went for her instead. She fled, with Skallagrim in pursuit. They came to the shore at the end of Digranes, and she ran off the edge of the cliff and swam away. Skallagrim threw a huge boulder after her which struck her between the shoulder blades. Neither the woman nor the boulder ever came up afterwards. That spot is now called Brakarsund (Brak's Sound).

Later that evening, when they returned to Borg, Egil was furious. By the time Skallagrim and the other members of the household sat down at the table, Egil had not come to his seat. Then he walked into the room and went over to Skallagrim's favourite, a man who was in charge of the workers and ran the farm with him. Egil killed him with a single blow, then went to his seat. Skallagrim did not mention the matter and it was let rest afterwards, but father and son did not speak to each other, neither kind nor unkind words, and so it remained through the winter.

The next summer Thorolf returned, as was recounted earlier. After spending the winter in Iceland, he prepared his ship in Brakarsund in the spring.

One day when Thorolf was on the point of setting sail, Egil went to see his father and asked him to equip him for a journey.

'I want to go abroad with Thorolf,' he said.

Skallagrim asked if he had discussed the matter with Thorolf. Egil said he had not, so Skallagrim told him to do so first of all.

When Egil raised the subject, Thorolf said there was no chance that 'I would take you away with me. If your own father doesn't feel he can manage you in his house, I can't feel confident about taking you abroad with me, because you won't get away with acting there the way you do here.'

'In that case,' said Egil, 'perhaps neither of us will go.'

That night, a fierce storm broke out, a south-westerly gale. When it was dark and the tide was at its highest, Egil went down to where the ship lay, went aboard and walked around the awnings. He chopped through all the anchor ropes on the seaward side of the ship. Then he rushed to the gangway, pushed it out to sea and cut the moorings fastening the ship to land. The ship drifted out into the fjord. When Thorolf and his men realized that the ship was adrift, they jumped in a boat, but it was much too windy for them to be able to do anything. The ship drifted over to Andakil and on to the spits there, while Egil went back to Borg.

When it became known, most people condemned the trick that Egil had played. But he answered that he would not hesitate to cause Thorolf more trouble and damage if he refused to take him away. Other people intervened in their quarrel, and in the end Thorolf took Egil abroad with him that summer.

On reaching his ship, Thorolf took the axe that Skallagrim had given to him, and threw it overboard into deep water, so that it never came up again.

Thorolf set off that summer and had a smooth passage, making land at Hordaland and heading north to Sognefjord. There, they heard the news that Brynjolf had died from an illness during the winter, and that his sons had shared out his inheritance among them. Thord had taken Aurland, the farm where his father had lived. He had sworn allegiance to the king and taken charge of his lands on his behalf.

Thord had a daughter named Rannveig, whose children were Thord and Helgi. Thord the younger also had a daughter named Rannveig, the mother of Ingirid whom King Olaf married. Helgi's son was Brynjolf, the father of Serk from Sognefjord and Svein.

41 Bjorn received another farm, a good and valuable one, and because he did not swear allegiance to the king, people called him Bjorn the Landowner. He was a man of considerable wealth and power.

After Thorolf landed, he went straight to see Bjorn, bringing his daughter Asgerd to the house with him. It was a joyful reunion. Asgerd was a fine and accomplished woman, wise and knowledgeable.

Thorolf went to see King Eirik. When they met, Thorolf delivered a greeting to him from Skallagrim, saying that he had been grateful for the gift the king had sent him, and presented him with a longship sail that he told him Skallagrim had sent. King Eirik was pleased with the gift, and asked Thorolf to stay with him for the winter.

Thorolf thanked the king for his offer, 'but I must go and see Thorir first. I have some pressing business to attend to with him.'

Then Thorolf went to see Thorir as he had said, and was warmly received there. Thorir asked Thorolf to stay with him.

Thorolf told him he would accept the offer: 'And there is a man with me who will stay wherever I do. He is my brother and has never been away from home before, so he needs me to keep an eye on him.'

Thorir said that Thorolf was free to have more men with him if he wanted – 'We regard it as an asset to have your brother, if he's anything like you.'

Thorolf went to his ship and had it pulled ashore and taken care of, then he and Egil went to stay with Thorir.

Thorir had a son named Arinbjorn, who was somewhat older than Egil. Arinbjorn was already an assertive character at an early age, and highly accomplished. Egil sought Arinbjorn's friendship and followed him around everywhere, but relations between the two brothers Thorolf and Egil were rather strained.

42 Thorolf Skallagrimsson asked Thorir what he would think if he asked for the hand of his niece Asgerd in marriage. Thorir answered favourably and said he would support him. Then Thorolf went north to Sognefjord, with a fine band of men, and reached Bjorn's house. He was welcomed warmly there and Bjorn invited him to stay as long as he wanted. Thorolf soon raised the matter with Bjorn and asked to marry his daughter Asgerd. Bjorn took the proposal favourably and it was easily settled, with the result that the pledges were made then and there and the date was set for the wedding, which was to be held at Bjorn's farm in the autumn. Thorolf went back to Thorir and told him the news of his journey. Thorir was pleased that the marriage had been arranged.

When the date came round for Thorolf to attend the wedding feast, he asked people to join him, inviting Thorir and Arinbjorn first, with their farmhands and more prominent tenants, a large party of worthy men. Just before the date when Thorolf was supposed to leave home, when his party had already arrived to accompany him, Egil fell ill and was unable to join them. Thorolf and his men had a large, well-equipped longship, and proceeded on their journey as planned.

43 There was a man called Olvir who worked for Thorir, managing his farm and the farmhands. He also collected debts and looked after his money. He was no longer young, but very active.

Olvir happened to have to go away to collect the rents that had been owing to Thorir since the spring. He went on a rowboat with twelve of Thorir's farmhands. By this time, Egil was recovering from his illness and was back on his feet. Feeling bored there after everyone had left, he approached Olvir and said he wanted to go with him. Olvir thought there was plenty of room on board for such a fine man to join them, so Egil went along too. Egil took his weapons, a sword, halberd and buckler. Once their ship was ready they set off, but encountered rough weather with strong, unfavourable winds. All the same, they proceeded vigorously, rowing when they needed to, and were drenched.

They happened to arrive at Atloy island in the evening and moored there. Just up from the shore was a large farm which King Eirik owned. It was run by a man called Atloy-Bard, a good steward who served the king well. He was not of a great family, but was highly thought of by King Eirik and Queen Gunnhild.

Olvir and his men hauled their ship up above the shoreline and went to the farm where they met Bard. They told him what their business was and asked to stay there for the night. Seeing how drenched they were, Bard led them into a fire-room which stood away from the other buildings. He had a large fire made up for them to dry their clothes.

When they had put their clothes back on, Bard returned.

'Now we will lay the table here,' said Bard. 'I know that you must feel like going to bed. You must be exhausted after that soaking you had.'

Olvir was pleased at the idea. A table was laid and they were given bread and butter, and large bowls of curds.

Bard said, 'It's a great shame there is no ale in the house to give you the welcome I would have preferred. You must get by with what there is.'

Olvir and his men were very thirsty and drank the curds. Afterwards Bard had whey served, and they drank that as well.

'I would gladly give you something better to drink if I had anything,' Bard said.

There were plenty of mattresses in the room, and he invited them to lie down and go to sleep.

44 King Eirik and Gunnhild arrived in Atloy the same night. Bard had prepared a feast for him, because a sacrifice was being made to the disir. It was a splendid feast, with plenty to drink in the main room.

The king asked where Bard was.

'I can't see him anywhere,' he said.

'Bard is outside,' someone told him, 'serving his guests.'

'Who are these guests that he feels more obliged to attend to than to be in here with us?' asked the king.

The man told him that Thorir the Hersir's men were there.

'Go to them immediately and call them in here,' the king said.

This was done, and they were told the king wanted to meet them.

When they entered, the king welcomed Olvir, offering him a place at table opposite him in the high seat, with his men further down. They took their seats, and Egil sat next to Olvir.

Then the ale was served. Many toasts were drunk, each involving a whole ale-horn. As the night wore on, many of Olvir's companions became incapacitated; some of them vomited inside the main room, while others made it through the door. Bard insisted on serving them more drink.

Egil took the drinking-horn that Bard had given to Olvir and finished it off. Saying that Egil was clearly very thirsty, Bard gave him another full horn at once and asked him to drink that too. Egil took the horn and spoke a verse:

8. You told the trollwomen's foe   *trollwomen's foe*: noble man
    you were short of feast-drink
    when appeasing the goddesses:
    you deceived us, despoiler of graves.
    You hid your plotting thoughts
    from men you did not know
    for sheer spite, Bard:
    you have played a bad trick on us.

Bard told Egil to stop mocking him and get on with his drinking. Egil drank every draught that was handed to him, and those meant for Olvir too.

Then Bard went up to the queen and told her that this man was bringing shame on them, always claiming to be thirsty no matter how much he drank. The queen and Bard mixed poison into the drink and brought it in. Bard made a sign over the draught and handed it to the serving woman, who took it to Egil and offered him a drink. Egil took out his knife and stabbed the palm of his hand with it, then took the drinking-horn, carved runes on it and smeared them with blood. He spoke a verse:

9.   I carve runes on this horn,
     redden words with my blood,
     I choose words for the trees
     of the wild beast's ear-roots;   *ear-roots*: part of the head; their *trees*:
     drink as we wish this mead   horns
     brought by merry servants,
     let us find out how we fare
     from the ale that Bard blessed.

The horn shattered and the drink spilled on to the straw. Olvir was on the verge of passing out, so Egil got up and led him over to the door. He swung his cloak over his shoulder and gripped his sword underneath it. When they reached the door, Bard went after them with a full horn and asked Olvir to drink a farewell toast. Egil stood in the doorway and spoke this verse:

10. I'm feeling drunk, and the ale
     has left Olvir pale in the gills,
     I let the spray of ox-spears   *ox-spears*: drinking-horns
     foam over my beard.
     Your wits have gone, inviter
     of showers on to shields;
     now the rain of the high god   *rain*: i.e. of spears, perhaps of poetry
     starts pouring upon you.   (or vomit?)

Egil tossed away the horn, grabbed hold of his sword and drew it. It was dark in the doorway; he thrust the sword so deep into Bard's stomach that the point came out through his back. Bard fell down dead, blood pouring from the wound. Then Olvir dropped to the floor, spewing vomit. Egil ran out of the room. It was pitch-dark outside, and he dashed from the farm.

People left the room and saw Bard and Olvir lying on the floor together, and imagined at first that they had killed each other. Because it was dark, the king had a light brought over, and they could see that Olvir was lying unconscious in his vomit, but Bard had been killed, and the floor was awash with his blood.

The king asked where that huge man was who had drunk the most that night, and was told that he had gone out in front of Olvir.

'Search for him,' ordered the king, 'and bring him to me.'

A search was made for him around the farm, but he was nowhere to be found. When the king's men went into the fire-room where they had been eating that night, many of Olvir's men were lying there on the floor and others up against the wall of the house. They asked whether Egil had been there. They were told he had run in and taken his weapons, then gone back out.

Then they went into the main room and reported this to the king, who ordered his men to act quickly and take all the ships that were on the island, 'and tomorrow when it is light we will comb the whole island and kill that man'.

45 Egil went by night, heading for the place the ships were, but wherever he came to the beach, there were people. He kept on the move for the whole night, unable to find a ship anywhere.

When dawn began to break, he was on a promontory and could see an island off the shore, across a very long strait. He decided to take off his helmet and sword, and broke the head off his spear and threw the shaft out to sea, then wrapped his weapons in his cloak to make a bundle that he tied to his back. Then he leapt into the sea and swam without stopping until he reached the island, which is called Saudoy, a small island covered with low shrub. A great number of livestock were kept there, cows and sheep, from the king's farm on Atloy. On reaching the island Egil wrung out his clothes and made ready; it was daylight by then and the sun was up.

King Eirik had Atloy combed to look for Egil as soon as it was light. This was a lengthy task because it was a large island, and he was nowhere to be found.

Then the king sent parties out to other islands to look for him. It was late in the evening when twelve men went to Saudoy in a skiff to look for Egil and to take some livestock back with them to slaughter. Egil saw the ship approaching the island, and he lay down in the shrub to hide before the ship landed.

Nine men went ashore and split up into search parties of three each, leaving three men to guard the ship. When they went behind a hill which blocked their view of the ship, Egil stood up, his weapons at the ready. He went straight to the waterfront and along the beach. The men guarding the ship did not notice Egil until he was upon them. He killed one of them with a single blow. Another took to his heels and ran up a slope. Egil swung at him, chopping off his leg. The third leapt into the boat and pushed it out to sea, but Egil grabbed the moorings, pulled the boat back in and jumped into it. They did not exchange many blows before Egil killed him and threw him overboard. He took hold of the oars and rowed the boat away for the rest of the night and the following day, not stopping until he had reached Thorir the Hersir.

Olvir and his men were incapable of doing anything at first after the feast. When they started to feel better, they set off for home. The king allowed them to leave without recrimination.

The men who were stuck on Saudoy spent several nights there; they slaughtered animals to eat and built a big fire to cook them, on the part of the island that faced Atloy, and to serve as a beacon. When this was seen from Atloy, people rowed over to bring the survivors back. By then the king had left Atloy for another feast.

To return to Olvir, he arrived home before Egil, but Thorolf and Thorir were already there. Olvir told them the news about the killing of Bard and everything that had happened, but he knew nothing of Egil's whereabouts after that. Thorolf became very upset, and Arinbjorn too. They did not expect Egil to return. But in daylight the next morning, Egil was discovered lying in his bed. When he heard of this, Thorolf got up and went to see Egil, and asked how he had managed to escape or whether anything of note had happened on his travels. Then Egil spoke a verse:

11.   Great in my deeds, I slipped
       away from the realm of the lord
       of Norway and Gunnhild
       – I do not boast overly –
       by sending three servants
       of that tree of the Valkyrie   *tree of the Valkyrie*: warrior, i.e. the king
       to the otherworld, to stay
       in Hel's high hall.   *Hel*: goddess of death

Arinbjorn applauded the deeds and said it was his father's duty to make terms with the king.

Thorir said people might well agree that Bard deserved to be killed.

'But you, Egil, have inherited your family's gift for caring too little about incurring the king's wrath, and that will be a great burden for most people to bear,' he said. 'But I will try to achieve a settlement between you and King Eirik.'

Thorir soon went to see the king, while Arinbjorn stayed at home and kept watch for himself and Egil, saying they should all meet the same fate. When Thorir saw the king he made an offer on Egil's behalf and proposed pledges for the judgement that the king would pass. King Eirik was so furious that it was virtually impossible to talk to him, and he said his father would be proved right when he had said that pledges could hardly be made on behalf of those kinsmen. He told Thorir to make sure that Egil did not stay in his realm for long.

'But for your sake, Thorir, I will accept money for the death of these men,' he said.

The king set the compensation for the men who had been killed at an amount that he saw fit, and they parted ways. Thorir went home then, and Thorolf and Egil spent the winter with him and Arinbjorn, and were treated well.

46 In the spring, Thorolf and Egil equipped big longships and took on a crew to go raiding in the Baltic that summer. They won a huge amount of booty and fought many battles there, and the same summer they also went to Courland where they lay offshore for a while. They offered the people there a fortnight's truce and traded with them, and when the truce was over they began plundering again. The Courlanders had gathered forces on land, but Thorolf and Egil raided various places that seemed most attractive.

One day they put in to an estuary with a large forest on the upland above it. They went ashore there and split up into parties of twelve men. They walked through the woodland and it was not far until the first settlement began, fairly sparse at first. The Vikings began plundering and killing people at once, and everyone fled from them. The settlements were separated by woods. Meeting no resistance, the raiders split up into smaller bands. Towards the end of the day, Thorolf had the horn sounded to call the men back, and they returned to the woods from wherever they were, since the only way to check whether they were all there was to go to the ships. When they took the count, Egil and his party had not returned. By then night was falling and they did not think there was any point in looking for him.

Egil had crossed a wood with twelve men and found great plains which were settled in many places. A large farm stood nearby them, not far from the wood, and they headed for it. When they reached it they ran inside, but found nobody there. They seized all the valuables they could take with them, but there were so many buildings to search that it took them a fairly long time. When they came out again and headed away from the farm, a large band of men had gathered between them and the wood, and was advancing upon them.

A high stockade extended from the farm to the wood. Egil said they should skirt it to prevent them being attacked from all sides, and his men did so. Egil led the way, with all of them so close together that no one could get between them. The Courlanders shot arrows at them but did not engage in hand-to-hand fighting. As they skirted the stockade, Egil and his men did not realize at first that there was another stockade on the other side of them, narrowing to a bend where they could not proceed any farther. The Courlanders pursued them into this pen. Some attacked them from the outside by lunging with their swords and spears through the fences, while others rendered them harmless by throwing blankets over their weapons. They suffered wounds and were captured, and all were tied up and led back to the farm.

The farm was owned by a powerful and wealthy man who had a grown-up son. They talked about what to do with the prisoners. The farmer advocated killing them one after the other, but his son said that since night was falling, they would not be able to enjoy torturing them, and asked him to wait until morning. The prisoners were thrown into one of the buildings, tightly bound. Egil was tied hand and foot against a post. Then the house was locked up tight, and the Courlanders went into the main room to eat, make merry and drink. Egil wriggled and pressed against the post until it came free of the floor. Then the post fell over. He slipped himself off it, loosened the binding on his hands with his teeth, and when his hands were free he untied his feet. Then he released his companions.

When they were all free, they looked around the building for the most suitable place to escape. The walls of the building were made of large logs, with flat timber panelling at one end. They rammed it, broke down the

panelling and found themselves in another building, with timber walls as
well.

Then they could hear voices coming from below. They searched around
and found a trap-door in the floor, and opened it. Underneath it was a deep
pit where they could hear voices. Egil asked who was there, and a man
called Aki spoke to him. Egil asked him if he wanted to come out of the pit,
and he said all of them certainly did. Egil and his men lowered the ropes
they had been tied up with down into the pit, and hauled three men up.

Aki told them that these were his sons, and that they were Danes and
had been captured the previous summer.

'I was well looked after during the winter,' he said. 'I was put in charge
of tending the cattle for the farmers here, but the boys disliked being made
to work as slaves. In the spring we decided to run away, but then we were
caught and put in this pit.'

'You must be familiar with the layout of the buildings,' Egil said. 'Where's
the best place to get out?'

Aki told them there was another panelled wall: 'Break it down, and you
will be in the barn where you can walk out as you please.'

Egil and his men broke down the panelling, entered the barn and got out
from there. It was pitch-dark. Their companions told them to run for the
woods.

Egil said to Aki, 'If you are familiar with the houses around here, you
must be able to show us some booty.'

Aki said there were plenty of valuables they could take, 'and a large loft
where the farmer sleeps. There's no lack of weapons inside.'

Egil told them to show them the loft. When they went up the stairs they
saw that the loft was open and there were lights inside, and servants were
making the beds. Egil told some of his men to stay outside and make sure
that no one escaped. He ran into the loft and snatched up some weapons
there, for there was no lack of them, and they killed everyone who was
inside. His men armed themselves fully. Aki went over to a hatch in the
floorboards and opened it, saying that they should go down into the room
below. They took a light and went down. The farmer's treasure-chests were
kept there, with valuable articles and much silver, and they took all they
could carry and left. Egil picked up a large chest and carried it under his
arm, and they headed for the woods.

In the woods, Egil stopped and said, 'This is a poor and cowardly raid.
We have stolen all the farmer's wealth without his knowing. Such shame

will never befall us. Let's go back to the farm and let people know what has happened.'

Everyone tried to dissuade him, saying that they wanted to go to the ship. But Egil put down the chest, and dashed off towards the farm. When he reached it he could see servants leaving the fire-room, carrying trenchers into the main room. Egil saw a great fire in a fire-room with cauldrons on top of it. He went over to it. Large logs had been brought inside and the fire was made in the customary manner, by lighting the end of a log and letting it burn all the way down to the others. Egil grabbed the log, carried it over to the main room and thrust the burning end under the eaves and up into the rafters. Some pieces of wood lay in the yard, and he carried them to the door of the main room. The fire quickly kindled the lining of the roof. The first thing the people knew who were sitting there drinking was that the rafters were ablaze. They ran to the door but there was no easy escape there, because of both the piled wood blocking the door and Egil guarding it. He killed them in the doorway and just outside. It was only moments before the main room flared up and caved in. Everyone else was inside and trapped, while Egil went back to the woods and rejoined his companions. They went to the ship together. Egil claimed as his private booty the treasure-chest he had taken, which turned out to be full of silver.

Thorolf and the others were relieved when Egil came back to the ship, and they left when morning broke. Aki and his sons were in Egil's party. They all sailed to Denmark later that summer and sat in ambush for merchant ships, robbing wherever they could.

47   Harald Gormsson had ascended to the throne of Denmark on the death of his father, King Gorm. Denmark was in a state of war, and Vikings lay off its shores in large numbers. Aki was familiar with both the sea and land there. Egil pressed him to find out about places where large amounts of booty could be taken.

When they reached Oresund, Aki told him there was a large town called Lund on the shore where they could expect to find some booty, but would probably encounter resistance from the townspeople. The men were asked whether they should go ashore and raid there, and there was much disagreement. Some advocated mounting an attack, but others argued against it. Then the question was put to the steersmen. Thorolf favoured going ashore. Then Egil was asked his opinion, and he spoke a verse:

12.   Let us make our drawn swords glitter,
        you who stain wolf's teeth with blood;
        now that the fish of the valleys thrive,   *fish of the valleys*: snakes; when
        let us perform brave deeds.   they *thrive*: summer
        Each man in this band
        will set off for Lund apace,
        there before sunset we will
        make noisy clamour of spears.

Then Egil and his men made ready to go ashore and went towards the town. When the townspeople became aware of the threat, they marched to face Egil's men. A wooden fortress surrounded the town, on which they posted men to defend it. Then battle ensued. Egil entered the fortress first, and the townspeople fled. Egil and his men inflicted heavy casualties, plundered the town and set fire to it before leaving. Then they returned to their ships.

48 Thorolf took his men north of Halland, and they moored in a harbour when the weather hindered their journey, but they did not raid there. Living just inland was an earl called Arnfinn. When he learned that Vikings had landed, he sent men to meet them and find out whether their mission was peaceful or warlike.

When the messengers met Thorolf and told him their errand, he said they had no need to raid and plunder in what was not a rich country anyway.

The messengers returned to the earl and told him the outcome of the meeting. When the earl heard that he did not need to gather any forces, he rode down to meet the Vikings without taking any men with him. They got on well together, and the earl invited Thorolf to a feast with any men he wanted to bring with him. Thorolf promised to come.

At the appointed time, the earl had some chargers sent down to them. Both Thorolf and Egil went along, and took thirty men with them. The earl welcomed them kindly when they arrived, and they were shown into the main room. The ale was already on the tables and they were served with drink. They sat there until night.

Before the time came to put away the tables, the earl said that they should cast lots to pair off the men and women who would drink together, as far as numbers allowed, and the remainder would drink by themselves. They all cast their lots into a cloth and the earl picked them out. He had an attractive and nubile daughter who drew lots with Egil to sit together for the evening. She walked around, keeping herself amused, but Egil got up and went to the place she had been sitting during the day. When people took their seats, the earl's daughter went to her place. She spoke a verse:

13.   What do you want my seat for?
       You have not often fed
       wolves with warm flesh;
       I'd rather stoke my own fire.
       This autumn you did not see ravens
       screeching over chopped bodies,
       you were not there when
       razor-sharp blades clashed.

Egil took hold of her and sat her beside him, and spoke a verse:

14.   I have wielded a blood-stained sword
       and howling spear; the bird
       of carrion followed me   *bird of carrion*: raven
       when the Vikings pressed forth;
       In fury we fought battles,
       fire swept through men's homes,
       we made bloody bodies
       slump dead by city gates.

They drank together that night and got on well together. It was a fine feast, and there was another the next day. Then the Vikings went to their ships. They left in friendship and exchanged gifts with the earl. Thorolf and Egil took their men to the Branno Islands, where Vikings used to lie in wait in those days for the many trading ships that sailed through them.

Aki and his sons went home to his farmlands. He was a wealthy man who owned many farms in Jutland. They left Thorolf and Egil on close terms, and each promised the other firm friendship.

When autumn arrived, Thorolf and Egil sailed north to Norway and put in at Fjordane, where they went to see Thorir the Hersir. He welcomed them warmly, and his son Arinbjorn even more so. Arinbjorn invited Egil to stay there for the winter, and he accepted gratefully.

But Thorir considered this a rather rash invitation when he heard about it.

'I do not know what King Eirik will think about it,' he said, 'because after Bard was killed, he said he did not want Egil in this country.'

'Father, you can easily use your influence with the king to stop him objecting to Egil's staying here. You can invite Thorolf, your kinsman by marriage, to be here, and Egil and I will both stay in the same place for the winter.'

From what Arinbjorn said, Thorir could see he intended to have his own way. The two of them invited Thorolf to stay for the winter, and he accepted the offer. Twelve men spent the winter there.

There were two brothers called Thorvald the Overbearing and Thorfinn the Strong, close relatives of Bjorn the Landowner, and many who had been brought up with him. They were big, strong men, great fighters and assertive. They had gone with Bjorn on his Viking raids, and when he settled down the brothers joined Thorolf and went raiding with him. They sat in the prow of his ship, and when Egil took over command of his own ship, Thorfinn manned the prow. The brothers went everywhere with Thorolf and he favoured them above the rest of his crew. They joined his men that winter, and sat next to Thorolf and Egil at table. Thorolf sat in the high seat, sharing drink with Thorir, while Egil's drinking partner was Arinbjorn. Guests left their seats and took to the floor every time a toast was drunk.

In the autumn, Thorir the Hersir went to see King Eirik, who gave him a fine welcome. Thorir began by asking him not to take offence at the fact that Egil was staying with him for the winter.

The king answered favourably, saying that Thorir could have whatever he wanted from him, 'although things would be different if someone else had taken Egil in'.

But when Gunnhild heard what they were talking about, she said, 'I think that once again you are allowing yourself to be too easily persuaded and are quick to forget being wronged. You'll go on favouring Skallagrim's sons until they kill a few more of your close kinsmen. Even though you happen to think Bard's killing was insignificant, I don't.'

The king said, 'More than anyone else, Gunnhild, you doubt my courage, and you used to be fonder of Thorolf than you are now. But I will not go back on my word once I have given it to him and his brother.'

'Thorolf was welcome here until Egil spoiled things for him,' she said. 'Now there is no difference between them.'

Thorir went home when he was ready, and told the brothers what the king and queen had said.

49 Gunnhild had two brothers called Eyvind Braggart and Alf Askmann, sons of Ozur Snout. They were big, powerful men and great fighters, and held in very high regard by King Eirik and Gunnhild, although they were not popular with most people. They were young at this time, but fully grown.

That spring, a huge sacrificial feast was arranged for the summer at Gaular, where there was a fine main temple. A large party attended from the Fjordane, Fjaler and Sognefjord provinces, most of them men of high birth. King Eirik went there too.

Gunnhild said to her brothers, 'I want you to take advantage of the crowd here and kill one of Skallagrim's sons, or preferably both.'

They said they would do so.

Thorir the Hersir made ready for the journey. He called Arinbjorn to talk to him.

'I am going to the sacrifice,' he said, 'and I don't want Egil to go. I know about Gunnhild's conniving, Egil's impetuousness and the king's severity, and we cannot keep an eye on all three at once. But Egil will not be dissuaded from going unless you stay behind too. Thorolf will be going with me, and their other companions. Thorolf will make a sacrifice and seek good fortune for himself and his brother.'

Arinbjorn told Egil afterwards that he would be staying at home.

'The two of us will stay here,' he said.

Egil agreed.

Thorir and the others went to the sacrifice and a sizeable crowd gathered there, drinking heavily. Thorolf followed Thorir everywhere he went, and they were never separated, neither by day nor by night.

Eyvind told Gunnhild he hadn't had a chance to get at Thorolf.

She ordered him to kill one of his men instead, 'rather than all of them escaping'.

One night the king had gone to bed, and so had Thorir and Thorolf, but Thorfinn and Thorvald were still up. Eyvind and Alf came and sat down with them and made merry, drinking from the same horn at first, then in pairs. Eyvind and Thorvald drank together from one horn, and Alf and Thorfinn from the other. As the night wore on they started cheating over the drinking, and a quarrel broke out that ended in abuse. Eyvind leapt to his feet, drew his short-sword and stabbed Thorvald, delivering a wound that was more than enough to kill him. Then the king's men and Thorir's men both leapt to their feet, but none of them was armed because they were in a sacred temple, and people broke up the fighting among those who were the most furious. Nothing else of note happened that night.

Because Eyvind had committed murder in a sacred place he was declared a defiler and had to go into outlawry at once. The king offered compensation for the man he had killed, but Thorolf and Thorfinn said they had never accepted compensation from anyone, refused the offer and left. Then Thorir, Thorolf and the rest went home.

King Eirik and Gunnhild sent Eyvind south to King Harald Gormsson in Denmark, because he had been banished from wherever Norwegian laws applied. The king welcomed him and his companions warmly. Eyvind had taken a big longship to Denmark with him and the king put him in charge of defending the land from Vikings. Eyvind was a great warrior.

The winter came to an end and spring arrived, and Thorolf and Egil made ready to go on Viking raids again. When they had prepared themselves they headed for the Baltic again, but on reaching Vik they sailed south past Jutland to plunder there. Afterwards they went to Frisia and stayed much of the summer there, then went back to Denmark.

One night when they were moored at the border between Denmark and Frisia, and were getting ready for bed, two men boarded Egil's ship and said they needed to talk to him. They were led in to see Egil.

The men said they had been sent by Aki the Wealthy to tell him that 'Eyvind Braggart is moored off the coast of Jutland and plans to ambush you when you come back from the south. He has gathered such a large force that you won't stand a chance if you confront all of it at once. Eyvind himself is in command of two light ships and is not far away.'

When he heard this news, Egil ordered his men to lift the awnings and not make any noise. They did so. At dawn they came upon Eyvind and his men where they were anchored. They attacked them with a volley of rocks and spears. Many of Eyvind's men were killed, but Eyvind himself jumped overboard and swam to land, along with some others who also escaped.

Egil and his men seized their ships, clothes and weapons, then returned to Thorolf. He asked Egil where he had been, and where he had got the ships they were sailing. Egil told him they had taken them from Eyvind Braggart. Then Egil spoke a verse:

15.   A mighty fierce attack
       we made off Jutland's shores.
       He fought well, the Viking
       who guarded the Danish realm,
       until swift Eyvind Braggart
       and his men all bolted
       from their horse of the waves   *horse of the waves*: ship
       and swam off the eastern sand.

Thorolf said, 'I think what you have done will make it inadvisable for us to go to Norway this autumn.'

Egil said it was well for them to look for another place.

50   In the days of King Harald Fair-hair of Norway, Alfred the Great reigned over England, the first of his kinsmen to be sole ruler there. His son Edward succeeded him on the throne; he was the father of Athelstan the Victorious, who fostered Hakon the Good. At this time, Athelstan succeeded his father on the throne. Edward had other sons, Athelstan's brothers.

After Athelstan's succession, some of the noblemen who had lost their realms to his family started to make war upon him, seizing the opportunity to claim them back when a young king was in control. These were British,* Scots and Irish. But King Athelstan mustered an army, and paid anyone who wanted to enter his service, English and foreign alike.

Thorolf and Egil sailed south past Saxony and Flanders, and heard that the king of England was in need of soldiers, and that there was hope of much booty there. They decided to go there with their men. In the autumn they set off and went to see King Athelstan. He welcomed them warmly and felt that their support would strengthen his forces greatly. In the course of their conversations he invited them to stay with him, enter his service and defend his country. It was agreed that they would become King Athelstan's men.

England had been Christian for a long time when this happened. King Athelstan was a devout Christian, and was called Athelstan the Faithful. The king asked Thorolf and Egil to take the sign of the cross, because that was a common custom then among both merchants and mercenaries who

---

* I.e. Welsh and possibly other native peoples.

dealt with Christians. Anyone who had taken the sign of the cross could mix freely with both Christians and heathens, while keeping the faith that they pleased. Thorolf and Egil did so at the king's request, and both took the sign of the cross. Three hundred of their men entered the king's service.

51   Olaf the Red was the king of Scotland. He was Scottish on his father's side and Danish on his mother's, a descendant of Ragnar Shaggy-breeches. He was a powerful man; the realm of Scotland was considered to be one-third of the size of England.

Northumbria was considered to be one-fifth of the English realm. It is the northernmost district, next to Scotland in the east, and had belonged to Danish kings in times of old. The main town is York. Northumbria belonged to King Athelstan, and he had appointed two earls to rule it, named Alfgeir and Godric. They stayed there to defend it against aggression by Scots and by Danes and Norwegians, who raided heavily and made a strong claim on the land, since the only people there of any standing were of Danish descent on their father's or mother's side, and there were many of each.

Two brothers called Hring and Adils ruled Britain.* They paid tribute to King Athelstan, and accordingly, when they went to battle with the king, they and their men were in the vanguard, with the king's standard-bearers. These brothers were great warriors, even though they were no longer young men.

Alfred the Great had deprived all the tributary kings of their rank and power. Those who had been kings or princes before were now titled earls. This arrangement prevailed throughout his lifetime and that of his son Edward, but when Athelstan ascended to the throne at an early age he was considered a less imposing figure and many people who had once served the king became disloyal.

52   King Olaf of Scotland gathered a great army and went south to England, and on reaching Northumbria he began plundering. When the earls who ruled there heard this, they mustered troops and went to face the king. A great battle ensued when they met, which ended in a victory for King Olaf, while Godric was killed and Alfgeir fled, together with the majority of the troops that had accompanied them and managed to escape from the fighting. Since Alfgeir offered no resistance, King Olaf conquered the whole

* I.e. Wales and neighbouring territories.

of Northumbria. Alfgeir went to meet King Athelstan and told him of his misfortunes.

Hearing that such a huge army had entered his land, Athelstan dispatched messengers at once, gathered forces and sent word to the earls and other leaders. The king set off straight away with the troops he mustered and went to face the Scots.

When word spread that King Olaf had won a battle and taken control of a large part of England, acquiring a much greater army than Athelstan, many powerful men joined him. Hring and Adils heard this when they had gathered a large force and joined his side, making an enormous army.

When King Athelstan heard all this, he met his chieftains and counsellors to ask what the best course of action would be, and gave everyone a full account of what he had heard about the deeds of the Scottish king and his large band of men. They were unanimous that Earl Alfgeir had done terribly and deserved to be stripped of his rank. A plan was decided whereby King Athelstan would go back to the south of England and move northwards across the whole country gathering troops, because they saw that it would be a slow process mustering forces on the scale they needed unless the king himself were to lead the army.

The king appointed Thorolf and Egil as leaders of the army that had rallied there. They were to be in charge of the forces that the Vikings had brought to the king; Alfgeir was still in control of his own troops. The king appointed other men to lead the other divisions as he saw fit. When Egil returned to his companions after the meeting, they asked him what news he had to report about the king of the Scots. He spoke a verse:

16.   Olaf turned one earl in flight
       in a sharp encounter,
       and felled another; I have heard
       this warrior is hard to face.
       Godric went far astray
       on his path through the battlefield;
       the scourge of the English subdues
       half of Alfgeir's realm.

After that they sent messengers to King Olaf, saying that King Athelstan challenged him to a battle and proposed Wen Heath* by Wen Forest as a

---

* The site of this battle has not been satisfactorily identified.

site; he wanted them to stop raiding his realm, and the victor of the battle should rule England. He proposed meeting in battle after one week, and that the first to arrive should wait one week for the other. It was a custom then that if a king had been challenged to a pitched battle, he incurred dishonour if he went on raiding before it had been fought. King Olaf responded by stopping his armies and ceasing his attacks until the appointed day for the battle. Then he moved his troops to Wen Heath.

There was a fortress north of the heath where King Olaf stayed and kept the greater part of his army, because beyond it lay a large stretch of countryside which he considered well suited for transporting provisions for his army. He sent his men up to the heath which had been appointed as the battlefield, to camp there and prepare themselves before the other army arrived. When they reached the place chosen for the battlefield, hazel rods had already been put up to mark where it would be fought. The site had to be chosen carefully, since it had to be level and big enough for large armies to gather. At the site of the battlefield there was a level moor with a river on one side and a large forest on the other.

King Athelstan's men had set up camp over a very long range at the narrowest point between the forest and river. Their tents stretched all the way from the forest to the river, and they had made camp so as to leave every third tent empty, with only a few men in each of the others.

When King Olaf's men arrived, Athelstan's troops had gathered at the front of the camp, preventing them from entering the area. Athelstan's troops said that their tents were so full of men that there was nowhere near enough room for them all. The tents were on such high ground that it was impossible for Olaf's men to see past them and tell whether they were closely pitched, so they assumed that this must be a great army.

King Olaf's men pitched their tents north of the hazel rods that marked out the battlefield, on a fairly steep slope. Every day, moreover, Athelstan's men said their king was either on his way then or had reached the fortress south of the moor. Troops joined them day and night.

Once the appointed time had passed, Athelstan's men sent messengers to King Olaf to tell him that their king was ready to do battle and had a great army with him, but that he wanted to avoid inflicting casualties on the scale that seemed likely. Instead, he told them to return to Scotland, offering to give them a shilling of silver for every plough in all his realm as a pledge of friendship between them.

King Olaf began preparing his army for battle when the messengers arrived, and intended to set off. But when they had delivered their message, he called a halt for the day and discussed it with the leaders of his army. They were divided over what to do. Some were eager to accept the offer, claiming that it would earn them great renown to return after exacting such a payment from Athelstan. Others discouraged him, saying that Athelstan would offer much more the second time if they turned this gesture down. This was what they decided to do.

The messengers asked King Olaf for time to meet King Athelstan again and find out if he was prepared to pay more to keep the peace. They asked for a day's leave to ride home, another day to discuss the matter and a third to come back, and the king agreed. The messengers went home and returned on the third day as had been settled, to tell King Olaf that King Athelstan was prepared to repeat his earlier offer, with an extra payment to the troops of one shilling for every free-born man, a mark for every leader of twelve men or more, a mark of gold for every captain and five marks of gold for every earl.

Olaf had the offer put to his men, and once again some were against it and others were eager to accept. In the end the king pronounced that he would accept the offer on condition that King Athelstan would give him Northumbria too, with all the dues and tributes that went with it.

The messengers asked for another three days' leave, and also for some of Olaf's men to go with them to hear King Athelstan's reply about whether or not he would accept this option, saying that they expected he would let little or nothing stand in the way of achieving a settlement. King Olaf agreed, and sent his men to King Athelstan. The messengers rode together and met King Athelstan in the nearest fortress on the southern side of the moor.

King Olaf's men delivered their message and offer of a settlement. Athelstan's men also told him the offer they had made to King Olaf, adding that wise men had advised them to delay the battle until King Athelstan arrived.

King Athelstan made a quick decision on the matter, telling the messengers, 'Send word from me to King Olaf that I want to give him leave to return to Scotland with his troops and repay all the money which he wrongly took in this country. Let us then declare peace between our countries, and promise not to attack each other. In addition, King Olaf will swear allegiance to me, and rule Scotland in my name as my tributary king. Go back and tell him the way things stand.'

That same evening the messengers went back and reached King Olaf in the middle of the night. They woke him up and told him King Athelstan's reply at once. The king had his earls and other leaders called over, then had the messengers repeat the outcome of their mission and King Athelstan's reply. When they heard it they were unanimous that the next step would be to prepare for battle. The messengers added that Athelstan had a huge army and had arrived in the fortress where they had been that same day.

The Earl Adils said, 'What I told you is coming to pass, King: you will find the English are cunning. While we have spent so much time sitting here waiting, they have mustered all their forces, but their king was nowhere around when we arrived here. They have been gathering a huge army since we put up camp here. My advice now is that I ride to battle with my brother this very night, with our troops. There is a chance that they will not be on their guard now that they have heard their king is nearby with a great army. We will mount an attack on them, and when they flee they will be routed and prove all the less courageous to fight us afterwards.'

The king considered this a fine plan – 'We will make our army ready at daybreak and join you.'

After deciding on this plan of action, they called an end to their meeting.

53 Earl Hring and his brother Adils prepared their army and set off southwards towards the moor the same night. At daybreak, Thorolf and Egil's guards saw the army approaching. Trumpets were sounded and the troops put on their armour, then formed into two columns. Earl Alfgeir commanded one of the columns with the standard at its head. In the column were the troops he had taken with him, together with others who had joined them from the countryside. It was a much larger band than the one under Thorolf and Egil's command.

Thorolf was equipped with a broad, thick shield and a tough helmet on his head, and was girded with a sword which he called Long, a fine and trusty weapon. He carried a thrusting-spear in his hand. Its blade was two ells long and rectangular, tapering to a point at one end but thick at the other. The shaft measured only a hand's length below the long and thick socket which joined it to the blade, but it was exceptionally stout. There was an iron spike through the socket, and the shaft was completely clad with iron. Such spears were known as 'scrapers of mail'.

Egil was equipped like Thorolf, girded with a sword that he called Adder and had received in Courland, an outstanding weapon. Neither of them wore a coat of mail.

They raised the standard, which Thorfinn the Strong carried. All their troops had Viking shields and other Viking weaponry, and all the Vikings who were in the army were in their column. Thorolf and his men gathered near the wood, while Alfgeir's went along the riverside.

Realizing that they would not be able to take Thorolf by surprise, Earl Adils and his brother began to group into two columns as well, with two standards. Adils grouped his troops to face Earl Alfgeir, and Hring against the Vikings. Then battle began, and both sides marched forward bravely.

Earl Adils pressed forward until Alfgeir yielded ground. Then they advanced all the more bravely, and it was not long before Alfgeir fled. What happened to him was that he rode away south along the moor, with a band of men with him. He rode until he approached the fortress where the king was staying.

Then Earl Alfgeir said, 'I do not want to go to the town. We were showered with abuse the last time we returned to the king after suffering defeat at King Olaf's hands, and King Athelstan will not think our qualities have improved on this expedition. I won't expect him to show me any honour.'

Then he set off for the south of England and what happened on his journey was that he rode night and day until he and his men reached Earlsness* in the west. He took a ship over the channel to France, where one side of his family came from, and he never returned to England.

Adils pursued the fleeing troops a short way at first, then returned to the site of the battle and mounted an attack.

Seeing this, Thorolf swung round to face the earl and ordered his men to bring his banner there, keep on the alert and stay close together.

'We will edge our way towards the forest,' he said, 'and use it to cover us from the rear, so that they cannot attack us from all sides.'

They did so and skirted the forest. A tough battle ensued. Egil attacked Adils and they fought hard. Despite the considerable difference in numbers, more of Adils' men were killed.

Then Thorolf began fighting so furiously that he threw his shield over his back, grabbed his spear with both hands and charged forward, hacking and thrusting to either side. Men leapt out of the way all around, but he killed many of them. He cleared a path to Earl Hring's standard, and there was no holding him back. He killed Earl Hring's standard-bearer and chopped down the pole. Then he drove the spear through the earl's coat of mail, into his chest and through his body so that it came out between his shoulder

---

* Unidentified; apparently in Wales.

blades, lifted him up on it above his own head and thrust the end into the ground. Everyone saw how the earl died on the spear, both his own men and his enemies. Then Thorolf drew his sword and hacked to either side, and his men attacked. Many British and Scots were killed then, and others turned and fled.

When Earl Adils saw his brother's death, the heavy casualties in his ranks and the men who were fleeing, he realized that the cause was lost. He turned to flee as well and ran for the forest, where he hid with his band. All the troops who had been with them fled too. They sustained heavy casualties and they scattered far and wide across the moor. Earl Adils had thrown down his standard and no one could tell whether it was he who was fleeing, or someone else. Night soon began to fall, and Thorolf and Egil returned to their camp just as King Athelstan arrived with all his army, and they put up their tents and settled down.

Shortly afterwards, King Olaf appeared with his army. They put up their tents and settled for the night where their men had already made camp. King Olaf was told that both his earls, Hring and Adils, had been killed along with many other men.

54 King Athelstan had settled for the night in the fortress mentioned earlier where he had heard about the battle on the moor. He and his whole army made ready at once and went north along the moor, where they heard clear accounts of the outcome of the battle. Thorolf and Egil went to meet the king, and he thanked them for their courage and the victory they had won, pledging them his total friendship. They remained there together for the night.

King Athelstan woke his men early the next morning. He spoke to his leaders and described how his troops were to be arranged. He ordered his band to lead the way, spearheaded by the finest fighters, and put Egil in command of it.

'Thorolf will stay with his men and some others that I will place there,' he said. 'This will be our second column and he will be in charge of it, because the Scots tend to break ranks, run back and forth and appear in different places. They often prove dangerous if you do not keep on the alert, but retreat if you confront them.'

Egil answered the king, 'I do not want to be separated from Thorolf in battle, but I think we should be assigned where we are needed the most and the fighting is the heaviest.'

Thorolf said, 'Let the king decide where he wants to assign us. We will support him as he wishes. I can take the place you have been assigned, if you want.'

Egil said, 'You can decide, but this is an arrangement I will live to regret.'

The men formed columns as the king had ordered and raised the standards. The king's column stood on the plain and faced towards the river, and Thorolf's skirted the forest above it.

King Olaf saw that Athelstan had arranged his troops, and he began doing the same. He formed two columns as well, and moved his standard and the column that he commanded, to face King Athelstan and his men. Both armies were so big that it was impossible to tell which was the larger. King Olaf's other column moved closer to the forest to face the men who were under Thorolf's command. It was led by Scottish earls and was very large, mostly consisting of Scots.

Then the troops clashed and a great battle soon ensued. Thorolf advanced bravely and had his standard carried along the side of the forest, intending to approach the king's men from their vulnerable side. He and his men were holding their shields in front of them, using the forest as cover to their right. Thorolf advanced so far that few of his men were in front of him, and when he was least expecting it, Earl Adils and his men ran out of the forest. Thorolf was stabbed with many spears at once and died there beside the forest. Thorfinn, his standard-bearer, retreated to where the troops were closer together, but Adils attacked them and a mighty battle ensued. The Scots let out a cry of victory when they had felled the leader.

When Egil heard their cry and saw Thorolf's standard being withdrawn, he sensed that Thorolf could not be following it. He then ran out between the columns, and as soon as he met his men he found out what had happened. He urged them to show great courage, and led the way. Holding his sword Adder, he advanced bravely and chopped to either side, and killed many men. Thorfinn carried the standard directly behind Egil, and the rest of the men followed it. A fierce battle took place, and Egil fought on until he came to Earl Adils. They exchanged a few blows before Adils was killed, and many men around him too, and when he died the troops he had led fled the field. Egil and his men pursued them, killing everyone they could catch, and it was pointless for anyone to ask for his life to be spared. The Scottish earls did not remain very long when they saw their companions fleeing, and ran away themselves.

Egil and his men headed for the king's column, came upon them from their vulnerable side and soon inflicted heavy casualties. The formation broke up and disintegrated. Many of Olaf's men fled, and the Vikings let out a cry of victory. When King Athelstan sensed that King Olaf's column was giving way, he urged his own men forward and had his standard brought forward, launching such a fierce assault that they broke ranks and suffered heavy losses. King Olaf was killed there, along with the majority of his men, because all those who fled were killed if they were caught. King Athelstan won a great victory there.

55 King Athelstan left the scene of the battle and his men pursued those who had fled. He rode back to the fortress without stopping for the night until he reached it, while Egil pursued the fleeing troops for a long time, killing every one of them that he caught. Then he returned to the scene of the battle with his band of men and found his dead brother Thorolf. He picked up his body and washed it, then dressed the corpse according to custom. They dug a grave there and buried Thorolf in it with his full weaponry and armour. Egil clasped a gold ring on to each of his arms before he left him, then they piled rocks over the grave and sprinkled it with earth. Then Egil spoke a verse:

17. The slayer of the earl, unfearing,
     ventured bravely forth
     in the thunder god's din: *thunder god's din*: battle
     bold-hearted Thorolf fell.
     The ground will grow over
     my great brother near Wen;
     deep as my sorrow is
     I must keep it to myself.

     And he spoke another verse:

18. I piled body-mounds, west of where
     the poles marked the battlefield.
     With black Adder I smote Adils
     in a heavy shower of blows.
     The young Olaf made
     thunder of steel with the English;   *thunder of steel*: battle
     Hring entered the weapon-fray
     and the ravens did not starve.

Then Egil went with his band of men to see King Athelstan, and approached him where he was sitting and drinking. There was much revelry. And when the king saw Egil arrive, he gave an order to clear the lower bench for his men, and told Egil to sit in the high seat there, facing him.

Egil sat down and put his shield at his feet. He was wearing a helmet and laid his sword across his knees, and now and again he would draw it half-way out of the scabbard, then thrust it back in. He sat upright, but with his head bowed low. Egil had very distinctive features, with a wide forehead, bushy brows and a nose that was not long but extremely broad. His upper jaw was broad and long, and his chin and jawbones were exceptionally wide. With his thick neck and stout shoulders, he stood out from other men. When he was angry, his face grew harsh and fierce. He was well built and taller than other men, with thick wolf-grey hair, although he had gone bald at an early age. When he was sitting in this particular scene, he wrinkled one eyebrow right down on to his cheek and raised the other up to the roots of his hair. Egil had dark eyes and was swarthy. He refused to drink even when served, but just raised and lowered his eyebrows in turn.

King Athelstan was sitting in the high seat, with his sword laid across his knees too. And after they had been sitting there like that for a while, the king unsheathed his sword, took a fine, large ring from his arm and slipped it over the point of the sword, then stood up and walked across the floor and handed it over the fire to Egil. Egil stood up, drew his sword and walked out on to the floor. He put his sword through the ring and pulled it towards him, then went back to his place. The king sat down in his high seat. When Egil sat down, he drew the ring on to his arm, and his brow went back to normal. He put down his sword and helmet and took the drinking-horn that was served to him, and finished it. Then he spoke a verse:

19.	The god of the armour hangs	*god of the armour*: warrior, king
	a jangling snare upon my clutch,	*jangling snare*: ring
	the gibbet of hunting-birds,	*gibbet of hunting-birds*: arm
	the stamping-ground of hawks.	
	I raise the ring, the clasp that is worn	
	on the shield-splitting arm,	
	on to my rod of the battle-storm,	*rod of the battle-storm*: sword
	in praise of the feeder of ravens.	*feeder of ravens*: warrior, i.e. Athelstan

From then onwards, Egil drank his full share and spoke to the others.

Afterwards, the king had two chests brought in, carried by two men each. They were both full of silver.

The king said, 'These chests are yours, Egil. And if you go to Iceland, you will present this money to your father, which I am sending him as compensation for the death of his son. Share some of the money with Thorolf's kinsmen, those you regard as the best. Take compensation for your brother from me here, land or wealth, whichever you prefer, and if you wish to stay with me for longer I will grant you any honour and respect that you care to name yourself.'

Egil accepted the money and thanked the king for his gift and friendship. From then on he began to cheer up, and spoke a verse:

20.   For sorrow my beetling brows
      drooped over my eyelids.
      Now I have found one who smoothed
      the wrinkles on my forehead:
      the king has pushed the cliffs   *cliffs*: eyebrows
      that gird my mask's ground,   *mask's ground*: face
      back above my eyes.
      He grants bracelets no quarter.

Afterwards the men who were thought likely to survive had their wounds dressed.

Egil remained with King Athelstan for the winter after Thorolf's death, and earned great respect from him. All the men who had been with the brothers and survived the battle stayed with him. Egil composed a drapa in praise of the king which includes the following verse:

21.   The wager of battle who towers
      over the land, the royal progeny,
      has felled three kings; the realm
      passes to the kin of Ella.   *Ella*: (probably) king of Northumbria,
      Athelstan did other feats,   d. 867.
      the high-born king subdues all.
      This I swear, dispenser   *wave-fire*: gold; its *dispenser*: generous
      of golden wave-fire.   man, king

      This is the refrain in the drapa:

22.   Even the highland deer's paths   *highland deer's paths*: Scotland
      belong to mighty Athelstan now.

As a reward for his poetry, Athelstan gave Egil two more gold rings weighing a mark each, along with an expensive cloak that the king himself had worn.

When spring came, Egil announced to the king that he intended to leave for Norway that summer and find out about the situation of Asgerd, 'who was my brother Thorolf's wife. They have amassed plenty of wealth, but I do not know whether any of their children are still alive. I must provide for them if they are alive, but shall inherit everything if Thorolf has died childless.'

The king said, 'While it is your decision, of course, to leave here if you feel you have duties to attend to, Egil, I would prefer you to do otherwise; stay here permanently and accept anything you care to name.'

Egil thanked the king for this offer: 'I must leave immediately,' he said, 'as is my duty. But I am more likely than not to return to collect what you have promised me, when I can arrange it.'

The king invited him to do so. Then Egil made ready to leave with his men, although many remained behind with the king. Egil had a great longship with a hundred men or more on board. And when he was ready to set off and a fair wind got up, he put out to sea. He and King Athelstan parted in great friendship. He asked Egil to come back as quickly as he possibly could. Egil said he would do so.

Then Egil headed for Norway, and when he reached land he sailed straight to Fjordane. He was told that Thorir the Hersir had died and that his son Arinbjorn had succeeded to his titles and become one of the king's men. Egil went to meet Arinbjorn and was well received by him. Arinbjorn invited him to stay there, and Egil accepted the offer. He had his ship pulled up on the beach, and his men were given places to stay. Arinbjorn took Egil and eleven other men into his house, and he spent the winter with him.

56 Berg-Onund, son of Thorgeir Thorn-foot, had married Bjorn the Landowner's daughter Gunnhild, and she was living with him at Ask. Asgerd, now Thorolf Skallagrimsson's widow, was staying with her kinsman Arinbjorn. She and Thorolf had a young daughter named Thordis, who was with her mother. Egil told Asgerd of Thorolf's death and offered to provide for her. Asgerd was very upset at the news but she answered Egil fittingly, and played the matter down.

As autumn progressed, Egil grew very melancholy and would often sit down with his head bowed into his cloak.

Once, Arinbjorn went to him and asked what was causing his melancholy – 'Even though you have suffered a great loss with your brother's death, the manly thing to do is bear it well. One man lives after another's death. What poetry have you been composing? Let me hear some.'

Egil told him this was his most recent verse:

23. The goddess of the arm where hawks perch,   *goddess of the arm*: woman
     woman, must suffer my rudeness;
     when young I would easily dare
     to lift the sheer cliffs of my brow.   *lift . . . my brow*: i.e. look up
     Now I must conceal in my cloak
     the outcrop between my brows   *outcrop between my brows*: nose
     when she enters the poet's mind,
     head-dress of the rock-giant's earth.   *head-dress of the rock-giant's earth*: woman (possibly also a play on As-gerd, which means 'God-fence' but its components can also be read as 'hill-head-dress')

Arinbjorn asked who this woman was that he was making love poems about – 'There seems to be a clue about her name concealed in the verse.'

Then Egil spoke this verse:

24. I seldom hide the name
     of my female relative
     in the drink of the giant's kin;   *drink of the giant's kin*: poetry
     sorrow wanes in sea-fire's fortress.   *sea-fire*: gold; its *fortress*: woman
     Some who stir the din
     of valkyries' armour   *valkyries' armour*: battle
     have poetic fingers that feel
     the essence of the war-god's wine.   *war-god*: Odin; his *wine*: poetry

'This is a case where the saying applies that you can tell anything to a friend,' said Egil. 'I will answer your question who the woman is that I make poems about. It is your kinswoman Asgerd, and I would like your support in arranging this marriage.'

Arinbjorn said he thought this was a fine idea, 'and I will certainly put in a word to bring the match about'.

Afterwards, Egil put his proposal to Asgerd, but she referred it for the advice of her father and her kinsman Arinbjorn. Then Arinbjorn discussed it with Asgerd, and she gave the same answer as before. Arinbjorn urged her to accept the offer of marriage. After that, Arinbjorn and Egil went to see Bjorn and Egil made a proposal to marry his daughter. Bjorn responded favourably, saying that it was up to Arinbjorn to decide. Arinbjorn favoured it strongly, so in the end they became betrothed, and their wedding was arranged to be held at Arinbjorn's house. When the appointed time came, a lavish feast was held there, and Egil took her for his wife. He remained in good spirits for the rest of the winter.

In the spring, Egil equipped a merchant ship to sail to Iceland. Arinbjorn had advised him not to stay in Norway while Queen Gunnhild held such power.

'She is very ill-disposed towards you,' Arinbjorn said, 'and it made things much worse when you ran into Eyvind off Jutland.'

When Egil was ready and a favourable wind got up, he sailed out to sea and had an easy passage. He reached Iceland in the autumn and headed for Borgarfjord. He had been away for twelve years. Skallagrim was growing very old by then, and was delighted when Egil returned. Egil went to stay at Borg, taking with him Thorfinn the Strong and many of his men. They spent the winter with Skallagrim. Egil had an enormous amount of wealth, but it is not mentioned whether he ever shared the silver that King Athelstan had presented to him, either with Skallagrim or anyone else.

That winter, Thorfinn married Skallagrim's daughter Saeunn, and the following spring Skallagrim gave them a place to live at Langarfoss, and the land stretching inshore from the Leirulaek brook between the Langa and Alfta rivers, all the way up to the mountains. Thorfinn and Saeunn had a daughter named Thordis, who married Arngeir from Holm, the son of Bersi the Godless. Their son was Bjorn, Champion of the Hitardal people.

Egil stayed with Skallagrim for several winters, and looked after the property and ran the farm just as much as Skallagrim did. Egil went balder than ever.

Then the district began to be settled in many places. Hromund, brother of Grim the Halogalander, was living at Thverarhlid with the crew of his ship. Hromund was the father of Gunnlaug, whose daughter, Thurid Dylla, was the mother of Illugi the Black.

57 One summer when Egil had been at Borg for many years, a ship arrived in Iceland from Norway, bringing the news that Bjorn the Landowner was dead. It was also reported that Bjorn's son-in-law, Berg-Onund, had taken all his wealth. He had taken all the valuables to his own home, and had put tenants on the farms and was collecting rent from them. He had also seized all the lands that Bjorn had owned.

When Egil learned of this, he asked in detail whether Berg-Onund would have done this on his own initiative, or with the backing of more powerful people. He was told that Onund was a good friend of King Eirik, and even closer to Queen Gunnhild.

Egil let the matter rest for the autumn. But at the end of winter and in early spring, Egil had the ship brought out that he owned and that had been standing in a shed at Langarfoss, equipped it to go to sea and gathered a crew. His wife Asgerd went on the journey, but Thorolf's daughter Thordis stayed behind. Egil put out to sea when he was ready, and nothing of note happened until he reached Norway. He went straight to see Arinbjorn at the first opportunity. Arinbjorn welcomed Egil and invited him to stay, which he accepted. Asgerd went there with him, along with several people.

Egil soon brought up the subject with Arinbjorn of collecting the property he laid claim to in that country.

'It does not look too promising,' Arinbjorn said. 'Berg-Onund is tough and troublesome, unfair and greedy, and now the king and queen are giving him much support. As you are aware, Gunnhild is your greatest enemy, and she will not urge Onund to settle up.'

Egil said, 'The king will allow me to win my lawful rights in this case, and with your support I won't hesitate about taking Onund to law.'

They decided that Egil should equip a boat, which he manned with a crew of almost twenty. They headed south for Hordaland, landed at Ask and went to the house to ask for Berg-Onund. Egil presented his case and demanded his share of Bjorn's inheritance from Onund, saying that both daughters had equal rights to inherit from Bjorn by law.

'Even if it seems to me that Asgerd might be considered of much higher birth than your wife Gunnhild,' he added.

'You've certainly got some nerve, Egil,' Onund snapped back. 'You've been outlawed by King Eirik, then you come back here to his country to pester his men. You can be sure that I have got the better of plenty of people like you, Egil, even when I have considered there to be much less reason than you with your claim on an inheritance for your wife, because everyone knows she's the daughter of a slave-woman.'

Onund delivered a long string of abuse.

When Egil saw that Onund was not prepared to make any settlement, he summonsed him to appear at an assembly and to be judged according to laws of the Gula Assembly.

Onund said, 'I'll be at the Gula Assembly, and if I have my way you won't be leaving there in one piece.'

Egil said he would risk going to the assembly, whatever happened – 'come what may of our dealings'.

Egil and his men went away, and when he returned home he told Arinbjorn about his journey and Onund's answers. Arinbjorn was furious at hearing his aunt Thora called a slave-woman.

Arinbjorn went to see King Eirik and put the matter to him.

The king took the matter quite badly, saying that Arinbjorn had taken Egil's side for a long time: 'It is for your sake that I have allowed him to stay in this country, but that will prove more difficult if you support him whenever he encroaches on my friends.'

Arinbjorn said, 'You should allow us to claim our rights in this case.'

The king was stubborn about the whole business, but Arinbjorn could tell that the queen was even more averse to it. Arinbjorn went back and said the outlook was quite bleak.

Winter passed and the time came round to attend the Gula Assembly. Arinbjorn took a large band of men with him, and Egil was among them. King Eirik was there too, and had a large band with him. Berg-Onund and his brothers were in the king's party, and had many men with them. When the time came to discuss the cases, both sides went to the place where the court was held, to present their testimonies. Onund was bragging.

The court was held on a flat plain, marked out by hazel poles with a rope around them. This was known as staking out a sanctuary. Inside the circle sat the court, twelve men from the Fjordane province, twelve from Sognefjord province and twelve from Hordaland province. These three dozen men were to rule on all the cases. Arinbjorn selected the members of the Fjordane court, and Thord from Aurland those from Sognefjord, and they were all on the same side.

Arinbjorn had taken a large band of men to the assembly, a fully-manned fast vessel and many small boats, skiffs and ferries owned by farmers. King Eirik had a large party there too, six or seven longships and many farmers.

Egil began his statement by demanding that the court rule in his favour against Onund. He recounted his grounds for claiming Bjorn Brynjolfsson's inheritance. He said that his wife Asgerd deserved to inherit from her father Bjorn, being descended entirely from landowners and ultimately of royal stock. He demanded that the court rule that Asgerd should inherit half of Bjorn's estate, both money and land.

When Egil finished his speech, Berg-Onund spoke.

'My wife Gunnhild is the daughter of Bjorn and Olof, Bjorn's lawful wife,' he said. 'Gunnhild is therefore Bjorn's legal heiress. I claimed ownership of everything Bjorn owned on the grounds that Bjorn had only one other daughter and she had no right to the inheritance. Her mother was captured and made a concubine without her kinsmen's approval, and taken from one country to another. And you, Egil, want to act as unreasonably and overbearingly here as you do everywhere else you go. But you do not stand to gain by it this time, for King Eirik and Queen Gunnhild have promised me that every case of mine in their realm will be ruled in my favour. I present irrefutable evidence to the king and queen and members of the court to prove that Thora of the Embroidered Hand, Asgerd's mother, was captured from her brother Thorir's home and on another occasion from Brynjolf's in Aurland. She travelled from one country to the next with Bjorn and some Vikings and outlaws who had been exiled by the king, and while she was away she became pregnant with Asgerd by Bjorn. It is astonishing that you, Egil, intend to ignore all King Eirik's rulings. For a start, you are here in this country after Eirik outlawed you, and what is more, even though you have married a slave-woman, you claim she has a right to an inheritance. I demand of the members of the court that they award me all of Bjorn's inheritance, and declare Asgerd a king's slave-woman, because she was begotten when her mother and father were under king's outlawry.'

Then Arinbjorn spoke: 'We will bring forth witnesses who will swear on oath that my father Thorir and Bjorn stated in their settlement that Asgerd, Bjorn and Thora's daughter, was deemed one of her father's heiresses, and also that you, king, granted him the right to live in this country, as you know for yourself, and that everything was settled that had once prevented them from reaching an agreement.'

The king took a long time answering his speech.

Then Egil spoke a verse:

25. This man pinned with thorns claims   *thorns*: brooches
     that my wife, who bears my drinking-horn,
     is born of a slave-woman;
     Selfish Onund looks after himself.
     Spear-wielder, my brooch-goddess   *brooch-goddess*: woman, wife
     is born to an inheritance.
     This can be sworn to, descendant
     of ancient kings: accept an oath.

Arinbjorn then had twelve worthy men testify that they had heard the
terms of Thorir and Bjorn's settlement, and they all offered to swear an oath
on it for the king and the court. The court wanted to take their oaths, if the
king did not forbid it. The king replied that he would neither order it nor
forbid it.

Then Queen Gunnhild spoke: 'How peculiar of you, King, to let this big
man Egil run circles around you. Would you even raise an objection if he
claimed the throne out of your hands? You might refuse to make any ruling
in Onund's favour, but I will not tolerate Egil trampling over our friends
and wrongly taking this money from Onund. Where are you now, Alf
Askmann? Take your men to where the court is sitting and prevent this
injustice from coming to pass.'

Askmann and his men ran to the court and cut the ropes where the
sanctuary had been staked out, broke the hazel poles and drove the court
away. Commotion broke out at the assembly; no one carried arms there.

Then Egil said, 'Can Berg-Onund hear me?'

'I'm listening,' he replied.

'I challenge you to a duel, here at the assembly. The victor will take all
the property, the lands and the valuables, and you will be a figure of public
scorn if you do not dare.'

Then King Eirik said, 'If you're looking for a fight, Egil, we can arrange
one for you.'

Egil answered, 'I'm not prepared to fight the king's forces and be outnumbered, but I will not run away if I am granted a fight on equal terms. I
will give you all the same treatment.'

Then Arinbjorn said, 'Let's leave, Egil. We've no business here for the
time being.'

Arinbjorn went away, taking all his men with him.

Egil turned round and said in a loud voice, 'Testify to this, Arinbjorn,

Thord and all who hear me now, landholders and men of law and common people, that I forbid that the lands once owned by Bjorn Brynjolfsson will be lived on, worked on and used for any purpose. This I forbid you, Berg-Onund, and all other men, foreign or native, of high or low birth, and anyone who does so I pronounce to have broken the laws of the land, incurred the wrath of the gods and violated the peace.'

After that, Egil left with Arinbjorn. They went to their ships, crossing a hill some distance away which prevented them from being seen in the assembly place.

When they reached the ships, Arinbjorn addressed his men: 'You are all aware how this assembly turned out. We failed to win our rights and the king is so furious that I expect him to deal out the harshest treatment to our men if he has the chance. I want everyone to board his ship and go home immediately. Let no man wait for any other.'

Then Arinbjorn boarded his ship and said to Egil, 'You board the boat that is tied to the seaward side of the longship and get away as quickly as possible. Travel by night if you can, not by day, and lie low, because the king will try to find a way to make your paths cross. Whatever may happen, come to me when all this is over.'

Egil did as Arinbjorn had told him. Thirty of them boarded the boat and rowed as fast as they could. It was an exceptionally fast craft. A large number of Arinbjorn's men rowed out of the harbour in boats and ferries, and the longship commanded by Arinbjorn went last, being the hardest to row. The boat that Egil was in soon went ahead of the others. Then Egil spoke a verse:

26.   Thorn-foot's false heir ruined
       my claim to the inheritance.
       From him I earn only
       threats and hectoring,
       whenever I may repay his robbing
       my lands where oxen toil.
       We disputed great fields
       that serpents slumber on: gold.

King Eirik had heard Egil's departing words to the assembly, and was furious. But since everyone had gone to the assembly unarmed, he did not attack him there. He ordered his men to board their ships, and they did so.

When they reached the shore, the king arranged a meeting to describe his plan: 'We will take down the awnings from our ships and row after Arinbjorn and Egil. Then we will execute Egil and spare no one who takes his side.'

They boarded their ships, quickly made ready to put to sea and rowed to where Arinbjorn's ships had been moored, but they had already left by then. The king ordered his men to row after them through the northern part of the sound, and when he entered Sognefjord, Arinbjorn's men were rowing into the Saudungssund sound. He pursued them and caught up with Arinbjorn's ships in the sound. Drawing up beside them, they called out and the king asked if Egil was on board.

Arinbjorn replied, 'Egil is not here, as you will soon find out for yourself, my lord. The men on board are all known to you, and you won't find Egil below deck if you look there.'

The king asked Arinbjorn about Egil's most recent whereabouts. He replied that Egil was on board a boat with thirty men, rowing out to Steinssund.

Then the king ordered his men to row along the channels that were farthest inland, and try to cut Egil off. They did so.

There was a man from Oppland called Ketil the Slayer, a member of King Eirik's court. He navigated and steered the king's ship. Ketil was a big, handsome man and a relative of the king's. Many people said there was a close resemblance between them.

Egil had left his ship afloat and moved the cargo before he went to the assembly. After leaving Arinbjorn, he and his men rowed to Steinssund to their ship, and boarded it. The boat was left to float between ship and shore, with its rudder ready and the oars tied in place in the rowlocks.

The following morning, when day had scarcely broken, the guards noticed several ships rowing up to them, and when Egil woke up he got straight to his feet and ordered all his men to board the boat. He armed himself quickly, and so did all the others. Egil took the chests of silver that he had been given by King Athelstan and took with him everywhere. They boarded the boat and rowed on the shore side of the warship closest to land; it was King Eirik's.

Because all this happened so quickly and there was still little daylight, the ships sailed past each other. When they stood aft to aft Egil threw a spear, striking the helmsman, Ketil the Slayer, through the middle. King Eirik called out an order to his men to row after Egil. When the ships passed the merchant vessel, the king's men boarded it. All of Egil's men who had stayed behind there and not boarded the boat were killed, if the king's men caught them; some fled to land. Ten of Egil's men died there. Some of the ships rowed after Egil and others plundered the merchant vessel. They took all the valuables they found on board, then burned it.

The party pursuing Egil rowed vigorously, with two men on each oar. They had plenty of men on board, while Egil had a small crew of eighteen men on his boat, and the king's men began to catch them up. Inland from the island was a fairly shallow fording-point to another island. It was low tide. Egil and his men headed for the shallow channel, and the warships ran aground there and lost sight of them. Then the king turned back for the south, while Egil headed north to see Arinbjorn. He spoke a verse:

27.   The mighty wielder of swords
      that flame in battle
      has felled ten of our men,
      but I acquitted myself,
      when the stout branch wetted   *branch*: spear
      with the war-goddess's wound-sea,   *wound-sea*: blood
      dispatched by my hand, flew straight
      between Ketil's curved ribs.

Egil went to see Arinbjorn and told him the news.

Arinbjorn replied that Egil could not have expected anything else from his dealings with King Eirik, 'But you will not lack for money, Egil. I will compensate you for your ship and give you another that will provide you with an easy passage to Iceland.'

Asgerd, Egil's wife, had stayed at Arinbjorn's house while they were at the assembly.

Arinbjorn gave Egil a very seaworthy ship and had it loaded with timber. Egil prepared the ship to put out to sea, and had almost thirty men with him again. He and Arinbjorn parted in great friendship, and Egil spoke a verse:

28.   Let the gods banish the king,
      pay him for stealing my wealth,
      let him incur the wrath
      of Odin and the gods.
      Make the tyrant flee his lands,
      Frey and Njord; may Thor
      the land-god be angered at this foe,
      the defiler of his holy place.

58   When Harald Fair-hair began to age he appointed his sons as rulers of Norway, and made Eirik king of them all. After he had been king of Norway for seventy years, Harald handed over the kingdom to Eirik. At that time, Gunnhild bore Eirik a son, whom Harald sprinkled with water and named after himself, adding that he should become king after his father if he lived long enough. King Harald then withdrew to live a quieter life, mainly staying at Rogaland or Hordaland. Three years later, King Harald died at Rogaland, and was buried in a mound at Haugesund.

After his death, a great dispute developed between his sons, for the people of Vik took Olaf as their king, and the people of Trondheim took Sigurd. Eirik killed both of his brothers in battle at Tunsberg a year after Harald's death. He took his army eastwards from Hordaland to Oslo to fight his brothers the same summer that Egil and Berg-Onund clashed at the Gula Assembly and that the events just described took place.

Berg-Onund stayed at home on his farm while the king went on his expedition, since he felt wary of leaving it when Egil was still in the country. His brother Hadd was with him.

There was a man called Frodi, a relative and foster-son of King Eirik. He was a handsome man, young but well built. King Eirik left him behind to provide Berg-Onund with extra support. Frodi was staying at Aarstad, on the king's farm, and had a band of men there with him.

King Eirik and Gunnhild had a son called Rognvald. He was ten or eleven years old at this time, a promising and attractive lad. He was staying with Frodi when all this happened.

Before sailing off on his expedition, King Eirik declared Egil an outlaw throughout Norway, whom anyone might kill with impunity. Arinbjorn accompanied the king on his expedition, but before he left, Egil set sail for the fishing camp called Vitar which lies off Alden, well away from travel routes. There were fishermen there who were good sources for the latest news. When he heard that the king had declared him an outlaw, Egil spoke this verse:

29.   Land spirit, the law-breaker
      has forced me to travel
      far and wide; his bride deceives
      the man who slew his brothers.
      Grim-tempered Gunnhild must pay
      for driving me from this land.
      In my youth, I was quick to conquer
      hesitation and avenge treachery.

The weather was calm, with a wind from the mountains at night and a sea breeze during the day. One night Egil and his men put out to sea, and the fishermen who had been appointed to spy on Egil's travels rowed to land. They reported that Egil had put out to sea and had left the country, and had the word passed on to Berg-Onund. When Onund heard this, he sent away all the men he had been keeping as a safeguard there. Then he rowed to Aarstad and invited Frodi to stay with him, telling him that he had plenty of ale there. Frodi went with him and took several men along. They held a fine feast there and made merry, with nothing to fear.

Prince Rognvald had a small warship with six oars on either side and painted above the plumbline. He always had the ten or twelve men on board who followed him everywhere. And when Frodi left, Rognvald took the boat and twelve of them rowed out to Herdla. The king owned a large farm there, run by a man called Beard-Thorir; Rognvald had been fostered there when he was younger. Thorir welcomed the prince and provided plenty to drink.

Egil sailed out to sea at night, as written earlier, and the next morning the wind dropped and it grew calm. They let the ship drift before the wind for a few nights.

Then, when the sea breeze got up, Egil said to his crew, 'Now we will sail to land, because it is impossible to tell where we would make land if a gale came in from the sea. Most places here are fairly hostile.'

The crew said Egil should decide where they went. Then they hoisted sail and sailed to the fishing camp at Herdla. Finding a good place to anchor, they put up the awnings and moored there for the night. On their ship they had a small boat, which Egil boarded with two men. He rowed over to Herdla by cover of night, and sent a man on to the island to ask for news.

When he returned, he reported that Eirik's son Rognvald was at a farm there with his men: 'They were sitting drinking. I met one of the farmhands who was blind drunk, and he said they didn't plan to drink any less than was being drunk at Berg-Onund's house, where Frodi was with four of his men.'

Apart from Frodi and his men, he said, the only people there were those who lived on the farm.

Then Egil rowed back to his ship and told his men to get up and take their weapons. They did so. They anchored the ship, and Egil left twelve men to guard it, then got into the smaller boat. There were eighteen of them in all, and they rowed through the sounds. They timed their landing to reach Fenring at night and put in at a concealed cove there.

Then Egil said, 'Now I want to go up on to the island and see what I can find out. Wait for me here.'

Egil had his customary weapons, a helmet and shield, and was girded with a sword and carried a halberd in his hand. He went up on to the island and along the side of a wood, wearing a long hood over his helmet. He arrived at a place where there were several young lads with big sheepdogs. Once they had started talking, he asked where they were from and why they were there with such huge dogs.

'You must be pretty stupid,' they answered. 'Haven't you heard about the bear that's roaming around the island, causing all sorts of damage and killing people and animals? A reward's being offered for catching it. Here at Ask, we stay up every night watching over our flocks that are kept in these pens. Why are you going around armed at night, anyway?'

'I'm afraid of the bear too,' Egil replied, 'and not many people seem to go around unarmed at the moment. The bear has been chasing me for much of the night. Look, it's over at the edge of the wood. Is everyone at the farm asleep?'

One lad said that Berg-Onund and Frodi would still be up drinking – 'They sit up all night.'

'Tell them where the bear is,' said Egil. 'I must hurry back home.'

He walked away while the boy ran back to the farm and into the room where they were drinking. By that time, all but three of them had gone to sleep: Onund, Frodi and Hadd. The boy told them where the bear was, and they took their weapons that were hanging there and ran straight outside and into the woods. A strip of land with patches of bushes jutted out from the woods. The boy told them that the bear was in the bushes, and when they saw the branches moving, they assumed that the bear was there. Berg-Onund told Hadd and Frodi to get between the bushes and the main part of the wood, to prevent the bear from reaching it.

Berg-Onund ran up to the shrubs. He was wearing a helmet, carried a shield in one hand and a spear in the other, and was girded with a sword. But it was Egil, not a bear, that was hiding in the shrubs, and when he saw Berg-Onund he drew his sword. There was a strap on the hilt which he pulled over his hand to let the sword hang there. Taking his spear, he rushed towards Berg-Onund. When Berg-Onund saw this he quickened his pace and put the shield in front of him, and before they clashed they threw their spears at each other. Egil darted his shield out to block the spear, at such an angle that the spear glanced off and stuck into the ground. His own spear struck the middle of Onund's shield and sank in so deep that it stuck there, making it heavy for Onund to hold. Then Egil quickly grabbed the hilt of his sword. Onund began to draw his sword, but had only pulled it half-way out of its sheath by the time Egil ran him through with his sword. Onund recoiled at the blow, but Egil drew his sword back swiftly and struck at Onund, almost chopping his head off. Then Egil took his spear out of the shield.

Hadd and Frodi ran over to Berg-Onund when they saw he had been felled. Egil turned to face them. He lunged at Frodi with his spear, piercing his shield and plunging it so deep into his chest that the point came out through his back. He fell over backwards dead on the spot. Then Egil took his sword and set on Hadd, and they exchanged a few blows before Hadd was killed.

The boys came over, and Egil said to them, 'Stand guard over your master Onund and his companions and make sure that the animals or birds do not eat their carcasses.'

Egil proceeded on his way and had not gone far when his men came from the opposite direction. There were eleven of them, and six others were guarding the ship. They asked what he had been doing. He spoke a verse:

30.   Too long I was short-changed
       by that tree of the glowing den   *tree*: man
       of the heather-fjord's fish;   *heather-fjord*: earth; its *fish*: serpent
       I guarded my wealth better once,   which guards gold
       until I dealt out mortal wounds
       to Berg-Onund, Hadd and Frodi too.
       Odin's wife, the earth,
       I clad in a cloak of blood.

Then Egil said, 'Let us go back to the farm and acquit ourselves like true warriors: kill everyone we can catch and take all the valuables we can carry.'

They went to the farmhouse and stormed it, killing fifteen or sixteen men. Some ran away and escaped. They took all the valuables and destroyed what they could not take with them. They drove the cattle down to the shore and slaughtered them, filled their boat, then proceeded on their way, rowing out through the sounds.

Egil was so furious that no one dared talk to him. He was sitting at the helm of the boat.

When they headed out into the fjord, Prince Rognvald and his twelve men rowed into their path in the painted warship. They had heard that Egil's boat was near the fishing camp at Herdla, and wanted to spy on his whereabouts for Onund. Egil recognized the warship as soon as he saw it. He steered straight for it and rammed its side with the prow of his own boat. The warship gave such a jolt that the sea flooded over one side and filled it. Egil leapt aboard, clutched his halberd and urged his men to let no one on the ship escape alive. Meeting no resistance, they did just that: everyone on the ship was killed, and none escaped. Rognvald and his men died there, thirteen of them in all. Egil and his men rowed to the island of Herdla. Then Egil spoke a verse:

31.   We fought; I paid no heed
        that my violent deeds might be repaid.
        My lightning sword I daubed with the blood
        of warlike Eirik and Gunnhild's son.
        Thirteen men fell there,
        pines of the sea's golden moon,   *sea's ... moon*: gold; its *pines* (trees): men
        on a single ship; the bringer
        of battle is hard at work.

When Egil and his men reached Herdla they ran straight up to the farmhouse, fully armed. Seeing them, Thorir and his people ran away from the farm at once, and everyone capable of escaping did so, men and women alike. Egil and his men took all the valuables they could find, then went to their ship. It was not long until a favourable wind got up from the land, and they made ready to sail. When their sails were hoisted, Egil went back on to the island.

He took a hazel pole in his hand and went to the edge of a rock facing inland. Then he took a horse's head and put it on the end of the pole.

Afterwards he made an invocation, saying, 'Here I set up this scorn-pole and turn its scorn upon King Eirik and Queen Gunnhild' – then turned the horse's head to face land – 'and I turn its scorn upon the nature spirits that inhabit this land, sending them all astray so that none of them will find its resting-place by chance or design until they have driven King Eirik and Gunnhild from this land.'

Then he thrust the pole into a cleft in the rock and left it to stand there. He turned the head towards the land and carved the whole invocation in runes on the pole.

After that, Egil went to his ship. They hoisted the sail and put out to sea.

The wind began to get up and a strong, favourable wind came. The ship raced along, and Egil spoke this verse:

32.   With its chisel of snow, the headwind,
      scourge of the mast, mightily
      hones its file by the prow
      on the path that my sea-bull treads.   *sea-bull*: ship
      In gusts of wind, that chillful
      destroyer of timber planes down   *destroyer of timber*: wave, imagined
      the planks before the head   as a file
      of my sea-king's swan.   *sea-king's swan*: ship

After that they sailed out to sea and had a smooth passage, making land in Iceland in Borgarfjord. Egil headed for harbour there and brought his cargo ashore. He went home to Borg, while his crew found other quarters to stay in. By this time Skallagrim was old and fragile with age, so Egil took charge of the property and maintaining the farm.

59   There was a man called Thorgeir Lamb. He was married to Thordis, who was the daughter of Yngvar and the sister of Bera, Egil's mother. Thorgeir lived inland from Alftanes, at Lambastadir, and had come to Iceland with Yngvar. He was wealthy and well respected. His son, Thord, had inherited Lambastadir from his father and was living there when Egil came to Iceland.

That autumn, some time before winter, Thord rode over to Borg to meet his kinsman Egil and invite him to a feast. He had brewed some ale at home. Egil promised to go along and the time was set for a week later. When this came around, he made ready to go, and his wife, Asgerd, with him. They were ten or twelve in all.

And when Egil was ready, Skallagrim came out with him, embraced him before he mounted his horse and said, 'You seem to be taking your time about paying me the money that King Athelstan sent me, Egil. How do you intend to dispose of it?'

Egil said, 'Are you very short of money, father? I wasn't aware. I will let you have silver as soon as I know that you need it, but I know you have kept a chest or two aside, full of silver.'

'You seem to think we have already divided our money equably,' said Skallagrim. 'So you won't mind if I do as I please with what I have put aside.'

Egil said, 'Don't pretend you need to ask my permission, because you will do as you please, whatever I say.'

Then Egil rode off to Lambastadir. He was given a warm and friendly welcome and was to stay there for the next three nights.

The same evening that Egil left home, Skallagrim had his horse saddled, then rode away from home when everyone else went to bed. He was carrying a fairly large chest on his knees, and had an iron cauldron under his arm when he left. People have claimed ever since that he put either or both of them in the Krumskelda Marsh, with a great slab of stone on top.

Skallagrim came home in the middle of the night, went to his bed and lay down, still wearing his clothes. At daybreak next morning, when everybody was getting dressed, Skallagrim was dead, sitting on the edge of his bed, and so stiff that they could neither straighten him out nor lift him no matter how hard they tried.

A horse was saddled quickly and the rider set off at full pelt all the way to Lambastadir. He went straight to see Egil and told him the news. Egil took his weapons and clothes and rode back to Borg that evening. He dismounted, entered the house and went to an alcove in the fire-room where there was a door through to the room in which were the benches where people sat and slept. Egil went through to the bench and stood behind Skallagrim, taking him by the shoulders and tugging him backwards. He laid him down on the bench and closed his nostrils, eyes and mouth. Then he ordered the men to take spades and break down the south wall. When this had been done, Egil took hold of him by the head and shoulders, and the others by his legs. They carried him like this right across the house and out through where the wall had been broken down. They carried him out to Naustanes without stopping and covered his body up for the night. In the morning, at high tide, Skallagrim's body was put in a ship and they rowed with it out to Digranes. Egil had a mound made on the edge of the promontory, where Skallagrim was laid to rest with his horse and weapons and tools. It is not mentioned whether any money was put into his tomb.

Egil inherited his father's lands and valuables, and ran the farm. Thordis, Asgerd's daughter by Thorolf, was with him there.

60   King Eirik ruled Norway for one year after the death of his father, before another of King Harald's sons, Hakon, arrived in Norway from England, where he had been fostered by King Athelstan. This was the same summer that Egil Skallagrimsson went to Iceland. Hakon went north to

Trondheim, and was accepted as king there. That winter, he and Eirik were joint kings of Norway. The following spring, they both gathered armies, and Hakon's was by far the more numerous. Eirik saw that he had no option but to flee the country, and left with his wife, Gunnhild, and their children.

Arinbjorn the Hersir was King Eirik's foster-brother, and foster-father to his children. King Eirik was fondest of him among all his landholders, and had made him the chieftain of all the Fjordane province. Arinbjorn left the country with the king, and they began by crossing over to the Orkneys. There the king gave his daughter Ragnhild in marriage to Earl Arnfinn. Then he travelled south with all his men to Scotland and raided there, and from there he continued southwards to England and raided there as well.

When King Athelstan heard this he gathered a great force and went to face Eirik. When they met, an agreement was settled whereby King Athelstan would appoint Eirik to rule Northumbria and defend his kingdom from the Scots and Irish. King Athelstan had made Scotland a tributary kingdom after the death of King Olaf, but the people there were invariably disloyal to him. King Eirik generally stayed in York.

It is said that Gunnhild had a magic rite performed to curse Egil Skalla-grimsson from ever finding peace in Iceland until she had seen him. That summer, after Hakon and Eirik had met and disputed the control of Norway, an embargo was placed on all travel from that country, so no ships sailed for Iceland then, and there was no news from Norway.

Egil Skallagrimsson remained on his farm. In his second year at Borg after Skallagrim's death, Egil grew restless and became increasingly melancholy as the winter progressed. When summer came, Egil announced that he was going to prepare his ship to sail abroad. He took on a crew, planning to sail to England. There were thirty men on board. Asgerd would remain behind to look after the farm, while Egil planned to go to see King Athelstan and collect what he had promised when they parted.

Egil was slow in getting ready, and by the time he put to sea it was too late for favourable winds, with autumn and bad weather approaching. They sailed north of Orkney. Egil did not want to stop there, since he assumed King Eirik was ruling the islands. They sailed southwards along the coast of Scotland in a heavy storm and crosswinds, but managed to tack and head south of Scotland to the north of England. In the evening, when it began to get dark, the storm intensified. Before they knew it, the waves were breaking on shoals both on their seaward side and ahead of them, so the only course of action was to make for land. They did so, running their ship aground in the mouth of the Humber. All the men were saved and most of their possessions, but the ship was smashed to pieces.

When they met people to talk to, they heard something that Egil thought rather ominous: King Eirik Blood-axe and Gunnhild were there, rulers of the kingdom, and he was staying not far away in York. He also heard that Arinbjorn the Hersir was with the king and on good terms with him.

After he had found out all this news, Egil made his plans. He did not feel he had much chance of getting away even if he were to try to hide and keep under cover all the way back out of Eirik's kingdom. Anyone who saw him would recognize him. Considering it unmanly to be caught fleeing like that, he steeled himself and decided the very night that they arrived to get a horse and ride to York. He arrived in the evening and rode straight into town. He was wearing a long hood over his helmet, and was fully armed.

Egil asked where Arinbjorn's house was in the town; he was told, and rode to it. When he reached the house, he dismounted and spoke to someone who told him that Arinbjorn was sitting at table.

Egil said, 'I would like you to go into the hall, my good man, and ask Arinbjorn whether he would prefer to talk to Egil Skallagrimsson indoors or outside.'

The man said, 'It's not much bother for me to do that.'

He went into the hall and said in a loud voice, 'There's a man outside, as huge as a troll. He asked me to come in and ask whether you would prefer to talk to Egil Skallagrimsson indoors or outside.'

Arinbjorn replied, 'Go and ask him to wait outside. He won't need to wait for long.'

He did as Arinbjorn said, went out and told Egil what he had said.

Arinbjorn ordered the tables to be cleared, then went outside with all the people from his household. He greeted Egil and asked him why he had come.

Egil gave him a brief account of the highlights of his journey – 'And now you will decide what I should do, if you want to help me in any way.'

'Did you meet anyone in town who may have recognized you before you came to the house?' asked Arinbjorn.

'No one,' said Egil.

'Then take up your arms, men,' said Arinbjorn.

They did so. And when Egil, Arinbjorn and all his men were armed, they went to the king's residence. When they reached the hall, Arinbjorn knocked on the door and asked to be let in, after identifying himself. The guards opened the door at once. The king was sitting at table.

Arinbjorn said twelve men would go inside, and nominated Egil and ten others.

'Egil, now you must go and offer the king your head and embrace his foot. I will present your case to him.'

Then they went inside. Arinbjorn went up to the king and greeted him. The king welcomed him and asked what he wanted.

Arinbjorn said, 'I have brought someone here who has travelled a long way to visit you and wants to make a reconciliation with you. It is a great honour for you, my lord, when your enemies come to see you voluntarily from other countries, feeling that they cannot live with your wrath even in your absence. Please treat this man nobly. Make fair reconciliation with him for the great honour he has shown you by crossing many great seas and treacherous paths far from his home. He had no motivation to make the journey other than goodwill towards you, because he could well spare himself from your anger in Iceland.'

Then the king looked around and saw over the heads of the other men that Egil was standing there. The king recognized him at once, glared at him and said, 'Why are you so bold as to dare to come to see me, Egil? We parted on such bad terms the last time that you had no hope of my sparing your life.'

Then Egil went up to the table and took the king's foot in his hand. He spoke a verse:

33.	I have travelled on the sea-god's steed	*sea-god's steed*: ship
	a long and turbulent wave-path	
	to visit the one who sits	
	in command of the English land.	
	In great boldness, the shaker	*shaker of the wound-flaming*
	of the wound-flaming sword	*sword*: warrior (Egil)
	has met the mainstay	
	of King Harald's line.	

King Eirik said, 'I have no need to enumerate all the wrongs you have done. They are so great and so numerous that any one of them would suffice to warrant your never leaving here alive. You cannot expect anything but to die here. You should have known in advance that you would not be granted any reconciliation with me.'

Gunnhild said, 'Why not have Egil killed at once? Don't you remember, King, what Egil has done to you: killed your friends and kinsmen and even your own son, and heaped scorn upon your own person. Where would anyone dare to treat royalty in such a way?'

'If Egil has spoken badly of the king,' Arinbjorn said, 'he can make recompense with words of praise that will live for ever.'

Gunnhild said, 'We do not want to hear his praise. Have Egil taken outside and executed, King. I neither want to hear his words nor see him.'

Then Arinbjorn replied, 'The king will not be urged to do all your scornful biddings. He will not have Egil killed by night, because killing at night is murder.'

The king said, 'Let it be as you ask, Arinbjorn: Egil will live tonight. Take him home with you and bring him back to me in the morning.'

Arinbjorn thanked the king for his words: 'I hope that Egil's affairs will take a turn for the better in future, my lord. But much as Egil may have wronged you, you should consider the losses he has suffered at the hands of your kinsmen. Your father King Harald had his uncle Thorolf, a fine man, put to death solely on the grounds of slander by evil men. You broke the law against Egil yourself, King, in favour of Berg-Onund, and moreover you wanted him put to death, and you killed his men and stole all his wealth. And then you declared him an outlaw and drove him out of the country. Egil is not the sort of man to stand being provoked. Every case should be judged in light of the circumstances,' Arinbjorn said. 'I will take Egil home to my house now.'

This was done. When the two men reached the house they went up to one of the garrets to talk things over.

Arinbjorn said, 'The king was furious, but his temper seemed to calm down a little towards the end. Fortune alone will determine what comes of this. I know that Gunnhild will do her utmost to spoil things for you. My advice is for you to stay awake all night and make a poem in praise of King Eirik. I feel a drapa of twenty stanzas would be appropriate, and you could deliver it when we go to see the king tomorrow. Your kinsman Bragi did that when he incurred the wrath of King Bjorn of Sweden: he spent the whole night composing a drapa of twenty stanzas in his praise, and kept his head as a reward. We might be fortunate enough in our dealings with the king for this to make a reconciliation between you and him.'

Egil said, 'I will follow the advice you offer, but I would never have imagined I would ever make a poem in praise of King Eirik.'

Arinbjorn asked him to try, then went off to his men. They sat up drinking until the middle of the night. Arinbjorn and the others went off to their sleeping quarters, and before he got undressed, he went up to the garret to Egil and asked how the poem was coming along.

Egil said he hadn't composed a thing: 'A swallow has been sitting at the window twittering all night, and I haven't had a moment's peace.'

Arinbjorn went out through the door that led to the roof. He sat down near the attic window where the bird had been sitting, and saw a shape-shifter in the form of a bird leaving the other side of the house. Arinbjorn sat there all night, until daybreak. Once Arinbjorn was there, Egil composed the whole poem and memorized it, so that he could recite it to him when he met him the next morning. Then they kept watch until it was time to meet the king.

61 King Eirik went to table as usual with a lot of people. When Arinbjorn noticed this, he took all his men, fully armed, to the hall when the king was sitting down to dine. Arinbjorn asked to be let in to the hall and was allowed to enter. He and Egil went in, with half their men. The other half waited outside the door.

Arinbjorn greeted the king, who welcomed him.

'Egil is here, my lord,' he said. 'He has not tried to escape during the night. We would like to know what his lot will be. I expect you to show us favour. I have acted as you deserve, sparing nothing in word and deed to enhance your renown. I have relinquished all the possessions and kinsmen and friends that I had in Norway to follow you, while all your other landholders turned their backs on you. I feel you deserved this from me, because you have treated me outstandingly in many ways.'

Then Gunnhild said, 'Stop going on about that, Arinbjorn. You have treated King Eirik well in many ways, and he has rewarded you in full. You owe much more to the king than to Egil. You cannot ask for Egil to be sent away from King Eirik unpunished, after all the wrongs he has done him.'

Arinbjorn said, 'If you and Gunnhild have decided for yourselves, King, that Egil will not be granted any reconciliation here, the noble course of action is to allow him a week's grace to get away, since he came here of his own accord and expected a peaceful reception. After that, may your dealings follow their own course.'

Gunnhild replied, 'I can tell from all this that you are more loyal to Egil than to King Eirik, Arinbjorn. If Egil is given a week to ride away from here in peace, he will have time to reach King Athelstan. And Eirik can't ignore the fact that every king is more powerful than himself now, even though not long ago King Eirik would have seemed unlikely to lack the will and character to take vengeance for what he has suffered from the likes of Egil.'

'No one will think Eirik any the greater for killing a foreign farmer's son who has given himself into his hands,' said Arinbjorn. 'If it is reputation that he is seeking, I can help him make this episode truly memorable, because Egil and I intend to stand by each other. Everyone will have to face the two of us together. The king will pay a dear price for Egil's life by killing us all, me and my men as well. I would have expected more from you than to choose to see me dead rather than to grant me the life of one man when I ask you for it.'

Then the king said, 'You are staking a great deal to help Egil, Arinbjorn. I am reluctant to cause harm to you if it should come to this, that you prefer to lose your own life than to see him killed. But Egil has done me plenty of wrong, whatever I may decide to do with him.'

When the king had finished speaking, Egil went before him and delivered his poem, reciting it in a loud voice, and everyone fell silent at once:

1.   West over water I fared,
        bearing poetry's waves to the shore   *waves*: i.e. the mead of poetry
        of the war-god's heart;   *war-god*: Odin, also the god of poetry
        my course was set.
        I launched my oaken craft
        at the breaking of ice,
        loaded my cargo of praise
        aboard my longboat aft.

2.   The warrior welcomed me,
        to him my praise is due.
        I carry Odin's mead
        to England's meadows.
        The leader I laud,
        sing surely his praise;
        I ask to be heard,
        an ode I can devise.

3.   Consider, lord –
      well it will befit –
      how I recite
      if my poem is heard.
      Most men have learned
      of the king's battle deeds
      and the war-god saw
      corpses strewn on the field.

4.   The clash of swords roared
      on the edge of shields,
      battle grew around the king,
      fierce he ventured forth.
      The blood-river raced,
      the din was heard then
      of metal showered in battle,
      the most in that land.

5.   The web of spears
      did not stray from their course
      above the king's
      bright rows of shields.
      The shore groaned,
      pounded by the flood
      of blood, resounded
      under the banners' march.

6.   In the mud men lay
      when spears rained down.
      Eirik that day
      won great renown.

7.   Still I will tell
      if you pay me heed,
      more I have heard
      of those famous deeds.
      Wounds grew the more
      when the king stepped in,
      swords smashed
      on the shields' black rims.

8. Swords clashed, battle-sun   *battle-sun, whetstone's saddle*: sword
    and whetstone's saddle;
    the wound-digger bit
    with its venomous point.
    I heard they were felled,
    Odin's forest of oaks,   *forest of oaks*: men
    by scabbard-icicles   *scabbard-icicles*: swords
    in the play of iron.

9. Blades made play
    and swords bore down.
    Eirik that day
    won great renown.

10. Ravens flocked
    to the reddened sword,
    spears plucked lives
    and gory shafts sped.
    The scourge of Scots
    fed the wolves that trolls ride,   *wolves*: (in myth seen as ridden by
    Loki's daughter, Hel,   trollwomen)
    trod the eagle's food.   *eagle's food*: corpses

11. Battle-cranes swooped
    over heaps of dead,
    wound-birds did not want
    for blood to gulp.
    The wolf gobbled flesh,
    the raven daubed
    the prow of its beak
    in waves of red.

12. The troll's wolfish steed   *troll's ... steed*: wolf
    met a match for its greed.
    Eirik fed flesh
    to the wolf afresh.

13. The battle-maiden keeps
the swordsman awake
when the ship's wall
of shields breaks.
Shafts sang
and points stung,
flaxen strings shot
arrows from bows.

14. Flying spears bit,
the peace was rent;
wolves took heart
at the taut elm bow.
The war-wise king fended
a deadly blow,
the yew-bow twanged
in the battle's fray.

15. Like bees, arrows flew
from his drawn bow of yew.
Eirik fed flesh
to the wolf afresh.

16. Yet more I desire
that men realize
his generous nature;
I urge on my praise.
He throws gold river-flame   *river-flame*: gold
but holds his lands
in his hand like a vice,
he is worthy of praise.

17. By the fistful he gives
the fire of the arm.   *fire of the arm*: gold
Never sparing rings' lives   *never sparing rings' lives*: i.e. throwing
he gives riches no rest,   them away, being generous
hands gold out like sand
from the hawk's coast.   *hawk's coast*: wrist
Fleets take cheer
from the grindings of dwarfs.   *grindings of dwarfs*: gold

18.   The maker of war
       sheds beds for spears   *beds for spears*: shields
       from his gold-laden arm,
       he spreads brooches afar.
       I speak from the heart:
       Everywhere he is grand,
       Eirik's feats were heard
       on the east-lying shore.

19.   King, bear in mind
       how my ode is wrought,
       I take delight
       in the hearing I gained.
       Through my lips I stirred
       from the depths of my heart
       Odin's sea of verse
       about the craftsman of war.

20.   I bore the king's praise
       into the silent void,
       my words I tailor
       to the company.
       From the seat of my laughter   *seat of laughter*: mind
       I lauded the warrior
       and it came to pass
       that most understood.

62   King Eirik sat upright and glared at Egil while he was reciting the poem.
       When it was over, the king said, 'The poem was well delivered.
Arinbjorn, I have thought about the outcome of my dealings with Egil. You
have presented Egil's case so fervently that you were even prepared to enter
into conflict with me. For your sake, I will do as you have asked and let Egil
leave, safe and unharmed. You, Egil, will arrange things so that the moment
you leave this room, neither I nor my sons will ever set eyes upon you again.
Never cross my path nor my men's. I am letting you keep your head for the
time being. Since you put yourself into my hands, I do not want to commit a
base deed against you. But you can be sure that this is not a reconciliation with
me or my sons, nor any of my kinsmen who wants to seek justice.'

Then Egil spoke a verse:

34. Ugly as my head may be,
     the cliff my helmet rests upon,
     I am not loathe
     to accept it from the king.
     Where is the man who ever
     received a finer gift
     from a noble-minded
     son of a great ruler?   *great ruler*: King Harald Fair-hair

Arinbjorn thanked the king eloquently for the honour and friendship he
had shown him. Then Arinbjorn and Egil rode back to his house. Arinbjorn
had horses made ready for his men, then with one hundred of them, all fully
armed, he rode off with Egil. Arinbjorn rode with the party until they
reached King Athelstan, who welcomed them. The king invited Egil to stay
with him for as long as he wished and be in great honour, and asked how
he had got on with King Eirik.

Then Egil spoke a verse:

35. That niggard with justice, maker
     of blood-waves for ravens,
     let Egil keep his black-browed eyes;
     my relative's courage availed me much.
     Now as before I rule
     the noble seat that my helmet,
     the sea-lords's hat, is heir to,   *sea-lords's hat*: cliff
     in spite of the wound-dispenser.   *wound-dispenser*: warrior (king)

When they parted ways, Egil gave Arinbjorn the two gold rings weighing
a mark each that King Athelstan had given him, while Arinbjorn gave Egil
a sword called Dragvandil (Slicer). Arinbjorn had been given it by Egil's
brother Thorolf. Before him, Skallagrim had been given it by Egil's uncle
Thorolf, who had received it from Grim Hairy-cheeks, the son of Ketil
Haeng. Ketil had owned the sword and used it in duels, and it was exceedingly
sharp. Egil and Arinbjorn parted in the greatest friendship. Arinbjorn returned
to King Eirik in York, where Egil's companions and crew were left in peace
to trade their cargo under his protection. As the winter progressed, they
went south to meet Egil.

63   There was a landholder in Norway called Eirik the All-wise, who was married to Thora, Thorir's daughter and Arinbjorn's sister. He owned land in Vik, in the east, and was very wealthy, distinguished and wise of mind. Their son, Thorstein, had been brought up at Arinbjorn's home, and although still young he was fully developed. He had gone west to England with Arinbjorn.

The same autumn that Egil went to England, word arrived from Norway that Eirik the All-wise had died and the royal agents had seized his inheritance in the king's name. When Arinbjorn and Thorstein heard this news, they decided that Thorstein should go to Norway to claim his inheritance.

As spring drew on and people who planned to sail abroad began to make their ships ready, Thorstein went south to London to see King Athelstan. He presented the king with tokens and a message from Arinbjorn, and also gave a message to Egil asking him to propose that the king should use his influence with his foster-son Hakon to help Thorstein win back his inheritance and property in Norway. King Athelstan needed little persuasion, saying that he knew Arinbjorn as a fine person.

Then Egil went to speak to King Athelstan and told him of his plans.

'I want to go over to Norway this summer,' he said, 'to collect the property that King Eirik and Berg-Onund robbed me of. Berg-Onund's brother, Atli the Short, has it in his possession now. I know I would win justice in the matter with a message from you to back me up.'

The king said that it was up to Egil to decide where he went, 'But I would greatly prefer it if you stayed with me to defend my kingdom and command my armies. I shall grant you great revenues.'

Egil said, 'This is a very attractive offer, and I accept it rather than refuse it. But first I must go to Iceland to collect my wife and the wealth I own there.'

King Athelstan gave Egil a good merchant vessel, and a cargo to go with it. The bulk of it was wheat and honey, and there was greater wealth still in other goods. When Egil was preparing his ship for the voyage, Arinbjorn's kinsman Thorstein joined his crew. Thorstein was the son of Eirik, as mentioned before, but was later known as Thora's son. When they were ready they all sailed away. King Athelstan and Egil parted in great friendship.

Egil and his crew had a smooth journey, made land in Norway at Vik in the east and headed all the way in to Oslo fjord. Thorstein owned a farm in the uplands there, stretching all the way to the province of Raumarike. When Thorstein reached land, he laid a claim to his inheritance against the king's agents who had occupied his farm. Many people helped Thorstein, and charges were brought. Thorstein had many kinsmen of high birth. In the end the matter was referred to the king for a ruling, and Thorstein took over safeguarding the property his father had owned.

Egil spent the winter with Thorstein, and there were twelve of them there in all. Wheat and honey were brought to his house, there was much celebration during that winter and Thorstein lived grandly with plenty of provisions.

64 Hakon, King Athelstan's foster-son, was ruling Norway at this time, as described earlier. The king spent that winter in Trondheim in the north.

As the winter wore on, Thorstein set off on his journey, accompanied by Egil. They had almost thirty men with them. When they had made their preparations, they went first to Oppland, then north over the Dovrefjell Mountains to Trondheim, where they went to see King Hakon. They delivered their messages to the king. Thorstein described the whole matter and produced witnesses to the fact that he owned the entire inheritance he had claimed. The king took the matter favourably, allowing Thorstein to recover his property and thereby become one of the king's landholders, as his father had been.

Egil went to see King Hakon and presented his own case, along with a message and tokens from King Athelstan. He enumerated the property once owned by Bjorn the Landowner, in the form of both land and money, and claimed half of it for himself and his wife, Asgerd. Supporting his case with witnesses and oaths, he said that he had presented the case to King Eirik as well, adding that he had not been given justice because of Eirik's severity and Gunnhild's incitements. Egil recounted the whole episode that had taken place at the Gula Assembly, and asked the king to grant him justice in the matter.

King Hakon answered, 'I have heard that my brother Eirik and his wife, Gunnhild, both think you have thrown a stone that was too heavy for you in your dealings with them, Egil. I think you ought to be quite contented if I do not involve myself in this matter, even though Eirik and I did not have the good fortune to agree with each other.'

Egil replied, 'You cannot keep quiet about such a great matter, King, because everyone in this country, native and foreign, must obey your orders. I have been told that you are establishing a code of law and rights for every man in this country, and I am certain that you will allow me to secure these rights like anybody else. I consider myself a match for Atli the Short in both strength and kinsmen here. As far as my dealings with King Eirik are concerned, I can tell you that I went to see him and when we parted he told me to go in peace wherever I wanted. I will offer you my allegiance and service, Lord. I know that you have men here with you who do not look any more fearsome in battle than I am. I have an intuition that it will not be very long before you cross paths with King Eirik again, if you both live to see the day. I would not be surprised if the time comes when you feel Gunnhild has rather too many ambitious sons.'

'You will not enter my service, Egil,' said the king. 'You and your kinsmen have carved too deep a breach in my family for you to be able to settle down in this country. Go out to Iceland and look after your inheritance from your father there. You will not suffer harm at the hands of myself or my kinsmen there, but you can expect my family to remain the most powerful in this country for the rest of your days. For King Athelstan's sake, however, you will be left in peace here and win justice and your rights, because I know how fond King Athelstan is of you.'

Egil thanked the king for his words and asked to be given tokens of proof to show to Thord at Aurland or his other landholders in Sognefjord and Hordaland. The king said he would do so.

65 Once they had finished their business with the king, Thorstein and Egil made preparations for their journey. They set off. On their way south over Dovrefjell, Egil said he wanted to go up to Romsdal and then back south along the coast.

'I want to finish my business in Sognefjord and Hordaland, because I want to make my ship ready to leave for Iceland this summer,' he said.

Thorstein told him to go his way as he pleased. He and Egil parted, and Thorstein went south through Dalene and all the way to his lands. He produced the king's tokens and gave his message to the agents to hand over all the possessions that they had seized and Thorstein had laid claim to.

Egil went on his way with eleven men. Arriving in Romsdal, they arranged transport; then they went south to More. Nothing happened on their journey until they reached Hod Island and stayed at a farm there called Blindheim. It was a fine farm and a landholder called Fridgeir lived there. He was a young man and had recently received his inheritance from his father. His mother was Gyda, the sister of Arinbjorn the Hersir, a fine and determined woman. She ran the farm with her son Fridgeir, and they lived in style. Egil and his men were well received there. In the evening, Egil sat next to Fridgeir, with Egil's companions farther down the table. There was plenty of drinking and a splendid feast.

Gyda, the lady of the house, went to talk to Egil that night. She asked about her brother Arinbjorn and other kinsmen and friends of hers who had gone to England with him, and Egil answered her questions. She asked Egil whether anything noteworthy had happened on his travels, and he gave her a straightforward account. Then he spoke a verse:

36.   I could not stand the ugly
land-claimer's wrath;
no cuckoo will alight knowing
that the squawking eagle prowls.
There, as before, I benefited
from the bear of the hearth-seat.   *bear*: *Arinbjorn* means 'hearth-bear'
No one need give up who boasts
such a loyal helper on his travels.

Egil was in good spirits that evening, but Fridgeir and the people on the farm were fairly subdued. Egil saw a beautiful and well-dressed girl there, and was told she was Fridgeir's sister. She was unhappy and wept all the evening, which the visitors thought was peculiar.

They spent the night there. The next morning there was a gale and the seas were too heavy for sailing; they needed a ship to take them from the island. Fridgeir and Gyda went to talk to Egil, inviting him to stay there with his companions until the weather was good enough to sail away, and offering him any transport he needed. Egil accepted and they spent three nights there weather-bound, amid great celebrations. After that the wind calmed down. Egil and his men got up early that morning and made their preparations to leave, then went off to eat and were served with ale, and they sat at table for a while. Then they took their cloaks, and Egil stood up, thanked the farmer and his mother for what they had provided and went outside. Fridgeir and Gyda accompanied them on their way, until she took her son aside and whispered something to him.

While he stood and waited, Egil asked the girl, 'What are you crying about? I have never seen you happy for a moment.'

Unable to answer, she cried all the more.

Fridgeir answered his mother in a loud voice, 'I don't want to ask them to do that. They're ready to leave now.'

Then Gyda went up to Egil and said, 'I will tell you what is going on here. There is a man called Ljot the Pale, a berserk and a dueller who is very much loathed. He came here and asked for my daughter's hand in marriage, but we turned him down on the spot. So he challenged my son Fridgeir to a duel. He'll be coming to fight him at Valdero Island tomorrow. I'd like you to go to the site of the duel with Fridgeir, Egil. If Arinbjorn were here, we would prove that we do not put up with overbearing behaviour from such a man as Ljot.'

'For the sake of your brother Arinbjorn it is my duty to make this journey with Fridgeir,' answered Egil, 'if he thinks I can help him in any way.'

'That is noble of you,' Gyda said. 'Let us go into the main room and spend the day here together.'

Egil and his men went into the main room and started drinking. They sat there all day, and in the evening Fridgeir's friends who were to accompany him arrived and there was a great gathering and feast that night.

The next day, Fridgeir prepared himself to set off, with a large band of men. Egil was with them. It was good weather for sailing, and they set off and reached Valdero island. There was a fine field a short way from the shore where the duel was to be held. Stones had been arranged in a circle to mark out the site.

Ljot arrived with his men and got ready for the duel. He had a shield and a sword. Ljot was a huge, strong man. And when he entered the arena, a berserk fury came over him and he started howling menacingly and biting at his shield. Fridgeir was not a big, strong man, but slim and handsome and unaccustomed to fighting. Seeing Ljot, Egil spoke a verse:

37.   Fridgeir is not fit to fight a duel
       with a maker of valkyries' showers   *valkyries' showers*: battle
       who bites his shield's rim
       and invokes the gods
       – we'll ban the man from the maiden.
       That awful character throws
       fated glances at us; men,
       let us go to the duelling-place.

Ljot saw Egil standing there and, hearing his words, spoke to him: 'Come here into the arena, big man, and fight me if you are so eager to do so. Let us test our strength. It will be a much more even fight than with Fridgeir, because I do not imagine I will grow in stature by taking his life.'

Then Egil spoke a verse:

38.   It is not right to refuse
      Ljot his little request.
      I will sport with the pale man
      with my armour-prodder.
      Prepare for a fight, I give him
      no hope of mercy.
      Man, we must make shields
      skirmish on this island.

After that, Egil made ready for his duel with Ljot. He held the shield he always carried and was girded with his sword Adder and held his other sword called Slicer in his hand. When he entered the arena marked out for the duel, Ljot was still not ready. Egil shook his sword and spoke this verse:

39.   Let polished hilt-wands clash,
      strike shields with brands,   *brands*: i.e. swords
      test our swords' shine on shields,
      redden them with blood.
      Hack Ljot's life away,
      play the pale man foul,
      silence the troublemaker
      with iron, feed eagle flesh.

Then Ljot entered the arena and they went for each other. Egil struck at Ljot, who parried with his shield, but Egil dealt such a succession of blows that Ljot was unable to strike back. Every time Ljot yielded ground to give himself room to deliver a blow, Egil followed him just as quickly, striking furiously. Ljot went outside the circle of stones and all over the field. The fight went on like this at first, until Ljot asked to rest, and Egil granted him that. They stopped to rest, and Egil spoke this verse:

40.   The thruster of spear-burners   *spear-burners*: swords
      seems to back off from my force,
      the ill-fated wealth-snatcher
      fears my fierce onslaught.
      The spear-dewed stave falters   *spear-dew*: blood; its *stave*: warrior
      and fails to strike.
      He who asks for doom is sent
      roaming by old bald-head.

According to the laws of duelling in those days, a man who challenged someone for anything and won would collect the stake, but if he lost he would pay a sum that had been determined beforehand. If he was killed in the duel, he would forfeit all his property and his slayer would inherit it. The laws also said that if a foreigner died with no heirs in that country, his inheritance would pass to the king.

Egil told Ljot to get ready – 'I want us to finish this duel now.'

Then Egil ran at him and struck at him. He dealt such a blow that Ljot stumbled and dropped his shield. Egil struck Ljot above the knee, chopping off his leg. Ljot dropped dead on the spot.

Egil went over to Fridgeir and the others, and was thanked kindly for his deed. Then Egil spoke a verse:

41. The feeder of wolves fell,   *feeder of wolves*: warrior
      worker of evil deeds.
      The poet chopped Ljot's leg off,
      I brought Fridgeir peace.   *Fridgeir* means 'peace-spear'
      I do not ask a reward
      from the splasher of gold for that.   *splasher of gold*: generous man
      The spears' din was fun enough,   *spears' din*: battle, fight
      the fight with the pale man.

Most people did not mourn Ljot's death, because he had been such a troublemaker. He was Swedish and had no kinsmen in Norway, but had gone there and grown wealthy by duelling. After challenging many worthy men to duels, he had killed them and claimed their farms and lands, and had great wealth in both property and money.

Egil went home with Fridgeir after the duel. He stayed there for a while before going south to More. Egil and Fridgeir parted in great friendship, and Egil asked him to claim the land that Ljot had owned. Then Egil went on his way and arrived in Fjordane. From there, he went to Sognefjord to meet Thord at Aurland, who gave him a good welcome. Egil stated his business and King Hakon's message, and Thord responded favourably to what he said, promising his assistance in the matter. Egil stayed with Thord for much of the spring.

66 Egil made his journey south to Hordaland, taking a rowboat and thirty men on board. One day they arrived at Ask on Fenring. Egil took twenty men up to the farm with him, and left ten to guard the ship. Atli the Short was there with several men. Egil had him called out, with a message saying that Egil Skallagrimsson had a matter to attend to with him. Atli took his weapons; so did all the men who were fit to fight, and they went outside.

'I am told you have been keeping the money that belongs by rights to me and my wife, Asgerd,' Egil said. 'You have heard it mentioned that I claimed an inheritance from Bjorn the Landowner that your brother Berg-Onund withheld from me. Now I have come to collect this property, the lands and money, and demand that you relinquish it and make it over to me at once.'

Atli replied, 'We've been hearing for a long time that you are overbearing, Egil, and now I'm being given a taste of this myself, if you intend to claim the money from me that King Eirik awarded to my brother Onund. King Eirik's word was law in this country then. I thought you would have come here to offer me compensation for killing my brothers and plundering the property here at Ask. I can answer your case if you intend to pursue the matter, but I cannot give any answers here.'

'I will offer you what I offered Onund,' Egil replied. 'To have the case settled according to the laws of the Gula Assembly. I think your brothers forfeited their immunity by their acts, when they deprived me of justice and my rights and seized my property. I have permission from the king to seek redress by law. I will summons you before the Gula Assembly and have a ruling made on the case.'

'I'll go to the Gula Assembly,' said Atli, 'and we can discuss it there.'

Then Egil and his companions left. He went north to Sognefjord and in to Aurland, where he stayed with his kinsman Thord until the Gula Assembly.

When people arrived for the assembly, Egil was there too. Atli the Short had also arrived. They began stating their cases, presenting them to the men who were to rule upon them. Egil lodged a claim for the money, while Atli defended himself with the sworn testimony of twelve witnesses that he did not have Egil's property in his keeping.

When Atli went to the court with his witnesses, Egil went up to him with his own men and said that he would not accept his oath in place of his money: 'I offer you a different type of justice, a duel here at the assembly, staking the money for the winner to take.'

What Egil said was law too, under the ancient custom that every man had the right to challenge another to a duel, whether to prosecute a case or defend it.

Atli said he would not refuse a duel with Egil – 'You took the words right out of my mouth. I have plenty of grounds for taking vengeance on you. You have killed my two brothers, and I would be a long way from achieving justice if I chose to hand over my money to you in defiance of the law, instead of taking up your offer of a fight.'

Egil and Atli shook hands to confirm their duel for the stake of the lands they had been disputing.

After that they prepared themselves for the duel. Egil came forward wearing a helmet on his head and carrying a shield in front of him, with a halberd in his hand and his sword Slicer tied to his right hand. It was the custom among duellers to have their swords at hand to have them ready when they wanted them, instead of needing to draw them during the fight. Atli was equipped in the same way as Egil. He was strong and courageous, an experienced dueller, and skilled in the magic arts.

Then a huge old bull was brought out, known as the sacrificial bull, for the victor to slaughter. Sometimes there was one bull, and sometimes each of the duellers brought his own.

When they were ready for the duel, they ran at each other and began by throwing their spears. Neither stuck in the shields; the spears both fell to the ground. Then they both grabbed their swords, closed in and exchanged blows. Atli did not yield. They struck hard and fast, and their shields soon began to split. When Atli's shield was split right through, he tossed it away, took his sword in both hands and hacked away with all his might. Egil struck him a blow on the shoulder, but his sword did not bite. He dealt a second and third blow, finding places to strike because Atli had no protection. Egil wielded his sword with all his might, but it would not bite wherever he struck him.

Egil saw that this was pointless, because his own shield was splitting through by then. He threw down his sword and shield, ran for Atli and grabbed him with his hands. By his greater strength, Egil pushed Atli over backwards, then sprawled over him and bit through his throat. Atli died on the spot. Egil rushed to his feet and ran over to the sacrificial bull, took it by the nostrils with one hand and by the horns with the other, and swung it over on to its back, breaking its neck. Then Egil went over to his companions. He spoke this verse:

42. Black Slicer did not bite
the shield when I brandished it.
Atli the Short kept blunting
its edge with his magic.
I used my strength against
that sword-wielding braggart,
my teeth removed that peril.
Thus I vanquished the beast.

Then Egil acquired all the lands he had fought over and had claimed as his wife Asgerd's inheritance from her father. Nothing else of note is said to have happened at the assembly. Egil went first to Sognefjord to make arrangements for the property that he had won the title to, and stayed there well into the spring. Then he set off east for Vik with his companions, went to see Thorstein and stayed with him for a while.

67 Egil prepared his ship that summer and put to sea when he was ready. He headed for Iceland and had a smooth crossing, sailing in to Borgarfjord and landing his ship close to his farm. He had the cargo carried home, then drew the ship up on the beach. Egil spent that winter on his farm. He had taken great riches to Iceland with him and was now very wealthy, and he ran his farm lavishly.

Egil was not the type to interfere in other people's affairs, and generally did not act aggressively in Iceland. Nevertheless, no one dared to meddle in his affairs. Egil then spent a good number of years on his farm.

Egil and Asgerd had children whose names were these: Bodvar was their first son, and Gunnar the second, and their daughters were Thorgerd and Bera. Their youngest was Thorstein. All Egil's children were promising and intelligent. Thorgerd was the eldest of Egil's children, followed by Bera.

68 Egil received word from Norway that Eirik Blood-axe had been killed on a Viking raid in Britain, Gunnhild and their sons had gone to Denmark and all the men who had accompanied them had left England. Arinbjorn had gone back to Norway. He had been granted the lands and revenues he had previously had and was on very friendly terms with King Hakon, so Egil thought it was a desirable prospect to go to Norway once more. Word also arrived that King Athelstan had died and England was being ruled by his brother Edmund.

Egil began preparing his ship and gathering a crew. Onund Sjoni, the son of Ani from Anabrekka, joined them. He was well built and the strongest man in his district. Not everyone agreed that he was not a shape-shifter. Onund had often travelled to other countries. He was somewhat older than Egil, and they had long been good friends.

When Egil was ready, he put to sea, and they had a smooth voyage, arriving half-way up the Norwegian coast. When they sighted land they headed for Fjordane. On land, they heard the news that Arinbjorn was at home on his farm. Egil took his ship there and docked close to Arinbjorn's farm.

Then Egil went to see Arinbjorn, and they greeted each other with great warmth. Arinbjorn invited Egil to stay with him, along with any of his companions as he pleased. Egil accepted the offer and had his ship drawn up and found places for the crew to stay; he and eleven others went to stay with Arinbjorn. He had had a very ornate sail made for a longship and gave it to Arinbjorn, together with other fitting gifts. Egil spent the winter there in great comfort, but also made a trip south to Sognefjord to his lands and stayed there for a considerable time before returning north to Fjordane.

Arinbjorn held a great Yule feast to which he invited his friends and neighbours from the district. It was a splendid feast and well attended. He gave Egil a customary Yuletide gift, a silk gown with ornate gold embroidery and gold buttons all the way down the front, which was cut especially to fit Egil's frame. He also gave him a complete set of clothes, cut from English cloth in many colours. Arinbjorn gave all manner of tokens of friendship at Yuletide to the people who visited him, since he was exceptionally generous and firm of character.

Then Egil made a verse:

43.   From kindness alone
        that noble man gave the poet
        a silk gown with gold buttons;
        I will never have a better friend.
        Selfless Arinbjorn has earned
        the stature of a king
        – or more. A long time will pass
        before his like is born again.

69 After the Yuletide feast, Egil grew so depressed that he did not speak
a word. Noticing this, Arinbjorn spoke to him and asked why he was
so depressed.

'I want you to tell me whether you are ill or if there is some other reason,'
he said, 'so that we might find a remedy.'

Egil said, 'I'm not suffering from an ailment. I'm just very anxious about
how to claim the property I won when I killed Ljot the Pale up north in
More. I have heard that the king's agents have seized all the property and
claimed it in the king's name. I would like your assistance in recovering it.'

'I don't think there's a law in this country that prevents you from acquiring
that property,' said Arinbjorn, 'but it seems to have been put in very secure
hands. The king's palace is an easy place to enter but hard to leave. I have
had a lot of trouble claiming debts from those overbearing characters, even
when I enjoyed much closer confidence with the king – but my friendship
with King Hakon is only recent. But I must do as the old saying has it:
"Tend the oak if you want to live under it."'

'I am interested in putting to the test,' replied Egil, 'whether the law is
on our side. Maybe the king will grant me what is mine by rights here,
because I am told he is a just man and abides by the laws he himself has
established in this country. I have more than half a mind to go and see the
king and put the matter to him.'

Arinbjorn said he did not feel eager to do so – 'I don't expect there's
much chance of reconciling your temper and rashness with the king's
disposition and severity, because I don't think he is a friend of yours or feels
any reason to be, either. I'd prefer we drop the matter and not bring it up
again. But if you really want, Egil, I will go to see the king and put the
matter to him.'

Egil expressed his thanks and gratitude and was eager to try that course.
At this time, Hakon was in Rogaland, but he sometimes stayed in Hordaland
instead, so it was not difficult to go to see him. This was shortly after the
two men's conversation.

Arinbjorn made preparations for his journey, and explained to everyone
that he was going to see the king. He manned a twenty-seater rowboat that
he owned, with men from his household, but Egil remained behind at
Arinbjorn's wish. Once he was ready, Arinbjorn set off and had a smooth
journey. He met King Hakon and was given a good welcome.

After he had been there for a short while, he stated his errand to the king, telling him that Egil Skallagrimsson was in the country and laid claim to all the money once owned by Ljot the Pale.

'I have been told that the law is in Egil's favour, King, but that your agents have taken the money and claimed it in your name. I beseech you to grant justice to Egil.'

After a long pause the king answered him: 'I do not know why you are presenting such a claim on Egil's behalf. He came to see me once, and I told him I did not want him staying in this country for reasons that you are well aware of. Egil has no need to make such a claim to me, as he did to my brother Eirik. And I will tell you one thing, Arinbjorn: you may only stay in this country on condition that you do not value foreigners more highly than myself or my words. I know your loyalty lies with your foster-son, my nephew Harald Eiriksson. The best course for you would be to go abroad to stay with him and his brothers, because I have a strong suspicion that men like you will prove unreliable if a confrontation arises between me and Eirik's sons.'

Since the king was absolutely firm, Arinbjorn realized it was futile to argue about the matter further, and made preparations to go home. The king was rather angry and abrupt to Arinbjorn after he found out the reason for his visit. Nor was it in Arinbjorn's character to humble himself before the king. They parted at this point.

Arinbjorn returned home and told Egil how his errand had turned out.

'I will not be asking the king's favour over such matters again,' he added.

Egil was very sullen at this news, feeling he had lost a great amount of money that was his by rights.

A few days later, when Arinbjorn was in his room early one morning and there were not many people about, he had Egil called in to him.

When he arrived, Arinbjorn opened a chest and handed over forty marks of silver to him, with the words, 'I'm paying you this money for the lands owned by Ljot the Pale, Egil. It seems fair to me to let you have this reward from my kinsman Fridgeir and myself for saving his life from Ljot. I know you did it as a favour to me and it's my duty to make sure that you are not deprived of what is yours by law.'

Egil accepted the money and thanked Arinbjorn. He regained his good spirits.

70   Arinbjorn spent the winter on his lands, and the following spring he announced that he wanted to go on some Viking raids. He owned a good selection of ships and prepared three longships for the journey that spring, all of them large, and took a crew of three hundred with him. The ship he went on was well manned with people from his household and many local farmers' sons. Egil joined him at the helm of one of the ships, taking many of the band of men he had brought with him from Iceland. Egil sent the merchant ship he had brought from Iceland on to Vik, where he took on men to guard its cargo. Arinbjorn and Egil sailed their longships south along the coast, heading with their men for Saxony, where they stayed during the summer and won great wealth. When autumn arrived they went north on more raids, and moored their ships off Frisia.

One night when the weather was calm they anchored in a large estuary, since there were few places to harbour there, and the tide was far out. On shore were great rolling plains, with a forest a short distance away. It had been raining heavily and the fields were wet.

Then they set off for land, leaving one-third of the men behind to guard the ships. They went along the riverbank, with the forest on their other side, and soon came across a village where a lot of farmers lived. All the villagers ran for their lives when they noticed the raiders, and the Vikings set off in pursuit. Then they found another village, and a third. Everyone who was able to do so fled from them. The land was flat, with great plains. Ditches had been dug in many places and were full of water. These were meant to separate the fields and meadows, but in some places there were bridges for crossing over, made of logs with planks on the floor. All the villagers fled to the forest.

Once the Vikings had ventured quite deep inland, the Frisians mustered forces in the woods, and when there were more than three hundred of them they set off to confront the Vikings and fight them. A fierce battle ensued, and in the end the Frisians fled and the Vikings chased after them. The fleeing villagers spread out in all directions, and so did their pursuers. Eventually they all split up into groups of a few men.

With a few men of his own, Egil set off in hot pursuit after a large group. The Frisians reached a ditch and crossed it, then took the bridge away. When Egil arrived with his men on the other side, he took a run up and leapt over, but it was too far for the others, and none of them tried. Seeing this, the Frisians attacked Egil, and he defended himself. Eleven of them attacked him, but eventually he killed them all. After that, Egil put the bridge back in place and crossed over the ditch again, to find that all his men had gone back to the ships. He was near the forest then, so he skirted it on his way back to the ship to provide himself with cover if he needed it.

The Vikings took a great deal of plunder inland and cattle as well. When they reached their ships, some of them slaughtered the cattle or took their booty out to the ships, while the others formed a wall of shields in front of them, because a large band of Frisians had come back down to the shore and they were firing arrows at them. Then the Frisians received more support. And when Egil reached the shore and saw what was going on, he ran towards the crowd at full pelt with his halberd in front of him and his shield thrown over his back. As he lunged out with his halberd, everyone jumped back and cleared the way for him through the column. Then he headed down towards his men, who had given him up for dead.

They went back to their ships and sailed off to Denmark. When they reached Limfjord and anchored off Hals, Arinbjorn called a meeting with his men to tell them about his plans.

'I'm going to meet Eirik's sons,' he said, 'and I'll take anyone with me who wants to come. I have heard that the brothers are here in Denmark with great armies. They go raiding in the summer but stay in Denmark during the winter. If anyone would prefer to go back to Norway instead of coming with me, I will give my permission. It seems advisable for you to go back to Norway, Egil, and then set straight off back to Iceland when we part.'

The men switched ships, and those who wanted to go back to Norway joined Egil. Many more chose to go with Arinbjorn. Egil and Arinbjorn parted with kindness and friendship. Arinbjorn went to see Eirik's sons, and they joined the army of Harald Grey-cloak, his foster-son, and stayed with him for the rest of their lives.

Egil went north to Vik and entered Oslo fjord. The merchant ship was there that he had sent south that spring, together with its cargo and crew.

Thorstein, Thora's son, went to see Egil and invited him to stay for the winter, along with any of his men that he chose. Egil accepted the offer and had his ships drawn up and the cargo taken to town for storage. Some of the men who had been with him stayed, while others returned to their homes in the north. Egil stayed with Thorstein; ten or twelve of them were there in all. He spent the winter there amid great celebrations.

71 King Harald Fair-hair had brought Norway under his rule as far east as Varmland. The first person to control Varmland was Olaf Wood-carver, father of Halfdan White-leg, who was the first of his family to become king of Norway. King Harald was directly descended from him and all the line had ruled Varmland, collecting tribute there and appointing men to govern it.

In King Harald's old age, Varmland was governed by Earl Arnvid. As was the case in many places, the tribute proved more difficult to collect then than when Harald was younger, now that his sons were disputing control of Norway. There was little supervision of the more remote tributary lands.

Once King Hakon ruled in peace, he sought to re-establish his rule throughout the lands that his father had reigned over. King Hakon sent a band of twelve men east to Varmland. After collecting tribute from the earl, they were going through Eideskog Forest when they were ambushed by robbers and all were killed. The same happened to other men that King Hakon sent to Varmland: they were killed and the money went missing. Some people claimed Earl Arnvid was sending his own men to ambush the king's men and bring the money back to him.

So while King Hakon was staying in Trondheim, he sent a third party there. They were told to go east to Vik and see Thorstein, Thora's son, with an ultimatum ordering him to go to Varmland and collect the tribute for the king, or be banished from the realm. By then, the king had heard that Thorstein's uncle Arinbjorn was in Denmark with Eirik's sons, and also that they had a large army there and went raiding during the summers. King Hakon did not feel that any of them could be trusted, because he expected hostilities from Eirik's sons if they ever acquired a large enough force to rebel against him. He dealt out the same treatment to all Arinbjorn's kinsmen, relatives by marriage and friends: he banished many of them and issued others with ultimatums. Thorstein was told this distrust was the main reason that the king issued the ultimatum to him.

The messenger who brought the command from the king was a widely travelled man. He had spent long periods in Denmark and Sweden and was familiar with the routes and knew all about the people there too. He had also been all over Norway. When he had presented Thorstein Thoruson with the order, Thorstein told Egil about the messengers' errand and asked how he should respond.

'It seems obvious to me that the king wants you out of the country like the rest of Arinbjorn's family,' said Egil. 'It's a dangerous mission for a man of your standing. I advise you to call the king's messengers in to talk to you, and I'll be there when you do. Then we'll see what happens.'

Thorstein did as Egil said, and brought them in to talk to him. The messengers gave a straight account of the reason for their visit, and of the king's order that Thorstein should either undertake the journey or else be made an outlaw.

Then Egil said, 'I can see what lies behind this business of yours. If Thorstein doesn't want to go on the mission, you will go and collect the tribute yourselves.'

The messengers said that he had guessed correctly.

'Thorstein will not be going on this mission,' Egil declared. 'A man of his standing is not obliged to undertake such a paltry voyage. On the other hand, Thorstein will do his duty to follow the king in Norway and abroad if the king demands it of him. If you want to take some of Thorstein's men with you on the mission he will grant you that, along with anything you ask him to provide for the journey.'

The messengers discussed the offer among themselves and agreed to it, provided Egil would join them.

'The king hates him and would be pleased with our mission if we could arrange to have him killed,' they said. 'Then he can drive Thorstein out of the country too if he sees fit.'

Then they told Thorstein that they wouldn't mind the plan if Egil went with them and Thorstein stayed behind.

'Let it be done, then,' said Egil. 'I will take Thorstein's place on the mission. How many men do you think you need to take from here?'

'There are eight of us,' they said, 'and we would like four more from here, to make twelve.'

Egil said this would be done.

Onund Sjoni and some of Egil's men had gone down to the sea to see about their ships and the cargo they had put in storage that autumn, and had not returned yet. Egil thought that was a great setback, because the king's men were impatient about going on the journey and did not want to wait.

72   Egil and the three men who were going with him made preparations for their journey. They took horses and sleighs, and so did the king's men. There had been heavy snows which had altered all the routes that could be taken. Once they were ready they set off and drove inland. On

their way to Eid it snowed so much one night that it was impossible to make out where the trails were. The next day they made slow progress, because they kept sinking into the snowdrifts whenever they left the trail.

In the course of the day they paused to rest their horses near a wooded ridge.

'The trail forks here,' they told Egil. 'The farmer who lives beneath the ridge is named Arnald and he's a friend of ours. We will go and stay with him, and you should go up on the ridge. When you get there you'll soon see a big farm where you are sure of a place to stay. A very wealthy man called Armod Beard lives there. We will meet up again early tomorrow morning and go to Eideskog in the evening. A farmer lives there, a good man called Thorfinn.'

Then they parted. Egil and his men went up on the ridge. As for the king's men, as soon as they were out of Egil's sight, they put on skis they had brought with them, then went back as fast as they could. Travelling day and night, they went to Oppland and north from there across Dovrefjell, and did not stop until they reached King Hakon and told him about how things had gone.

Egil and his companions crossed the ridge that evening and lost their way at once in the heavy snows. Their horses repeatedly sank down into drifts and had to be pulled out. There were rocky slopes and brushwood which were difficult to negotiate. The horses caused them a long delay, and it was extremely hard going on foot too. Exhausted, they made their way down from the ridge at last, saw a big farm and headed for it.

When they arrived in the fields in front of the farmhouse, they saw Armod and his men standing outside. They exchanged greetings and asked each other if there was any news. When he heard that these men were envoys from the king, Armod invited them to stay, and they accepted. Armod's farmhands took their horses and baggage, while the farmer invited Egil and his men to go in to the main room, and they did so. Armod gave Egil a seat on the lower bench and seated his companions farther down the table. They spoke at length about their tough journey that night, and the people who lived there were astonished that they had made it at all, saying that the ridge could not even be crossed when it was free of snow.

'Don't you think the best thing I can provide you with now is to lay the tables and give you a meal for the night, and then you can go to bed?' asked Armod. 'You'll get the best night's rest that way.'

'That would be fine,' said Egil.

Then Armod had the tables laid for them, and large bowls of curds were brought in. Armod gave the impression he was upset at not having any ale to serve them. Because Egil and his men were so thirsty after their ordeal, they picked up the bowls and gulped down the curds, Egil much more than the others. No other food was served.

Many people were living and working on the farm. The farmer's wife sat on a cross-bench with some other women beside her. Their daughter, aged ten or eleven, was on the floor. The wife called over to her, and whispered in her ear. Then the girl went round to where Egil was sitting at the table. She spoke this verse:

44.   My mother sent me
       to talk to you
       and bring Egil word
       to keep on his guard.
       The maid of the ale-horn
       said treat your stomach
       as if you expect
       to be served something better.

Armod slapped the girl and told her to keep quiet – 'You're always saying things at the worst of times.'

The girl went away, and Egil put down the bowl of curds, which was almost empty. Then the bowls were taken away and the men of the household went to their seats as well. Tables were laid across the whole room and the food was spread out on them. Choice food was served to Egil and his men, and everyone else.

Then the ale was brought in, an exceptionally strong brew. Each man was given a horn to drink from, and the host made a special point of letting Egil and his men drink as much as possible. Egil drank incessantly for a long time at first, and when his companions became incapacitated, he drank what they could not finish as well. This continued until the tables were cleared.

Everyone became very drunk, and for every toast that Armod drank he said, 'I drink this to your health, Egil.'

The men of the household drank to his companions' health, with the same words. A man was given the job of keeping Egil and his companions served with one toast after another, and he urged them to drink it up at once. Egil told his companions they should not drink any more, and he drank theirs for them too when there was no way to avoid it.

Egil started to feel that he would not be able to go on like this. He stood up and walked across the floor to where Armod was sitting, seized him by the shoulders and thrust him up against a wall-post. Then Egil spewed a torrent of vomit that gushed all over Armod's face, filling his eyes and nostrils and mouth and pouring down his beard and chest. Armod was close to choking, and when he managed to let out his breath, a jet of vomit gushed out with it. All Armod's men who were there said that Egil had done a base and despicable deed by not going outside when he needed to vomit, but had made a spectacle of himself in the drinking-room instead.

Egil said, 'Don't blame me for following the master of the house's example. He's spewing his guts up just as much as I am.'

Then Egil went over to his place, sat down and asked for a drink. Then he blared out this verse:

45. With my cheeks' swell I repaid
     the compliment you served.
     I had heavy cause to venture
     my steps across the floor.
     Many guests thank favours
     with sweeter-flavoured rewards.
     But we meet rarely. Armod's beard
     is awash with dregs of ale.

Armod leapt to his feet and ran out, but Egil asked for more to drink. The farmer's wife told the man who had been pouring out the drinks all evening to keep serving them so they would not lack drink for as long as they wanted. He took a large horn, filled it and carried it over to Egil. Egil quaffed the drink, then spoke this verse:

46. Drink every toast down,
     though the rider of the waves   *rider of the waves*: seaman
     brings brimful horns often
     to the shaper of verse.
     I will leave no drop
     of malt-sea, even if the maker   *malt-sea*: ale
     of sword-play brings me
     horns until morning.

Egil went on drinking for some time, polishing off every drinking-horn that was brought to him, but there was not much merry-making in the room even though a few other men were still drinking. Then Egil and his companions stood up and took their weapons from the wall where they had hung them, went to the barn where their horses were being kept, lay down in the straw and slept the night there.

73   Egil got up at daybreak the next morning. He and his companions prepared to leave, and when they were ready they went back to the farm to look for Armod. When they found the chamber where Armod was sleeping with his wife and daughter, Egil flung the door open and went over to his bed. He drew his sword, seized Armod by the beard with his other hand and tugged him over to the side of the bed. Armod's wife and daughter both jumped up and implored Egil not to kill him.

Egil said he would spare him for their sake – 'That is the fair thing to do, but if he were worth the bother I would kill him.'

Then he spoke a verse:

47.   His wife and daughter aid
the foul-mouthed man
who twines arms with rings.   *twines arms with rings*: i.e. is generous;
I do not fear this battle-maker.   a conventional image used ironically
You will not feel deserving
of such dealings from the poet
for that drink you served him.
Let us be gone far on our way.

Then Egil cut off Amrod's beard close to the chin, and gouged out one of his eyes with his finger, leaving it hanging on his cheek. After that, Egil went off to his companions.

They went on their way and arrived at Thorfinn's farm early in the morning. He lived in Eideskog. Egil and his men asked for breakfast and somewhere to rest their horses. Thorfinn granted them that, and Egil and his men went into the main room.

Egil asked Thorfinn if he knew anything about his companions.

'We arranged to meet here,' he said.

Thorfinn replied, 'Six men came by here some time before daybreak, all heavily armed.'

One of Thorfinn's farmhands added, 'I went out to gather timber in the night and came across six men who were going somewhere. They were

Armod's farmhands and it was well before daybreak. I don't know whether these were the same six you mentioned.'

Thorfinn said the men he met had been travelling later than when the farmhand brought the cartload of timber back.

When Egil and his men sat down to eat, he saw a sick woman lying on the cross-bench. Egil asked Thorfinn who the woman was and why she was in such a poor state.

Thorfinn said she was his daughter Helga – 'She has been weak for a long time.'

She was suffering from a wasting sickness, and could not sleep at night because of some kind of a delirium.

'Has anyone tried to find out the cause of her illness?' Egil asked.

'We had some runes carved,' said Thorfinn. 'The son of a farmer who lives close by did it, and since then she's been much worse. Do you know any remedy, Egil?'

Egil said, 'It might not do any harm if I try something.'

When Egil had eaten his fill he went to where the woman was lying and spoke to her. He ordered them to lift her out of her bed and place clean sheets underneath her, and this was done. Then he examined the bed she had been lying in, and found a whalebone with runes carved on it. After reading the runes, Egil shaved them off and scraped them into the fire. He burned the whalebone and had her bedclothes aired. Then Egil spoke a verse:

48.   No man should carve runes
        unless he can read them well;
        many a man goes astray
        around those dark letters.
        On the whalebone I saw
        ten secret letters carved,   *linden tree*: woman
        from them the linden tree
        took her long harm.

Egil cut some runes and placed them under the pillow of the bed where she was lying. She felt as if she were waking from a deep sleep, and she said she was well again, but still very weak. But her father and mother were overjoyed. Thorfinn offered Egil all the provisions he thought he needed.

74   Egil told his companions that he wanted to continue on his journey and not wait any longer. Thorfinn offered to accompany Egil through the forest with his son Helgi, who was a brave lad. They told him they were certain Armod Beard had sent the six men to waylay them in the forest, and that there were likely to be more ambushes if the first failed. Thorfinn and three others offered to go with them. Then Egil spoke a verse:

49.   You know if I take four men,
         six will not manage to swap
         bloody blows of the battle-god's
         shield-piercer with me.   *battle-god's shield-piercer*: sword
         And if I have eight men,
         no twelve will strike fear
         into the dark-browed man's heart
         when the swords clash.

Thorfinn and his men decided to go to the forest with Egil, so there were eight of them in all. When they came to the ambush they saw some people there. Armod's six farmhands were lying in ambush, but when they saw eight men approaching, they did not think they had any chance against them, and stole away to the forest. When Egil and his men reached the spot where the spies had been, they could tell that danger was lurking. Egil told Thorfinn and his men to go back, but they wanted to go on. Egil refused and insisted that they go home, so in the end they did. They set off for home again, while Egil and his three men continued their journey.

As the day wore on, Egil and his men noticed six men in the woods, and guessed that they were Armod's farmhands. The spies jumped out and attacked them, but Egil fought back. When they clashed, Egil killed two of the attackers and the rest ran back into the forest.

Then Egil and his men proceeded on their way, and nothing else happened until they emerged from the forest and spent the night on a nearby farm with a farmer named Alf, who was nicknamed Alf the Wealthy. He was an old, wealthy man, but so unsociable that he could only bear having a few people working for him on the farm. Egil received a warm welcome there, and Alf was talkative to him. Egil asked him many things, and he answered them all. They talked mainly about the earl and the envoys of the king of Norway who had gone out to the east to collect tribute. From what Alf said, he was no friend of the earl's.

75 Early the next morning, Egil and his companions prepared to leave. As a parting gift, Egil gave Alf a fur coat which he accepted thankfully.

'I can have it made into a fur cape,' he said, as he invited Egil to visit him again on his way back.

They parted good friends, and Egil continued on his way. In the evening he reached Earl Arnvid's company and was well received there. He and his companions were given seats next to the head of the table.

After staying there for the night, Egil and his companions told the earl of their errand and the king's message, saying he wanted all the tribute from Varmland that had gone unpaid since Arnvid was appointed to rule there.

The earl told them he had already paid all the tribute to the king's envoys: 'I don't know what they did with it after that, whether they handed it over to the king or ran away with it to another country. Since you are carrying genuine tokens to prove the king sent you, I will pay all the tribute he is entitled to and hand it over to you. But I won't be held responsible for the way you look after it.'

Egil and his men stayed there for some while, and before they left, the earl paid the tribute over to them. Some of it was in silver and the rest in furs.

After Egil and his men had made their preparations to leave, they set off.

When they parted, Egil told the earl, 'We will give the king the tribute we have received from you, but you ought to realize that this is much less money than the king lays claim to here. And that's not counting the fact that he feels you should pay compensation for the lives of his envoys, because people are saying you had them killed.'

The earl said this rumour was untrue, and they parted.

Once Egil had left, the earl called in two brothers, both of them named Ulf.

He said to them, 'That big man, Egil, who was around here for a while – I think it will cause us a lot of trouble if he makes it back to the king. I can imagine the impression he will give about me to the king, judging from the accusations he threw around here about executing the king's men. You go after them and kill them all to stop them spreading such slander to the king. My advice is to ambush them in Eideskog. Take enough men with you, to be sure that none of them gets away and that you do not suffer any injuries at their hands.'

The brothers got ready to leave, taking thirty men with them. They entered the forest, where they were familiar with every trail, and kept watch for Egil's movements.

There were two routes through the forest. The shorter one involved crossing a ridge that had steep slopes and a narrow track over the top. The other route was to go round the ridge where there were large marshes, covered by felled logs to cross by, with a single track over them too. Fifteen men sat in ambush on each route.

76 Egil proceeded until he reached Alf's farm, where he stayed for the night and was well looked after. The next morning he got up before daybreak and prepared to leave. Alf came over to them when they were having breakfast.

'You're making an early start, Egil,' he said. 'But I wouldn't advise you to rush your journey. Be careful, because I expect people to be waiting in ambush for you in the forest. I do not have any men who would be any help to send with you, but I want to invite you to stay here with me until I can tell you it's safe to go through the forest.'

'It's nothing but nonsense to claim that we will be ambushed,' Egil replied. 'I will go on my way as I planned.'

Egil and his men made preparations to leave, but Alf tried to discourage him and told him to come back if he noticed tracks on the path, saying that no one had come back through the forest from the east since Egil went there, 'unless the people that I expect will be looking for you have been there'.

'How many of them do you think there are, assuming what you say is right?' asked Egil. 'We're not at their mercy, even if they outnumber us by a few men.'

'I went over near the forest with my farmhands,' said Alf, 'and we came across human tracks that extended into the forest. There must have been a lot of them together. If you don't believe what I'm saying, go there yourself and take a look at the tracks, but come back here if you think what I've told you is right.'

Egil went on his way, and when the party reached the road through the forest, they saw tracks left by both men and horses. Egil's companions said they wanted to turn back.

'We will go on,' Egil said. 'It doesn't surprise me that people have been travelling through Eideskog, because it's the route everyone takes.'

They set off again and the tracks continued, many of them, until they reached a fork in the road where the tracks also split up into two equal groups.

'It looks as though Alf may have been telling the truth,' said Egil. 'Let us be prepared to expect an encounter.'

Egil and his men took off their cloaks and all their loose clothing, and put them on the sleighs. He had taken along a long bast rope in his sleigh, since it was the custom on longer journeys to have a spare rope in case the reins needed mending. Then he took a huge slab of rock and placed it against his chest and stomach, then strapped it tight with the rope, winding it around his body all the way up to his shoulders.

Eideskog is heavily wooded right up to the settlements on either side of it, but deep inside it are bushes and brushwood, and in some places no trees at all.

Egil and his men took the shorter route that lay over the ridge. They were all carrying shields and wearing helmets, and had axes and spears as well. Egil led the way. The ridge was wooded at its foot, but the slopes up to the bluff were bare of trees.

When they were on the bluff, seven men leapt out of the trees and up the cliff after them, shooting arrows at them. Egil and his men turned around and blocked the whole path. Other men came down at them from the top of the ridge and threw rocks at them from above, which was much more dangerous.

Egil told them, 'You go and seek shelter at the foot of the bluff and protect yourselves as best you can, while I take a look on top.'

They did so. And when Egil reached the top of the bluff, there were eight men waiting there, who all attacked him at once. Without describing the blows, their clash ended with Egil killing them all. Then he went up to the edge of the bluff and hurled down rocks that were impossible to fend off. Three of the Varmlanders were left dead, while four escaped into the forest, hurt and bruised.

After that, Egil and his men returned to their horses and continued until they had crossed the ridge. The Varmlanders who had escaped tipped off their companions who were by the marshes. They headed along the lower path and emerged on the track in front of Egil and his men.

One of the brothers who were both named Ulf said to his men, 'Now we have to devise a scheme and arrange things to prevent them running away. The route here skirts the ridge, and there's a cliff above it where the marsh extends up to it. The path there is no wider than a single track. Some of us should go around the ridge and face them if they try to move forwards, and the rest should hide here in the forest and jump out behind them when they come past. We will make sure that no one gets away.'

They did as Ulf said. Ulf went around the cliff, taking ten men with him.

Egil and his men went on their way, unaware of this plan until they reached the single track, where they were attacked from behind by nine armed men. When Egil and his men fought back and defended themselves, others rushed up who had been in front of the ridge. Seeing this, Egil turned to face them. In a few quick blows he killed some of them, and the rest retreated to where the ground was more level. Egil pursued them. Ulf died there, and in the end Egil killed eleven men by himself. Then he pressed on to where his companions were holding eight men at bay on the path. Men were wounded on both sides. When Egil arrived, the Varmlanders fled at once into the nearby forest. Five of them escaped, all severely wounded, and three were killed on the spot.

Egil received many wounds, but none of them serious. They went on their way, and Egil tended his companions' wounds, none of which was fatal. Then they got on to their sleighs and rode for the rest of the day.

The Varmlanders who managed to escape took their horses and struggled back from the forest to the settlement in the east, where their wounds were tended to. There they got some men to go and see the earl and tell him about their misfortunes.

They reported that both brothers named Ulf were dead, and twenty-five men in all: 'Only five escaped with their lives, all of them wounded or injured.'

The earl asked about Egil and his men.

'We have no idea how many of them were wounded,' they replied. 'They attacked us with great bravery. When there were eight of us and four of them, we fled. Five of us made it to the forest and the other three died, and as far as we could see, Egil and his men hadn't taken a scratch.'

The earl said their expedition had turned out in the worst possible way.

'I could have put up with you suffering heavy losses if you had killed the Norwegians,' he said, 'but now when they go west of the forest and tell this news to the king of Norway we can expect the harshest treatment imaginable from him.'

77 Egil continued his journey until he emerged on the western side of the forest. He and his men went to Thorfinn at night and were warmly welcomed. Egil and his companions had their wounds dressed there, and they stayed for several nights. By then, Thorfinn's daughter Helga was back on her feet, cured of her ailment, and she and everybody else thanked Egil for that. The travellers rested their horses at the farm as well.

The man who had carved runes for Helga lived close by. It transpired that he had asked for her hand in marriage, but Thorfinn had refused him. Then the farmer's son had tried to seduce her, but she did not want him. After that he pretended to carve love runes to her, but did not know how to, and what he carved had caused sickness instead.

When Egil was ready to leave, Thorfinn and his sons accompanied him along the trail. There were ten or twelve of them in all. They travelled together all day as a precaution against Armod and his men. When word spread that Egil and his men had fought against overwhelming odds and won, Armod realized there was no hope that he might be able to put up a fight against him, so he stayed at home with all his men. Egil and Thorfinn exchanged gifts when they parted, and promised each other friendship.

Then Egil and his men continued on their way and nothing happened on the journey until they reached Thorstein. Their wounds had healed by then. Egil stayed there until spring. Thorstein sent envoys to King Hakon to deliver the tribute that Egil had collected in Varmland, and when they saw the king and handed it over, they told him what had happened on the expedition. The king realized then that his suspicions were true and Earl Arnvid had killed the two teams of envoys that he had sent to the east. The king told Thorstein he would be allowed to stay in Norway and be reconciled with him. Then the envoys went home. When they returned, they told him that the king was pleased with the expedition and had promised Thorstein reconciliation and friendship.

King Hakon travelled to Vik in the summer, and east from there to Varmland with a large army. Earl Arnvid fled from him, while the king exacted heavy levies from the farmers he considered to have wronged him, as reported by the collectors of the tribute. He appointed another earl and took hostages from him and the farmers.

On this voyage King Hakon travelled widely in Vastergotland and brought it under his rule, as is described in his saga and mentioned in the poems that have been composed about him. It is also said that he went to Denmark and raided many places. He disabled twelve Danish ships with just two of his own, granted his nephew Tryggvi Olafsson the title of king and made him ruler of Vik in the east.

Egil made his trading vessel ready and took on a crew, and as a parting gift he gave Thorstein the longship he had brought from Denmark that autumn. Thorstein presented Egil with fine gifts, and they promised each other great friendship. Egil sent messengers to his kinsman Thord at Aurland, granting him authority to manage the lands Egil owned in Sognefjord and Hordaland and asking him to sell them if buyers could be found.

When Egil and his men were ready to make their journey and a fair wind got up, they sailed out of Vik and along the coast of Norway, then out to sea for Iceland. They had a fairly smooth journey and arrived in Borgarfjord. Egil took his ship along the fjord to anchor it close to his farm, then had his cargo taken home and the ship pulled up. Egil went home to his farm, and everyone was pleased to see him. He stayed there for the winter.

78   By the time Egil returned from this voyage, the district was completely settled. All the original settlers had died by then, and their sons or grandsons were living in the district.

Ketil Gufa (Steam) came to Iceland when it was by and large settled. He spent the first winter at Gufuskalar on Rosmhvalanes. Ketil had sailed over from Ireland, and brought many Irish slaves with him. Since all the land on Rosmhvalanes was settled by that time, Ketil moved away to Nes and spent his second winter at Gufunes, but found nowhere to make his home. Then he went into Borgarfjord and stayed for the third winter at the place now called Gufuskalar, keeping his ship on the river Gufua, which comes down from the mountains there.

Thord Lambason was living at Lambastadir then. He was married and had a son named Lambi, who was fully grown by this time and big and strong for his age. In the summer when everyone rode off to the Thing, Lambi did so too. By then, Ketil had moved west to Breidafjord to look for a place to live.

Ketil's slaves ran away and came upon Thord at Lambastadir by night. They set fire to the houses, burning Thord and all his farmhands inside, broke into his sheds and brought all the cattle and goods outside. They rounded up the horses, loaded the booty on to them and rode out to Alftanes.

That morning around sunrise, Lambi returned home, having seen the flames during the night. There were several men with him. He rode off at once to search for the slaves, and people from other farms joined him. When the slaves saw they were being pursued, they discarded their booty and headed for shelter. Some ran to Myrar, and others towards the sea until they reached a fjord.

Lambi and his men pursued them and killed the slave named Kori at the place now known as Koranes. Skorri, Thormod and Svart dived into the sea and swam away from land. Lambi and his men looked around for some boats and rowed after them. They found Skorri on Skorrey Island, where they killed him, then rowed out to the skerry where they killed Thormod, which has been called Thormodssker (Thormod's skerry) ever since. They caught other slaves at places that are also named after them now.

Lambi lived at Lambastadir after this, and became a worthy farmer. He was a man of great might, but not a troublemaker.

Ketil Steam went west to Breidafjord and settled in Thorskafjord. Gufudal valley and Gufufjord are named after him. He married Yr, the daughter of Geirmund Dark-skin, and they had a son called Vali.

There was a man named Grim, the son of Sverting, and he lived at Mosfell at the foot of the moor called Heidi. He was wealthy and of good family. His half-sister was Rannveig, wife of Thorodd the Godi from Olfus, and their son was Skafti the Lawspeaker. Grim also became Lawspeaker later. He asked to marry Egil's niece and foster-daughter Thordis, the daughter of Thorolf. Egil loved Thordis no less dearly than his own children; she was a very attractive woman. Since Egil knew that Grim was a man of good birth and this was a good match, the marriage was settled. When Thordis married Grim, Egil handed over the inheritance her father had left to her. She went to Grim's farm and they lived at Mosfell for a long time.

79 There was a man named Olaf, the son of Hoskuld and grandson of Koll of Dalir. His mother Melkorka was the daughter of King Myrkjartan of Ireland. Olaf lived at Hjardarholt in Laxardal, in the valleys of Breidafjord. He was very wealthy, one of the most handsome men in Iceland at the time, and very firm-minded.

Olaf asked to marry Egil's daughter Thorgerd, who was a very fine woman, wise, rather strong-tempered, but usually quiet. Egil knew from Olaf's background that this was a splendid offer of marriage, and so she married him and went to live with him at Hjardarholt. Their children were Kjartan, Thorberg, Halldor, Steindor, Thurid, Thorbjorg and Bergthora, who became the wife of Thorhall Oddason the Godi. Thorbjorg was married first to Asgeir Knattarson and later to Vermund Thorgrimsson. Thurid married

Gudmund, son of Solmund, and their sons were Hall and Killer-Bardi.

Ozur, the son of Eyvind and brother of Thorodd from Olfus, married Egil's daughter Bera.

By this time, Egil's son Bodvar was grown up. He was exceptionally promising and handsome, big and strong like Egil and Thorolf at his age. Egil loved him dearly, and Bodvar was likewise very attached to his father.

One summer there was a ship moored on Hvita and a large market was held there. Egil had bought a lot of timber and arranged for it to be shipped back to his farm. The men of his household went out to fetch it from Hvita on an eight-oared vessel that Egil owned. On this occasion Bodvar had asked to go with them, and they allowed him to. He went down to Vellir with the farmhands, and there were six of them on the eight-oared ship. When they were ready to put to sea, high tide was in the afternoon, and since they had to wait for it they did not set out until late in the evening. A wild south-westerly gale got up, against the current of the tide, and the sea grew very rough in the fjord, as often happens. In the end their ship sank beneath them, and they were all lost at sea. The following day the bodies were washed up. Bodvar's body came ashore at Einarsnes, and some of the others farther south where the ship drifted to land, too; it was found washed ashore at Reykjarhamar.

Egil heard the news that day and rode off immediately to search for the bodies. He found Bodvar's body, picked it up and put it across his knees, then rode with it out to Digranes to Skallagrim's burial mound. He opened the mound and laid Bodvar inside by Skallagrim's side. The mound was closed again, which took until sunset. After that, Egil rode back to Borg, and when he got home he went straight to his normal sleeping-place in his bed-closet, lay down and locked the door. No one dared to ask to speak to him.

It is said that when Bodvar was buried, Egil was wearing tight-fitting hose and a tight red fustian tunic laced at the sides. People say that he became so swollen that his tunic and hose burst off his body.

Later that day, Egil kept his bed-closet locked, and took neither food nor drink. He lay there that day, and the following night. No one dared to speak to him.

On the third day, when it was daylight, Asgerd sent a messenger off on horseback. He galloped westwards to Hjardarholt and when he arrived in mid-afternoon he told Thorgerd the whole story. He also gave her a message from Asgerd asking her to come to Borg as quickly as possible.

Thorgerd had a horse saddled at once and set off with two men. They rode that evening and into the night until they reached Borg. Thorgerd went straight into the fire-room. Asgerd greeted her and asked whether they had eaten their evening meal.

Thorgerd replied in a loud voice, 'I have had no evening meal, nor will I do so until I go to join Freyja*. I know no better course of action than my father's. I do not want to live after my father and brother are dead.'

She went to the door to Egil's bed-closet and called out, 'Father, open the door, I want both of us to go the same way.'

Egil unfastened the door. Thorgerd walked in to the bed-closet and closed the door again. Then she lay down in another bed there.

Then Egil said, 'You do well, my daughter, in wanting to follow your father. You have shown great love for me. How can I be expected to want to live with such great sorrow?'

Then they were silent for a while.

Then Egil said, 'What are you doing, my daughter? Are you chewing something?'

'I'm chewing dulse,'† she replied, 'because I think it will make me feel worse. Otherwise I expect I will live too long.'

'Is it bad for you?' asked Egil.

'Very bad,' said Thorgerd. 'Do you want some?'

'What difference does it make?' he said.

A little later she called out for some water to drink, and she was brought something to drink.

Then Egil said, 'That happens if you eat dulse, it makes you even thirstier.'

'Would you like a drink, father?' she asked.

She passed him the animal horn and he took a great draught.

Then Thorgerd said, 'We've been tricked. This is milk.'

Egil bit a lump from the horn, as much as he could get his teeth into, then threw the horn away.

Then Thorgerd said, 'What will we do now? Our plan has failed. Now I want us to stay alive, father, long enough for you to compose a poem in Bodvar's memory and I will carve it on to a rune-stick. Then we can die if we want to. I doubt whether your son Thorstein would ever compose a

* Join the goddess, by dying.
† Edible seaweed.

poem for Bodvar, and it is unseemly if his memory is not honoured, because I do not expect us to be sitting there at the feast when it is.'

Egil said it was unlikely that he would be able to compose a poem even if he attempted to.

'But I will try,' he said.

Another of Egil's sons, called Gunnar, had died shortly before.

Then Egil composed this poem:

1. My tongue is sluggish
    for me to move,
    my poem's scales
    ponderous to raise.
    The god's prize
    is beyond my grasp,
    tough to drag out
    from my mind's haunts.

    god's prize: poetry. The dwarfs made the mead of poetry from the blood of a wise man, and a giant held them to ransom for it. Odin was given a drink of the mead by the giantess who guarded it, then flew back to the gods and spat it out for them.

2. Since heavy sobbing
    is the cause –
    how hard to pour forth
    from the mind's root
    the prize that Frigg's
    progeny found,
    borne of old
    from the world of giants,

    Frigg's progeny: the gods; their *prize* . . . *borne . . . from the world of giants*: poetry

3. unflawed, which Bragi
    inspired with life
    on the craft
    of the watcher-dwarf.
    Blood surges
    from the giant's wounded neck,
    crashes on the death-dwarf's
    boathouse door.

    Bragi: god of poetry

    Blood: sea, made from the blood of a giant; also the mead of poetry.

    boathouse door: rocks, cliffs; also the gates of Hel (i.e. loss hinders Egil's verse-making).

4. My stock
    stands on the brink,
    pounded as plane-trees
    on the forest's rim,
    no man is glad
    who carries the bones
    of his dead kinsman
    out of the bed.

5. Yet I will
    first recount
    my father's death
    and mother's loss,
    carry from my word-shrine
    the timber that I build
    my poem from,
    leafed with language.

6. Harsh was the rift
    that the wave hewed
    in the wall
    of my father's kin;
    I know it stands
    unfilled and open,
    my son's breach
    that the sea wrought.

7. The sea-goddess
    has ruffled me,
    stripped me bare
    of my loved ones:
    the ocean severed
    my family's bonds,
    the tight knot
    that ties me down.

8. If by sword I might
    avenge that deed,
    the brewer of waves   *brewer of waves*: sea-god
    would meet his end;

smite the wind's brother   *wind's brother*: sea
that dashes the bay,
do battle against
the sea-god's wife.

9. Yet I felt
    I lacked the might
    to seek justice against
    the killer of ships,   *killer of ships*: sea
    for it is clear
    to all eyes,
    how an old man
    lacks helpers.

10. The sea has robbed
    me of much,
    my kinsmen's deaths
    are harsh to tell,
    after the shield
    of my family
    retreated down
    the god's joyful road.   *road*: i.e. to death

11. Myself I know
    that in my son
    grew the makings
    of a worthy man,
    had that shield-tree   *shield-tree*: man, warrior
    reached manhood,
    then earned the claim   *earned the claim of war's arms*: become a
    of war's arms.   warrior; or be claimed (in death) by
                                             the war-god

12. Always he prized
     his father's words
     highest of all, though
     the world said otherwise.
     He shored me up,
     defended me,
     lent my strength
     the most support.

13. My lack of brothers
     often enters my thoughts   *moon-bears*: giants; their *winds*: thoughts (this
     where the winds   image occurs elsewhere, but its original
     of moon-bears rage,   justification (myth?) is now lost).
     I think of the other   *the other*: Thorolf?
     as the battle grows,
     scout around
     and wonder

14. which other valiant
     warrior stands
     by my side
     in the peril;
     I often need him
     when facing foes.
     When friends dwindle
     I am wary to soar.

15. It is rare to find
     one to trust
     amongst men who dwell
     beneath Odin's gallows,   *Odin's gallows*: the tree of life
     for the dark-minded   (Yggdrasil) where Odin sacrificed
     destroyer of kin   himself to himself in order to gain
     swaps his brother's   wisdom
     death for treasure.

16.   I often feel
      when the ruler of wealth
      . . .   [defective verse]

17.   It is also said
      that no one regains
      his son's worth
      without bearing
      another offspring
      that other men
      hold in esteem
      as his brother's match.

18.   I do not relish
      the company of men
      though each of them might
      live in peace with me:
      my wife's son
      has come in search
      of friendship
      to One-Eye's hall.   *One-Eye*: Odin; his *hall*: Valhalla

19.   But the lord of the sea,
      brewer of storms,
      seems to oppose me,
      his mind set.
      I cannot hold
      my head upright,
      the ground of my face,
      my thoughts' steed

20.   ever since the raging
      surf of heat   *surf of heat*: fever
      snatched from the world
      that son of mine
      whom I knew
      to shun disgrace,
      avoid words
      of ill repute.

21.   I remember still
       when the Gauts' friend   *Gauts' friend*: Odin
       raised high
       to the gods' world
       the ash that grew
       from my stock,
       the tree bearing
       my wife's kin.

22.   I was in league
       with the lord of spears,   *lord of spears*: Odin
       pledged myself loyal
       to believe in him,
       before he broke off
       his friendship with me,
       the guardian of chariots,
       architect of victory.

23.   I do not worship
       Vilir's brother,   *Vilir*: one of Odin's two brothers who
       guardian of the gods,   were minor deities
       through my own longing,
       though in good ways too
       the friend of wisdom
       has granted me
       redress for affliction.

24.   He who does battle   *hell-wolf*: Fenrir, the wolf that kills
       and tackles the hell-wolf   Odin in the Doom of the Gods
       gave me the craft   *craft*: poetry
       that is beyond reproach,
       and the nature
       that I could reveal
       those who plotted against me
       as my true enemies.

25.   Now my course is tough:
       Death, close sister
       of Odin's enemy,   *sister of Odin's enemy*: Death (Hel) was
       stands on the ness: the sister of the wolf Fenrir, whom
       with resolution   Odin fought; their father was Loki, the
       and without remorse   treacherous god
       I will gladly
       await my own.

Egil began to recover his spirits as he proceeded to compose the poem, and when it was finished, he delivered it to Asgerd and Thorgerd and his farmhands, left his bed and sat down in the high seat. He called the poem The Loss of My Sons. After that, Egil held a funeral feast according to ancient custom. When Thorgerd went home, Egil presented her with parting gifts.

80   Egil lived at Borg for a long time and grew to an old age. He is not said to have been involved in disputes with anyone in Iceland. Nor is anything told about him duelling or killing anyone after he settled down in Iceland.

People also say that Egil did not leave Iceland after the incidents that were described earlier, the main reason being that he could not stay in Norway because of the wrongs that the king felt he had done him, as narrated before. Egil lived lavishly, for he did not lack the means to do so, and he had the temperament as well.

King Hakon, King Athelstan's foster-son, ruled Norway for a long while. In Hakon's later years, King Eirik's sons went to Norway and disputed the control of the realm with him. They fought several battles and Hakon invariably won. Their last battle was in Hordaland, at Stord in Fitjar. King Hakon won the battle, but was fatally wounded, and Eirik's sons took over the kingdom afterwards.

Arinbjorn the Hersir was with Eirik's son Harald, and became his counsellor and was granted great revenues by him. He was in charge of his forces and defences. Arinbjorn was an outstanding and victorious warrior. He lived on the revenues from the Fjordane province.

Egil Skallagrimsson received word that there was a new king in Norway and that Arinbjorn had returned to his lands there and was held in high respect. Then Egil composed a poem in Arinbjorn's praise and sent it to him in Norway, and this is the beginning of it:

1.   I am quick to sing
a noble man's praises.
but stumble for words
about misers;
freely I speak
of a king's deeds,
but stay silent
about the people's lies.

2.   Replete with taunts
for bearers of lies,
I sing the favours
of my friends;
I have visited many
seats of mild kings,
with the ingenuous
intent of a poet.

3.   Once I had
incurred the wrath
of a mighty king
of Yngling's line;
I drew a bold hat
over my black hair,
paid a visit
to the war-lord

Yngling: ancestor of the kings of Norway

4.   where that mighty
maker of men
ruled the land from beneath
his helmet of terror;
In York
the king reigned,
rigid of mind,
over rainy shores.

5. The shining glare
    from Eirik's brow
    was not safe to behold
    nor free from terror;
    when the moons
    of that tyrant's face   *moons of . . . face*: eyes
    shone, serpent-like,
    with their awesome glow.

6. Yet I ventured
    my poem to the king,
    the bed-prize that Odin   *bed-prize . . . slithered*: Odin stole the
    had slithered to claim,   mead of poetry after entering the
    his frothing horn   giantess Gunnlod's chamber in the
    passed around   guise of a serpent; *frothing horn*: mead
    to quench   of poetry
    all men's ears.

7. No one praised
    the beauty of the prize
    my poetry earned
    in that lavish house
    when I accepted from the king
    in reward for my verse
    my own sable head
    to stand my hat on.

8. My head I won
    and with it the two
    dark jewels   *jewels*: i.e. eyes
    of my beetling brow,
    and the mouth
    that had delivered
    my head's ransom
    at the king's knee.

9.   A field of teeth there
     and my tongue I took back,
     and my flapping ears
     endowed with sound;
     such a gift
     was prized higher
     than earning gold
     from a famous king.

10. By my side, better
     than every other
     spreader of treasure,
     stood my loyal friend
     whom I truly trusted,
     growing in stature
     with his every deed.

11. Arinbjorn,
     paragon of men,
     who lifted me alone
     above the king's anger:
     the king's friend,
     who never told untruth
     in the warlike
     ruler's hall.

12. And ...   [defective verse]
     ... the pillar,
     glorifier
     of my deeds,
     which ...

     ...

     ... the scourge
     of Halfdan's line.

13. I would be deemed
     a thief from my friend
     and undeserving
     of Odin's horn,
     unworthy of praise
     and a breaker of oaths
     if I omitted
     to repay his favour.

14. Now it is clear
     where to present
     my praise of the mighty
     leader of men
     before the people,
     to their many eyes,
     the tortuous path
     that my verse treads.

15. The stuff of my praise
     is soon honed
     by my voice's plane
     for my friend,
     Thorir's kinsman,
     for double, triple
     choices lie
     upon my tongue.

16. First I will name –
     as most men know
     and is ever borne
     to people's ears –
     how generous
     he always seemed,
     the bear whose land
     the birch fears.

land the birch fears: fire, hearth; the
name *Arinbjorn* means 'hearth-bear'

17. All people
watch in marvel
how he sates
men with riches;
Frey and Njord
have endowed
rock-bear
with wealth's force.

18. Endless wealth
flows to the hands
of the chosen son
of Hroald's line
his friends ride
from far around
where the world lies beneath
the sky's cup of winds.

19. Crowned from ear
to ear like a king
he owned
a drawn line,   (defective and cryptic verse, a
dear to the gods   conjectural reading. *drawn line*: the
with his flock of men,   sword Dragvandil, 'Slicer'?)
friend of the sacred
and pillar of the poor.

20. His deeds will
outlast most men's
even those who are
blessed with wealth;
givers' houses are
few and far between,
a legion's spears   *a legion's spears need many shafts*: it is
need many shafts.   not easy to tend to every man's
                                 problem

21. No man went
     to the longboat   *longboat*: house
     where Arinbjorn's
     bed lay at rest
     led by mockery
     or bitter words,
     or his spear's
     grip empty.   *spear's grip*: hands

22. The man in Fjordane
     shows money no love:
     he banishes rings
     that drip like fruit,   *drip like fruit*: Draupnir, Odin's ring,
     defies the ring-clad   dripped eight identical rings every
     verse-brew's thief,   ninth night; *verse-brew's thief*: Odin,
     hacks treasures in half,   who stole the mead of poetry
     imperils brooches.

23. The acre
     of his ample life
     was much sown
     with the seeds of war.
     . . .   [defective verse]

24. It would be unjust
     if that spreader of wealth
     had cast overboard
     on to the course
     where the sea-god's steeds   *sea-god's steeds*: ships; their *course*: sea
     trample and race
     the many favours
     he has done for me.

25. I awoke early
     to stack my words
     as my speech's slave   *speech's slave*: tongue
     did its morning's work.
     I have piled a mound
     of praise that long
     will stand without crumbling
     in poetry's field.

81 There was a man named Einar, the son of Helgi Ottarsson and the
    great-grandson of Bjorn the Easterner who settled in Breidafjord. Einar
was the brother of Osvif the Wise. Even at an early age, Einar was large
and strong and a man of great accomplishments. He began composing poetry
when he was young and was fond of learning.

One summer at the Althing, Einar went to Egil Skallagrimsson's booth
and they began talking. The conversation soon turned to poetry and they
both took great delight in the discussion.

After that, Einar made a habit of talking to Egil and a great friendship
developed between them. Einar had just come back from a voyage abroad.
Egil asked Einar about recent news and his friends in Norway, and also
about the men he regarded as his enemies. He also often asked about the
leading men there. Einar asked in return about Egil's voyages and exploits;
Egil enjoyed talking about them and they got on well together. Einar asked
Egil to tell him where his toughest ordeal had been, and Egil spoke a verse:

50. I fought alone with eight,
     and twice with eleven.
     I fed the wolf with corpses,
     killed them all myself.
     Fiercely we swapped
     blades that shiver through shields.   *blades that shiver through shields*: swords
     From the tree of my arm
     I tossed the plated fire of death.   *plated fire of death*: sword

Egil and Einar promised each other friendship when they parted. Einar
spent a long time in other countries with men of rank. He was generous but
usually had scant means, and he was a firm character and a noble man. He
was one of Earl Hakon Sigurdarson's men.

At that time there was much unrest in Norway. Earl Hakon was at war with Eirik's sons and many people fled the country. King Harald Eiriksson died in Denmark, at Hals in Limfjord, when he was betrayed. He fought against Harald, the son of Canute, who was called Gold-Harald, and against Earl Hakon.

Arinbjorn the Hersir died with Harald Eiriksson in that battle. When Egil heard of Arinbjorn's death, he composed this verse:

51.   Their numbers are dwindling, the famous
       warriors who met with weapons
       and spread gifts like the gold of day.
       Where will I find generous men,
       who beyond the sea that, nailed with islands,
       girds the earth, showered snows of silver
       on to my hands where hawks perch,
       in return for my words of praise?

The poet Einar Helgason was nicknamed Skalaglamm (Bowl-rattle). He composed a drapa about Earl Hakon called Lack of Gold, which was very long. For a long time the earl was angry with Einar and refused to listen to it. Then Einar spoke a verse:

52.   I made mead for the battle-father   *mead*: poetry; *battle-father*: Odin,
       while everyone slept, about the noble   god of poetry and battle
       warrior who rules the lands –
       and now I regret it.
       I think that the spreader of treasure,
       the renowned leader, considers few
       poets worse than me; I was
       too eager to come to see him.

And he spoke another verse:

53.   Let us seek to meet the earl who dares
       to make meals for the wolf with his sword,
       adorn the ship's oar-sides
       with ornate victory shields;
       the warrior who swings his sword
       like a serpent inflicting wounds

will not turn his hand
to rebuff me when I find him.

The earl did not want Einar to leave then, but listened to his poem and afterwards gave him as a reward a shield, which was an outstanding treasure. It was adorned with legends, and between the carvings it was overlaid with gold and embossed with jewels. Then Einar went to Iceland to stay with his brother Osvif.

In the autumn, Einar rode over to Borg and stayed there. Egil was not at home, having gone north, but was expected shortly. Einar stayed three nights waiting for him; it was not the custom to stay more than three nights on a visit. Einar then prepared to leave, and when he was ready to go he went to Egil's bed and hung up his precious shield there, and told the people of the household that it was a present for Egil.

After that, Einar rode away, and Egil came home the same day. When he went to his bed he saw the shield and asked who owned such a treasure. He was told that Einar Skalaglamm had been there and given him the shield as a present.

Then Egil said, 'That scoundrel! Does he expect me to stay awake making a poem about his shield? Fetch my horse, I will ride after him and kill him.'

Then he was told that Einar had ridden away early that morning – 'He will have reached Dalir by now.'

Then Egil made a drapa, which begins with this verse:

54.   It is time to light up with praise
      the bright bulwark I was given.   *bright bulwark*: shield
      The sender of generosity's message
      reached me at my home.
      I will steer the reins well
      of the sea-king's horse,   *sea-king's horse*: ship
      my dwarf's ship of verse.   *dwarf's ship*: poetry
      Listen to my words.

Egil and Einar remained friends all their lives. It is said of the fate of the shield that Egil took it with him when he went north to Vidimyri with Thorkel Gunnvaldsson, who was going to fetch his bride there, and Bjorn the Red's sons Scarf and Helgi. The shield was dilapidated by then; it had been thrown into a tub of whey. Afterwards Egil had the fittings taken off, and there were twelve ounces of gold in the overlays.

82   Thorstein, Egil's son, was a very handsome man when he grew up, with fair hair and a fair complexion. He was tall and strong, although not on his father's scale. Thorstein was a wise and peaceful man, a model of modesty and self-control. Egil was not very fond of him. Thorstein, in turn, did not show his father much affection, but Asgerd and Thorstein were very close. By this time, Egil was growing very old.

One summer, Thorstein rode to the Althing, while Egil stayed at home. Before Thorstein left home, he and Asgerd decided to take Arinbjorn's gift, the silk cloak, out of Egil's chest, and Thorstein wore it to the Thing. It was so long that it dragged along the ground and the hem got dirty during the procession to the Law Rock. When he returned home, Asgerd put the gown back where it had come from. Much later, when Egil opened his chest, he discovered that the gown was ruined, and asked Asgerd what the explanation was. She told him the truth, and Egil spoke a verse:

55.   I had little need of an heir
      to use my inheritance.
      My son has betrayed me
      in my lifetime, I call that treachery.
      The horseman of the sea   *horseman of the sea*: seafarer, man
      could well have waited
      for other sea-skiers   *sea-skiers*: seafarers
      to pile rocks over me.

Thorstein married Jofrid, the daughter of Gunnar Hlifarson. Her mother was Helga, who was the daughter of Olaf Feilan and sister of Thord Bellower. Jofrid had previously been married to Thorodd, son of Tungu-Odd.

Shortly after this, Asgerd died. Then Egil gave up his farm and handed it over to Thorstein, and went south to Mosfell to his son-in-law Grim, because he was fondest of his step-daughter Thordis of all the people who were alive.

One summer a ship arrived in Leiruvog, with a man called Thormod at the helm. He was Norwegian and lived on the farm of Thora's son Thorstein the Hersir. He brought with him a shield that Thorstein had sent to Egil Skallagrimsson, a fine piece of work. Thormod gave Egil the shield and he accepted it with thanks. Later that winter, Egil composed a drapa in honour of the shield he had been given, which he called the Drapa of the Shield. It begins with the verse:

56.   Hear, king's subject, my fountain
       of praise from long-haired Odin,
       the guardian of sacrificial fire:
       may men pledge silence.
       My words of praise, my seed sown   *seed sown from the eagle's mouth*:
       from the eagle's mouth, will often   poetry, stolen by Odin in the
       be heard in Hordaland, O guider   guise of an eagle
       of the wave-cliffs' raven.   *wave-cliffs' raven*: ship

Egil's son Thorstein lived at Borg. He had two sons outside wedlock, Hrifla and Hrafn, and ten children with Jofrid after they were married. One of their daughters was Helga the Fair, whose love Hrafn the Poet and Gunnlaug Serpent-tongue contested. Grim was their oldest son, followed by Skuli, Thorgeir, Kollsvein, Hjorleif, Halli, Egil and Thord. They had another daughter named Thora, who married Thormod Kleppjarnsson. A great family is descended from Thorstein's children, including many great men. Everyone descended from Skallagrim is said to belong to the Myrar clan.

83   Onund Sjoni was living at Anabrekka when Egil lived at Borg. His wife was Thorgerd, the daughter of Bjarni the Stout from Snaefellsstrond. Their children were Steinar, and Dalla, who married Ogmund Galtason and had two sons named Thorgils and Kormak. When Onund grew old and began to go blind, he handed over his farm to his son Steinar. The two of them were very wealthy. Steinar was exceedingly large and strong, an ugly man, stooping, with long legs but a short trunk. He was a great troublemaker, overbearing, difficult to deal with and ruthless, and very quarrelsome.

When Egil's son Thorstein was living at Borg, he and Steinar did not get along. South of the Hafslaek Brook is a marsh called Stakksmyri which is submerged in winter, but in spring when the ice has thawed it is such good pasture for cows that it was considered worth a whole haystack. Hafslaek had marked the boundary between farms since early times. During the spring, Steinar's cattle grazed heavily on Stakksmyri when they were driven out from Hafslaek. Thorstein's farmhands complained, but Steinar paid no heed to them, and there the matter rested for the first summer.

The following spring, Steinar continued to graze his cattle there. Thorstein talked calmly to him about it and asked him to graze his cattle within the old boundaries. Steinar replied that cattle would always go wherever they pleased. He spoke quite forcefully on the matter, and they exchanged harsh words. Then Thorstein had the cattle driven back over the brook. When Steinar realized this, he sent his slave Grani to watch over the cattle at Stakksmyri, and he stayed there every day. This was towards the end of summer, and all the pasture south of Hafslaek was completely grazed.

One day Thorstein went up on to a rock to take a look around and, seeing where Steinar's cattle were heading, he went out to the marsh. It was late in the day. He could see that the cattle had gone a long way up the tract between the hills. Thorstein ran out to the meadows, and when Grani saw this, he drove the cattle as hard as he could back to the milking-pens. Thorstein went after them and met Grani at the gate to the farm. Thorstein killed him there, and the spot at the hayfield wall has been called Granahlid (Grani's Gate) ever since. Thorstein pulled down the wall to cover his body, then went back to Borg. The women found Grani lying there when they went out to the milking-pens, and returned to the farmhouse to tell Steinar what had happened. Steinar buried him up in the hills, then appointed another slave, whose name is not mentioned, to go with the cattle. Thorstein pretended to ignore the grazing cattle for the rest of the summer.

Early in the winter, Steinar went out to Snaefellsstrond and spent some time there. He saw a slave named Thrand there, a very large and strong man. Steinar offered a high price to buy the slave; his owner valued him at three marks of silver, which was twice the value of an ordinary slave. The deal was made and he took Thrand home with him.

When they returned home, Steinar said to Thrand, 'It so happens that I want you to do some work for me, but all the jobs have been shared out already. I want to ask you to do a job which will not be very difficult for you. You will watch over my cattle. I think it is important that they are grazed well, and I want you to rely solely on your own judgement about where the best pasture is on the marsh. I'm a poor judge of character if you don't turn out to have the courage or strength to stand up to any of Thorstein's farmhands.'

Steinar gave Thrand a big axe, measuring almost one ell across the head of the blade and razor-sharp.

'From the look of you, I can't tell how highly you would think of the fact that Thorstein is a godi, if the two of you met face to face,' Steinar added.

Thrand answered, 'I don't owe Thorstein any loyalty, but I think I realize what the job is you're asking me to do. You don't reckon you have much to lose in me. But when Thorstein and I put our strength to the test, whichever of us wins will be a worthy victor.'

Then Thrand started tending the cattle. Although he had not been there long, Thrand realized where Steinar had sent his cattle, and he sat watching over them in Stakksmyri.

When Thorstein noticed this, he sent one of his farmhands to see Thrand and tell him where the boundary between his land and Steinar's lay. The farmhand met Thrand and gave him the message to keep his cattle on the other side, since they were on Thorstein Egilsson's side.

'I don't care whose land they are on,' said Thrand. 'I will keep the cattle where I think the best pasture is.'

They parted, and the farmhand went home and told Thorstein what the slave had replied. Thorstein let the matter rest, and Thrand started watching over the cattle day and night.

84 One morning Thorstein got up at sunrise and went up to the top of a rock. Seeing where Steinar's cattle were, he walked over to the marsh until he reached them. A wooded cliff overlooks Hafslaek, and Thrand was sleeping barefoot on the top of it. Thorstein went up to the top of the cliff, carrying an axe which was not very large, and no other weapon. He prodded Thrand with the shaft of the axe and ordered him to wake up. Thrand leapt to his feet, grabbed his axe with both hands and raised it. He asked Thorstein what he wanted.

Thorstein said, 'I want to tell you that this is my land, and your pasture is on the other side of the brook. I'm not surprised you don't realize where the boundaries lie here.'

'I don't care whose land it is,' Thrand replied. 'I will let the cattle be where they prefer.'

'I'd rather be in charge of my own land than leave that to Steinar's slaves,' said Thorstein.

'You're more stupid than I thought, Thorstein, if you want to risk your honour by seeking a place to sleep for the night under my axe,' said Thrand. 'I'd guess I have twice your strength, and I don't lack courage either. And I'm better armed than you.'

Thorstein said, 'That's a risk I'm prepared to take if you don't do anything about the cattle grazing. I trust there's as much difference between our fortunes as there is between our claims in this matter.'

Thrand said, 'Now you'll find out whether I'm scared of your threats, Thorstein.'

Then Thrand sat down to tie his shoe, and Thorstein raised his axe high in the air and struck him on the neck, so that his head fell on to his chest. Thorstein piled some rocks over his body to cover it up and went back home to Borg.

That day Steinar's cattle were late coming back. When there seemed to be no hope left of them returning, Steinar took his horse and saddled it. He rode south to Borg, fully armed, and spoke to some people when he arrived. He asked about Thorstein and was told he was indoors. Steinar told them he wanted Thorstein to come outside to attend to some business. When Thorstein heard this, he picked up his weapons and went to the door. Then he asked Steinar what he wanted.

'Did you kill my slave Thrand?' Steinar asked.

'That's right,' said Thorstein. 'You don't need to imagine that anyone else did.'

'I can see you're set on defending your land with a firm hand, since you've killed two of my slaves,' replied Steinar. 'But I don't consider that much of a feat. If you're so determined to defend your land bravely, I can give you a much more worthy option. From now on I won't rely on anyone else to look after my cattle, and you can rest assured that they'll remain on your land both day and night.'

'It so happened that last summer I killed the slave you sent to graze the cattle on my land,' said Thorstein. 'Then I let you have all the pasture you wanted right up until winter. Now I have killed another of your slaves for the same reason I killed the first one. You can have all the pasture you want for the coming summer, but after that, if you graze your cattle on my land and send men to drive your cattle here, I will kill every single one who herds them, even if it is you yourself. I will go on doing this every summer for as long as you keep on grazing them there.'

Then Steinar rode off back to Brekka and on to Stafaholt shortly afterwards. A godi called Einar lived there. Steinar asked for his support and offered to pay him for it.

Einar said, 'My support will make little difference to you unless other men of standing back you up in this matter.'

After that Steinar rode up to Reykjadal to see Tungu-Odd, asked him for support and offered to pay him for it. Odd took the money and promised his support in helping Steinar to secure his rights against Thorstein. Then Steinar rode home.

That spring Odd and Einar went with Steinar to Borg to announce their summons, taking a large band of men with them. Steinar summonsed Thorstein for killing his slaves and demanded a penalty of lesser outlawry for each of them, which was the punishment for killing a man's slaves unless compensation was paid before the third sunrise. Double lesser outlawry was considered equal to full outlawry.

Thorstein brought no counter-charges, but sent some men off to Nes shortly afterwards. They went to Grim at Mosfell and told him the news. Egil showed little interest, but asked secretly in detail about Thorstein's dealings with Steinar and about the men who had supported Steinar in the case. Then the messengers went back home, and Thorstein was pleased with their journey.

Thorstein Egilsson took a very large party to the Spring Assembly and arrived the night before everybody else. They pitched tents over their booths, and so did his thingmen who had booths there. When they had set everything up, Thorstein sent word to his supporters to build great walls for a booth, which he then covered with a much larger tent than all the others there. No men were in that booth.

Steinar rode to the assembly with very many men. Tungu-Odd was in charge of a large band of his own men, and Einar from Stafaholt also brought a large party. They pitched their tents over their booths. It was a very well-attended assembly. When the cases were presented, Thorstein made no offer of a settlement on his own behalf, and told anyone who tried to arrange one that he would wait to hear the ruling, since he set little store by Steinar's charges of killing his slaves after all they had done to deserve it. Steinar made a great show about his case, claiming that his charges were valid and that he had ample support to win his rights, and was very aggressive about the whole matter.

The same day all the men went to the Assembly Slope to plead against the charges before they went before the courts in the evening. Thorstein was there with his party. He had the most influence over the conduct of proceedings there, just as Egil had done when he was a godi and chieftain. Both sides were fully armed.

From the assembly, a band of men was seen riding alongside the river Gljufura, their shields glinting. They rode into the assembly led by a large man wearing a black cloak and gilded helmet and carrying a shield decorated with gold by his side. In his hand he held a barbed spear with its socket embossed with gold, and he was girded with a sword. Egil Skallagrimsson had arrived with eighty men, all armed for battle. It was an elite band of men, for Egil had brought along the finest farmers' sons from the south side of Nes, those whom he considered most warlike. Egil rode with his party over to the booth where Thorstein had already pitched tents which were standing empty. They dismounted from their horses.

When Thorstein recognized his father, he went up to him with all his men and welcomed him warmly. Egil and his men had all the gear they had brought with them carried into the booth, and drove the horses out to graze. Once this was done, Egil and Thorstein went up the Assembly Slope with all their men and sat down in their usual places.

Then Egil stood up and said in a loud voice, 'Is Onund Sjoni here on the slope?'

Onund said he was, 'And I am pleased that you have come, Egil. It will make a great contribution towards solving this dispute.'

Egil asked, 'Are you responsible for the charges your son Steinar has brought against my son Thorstein and the forces he has gathered to have Thorstein declared an outlaw?'

'Their quarrel is none of my doing,' said Onund. 'I have spent a lot of words telling Steinar to make a reconciliation with Thorstein, because I have always been reluctant to bring any dishonour upon your son Thorstein. The reason is our lifelong friendship, Egil, ever since we were brought up here together.'

'It will soon emerge,' said Egil, 'whether you are speaking earnest or empty words, although I consider the latter less likely. I remember the days when neither of us could have imagined that we would quarrel with each other or need to restrain our sons from committing such folly as I hear is in the offing now. It seems advisable to me, for as long as we live and witness their dispute, that we should take charge of the matter ourselves and settle it, without letting Tungu-Odd and Einar pit our sons against each other like horses at a fight. They can find a better way to earn their living than involving themselves in this.'

Onund stood up and said, 'What you say is right, Egil. It is unfitting for us to attend an assembly where our sons are quarrelling. We will never incur the shame of being so weak in character that we cannot reconcile them. Steinar, I want you to grant me charge of this case and allow me to pursue it as I please.'

'I don't know whether I want to drop my case,' said Steinar, 'after seeking the support of great men. I want to settle the matter immediately to Odd and Einar's satisfaction.'

Then Odd and Steinar conferred, and Odd said, 'I will grant you the support I promised you, Steinar, to win your rights or a settlement that you are prepared to accept. It will be largely your responsibility if Egil rules on the matter.'

Then Onund said, 'I don't want to leave the matter up to Odd's tongue to decide, for he has neither treated me well nor badly. But Egil has done many fine things for me. I trust him better than other people, and I will have my own way now. You will be better off not having to tackle all of us. I have made the decisions on our behalf until now, and that's the way it will stay.'

'You are very insistent about it, Father,' said Steinar, 'but I expect we will regret it later.'

Then Steinar handed over charge of the case to Onund, who was to prosecute or settle, as the law stipulated.

Once Onund had taken charge of the case, he went to see Thorstein and Egil.

Onund said, 'I will leave it up to you to rule and judge here, Egil, just as you please, because I trust you most to decide on these matters of mine and all others.'

Then Onund and Thorstein shook hands and named witnesses, adding that Egil Skallagrimsson alone should rule on the case at that assembly as he saw fit, without reservations, and so the matter ended. Everyone went back to the booths. Thorstein had three oxen brought to Egil's booth and had them slaughtered to provide him with a feast at the assembly.

When Tungu-Odd and Steinar returned to their booths, Odd said, 'You and your father have decided how your case will be concluded, Steinar. Now I am free of all obligation to grant you the support that I promised you, because we agreed that I should help you to pursue your case or bring it to a conclusion that you found favourable, however Egil's settlement turns out.'

Steinar told Odd he had supported him well and nobly, and that they would be closer friends than before.

'I declare that you are free of all your earlier obligations to me,' he said.

That evening the courts met, and nothing eventful is said to have happened then.

85   Egil Skallagrimsson went to the Assembly Slope the following day together with Thorstein and all their men. Onund and Steinar were there too, and Tungu-Odd and Einar.

When everyone had stated their cases, Egil stood up and asked, 'Are Steinar and his father Onund here and able to hear what I am saying?'

Onund said they were there.

'Then I will pronounce the settlement between Steinar and Thorstein: I will begin my statement with my father Grim's arrival in Iceland, when he took all the land in Myrar and around the district and made his home at Borg. He designated that land for his farm, but gave his friends the outlying lands which they settled later. He gave Ani a place to live at Anabrekka, where Onund and Steinar have lived until now. We all know, Steinar, where the boundary lies between Borg and Anabrekka: the brook at Hafslaek separates them. It was not by accident that you grazed your cattle on Thorstein's land, Steinar, and seized his property, expecting him to be such a disgrace to his family that he would let you get away with robbing him. You are well aware, Steinar and Onund, that Ani accepted that land from my father Grim. When Thorstein killed two of your slaves, it is obvious to everyone that they fell by their own doing and do not qualify for compensation; even if they were free men, they would be considered criminals and thereby not qualify for compensation. Yet since you, Steinar, planned to rob my son Thorstein of his land, which he took over with my approval and I had inherited from my father, you will forfeit your land at Anabrekka and be paid nothing for it. Furthermore, you will not make your home or accept lodging in this district on the south side of the river Langa, and leave Anabrekka before the end of the Moving Days, and be rightfully killed by Thorstein or any man who is ready to grant Thorstein his assistance after that time if you refuse to leave or to abide by any of these stipulations I have made towards you.'

When Egil sat down, Thorstein named witnesses to his settlement.

Then Onund Sjoni said, 'Everyone will agree, Egil, that the settlement you have made and delivered here is unjust. For my part, I have made every effort to prevent the trouble between them, but from now on I will not restrain myself from any inconvenience I can cause to Thorstein.'

'On the contrary,' said Egil, 'I expect you and your son's lot to worsen, the longer that our quarrel lasts. I would have thought you realized, Onund, that I have always held my own against people like you and your son. And Odd and Einar, who were so interested in this matter, have received the honour they deserve from it.'

86 Thorgeir Blund, Egil's nephew, was at the assembly and had supported Thorstein strongly in the case. He asked Egil and Thorstein to grant him some land in Myrar; he had been living on the south side of Hvita, below the lake called Blundsvatn (Snooze Lake). Egil took his request well, and Thorstein urged his father to let him move there. They gave Thorgeir Anabrekka to live in, while Steinar moved his home to the other side of Langa and settled at Leirulaek. Egil rode off home to Nes, and he and his son parted on warm terms.

There was a man named Iri who was a member of Thorstein's household, very swift of foot and exceptionally sharp-sighted. Although he was a foreigner and a freedman, he was in charge of watching over Thorstein's sheep, which mainly involved rounding up the sheep that were unsuitable for milking, and driving them up to the mountains in spring and rounding them up again for penning in autumn. After the Moving Days, Thorstein had the sheep rounded up which had been left behind in the spring and planned to drive them up in the mountains. Iri was in the fold, but Thorstein and his farmhands, eight of them altogether, rode off to the mountains.

Thorstein built a fence right across Grisartunga between Langavatn and Gljufura and sent a number of men to work on it in the spring. After inspecting his farmhands' work, he rode home, and as he was passing the site of the assembly, Iri came running up from the opposite direction and said he wanted to talk to him in private. Thorstein told his companions to ride ahead while they talked.

Iri told Thorstein that they had been up to Einkunnir earlier that day to keep an eye on the sheep.

'And in the woods above the winter track,' he said, 'I saw the glint of twelve spears and several shields.'

Thorstein answered in a loud enough voice for his companions to hear him clearly: 'Why does he want to see me so badly that I can't even ride home? Olvald must know that I'm unlikely to refuse to speak to him when he's ill.'

Iri ran up the mountain as fast as he could.

Then Thorstein said to his companions, 'I want to make a detour and ride south to Olvaldsstadir. Olvald sent me word asking me to meet him. He'll think I owe him at least that for the ox he gave me last autumn, to go and see him when he thinks it's important.'

After that, Thorstein and his men rode south across the marshland above Stangarholt, then south to Gufa and along the riding path that skirts the river. On their way down from Vatn they saw a large number of bulls on the south side of the river, and a man there with them. It was Olvald's farmhand. Thorstein asked him if everybody was well, and he said that they all were, and Olvald was in the woods chopping timber.

'Then go and tell him to go to Borg if he has any business with me,' said Thorstein. 'I will ride home now.'

And then he did that.

Later, word went around that Steinar Sjonason had been lying in wait on Einkunnir with eleven men that same day. Thorstein pretended not to know, and everything remained quiet afterwards.

87 There was a man named Thorgeir, a kinsman and close friend of Thorstein's. At that time he was living at Alftanes. Thorgeir was in the habit of holding a feast every autumn. He went to see Thorstein Egilsson to invite him. Thorstein accepted the invitation, and Thorgeir went back home.

On the appointed day, Thorstein made his preparations for the journey; this was four weeks before winter. A Norwegian and two of his farmhands went with him. Thorstein had a ten-year-old son named Grim who went with them too, so that there were five of them when they rode out to Foss to cross Langa, then straight on to the river Aurridaa.

On the other side of the river was a long and narrow wood through which the path lay, and meadows west of the trees, belonging to several farms. Steinar, Onund and their farmhands were working there. When they recognized Thorstein they ran for their weapons and set off in pursuit. And when Thorstein saw Steinar chasing them, he and his men rode from Langaholt towards a high, narrow hill which was nearby. Thorstein and his men dismounted and set off up the hill, and he told the boy Grim to stay clear of their encounter and go into the woods. When Steinar and the others reached the hill, they attacked Thorstein and his men and a battle ensued. There were six grown men on Steinar's side, as well as his ten-year-old son. People from nearby farms who were working in the meadows saw the two sides clash and ran over to separate them. By the time the fight was broken up, both of Thorstein's farmhands had been killed. One of Steinar's farmhands was dead and some of the others wounded.

After the battle had been broken up, Thorstein went to look for Grim. They found him severely wounded, with Steinar's son lying dead beside him.

As Thorstein jumped on his horse, Steinar called out to him, 'Are you running away now, Thorstein the White?'

Thorstein replied, 'You'll run further before the week is past.'

Then Thorstein and his men rode over the marshland, taking Grim with them. When they reached the hillock that stands there, the boy died. They buried him on the hillock, and it was called Grimsholt afterwards; the hill where they had fought is called Orustuhvol (Battle Hill).

That evening, Thorstein rode out to Alftanes as he had planned, stayed at the feast for three days and then prepared to go back home. People offered to accompany him, but he refused, and set off with the Norwegian.

Steinar rode out towards the shore on the day that he knew he could expect Thorstein to be riding home. He sat down on the sand banks that start below Lambastadir, and was armed with a sword called Skrymir, an outstanding weapon. He stood on the bank with his sword drawn, his eyes focused on Thorstein whom he saw riding along the edge of the sands.

Lambi, who lived at Lambastadir, saw what Steinar was doing. He set off from home and down to the sand bank, and when he reached Steinar he grabbed his arms from behind. Steinar tried to shake him off, but Lambi held him tight, and they struggled down from the bank and on to level ground just as Thorstein and his companion rode past along the track below. Steinar had ridden his horse there and had tethered it; the horse freed itself and galloped off along the shore. This surprised Thorstein and his companion when they saw it, because they had not noticed Steinar's movements. Not seeing Thorstein ride past, Steinar worked his way back to the sand bank, and when they reached the edge Lambi caught him off his guard and pushed him off it. He tumbled on to the sands, Lambi ran home and when Steinar got to his feet he chased after him. When Lambi reached the door of his house he ran inside and slammed it. Steinar swung a blow at him, but his sword stuck tight in the rafters. That was the end of their dealings, and Steinar went home.

The day after Thorstein came back home he sent his farmhand off to Leirulaek to tell Steinar to move house beyond Borgarhraun and be gone by the next evening with everything he had, or he would take advantage of his greater power, 'and if I do, then you won't have the chance to leave'.

Steinar moved out to the coast at Snaefellsstrond and set up a farm at the place called Ellidi, and that was the end of his dealings with Thorstein Egilsson.

Thorgeir Blund lived at Anabrekka and quarrelled with Thorstein about everything he could.

On one occasion when Egil and Thorstein met they talked at great length about their kinsman Thorgeir Blund and agreed entirely about him. Then Egil spoke this verse:

57.   In the past I pulled the land
    out of Steinar's hands with words
    thinking I was working
    in Thorgeir's favour.
    My sister's son failed me,
    gave me golden promises,
    yet Snooze, to my astonishment,
    could not refrain from causing harm.

Thorgeir Blund left Anabrekka and went south to Flokadal, because even though he was prepared to back down, Thorstein refused to have anything to do with him.

Thorstein was a straightforward, just and unimposing man, yet stood firm if others imposed on him and proved a tough opponent when challenged. He and Tungu-Odd were on cold terms after Steinar's case.

Odd was the chieftain of Borgarfjord on the south side of Hvita then. He was the godi of the temple to which everyone living south of Skardsheidi paid tribute.

88   Egil Skallagrimsson lived a long life, but in his old age he grew very frail, and both his hearing and sight failed. He also suffered from very stiff legs. Egil was living at Mosfell with Grim and Thordis then.

One day Egil was walking outdoors alongside the wall when he stumbled and fell.

Some women saw this, laughed at him and said, 'You're completely finished, Egil, now that you fall over of your own accord.'

Grim replied, 'Women made less fun of us when we were younger. And I expect they find little of value in our womanizing now.'

Egil said that things had reached that pass, and he spoke a verse:

58.   My head bobs like a bridled horse
       it plunges baldly into woe.
       my middle leg both droops and drips
       while both my ears are dry.

Egil went completely blind. One winter day when the weather was cold, he went to warm himself by the fire. The cook said it was astonishing for a man who had been as great as Egil to lie around under people's feet and stop them going about their work.

'Don't grudge me that I warm myself through by the fire,' said Egil. 'We should make room for each other.'

'Stand up,' she said, 'and go off to your bed and leave us to get on with our work.'

Egil stood up, went off to his bed and spoke this verse:

59.   Blind I wandered to sit by the fire,
       asked the flame-maiden for peace;
       such affliction I bear on the border
       where my eyebrows cross.
       Once when the land-rich king
       took pleasure in my words
       he granted me the hoard
       that giants warded, gold.

Another time Egil went over to the fire to keep warm, and someone asked him if his legs were cold and told him not to stretch them out too close to the fire.

'I will do that,' said Egil, 'but I don't find it easy to control my legs now that I cannot see. Being blind is dismal.'

Then Egil spoke a verse:

60.   Time seems long in passing
       as I lie alone,
       a senile old man
       on the king's guard.   *king's guard*: his back? a bed? his chest?
       My legs are two
       frigid widows,
       those women
       need some flame.

This was at the start of Earl Hakon the Powerful's reign. Egil Skallagrims-son was in his eighties then and still active apart from his blindness.

In the summer, when everyone was preparing to ride to the Thing, Egil asked Grim to ride there with him. Grim was reluctant.

When Grim spoke to Thordis, he told her what Egil had asked of him.

'I want you to find out what lies behind this request of his,' he said.

Thordis went to see her kinsman Egil, who by that time had no greater pleasure in life than talking to her.

When she saw him she asked, 'Is it true that you want to ride to the Thing, kinsman? I'd like you to tell me what you're planning.'

'I will tell you what I've been thinking,' he said. 'I want to go to the Thing with the two chests full of English silver that King Athelstan gave to me. I'm going to have the chests carried to the Law Rock when the crowd there is at its biggest. Then I'll toss the silver at them and I'll be very much surprised if they all share it out fairly amongst themselves. I expect there'll be plenty of pushing and shoving. It might even end with the whole Thing breaking out in a brawl.'

Thordis said, 'That sounds like a brilliant plan. It will live for as long as people live in Iceland.'

Then Thordis went to talk to Grim and tell him about Egil's plan.

'He must never be allowed to get away with such a mad scheme,' said Grim.

When Egil brought up the subject of riding to the Thing with Grim he would have none of it, so Egil stayed at home while the Thing was held. He was displeased and wore a rather grumpy look.

The cattle at Mosfell were kept in a shieling, and Thordis stayed there while the Thing took place.

One evening when everyone was going to bed at Mosfell, Egil called in two of Grim's slaves.

He told them to fetch him a horse, 'because I want to go to bathe in the pool'.

When he was ready he went out, taking his chests of silver with him. He mounted the horse, crossed the hayfields to the slope that begins there and disappeared.

In the morning, when all the people got up, they saw Egil wandering around on the hill east of the farm, leading a horse behind him. They went over to him and brought him home.

But neither the slaves nor the chests of treasure ever returned, and there are many theories about where Egil hid his treasure. East of the farm is a gully leading down from the mountain. It has been noticed that English coins have been found in the gully when the river recedes after floods caused by sudden thaws. Some people believe Egil must have hidden his treasure there. Then there are large and exceptionally deep marshes below the hayfields at Mosfell, and it is claimed that Egil threw his treasure into them. On the south side of the rivers are hot springs with big pits nearby, where some people believe Egil must have hidden his treasure, because a will-o'-the-wisp is often seen there. Egil himself said he had killed Grim's slaves and hidden his treasure somewhere, but he never told a single person where it was.

In the autumn Egil caught the illness that eventually led to his death. When he died, Grim had his body dressed in fine clothes and taken over to Tjaldanes, where a mound was made that Egil was buried in, along with his weapons and clothes.

89 Grim from Mosfell was baptized when Christianity was made the law in Iceland and he had a church built at Mosfell. It is said that Thordis had Egil's bones moved to the church. This is supported by the fact that when a cemetery was dug, after the church that Grim had had built at Hrisbru was taken down and set up at Mosfell, human bones were found under the site of the altar. They were much larger than normal human bones, and on the basis of old accounts people are certain they must have belonged to Egil.

Skafti Thorarinsson the Priest, a wise man, was there at the time. He picked up Egil's skull and put it on the wall of the churchyard. The skull was astonishingly large and even more incredible for its weight. It was all ridged on the outside, like a scallop shell. Curious to test its thickness, Skafti took a fair-sized hand-axe in one hand and struck the skull with it as hard as he could, to try to break it. A white mark was left where he struck the skull, but it neither dented nor cracked. This goes to prove that such a skull would not have been easy for weak men to damage when it was covered with hair and skin. Egil's bones were buried by the edge of the churchyard at Mosfell.

90   Thorstein, Egil's son, was baptized when Christianity came to Iceland and he had a church built at Borg. He was a devout and orderly man. He grew to an old age, died of illness and was buried at Borg in the church he had had built there.

A great family is descended from Thorstein which includes many prominent men and poets. Thorstein's descendants belong to the Myrar clan, as do all other descendants of Skallagrim. For a long time it was a family trait to be strong and warlike, and some members were men of great wisdom. It was a family of contrasts. Some of the best-looking people ever known in Iceland belonged to it, such as Thorstein Egilsson, his nephew Kjartan Olafsson, Hall Gudmundarson and Thorstein's daughter Helga the Fair, whose love Gunnlaug Serpent-tongue and Hrafn the Poet contested. But most members of the Myrar clan were exceptionally ugly.

Of Thorstein's sons, Thorgeir was the strongest but Skuli was the greatest. He lived at Borg after his father's day and spent a long time on Viking raids. He was at the stem of Earl Eirik's ship Iron-prow in the battle where King Olaf Tryggvason was killed. Skuli fought seven battles on his Viking raids and was considered to be outstandingly resolute and brave. He went to Iceland afterwards and farmed at Borg, where he lived until his old age, and many people are descended from him. And here this saga ends.

Translated by BERNARD SCUDDER

THE SAGA OF THE PEOPLE OF VATNSDAL

Vatnsdæla saga

Time of action: 875–1000
Time of writing: 1270–1320

The Saga of the People of Vatnsdal begins in Norway, as do most sagas of Icelanders, though its strange and sombre opening has more in common with scenes from legendary sagas. The birth of Ingimund, patriarch of the people of Vatnsdal, serves as an affirmation of the power of reconciliation within a community, for the wife of his father Thorstein was the sister of a man whom he had killed. Ingimund fights on the king's side in the battle of Havsfjord and, like other settlers such as Ketil Flat-nose, consents only reluctantly to abandon his estate and social position as he looks towards a new life in Iceland. A hidden talisman, the gift of King Harald Fair-hair, guides him to his new home in Vatnsdal, and the sense of a protective good fortune continues to accompany his lineage as they live their lives in the beautiful Vatnsdal countryside.

The events of the saga span five generations, but the narrative focus falls especially on the third of these, the sons of Ingimund and the conflicts in which they engage as they play their part in the creation myth of a region and a dynasty. On the death of Ingimund, his five sons divide among themselves the various tokens of family nobility: the farm, the ship and the wealth resulting from its trading voyages, the godord in which the family's social authority is vested and the sword which symbolizes how all these elements can be defended. This weapon is shared by two of the sons, who take turns at wearing it at public gatherings. The saga explores the way in which successive generations handle these emblems of their family's claim to distinction, as they strive to maintain order among volatile kinsfolk, and within the broader and often turbulent community.

In its presentation of character the saga is generally clear and succinct.

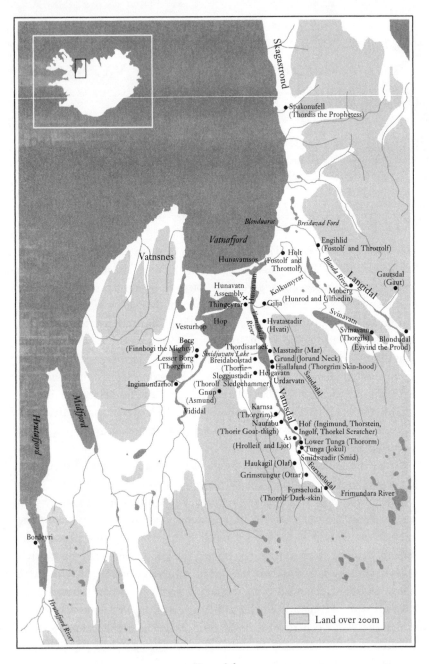

Vatnsdal

Ingimund's Ancestors and Family in Vatnsdal

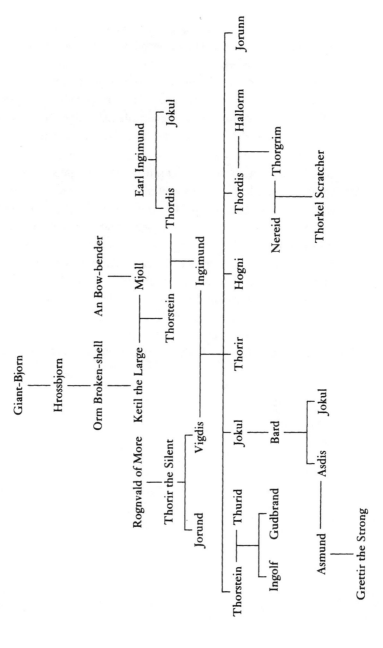

Its author's sympathies, while never stated directly, are there for all to see: he even seems to relish the grotesque and sometimes comic aspect of the rogues and wretches whom his heroes encounter. The cast of characters is richly variegated, and the saga moves swiftly from one colourful episode to another, with its Viking expeditions, sea battles, pagan temples, berserk fits, witches and sorcerers, monstrous cats, murderous attacks and beautiful women. At times the narrative rises to classic splendour, as in the magnificent scene of Ingimund's death (chs. 22–3). The ethic of the saga is undogmatically Christian, as the servants of good overcome the manifestations of a darker world, and heathen notions of fate and self-reliance merge seamlessly with a divine providence which watches over all of noble spirit.

Some scholars have been tempted to think that *The Saga of the People of Vatnsdal*, with its learned style and its sense that nobility and goodness will always defeat malevolent forces in this world and the next, may have links with the Benedictine monastery and literary centre at Thingeyrar in the district in which the main action of the saga takes place.

The Saga of the People of Vatnsdal is thought to have been written around the year 1300, but is only preserved in later manuscripts; the oldest vellum fragment (AM 445 b 4to) is dated 1390–1425. It is translated here by Andrew Wawn from the text in *Íslenzk fornrit*, vol. 8 (Reykjavík, 1939).

1   There was a man named Ketil, nicknamed the Large. He was a mighty
     man, and lived on a farm called Romsdal, in the north of Norway. He
was the son of Orm Broken-shell, who was the son of Hrossbjorn, son of
Giant-Bjorn from the north of Norway. There were district-kings in Norway
when the events of this saga took place. Ketil was a noble and wealthy man,
of great strength, and very brave in all his exploits. He had been away
raiding during the early part of his life, but as the years caught up with him
he settled down on his estates. He married Mjoll, the daughter of An
Bow-bender. By her Ketil had a son called Thorstein. He was good-looking
though nothing out of the ordinary in terms of size or strength – his bearing
and talents were up to the high standard of other young men at that time.
Thorstein was eighteen years old when these events took place.

At this time people had come to believe that there must be robbers or
felons on the road which lay between Jamtland and Romsdal, because no
one who set out along that highway ever came back; and even with fifteen
or twenty people travelling together, not one had returned home. Thus
people concluded that some extraordinary being must be living out there.
Ketil's men suffered least from this harassment, both in terms of loss of life
and damage to property, and there was a good deal of reproachful talk to
the effect that the man who was chieftain of the region was proving no sort
of leader, in that no measures had been taken against such outrages. People
claimed that Ketil had aged greatly; he showed little reaction, but pondered
what had been said.

2   On one occasion* Ketil said to Thorstein his son, 'The behaviour of
     young men today is not what it was when I was young. In those days
men hankered after deeds of derring-do, either by going raiding or by

---

* A feast; see the opening of ch. 3.

winning wealth and honour through exploits in which there was some element of danger. But nowadays young men want to be stay-at-homes, and sit by the fire, and stuff their stomachs with mead and ale; and so it is that manliness and bravery are on the wane. I have won wealth and honour because I dared to face danger and tough single combats. You, Thorstein, have been blessed with little in the way of strength and size. It is more than likely that your deeds will follow suit, and that your courage and daring will match your size, because you have no desire to emulate the exploits of your ancestors; you reveal yourself to be just as you look, with your spirit matching your size. It was once the custom of powerful men, kings or earls – those who were our peers – that they went off raiding, and won riches and renown for themselves, and such wealth did not count as part of any legacy, nor did a son inherit it from his father; rather was the money to lie in the tomb alongside the chieftain himself. And even if the sons inherited the lands, they were unable to sustain their high status, if honour counted for anything, unless they put themselves and their men at risk and went into battle, thereby winning for themselves, each in his turn, wealth and renown – and so following in the footsteps of their kinsmen. I believe that the old warriors' ways are unknown to you – I wish I could teach them to you. You have now reached the age when it would be right for you to put yourself to the test, and find out what fate has in store for you.'

Thorstein answered, 'If ever provocation worked, this would be provocation enough.'

He stood up and walked away and was very angry.

A great forest lay between Romsdal and Oppland, through which a highway ran, though it was then impassable because of the felons who were thought to be lying in wait, though no one could say anything for sure about this. At that time it seemed quite an achievement to come up with any solution to the problem.

3   It was shortly after father and son had talked together that Thorstein left the drinking on his own. His uppermost thought was to put his father's luck to the test, and no longer to endure his taunting but to place himself at some risk. He took his horse and rode off on his own to the forest, to the place which he thought offered the greatest likelihood of encountering the felons, even though there seemed little hope of success against the kind of mighty force which he thought would be there. By this time, however, he would rather have laid down his life than have a wasted journey.

He tethered his horse at the edge of the forest, and proceeded on foot and found a path which led off the main track; and after he had walked for quite some time, he came across a large and well-built house in the forest. Thorstein felt sure that the owner of the building was whoever had made the highway impassable for people. Thorstein then went into the hall, and there came across huge chests and many a treasure. There was a great pile of firewood and opposite this were sacks of wares and goods of every kind. Thorstein saw a bed there, far larger than any he had ever seen before. It seemed to him that the person who fitted into such a bed must be quite a size. The bed had splendid curtaining. There was also a table laid with clean linen, rich delicacies and the finest drink; Thorstein did not touch these things. He then sought some means whereby he would not immediately catch the eye of whoever lived in the house because, before they saw or spoke to each other, Thorstein wanted to find out what he was up against. He then made his way between the sacks and into the pile of goods and sat down there.

Later, well into the evening, he heard a great din outside, and a man then came in, leading a horse behind him. He was of massive size, with shoulder-length locks of fair hair. Thorstein thought him a very handsome fellow. Then the man stirred up the fire, having first led his horse to its stall. He put out a washing basin, washed his hands and dried them on a white cloth. From a cask he poured fine drink into a large goblet, and then he began to eat. Everything about this man's behaviour seemed to Thorstein very refined and remarkable. He was much larger than Ketil, his father, and seemed, as indeed he was, a mountain of a man.

When the hall-dweller had finished eating, he sat by the fire, gazed into it and said: 'There's been some disturbance here; the fire has burned down more than I expected; I think that it has been stirred recently. I don't know what this means; it may be that men have come here, and have designs on my life – and not without reason. I will go and search the house.'

He then took up a smouldering brand, and went off searching, and came to where the pile of goods stood. It was so arranged that someone could get from this pile to the big chimney which opened into the hall. By the time the robber searched the pile, Thorstein was outside, and the hall-dweller could not find him, because it was not Thorstein's destiny to be killed there. The hall-dweller searched the house three times and found nothing.

Then he said, 'I will leave things as they are for now; the shape of events is not clear, and it may work out in my affairs, as the saying goes, that "bad counsel turns out badly".'

He then went to his bed and took off his short-sword. Thorstein regarded this sword as a great treasure and very likely to cut well, and he felt that the weapon would serve his purpose if he could get hold of it. He recalled his father's incitement – that strength and daring would be needed to accomplish this or any other bold deeds, but that glory and glittering coins would be the reward, and he would then be deemed to have done better than by sitting at his mother's hearth. He then also recalled that his father had said that he was no better at wielding a weapon than a daughter or any other woman, and that it would better serve his kinsmen's honour if there were a gap in the family line rather than having him. This drove Thorstein on, and he looked for an opportunity to avenge single-handedly the wrongs done to many people; yet, on the other hand, it seemed to him that the man would be a great loss.

In time the hall-dweller fell asleep and Thorstein tested how soundly he slept by making a noise. At this the man woke up and turned on to his side. More time passed and Thorstein tried again and once more the man stirred, though less than before. On the third occasion Thorstein approached and struck a mighty blow on the bed-post – and found that all was quiet with the man. Then Thorstein stirred up some flames in the fire and approached the bed; he wanted to see if the man was still there. Thorstein saw him lying there – he was sleeping face upwards in a gold-embroidered silk shirt. Thorstein then drew the short-sword and thrust at the mighty man's chest and dealt him a deep wound. The man turned sharply and grabbed hold of Thorstein and pulled him up on to the bed alongside himself, and the sword remained in the wound – so strongly had Thorstein struck him that the sword-tip was stuck in the bed. This man was amazingly strong, however, and let the sword stay where it was; and Thorstein lay between him and the bed panel.

The wounded man said, 'Who is this man who has dealt me such a blow?'

He answered, 'My name is Thorstein, and I am the son of Ketil the Large.'

The man said, 'I thought that I knew your name before, but I feel that I have in no way deserved this from you and your father, for I have done you both little or no harm. You have been rather too hasty and I rather too slow because I was ready to go away and abandon my wicked ways; but now I have complete power over you as to whether I let you live or die. If I treat you as you deserve and have laid yourself open to, then no one would be able to say a word about our dealings. But I think that the wisest course would be to spare your life, and it may be that I may derive some benefit from you if things work out well. I want now to tell you my name. I am Jokul, son of Ingimund, earl of Gotland; and in the manner of sons of mighty men, I won riches for myself, though in a rather violent way, but now I was ready to leave. If this gift of your life seems worth anything to you, then go and meet my father, but speak first with my mother who is named Vigdis and tell her on her own of our dealings and give her my loving greetings and ask her to seek reconciliation and friendship on your behalf with the earl so that he will let you marry Thordis, his daughter and my sister. Here now is gold which you must take as a token that it is I who send you. And though the news about me will seem a great grief to her, I believe that she will pay more heed to my love and message than to your deserts; something tells me that you will be a man of good fortune. And if you or your boys are blessed with sons, do not allow my name to die out – it is from this that I hope to derive some benefit, and I want this in return for sparing your life.'

Thorstein told him to do what he liked about sparing his life and any other matters, and said that he would not plead for anything. Jokul said that his life was now in his hands – 'but you must have been sorely provoked into this by your father, and his plan has touched me to the quick, and I see that you would be quite content even if both of us were to die, but a greater future is in store for you. With you at their head no one will be without leadership, because of your daring and manliness, and my sister will be better looked after if you take her as your wife than if Vikings seize her as some spoil of war. Moreover, even if you are invited to rule in Gotland, return instead to your estate in Romsdal, because my father's kinsmen will not grant you authority after his death, and it may be that terrible killings would lie in store for your kith and kin, and men would lose their innocent kinsmen. Do not mention my name in public except to your father and my kinsmen, because my life has been an ugly one and now has the reward it deserves, and that's the way it goes with most wrongdoers. Take the gold here and keep it as a token, and draw out the short-sword – after this our conversation will not be a long one.'

Thorstein then drew out the short-sword and Jokul died.

4   After these events, Thorstein rode home, and as he approached the farm, he saw many men riding towards him, and he spotted his father and many people whom he knew and all were on their way to look for him; and when they met each other, Ketil greeted his son warmly and felt that he had reclaimed him from death's door – 'I straight away rued the words which I spoke to you in taunt and reproach.'

Thorstein answered and said that little had his father known whether or when he would return home, but that good fortune had sustained his cause so that he had returned safe and sound.

Though they bandied heated words, they were soon fully reconciled. Thorstein then told his father about everything that had happened on his journey. Thorstein received great praise from everyone for this exploit, as was to be expected. Later Thorstein had the assembly summoned and all the householders in the region attended.

At this assembly Thorstein stood up and said, 'It can now be made known to all of you that the fear of highway robbers which has troubled us here for some time, with people unable to go on their journeys – that fear is now removed and at an end. The main reason for my calling this assembly is that I want every man to take the items which belong to him, and I will keep whatever is left.'

This was greeted with acclaim by those present, and Thorstein gained great honour from all his efforts. People did not come to know the name of the highwayman, because it was little noised abroad.

5   One day Thorstein said to his father that he intended to travel east to meet Earl Ingimund as he had promised Jokul.

Ketil said that it was not advisable to put himself into the hands of his enemies and asked him rather to stay at home – 'and though the earl might not want to hurt you, it may be, however, that some people will be hostile to you and not well disposed'.

Thorstein replied, 'I will carry out my promise to Jokul; and even if I bring neither foot back in one piece, I will go there just the same.'

Then Thorstein made preparations and journeyed to Gotland and proceeded until, early one day, he came to the earl's home. The earl had gone hunting, as was the custom of great men. Thorstein went into the drinking room and seated himself on a bench along with his retinue. Then the earl's wife entered the room and looked at the people who had arrived and saw that they must be foreigners. She asked who they were.

Thorstein said that he was a Norwegian – 'and I have a private message for you; let us walk together, just the two of us'.

They did so.

Thorstein then said, 'I have some news to report to you – the killing of Jokul, your son.'

She answered, 'This may seem grievous news to me, but it is not unexpected, because of his scheming and his wicked deeds. But what is it that has made you tell this tale of woe and travel all this way?'

Thorstein replied, 'There is much which leads me to do this; I promised him faithfully when we parted that I would seek you out and tell the truth about our parting. There is no hiding the fact that I was his killer, for our men were unwilling to sit meekly under his control because of his killings and robberies, and yet, to speak to you in good faith, I came under his sway and he had the chance to kill me had he wished to do so, but he spared my life, and laid on me the obligation to go and seek you out with a message from him, and you can see that it would have been easier for me to stay at home than to take a chance on your forgiveness. Now I have gold here which he said you would recognize and he told me to bring it as a token, so that you might make my peace with the earl with the proposition that I take Thordis your daughter as my wife. Jokul also said that he believed you would pay more heed to his message and wishes than to my actions.'

Vigdis blushed deeply at this and said, 'You must be a bold man, but I think that you are telling the truth about your meeting with my son; and if Jokul spared your life, then it is my decision that you will keep it, because you have the look of a lucky man about you; and, for the sake of my son Jokul's request, I will plead your cause with the earl, but first you must hide yourself.'

When the earl came home, the queen went to meet him and said, 'There is some news to tell you which touches us both.'

The earl replied, 'You must be talking about the death of Jokul my son.'

She said that this was the case.

The earl said, 'He will not have died of any sickness.'

She replied, 'It is true that he was killed, and before that he showed great nobility; he spared the life of his killer, and sent him here into our power with trustworthy tokens so that you might pardon and forgive his offences, grievous though they are. The man might also become a source of strength for you if you ennoble him by marriage and give him your daughter as Jokul proposed. Jokul also believed that you would show some respect to his last wish. You can also see how faithful the man has been to his promises, in that he has come from his own home estate into a hostile land here and into our power. Now, for the sake of my words and of your son's wishes, I hope that you will do as I request, and examine the tokens here.' She showed him the gold.

Then the earl sighed wearily and said, 'You have spoken a good deal – and very boldly at that – that I should honour the man who has killed my son; such a man deserves death rather than a friendly gift.'

The queen replied, 'My lord, you ought to consider what else there is to take account of – the word of Jokul, and the integrity of this man in placing himself at your mercy; also, your advanced years, and your need for someone to manage things on your behalf, and this fellow may prove well suited for this. Just as Jokul granted Thorstein his life, having had the power to do anything with him, and just as Thorstein received good fortune at Jokul's hands, unpromisingly as he was situated, so is it now clear that we ought not to destroy that victory or this man's luck, or the noble purpose of our son; and it is a great achievement to act as Jokul did in sparing the life of a man who has done us such harm, and it would be the greatest possible disgrace to harm him, now that he has come into our power.'

The earl said, 'You support this man very strongly, and think that he has a promising look about him; I will certainly see him, and judge for myself what I think he is worth, and it will matter a lot to him whether or not I like the look of him.'

Then Thorstein was led forward and stood before the earl, and the queen had so contrived it that most of Ingimund's anger had left him.

Thorstein said, 'My lord, my whole fate is in your hands. You now know the message which I have brought here. I wish to ask you to be reconciled with me, but I have no fear of anything else which you may wish to have done. It is the custom of leaders to spare the lives of those who voluntarily place themselves at their mercy.'

The earl said, 'I like the look of you sufficiently to spare your life. It may also be the best way of atoning for my son that you take his place, if you are willing to live here with me, because you have the mark of good fortune about you. It is dishonourable to harm a man who places himself in another man's power.'

Thorstein thanked the earl for sparing his life, and stayed there for a while, and the two men got to know each other. The earl soon found out that Thorstein was a wise man, remarkable in every way.

On one occasion, Thorstein said to the earl, 'Now I want to know, my lord, what are my chances of becoming your son-in-law?'

The earl replied, 'I have no wish to refuse this, because it may be that it will work to the good fortune of our family. But I want you to live here with us.'

Thorstein said, 'I agree to this while you are alive, and am grateful to you; but your men will not grant me respect after your days are up, and each man must then fashion his own destiny.'

The earl said that this was fittingly spoken.

6   Shortly afterwards, Thorstein rode home and told his father about all
     the plans and asked him to travel back there with him, and Ketil did
so. The earl prepared a feast, and Thorstein attended with the Romsdal
people and many men of distinction and the feast was splendid with its fine
fare. It drew to a close with the greatest honour and with lavish gifts, and
Ketil and the earl parted on the friendliest of terms. Thorstein stayed on
there with his wife. He always heard the earl address him in a friendly way.
A strong love soon developed between Thorstein and Thordis.
     It is said that one evening men came to the earl with the news of the
death of Ketil the Large, and also that men wanted Thorstein to return to
his family estate and authority. Thorstein reported this news to his wife and
the earl. She told him that it was his decision and said that it was her wish
to go along with whatever he wanted. He said that above all he wanted to
return home, reckoning that his inheritance there would be the source of
least envy, and that everyone would grant him full honour. The earl agreed
with this plan of action, and said that it was more likely that Thorstein
would secure advancement at home than among strangers. Shortly after this
the earl fell ill.
     He summoned Thorstein, his son-in-law, and also his daughter, and said,
'Prepare now for your journey away from here, so that it can be honoured
with great riches, and our kinsmen should be content with the fact that all
control of the land here is handed over to them along with everything that
goes with it. And if you are blessed with a son, let him take my name.'
     Thorstein said that this should be so, but declared that he would not seek
the title of earl, because his kinsmen were untitled.

7   Earl Ingimund died shortly afterwards, and Thorstein went home to
     his estates and took over his father's inheritance. He went raiding each
summer and won wealth and honour, and stayed at home on his estate
during the winters, and was reckoned a very worthy man.
     There was a man named Ingjald who lived on Hefne, an island in
Halogaland in the north. He was a worthy farmer and went raiding by
summer, but did not stir during the winters. Ingjald and Thorstein were
good friends. Ingjald was a good farmer and a man of many talents. Thorstein
and his wife had a son, and when the boy was born, he was presented to his
father.
     Thorstein looked at him and said, 'This boy will be named Ingimund

after his mother's father, and I expect that he will enjoy good fortune because of his name.'

The boy was very mature from an early age.

Ingjald and Thorstein held a feast together each autumn, when they returned home from their Viking raids.

Once when Ingjald was feasting with Thorstein, the boy Ingimund ran up to Ingjald. Ingjald then said, 'You are a lucky-looking boy, and because of my friendship with your father, I want to invite you to my home and foster you in the best way I can.'

Thorstein said that he would accept the offer, and the boy went home with Ingjald. Ingjald had a son named Grim, and another one named Hromund. They were promising young men and became Ingimund's foster-brothers. Thorstein and Ingjald continued as before with their visits and feasts, and men felt that in Thorstein they had compensation for the loss of Ketil, even though he was neither as big nor as strong.

It was on one occasion, when Ingimund met his father, that he said, 'You have secured good fostering for me, but now I would like you to give me a ship; I want to go raiding this summer just like my ancestral kinsmen. I am now of an age when I can do this successfully, and I want the two of us to pay for this journey and not my foster-father, though I know that I can have anything I want from him.'

Thorstein said that this was a very proper request, 'and I will get you a ship'.

Ingimund said that nothing less would do and went home and told his foster-father.

Ingjald answered, 'It is a good plan, and I will get another ship for Grim, and the two of you can set out together – with due care and caution. Beware of going where an overwhelming force would oppose you. There is more honour in accumulating little by little than in reaching for the sky and ending up flat on your face.'

In due course Ingimund and Grim set off on their raiding expedition and prospered in their life as Vikings. They did not attack where it made no sense, and had acquired five ships by the autumn, all of them well equipped with weapons, crew and all battle-gear. It soon became clear that Ingimund was a brave man in action and a good sort, trusty and tough with a weapon, loyal and kind, staunch with his friends – he was the sort of man that the greatest chieftains of old must have been. He told Grim that he intended to go home to his father that autumn and remain there for a period over the winter with twenty men, and that is what happened.

It was apparent, however, that Thorstein sensed a certain haughtiness and a lack of due caution during their time there.

Ingimund said, 'It does not seem so to me, and you ought not to say this; and it would be more suitable for you to ask for anything you want from our winnings as was the old warrior custom, and enjoy that with due honour. It would be very appropriate for you now to offer us hospitality out of our own provisions.'

Thordis said, 'This is well and nobly spoken, and just as your grandfather would have done.'

Thorstein said, 'I will do this, and this is admirably spoken.'

They remained there that winter up to Yuletide, and the hospitality was warm and friendly. Everyone thought a great deal of Ingimund, both his manner and appearance. He was talented in all games and very able in every accomplishment and not at all aggressive towards lesser men, but tough and combative with his enemies.

After Yuletide, Ingimund said to his father, 'Now we warriors are off to my foster-father's home, and we will stay there for what is left of the winter, because he will be pleased to have us there.'

Thorstein said, 'I think it would be a good idea for you to remain with us this winter, kinsman.'

Ingimund said that he had decided to follow his own plan of action, and so they did. Ingjald welcomed them very warmly and his pleasure showed on his face; and they stayed there throughout the rest of the winter.

When spring came, Ingimund said that he wanted them to get ready for their raiding trip, and claimed that they were better prepared in every way than before. Ingjald said that this was true. They then set off raiding for a second summer and seized large amounts of booty from pirates and robbers, who had pillaged the goods of farmers and merchants. They carried on like this through the summer.

Then Ingimund said, 'If there are no great trials on our travels, there is nothing else for it but to continue boldly with the raiding.'

Everyone obeyed his every beck and call.

Well on into autumn, they came to Sviasker. There were Vikings there, and both sides prepared for battle, and they fought first with arrows and stones. The forces differed little in size. Many men were wounded on both sides. Ingimund won great fame that day, and certainly those who were his men believed that they were in the service of a fine leader.

And when it grew dark, there was a lull in the battle.

Then Ingimund said, 'Let it not be thought that we are easing off, even though this skirmish may have had some rather dangerous moments.'

Then a man stood up in one of the Viking ships. He was both big and brave.

This man said, 'Who are these men, who have fought against us today; it is discourteous that no word has been exchanged. So far as I know, there have been no previous disputes between us.'

Ingimund replied, 'If you are asking about the leaders of our troop, then one is called Ingimund and the other is Grim; but who are you?'

He answered, 'Saemund is my name; I am leader of this troop, a Sognefjord man by birth. I know about you two kinsmen and, in that we are men from the same country, it would be more fitting for us to join forces than to fight each other. We have heard only good things about you. We want to talk about becoming friends with you, though not because we need to sue for peace on account of any difference in size between our forces.'

Ingimund replied, 'We are willing to consider the matter carefully, and will not speak ill of it. For our part, we are not inclined to oppose you when there is no guarantee of success, but would like to have secure peace and friendship with you.'

They then made a truce and established peace between each other, and thereafter remained together for the rest of the summer, and things went well for them as regards riches and renown; and they sailed around Sognefjord during the autumn.

Saemund then said that there they must part company, but they would meet again as friends next summer. Ingimund agreed to this. Saemund then sailed into the fjord, and Ingimund sailed north along the coast, and had many ships and much wealth. He returned to his father with fifty men.

Grim said, 'Don't you feel, foster-brother, that your father will think that there are enough guests?'

He said that he thought that the numbers were close to what was right and proper. Thorstein went to meet his son, and offered him the warmest hospitality. Ingimund said that he would accept this.

Thorstein entertained them splendidly through the winter and declared that he was very happy to have such a son, and said that early on he had spotted in him the luck of the family, 'and as I see you mature, so will you enjoy more esteem from me'.

Ingimund stayed there over the winter, and his honour seemed to be much on the increase; and the more plentiful his provisions, the more he engaged in gift-giving and other generous acts.

When spring came, the foster-brothers discussed their travels. Grim said that he had no wish to change and would follow him. They then set off raiding and Saemund met up with them as agreed, and they all went together during the summer. They stayed as a group in the western seas for three successive summers and won wealth and great fame. Ingimund excelled in sound advice, good sense and nobility, and their fellowship was outstanding in every way. Ingimund wintered with his father. Thorstein felt that he could never honour his son Ingimund sufficiently when he saw the kind of man he wanted to become.

8   It is said that in the last summer that Ingimund and Saemund held fellowship together, they returned with far more booty than ever before, and it so happened at the same time in Norway that an army had assembled in the east by Jaeren, and nearly all the arms-bearing men of the country were then assembled in two locations. On one side was Harald, nicknamed Tangle-hair.* He fought against the local chieftains, and the battle he fought at Havsfjord was his last before he brought the whole country under his control.

At that moment Ingimund and Saemund landed, as was said earlier, close to the spot where the troops were assembled.

Then Ingimund said, 'Great news is in prospect now, because all the mightiest men in the land are committed here; but I think that King Harald is the worthiest of them, and he is a man after my own heart and I want to offer him my support, because some help is always better than none.'

Saemund said that he would not risk his life for the king's sake; and he took no part in the battle.

Ingimund replied, 'You can see, foster-brother, that the king's strength is great, and you may judge whether things will go better for those who stand by him, or with those who are set against him. As I see it, he will reward well those who show him honour and support, and it seems to me uncertain as to what might lie ahead if his wishes are not followed; and this will be the parting of the ways for us.'

Then Saemund and his men sailed into and along Sognefjord, and Ingi-

* See footnote on p. 9.

mund sailed into Havsfjord and joined King Harald's fleet. The most important leaders opposing King Harald were Thorir Long-chin and Asbjorn the
Fleshy. Their forces were large in number and tough. Ingimund tied up
alongside the raised deck of the king's ship and greeted the king thus: 'Hail,
my lord, hail.'

The king replied, 'You greet me handsomely, but who are you?'

'My name is Ingimund and I am the son of Thorstein, and I have come
here because I want to offer you my support, and we believe that those who
support you will fare better than those others who rise up against you. I am
newly returned from raiding with several ships.'

The king received his greeting warmly, and said that he had heard good
things about him, 'and I would want you rewarded for your efforts, because
I will bring all Norway under my control, and I will treat those who wish
to serve me very differently from those who now flee to the ranks of our
enemies, or to their estates, as I have heard that Saemund, your companion,
has done; and I declare that there is greater manliness to be seen in the kind
of actions which you have taken'.

Ingimund said that there were many good points about Saemund.

9   After that, horns sounded throughout the troops and men prepared
themselves, each as best he could. This was King Harald's greatest
battle. With him were Rognvald of More and many other great chieftains
and those berserks known as 'Wolf-skins' – they used wolf-skin cloaks for
corslets and defended the bow of the king's ship, and the king himself
defended the stern with the greatest bravery and valour. Many a mighty
blow could be seen there. Many and great deeds were done there in a short
time, with blows and spear-thrusts along with fierce stone-throwing. Before
long many men had fallen on both sides. Ingimund supported King Harald
valiantly and won great praise for himself. The battle ended, as is well
known to many and has become very famous, with King Harald winning a
great victory and becoming thereafter sole ruler over all Norway. He
rewarded all those chieftains who had supported him, and also all his other
followers with the greatest generosity.

He rewarded Rognvald with an earldom and said, 'You have shown great
courage in your support of me; you have also lost your son for my sake,
and he cannot be restored to you, but I can reward you with honours – first
by making you an earl, and also by giving you those islands which lie over
the sea to the west, and are called the Orkney Islands. You will have those

islands as compensation for your son; and you will receive many another honour from me.'

The king was as good as his word. Rognvald sent his son Hallad west, but he was unable to defend the islands against the Vikings. He then sent his son Turf-Einar, saying that he felt sure that he could hold the islands. He was the first earl in the Orkney Islands, and all the Orkney earls are descended from him.

King Harald gave substantial grants of land to many people in return for their support, and it made a big difference whether men had been for or against him, in that he rewarded his supporters in a variety of ways, but those others, who had been opposed to him, he drove from the land, or maimed or killed, so that none of them received any reparation.

Then the king said to Ingimund, 'You have shown me great friendship, and added to your renown. I will always be a friend to you; and your share of the spoils will be three ships and their crews. Along with this you will have the war gear of all those Vikings against whom you fought and, as a token that you were present at Havsfjord, you will have as a gift the talisman* which Asbjorn the Fleshy owned, and which he valued the most. That will be a better token of this battle than great riches would be, and it is an honour for you to receive it from our hand. And when we have put our kingdom in order, then I will reward your support with a feast and with gifts of friendship.'

Ingimund thanked the king for his gifts and generous words, and with that they parted. The king also said that he would be mindful of Saemund because of his designs and treason against him.

10   Ingimund met Saemund soon after the battle of Havsfjord and said to him that his prophecy about the conflict had turned out to be not far off the mark: 'I know also because of the words of the king, that it is not your lot to live in peace, and I think it would be a good idea for you to go away, because the king will carry out his threat, but I would like to spare you from a harsher fate because of our friendship. It seems to me not a bad idea for you to head for Iceland, as many worthy men do these days who cannot be sure of defending themselves against the power of King Harald.'

Saemund said, 'In this, as in everything else, you show your good faith and friendship, and I will take your advice.'

Ingimund urged him to do so, 'but it would have been better if you had

---

* Refers to the amulet described by the Lapp woman in ch. 10.

followed me at Havsfjord; you would not now need to head for that desolate outcrop'.

Saemund said that in many ways his words were not far from the truth. He then secretly sold his land and made ready to depart, and thanked Ingimund for his advice and pledged continuing friendship. Saemund then journeyed to Iceland and landed in Skagafjord; in all directions at that time there was land still to be settled. He set out carrying fire, in accordance with the old custom, and laid claim to land which is now called Saemundarhlid in Skagafjord and became a formidable man. He had a son named Geirmund and his daughter was Reginleif, who married Thorodd Helmet. Their daughter was Hallbera, mother of Gudmund the Powerful of Modruvellir, and of Einar of Thvera.

Ingimund, in great honour, visited his father after the battle of Havsfjord. Thorstein welcomed him with open arms and said to him that through good fortune he had turned his affairs around. He said that this was to be expected, 'because you are the grandson of earl Ingimund, the noblest of men'.

He remained there over the winter, and during that time Ingjald came to Thorstein and there was a happy reunion.

Ingjald said that things had turned out for Ingimund as he had prophesied, 'and I have now prepared a feast for you, my foster-son, with all the resources which I have at my disposal'.

Ingimund said that he would be present.

Ingjald returned home and invited many people to the feast. All those invited duly attended. Ingjald and his men prepared a magic rite in the old heathen fashion, so that men could examine what the fates had in store for them. A Lapp enchantress was among those present. Ingimund and Grim arrived at the feast along with a large retinue. The Lapp woman, splendidly attired, sat on a high seat. Men left their benches and went forward to ask about their destinies. For each of them she predicted that which eventually came to pass, but each took the news in a different way.

The foster-brothers sat in their places and did not go up to enquire about the future; they placed no trust in her predictions.

The seeress said, 'Why do those young men not ask about their futures, because they seem to me to be the most outstanding of the men assembled here?'

Ingimund answered, 'It is not important for me to know my future before it happens, and I do not think that my future life lies at the roots of your tongue.'

She answered, 'I will nevertheless tell you without being asked. You will settle in a land which is called Iceland; it is as yet not widely settled. There you will become a man of honour and live to a great age. Many of your kinsfolk will be noble figures in that land.'

Ingimund answered, 'That is all very well, seeing that I have made up my mind never to go to that place, and I won't be a successful merchant if I sell my many fine ancestral lands and head off to that wilderness.'

The Lapp woman answered, 'What I am saying will come to pass and, as a sign of this, an amulet is missing from your purse – the gift which King Harald gave you at Havsfjord – and it now lies in the wood where you will settle, and on this silver amulet the figure of Frey is carved and when you establish your homestead there, then my prophecy will be fulfilled.'

Ingimund answered, 'If it were not for offending my foster-father, you would receive your reward on your skull; but because I am not an aggressive or irritable man, we will let it pass.'

She said that there was no need for angry words. Ingimund said that ill fortune had brought her there. She said that things would turn out as she had stated, whether he liked it or not.

She went on – 'the destinies of Grim and of his brother Hromund also lie in Iceland; and they will both become worthy farmers'.

The next morning Ingimund searched for the amulet and could not find it. That did not seem to him a good omen.

Ingjald told him to cheer up and not let this get him down or stand in the way of the festivities, and said that many worthy men now regarded it as no shame to go to Iceland – 'Even though I did invite the Lapp woman here, I intended nothing but good.'

Ingimund said that he could not thank him for that, 'but our friendship will never come to an end'.

Ingimund then went home to his father and remained there through the winter.

When spring came, he asked his foster-brothers what they thought of heading off on a voyage.

Grim said that he thought there was nothing to be gained from fighting against fate, 'and I am off to Iceland this summer along with my brother, and many consider this no shame even though they are of noble birth. I have heard good things about the land – that livestock feed themselves during the winters, that there are fish in every river and lake, and great forests, and that men are free from the assaults of kings and criminals.'

Ingimund said, 'I will not go there, and this will be the parting of the ways for us.'

Grim said that this may be so, 'but it would not surprise me if we were to meet each other in Iceland, because it is not possible to fly from fate's decree'.

Ingimund said that their parting was certainly a loss for him.

Grim set sail that summer along with his brother; they reached Borgarfjord and put in at Hvanneyri. Grim said that he thought he would take that land as his own and settle on it. He claimed so much land that many farms now occupy what was once his estate. Hromund said that he would head for the hills and settle happily on the mountain ends. Grim said that things had worked out well, in that they would have the best of the high ground but also the benefits of the sea. Hromund settled at Thverarhlid and was considered a remarkable man, blessed with good offspring; Illugi the Black was descended from him. Grim also was fortunate in his kinsfolk, and many worthy people are descended from him though they are not named here.

II During that summer when the brothers set sail for Iceland, Ingimund went to his father and stayed with him. Thorstein began to age.

On one occasion, Thorstein said to Ingimund, 'It is now good to die knowing that one's son is such a lucky man. The thing which I hold best in my life is that I have not been aggressive towards others; and it is very likely that my life will come to an end in the same peaceful manner because I feel a sickness coming on. Now, kinsman, I want to let you know how my affairs stand. It would not seem to me strange were you to find yourself moving from these ancestral lands, and I do not allow this to trouble me.'

Ingimund said that he would commit himself to act in accordance with Thorstein's instructions. Thorstein said that he believed Ingimund would be regarded as a great man wherever he settled. Thorstein then prophesied many things for him and died shortly afterwards. He was given a fitting burial in the ancient heathen way. Ingimund took over the management of the estate and all its effects. He intended to make his home there and did not stir for a while.

12 King Harald Fair-hair, the greatest of all the old kings of Scandinavia, had now established complete peace and stability. He then remembered what he had promised his friends and prepared lavish feasts for them with all due honours.

He issued a special invitation to Ingimund, and when he arrived, the king welcomed him warmly and said, 'I understand that your situation is in many ways an honourable one, but you nevertheless lack one thing, in that you are unmarried; but I have thought of a match for you. It was in my mind when you risked your life for mine. Earl Thorir the Silent has a daughter called Vigdis; she is the most beautiful of women and very wealthy. I will arrange this marriage for you.'

Ingimund thanked the king and said that he was keen on the idea. The king held a feast of great splendour and honour, and then men returned home. After that Ingimund prepared for the wedding and when things were ready King Harald arrived and many other men of distinction. Ingimund married Vigdis as arranged. The marriage went off with great splendour. The king paid for costly gifts and other honours.

Ingimund said to the king, 'Now I am very happy with my marriage, and it is a great honour to be the object of your goodwill, but I have in mind what the Lapp woman prophesied for me about a change in my life, because I have no wish that it should ever be the case that I leave my family estate.'

The king answered, 'I cannot deny that the prophecy may have some purpose, and that Frey might wish his amulet to come to rest in the place where he wants his seat of honour to be established.'

Ingimund said that he was eager to know whether he could find the amulet after the digging was done for his high-seat pillars – 'It may be that all this has not happened for nothing. It is, therefore, to be no secret, my lord, that I now propose to send for those Lapps who can show me the extent of the region and the lie of the land where I will be living; and I intend to send them to Iceland.'

The king said that he could do that, 'but I think that you will end up in Iceland, and it is a matter of concern whether you go with my blessing or keep the decision to yourself, which is very much the fashion nowadays'.

'It would never be the case that I would go without your permission.'

Afterwards he and the king parted. Ingimund went home and remained on his farm. He sent for the Lapps, and three of them came from the north. Ingimund said that he wanted to make a bargain with them – 'I will give you butter and tin, and you are to undertake an errand for me in Iceland and search for my amulet and report back to me about the lie of the land.'

They answered, 'This is a hazardous mission for Lapp messengers to undertake, but in response to your request we want to make an attempt. You must now shut us up together in a shed and our names must not be revealed.'

This was duly done. And when three nights had passed, Ingimund went to them.

They stood up and sighed deeply and said, 'It has been hard for us, and we have had much toil and trouble, but nevertheless we have returned with these tokens so that you may recognize the land from our account, if you go there; but it was very difficult for us to search for the amulet, and the spell of the Lapp woman was a powerful one because we placed ourselves in great jeopardy. We arrived at a spot where three fjords open up to the north-east and in one fjord there were big lakes to be seen. We later entered a long valley and there at the foot of a mountain were some wooded areas. It was a habitable hillside, and there in one of the woods was the amulet, but when we tried to pick it up, it flew off into another wood, and as we pursued it, it always flew away, and some sort of cover always lay over it, so that we could not get hold of it; and so it is that you yourself must go there.'

Ingimund said that he would be heading off there soon and declared that it was useless to fight against this. He looked after the Lapps well and they left, and he stayed quietly on his estate and was a very wealthy and worthy man. Afterwards he met the king and told him what he had done and what he was planning. The king said that this came as no surprise to him and that it was difficult to go against the way things must be.

Ingimund said that this was true – 'I have now tried every way.'

The king said, 'Whichever land you live in, you will be an honoured man.'

As before, the king showed him all due honour.

After this Ingimund held a splendid feast and invited his friends and the chieftains, and at the feast he asked for silence and said, 'I have decided on a change in my life; I am thinking of going to Iceland, more because of destiny and the decree of mighty forces than out of any personal desire. Anyone wishing to accompany me may do so; those others wishing to remain behind are free to do so, and both groups will remain equally our friends, whatever they choose to do.'

There was much acclaim for his speech, and people said that the departure of such a man was a great blow, 'but there are few things more powerful than destiny'. Many made ready to go with Ingimund – people of great worth, both farmers and men without land.

13   This was the time of greatest emigration to Iceland, and it was then that Vigdis gave birth to a child. It was a boy, and he was very fine-looking.

Ingimund gazed at the child and said, 'That boy has a thoughtful look in his eye, and I don't need to search far for a name. He will be named Thorstein, and it is my hope that good luck will go with the name.'

The boy was good-looking and accomplished from an early age, even-tempered, witty, far-sighted, steadfast in friendship and moderate in everything.

They had a second son. He was also presented to his father and Ingimund had to choose a name for him.

He looked at him and said, 'This boy is hefty and sharp-sighted. If he survives, few will be his match, and he will be no great shakes at controlling his temper; but he will be true to his friends and kinsmen, and a great warrior, if I am any judge. Our kinsman Jokul must be remembered, as my father requested of me, and he will be named Jokul.'

The boy grew up to be a formidable figure in size and strength. He was taciturn, tough, difficult to deal with, stern-minded and brave in every way.

The third son of Ingimund's marriage was named Thorir. He was a fine-looking fellow, a big man with very much the mind of a merchant. The fourth was named Hogni; a fifth child was Smid – he was a concubine's son. Thorstein was the wisest of all the brothers. Ingimund's first daughter was called Thordis, named after his mother; there was a second daughter named Jorunn.

There was a man named Jorund, the son of Earl Thorir the Silent, Vigdis's brother. He made it known that he would be going to Iceland with Ingimund, saying that it was for reasons both of friendship and kinship. Ingimund said that he was well pleased with this. There was a man named Hvati and another called Asmund, both of them Ingimund's slaves. There was a man named Fridmund, another was named Thorir, a third Refkel, a fourth Ulfkel, a fifth Bodvar. These men prepared to leave for Iceland with Ingimund, and all of them were very wealthy.

14   Ingimund set sail with his company as soon as he was ready, had a good voyage and arrived off the west coast of Iceland, and sailed on into Borgarfjord to Leiruvog. News of the ship's arrival soon spread.

Grim rode to the ship and greeted his foster-brother warmly, and said that he was very pleased about his arrival, 'and so it is with you here now that, as the saying goes, it is very hard to fly in the face of fate'.

Ingimund said that this was true – 'It cannot be resisted, foster-brother.'

Grim said, 'I invite you and all your company to my home, and you may have anything of mine that you want, whether land or other valuables.'

Ingimund thanked him for the offer and said that he would stay with him over the winter, 'but because I have changed my life by undertaking this voyage, I must in due course set off to look for the place which was revealed to me as my settlement'.

Ingimund and his wife and sons went to Hvanneyri, and all his followers were everywhere in the vicinity. Grim looked after them nobly and did everything he could to honour them over the winter. And when spring came, then as earlier Grim made available to them everything which he owned, whether land or other resources.

Ingimund said that, as was to be expected, he had been treated as well as could be, 'but I must head north, though we will avail ourselves of your help with transportation and provisions'.

Grim said that this should be so, and so also did Hromund, because they had all welcomed the worthy Ingimund warmly.

He journeyed north that summer in search of land, and went up Nordurardal and came down into an uninhabited fjord. On the day they travelled along the fjord, two sheep ran down the mountain side towards them. They were rams.

Then Ingimund said, 'It seems only right that this fjord should be called Hrutafjord (Rams' fjord).'

After they came to the fjord, a thick fog descended. They came to a headland, and found there a big wooden plank, newly washed ashore.

Ingimund then said, 'It must be intended that we should give this place a name – one that will last – and so let us call the headland Bordeyri (Plank headland).'

Summer was passing, for there was a great deal to move and they had set out late, and winter was almost upon them when they came to a valley with willow scrub growing all over it.

Then Ingimund said, 'This valley is overgrown with willow; let us call it Vididal (Willow valley), and I think that this looks just the place for our winter quarters.'

They stayed there for a second winter and built themselves a hall which is now called Ingimundarhol (Ingimund's hill).

Then Ingimund said, 'Our home here may not be as cheery as the one in Norway, but we need not to think about that because there are many good men assembled here for some fun, and so let us enjoy ourselves as far as our resources allow.'

Everyone agreed with this. They remained there throughout the winter, and played games and had all kinds of merriment.

15 And when spring came, and the snow had melted a little from the slopes, Ingimund said, 'I am curious to know if anyone can climb to the top of a high mountain and see if there is any less snow visible elsewhere, because it does not seem to me that we can start a settlement in this valley; it is a poor exchange for Norway.'

Men then climbed up one high mountain and from it they could see far and wide.

They returned and told Ingimund that those mountains which lay to the north-east were quite without snow, 'and they are lovely to look on, but here where we are it is as if the same storm is always with us, and we can see that over there the quality of the land is much better'.

Ingimund replied, 'Well and good, then, and we may yet hope that some greenness awaits us. This may turn out to be our lot.'

They made themselves ready early in the spring and, as they approached Vatnsdal to the north, Ingimund said, 'This must confirm the Lapps' prophecy for I now recognize the lie of the land from their description; this must be the place intended for us, and how very good it now looks. I see a spacious land, and if its qualities match its size, it may be that here is a fine place to settle.'

And when they came to Vatnsdalsa river, Vigdis, the wife of Ingimund, then said, 'I must take a rest here, because I feel unwell.'

Ingimund replied, 'May all go well with you.'

Then Vigdis gave birth to a girl; she was named Thordis.

Ingimund said, 'This place will be called Thordisarholt (Thordis's wood).'

Then people set off up the valley and saw there fine land with good grass and woods. It was lovely to behold; people's faces brightened. Ingimund claimed all Vatnsdal above the lakes Helgavatn and Urdarvatn. The Thordis-arlaek stream flows from the west into Smidjuvatn lake. Ingimund chose a site for his home in a very beautiful vale and prepared to build his homestead. He built a great temple a hundred feet long, and when he dug holes for the high-seat pillars, then he found the amulet as had been prophesied.

Then Ingimund said, 'Though it is true to say that one cannot fight against fate, yet we may now settle here in good spirits. This farm will be called Hof (Temple).'

Ingimund's men spread themselves all over the valley and took settlement sites as he directed.

That autumn there was a good deal of ice, and when men walked out on to it, they found a she-bear and with her were two cubs. Ingimund was with them on this trip and said that the lake should be called Hunavatn (Cubs' lake), 'and the fjord into which all the waters flow will be called Vatnafjord'.

After that Ingimund went home. He built a splendid homestead and soon became chieftain of the Vatnsdal people and of the adjoining areas. He owned a good many livestock, both cows and sheep and other beasts. That same autumn some sheep went astray and were found the following spring in the woods – this place is now called Saudadal (Sheep valley). The excellence of the land at this time can be judged from the fact that all the sheep fed themselves out of doors. It is also said that some pigs went missing from Ingimund's land and were not found until the autumn of the following year, and by that time there were a hundred of them in all; they had become wild. A big old boar followed them around and was called Beigad. Ingimund gathered men together to round up the swine and declared that it could truly be said that there were two heads on every one of them. They chased after the swine, and drove them to the lake which is now called Svinavatn (Swine lake), and wanted to head them off there, but the boar jumped into the water, swam across and grew so tired that his trotters dropped off. He reached a hill which is now called Beigadarhol (Beigad's hill) and died there. By now Ingimund felt comfortable in Vatnsdal. Many districts had been settled; they also adopted laws and established rights.

16 When Ingimund had lived for some time at Hof, he announced that he was going abroad to collect building-wood for himself, because he said that he wanted to live in fine style there, and that he expected King Harald to greet him warmly. Vigdis said that good was to be expected from the king. He appointed men to look after the estate, along with Vigdis. Ingimund took the bears along with him.

The journey went well for him and he arrived in Norway. He asked where King Harald was; the country was then at peace. And when he found King Harald he was warmly welcomed. The king invited him to stay with him and Ingimund accepted. Throughout the winter he was entertained with great honour by the king. The king asked what the good points were about the new land.

He spoke well of it, 'and it is my main object now to get some building timber'.

The king said, 'Good for you. I grant you permission to have whatever timber you want cut from our forests, and I will have it moved to the ship, and you need have no concerns on that score; and you will stay here with me.'

Ingimund said, 'My lord, you can see here before you a bear which I captured in Iceland, and I would like you to accept it from me.'

The king answered, 'I will certainly accept it and offer you my thanks.'

They exchanged many gifts over the winter, and when spring came, Ingimund's ship was loaded with the cargo which he had selected, and with the choicest timber to be found.

The king said, 'I see, Ingimund, that you have no intention of travelling again to Norway; you should take enough timber with you now to meet your needs, but a single ship cannot carry it. Here are some other ships to look at. Select whichever one you want.'

Ingimund said, 'Select one for me, my lord. That will ensure the best possible luck.'

'So be it; I know them best. Here is a ship called Stigandi (High Stepper) which we consider the best ship of all upwind under sail and better voyaging than any of the others, and this is the one which I choose for you. It is a fine vessel, though not a large one.'

Ingimund thanked the king for the gift. He then took his leave with many tokens of friendship.

He soon discovered how fast a ship Stigandi was.

Then Ingimund said, 'The king's choice of ship for me was a good one, and rightly is it called Stigandi, stepping through the waves as it does.'

They arrived off the coast of Iceland, and then sailed first to the north, and then westwards. No one had done this before. Ingimund brought both ships into Hunavatnsos and there assigned all the place names which have lasted ever since. The place where the ship beached was called Stigandahrof (Stigandi's Shed). News of Ingimund's arrival spread widely, and all were pleased that he had returned. Ingimund had an excellent farm with ample resources. He now greatly improved his homestead, because he had enough building materials. He also acquired for himself a godord and authority over men.

Jorund Neck was the second most prominent man who came out to Iceland with Ingimund; on the advice of his kinsman Ingimund, he settled land beyond Urdarvatn and all the way to Mogilslaek, and lived at Grund below Jorundarfell in Vatnsdal. He was powerful, and so was his family. His son was a worthy man named Mar who lived in Masstadir in Vatnsdal. He and Ingimund's sons grew up at the same time. The valley became widely settled. There was a man named Hvati who journeyed out to Iceland with Ingimund and claimed the land from Mogilslaek to Gilja. Asmund took land beyond Helgavatn and around the Thingeyrar district. Saudadal lies to the east of Vatnsdal, and then Svinadal, and in that valley lie Svinavatn and Beigadarhol.

There was a man called Thorolf Dark-skin. He settled in Forsaeludal. He was a big troublemaker and an unpopular man. He caused much friction and disruption in the district. He built a fortification for himself in the south by Fridmundara river, a short distance from Vatnsdalsa, and next to a ravine; a headland ran between the ravine and the river, and at its edge was a great cliff. The suspicion was that he offered up human sacrifice, and no man in all the valley was disliked more than he was. The place where Hvati lived was called Hvatastadir, and Asmund lived at Gnup. There was a man named Ottar, who lived at Grimstungur. He married Asdis, daughter of Olaf from Haukagil. Their son was Hallfred the Troublesome Poet, and his daughter was named Valgerd, a very showy, good-looking woman.

17   And so time passed. Ingimund grew somewhat elderly, but always kept up his generous hospitality. Nothing is said here of his dealings at the assembly – that he pursued great lawsuits against men – because he got on well with most people and was not aggressive. There were good people aplenty in the vicinity, but it was he who enjoyed the most honour, and his goodwill, generosity and clear head helped sustain this. His sons grew up and were all accomplished in the ways already described.

One summer it is said that a ship owned by some Norwegians came into Hunavatnsos. The skipper was called Hrafn. He was taciturn by nature, burly, difficult to deal with, and a self-made man; he had been on Viking raids for a long time, and was well off for weapons and war-clothing. It was Ingimund's custom to be the first man to meet any ship, and to select from its wares whatever he fancied; and he did so on this occasion – he met with the skipper for a talk, and offered him the hospitality of his home if he wanted it. Hrafn said that there was nothing better on offer, and went home with Ingimund, and continued to act as before, and kept very much to himself. There had been many a man staying with Ingimund whom he had liked better, because Hrafn was no loyal follower and the two men had nothing in common. Hrafn always had a fine sword in his hand. Ingimund often ran his eyes over it, and once asked to see it. Hrafn said that he could. Ingimund took hold of it and drew it. The weapon seemed to him worth no less now, and he asked if he would like to sell it. Hrafn declared that he was not so hard up that he would hand over a weapon; but he said that the farmer would have payment for his hospitality. Hrafn said that he had been in places where he had needed weapons and might find himself in such places again. Ingimund was very angry and felt that he had been insulted, and he pondered what he ought to do.

On one occasion when he went to his temple, he arranged it so that the Norwegian went with him. Ingimund then spoke to him in a casual way about the topic which he found pleased him most – Hrafn always wanted to talk about his Viking adventures and raids. Ingimund went on ahead into the temple, and the next thing he knew was that Hrafn had rushed into the temple with his sword.

Ingimund turned towards him and said, 'It is not our custom to carry weapons into the temple, and you are exposing yourself to the wrath of the gods, and this is intolerable unless some amends is made.'

Hrafn answered, 'You have waited and plotted here for a long time; but if I have broken your laws, then I think it right that you should deal with it, because you are said to be a just man.'

Ingimund said that it would be suitable amends for Hrafn to honour the gods, and said that it would help his cause most that he had not acted wilfully – 'and therefore there is less likelihood of vengeance', and said justice would be best served if Hrafn were to hand over the sword to him, because Ingimund could then say that he owned and had control of it, and in this way assuage the wrath of the gods.

Hrafn said that Ingimund had had a good deal of money off him already, and this business seemed to him no better – 'your other dealings do you more credit'.

He went away during the summer and is out of this saga. Father and son owned this sword for as long as they lived, and they called it Aettartangi.

There was a man named Eyvind, known as 'the Proud'. He came out from Norway with Ingimund and returned there one summer together with Thororm; the two men were friends. Ingimund lent them Stigandi and said that, even though he was not going himself, he was curious to know whether the ship could stride the waves. Ingimund was a popular figure with all good men. The next summer they sailed back into Blonduaros from Norway and were able to tell Ingimund that the ship could not have been better. They had had a very good trading voyage. Eyvind lived at Blondudal, and Gaut in Gautsdal.

18   There was a man named Hrolleif, nicknamed 'the Tall'. He came from Norway with his mother, who was named Ljot, and made land by the Hvita river. Her disposition was not much admired, and in her behaviour she was a law unto herself, as was only to be expected because she had little enough in common with most ordinary good-natured folk. Her son's temperament matched her own. Hrolleif was the nephew of Saemund, foster-brother of Ingimund. Mother and son journeyed to Skagafjord to meet him, and spoke about themselves and told him that he was their kinsman.

In reply Saemund said that he could not deny his kinship with Hrolleif, 'but I fear that you have a worse mother than father, and I am very much afraid that you take more after her side of the family than your father's'.

Hrolleif said that he deserved better than such ill-natured tittle-tattle. Saemund said that he would offer them winter quarters. Hrolleif was a very strong man but misused his strength against lesser men; he was provocative and overbearing and, under his mother's influence, repaid good with bad. He got on badly with Geirmund, the son of Saemund, in both games and other dealings, and a coolness developed between the two kinsmen.

On one occasion, Geirmund said to his father, 'This kinsman of ours pays for his board with those things of which he has an abundance, but which ill become most people – threats and harsh words along with cruel deeds. Some have received broken bones or other injury from him, and no one dares to speak out.'

Saemund said that Hrolleif certainly repaid his hospitality in a worse way than had been bargained for, 'and I can stand it no longer'.

Hrolleif said that it was disgraceful to whinge about such trifling matters, and not to support one's kinsmen – 'I will certainly not put up with beggars kicking me in the teeth.'

Saemund said, 'You may say so but, as I suspected, in disposition you resemble Ljot, your mother, more than our kinsfolk. I have thought of a good estate and homestead for you, out on Hofdastrond beyond Hofdi, to the north of Unadal. My advice is that you try to get along with those who live nearby you there, Thord the farmer at Hofdi and Uni in Unadal and other settlers, and ask permission to make a home.'

Hrolleif said that he felt disinclined to go grovelling to the likes of them. Hrolleif and his mother went off to that valley and settled in a place since then known as Hrolleifsdal. They had little interest in making friends with other people, made threats and menacing remarks and showed a scowling face to their neighbours in all their dealings. People soon came to hate them in return, and felt that Saemund had sent a nasty piece of driftwood floating their way. At first people thought it wrong to complain, since Hrolleif was Saemund's kinsman. But then, after their disposition was fully understood, people wanted to be rid of them, and wished that they had never come.

Uni was a wealthy man and had a son named Odd; he was in his prime. Uni's daughter was named Hrodny; she was a good-looking and hard-working woman. Soon Hrolleif went to meet Uni and said that it was impossible to be cheerful or content in that tiny valley even though men had such entertainment as they could devise.

'I now consider that it would be right and proper,' he said, 'to secure bonds of kinship between us by my marrying your daughter. It may be that our dealings would then improve.'

Uni said that Hrolleif did not have the disposition to win a good woman – 'There is nothing about yourself which suggests that you have; my daughter is not without prospects, and I refuse your request.'

Hrolleif said that he was acting in a way which was less than wise, 'and she will be my mistress, which is plenty good enough for her'.

After that Hrolleif got into the habit of going there and sitting in conversation with Hrodny. This went on for some time, against the wishes of her family.

19   On one occasion, when Hrolleif was preparing to go home, Uni spoke with his son Odd: 'It seems to me no ordinary lack of action that has led us to do nothing about this man's visits; we took more risks in our youth, when I fought with Kolbein, and got the better of him; and he was a chieftain and a force to be reckoned with, whereas this fellow comes on his own to shame us.'

Odd said that it was not easy to deal with this dreadful creature, and the sorcery of his mother – 'Men say that he has a cloak which no weapon can bite into. But first I will meet with Hrolleif,' and so he did.

They met each other up on the mountain separating the valleys.

Odd said, 'You are forever using this path, but we feel it would be better for you to make this journey less often.'

Hrolleif answered, 'Since I was nine years old, I have always organized my own journeys, and will continue to do so. I will pay no heed to your words, and it seems to me that my path is no more difficult with you shadowing my every step.'

Odd said that it would have been possible to come up with a better answer.

Hrolleif came home and told his mother that he would now take a slave from his work, 'and he will accompany me on house-visits, because Uni and his family are beginning to get annoyed with me'.

In reply Ljot said that there was no more important work for a slave than to go with him, 'and pay no attention to the behaviour of those rustics, and go clad in your cloak as soon as you like and see how it does'.

Odd then met his father and said that he wished to meet Saemund and tell him about the problem. Uni said that he little relished all the delay which would ensue.

Odd went to see Saemund and said, 'Thanks to you an ill-starred gift has come our way in the form of your kinsman Hrolleif, and we have to put up with many insults from him and we have not reacted strongly, because he is your kinsman.'

Saemund said that this came as no surprise, 'and it would be no bad thing if such men were eliminated'.

Odd said that Saemund would view things differently if this were done, 'and yet we have this man who wishes to harm everyone, and it is out of respect for you that no action is ever taken'.

Odd went home.

Uni said, 'It seems to me that Hrolleif is not cutting back on his visits, and I reckon that it all comes down to you, kinsman Odd, because you are young and fit for anything, and I am worn out by age. Even though he is a tough customer, and his mother has magic powers, things cannot be left as they are now.'

Odd replied and said that he would look for some remedy. One evening Odd and four other men prepared to ambush Hrolleif. He and the slave were riding together.

Odd jumped up and said, 'It may be that your journeying is at an end for the time being, Hrolleif. It may also be that your wickedness has tied your feet in knots.'

Hrolleif said that it was not yet clear which of them would have most to crow about when they parted company, 'though you have more men with you than I do. I don't think it would be a bad thing if some people here were to shed blood.'

Then they ran at each other and fought. Hrolleif was a tough and very strong man. He was also wearing the cloak which his mother had made for him and which iron could not pierce.

It can be said that Odd slew Ljot, Hrolleif's companion, and then turned against Hrolleif saying, 'The weapons bite you feebly, Hrolleif, and you are evil in all sorts of ways, skilled in sorcery and foul-mannered in other matters.'

Then Odd slashed at Hrolleif's foot, and struck where the cloak did not protect him. Odd then said, 'The magic cloak failed to protect you just then.'

Hrolleif cut at Odd and gave him his death wound; he killed another man, and three others took flight.

This took place late in the evening on the ground above Uni's farm. Hrolleif came home and told his mother that the fight had gone badly for those who stood against him. She showed how glad she was that neither farmers nor their sons, people assailing Hrolleif with hostile words, would be determining her son's travels.

Hrolleif said that he had repaid Odd for the time 'when he abused me most and said that I was in no way the equal of brave men, but I prophesied for him what has now come to pass, that his shame would increase in the wake of our meeting; and so it has now turned out for him'.

20 Uni went to visit Thord from Hofdi and told him of his plight following the killing of his son Odd, 'and I would like to have your support to right this wrong. Your honour is also much at stake in this, to ensure that such rough-necks do not prosper here in the district.'

Thord said that he was right – 'a big problem has arisen for us, and yet it is Saemund above all who is responsible for dealing with his kinsman's wickedness and removing him from the district'.

They then went to meet with Saemund and asked him to put the matter right and said that nothing less than this would be worthy of him. Saemund said that this would be done. Hrolleif's home was seized and he and his mother went to stay with Saemund, and men were found to look after the estate. And at a peace-meeting in the spring, the case was settled with Uni taking Hrolleif's land as compensation, and Hrolleif being outlawed from all lands whose waters flowed into Skagafjord.

Saemund now recalled his long-standing friendship with Ingimund; and when they met, Saemund said, 'The situation is, foster-brother, that a man has come to me who in disposition does not seem easy to deal with, but he is nevertheless my kinsman and is called Hrolleif. I would now like you to take him in, along with his mother, and find them a home near where you live.'

Ingimund replied, 'The reports about them are not good, and I am reluctant to look after them, but you will think it disobliging and ungenerous if I refuse, although it does not particularly suit us because I have several sons who are by no means easy to get on with.'

Saemund said in answer to this that he was a lucky man and would bring luck to most people. Ingimund said that this would have been well tested if all turned out well. Then Hrolleif and his mother Ljot went to Ingimund with little in the way of praise to recommend them.

21   Hrolleif and his mother stayed with Ingimund for two or three years. They no more changed their ways in dealing with the sons of Ingimund than they did with other men. The sons took this badly, and Jokul worst of all, because he and Hrolleif had so many tough games together which almost led to injury, and Jokul declared that Hrolleif had been Saemund's ill-starred gift, 'and yet things will be all right,' he said, 'if they don't get any worse'; and declared that this devil incarnate would never prevail over them.

There was no difference between them in size or strength, for both were very powerful.

Ingimund said, 'You do wrong, Hrolleif, in not controlling your temper and in not repaying good with good. I can now see that this arrangement will not work as it stands, and I will find you a farmstead, on the other side of the river, at As.'

Hrolleif said that this would be no more unfriendly 'than staying here with your ill-natured sons'.

'I am sorry to give up on you,' said Ingimund, 'because I have never done this before, having once taken someone in.'

Thorstein said that he reckoned things would turn out worse later. Ingimund settled Hrolleif and his mother Ljot on the farm at As, and they lived there for a long time, and Hrolleif thought himself in every way the equal of Ingimund's sons.

At that time two brothers arrived from Norway – one was named Hallorm and the other Thororm; they were wealthy men. They stayed with Ingimund over the winter. Hallorm made a request and asked to marry Thordis, Ingimund's daughter, and he received a favourable answer. Ingimund said that great strength would accrue to him on account of Hallorm's wealth, and Thordis was given to him in marriage, and the dowry which went with her was the land at Karnsnes. They had a son named Thorgrim. Thororm lived in Lower Tunga in Vatnsdal; this was later called Thorormstunga.

22   There was said to be good fishing in Vatnsdal, of salmon and other fish. The brothers, Ingimund's sons, divided the work between them because in those days it was customary for important men's sons to have some sort of occupation. Four brothers, Thorstein, Jokul, Thorir and Hogni, took their turns with the fishing – Smid had other work to do. The brothers went into the river and their catches were good. Hrolleif carried on behaving just as usual; relations were bad with everyone in the vicinity. It had not been on the advice of friends that Ingimund had ever taken up with him. The sons of Ingimund took it very badly when Hrolleif had the best of what was theirs, and caused only trouble in return; they said that their father had made a great mistake in taking him in. They owned the fishing rights between them, the Hof men and Hrolleif. It was laid down that Hrolleif was free to fish if neither Ingimund's sons nor their men were present, but he took no notice of this arrangement because he set greater store by his own wishes and wickedness than by anything that had been agreed.

On one occasion, when Ingimund's workmen came down to the river, they told Hrolleif to clear his nets out of the way for them. Hrolleif said that he would pay no heed to this, no matter what such thralls might say. They answered by telling him that it would be better not to pick a fight with the Hof men, saying that it would not turn out well for him even though he might get away with it with other folk. Hrolleif told them to move themselves, wretched slaves that they were, and not to threaten him with other men. He drove them off shamefully and without justification.

They said, 'You are wrong in behaving like this, when you are so much in Ingimund's debt. He received you, gave you both a place to live and fishing rights, and many other benefits, whereas before this you did not seem fit company for worthy men.'

Hrolleif said that he did not have to vacate the river at the behest of wretched slaves and let fly with a stone at one of them so that he lay on the ground stunned; Hrolleif said that it did not do for their tongues to wag so freely.

When they returned home the household was seated at the table; they rushed in. Ingimund asked why they had arrived with such a commotion. They said that they had been driven from the river by Hrolleif with blows and harsh words.

Jokul answered, 'He must want to become the Vatnsdal godi and to treat us like he treated others before, but it will never be the case that this devil of a man will lord it over us.'

Thorstein said that Hrolleif had gone too far, but that it was best to deal with this calmly – 'and it was a mistake ever to have had anything to do with Hrolleif'.

'There is much truth in this,' said Ingimund, 'but nevertheless you would do well to reach a settlement with him because you have more at stake. He is a man out of Hel,* and you can be sure of trouble from him.'

Jokul said that he would soon see whether Hrolleif would leave the river, and sprang up from the table and rushed out.

Ingimund said, 'Thorstein, my son, I trust you best to keep calm in everything; go along with your brothers.'

Thorstein said that he was not sure how easy it would be to control Jokul – 'and I will not stand idly by if he gets into a fight with Hrolleif'.

When they came to the river, they saw that Hrolleif was fishing there.

Then Jokul said, 'Get out of the river, you villain, and don't you dare tangle with us, or else we will have it out between us once and for all.'

Hrolleif said, 'All the same, though there are three or four of you, I will go about my business despite your cursing.'

Jokul said, 'You, evil creature, must have faith in your mother's witchcraft, if you on your own intend to dispute the fishing against all of us.'

Jokul then waded into the river towards him, but Hrolleif stood his ground.

Thorstein said, 'Stop being so stubborn, Hrolleif; it will be the worse for you if we do not get our rights from you. It may be that others will have to pay the price. It simply will not do for you to lord it over men with your evil deeds.'

Then Jokul said, 'Let's kill the devil.'

Hrolleif then made for the riverbank at a point where there were some

---

* Hel is the old Icelandic word for the place of the dead, corresponding to the Greek Hades. *Heljarmenni* were often associated with unusual strength and malevolence.

stones, and threw these at them and they returned fire across the river; and some hurled spears at him, but Hrolleif was never in danger. Jokul wanted to cross the river and attack him at another place, and said it would be no ordinary humiliation if they failed to overcome him.

Thorstein said, 'My advice is different – hold back here and remain in control rather than tangle with mother and son, because I believe that she is nearby. Coping with their sorceries would not be like fighting against honourable men.'

Jokul said that this would never worry him and sought to advance, while his brothers threw stones and spears at Hrolleif.

Then a man came running back to Hof and told Ingimund that things had come to a parlous state and that the men were fighting each other across the river, 'and your neighbour is like few others'.

Ingimund said, 'Get my horse ready, and I will ride out there.'

He was by then old and almost blind. He had given up the management of his affairs and also the farm itself. A boy was found to attend him. Ingimund was wearing a black cape. The boy led him on horseback.

When they came to the riverbank, his sons saw him.

Thorstein said, 'Our father has arrived; let us withdraw; he will want us to follow his wishes, but I am worried about his coming here,' and he urged Jokul to restrain himself.

Ingimund rode into the river and said, 'Leave the river, Hrolleif, and think about what is right and proper for you.'

When Hrolleif saw him, he hurled a spear at him, and it hit him in the midriff.

And when Ingimund received the wound, he rode back to the bank, and said, 'You, boy, lead me home.'

He did not meet his sons and when they arrived home, the evening was well advanced.

As Ingimund came to dismount, he said, 'I am now stiff; we old men grow shaky on our feet.'

When the boy helped him down, there was a sucking noise from the wound. At that moment the boy saw that the spear had gone right through him.

Ingimund said, 'You have been loyal to me for a long time; do now what I ask of you; it is more than likely that I will be asking few things of you after this. Go now and tell Hrolleif that before morning comes I think it likely that my sons will be on his trail to see about avenging their father;

and he should be sure to have left by daybreak. I am no better avenged by his death and, no matter what happens later, as long as I have any say in things, it is right for me to protect the person whom I have previously agreed to help.'

He snapped off the shaft from the spear head and went inside with the help of the boy and sat down on his high seat and asked him not to kindle a light before his sons arrived home.

The boy returned to the river and saw the many salmon which Hrolleif had caught there.

The boy said, 'Truly is it said that you are the most miserable dog of a man. You have done something for which we can never look for compensation; you have dealt my master Ingimund his death wound, and he asked me to say that you should not stay at home until morning, and said that he believed his sons would seek to avenge their father's death on you; and I am doing this more at his request than out of any wish that my words should save you from the brothers' axes.'

Hrolleif answered, 'I believe what you say, and you would not have left here in one piece if you had not passed on this news.'

23   To return to Ingimund's sons, they headed home in the evening and agreed among themselves that Hrolleif was a most despicable man.

Thorstein said, 'We do not yet know exactly what evil we may have suffered from him, but I have an uneasy feeling about our father's journey.'

They arrived home and Thorstein went into the fire-hall and, stumbling, stuck out his hand and said, 'Why is the floor wet, mistress?'

She replied, 'I think that something may have run from the clothes of Ingimund, my master.'

Thorstein answered, 'This is as slippery as blood; kindle a light at once,' and this was done.

Ingimund was sitting in his high seat and was dead. The spear stood there piercing him right through.

Jokul said, 'It is terrible to know about a noble man like this, that a wretch like Hrolleif should have done him to death; let us be off at once and kill him.'

Thorstein said, 'You know nothing of our father's goodness if he has not helped Hrolleif to escape; where is the boy who went with him?'

He was nowhere to be seen.

Thorstein said, 'I don't think we can expect Hrolleif to be at home, and we must have a plan in searching for him and not rush in headlong; and we can take comfort in the huge difference that there is between my father and Hrolleif, and for this my father will be rewarded by him who created the sun and all the world, whoever he is – we can be sure that someone must have been its creator.'

Jokul was so furious that they could hardly control him. At that moment the boy came in and told them of his errand. Jokul said that it had been wrong.

Thorstein said, 'We must not be angry with him, because he did what our father wanted.'

Ingimund was laid in the small boat from the ship Stigandi and afforded every honour, as was then customary with noble men. This was then reported far and wide, and it seemed – as indeed it was – great and grave news.

Thorstein said to his brothers, 'I think it would be a good idea for us not to sit in our father's seat, whether at home or as other men's guests, while he remains unavenged.'

They kept to this, and were little in evidence at games or other gatherings of men.

But when Eyvind the Proud heard this, he said to his foster-son, 'Go and tell my friend Gaut what I am going to do; it seems to me that he ought to do the same.'

He then drew a short-sword from under his cloak, and had himself fall on it and so died.

And when Gaut heard of this he said, 'Life is not worth living for the friends of Ingimund, and I will follow the example of my friend Eyvind,' and put his sword to his breast and killed himself.

Eyvind's sons were called Hermund and Hromund the Lame, who will be mentioned later.

24 Let this pass for now; something must be said about Hrolleif. He met his mother and told her the news. She said that no one lived beyond their allotted span, and that Ingimund had enjoyed a long life.

'My advice is,' she said, 'that, first, you must get away from here because blood nights are the most furious. Come and see me here when I judge it most likely that some benefit will arise from my plotting, but I cannot tell which will prevail, Thorstein's guile and good luck or my scheming.'

Then Hrolleif went north to Skagafjord and came to Saemundarhlid; Saemund was dead by then and Geirmund was in charge of the estate. His brother was named Arnald. Geirmund asked what the news was. Hrolleif said that he had to report the death of Ingimund from Hof.

'There's an able man gone; what was the cause of his death?'

Hrolleif said, 'He was used as a target,' and then described the whole incident.

Geirmund replied, 'I can see that you are an utter wretch; be off with you, evil creature, and never come here again.'

Hrolleif said that he would not leave, 'and I will be killed here, to your great shame; I still remember the fact that my father fell when in the service of your father and Ingimund, and this came about because of you and your men'.

Geirmund said that falling in battle was the lot of brave men, 'but I will hand you over the moment that the sons of Ingimund arrive'.

Hrolleif said that he had expected as much, or worse. He hid there in a harness shed.

The sons of Ingimund remained at home during the winter; they sat on the lower bench and went to no games nor assembly meetings and were very downcast.

And shortly before the summer, Thorstein summoned his brothers for a discussion and said, 'I think we are all agreed that it seems high time for us to seek to avenge our father, but this is not very easily done. I think it would be a good idea that whoever has the wit to take on the task should choose as a reward one valuable item from our inheritance.'

They said that this was their wish, 'and you are the best suited of any of us because of your good sense'.

25 One morning Thorstein was up early and said to his brothers, 'Let us now make preparations for journeying north into the country, no matter what tasks await us there.' They were five brothers in all and no one else. Late one evening they came to where Geirmund lived and he welcomed them warmly, and they enjoyed fine hospitality during their night's stay.

In the morning Thorstein said to his brothers, 'You will play at a board game today and I will talk with Geirmund.'

They did so.

Thorstein said to Geirmund, 'We brothers have come here because we are looking for Hrolleif, whom we think is here with you. You are under a big obligation to help us, as it was you and your family who sent our father this wretch from whom so much harm has come, even though this was not your wish. He has no good kinsmen to look to except you.'

Geirmund replied, 'All this is true and you have searched shrewdly, but Hrolleif is not here now.'

Thorstein said, 'I believe it more true to say that he is sitting in your shed. Take this hundred of silver, and have him leave, and I will so arrange it that he is not seized while in your safe custody here, so that no blame can be laid at your door; but we will seek him out, even though it is little enough revenge for our father. Tell him that you do not feel safe in protecting him against us, and in bearing the brunt of our hostility, when you would otherwise enjoy our friendship.'

Geirmund answered, 'Now I will admit that he is here, and everyone may make of this what he wishes; I will do as you suggest and tell him to go away, and you may then look for him, when he is no longer with me.'

'So be it,' said Thorstein.

Then Geirmund met with Hrolleif and said, 'The sons of Ingimund have come here and are looking for you. You may no longer stay here with me, because I will not put myself or my assets at risk on account of you and your evil cause; the brothers are both shrewd and aggressive.'

Hrolleif replied, 'It was to be expected that you would behave shamefully, and no thanks are due to you for your assistance.'

Geirmund said, 'Be off with you, at once.'

He met Thorstein later and said, 'I think it would be best for me if you were to do nothing in haste and remain here today.'

Thorstein said that this should be so.

Then next day they got ready and went west over the mountains; and there had been a thaw and they saw a man's footsteps in the snow.

Then Thorstein said, 'Let us now sit down, and I will tell you of my conversation with Geirmund. I was aware that Hrolleif was there.'

Jokul said, 'You're a strange man; you were content to sit and do nothing, and your father's killer was right by you. If I'd known that, things would not have remained altogether quiet.'

Thorstein said that this was not unexpected, 'but it looked better not to show up Geirmund in this. We will travel in day-long journeys and see if we can make it to the west no later than Hrolleif does, because his footsteps must point towards his home, and Ljot, his mother, will now be sacrificing to celebrate the beginning of summer, as is her custom in accordance with their faith, and there will be no revenge achieved if the sacrifice has already been made.'

Jokul said, 'Let's hurry then.'

He led the way for them all.

He then looked back and said, 'Woe betide those men who are as feeble in size and speed as Thorstein, my brother; vengeance will escape us if we don't move quickly.'

Thorstein replied, 'It is not yet clear that my plans and schemes will be worth any less than your witless rushing around.'

Late in the evening they descended to the farm at Hof, and men were sitting at table there.

26 Thorstein met his shepherd outside and said, 'Go to As and knock on the door and take note of how quickly the door is answered, and recite a verse while you are waiting. Announce it as your errand that you are enquiring about stray sheep, and you will be asked whether we have returned home, and you must say that we have not.'

The shepherd set off and came to As and knocked on the door, and no one answered before he had recited twelve verses. Then a farmhand came out and asked what the news was and whether the brothers had arrived home. He said that they had not, and asked about his sheep. The farmhand said that they had not come there.

The shepherd returned home and told Thorstein how many verses he had recited.

Thorstein said that he had stood outside long enough for a great deal to have gone on inside in the meantime, 'but did you go in at all?'

He said that he had gone in and looked around.

Thorstein asked, 'Was there a bright fire in the hearth or not?'

He answered, 'It looked rather as if it had been kindled just a short time before.'

Thorstein said, 'Did you see anything strange in the house?'

He said that he had seen a great pile of things and there was red clothing sticking out from underneath.

Thorstein said, 'It must have been Hrolleif and his sacrificial garments that you saw. We must now go and search there. Let us get ready at once and take on this risk, whatever happens.'

They journeyed and came to As and there was no one outside. They saw firewood piled against the wall on both sides of the gable. They also saw a little hut standing in front of the door, and a gap between it and the door to the main building.

Thorstein said, 'That must be the place of sacrifice, and Hrolleif is meant to go there when his mother has completed her rites and all her witchcraft – but I don't much like it all. Go now and wait round the corner by the house and I will sit up above the door with a stick in my hand; and if Hrolleif comes out, I will then throw the stick towards you, and you must all then run over to me.'

Jokul said, 'It's easy to see, brother, that you want to gain honour from this as from everything else, but I won't have it, and I will sit with the stick.'

Thorstein said, 'You want your own way, even though things will not go any better, because it seems to me that you are liable to be the cause of some mishap.'

Jokul positioned himself in the pile of firewood, and soon a man came out and looked around by the door, and did not see the men who had come there. Then a second man came out and a third, and this was Hrolleif. Jokul recognized him clearly and gave a violent start, and the log pile collapsed, but he was still able to throw the stick to his brothers, and jumped down and managed to grab Hrolleif so that he could not run away. There was no difference in their strength, and they both rolled down the bank, each lying alternately on top and underneath.

When the brothers approached, Hogni said, 'What monster is this coming towards us here? I do not know what it is.'

Thorstein replied, 'This is Ljot the old witch – look how bizarrely she has got herself up.'

She had pulled her clothes up over her head and was walking backwards, with her head thrust between her legs. The look in her eyes was hideous – the way she could dart them like a troll.

Thorstein said to Jokul, 'Kill Hrolleif now; you have wanted to do this for a long time.'

Jokul said, 'I'm quite ready for it now.'

He then hacked off his head and told him that he would never haunt them again.

'Well, well,' said Ljot, 'I came very near to being able to avenge my son Hrolleif, and you sons of Ingimund are very lucky men.'

Thorstein replied, 'What is the clearest sign of that?'

She said that she had intended to change the whole lie of the land there, 'and all of you would have run wild and been driven crazy with fear out among the wild animals, and that is how things would have turned out if you had not spotted me before I saw you'.

Thorstein said that it was no surprise that their respective luck had changed. Then Ljot the witch died in her rage and sorcery, and mother and son are now out of the saga.

27 After the killing of Hrolleif and Ljot the brothers returned home, and folk were pleased to see them.

Somewhat later, Thorstein said to his brothers, 'Now I think I am entitled to choose some valuable item from our possessions.'

They agreed that this was the case.

'Then I choose the homestead at Hof and the land along with its livestock.'

They said that this was hardly just a single item and felt that it looked rather greedy.

Thorstein said that everything ought to go together, land and livestock, 'and though this seems to you somewhat greedy, it should be borne in mind that, for one thing, our honour will be at its greatest when we are most united, and, secondly, I have the most foresight in this matter. There are plenty of other precious things here, and I happily grant them to you.'

The share-out then took place. Hogni received the ship Stigandi because he was a merchant. Thorir Goat-thigh received the godord, and Jokul was given the sword Aettartangi. He had the sword with him at games meetings and horse-fights, and Thorstein carried it at Autumn meetings and law meetings, because this was the way that Jokul wanted it. Similarly, Thorir said that although the godord was his, he would allow Thorstein to have all the honour from their law cases.

Thorstein said, 'It is clear to me that you brothers want to find ways of honouring me in everything; and though I have chosen the homestead for myself, I would be happy to grant you some valuables in return. It seems to me a good idea that we should now move our seats to where our father's high seat was.'

They did so. Thorstein became chieftain of the Vatnsdal people and Vesturhop and over all the areas where his father Ingimund had exercised authority. Thorstein married a woman named Gyda who was the daughter of Solmund, the son of Gudmund. He was the father of Killer-Bard. At that time it was thought that being associated with the Vatnsdal people was a likely source of honour. Jokul lived at Tunga and Smid at Smidsstadir, and Thorir Goat-thigh at Nautabu, which is now called Undunfell.

28 It is now time to tell of the man who was mentioned earlier, and was called Thorolf Sledgehammer. He developed into an extremely unruly individual. He was a thief and also much inclined towards other troublemaking. It seemed to folk that his settling in the area was a very bad thing and that no sort of evil from him would come as any surprise. Though he was without followers, he was the owner of creatures on whom he relied for protection – these were twenty cats; they were absolutely huge, all of them black and much under the influence of witchcraft.

At this time men went to Thorstein and told him of their difficulties – they said that all governance in the region was in his hands, and that Thorolf had stolen from lots of people and done many other wicked deeds.

Thorstein said that what they said was true, 'but it is not easy to deal with this man of Hel and his cats, and I'll spare all my men that'.

They said that he could hardly retain his honour if nothing were done. After that Thorstein assembled some men and wanted the backing which came with their numbers. With him were all his brothers and his Norwegian follower. They went to Sleggjustadir. Thorolf would have no dealings with them; he could never abide the company of good men.

He went inside when he saw the troop of men arriving on horseback and said, 'Now there are guests to receive, and I intend to have my cats take care of this, and I will put them all outside in the doorway, and the men will be slow to gain entry with them defending the entrance.'

He then fortified them greatly by magic spells and after this they were simply ferocious in their caterwauling and glaring.

Jokul said to Thorstein, 'Now you must come up with a good plan; you did right in not allowing that monster to remain in peace any longer.'

There were eighteen men in the party.

Thorolf said, 'I will now make a fire, and I do not mind if it smokes, because the coming of the Vatnsdal men will not be peaceful.'

He put a kettle over the fire and placed wool and all sorts of rubbish underneath it, and the house filled with smoke.

Thorstein went to the door and said, 'We ask you to come out, Thorolf.'

He said that he knew their visit meant only one thing, and that was not at all friendly. Then at once the cats began to howl and behave monstrously.

Thorstein said, 'They are a gruesome lot.'

Jokul replied, 'Let's get in there, and not worry about these cats.'

Thorstein said that they should not, 'because it is more likely that we would be unable to keep our troop safely together, what with the cats and

Thorolf's weapons and everything else, because he is a formidable warrior; I think it would be better for him to give himself up and come out, because he has more fuel for his fire than he may find comfortable while he remains inside'.

Thorolf moved the kettle from the fire and pressed the wool down on the fire, and choking smoke billowed out so that Thorstein and his men could not get near the door.

Then Thorstein said, 'Watch out that the cats don't get hold of you, and let us throw fire against the house.'

Jokul seized a great burning brand and threw it against the door, and the cats fled, and with that the door slammed shut. The wind blew against the house, and the fire began to grow bigger.

Thorstein said, 'Let us stand by the hayfield wall, where the smoke is thickest, and see what he does, because he has more fuel for a fire than may be helpful to him in the long run.'

In this Thorstein was pretty close to the mark.

At that moment Thorolf leapt out with two chests full of silver and went through the smoke, and when he reappeared, the Norwegian stood facing him and said, 'Here comes the monster now – what a mean-looking creature he is.'

The Norwegian ran after him down to the Vatnsdalsa river. Thorolf came to a place where there was a deep hole or mire.

Thorolf then turned towards the Norwegian and grabbed at him and dragged him under his arm and said, 'So you want to have a race against me; but now we can both go together,' and he leapt into the mire and they sank so that neither reappeared.

Thorstein said, 'This has turned out very badly, now that my Norwegian companion has perished, but it will be some redress that Thorolf's wealth will end up as compensation for him'; and so it did.

The place where Thorolf lived has been called Sleggjustadir ever since, and cats have always been sighted there, and the place has often seemed ill-fated since then. This farm is down the valley from Helgavatn.

29 Mar Jorundarson moved his homestead from Grund to Masstadir. Relations between him and the sons of Ingimund were good. One autumn there was news that Mar had lost some sheep; they were searched for far and wide and not found. There was a man named Thorgrim, known as Skin-hood. He lived in Hjallaland. He was very skilled in magic but mean in other ways.

There was a good deal of talk about the disappearance of sheep, for the valley seemed mostly settled by honest folk. One evening, when the shepherd came home, Mar asked him if there was any news.

He said that his sheep had been found, and no harm had befallen them, 'but there is something more to add. I have found a plot of land in the woods, and the soil is very good, and it is there that the sheep have been and they are now very fat.'

Mar asked, 'Is this on my land or someone else's?'

The shepherd said that he thought it would prove to be his – 'but it lies next to land belonging to the sons of Ingimund; it can only be approached from your own property'.

Mar had a look at this choice piece of land, and thought well of it and took it as his own. Thorgrim said that he thought they could keep the land from the sons of Ingimund.

Thorstein heard about this and said, 'It seems to me that our kinsman Mar judges this in his own way and scarcely grants us our legal due.'

A little later Jokul met his brother Thorstein and they discussed many matters.

Jokul said that it would be a disgrace if men were to rob them right there in the valley, 'and that wretch Thorgrim Skin-hood quite unjustifiably takes it upon himself to irritate us, and it would be right and proper for him to be repaid for this'.

Thorstein said that he was no one worth sparing, 'but I do not know whether he is yet at our mercy'.

Thorstein suggested that they should go to meet with Thorgrim; Jokul said that he was ready. When Thorgrim became aware of this, he went to meet with Mar; they greeted each other warmly.

Thorgrim said that he had come running from an attack, 'and the sons of Ingimund will be heading this way'.

Mar asked what he knew about all this.

Thorgrim replied, 'They are now making their way to my farm and want to kill me, but it will always appear that I know more than other men.'

When they came to the farm, Thorstein said, 'We are here dealing with a tricky customer in Thorgrim, because he will not be home.'

Jokul said, 'Let's do some damage here, nevertheless.'

Thorstein said that he did not want to – 'I do not want it said that we seized his goods, but couldn't seize the man himself,' and with that they went home.

On another occasion Thorstein said again to his brothers, 'I am curious to see whether we can find Thorgrim.'

'I'm ready to go this minute,' said Jokul.

Again Thorgrim went to meet Mar and said, 'The sons of Ingimund have not yet forgotten me; I want you now to come back with me, and they will see for themselves that I am not afraid to wait for them at home.'

Mar went back home with him.

Then the sons of Ingimund approached the farm and met up with Mar in the hayfield.

Thorstein said, 'Mar, our kinship is not working out as it should do; I would like each of us to have respect for the other and not to support those troublemakers who want to quarrel with us.'

Mar said that theirs was obviously a hostile visit; he declared that he would not give up his share on their account. Jokul said that it was evident that Mar and his men wanted to test their strength against them.

Thorstein said that he was reluctant to quarrel with his kinsfolk, 'but it is not unlikely that it may come to that if we do not get our rights'.

They departed, because they could not get at Thorgrim because of his sorcery and the presence of Mar; and for some time after this the situation was that either Thorgrim had disappeared from his home, or Mar was present there with plenty of men.

At that time Hogni Ingimundarson came out to Iceland in his ship Stigandi and stayed with Thorstein over the winter and told remarkable tales of his travels while he had been away; he also said that he had never known as fine a ship as Stigandi.

There was much talk around the region of the goings-on between the kinsmen. Jokul often met his brother Thorstein and claimed that he still wanted to give in to Mar.

Thorstein said, 'That's the way it has been up to this point, but now we will waylay Thorgrim, even though something tells me that this is not a specially good idea.'

One day the brothers prepared to leave home; there were twenty-five of them in all, including the five brothers.

Then Thorgrim said, 'There is now trouble afoot; the sons of Ingimund will be here at any moment.'

He gathered up his clothes and rushed out.

He met Mar and told him that the sons of Ingimund were on their way, 'and they intend grim-heartedly to seize us, and we had better be ready to make them regret their attack'.

Mar assembled some men. Hromund, son of Eyvind the Proud, a mighty warrior who married Mar's daughter, was with them at the farmstead. He said that it was clear that the Hof men would try their luck against them. There were forty of them in all, not counting Mar's two nephews, who were promising young men.

Thorgrim said, 'The best plan is to go out and confront Ingimund's sons,' and they did so.

Thorstein saw this and said, 'Now we have the chance to prove ourselves, and I think it best for everyone to give it everything they have.'

Jokul then drew Aettartangi and said that he liked the idea of testing it on the necks of Mar's followers. The two sides met at Karnsnes.

Thorgrim told Mar that he would hide himself – 'and it may be that I will be no less useful than if I were standing right by you, but I don't trust myself in a fight'.

Mar did not reply.

The battle then began, and when it had been under way for some time, Jokul said, 'I can't say much for the biting power of Aettartangi.'

Thorstein replied, 'It is the same with us, and yet our men are being wounded.'

Jokul was right in the thick of things and hacked away with both hands. He was formidably strong and quite without fear. He struck blows which bruised but did not cut.

'Has your good luck changed, Aettartangi, or what?'

Thorstein replied, 'It appears to me that men whom I have struck down stand up again; can you see anything of Thorgrim?'

They said that he was nowhere to be seen.

Thorstein told Jokul to leave the battle and find out whether he could catch sight of him, 'and you, kinsman Hogni, carry on with the fight in the meantime'.

Hogni said that he would.

They then went off in search of Thorgrim.

Jokul said, 'I see where the monster shows his face above ground.'

Thorstein said, 'There lies the fox in his lair,' and Thorgrim eyed them from where he lay – this was near the river.

Jokul and both brothers rushed towards him; Thorgrim raced towards the river. Jokul got near enough for his sword to catch him, and it cut off whatever it made contact with, that is both his buttocks right to the backbone. The place where he ran into the water has since been known as Hufuhyl ([Skin-]hood's pool).

Jokul said, 'Now Aettartangi has bitten.'

Thorstein said, 'I fancy that it will do so from now on.'

The events of the battle must now be related. Hromund went hard at Hogni and there was a ferocious exchange of blows; it ended up with Hogni falling at Hromund's feet. At that moment Jokul arrived; he was again seized with his great fury and attacked Hromund savagely. His sword did not fail to bite, and neither did the weapons of others in the fight. Jokul struck at Hromund's foot and gave him such a wound that he was maimed for the rest of his life and became known as Hromund the Lame. The cousins of Mar fell in the fight. Eventually men from nearby farms noticed the battle raging there and went to separate those involved. Thorgrim of Karnsa was first on the scene, along with other farmers; he was a kinsman of the sons of Ingimund. The two sides were separated; many were injured and all were exhausted.

Thorgrim said, 'You, Mar, have shown great stubbornness in going against the brothers, but they are more than a match for you. My advice is that you surrender to them and offer Thorstein self-judgement.'

He said that this was good advice, and they were reconciled in this way. Thorstein said that he would not deliver his judgement before the next assembly. Men then made their way home from the battle.

When the assembly took place at which Thorstein wished to announce the terms of settlement, the Hof people had many supporters there.

Thorstein then said, 'It is well known to people in this region how the conflict between me and my kinsman Mar turned out; and also that the case is now for me to arbitrate. My judgement is that the killing of Hogni, my brother, be taken as equivalent to those wounds, great and small, suffered by Mar's followers. For the killing of Hogni, Hromund is to be outlawed between Hrutafjord river and Jokulsa river in Skagafjord, and is to receive no compensation for his permanent injury. Mar will be the owner of Hjallaland, because it can only be approached from his land, but he will pay us brothers the sum of one hundred of silver. Thorgrim Skin-hood will receive no compensation for his injury, and he deserves something worse.'

Men then went home and were reconciled in this affair. Thorgrim Skin-hood left the region and settled in the north at Melrakkasletta, and remained there until he died.

Thorstein had two sons; one was named Ingolf, a very handsome man, and the other was Gudbrand, also a good-looking fellow. Ingimund's daughter Jorunn married Asgeir Scatter-brain, the father of Kalf, and of the same Hrefna who married Kjartan Olafsson, and also of Thorbjorg, who was called Pride of the Farm.

30 Of Thorolf Dark-skin it can be said that to begin with he lived in Forsaeludal and men thought badly of him.

Thorstein from Hof approached him and said that he did not want him to settle there – 'unless you behave differently from the way you have up to now; if you don't, we will not put up with it'.

Thorolf said that it was very likely that Thorstein would decide whether or not he lived there, 'but I myself will decide on the way I live my life'.

He then moved his home and constructed a fortification for himself by Fridmundara river. Thorolf stole men's livestock and became the worst of thieves. He also had trenches for sacrifices and the belief was that he offered up both men and animals. He was not well off for supporters among honest men, but he had nine in all, every one of them as bad as or worse than he was. When they heard that Thorstein intended to attack them, there were some who had no wish to wait around and fled from the fortification. Men from the region met Thorstein and asked him to put an end to this man who was so disruptive in the neighbourhood that men could neither control nor tolerate him. He said that what they said was true; he then sent for his brothers Jokul and Thorir.

Thorir was prone to berserk fits from time to time; this seemed a great drawback in such a man because it did nothing for his reputation. Jokul said to Thorstein, 'You do well in not allowing any villains to cause trouble in this valley.'

Then nineteen of them set off together and when they sighted Thorolf's fortification, Thorstein said, 'I have no idea how so few of us can attack the fortification because of this river chasm.'

Jokul said, 'That's no great problem, and I'll give advice on how to do it. You, Thorstein, and the men with you must throw spears at Thorolf and his men and taunt them; and I will work my way up along the river with a few men and find out if it is possible to get into the fortification from the rear; they would then have to be on their guard against both of our groups.'

Thorstein said that this was a hazardous undertaking. Jokul then made his way up the river with a handful of men.

Thorolf and his men did not see this; he urged his men to give a good account of themselves, 'even though the brothers have mighty fetches with them; let us make for our hiding places if we find ourselves hard pressed'.

Jokul crossed the river above the fortification; in his hand he had a great axe which he owned. He then came to the fortification and managed to hook the axe on to it and then hauled himself up by the shaft and in this way entered the fortification. He went quickly in search of Thorolf, but he was nowhere to be seen. Jokul then managed to catch sight of Thorolf as he emerged from his sacrificial trench; he leapt down from the fortification, with Jokul in hot pursuit. Jokul's men sought out Thorolf's companions, pursuing them everywhere.

By then Thorolf had reached some marshy ground up along the river, and Jokul followed him. And when Thorolf saw that he could not escape, he sat down in the swamp and wept. This place has since been known as Gratsmyri (Crying mere). Jokul approached him and said that he was a great monster and villain, and yet had no courage. Jokul then dealt him his death blow. Thorstein attacked the fortification, because the criminals had regrouped. Jokul took a run at it and got into the fortification; and when those who were inside saw this, they feared for their lives, and two of them fled from Jokul as far as the end of the headland, and then he slew them both. The third leapt off the cliff. It seemed to people that no exploit had ever seemed braver than Jokul's on this occasion. The brothers made for home after this; they had done a great service for the region by killing Thorolf Dark-skin.

31 Thorstein from Hof was generous to his neighbours with the goods from his estate. There was free food for everyone and a change of horses and every other kind of help for a journey, and all men from other areas felt duty bound to go first and visit Thorstein and tell him what had been going on in the regions, and anything else that was new. The best of the Hof lands was known as Eyjarengi; Thorstein's workers had a tent there every summer.

One day they noticed ten men grazing their horses in the meadow, and there was a woman with them; they were all in coloured clothing. One of the men was wearing a cloak and a long gown of fine quality cloth. They watched what this man did. He drew his sword and cut off the bottom of the cloak which had become dirty during his riding, and he threw the strip of cloth away – it was the width of a hand – and, speaking so that they could hear, said that he had no wish to go around covered in muck. Thorstein's men had no contact with these people but felt that it was unseemly to graze horses in other men's meadows. A servant woman picked up the piece of cloth which the man had cut off, and said that this fellow could well be called an outrageous show-off.

In the evening Thorstein asked what the news was, and they said that there was none – apart from one small but strange occurrence. They then reported what they had seen and heard of these people and showed the strip which the man had cut from his gown.

Thorstein said that destroying one's valuable belongings, even if they were mud-splattered, and then grazing in another man's meadow were either the actions of some fool or crook, or of a formidable and arrogant man – 'These men have not visited me, as is the custom with travellers from far away. My guess is that this must have been Berg the Bold who arrived in Iceland this summer, the nephew of Finnbogi the Mighty from Borg in Vididal. He is mighty strong and the most mulish of men.'

As on other occasions when Thorstein hazarded a guess, he was pretty near the mark.

Berg came to Borg and Finnbogi greeted him warmly and asked him what the news was, and he told him what he knew. Finnbogi asked whether he had met Thorstein Ingimundarson. Berg said that he had not, but that Thorstein had ridden past below his hayfield wall. Finnbogi said that it was more usual to go and visit him first and tell him what the news was.

Berg said that he had no wish to demean himself in this way by seeking him out – 'because my errand had nothing to do with him'.

32 There was a man called Thorgrim who lived at Lesser Borg in Vididal. He was engaged to a woman named Thorbjorg, the daughter of Skidi. Thorgrim invited Finnbogi and Berg to the wedding; they said that they would attend. The wedding feast was to take place over the Winter Nights at Skidi's farm.

Thorgrim then met the sons of Ingimund and invited them to the wedding – 'because I feel that it will not be fully honoured unless you are present'.

They promised to make the journey.

The weather was not at all good, and it was tough going crossing the Vatnsdalsa river, and things went pretty badly for the Vididal people.

Finnbogi and Berg left their horses with a farmer who lived by the river. The river channel was open in the middle but great chunks of ice lay along the banks.

Berg said, 'I will carry people across,' and so he did, showing great strength in making the crossing.

There was a hard frost and his clothes froze on him. Skidi and the guests who were already there, Thorstein and his brothers, went out to meet the others who were arriving. Then fires were kindled and people's clothes were thawed out. Thorstein the farmer went around eagerly serving people, helping with their clothes, for he was the most considerate of men.

Finnbogi went inside first and was to sit on the high seat opposite Thorstein; then came Berg, who was clad in a long gown and an outer cloak made of skin. This stood out from him because he was completely frozen, and he took up a lot of space. He made for the fire and wanted to thaw out.

He walked past where Thorstein was and said, 'Make room for me, fellow.'

He barged past in such a rush that Thorstein lost his balance and almost fell into the fire.

Jokul saw this and was very angry; he had Aettartangi in his hand, sprang up, leapt at Berg, and struck him between the shoulders with the sword-boss so that he fell flat on his face; he said, 'What are you doing, you scoundrel; is not even our Vatnsdal godi to be spared?'

Berg sprang up and was seething with rage and took up his weapons. Then men came between them, but they were still on the verge of coming to blows because Berg was as unruly as could be. They were, however, kept apart.

Thorstein said, 'Trouble has now arisen once again because of my brother Jokul's quick temper; I wish to offer sufficient compensation to satisfy Berg's honour.'

Berg said that he was not short of money, and would take care of the revenge himself. Jokul said that Berg would always come off worse the more dealings they had with each other. Skidi requested that Finnbogi and his men should leave and have nothing more to do with the people there. Thorstein said that it would not do for the marriage to be disrupted – 'and so we brothers will ride with our men to Masstadir,' and this they did.

33 Berg announced the blow from the sword-boss at the Hunavatn Assembly and prepared the lawsuit. Men then came to the assembly and tried to find a settlement.

Berg said that he would not accept money as compensation and would only settle the case if Jokul were to crawl under three arches of raised turf, as was then the custom after serious offences, 'and by so doing show humility towards me'.

Jokul said that the trolls would take him before he would bow the knee to him in this way.

Thorstein said that the idea was worth considering, however, 'and I myself will go under the turf arch'.

Berg said that he would then be compensated.

The first arch reached up to the shoulder; the second up to the belt on a pair of breeches and the third up to the mid-thigh. Thorstein went under the first.

Then Berg said, 'I have now made the top man amongst the Vatnsdal people stoop like a swine.'

Thorstein replied, 'You had no need to say that, and the first result of those words is that I will not go under any more arches.'

Finnbogi said, 'That was certainly not the right thing for you to say, and it does little to redress Berg's humiliation at the hands of Jokul if things stay as they are. Everything else seems of little account to you Vatnsdal people; but I wish to challenge you, Thorstein, to a duel one week from today at the haystack wall which stands on the island below my house at Borg.'

Then Berg said, 'I wish to say the same thing to you, Jokul – that I challenge you to a duel at the time determined by Finnbogi, and you Hof-dwellers will then be the ones bending low.'

Jokul said, 'Listen to what this devil of a man says – that you should dare to match yourself against us or challenge me to a duel. I think that it wouldn't be too much for me even if I were to fight against both you and Finnbogi. And that's the way it will be; and I want to release my brother Thorstein, because it would be very bad if he were to come to any harm, as would be not unlikely were he and Finnbogi to come to blows, because Finnbogi is the most fearless of men; but neither one of us need be spared. Berg, the dog, bent lower when I hit him, so that he fell down. You must now turn up to the duel if you have a man's heart rather than a mare's. And if anyone fails to turn up, then a scorn-pole will be raised against him with this curse – that he will be a coward in the eyes of all men, and will never again share the fellowship of good folk, and will endure the wrath of the gods, and bear the name of a truce-breaker.'

With this their ways parted and each headed back to his homestead. News of this spread through the region. These duels were to take place at the same time as Thorstein was to hold a feast at Hof, as he did every autumn.

There was a woman named Helga; she came to Iceland with Berg and was his mistress. She was a large and imposing woman, gifted with foresight and prophecy, and wise in witches' ways.

She said to Berg, 'Things have turned out unhappily for you and your kinsmen in that you intend to try your luck against the sons of Ingimund. It must not go this way, because Thorstein is a proven man in both intelligence and luck, and it is rightly said of Jokul that no berserk is his equal anywhere in the Northern Quarter, and you are no match for him, powerful figure that you are; and whatever great disgrace you have already suffered at his hands, you will endure twice as much if you have any further dealings with him.'

Berg replied, 'Jokul has said so much that it has become intolerable for me.'

Helga replied, 'Even though you are so stupid that you cannot look after yourself, I will bring it about that this duel never takes place.'

'Why shouldn't you have the last word?' said Berg.

Finnbogi knew nothing of these plans.

34 It is said that the very morning on which they were to go to the duel, there was such a thick fall of snow and a frost that not a soul ventured out. Early that same morning there was a knock at the door at Hof. Thorstein went to answer it and greeted his brother Jokul.

He said, 'Thorstein, are you ready for the duel?'

He replied, 'Are you set on going, in view of the terrible weather?'

Jokul said, 'I certainly am.'

Thorstein replied, 'Come in first, brother, and wait to see if the weather improves.'

Jokul said that he had no wish to go in and have the snow which lay on him melt – 'and even if you don't want to, I will go all the same'.

Thorstein said, 'There will never be such a difference in courage between the two of us, that I stay behind, and you go – wait for me.'

Thorstein went inside and got himself ready and said to his guests that they should wait there and not leave until the weather was a lot better; he told the mistress of the house and his sons to serve the guests. The brothers set off together.

Then Thorstein said, 'What is your plan now?'

Jokul replied, 'I've never known it happen before that you would seek advice from me. If the need arises there's little enough advice on offer. Yet in this affair I'm not totally without ideas. We'll go to Undunfell, and Thorir our brother will come with us.'

They did so; they set off in that direction and came in the evening to Faxi-Brand's homestead – he was a friend of Jokul's. They stayed the night there. Brand had a horse with a coloured mane called Freyfaxi. He was fond of the horse and thought it a good one; it was fearless in fighting and when put to other uses. Many people felt sure that Brand placed special faith in Faxi. The next morning the same storm returned, only even worse. The brothers wanted to get on their way, even though the weather did not relent. Brand had covered a sledge with hides and harnessed Faxi to it and said that between the two of them they would find the way.

Jokul said, 'Thorstein and Thorir will sit on the sledge while Faxi-Brand and I walk in front.'

They arrived at the haystack wall early that day, and no one else was there.

That same morning Finnbogi said to Berg, 'Do you think that Jokul will have arrived for the duel?'

He said, 'I don't think so, because no one could travel in such weather.'

Finnbogi said, 'Jokul is not the man I think he is if he has not arrived there; and it would have been better not to have taken things this far with him, and thus not now to suffer a second humiliation on top of the first.'

'You have realized this too late,' said Helga, 'and bad as things are now, they will be worse later.'

'Do you think that Jokul has come?' said Berg.

'I will not think about that,' she said, 'but I do believe that, as things will turn out, he is more than a match for the two of you.'

The conversation was at an end, but they did not go outside.

The brothers waited until mid-afternoon, and at that time Jokul and Faxi-Brand went to Finnbogi's sheep-shed, which was right by the yard, and they took a post and set it on the ground by the wall. There were also horses there, which had gone to shelter during the storm. Jokul carved a man's head on the end of the post, and wrote in runes the opening words of the curse, spoken of earlier. Jokul then killed a mare, and they cut it open at the breast, and set it on the pole, and had it face towards Borg. They then set off home and stayed at Faxi-Brand's overnight. They were in good humour during the evening.

Jokul said, 'It is now the case, kinsman Thorstein, that you're much more popular than I am and have more friends, but as things have turned out my friends have helped no less than yours. It seems to me that Faxi-Brand has done us proud.'

'Brand has fully proved himself,' said Thorstein.

Brand said, 'It is good to help a man such as Jokul, because there are few like him.'

Faxi-Brand and Jokul claimed that there had been witches' weather and blamed it on Helga at Borg. The brothers returned home, and everyone was glad to see them again. News spread throughout the district as to the great humiliation which the men of Borg had once again suffered at the brothers' hands.

35 Some time shortly after this, Finnbogi and Berg assembled their men in Vididal, and there were thirty of them in all. Helga asked what they were intending to do. Finnbogi said that he was off to Vatnsdal.

'Yes,' said Helga, 'you must now be intending to avenge yourselves on the brothers, but I think that the more you tangle with them the unluckier you will be.'

'We will have to risk that,' said Finnbogi.

Helga replied, 'Be off with you; you will not be in any less of a hurry on your way home than you are now in setting out.'

The news soon got around and reached Thorstein at Hof. He sent word to his brothers and they came to see him; he told them what he had heard. It was decided that they should assemble their men and, on the day when Finnbogi and his forces were expected from Vididal, sixty men gathered at Hof. Their kinsman Mar from Masstadir was there, and Eyjolf from Karnsnes and other friends.

They then observed the approach of Finnbogi and his men.

Thorstein said, 'Let us now get on our horses and ride towards them, because I don't want them trampling over my land.'

They did this.

Jokul said, 'Let's ride hard and charge at them, so that they'll not be ready for us.'

Thorstein replied, 'We will not behave rashly; I will speak on our behalf and find out what they want, and it may be that little will need to be done; but I know, kinsman, that you are ready for anything.'

Jokul replied, 'It was to be expected that you wouldn't want my advice to prevail for long.'

'Things went well, kinsman,' said Thorstein, 'when we followed your advice, but it is little needed now.'

Finnbogi said to his men, 'There are men riding from Hof, quite a few of them, and it can very truly be said that few things surprise Thorstein. There are now two choices open to us and neither is good – either to ride off home with things as they stand, though this would be the greatest disgrace, or to risk a fight with them, but there is some danger in this when the odds are against us, as they seem to me to be.'

'Surely now is the time to risk something,' said Berg. 'We should certainly confront them.'

Finnbogi said, 'Let's dismount and tether our horses and keep close together, whatever happens.'

Thorstein and his men saw this, and they too dismounted and tied up their horses.

Then Thorstein said, 'Let us now go to meet them, and I will be our spokesman.'

Thorstein then asked, 'Who is the leader of these men who have come here?'

Finnbogi said that he was.

'What is your business here in the valley?'

'There are often small errands to be done around the countryside,' said Finnbogi.

Thorstein said, 'I believe that your errand of finding us brothers, planned when you left home, has now been accomplished – though differently from the way you had expected. If so, things have turned out well. I will now offer you two choices, Finnbogi, though not because it wouldn't have been more fitting for you to have been given just one. Either go back to Borg with matters as they stand, and stay there in your homestead; or, as the other choice, we will fight our duel, but in such a way that each of us may make use of his helpers; and then you will see how you get on, big and strong though you are. It will follow from this that you must leave Vididal in the spring and never again take up residence between Jokulsa river in Skagafjord and the Hrutafjord river; and understand that you must never again get into conflict with us brothers. You, Berg, have shown great hostility towards us. You played a boorish little trick on me when you arrived in the district – you grazed your horses in my meadow, and thought that I was such a petty-minded individual that I would worry about where your horses were eating the grass; and as for when my brother Jokul struck you – this you must bear without compensation because you refused it when it was offered. You will also keep out of those areas forbidden to Finnbogi, and the two of you will then have some reminders of your dealings with us. Choose one or the other – at once.'

Jokul stood next to Thorstein with Aettartangi at the ready. Finnbogi and Berg and their followers moved towards their horses, mounted and rode away, and did not stop until they arrived back at Borg. Helga was standing outside and asked them the news. They said that they had nothing to report.

'That may be the way it seems to you, but it won't seem that way to anyone else, seeing that the two of you have been outlawed from the locality as criminals; and now your ill fortune has reached its peak.'

Thorstein and his brothers rode back to Hof, each heading for his own home. Thorstein thanked them warmly for their support. He maintained his honour in this affair, as in all the others. In the spring Finnbogi sold his land at Borg and moved north to Strandir in Trekyllisvik and settled there. Berg went away, too, and the saga says nothing of what became of him; and thus ended the dealings of Finnbogi and Berg with the sons of Ingimund.

36 It is said that one summer a ship arrived in Hrutafjord. On board were two sisters Thorey and Groa. They both went to stay with Thorstein at Hof and were there through the winter, but in the spring they asked him to find them a permanent place to live. On Thorstein's advice Thorey bought some land and lived there, and Thorstein found a home for Groa nearby. Thorstein had to put up with scorn from his wife Thurid because he took an interest in Groa on account of her witchcraft. Groa bought some malt and prepared a feast and invited the sons of Ingimund to attend; and so the sisters were not held to be of such little importance. Groa also invited Mar of Masstadir and many other men from the region.

Three nights before Thorstein was due to set out from home on horseback, he dreamed that the fetch who had attended the kinsmen appeared before him and told him not to go to the feast. He said that he had promised to.

She said, 'It does not seem to me to be wise, and harm will befall you from this.'

And so it went on for three nights that she appeared and chided him and said that he must not go and touched his eyes.

It was the custom, whenever Thorstein was to set off on some journey, that on the day of his departure everyone who was to ride with him came to Hof. Jokul and Thorir arrived, along with those other men who were to go with him. Thorstein told them to return home; he said that he was sick. They did so.

That afternoon, when the sun had set, a shepherd noticed that Groa went out and walked backwards round her house and said, 'It will be difficult to resist the luck of the sons of Ingimund.'

She looked up at the mountain and waved a kerchief or cloth of hers in which she had wrapped much gold, and said, 'Let whatever is fated come to pass.'

She then went inside and shut the door behind her. There was then a rock-fall on the house and everyone inside died. And when this became known, the brothers drove her sister Thorey out of the district. Ever afterwards the place where Groa lived seemed haunted, and men had no wish to live there from that time on.

37 Thorgrim at Karnsa had a child by his mistress who was named Nereid, and on the command of his wife the child was put out to die. There was great friendship among the brothers, the sons of Ingimund, and they often met up with each other. One time Thorstein visited Thorir his brother and Thorir led him back out on to the highway. Then Thorstein asked Thorir which one of the brothers seemed to him to be the leading man.

Thorir said that there was no question about this – 'you are above us all in wise counsel and in good sense.'

Thorstein replied, 'Jokul is foremost in all matters of courage.'

Thorir said that he himself was the least of them, 'because a berserk fury always comes over me when I would least wish it to, and I wish, brother, that you could do something about this'.

'I have come here because I have heard that our kinsman Thorgrim has had his child left out to die on the instructions of his wife, and that is a wicked thing to do. It also seems to me a great pity that in your nature you are not like other men.'

Thorir said that he would do anything to be rid of it.

Thorstein said that he wanted to suggest a remedy – 'but what are you willing to do?'

Thorir said, 'Whatever you want.'

Thorstein said, 'There is one thing which I request, and that is the godord for my sons.'

Thorir said that they could have it.

Thorstein said, 'I will call on the one who has created the sun, because I believe him to be the mightiest, so that this affliction might leave you. In return, for his sake, I want to help with the child and bring it up, so that he who has created mankind, might later turn him to himself,* because I think that he is able to do this.'

They then jumped on their horses and rode to the place where they knew that the child was hidden; Thorir's slave had found it at Karnsa. They saw that its face had been covered, and that the child was pawing at it, and was by then almost at the point of death. They took the child and hurried home to Thorir, and he brought up the boy, and he was duly called Thorkel Scratcher;† and a berserk fit never again came over Thorir. And it was in this way Thorstein acquired the godord.

Olaf lived at Haukagil, and Ottar in Grimstunga; he married Asdis, daughter of Olaf, and at law meetings they shared the same booth. Thorstein's sons grew up and were accomplished men. Gudbrand was a big and strong fellow. Ingolf was the most handsome of men, and also hefty; his accomplishments surpassed those of most men.

At one Autumn Assembly many men came together and a game was arranged. Ingolf took part and again showed his skills. Once when he chased after his ball, it so happened that it flew towards Valgerd Ottarsdottir. She let her cloak fall on it, and they talked together for a while. She seemed to him a remarkably beautiful woman; and on each remaining day of the assembly, he came to talk with her. After that he was always paying her visits there.

This was not to Ottar's liking, and he came to talk to Ingolf and asked him not to continue behaviour which dishonoured them both, and said that he would rather give him the woman honourably than have him beguile her ignobly. Ingolf said that he would organize his visits as he saw fit, and said that there was no dishonour to Ottar in that. Ottar then met Thorstein and asked him to intervene in this with Ingolf, so that he would do as Ottar wished. Thorstein said that he would.

---

* That is, might later turn him (the child) to himself (the one who created the sun).

† The present translation takes the nickname to refer to the action of the child pawing at its face which had been covered with a cloth. Some scholars have suggested that the phrase refers to the puckering of the cloth over the passive child's mouth and nose as it breathes.

Thorstein said to Ingolf, 'Why is it that you are bent on dishonouring Ottar and shaming his daughter; you are behaving badly, and there will be discord between us if you don't do something about this.'

Ingolf then put an end to his visits, but composed some love-verses about Valgerd and then recited them. Ottar again went to see Thorstein and said that he could not accept Ingolf's versifying – 'it seems to me that you should come up with some remedy for this'.

Thorstein said that the verses were not to his liking, 'and I have said so, but to no effect'.

Ottar said, 'You can pay compensation on behalf of Ingolf or give us permission to take him to court.'

'I wish to urge you,' said Thorstein, 'not to pay any attention to all this, but you may prosecute him.'

Ottar journeyed to Hof and summoned Ingolf to the Hunavatn Assembly and prepared the case.

When Jokul heard of this, he was furious about it and said that it would be an absolute disgrace if kinsmen of theirs were to be made outlaws in their own lands, and said that Thorstein was growing very old; 'and though we are not well versed in the law, we will render this case void with our axe-hammers'.

When it was time for the Spring Assembly, Ingolf asked Thorstein to give advice in the case; otherwise he said that he would bury his axe in Ottar's head.

Thorstein said, 'I want you now to take over the godord and have the benefit of it,' and he did so.

When the case came to court, Ingolf and Jokul went and broke up the proceedings violently and the case collapsed. Shortly after the assembly, Ottar said to his father-in-law Olaf that he would not remain there any longer and would be selling his land. This he duly did, and moved his home south across the heath.

38 Not long after this Thorstein fell sick and died. Though Thorstein's death is mentioned first, Jokul was the first of the brothers to die, and it was Thorir who lived longest. Thorkel Scratcher was three years old when Thorir, his foster-father, died. Thorkel then went to Thororm's home and was fostered there. Men did not believe that they would be able to replace Thorstein and his brothers, but his sons were held to be following nicely in his footsteps. Ingolf seemed to women the most handsome, as this verse states:

All the grown-up girls
longed to go with Ingolf;
glum forever
was the one too young.

The brothers divided the inheritance among themselves. Ingolf lived at Hof, and Gudbrand at Gudbrandsstadir. Ingolf married Halldis, daughter of Olaf from Haukagil; she was younger than Asdis, whom Ottar married, and who was the mother of Valgerd and Hallfred the Troublesome Poet. Ingolf always went to meet Valgerd when on his way to or from the assembly. Ottar did not like this; she also made for him all the most elaborate clothing.

39 Some winters after the death of Thorstein Ingimundarson, Ottar, when riding from the assembly across Blaskog heath, came across an outlawed man called Thorir who had come from the East Fjords. He said that he had been outlawed in a lawsuit about a woman, and asked Ottar for hospitality. Ottar said that he would help him on one condition – 'if you go on an errand for me'.

He asked what this was.

Ottar replied, 'I want to send you north to Vatnsdal to Ingolf, so that you can try to kill him or either one of the brothers, because it is not unlikely, if things turn out as expected, that luck will not be on their side in this. If you go, then I will offer you help.'

He said that he was well able to handle this, 'for I do not lack courage'.

He went home with Ottar and they made an agreement that he would kill Ingolf – or Gudbrand if he could get to him more easily – and that Ottar should help him to get abroad.

He went north to Vatnsdal and arrived at Hof; he stayed there overnight and asked Ingolf for hospitality, saying that he was an outlaw. Ingolf said that he had no need of men from outside the region; he said that such people were easily found. He told him to leave at once and said that he did not like the look of him.

Thorir departed and came to Gudbrand; he took him in and Thorir stayed there for a time. One morning Gudbrand asked him to get him a horse, and walked outside with Thorir behind him. And as Gudbrand came to the threshold he bent down, and Thorir aimed a blow at him, and when he heard the axe whistling, he got himself through the doorway and Thorir's blow hit the beam which ran from the barge-rafter. The axe stuck fast in the beam, and Thorir ran away out of the yard with Gudbrand in pursuit. Thorir leapt over the river chasm, and lay there flat out. Gudbrand hurled his sword after him and it hit him in the midriff. He had tied the bridle around himself and the sword hit the bridle ring. Gudbrand jumped over the river and ran up to Thorir, but he was dead by then. He threw earth over him where he lay. There were notches made in the sword, and one was the size of a finger tip. The sword was later sharpened; it was the finest of weapons.

Gudbrand went to find his brother and told him what had happened and said that Ottar was behind this, and that they would have to be prepared for this sort of thing. Ingolf said that this was a shocking business, and they rode south to Borgarfjord and confronted Ottar with it, but he denied everything, and as at this time there were many people there, they were not able to seize him.

A settlement was sought and the matter was resolved by Ottar paying out a hundred of silver and with no price being set on Thorir's death. It was also part of this settlement that Ingolf should be slain unprotected by the law if he should come to visit Valgerd, unless Gudbrand was with him.

Then Ingolf said, 'You may think about this, Ottar – if there are any more unfriendly journeys to us than this one, there will be no compensation paid, and your treachery will then receive its due reward.'

He said that many would claim that there had been offences before this one was committed. They then parted company.

40 There was a man named Svart who brought his ship in to Minthakseyri; he was of Hebridean descent, a big strong man, not much blessed with friends and generally unpopular. He arrived with his ship badly damaged. And when men realized the sort of man he was, no one was prepared to offer him hospitality, and he went around the region until he came to Ottar's homestead where he asked for hospitality and help.

Ottar replied, 'It seems to me that you have been treated badly – a man such as yourself not being shown hospitality; and I want to offer you a welcome, because you are by no means an insignificant figure, and I think that you can offer me plenty of protection.'

Svart said that Ottar deserved this. Svart was not without money.

He had not been with Ottar long before his host said to him, 'I want to send you north to Hof in Vatnsdal. There is a man named Ingolf living there; he is my enemy and has done me many a wrong, and I never receive any redress from him. Though he is a gifted man, I feel that with my guidance you will have the luck to avenge these wrongs, because I think well of you.'

Svart said that he had experience of places where not everyone saw things the same way; he also said that it was more than likely that he would succeed on this errand because he had been on raiding trips and often been the only one to escape. There was a ship laid up in the Hvita, and Svart and Ottar came to a deal as follows – Svart should cut off Ingolf's hand or foot, or kill Gudbrand if he could not get at Ingolf, and Ottar would provide him with winter quarters, and then help him to get abroad. Svart would have to fend for himself if he did not get the job done, but could otherwise proceed to Ottar's homestead.

Ottar got himself some wares from the ship and gave them to Svart for safe-keeping; he found a man to go with him and also two horses, informed him about the homesteads, and told him which were the best roads for travelling to or from the north.

Svart rode until he came to Hvanndalir where he unloaded his horses, checked his wares, and the horses went off to graze. Svart arrived on foot at Hof early in the day, and Ingolf was outside making shafts for spears. Svart greeted Ingolf and said that his journey had not been without problems – his two horses had disappeared on the heath and his wares were still lying there, a chest and a leather sack. He asked Ingolf to assemble some men to go with him to look for the horses, or to carry his goods to his lodgings. He said that he wanted to move on north to Eyjafjord and that he had been in Hrafnagil some years ago.

Ingolf said that at this time there were few men round the farm – 'and I don't want to go with you at all; be off with you at once'.

'Then would you mind coming with me to the main track and directing me to the next farm,' and so it was that Ingolf went with him to the road; but some foreboding put Ingolf on his guard against him, because Svart always wanted to walk behind him. He was wearing a sword and in his hand he had a long, broad-bladed spear, its shaft reinforced with iron.

Svart asked for hospitality, and said that Ingolf could have whatever he wanted from his goods – 'you are a widely-renowned man and it is right and proper for you to take in travellers from afar, especially if they are not short of money to pay for their board'.

Ingolf said, 'I am not in the habit of taking in unknown men; they can cause a great deal of trouble, as is not unlikely in your case because you have a grim look about you,' and he showed him hastily off the premises and said that he had no wish to bargain with him. He then headed back home.

Svart set off and came to Gudbrand's home and spun him the same tale.

Gudbrand said, 'You strangers do no one any good, but I can have your goods brought here, and later we can settle your board and lodging as seems best.'

They went and found the goods, and thought that the horses had run off; but they were quickly found. Gudbrand had everything brought to his homestead and took Svart in.

When Ingolf heard this, he met with his brother and said that his dealings with Svart were risky – 'I wish that he would go away.'

Gudbrand said that he believed the man intended him no harm, and that he had shown no inclination to do anything wrong since he arrived.

Ingolf said, 'We don't look at this matter in the same way, because this fellow looks like a hired killer to me and he will prove to be bad news; I don't want him to be anywhere near you, because something tells me that he is evil, and it seems to me that forethought is better than afterthought.'

But things did not turn out this way and Svart remained there over the winter. During the spring, with summer approaching, Gudbrand moved his household up to the shieling, and things were so arranged that the mistress of the house rode on her own, Gudbrand and Svart rode together on one horse, with Svart at the rear. And when they came to the marshes now known as Svartsfell Marsh, the horse sank under their weight, and Gudbrand told Svart to slide back off the horse at that moment, and he did so; and when Svart saw that Gudbrand was not watching, he turned his spear towards him.

The housewife saw this and said, 'Watch out for that dog, who wants to betray and kill you.'

At that instant, Svart thrust Gudbrand through with his spear – under his arm and right into his torso. Gudbrand managed to draw his sword and swung at Svart and slashed him severely in the midriff.

The mistress of the house arrived at the shieling and reported the deaths of both men, and this was considered terrible news. Ingolf heard about this and said that things had turned out as he had feared. He prepared a lawsuit against Ottar to be heard at the Althing on the grounds of his plotting to kill both him and his brother. And when men came to the assembly, compensation terms were sought, though these were hard won from Ingolf. However, because many good men took part, and also because Ingolf had not kept to the terms of his settlement with Ottar regarding his visits to Valgerd, he finally accepted a settlement – three hundred of silver for the plot against Gudbrand; the breach of settlement with Ottar over Valgerd would then be disregarded.

With this agreed Ingolf and Ottar parted company and were reconciled. Ingolf and his wife had two sons named Surt and Hogni. Both of them were accomplished men. Ingolf was regarded as a great chieftain, in many ways following admirably in the footsteps of his father. By this time Olaf at Haukagil was ageing fast.

41 Outlaws and robbers were much in evidence at this time, both in the north and the south, so that people could hardly hold their own. One night they stole a great deal of food from Haukagil because there was plenty of everything to be had there. Olaf went and met Ingolf and told him of this. Ingolf prepared to set off from home with fourteen men. Olaf told him to be careful and said that his safe return home mattered more to him than the whereabouts of the food. They rode south over the heath and talked about the robbery at Olaf's homestead. The thieves had stolen goods worth fifteen hundred ells.

Ingolf and his men came across their tracks and followed them until they became confused because the tracks went off in two different directions. Then the men split up, eight in one party and seven in the other, and they searched in this way for a long time. A short distance from them were some shielings and they made for them. There they saw eighteen horses by one shieling and they concluded that it must be the thieves; and they said that the best idea would be to look for their own companions.

Ingolf said that in some ways this was inadvisable, 'because the thieves may then reach their cave, for it is only a short distance away, and they will be safe if they get there; and then our journey would be worthless – besides we are not sure where our men are'.

Ingolf jumped down off his horse and ran down into a nearby ravine, picked up two flat stones, and fixed one to his chest and the other between his shoulders, and so protected his exterior. In his hand he had the sword Aettartangi and then went into the shieling. It had two doors. Men say that Ingolf had the support of no more than one other man. Ingolf's companion then said that they should let his other men know what was going on. Ingolf said that he would guard the shieling doors, and his companion could go off after the other men.

The companion said that he would not leave him – 'it seems to me that your supporters here are by no means thick on the ground'.

Ingolf wanted to attack straight away and told his companion to follow him staunchly. The thieves laid into him as soon as he entered, but the stones which he was wearing protected him, and the blows glanced off him.

They then attacked Ingolf from all sides, but he defended himself bravely and well. Then he raised Aettartangi and the sword fell on the head of the man standing behind him so that he met his death, and it delivered a death blow to the man standing in front and thus Ingolf killed them both with a single blow. There was a fierce fight and, when it finished, Ingolf had killed five men, and his companion had also been struck down. They had by then come out of the shieling but Ingolf was severely wounded. His men approached him. The thieves then fled, and Ingolf's men seized the booty and fastened it on to the horses and then headed off back northwards.

Ingolf lay wounded that winter, and the wounds healed after a fashion. But in the spring, when the weather grew warmer, his wounds opened up again, so that he was brought to his death. And before Ingolf died, he asked to be buried on a different hill from the one on which his kinsmen were buried, and said that the girls of Vatnsdal would remember him better if his grave were close to the road. He then died. The place where he was buried is called Ingolfsholt. All men lamented greatly the death of Ingolf. He had lived on in great honour for twelve years after the death of his father. Ottar married his daughter Valgerd to a Stafholt man.

When Ingolf died, Vatnsdal was without a chieftain, because the sons of Ingolf were not able to assume the godord due to their age. Men sought to know what should be done. It was the law at this time that, while heirs were still young, whoever seemed best suited amongst the thingmen should look after the godord.

42 Thorkel Scratcher, son of Thorgrim, was both big and strong; he was twelve years old when these events were taking place. Thorgrim did not acknowledge him as his son, but Thorkel was much braver than Thorgrim's legitimate sons. Thorkel Silver from Helgavatn was a great shape-shifter and also wise in the ways of magic. He was very wealthy, without friends, disliked by many men, and yet a very worthy fellow.

The same day on which the meeting about the godord had been arranged at Karnsa, the wife of Thorkel Silver said, 'What do you intend to do today?'

Thorkel replied, 'Go to the meeting and be a godi by the time I return home this evening.'

'I do not want you to go,' she said, 'intending to become chieftain of the Vatnsdal people, because this will not be granted to you, and indeed you are not cut out for it.'

He replied, 'Your advice would count in other matters, but not in this.'

Klakka-Orm also intended to attend the meeting, and also Thorgrim from Karnsa, Ingimund's grandson. Thorgrim was considered best suited for the chieftain's role because of his kinship with the Vatnsdal people, but it was to be settled by lot, because many others thought themselves well suited. This meeting was set for the last month of winter at Klakka-Orm's homestead in Forsaeludal.

Thorkel Silver had a dream on the night before the meeting, and told his wife Signy that he thought he was riding down through Vatnsdal on a red horse, and he hardly seemed to be touching the ground, 'and I interpret this to mean that something red is burning ahead, and this bodes well for my honour'.

Signy said that she thought otherwise – 'this seems to me to be an evil dream'; and said that the horse was called Nightmare and a mare is a man's fetch; she said also that red can be seen if things are to turn out bloody, 'and it may be that you will be killed at the meeting if you intend to win the godord, because there are enough people who would begrudge you this'.

Thorkel acted as if he had not heard this, and prepared himself well for his journey as regards clothing and weapons, for he was a very showy fellow; and he arrived at the last moment.

Thorgrim arrived early in the day and sat on the high seat next to Orm; he had never acknowledged that he was the father of Thorkel Scratcher. Thorkel was playing on the floor with other children and was both big and strong and a very handsome youth. He stopped in front of Thorgrim and gazed at him for a very long time and at the small axe which he was holding. Thorgrim asked why this slave-woman's son was staring at him as he was. Thorkel said that it was no great thrill for him even though he was looking at him.

Thorgrim asked, 'What are you prepared to do, Scratcher, first in return for my giving you the axe, because I see that you like it very much; and also in return for my acknowledging kinship with you?'

Thorkel asked him to name his terms.

Thorgrim said, 'You must bury the axe in Silver's head, so that he never gets the Vatnsdal godord; it seems to me that you would then have shown yourself worthy of Vatnsdal kinship.'

Thorkel said that he would do this. Thorgrim instructed him that he should behave as badly as possible with the other boys. Silver always sat with his chin in his hand and his legs crossed. Thorkel was to rush off into the mud, and then hurry back inside and brush against Silver's clothing and see whether he became angry.

They now discussed the godord and reached no agreement; everyone wanted his own way. The lots were then placed in a small cloth and it was always Silver's lot which came up, because of his magic powers. Thorgrim then went off and met Thorkel Scratcher in the doorway with the boys.

Thorgrim said, 'I now want you to pay for the axe.'

Thorkel said, 'I long to own the axe, and I will now pay for it in full, though not in the way that you would wish.'

Thorgrim replied, 'More than one method of payment will be acceptable.'

Thorkel said, 'Do you want me to kill Silver now?'

'Yes,' said Thorgrim.

Silver's lot had secured the godord.

Thorkel Scratcher came into the main room and brushed past Silver and bumped into his foot; and Silver kicked him away and called him a slave-woman's son. Thorkel leapt up on to the seat right by him, and buried the axe in his head, and Thorkel Silver died instantly, and Thorkel said that he had not had to do too much to acquire the axe.

Thorgrim said that the boy had been sorely harassed, 'and he has not stood up to it well; but has now shown himself to be very much a Vatnsdal man, and I will now acknowledge that I am your father'.

Thorgrim then took over the godord and was called the Godi of Karnsa. A settlement was agreed for the killing of Silver because his sons were young. Thorkel went home to Karnsa with his father and asked permission to go abroad and find out how things would turn out if he met up with his kinsman Earl Sigurd, son of Hlodver. Thorgrim said that he should have whatever he wanted.

43 There was a Norwegian named Bjorn who owned a ship which was ready for sea. Thorkel Scratcher went abroad with him. They arrived in the Orkney Islands. At that time Sigurd was earl in the islands. Bjorn was known to the earl and asked him to offer hospitality to Thorkel and himself, and said that he was a man of good family, very worthy, and far superior

to Icelandic men. The earl said that he would offer them hospitality and asked about Thorkel's kinsfolk; Thorkel told him who he was but the earl paid little attention. The earl then made them welcome. Thorkel seemed stubborn in the eyes of the earl's men; he never left his place unless the earl went somewhere. He was very faithful to him.

Once, in the spring, the earl's men set off from the hall for the games, but the earl remained behind with a few men and said, 'You are more single-minded than most other men, Thorkel, in that you do not go off to the games; now what was it that you said to me about your kinsfolk?'

Thorkel spoke of his family, and the earl took this in and said, 'You must be related to me, but you are very slow in letting this be known.'

The earl's respect for him grew, and during the following summer he went raiding and asked Thorkel whether he wanted to go with him. He replied that he would like to go with him if this was the earl's wish.

They raided far and wide that summer. Once, when they made an attack in Scotland and returned to their ships, the earl asked how many men were missing. This was then looked into and Thorkel alone was missing; he had been on the earl's ship. The earl's men said that such a lazy lout was no loss. The earl asked them to go at once and look for him; and so they did. They found Thorkel by an oak tree in a forest clearing; two men were attacking him and four others lay dead by him. When the earl's men arrived, Thorkel's attackers fled. The earl asked what had delayed him.

Thorkel said, 'I have heard you say that men should run from ship to shore; but never that one should run back to the ships in such a way that each man abandons the next.'

The earl replied, 'You speak the truth, kinsman, and henceforth this is how things will be; anyone running away from the standard on land will have no share of the spoils.'

The earl asked whether the men who lay dead beside him were natives or his own men.

Thorkel said that they were natives.

He said that he had gone past a castle, 'and at the place where I was passing some stones fell from the walls, and inside there I found a sizeable store of treasure; and the men in the castle saw this and attacked me and our fight finished up in the way that you can see'.

Then, in front of his men, the earl commended Thorkel's bravery. He then asked how much treasure there was. Thorkel said that it was worth twenty marks of silver. The earl said that Thorkel and no one else should have it all. Thorkel said that the earl should have it all, including his own share. The earl then said that they should both have it, and this treasure was not shared out.

The earl held Thorkel in much esteem because of that exploit. He was with the earl for two winters, and then Thorkel felt a longing to go to Iceland and told the earl this.

He replied, 'I believe that you will be a source of honour to your kinsfolk.'

He became one of the earl's men, and the earl gave him a gold-inlaid axe and fine clothing and said that he should remain his friend. The earl gave him a trading ship along with whatever cargo he might choose. The earl sent a gold ring weighing half a mark to Thorgrim to pay for Nereid's freedom. As a gesture of kinship he sent to Nereid a complete and splendid woman's outfit. Thorkel then set sail and his journey went well. He brought his ship into Hunavatnsos. Thorgrim the Godi of Karnsa rode to the ship and greeted his son warmly and invited him to stay with him, and Thorkel accepted. Thorgrim granted Nereid her freedom just as the earl had requested. A little later Thorgrim fell sick and died and, in accordance with the law, his legitimate sons inherited his estate.

Thororm was the brother of Klakka-Orm, father of Thorgrim, who was the father of Thorkel. Thororm went to meet Thorkel and invited him to his homestead; and he accepted the invitation. Thorkel was an agreeable and good-humoured man.

44 There was a man called Thorgils who lived at Svinavatn; he had a wife and they had four sons, of whom two are mentioned by name – Thorvald and Orm. The brother of Thorgils had a son named Glaedir; his mother was the sister of Gudmund the Powerful of Modruvellir. Glaedir was a flamboyant individual, a chatterbox, a dimwit and a great blusterer. Father and son, Thorgils and Thorvald, went to Klakka-Orm to ask for the hand of Sigrid, his daughter. This was well received, and the wedding feast was fixed for the Winter Nights in Forsaeludal. There were few men at home and much work to do, both searching for sheep and pigs on the mountain, and in taking care of many another task. Thorkel offered to go up the mountain with the workmen. Orm said that he would like him to. They then set off, and made slow progress because the beasts were shy. No one searched more energetically than Thorkel. The swine seemed especially difficult to deal with. Thorkel was tireless in his efforts, and always volunteered for those tasks which other people thought were the worst.

When they were getting the food ready, Thorkel said, 'Would it not be a good idea for us to have some piglet to eat?'

Thorkel took one and prepared it for the table. They were all agreed that Thorkel was a help to them in everything. They returned home.

There was a man named Avaldi who was with Klakka-Orm; he was the son of Ingjald. He ran the farm and Hild his wife worked indoors; she was the daughter of Eyvind the Proud.

Shortly before the wedding was to take place, Glaedir came from the East Fjords and heard all the news and the plans.

Glaedir also said that he heard other news – 'and that is the mountain journey of Thorkel Scratcher – how he was chosen for herding the swine'.

He said that this was right and proper for a slave-woman's son, and said that he had killed a piglet which had only the previous night drunk from the teat, and had lain beside the boar – 'because he felt cold like any other bitch'.

Thorgils said, 'That is a foolish joke which you have made; Thorkel is said to have behaved in the most proper way, both there and elsewhere.'

'It seems to me that this has turned out shamefully for him,' said Glaedir.

Men arrived for the wedding.

Then Thorkel said to Orm, his foster-father, 'I will offer hospitality to people and be on hand for any work or arrangements.'

Orm said that he would gladly accept this offer. Thorkel organized the feast splendidly. Orm and his men sat on the upper high seat, and Thorgils and his followers sat opposite on the lower high seat. Thorkel saw to the guests attentively and dealt with them with due deference. The Svinadal folk laughed at him a good deal and said that the slave's son was now grand enough. Thorkel said that it would be more courteous to reward such hospitality with good humour and a cheery word rather than with ridicule or abuse.

Glaedir said that he had done many great deeds, 'and well may you boast mightily of the fact; it was but a short time ago that you killed the piglet which had sucked the teat for only one night – that is just your kind of job'.

Thorkel answered, 'My great deeds are few, Glaedir, and yet they amount to more than yours; you have no right to talk like that.'

Glaedir laughed at Thorkel in front of Thorvald and said that he was the dabbest of hands at food preparation. Thorvald said that Glaedir spoke unwisely. And in the evening men went to bed.

In the morning Thorkel went into an outside shed and sharpened the axe

Jarlsnaut (Earl's Gift) and then went to the porch. Glaedir was there taking a bath. At that moment men walked past him with a meat trough.

Then Glaedir said to Thorkel, 'You must have been at your farmwork this morning, and we will now enjoy your pig; and make sure that we are the ones who get the fattest bits; that is suitable work for the slave-woman's son.'

'Would it not be right to chop at the head first,' said Thorkel, 'and choose the pieces for yourself? I have never known you to be so greedy that you find it difficult to stuff yourself full.'

They were to ride home from the feast that day. Thorgils asked whether breakfast was ready. Thorkel said that it would be ready when it was cooked, and that this would not take long. He went out by the workmen's entrance and in by another door and took up his axe which stood by the door. And when Glaedir walked out, Thorkel followed after him and hacked at his head, and Glaedir met his death straight away.

Thorkel ran to the northerly door, because people were blocking the one to the south. There was food everywhere in the house. Thorgils had plenty of men with him, and they rushed all over the house, determined that Thorkel should not escape and intending to lay hands on him. Thorkel jumped among the benches. There was a narrow passageway through the house, and there were lockable bed-closets, and from any one of these a man could jump into the passageway. Thorkel looked towards where women sat donning their head-dresses, and ran to where Hild was. She asked him why he was in such a hurry. Thorkel told her what had happened. She told him to go into the passage right by where she was, and so he made his escape.

Thorgils said, 'Let's head for where the women are because it seemed to me that the man ran in that direction.'

Hild picked up an axe and said that none of them would take it from her. Thorgils believed that Thorkel must still be there, and told his men to carry a protective wad of clothing against the women. This was done, but Thorkel was not found.

Thorgils now saw that all this had been no more than a trick and delaying device, and he and his men then went outside, and when they did so they thought that they glimpsed a man down by the river. Thorgils ordered his men to search there, and this was done, but he was not found. Thorkel knew that there was a cave by the river which is now called Krofluhellir (Scratcher's Cave), and he hid there.

Thororm and Klakka-Orm looked for a settlement. Thorgils would not accept compensation, and they could not weaken his resolve; he and his men declared that there must be blood revenge for the killing of Glaedir. Thororm led the bridegroom's men away from the farm, all the time seeking a settlement but not finding one, and they parted on these terms.

Over the winter Thorkel was variously at Karnsa with his brothers or with other kinsmen, because everyone wanted to offer him some help and liked the idea that he would grow to manhood in the district, so that no outsiders would settle there and lord it over them. Then the Vatnsdal people went to seek help for him from Thordis the Prophetess, who lived at Spakonufell. She was a worthy woman and wise in many ways. They asked her for protection and help in Thorkel's case, and said that a great deal depended on her coming up with some plan. She said that she would.

Thorgils went to meet Gudmund the Powerful and said that he above all was duty bound to take up the case on behalf of his kinsman, 'but I will back you up'.

Gudmund said, 'This case does not seem to me to be that easy, because I think that Thorkel will grow to be a great man, with many a kinsman supporting him, and I have been told that what Thorkel did was not without provocation. You prepare the case now and I will take it on this summer at the assembly.'

During the spring Thorgils prepared the case for the Althing. The Vatnsdal people were thick on the ground, and so were their opponents. Thorgils rode to the Thing with a large troop of men. Thorkel also rode there with his kinsmen. Thordis the Prophetess rode with them, and had a booth for herself and her men. Gudmund then took up the case. The Vatnsdal men offered settlement terms, but Gudmund and his men would accept nothing short of outlawry.

Thororm met with Thordis and discussed the matter with her, because she was very wise and could see into the future and was thus chosen to act in major cases.

She then said, 'Thorkel must come here to my booth and we will see what happens.'

Thorkel did so.

Thordis said to Thororm, 'Go and offer terms to Gudmund, and suggest that I arbitrate the case.'

Thorkel gave Thordis two hundred of silver. Thororm suggested that Thordis should decide the case, but Gudmund refused and said that he had no wish to accept monetary compensation.

Thordis said, 'I cannot say that I am obliged to Gudmund.'

She then said to Thorkel, 'Go now in my black cloak and carry in your hand the staff which is called Hognud; would you dare to go among Gudmund's men dressed in this way?'

He said that at her bidding he would dare to do this. She said, 'Let us risk it, then. You will go to Gudmund and strike him three times on his left cheek with the staff; it does not seem to me that you are due for an early death, and I think that this may work.'

Thorkel came among Gudmund's men and no one saw him. He approached Gudmund and was able to bring about what he had been told to do.

Now the prosecution of the suit was held up, and the case was delayed. Thorgils said, 'Why is the case not proceeding?'

Gudmund said that it would soon proceed, but it did not, and the delay was such that the case became null and void for prosecution.

Thordis met the Vatnsdal men and told them to go to the court and offer money as compensation for the man, 'and it may be that they will accept it, and thus bring the case to a close'.

This they did; they went to the court, met Gudmund, and offered terms and monetary compensation.

Gudmund answered, 'I do not know what you are willing to offer but I place much store on the fact that in this case the person who was killed had by his own words made himself no longer inviolable.'

They said that they wished to make the offer for his sake, and they asked him to stipulate the amount.

When he realized how the case stood, and that it could not be prosecuted in law, then he accepted self-judgement from Thororm – he could stipulate whatever sum he wished, but banishment abroad and outlawry in the region were excluded. They agreed with a handshake to drop the case. Then Thordis sent Thorkel to Gudmund a second time to have the staff strike his right cheek; and he saw to this. Then Gudmund recovered his memory and thought it strange that it had ever left him.

Gudmund stipulated a hundred of silver for the killing of Glaedir, and the counter-charge collapsed and Thororm and Thordis paid over all the money, and, fully reconciled, they parted company. Thorkel went home to Spakonufell with Thordis.

Thorgils said to Gudmund, 'Why did you change your mind so suddenly about the case today?'

Gudmund replied, 'Because I could not think of a single word to say, and therefore I dried up; but it may be that I was pulling on a rope against a strong man.'

They then went home from the assembly.

45 The Vatnsdal people did everything possible to honour Thorkel Scratcher. They found him a wife; and assigned the godord to him, because Surt and Hogni the sons of Ingolf were then eleven and fifteen years old and could not receive their confirmation as chieftains from Thorkel; and Hofsland was bought for him; and so Thorkel became leader of the Vatnsdal people.

Ottar's men were dispersed in the north of the region but no attention was paid to this. Hallfred and Galti, the sons of Ottar, went north and so did some of his other children. Hallfred often visited Beard-Avaldi's homestead and talked with his daughter who was named Kolfinna. Gris Saemingsson married this woman but there were rumours about her and Hallfred, as is told in his saga. Once, when he came to Iceland – he was then a seaman – and Gris was at the assembly, Hallfred made his way to where Kolfinna was in a shieling, and slept with her there. And when Gris found out about this, he was extremely angry, and at once Hallfred went abroad that same summer.

At an Autumn Meeting in Vatnsdal there were many men present, and men put tented roofs on their booths because they would be there for two nights. Thorkel had the largest and most crowded booth. Beard-Avaldi and his son Hermund shared a booth. And while Galti Ottarsson was seeing to his affairs, he met Hermund who recalled the offences which Hallfred had committed against him and his men, and rushed at Galti and killed him and then returned to his father in the booth. And when Thorkel heard of the killing, he sprang to his feet along with his followers and wanted to avenge it.

Hild, the mother of Hermund, stood in the doorway and said, 'It would be a better idea, Thorkel, not to be in such a hurry; and it cannot have been in your mind, when we met previously, that you would kill my son in my presence.'

Thorkel replied, 'More things have now come to pass than we then expected; leave the booth now, because if you do so you will then not see your son killed before your eyes.'

She now understood, in fact, that what he said was meant to help Hermund and this ruse seemed to her both quick-witted and brave. She then took off her head-dress and decked out Hermund in it, and took his place on the bench so that no more women than were expected to went outside.

Thorkel told the women to make haste and hustled them on, saying, 'Don't stand about in this way, because the woman's ordeal is bad enough even if she doesn't see or hear the man killed.'

They wanted to rush in and kill Hermund straight away.

Thorkel then went to the doorway of the booth and said, 'See how it befits us not to kill men of our own region and thingmen; let us be reconciled instead.'

Terms were sought between them and they worked towards a settlement with which both sides were well satisfied, and the amounts of compensation paid were so large that those accepting them were properly honoured. Thorkel resolved this case in an honourable way, and all were very pleased. All disputes in the region were referred to him because, apart from Thorstein Ingimundarson, he seemed to be the most gifted of the Vatnsdal people.

46 Around this time Bishop Frederick, and Thorvald Kodransson, called the Far-traveller, came out to Iceland. Right after this another skip arrived, and on board were two berserks, both of them named Hauk. They were unpopular with men because they ordered them to give up their women or their wealth, or else challenged them to a duel. They howled like dogs and gnawed the ends of their shields and walked barefoot on burning coals. The bishop and Thorvald went around preaching the new religion, offering people a faith different from the one previously followed here. They stayed the first winter at Gilja. The Icelanders shunned this new-fangled faith which the bishop and his followers promoted. Kodran and his wife accepted the faith and were baptized at the outset. Olaf at Haukagil was so old that he lay in bed and drank from a horn.

During autumn, at the time of the Winter Nights, Olaf invited his friends to join him, especially Thorkel his kinsman. The bishop and Thorvald were present. Thorkel was the only one to give them a decent welcome, and let them be alone together in the house because they were of the other faith. On the first evening of the feast the approaching berserks were observed and people were very apprehensive about them. Thorkel asked the bishop if he could suggest any way in which the berserks might meet their death.

The bishop urged them to accept the faith and allow themselves to be baptized, and said that he would deal with these wicked ruffians 'with your help'.

Thorkel said, 'Everything would be better if you were to show the people a sign.'

'Have three fires kindled on the floor in the hall'; this was done.

Then the bishop blessed the fires.

He said, 'Now the benches must be packed with the most courageous men carrying great cudgels because steel will not cut them, and thus will the berserks be beaten to death.'

When the two Hauks arrived, they went inside, and walked through the first fire and then the second and they were severely burned and became very frightened of the fiery heat and wanted at once to make for the benches. They were then beaten to death and carried up along the ravine which has since been called Haukagil.

The bishop now felt that he had fulfilled his bargain with Thorkel, so that he would accept the new faith and allow himself to be baptized.

Thorkel said that he had no wish to accept any religion other than the one which 'Thorstein Ingimundarson and Thorir my foster-father held to; they believed in the one who made the sun and ruled all things.'

The bishop answered, 'I offer to you the same faith, but with the difference that you will believe in one God, Father, Son and Holy Spirit, and have yourself baptized in water in his name.'

It seemed to Thorkel very peculiar to have to bathe himself in water, and he said that he did not want to undergo this conversion just yet, but said that he thought it would be a good thing, 'and this change of faith will go from strength to strength here in this land. My kinsman Olaf the farmer is an old man; he will accept the new faith, and all the others who wish to, but I will still bide my time.'

Then Olaf was baptized and died in his white baptismal vestments, and more men were baptized at that same feast. Thorkel was baptized, as were all the Vatnsdal people, when Christianity was officially adopted in Iceland. Thorkel was a great chieftain; he had a church built on his farm and kept his faith well.

47 Two brothers, Fostolf and Throttolf, settled at Engihlid in Langadal; they were formidable figures. They took in a man to protect him and wanted to hide him at Kjol, a short distance from Reykjavellir, while they went to the assembly, where they would deal with his case. Two other brothers settled at Moberg in Langadal and they were named Hunrod and

Ulfhedin, the sons of Vefrod Aevarsson the Old. Ulfhedin was the more popular of the two.

There was a man named Thorolf, called Play-godi, who was with the brothers. Ulfhedin was a great friend of Dueller-Starri, and men say that, when Thorarin the Evil challenged Starri to a duel, Ulfhedin accompanied him to the duelling place; and on that journey the weather turned foul, and they believed it was a witch's storm.

There was a man named Bard who was called the Peevish; he also went with them. They asked him to call off the bad weather, because he had the wisdom of a magician. He asked them to join hands and make a circle; he then went round backwards three times, spoke in Irish and bade them all say 'yes' out loud – and this they did. He then waved a kerchief at the mountain and the weather relented.

Throttolf and Fostolf went to the assembly, as was said earlier, and their charge was meanwhile back in Thjofadal; he reckoned that less money would need to be paid out if he himself was not present. Hunrod and Thorolf Play-godi also rode to the assembly. A short way from Reykjavellir some horses bolted, and they searched far and wide and did not find them. They saw a man a short distance away from them, and believed that he was up to no good and that he must have taken their horses. They did not stop to ask but rushed at him and killed him. They then rode to the assembly and reported this to the brothers Throttolf and Fostolf. They were extremely displeased and demanded compensation, and said that they had made a settlement with the kinsmen on the man's behalf – they had made peace, and then paid over money for him. Hunrod said that he thought other payments were more pressing, and with that they rode from the assembly.

Throttolf and Fostolf purchased land at Kolkumyrar at a place called Holt. There was a man named Thorfinn, a kinsman of theirs, who lived at Breidabolstad in Vatnsdal. He had a journey to make to Skagastrond, and it so happened that Ulfhedin was heading in that direction, and with him was Thorolf Play-godi. When they arrived at the Breidavad ford at the Blanda river, Thorfinn and the brothers Fostolf and Throttolf were riding some little way behind.

Fostolf and his brother said that they were pleased to meet up with Ulfhedin – 'because those brothers killed our man this summer and we will ride after Ulfhedin'.*

* The edited Iceland text reads 'ride after them'. This may be an error; there is no indication that Hunrod was with his brother at this point.

Thorfinn said, 'I will not ride after him,' and he did not.

Fostolf and Throttolf then rode off in hot pursuit.

Thorolf Play-godi noticed this, and said, 'Let us ride on fast; the brothers are on our trail.'

'No,' said Ulfhedin, 'I won't do that because they would then accuse me of running away.'

Thorolf headed out into the river, but the brothers attacked Ulfhedin and he was left lying there afterwards. Then the brothers rode back and told Thorfinn what had happened. He said that they had dealt shamefully with a good man, and he returned home to Vatnsdal. Ulfhedin was fatally wounded.

Hunrod went to collect his brother, and carried him home, and Ulfhedin asked his brother to settle this affair after his death – he said that no revenge would be granted him, 'because I now recall the earlier journey,* and I know that none of those on that journey have died of sickness'.

Ulfhedin then died, but Hunrod did not behave as if he wanted a settlement and prepared the case for the Althing. Thorfinn offered a settlement and compensation, but Hunrod said that he would accept nothing except the outlawry of Fostolf and Throttolf; and this came to pass, and then he rode from the assembly. The brothers made a great fortification at Holt in Kolkumyrar and it was very difficult for Hunrod to attack them.

There was a freed slave named Skum who had accumulated money and grown wealthy. Hunrod spent it for him, and Skum went abroad, came to Norway and then travelled north to Trondheim. He acquired great wealth and stayed there; he became a rich man for the second time. Hunrod spent all his own money as well as Skum's, so that he ended up virtually penniless. He went to meet Thorkel the Vatnsdal godi and told him of his problem.

Thorkel said, 'It was bad advice to follow, not to accept compensation for your brother, when he told you earlier that you would gain nothing else; and now you have neither money nor revenge. However, because you have come to my home to ask for advice, then I will go with you and seek a settlement.'

Thorkel then met the brothers and asked whether they would settle with Hunrod if the chance arose; they reacted coolly to this and said that it was

---

* Perhaps a reference to Ulfhedin's journey to the duelling place early in this chapter; if so, the significance of Ulfhedin's recollection seems unclear.

no better to make a settlement with him now than when one was offered to him earlier.

Thorkel said, 'You must now do one of two things – go abroad, as stipulated earlier, or I will not advise you further.'

They said that his advice was well worth paying heed to, 'for the last thing that we want is to have you against us'.

They then went abroad and arrived in Trondheim.

Then Throttolf said, 'It is not as it should be that Hunrod, a good man, should have become penniless, mostly on our account, while his slave Skum grows as rich as Njord.'

Then they went and killed him, and seized all his money and sent it to Hunrod. A little later Throttolf travelled to Iceland and went to meet with Thorkel Scratcher and told him to seek a settlement between them and Hunrod. Thorkel said that he would. He then went to meet Hunrod, and through his wisdom and goodwill he brought about a full settlement, so that both sides were happy with what he had decreed.

Thorkel grew old and when he lay in his final illness, he summoned his friends, kinsmen and thingmen.

Thorkel then said, 'I wish to make it known to you that I have contracted a sickness, and it seems to me likely that it will result in the parting of our ways. You have had faith in my foresight and shown me respect and obedience; accept my thanks for this.'

With that he died and this was a great sorrow to his thingmen, and all men of the region, because he seemed – as was indeed the case – a great district leader, and a man blessed with great luck, and the man most like the old Vatnsdal men such as Thorstein and Ingimund. However, Thorkel surpassed them in that he was a man of the true faith, and loved God, and prepared himself for his death in a Christian way. And with that we make an end of the saga of the people of Vatnsdal.

Translated by ANDREW WAWN

THE SAGA OF THE PEOPLE OF LAXARDAL

Laxdæla saga

Time of action: 890–1030
Time of writing: 1250–70

The Saga of the People of Laxardal is vast in conception. Its story includes important characters from other major sagas, and its time span is well over a century. The grand sweep of its action – at whose centre is the greatest of all saga heroines, Gudrun Osvifsdottir – takes in the Viking realms in Britain and Ireland, and has been shaped by continental literary traditions and several types of saga. This is a family saga, describing the line of Ketil Flat-nose, and more particularly that of his daughter Unn the Deep-minded, the matriarchal settler of Dalir, in west Iceland. It is also a heroic tragedy, in which conflicting loyalties subvert the bonds of family and lead to enmity and vengeance; a dramatic account of social ambition that also probes the rights of women, the lowly-born and the illegitimate; the history of a regional feud over land, wealth and status; and above all the story of the life and loves of Gudrun, her feminine nature coming to terms with the tragic forces of the heroic man's world.

When Ketil flees King Harald in Norway, he and Unn head for the Viking kingdoms in Scotland and Ireland, rather than for Iceland; he is of high birth and does not intend 'to spend my old age in that fishing camp'. After Unn loses her husband and son – both kings – in successive battles, she marries her daughters into the Orkney and Faroese nobility. Unn settles in west Iceland, as authoritative a family head as any male settler, holding sway over the community and dispensing land to her kinsmen, other settlers and even freed slaves – among them, incidentally, the Irish grandfather of Gudrid Thorbjarnardottir, the heroine of the Vinland sagas. Although her gifts of land are inspired by Christian charity, they sow the seeds of conflict among later generations who will fight over boundaries and inheritances when

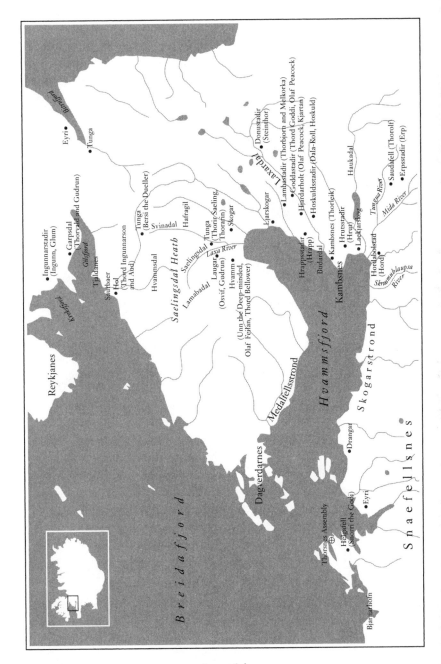

Laxardal

Family Ties in Laxardal

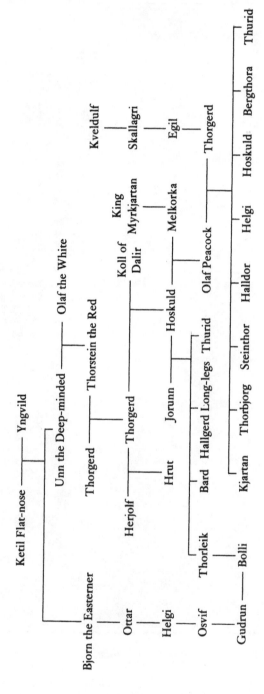

Gudrun's Family and Husbands

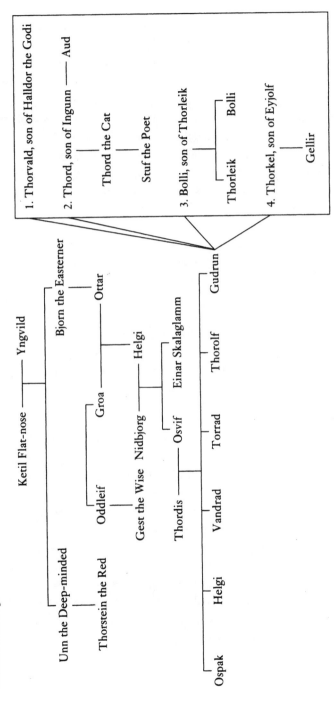

Iceland is fully populated. Not once but three times, fierce conflicts divide the community when half-brothers or foster-brothers clash (Hoskuld and Hrut, Thorleik and Olaf Peacock, Kjartan and Bolli), but we only see the full disintegration of Ketil Flat-nose's line with the rivalry between Kjartan and Bolli for the love of Gudrun. All three players in this love triangle are descendants of Ketil, five or six generations removed.

Unn's loss of husband and son and her attempts to shape her own fate establish certain themes that expand into Gudrun Osvifsdottir's tragedy, her four marriages and love for Kjartan. Gudrun's fate is also foretold in a dream, a familiar saga device. It is not the events of the plot as such that engage us, but rather its unravelling as a narrative of the predicament of individuals who are caught up in the relentless onward march of events and social change. Certainly the upheavals that Ketil Flat-nose's descendants experience do not stop when the settlers make new homes for themselves in Iceland. As a young Viking Age mother, Gudrun brings up her son to wreak vengeance on his father's killers, but she ends her life in Christian piety as an anchoress in a completely different ethical world.

The saga is symphonic in its structure, with subtle repetitions, parallels and echoes in gradually changing circumstances. And although the plot has striking similarities to the cycle of eddic poems about Brynhild, Sigurd, Gunnar and Gudrun, this is only one aspect of its literary context. The characterization highlights nobility, splendour and physical appearance, with a colour more akin to medieval romance than to brawny Viking heroism. Nonetheless, in their actions the male characters tend not to live up to the grandeur and hyperbole with which they are presented. At foreign courts their stature is aristocratic, but at home in Iceland they are farmers with few outlets other than words and smart clothes for their aspirations to nobility. This is a saga in which even slaves are high-born, descended from the kings of Ireland. The women in *The Saga of the People of Laxardal* are much more complex and memorable than the men, as if the men buckle beneath the weight of the heroic legacy they are forced to bear.

The Saga of the People of Laxardal belongs to the earliest group of sagas and was written shortly after the middle of the thirteenth century. By focusing on divisive claims to land, authority and rank it seems to mirror the issues of the fierce civil war that raged while it was being written. Arguments have been put forward claiming that the saga, with its focus on women as leaders or instigators, its firm grasp of female psychology, its close attention to the details of women's routine life and its insights into the position and lot of women – from the highest to the lowest ranks of life – must surely be the work of a woman author.

Many manuscripts of *The Saga of the People of Laxardal* have been preserved. The version in *Möðruvallabók* (AM 132 fol., dated 1330–70) is the only intact vellum manuscript, and all printed versions have been based upon it, with minor amendments and variant readings from other manuscripts. The saga is translated here by Keneva Kunz from the version printed in *Íslenzk fornrit*, vol. 5 (Reykjavík 1934), with a few variant readings from Kristian Kålund's critical edition (*Samfund til udgivelse af gammel nordisk litteratur*, vol. 19 (Copenhagen 1896)).

I   A man called Ketil Flat-nose, the son of Bjorn Buna, was a powerful
     hersir in Norway and came from a prominent family. He lived in
Romsdal in the Romsdal district, between South More and North More.
Ketil Flat-nose was married to Yngvild, the daughter of Ketil Ram, a man
of good family. They had five children: one of their sons was Bjorn the
Easterner, another Helgi Bjolan. One of their daughters, Thorunn Hyrna,
was married to Helgi the Lean. Helgi the Lean was the son of Eyvind the
Easterner and Rafarta, the daughter of Kjarval, the king of the Irish. Another
of Ketil's daughters, Unn the Deep-minded, was married to Olaf the White.
Olaf the White was the son of Ingjald, son of Frodi the Valiant, who was
killed by the descendants of Earl Sverting. Ketil's third daughter was called
Jorunn Manvitsbrekka.* Jorunn was the mother of Ketil the Lucky Fisher,
who settled at the farm Kirkjubaer. His son was Asbjorn, the father of
Thorstein who was the father of Surt, who was the father of Sighvat the
Lawspeaker.

2   During Ketil's later years King Harald Fair-hair grew so powerful in
     Norway that no petty king or other man of rank could thrive in
Norway unless he had received his title from the king. When Ketil learned
that the king had intended to offer him the same terms as others, namely to
submit to his authority without receiving any compensation for kinsmen
who had been killed by the king's forces, he called a meeting of his kinsmen
and addressed them, saying:
    'All of you know of our dealings with King Harald in the past, so there
is no need to go into that here, but all the more need to discuss the difficulties
at hand. Of King Harald's animosity towards us there is proof enough; it
seems to me we should expect little friendship from that direction. We seem

---

* The byname Manvitsbrekka is thought to suggest wisdom.

to have two choices before us: to flee the country or to be killed off, one by one. Although I would prefer to meet my death as my kinsmen have done, I do not wish to make a decision on my own which will make things difficult for all of you. I know only too well the character of my kinsmen and friends: you would not want us to go our separate ways despite the trials that following me would involve.'

Ketil's son Bjorn answered: 'I can tell you at once what I want to do. I want to follow the example of other worthy men and flee this country. I see little honour to be gained in sitting at home waiting for King Harald's henchmen to chase us off our lands, or even in meeting death at their hands.'

They applauded his words as being boldly spoken. Then they decided to leave the country, since Ketil's sons were greatly in favour of the idea and no one opposed it. Bjorn and Helgi wanted to go to Iceland, as they claimed they had heard many favourable reports of the country; there was enough good land available, they said, without having to pay for it. There were reported to be plenty of beached whales and salmon fishing, and good fishing every season.

To this Ketil answered, 'I do not intend to spend my old age in that fishing camp.'

Ketil said he preferred to travel to the west; there, he said, they seemed to live a good life. He knew the country well, for he had gone raiding through much of the area.

3   Afterwards Ketil held an excellent feast, and it was here that he gave his daughter Thorunn to Helgi the Lean in marriage. He then prepared to leave the country and sail westward. His daughter Unn went with him, along with many of his other kinsmen. Ketil's sons and their brother-in-law Helgi the Lean set out for Iceland the same summer. Bjorn Ketilsson made land in the bay of Breidafjord in the west and followed the southern shore of the bay until he reached a fjord stretching inland. A high mountain rose up from a headland on the far side of the fjord, with an island just offshore. Bjorn said they should stop there a while. He went ashore with several others and made his way along the coast. There was only a short distance between the mountains and the sea, and he thought it looked a good place to settle. In one inlet he found his high-seat pillars had drifted ashore, and they took this to be a sign of where they should settle.

Following this Bjorn took all the land between the Stafa river and Hraunsfjord and made his home at the place which has since been called Bjarnarhofn (Bjorn's Harbour). He was called Bjorn the Easterner. Bjorn's wife was Gjaflaug, the daughter of Kjallak the Old. Their sons were Ottar and Kjallak, whose son was Thorgrim, the father of Killer-Styr and Vermund. Kjallak's daughter was named Helga. She was married to Vestar of the Eyri farm, the son of Thorolf Blister-pate who settled at Eyri. Their son was Thorlak, the father of Steinthor of Eyri.

Helgi Bjolan made land in the south and took all the Kjalarnes headland between Kollafjord and Hvalfjord. He lived at Esjuberg into his old age.

Helgi the Lean made land in the north of Iceland and took all of Eyjafjord between the Siglunes and Reynisnes headlands. He lived at Kristnes. The people of Eyjafjord trace their descent from Helgi and Thorunn.

4   Ketil Flat-nose made land in Scotland, where he was well received by the men of high rank, being both renowned and of a prominent family. They offered to let him settle wherever he wished. Ketil and the rest of his kinsfolk made their homes there, with the exception of Thorstein, his grandson. He set off immediately to go plundering and raiding in many parts of Scotland, and was everywhere successful. He later made peace with the Scots and became the ruler of half of the Scottish kingdom. He married Thurid, the daughter of Eyvind and sister of Helgi the Lean. The Scots only kept the peace for a short time before breaking their pact with Thorstein. He was killed at Caithness, according to Ari Thorgilsson the Learned.

Unn was at Caithness when her son Thorstein* was killed. Upon learning that her son had been killed, and as her father had died as well, she felt her future prospects there were rather dim. She had a knorr built secretly in the forest. When it was finished, she made the ship ready and set out with substantial wealth. She took along all her kinsmen who were still alive, and people say it is hard to find another example of a woman managing to escape from such a hostile situation with as much wealth and so many followers. It shows what an exceptional woman Unn was.

Unn also took along with her many other people of note and from prominent families. One of the most respected was a man named Koll and called Dala-Koll. He came from a renowned family and was himself a hersir. Another man of both rank and distinction making the journey with Unn was named Hord.

Her preparations complete, Unn sailed to the Orkneys, where she stayed for a short while. There she arranged the marriage of Groa, Thorstein the Red's daughter. Groa was the mother of Grelod, who was married to Earl

_____
* Thorstein was also known by his byname 'the Red'.

Thorfinn, the son of Earl Turf-Einar and grandson of Rognvald, Earl of More. Their son was Hlodver, the father of Earl Sigurd, who was the father of Earl Thorfinn, from whom all the earls of Orkney are descended. Unn then sailed to the Faroe Islands, where she also stayed a while and arranged the marriage of Olof, another of Thorstein's daughters. The most prominent family in that country, the so-called Gotuskeggi clan, are descended from Olof.

5   Unn then made ready to leave the Faroe Islands, and told her sailing companions that she intended to sail to Iceland. With her she took Olaf Feilan, Thorstein the Red's son, and his sisters who were still unmarried. She set sail and had a smooth journey, making land at Vikrarskeid on the south shore. The ship was wrecked upon landing but all those aboard survived and managed to save their property. Taking twenty men with her, Unn set off to seek her brother Helgi. He came to meet her as she approached and offered to put her up along with nine others. She answered him angrily, saying she had hardly expected such stinginess of him, and departed. She then set off to visit her brother Bjorn in Breidafjord. When he learned of her coming, he went out to meet her with a large company, welcomed her warmly and invited her to stay with him along with all her companions, as he knew well his sister's grand style. This was much to her liking, and she thanked him for his generosity.

Unn stayed there over the winter, and was given generous treatment, as Bjorn was well off and unsparing with his wealth. In the spring she crossed Breidafjord, arriving at a promontory where they had a morning meal and which has since been known as Dagverdarnes (Morning Meal Point). The point juts out into the sea from the coast of Medalfellsstrond. Unn then sailed her ship into Hvammsfjord until she came to another promontory where she also made a brief stop. She lost a comb there and the point has since been called Kambsnes (Comb Point). Afterwards she travelled through all the valleys of Breidafjord and took as much land as she wished.

Unn sailed to the head of the fjord. Finding that her high-seat pillars had floated ashore there, she felt it was clear that this was where she should make her home. She had a farm built at the site, now called Hvamm, and lived there. The same spring that Unn was building her farm in Hvamm, Dala-Koll married Thorgerd, the daughter of Thorstein the Red. Unn held the marriage feast and gave Thorgerd all of Laxardal as a dowry. Koll set up a farm on the south bank of the Laxa river and was held in high esteem. Their son was Hoskuld.

6   Unn subsequently gave away portions of the land she had taken to various other men. To Hord she gave all of Hordadal, as far as the Skraumuhlaupsa river. He lived at Hordabolstad and was an important man with many notable descendants. His son was Asbjorn the Wealthy, who lived at Asbjarnarstadir in Ornolfsdal. He was married to Thorbjorg, the daughter of Skeggi of Midfjord. Their daughter was Ingibjorg who was married to Illugi the Black. Their sons were Hermund and Gunnlaug Serpent-tongue. They are known as the Gilsbakki family.

Unn spoke to her followers: 'For your services you will be rewarded; we have now no lack of means to repay you for your efforts and your loyalty. You are aware of the fact that I have made a free man of Erp, the son of Earl Meldoon. It was far from my intention that such a well-born man be called a slave.'

Unn then gave him land at Saudafell between the Tungua and Mida rivers. His children were Orm, Asgeir, Gunnbjorn and Halldis, who was married to Alf of Dalir. To Sokkolf she gave the valley Sokkolfsdal, where he lived into his old age.

One of her freed slaves, Hundi, who was of Scottish descent, was given the valley Hundadal. A fourth slave was named Vifil, and she gave him Vifilsdal.

Thorstein the Red had a fourth daughter, Osk, the mother of the wise Thorstein Surt (Black), who devised the 'leap week' in summer.* Thorhild, a fifth daughter, was the mother of Alf of Dalir, to whom many people trace their ancestry. Alf's daughter was Thorgerd, the wife of Ari Masson of Reykjanes. His father, Mar, was the son of Atli, son of Ulf the Squinter and Bjorg Eyvindardottir, the sister of Helgi the Lean. The people of Reykjanes are descended from them. Vigdis was the sixth daughter of Thorstein the Red. Her descendants are the people of Hofdi in Eyjafjord.

---

* The addition of an extra week to the summer season was an attempt to readjust the calendar to fit the solar seasons. As the settlers of Iceland had only fifty-two weeks to a year, or 364 days, their calendar was a day and a quarter short of the proper length. As the calendar and solar seasons became more and more out of joint, the idea of adding an extra week every six years in compensation was adopted.

7   Olaf Feilan was the youngest of Thorstein's children. He was a large, strong man, handsome and highly accomplished. Unn was fonder of him than anyone else and let it be known that she intended to leave all her property at Hvamm to Olaf after her death. As Unn grew weak with advancing age, she sent for Olaf and spoke to him:

'It has occurred to me, my grandson, that you should think of settling down and marrying.'

Olaf agreed and said he was ready to follow her advice on this matter.

Unn said, 'It would be best, I think, to hold your wedding feast at the end of this summer, when it is easiest to provide everything we need. If things turn out as I expect, our friends will attend in number, as this will be the last feast I will hold.'

Olaf answered: 'You have made me a generous offer, and the only wife I take will be one who will rob you of neither your property nor your authority.'

Olaf was married that same autumn to Alfdis and the wedding was celebrated at Hvamm. Unn went to great expense with the feast, to which she invited prominent people from distant districts. She invited her brothers Bjorn and Helgi Bjolan, both of whom attended with large followings. Koll, her granddaughter's husband, came as did Hord of Hordadal and many other men of distinction. There were large numbers of guests, even though nowhere near as many came as Unn had invited, since those who lived in Eyjafjord had a long distance to travel.

Old age was tightening its grip on Unn. She was not up and about until noon and retired to bed early in the evening. No one was allowed to consult her from the time she went to bed in the evening until she was dressed the next day. She replied angrily if anyone asked after her health. On the day the feast began Unn slept longer than usual, but was up when the guests began to arrive and went out to give her friends and kinsmen a proper welcome. She said they had shown their affection for her by making the long journey.

'I mean Bjorn and Helgi especially, but to all of you who have come, I give my thanks.'

Unn then entered the hall, followed by a large group of people. When the hall was filled, everyone was impressed by the magnificence of the feast. Unn then spoke:

'I call upon you, my brothers Bjorn and Helgi, and my other kins-men and friends, as witnesses. This farm, with all the furnishings you see around you, I hand over to the ownership and control of my grandson, Olaf.'

Unn then rose to her feet and said she would retire to her bedchamber. She urged them to enjoy themselves in whatever way they saw fit, and people could take pleasure in drinking. It is said that Unn was both tall and heavy-set. She walked briskly along the hall and people commented on her dignified bearing.

The evening was spent feasting until everyone went to bed. Olaf Feilan came to the sleeping chamber of his grandmother Unn the following day. As he entered the room, Unn was sitting upright among the pillows, dead. Olaf returned to the hall to announce the news. Everyone was impressed at how well Unn had kept her dignity to her dying day. The feast then continued, in commemoration of both Olaf's marriage and Unn's death. On the final day Unn was borne to the burial mound which had been prepared for her. She was placed in a ship in the mound, along with a great deal of riches, and the mound closed.

Olaf Feilan then took over the farm at Hvamm and its property with the consent of his kinsmen who had come to visit. When the feast concluded, Olaf gave generous parting gifts to his most respected guests. Olaf became an influential man and a great chieftain. He lived at Hvamm into his old age. The children of Olaf and Alfdis were Thord Bellower, who married Hrodny, the daughter of Skeggi of Midfjord. Their sons were Eyjolf the Grey, Thorarin Foal's-brow and Thorkel Kuggi. Olaf's daughter Thora was married to Thorstein Cod-biter, the son of Thorolf Moster-beard. Their sons were Bork the Stout and Thorgrim the father of Snorri the Godi. Another daughter, Helga, was married to Gunnar Hlifarson. Their daughter Jofrid was married first to Thorodd, the son of Tungu-Odd, and later to Thorstein Egilsson. Another of their daughters, Thorunn, was married to Herstein, the son of Thorkel Blund-Ketilsson. Olaf's third daughter, Thordis, was married to Thorarin Ragi's brother the Lawspeaker.

Olaf was living at Hvamm when his brother-in-law Dala-Koll became ill and died. Hoskuld, Koll's son, was still a youngster when his father died, but wise beyond his years. Hoskuld was a handsome and accomplished youth. He inherited his father's property and took over the running of the farm. His name was soon linked with the farm where Koll had lived, and it was called Hoskuldsstadir. Hoskuld was soon a well-liked farmer in the district, as he enjoyed the support of many who had been friends and relatives of his father, Dala-Koll.

His mother Thorgerd, Thorstein the Red's daughter, was still a young and good-looking woman. After the death of Koll she was unhappy in Iceland and told her son Hoskuld that she wished to take her portion of the property and go abroad. Hoskuld answered that he would deeply regret their parting, but would not oppose her in this or anything else. He proceeded to purchase for his mother a half-share in a ship which was beached at Dagverdarnes. Thorgerd arranged her passage, taking substantial wealth with her. She put out to sea and the ship had a good journey to Norway. In Norway Thorgerd had many relatives and numerous kinsmen of high birth. They welcomed her warmly and offered her whatever hospitality she cared to accept. Thorgerd accepted gladly, saying that she intended to settle in Norway.

Thorgerd did not remain a widow for long before a suitor named Herjolf asked for her hand. He had been granted the rank of landholder, and was wealthy and greatly respected. Herjolf was a large and powerful man. While not handsome, he was still an impressive-looking fellow, and the best of warriors. Under such circumstances, as a widow, Thorgerd was free to decide for herself, and on the advice of her kinsmen she decided not to refuse his offer.

Thorgerd married Herjolf and went to live at his farm; they cared deeply for one another. Thorgerd soon proved herself to be a woman of firm character. Herjolf's situation was now considered better than before as he enjoyed even greater respect after having married a woman like Thorgerd.

8   Soon after Herjolf and Thorgerd began their life together they had a son. The child was sprinkled with water and named Hrut. From his early childhood he was both big and strong for his age, and no man cut a better figure: tall, broad-shouldered and narrow at the waist, with well-formed arms and legs. Hrut was also very handsome, and in this respect took after his grandfather, Thorstein, and great-great-grandfather, Ketil. He was highly accomplished in all respects.

Herjolf fell ill and died, and was deeply mourned by everyone. Afterwards Thorgerd wanted to return to Iceland and see her son Hoskuld, whom she cared for more than anyone else. Hrut stayed behind with his kinsmen where he was in a favourable position. Thorgerd set out on the trip to Iceland and made her way to her son Hoskuld's farm in Laxardal. He gave his mother a fitting welcome. Thorgerd was wealthy and spent the remainder of her life with Hoskuld. A few years later she fell ill and died, and was buried in a mound. Hoskuld took over all her wealth, although his brother Hrut was entitled to half.

9   At this time Norway was ruled by King Hakon, foster-son of King Athelstan of England. Hoskuld was one of the king's men and spent alternate years at court and at home on his farm. He was a well-known person in both Norway and Iceland.

A man named Bjorn had settled in Bjarnarfjord, which cuts into the land north of Steingrimsfjord and is named after him. There is a ridge between the two fjords. Bjorn was a wealthy man and of good family. His wife was named Ljufa and they had a daughter named Jorunn, a good-looking woman, very proud, and no less clever. She was considered the best match in the entire West Fjords.

Hearing of this woman and also that Bjorn was the foremost farmer of the Strandir district, Hoskuld set out with a party of nine men to visit him in Bjarnarfjord. Hoskuld was well received, for Bjorn had heard others speak well of him. Eventually Hoskuld asked for his daughter's hand. Bjorn consented for his part, and said in his opinion his daughter could not wish for a better marriage, but referred the question to her.

When the question was put to Jorunn, she answered, 'Nothing I have heard of you, Hoskuld, would make me inclined to refuse you, and I think any woman married to you will be well cared for. In this, however, my father will have the deciding say, as I will abide by his wishes.'

The long and the short of it was that Jorunn was betrothed to Hoskuld with a large dowry. Their wedding was to be celebrated at Hoskuldsstadir. The question settled, Hoskuld rode home to his farm, where he remained until the date set for the wedding. Bjorn came south for the occasion, accompanied by a sizeable following. Hoskuld had also invited a great many guests from among both his friends and his kinsmen, and the wedding feast was a very grand one. Afterwards everyone returned home in a spirit of friendship and bearing worthy gifts.

Jorunn Bjarnardottir remained at Hoskuldsstadir and assumed her duties in running the farm along with Hoskuld. She soon showed herself to be both clever and experienced, and skilled at many things, though often somewhat headstrong. She and Hoskuld got along well together, but they seldom showed strong affection for each other.

Hoskuld soon became a great chieftain. He was both powerful and ambitious, and did not lack wealth. People felt him to be at least the equal of his father, Koll, in all respects. Not long after their marriage Hoskuld and Jorunn had a child. This son was named Thorleik and was the eldest of their children. A second son was named Bard. Their daughter Hallgerd was later called Long-legs. Another daughter was named Thurid. All their children were promising.

Thorleik was a big, strong man with striking features, who spoke little and was unruly. Judging from his character as a youngster people felt he would hardly prove to be easy to get along with. Hoskuld often said that Thorleik reminded him of his relatives in the Strandir district. Bard was exceptionally good-looking, strong and intelligent, and in character resembled more his father's side of the family. As a youngster Bard was even-tempered, and he grew up to be a popular man. Of all the children he was Hoskuld's favourite.

Hoskuld's situation was by this time extremely prosperous and he was highly respected. At this point Hoskuld married his sister Groa to Veleif the Old. Their son was Bersi the Dueller.

10   A man named Hrapp lived north of the Laxa river, across from Hoskuldsstadir. His farm, later called Hrappsstadir, is now deserted. Hrapp was the son of Sumarlidi and was called Killer-Hrapp. He was of Scottish descent on his father's side, but his mother's family had lived in the Hebrides, where he was born. A big, strong man, he was never willing to back down, even when facing an opponent who was considered more than his equal. He had fled from the Hebrides to Iceland and purchased the farm where he now lived because this same belligerence had led him to commit misdeeds for which he refused to make retribution. His wife was Vigdis Hallsteinsdottir and their son was named Sumarlidi.

Vigdis's brother was Thorstein Hallsteinsson, who lived at Thorsnes. Sumarlidi grew up there and was a promising youth. Thorstein had been married, but his wife had died by this time. He had two daughters, one named Gudrid and the other Osk. Gudrid was married to Thorkel Scarf who lived at Svignaskard, an important chieftain and wise man; he was the son of Red-Bjorn. Osk, Thorstein's other daughter, was married to a man named Thorarin who lived in Breidafjord. He was a robust and popular man who farmed with his father-in-law Thorstein, now an elderly man and much in need of help.

Most people cared little for Hrapp. He pushed his neighbours around and had on occasion hinted to them that they could expect trouble if they showed anyone else more respect than they did him. The farmers got together and agreed to approach Hoskuld and tell him of their difficulties.

Hoskuld told them to let him know if Hrapp did them any harm, 'for he'll deprive me of neither men nor means'.

11   A man named Thord Goddi lived on the north side of the Laxa river on a farm which has since been called Goddastadir. He was very wealthy and had no children. He had purchased the farm where he lived. As a neighbour of Hrapp's, he was often the victim of his aggression. Hoskuld gave him protection so that he could remain on his farm. Thord's wife Vigdis was the daughter of Ingjald, who was the son of Olaf Feilan and brother of Thord Bellower. On her mother's side she was the niece of Thorolf Red-nose of Saudafell. Thorolf was a noted warrior and a man of means; his kinsmen could always look to him for support. Vigdis had been married to Thord more for his wealth than his worth.

Thord had a slave, who had immigrated to Iceland with him, named Asgaut. He was a large and capable man, and, though he was called a slave, there were few among those called free men who could regard themselves as his equals. He was exceptionally loyal to his master. Thord had other slaves, but only Asgaut is mentioned by name.

A man named Thorbjorn, who was called Pock-marked, lived on the next farm up the valley from Thord. He was a man of wealth, much of it in gold and silver. He was a big man, very strong, and tight-fisted in his dealings with most people.

The buildings on Hoskuld's farm were far from his liking, as he felt them unworthy of a man in his situation. He purchased a ship from a man from the Shetland Islands which was beached at Blonduos. He made the ship ready and declared his intention to travel abroad, leaving Jorunn to look after his farm and children. They set out to sea, had favourable winds and made land in the south of Norway, in Hordaland, where the trading town of Bergen was later established. He had the ship drawn ashore there, as important kinsmen of his lived nearby, although they are not mentioned by name. King Hakon was then in Vik. Hoskuld did not proceed on to the king, as his kinsmen received him with open arms. Nothing of note occurred all that winter.

12   The coming summer was the occasion of a royal expedition east to the Brenno Islands. Intended to keep the peace in the region, the excursion was made every third summer, according to the law. An assembly of chieftains was called to choose the cases in which the kings were to pass judgement. Attending the assembly was regarded as an entertainment, as men attended from all the lands of which we have reports.

Hoskuld had his ship set afloat. He also wanted to attend the assembly, as he had not yet paid his respects to the king that winter. The assembly attracted a gathering of traders. People attended in large numbers, and there was plenty of entertainment, drinking and games, and festivities of all sorts. Nothing especially newsworthy occurred, but Hoskuld met many of his kinsmen who lived in Denmark.

One day, when Hoskuld was on his way to the festivities with several companions, he noticed a highly decorated tent some distance away from the others. Hoskuld went over and entered the tent, where a man sat dressed in costly clothing and wearing a Russian hat.

When Hoskuld asked him his name he replied that it was Gilli, 'but many know me better by my nickname; I am called Gilli the Russian'.

Hoskuld replied that he had often heard him mentioned and called him the richest of the merchants trading there.

Hoskuld then said, 'I suppose you can provide me with anything I might want to buy?'

Gilli asked what it was that he and his companions wished to buy.

Hoskuld said that he wanted to purchase a slave-woman, 'if you should happen to have one for sale'.

Gilli replied, 'You hope to put me on the spot by asking for something you assume I don't have. I wouldn't be too sure of that, however.'

Hoskuld then noticed an inner curtain drawn across the tent. When Gilli lifted the curtain Hoskuld saw twelve women sitting behind it. Gilli told Hoskuld to go inside and take a look, to see whether he cared to buy any of these women. Hoskuld did so. The women sat in a row across the width of the tent. When Hoskuld looked more closely he noticed one of the women sitting near the outer side of the tent. She was poorly dressed, but Hoskuld thought her to be a good-looking woman, as far as he could judge.

Hoskuld then spoke: 'Say I wanted to buy this woman, how much would she cost?'

Gilli answered: 'For her you will weigh out and pay me three marks of silver.'

'It seems to me,' said Hoskuld, 'that you value this slave-woman rather highly; that is the price of three.'

To this Gilli answered, 'Right you are, I do value her more highly than the others. Choose one of the eleven others instead, for one mark of silver; I will keep this one.'

Hoskuld said, 'Tell me first how much silver is in this purse on my belt,' and asked Gilli to bring out his scales while he sought his purse.

Gilli then said, 'I'm not out to trick you in this transaction – the woman has a major flaw and I wish you to know of it, Hoskuld, before we conclude the bargain.'

When Hoskuld asked what it was, Gilli replied: 'The woman cannot speak. I have tried in many ways to get her to speak, but never got so much as a word from her. To my mind, at least, she doesn't know how to speak.'

To this Hoskuld replied, 'Bring out your scale and we will see how much the money I have here weighs.'

This Gilli did, and weighed the silver, which proved to weigh three marks.

Hoskuld then said, 'Since that's the case, we'll call it a bargain. You take the silver, and I will take the woman. I must say you acted fairly, in not trying to trick me into a purchase.'

Hoskuld then went back to his own booth.

Hoskuld slept with the woman that same evening. The next morning, as they were dressing, Hoskuld spoke:

'There's not much sign of pride in this clothing which the wealthy Gilli has provided you with. But I suppose it's more of a burden for him to dress twelve than for me to dress one.'

Hoskuld then opened a chest from which he took fine women's clothing and gave it to her. Everyone remarked on how well fine clothing suited her.

When the leaders had concluded the business provided for by law, the assembly was dissolved. Hoskuld then approached King Hakon and offered his respectful greetings in a fitting manner.

The king looked hard at him and said, 'We would have received you well, Hoskuld, had you hailed us earlier, and so will it be even now.'

13   This said, the king welcomed Hoskuld affectionately and suggested he come aboard his ship – 'and dwell with us as long as you wish to stay in Norway'.

Hoskuld answered, 'For your offer, many thanks, but I have much work ahead of me this summer. My intention of acquiring building timber was the main reason for the delay in paying you my respects.'

King Hakon told Hoskuld to sail to Vik, where he spent some time as the king's man. The king gave him a supply of building timber and had it loaded aboard ship.

He then spoke to Hoskuld: 'I will not detain you here longer than you wish to stay, but it will be no easy task to find someone to take your place.'

The king then accompanied Hoskuld to his ship and spoke: 'You have proved the best of men, but I suspect that this will be the last time you sail from Norway under my rule.'

The king drew a gold ring, which weighed a full mark, from his arm and presented it to Hoskuld along with another treasure, a sword which was worth half a mark of gold. Hoskuld thanked the king for his gifts and all the honour he had shown him. He then boarded his ship and sailed out to sea.

The ship was favoured with good winds and made land on the south shore of Iceland. They sailed westward, skirting the peninsulas of Reykjanes and then Snaefellsnes, to enter the bay of Breidafjord. Hoskuld landed at the mouth of the Laxa river, had the cargo unloaded and the ship drawn up on the beach on the inland side of the river. There they constructed a boat shed for the ship, the remains of which are still visible. They built booths at the place now known as Budardal (Booth valley). Hoskuld then had the timber transported to his home, which was not difficult as it was no great distance away. Afterwards he and several other men rode home to be met with a warm reception, as might be expected. His property had also been well looked after in his absence.

Jorunn asked who the woman was accompanying him.

Hoskuld answered: 'You probably think I'm mocking you, but I do not know her name.'

Jorunn said, 'Unless the stories I've heard are lies, you must have spoken to her enough to have at least asked her name.'

Hoskuld said there was no denying that and told her the whole story. He asked her to show the woman respect and said he wanted her to live there at home with them.

Jorunn replied: 'I've no intention of wrangling with some slave-woman you have brought home from Norway who doesn't know how her betters behave, least of all since she is obviously both deaf and dumb.'

Hoskuld slept with his wife every night after returning home, and had little to do with his slave-woman. Everyone noticed the obvious air of distinction about her and realized that she was no fool. Late that winter Hoskuld's slave-woman gave birth to a boy. When Hoskuld was sought and the boy shown to him, he felt, as did others, that he had never seen a handsomer or more distinguished-looking child. Hoskuld was asked what the child should be called. He asked that the boy be named Olaf, as his uncle Olaf Feilan had died a short time earlier.

Olaf was an exceptional child and Hoskuld became extremely fond of the boy. The following summer Jorunn said that the slave-woman would either have to do her share of the farm work or leave. Hoskuld asked the woman to wait upon himself and Jorunn as well as look after her child. By the time the boy was two years old he spoke perfectly and ran about on his own like a child of four.

One morning Hoskuld had gone out on some farm business. The weather was good, and the sun still low in the sky. He heard voices and followed the sound to a place where a stream ran down the slope of the hayfield. There he saw two people whom he recognized: his son, Olaf, and the child's mother. He then realized that she was anything but dumb, as she had plenty to say to the boy. Hoskuld went over to them and asked her what her name was, saying that there was no point in pretending any longer. She agreed and they all sat down on the slope.

Then she spoke: 'If you wish to know my name, it is Melkorka.'

Hoskuld asked her for details of her family.

She answered: 'My father is Myrkjartan; he is a king in Ireland. I was taken captive there at the age of fifteen.'

Hoskuld said that she had too long concealed such noble birth.

Hoskuld then returned to the house and told Jorunn what he had learned. Jorunn said there was no way of knowing whether she spoke the truth, and that she had no use for people of dubious origin. Their discussion ended on this point. Jorunn treated the slave-woman no better than before, but Hoskuld was rather more kindly towards her from then on. Shortly afterwards, when Jorunn was getting ready for bed, Melkorka assisted her in removing her socks and shoes and laid them on the floor. Jorunn picked up the socks and struck her with them. Angered, Melkorka gave Jorunn a blow on the nose, causing it to bleed, before Hoskuld came in and separated them. After that he had Melkorka move to another farm farther up the valley which has been called Melkorkustadir ever since and is now deserted. It is on the south shore of the river. Melkorka set up household there with her son Olaf, and Hoskuld supplied her with everything she needed. As Olaf grew up it was obvious to everyone how exceptionally handsome and well mannered he was.

14   A man named Ingjald lived on the Saudeyjar Islands in Breidafjord. He was called the Godi of Saudeyjar. He was a wealthy man who liked to throw his weight around. His brother Hall was a big and capable man. He lacked wealth, though, and few men put much store by him. The brothers seldom agreed; Ingjald felt that Hall hardly conducted himself in the manner of worthy men, while Hall felt that Ingjald failed to do what he could to improve his lot.

On the Bjarneyjar Islands in the bay of Breidafjord was a fishing camp. This is a cluster of islands rich in supplies of food. People often went there for provisions and visited in large numbers every year. Wise men said it was important to maintain harmony in fishing camps, and it was said that catches would be poorer if there was dissension, advice which was heeded by most people.

Ingjald's brother, Hall, is said to have gone to the islands one summer to fish. He hired on a boat with a man called Thorolf. He was from Breidafjord and had barely a permanent home or any property, although he was a sturdy fellow. Hall stayed there some time and behaved as if he were superior to most of the others. One evening Hall and Thorolf returned to shore and set about dividing the day's catch. Hall intended both to divide the catch into two portions and then choose his portion first, because he felt himself superior. Not mincing his words, Thorolf refused to take less than his share. After a few angry exchanges, with each of them becoming more adamant, Hall picked up a gaff lying nearby and attempted to strike Thorolf in the head with it. At this point other people intervened and separated them, restraining Hall who struggled furiously but to no avail, at least for the moment. Their catch was left undivided and when Thorolf left the island that evening, Hall took the entire catch for himself, being the more influential of the two. Hall then found someone to replace Thorolf and continued fishing as before.

Thorolf was far from satisfied with this turn of events and felt he had been shamefully treated in the exchange. He continued to work in the islands, and awaited the chance to even the score. Hall paid no heed to him, thinking that no one would dare to raise a hand against him there on his home territory. One day Hall was out fishing in his boat with two others. The fish had been biting well, and the companions were in a cheerful frame of mind as they rowed home in the evening. Thorolf learned of Hall's movements that day and waited down by the landing in the evening as Hall and his companions came in to land. Hall rowed from the bow and jumped out as the ship approached shore to draw it up on the beach. Thorolf was close by and as Hall came ashore he swung at him. The blow struck Hall on the neck, close to the shoulder, and sent his head flying. Thorolf then turned to run away but Hall's companions fell upon him. News of Hall's killing spread throughout the islands and was considered a major event, as the man came from a prominent family, although he himself had hardly been luck's favourite.

Following this Thorolf sought to get away from the islands, as he could expect no one there to offer him protection after such a deed. Nor did he have any kinsmen from whom he could expect support, while there were powerful men close at hand who were certain to wait for the chance to take his life, among them Hall's brother Ingjald the Godi of Saudeyjar.

Thorolf managed to get passage to the mainland. He kept himself hidden as much as possible and nothing is said of his movements until he arrived at Goddastadir one evening. Vigdis, Thord Goddi's wife, was distantly related to Thorolf, and this was the reason for his visit to the farm. Thorolf had already heard something of the situation there, and that Vigdis was made of sterner stuff than her husband, Thord. He approached Vigdis directly upon arriving, told her of his plight and asked for her protection.

Vigdis answered his request, saying: 'We are, of course, related, and in my opinion you have done nothing to lower my opinion of you. But it does look like anyone who offers you protection does so at the risk of his own life and property, because such powerful men will be on your trail. My husband Thord,' she said, 'is no hero, and any help we women can offer is generally of little protection against such odds. All the same, I don't want to desert you completely, since you did come here for protection.'

Vigdis then led him to a storage shed and told him to wait there until she returned. She locked the shed, then went to Thord and said, 'A man by the name of Thorolf has come to stay with us. He is a distant relation of mine, and he needs to stay for some time, if you agree to it.'

Thord said he did not care to have anyone stay there. The fellow might rest until the following day, if he was not in any trouble, but if such was the case he must be off straight away.

Vigdis answered, 'I have already promised him lodging and do not intend to go back on my word, despite the fact that he is a man of few friends.'

She then told Thord of the killing of Hall and that it was Thorolf, who now sought shelter with them, who had slain him.

This news upset Thord greatly, and he said he knew for certain that Ingjald would make him pay a high price for the accommodation that was now offered Thorolf, 'since we have allowed the door to shut behind this man'.

Vigdis answered: 'Ingjald won't be making you pay for a single night's accommodation, for he'll be staying here all winter.'

Thord spoke: 'If you do this you put me in the utmost danger, and I am against letting such a troublemaker stay here.'

All the same, Thorolf spent the winter there.

Ingjald, who was to seek redress for his brother's killing, learned of it. He made ready an excursion into the valley late in the winter and set afloat a ferry he owned. They were a party of twelve. They sailed eastward under a strong north-westerly wind and made land at the mouth of the Laxa river. They drew the ferry ashore and headed for Goddastadir the same evening. Their arrival scarcely came as a surprise, but they were well received.

Ingjald drew Thord aside and told him of his reason for coming, that he had heard that Thorolf, his brother's killer, was there. Thord said that there was no truth to this.

Ingjald told him there was no point denying it – 'We'll make a deal, you hand the man over to me without causing me any trouble, and I have here three marks of silver which will be yours. I'll also forgive you any offence you have given me in sheltering Thorolf.'

Thord was tempted by the sight of the silver, as well as the chance to get off without paying for an offence which he had feared would cost him money.

Thord then spoke: 'I intend to keep our words a secret from the others, but you have yourself a bargain.'

They went to sleep until the night was almost at an end and daybreak only a short while off.

15   When Ingjald and his men rose up and got dressed, Vigdis asked Thord what he and Ingjald had been talking of the previous evening.

He said they had talked of many things, and had agreed that a search of the farm would be made and their part in the matter would be considered closed if Thorolf were nowhere to be found; 'I had Asgaut, my slave, take him away.'

Vigdis said she had no use for lies, nor for having Ingjald snooping around her household, but told him to have it his own way.

Ingjald made his search and failed to find his man. While this was going on Asgaut returned, and Vigdis asked him where he had left Thorolf.

Asgaut answered: 'I took him to our sheep sheds, as Thord told me to do.'

Vigdis spoke: 'Is there any place more directly in Ingjald's path on the way to his boat? There's little doubt that they planned this together yesterday evening. I want you to go there at once and take him away as quickly as possible. Take him to Saudafell, to Thorolf Red-nose. And if you do as I bid you, you will be rewarded. I will give you your freedom and the wealth you need to go wherever you wish.'

Asgaut agreed to this, went back to the sheep shed and found Thorolf. He told him to come quickly. Meanwhile Ingjald left Goddastadir, intending to collect his silver's worth. As they rode down from the farm they saw two men making their way towards them, Asgaut and Thorolf. It was still early in the morning and not yet fully light.

Asgaut and Thorolf were trapped, with Ingjald on the one side and the Laxa river on the other. The river was very high, with stretches of ice along both banks and a torrent of open water in the middle, making it treacherous to cross.

Thorolf spoke to Asgaut: 'It looks to me as if we have two choices. We can wait for them here on the bank and defend ourselves as long as our courage and strength last; more likely than not Ingjald and his men will put a quick end to us. Or we can take our chances with the river, a choice which is not without danger either.'

Asgaut told him to decide, and said he would not desert him 'whichever course you choose'.

Thorolf answered: 'We'll try the river.'

This they did, first ridding themselves of excess weight. They then made their way over the stretch of ice along the shore and set out to swim across the water. As they were both strong men, and fate intended them to live for some time yet, they managed to cross the river and climb up on the ice on the other side.

No sooner had they crossed the river than Ingjald and his men arrived at the bank opposite them.

Ingjald spoke to his men: 'What will we do now? Try the river or not?'

They told him to decide and said they would abide by his decision, but the river looked impassable to them.

Ingjald agreed – 'We won't attempt to cross.'

Not until Thorolf and Asgaut saw that Ingjald and his men did not attempt to cross the river did they stop to wring the water out of their clothes. They then made ready for their journey and, after walking all that day, arrived at Saudafell in the evening. They were received well, for everyone was put up at Saudafell. Asgaut went to Thorolf Red-nose the same evening and told him the whole story of their journey and that Thorolf's kinswoman, Vigdis, had sent his travelling companion to Thorolf for safe-keeping. He told him everything of Thord Goddi's dealings and produced the tokens which Vigdis had sent Thorolf.

Thorolf answered: 'These tokens are not to be mistaken, and I will certainly look after the man at her request. I think her conduct in this affair does great credit to Vigdis. It's all the more shame that a woman like her should be so poorly married. Stay here with us, Asgaut, as long as you wish.'

Asgaut said he did not intend to stay long. Thorolf then welcomed his namesake, who became one of his followers, and parted with Asgaut on good terms. Asgaut then headed homeward.

As for Ingjald, he turned back towards Goddastadir after leaving Thorolf. By that time men from the neighbouring farms, to whom Vigdis had sent word, had arrived and there were at least twenty men there. When Ingjald and his men returned to the farm, he summoned Thord and spoke to him.

'You have treated me badly, Thord,' he said, 'for I know it was you who helped this man escape.'

Thord replied that there was no truth in his accusations, and the whole scheme between Ingjald and Thord was revealed. Ingjald demanded the return of the silver which he had given Thord. Vigdis stood nearby, listening to their words, and said they had both got what they deserved.

She told Thord not to keep the money. 'For you, Thord,' she said, 'have come by it dishonourably.'

Thord replied that she obviously intended to have her way. Vigdis then went indoors and opened a chest of Thord's, where she found a heavy purse of money. She took the purse and went out, came up to Ingjald and told him to take his money. Ingjald's face brightened at the sight and he reached his hand out to take the purse. Vigdis swung the purse up into his face, striking him on the nose which bled so that drops of blood fell to the ground. While doing so she heaped abuse on him, adding that he would never again see this money, and told him to be off. Ingjald decided he had little choice but to leave as quickly as possible, and did so, hardly slowing his pace until he was at home once more. He was very displeased at the outcome of his journey.

16 Soon Asgaut returned home. Vigdis gave him a hearty welcome and asked him whether they had been well received at Saudafell. He gave her a glowing report and told her of Thorolf's concluding words. She was highly pleased at this.

'You, Asgaut,' she said, 'have carried out your task both loyally and well. Your reward will not be long in coming. I give you your freedom, so that from this day onward you may call yourself a free man. You will take the money which Thord accepted for the head of Thorolf, my kinsman; it will be better off in your hands.'

Asgaut praised her and thanked her for this gift.

The following summer Asgaut took passage on a ship which put out to sea from Dagverdarnes. They had a brief, stormy sailing and made land in Norway. Asgaut then travelled to Denmark and settled there and was considered a capable and decent fellow; his story ends here.

After the scheme between Thord Goddi and Ingjald the Godi of Saudeyjar to bring about the death of Thorolf, Vigdis's kinsman, Vigdis showed open enmity to Thord. She announced she was divorcing him and went to stay with her kinsmen, to whom she told the story. Thord Bellower, who was their leader, was not pleased about it, but no action was taken. Vigdis had taken nothing but her own belongings with her from Goddastadir. Her relatives at Hvamm made it known that they claimed half of the property in Thord Goddi's possession. He was very upset by this news and rode off at once to Hoskuld to tell him of his dilemma.

Hoskuld said, 'You've been stricken with fear before, even when you weren't pitted against such superior forces.'

Thord then offered Hoskuld money for his support and said he would not be petty about the payment.

Hoskuld said, 'We all know you can never stand by and look on happily while anyone else enjoys your wealth.'

Thord answered: 'You won't have to worry about that in this case, because I will gladly place you in charge of all my wealth. What's more, I'm offering to foster your son, Olaf, and make him my sole heir after my death, as I have no heirs in this country and I would rather the wealth went to him than for Vigdis's kinsmen to get their paws on it.'

Hoskuld agreed to this and they settled the agreement. Melkorka was not pleased, as she felt the fosterage was far from worthy enough. Hoskuld said she failed to see its advantages:

'Thord is an elderly man and has no children. All his wealth will go to Olaf; meanwhile, you can see the boy whenever you wish.'

After this Thord took over the raising of Olaf, who was then seven years old, and treated the boy with great affection. When news of this spread to those men who had unfinished business with Thord Goddi, they saw that it would make settling scores considerably more difficult.

Hoskuld sent Thord Bellower generous gifts and asked him not to take offence at the developments. Legally, he said, they had no right to demand payment on Vigdis's behalf, as Vigdis had not declared any grounds for her divorce which had been proven to be true and thus justified her departure.

'One can hardly blame Thord for trying to seek a way to rid himself of a man who threatened to cost him dearly and whose guilt surrounded him like juniper bushes around a rowan tree.'

When Hoskuld's message was conveyed to Thord Bellower, along with substantial gifts of money, he let himself be appeased. Any property Hoskuld was in charge of was well looked after, he said. He accepted the gifts and no action was taken, although relations were somewhat cooler between them after that.

Olaf grew up with Thord Goddi and turned into a big, strong man. He was so handsome that no man could be found to equal him. At the age of only twelve he rode to the Althing, and people coming from other districts were impressed at how fine a figure he cut. Olaf dressed well and bore fine weapons, all of which set him apart from other men. Thord Goddi's situation was much better after Olaf became his foster-son. Hoskuld gave his son the nickname Peacock. The name stuck and he was known by it from then on.

17   Hrapp was becoming increasingly difficult to deal with. By now he was so aggressive that his neighbours could hardly stand up to his attacks. Hrapp could not touch Thord after Olaf came of age. As he grew older, Hrapp's strength waned until he was confined to his bed, but his malicious nature remained the same. He summoned his wife Vigdis and spoke:

'I'm not one to catch every passing disease,' he said, 'and this illness will likely send us our separate ways. When I'm dead I want to be buried in the kitchen doorway. Have me placed in the ground upright, so I'll be able to keep a watchful eye over my home.'

He died soon afterwards.

Everything was done just as he had instructed, for she dared not go against his wishes. But if it had been difficult to deal with him when he was alive, he was much worse dead, for he haunted the area relentlessly. It is said that in his haunting he killed most of his servants. To most of the people living in the vicinity he caused no end of difficulty and the farm at Hrappsstadir became deserted. Vigdis, Hrapp's wife, fled to the west of Iceland to her brother Thorstein Surt, who offered her a home and took charge of her property.

Once again, the farmers called on Hoskuld to tell him of the difficulties Hrapp was causing and ask him to find some solution. This Hoskuld promised to do and, taking several men with him, went to Hrappsstadir to disinter Hrapp and move him somewhere far away from sheep and men alike. Hrapp's haunting decreased considerably after this. Sumarlidi, Hrapp's son, inherited his property, which was both of good quality and quantity. The following spring Sumarlidi set up a farm at Hrappsstadir, but went insane after having lived there only a brief while and died shortly afterwards. Vigdis, his mother, then inherited all the property, but she refused to live on the farm at Hrappsstadir so Thorstein Surt took charge of all the property. He was an elderly man by this time, but still strong and in good health.

18 In the meantime, Thorstein's kinsmen in the Thorsnes district, Bork the Stout and his brother Thorgrim, had become full-grown men. It was soon evident that the brothers intended to be the leading men of the district and enjoy the greatest respect. Thorstein saw this and, in order to avoid coming into conflict with them, declared his intention to move and set up house at Hrappsstadir in Laxardal. He made his preparations for the journey following the Spring Assembly and had his livestock herded along the coast.

Thorstein and eleven others boarded a ferry. Among them were his son-in-law Thorarin, his daughter Osk and Thorarin's daughter, Hild, who was then three years old. A strong south-westerly wind bore Thorstein's ship into a current known as Kolkistustraum (Coal-chest Current), the most dangerous of the Breidafjord currents. Their crossing was slow and difficult, mainly because the tide was ebbing and the wind against them. The rain came in showers, with strong winds gusting when the clouds broke and then calmer spells in between.

Thorarin was at the helm. He had the straps to control the rudder bound round his shoulders as there was little room to move about aboard ship. It was loaded with chests and cases, piled high, for they were not far from land. The boat made slow progress against the strong opposing current. They ran aground on a skerry but not hard enough to break through the hull of the ship. Thorstein told them to strike the sail quickly, take the long forks and attempt to push the ship afloat again. They tried this but without success, because the water on both sides of the ship was so deep that the forks could not reach the bottom. The only course was to await the incoming tide.

While they waited, and the tide continued to ebb around them, they saw a seal, much larger than most, swimming in the water nearby. It swam round and round the ship, its flippers unusually long, and everyone aboard was struck by its eyes, which were like those of a human. Thorstein told them to spear the seal and they tried, but to no avail.

Finally, the tide began to come in. When it had reached the point where the ship was about to float free, a great storm struck which capsized the ship. Everyone aboard was drowned except one man who managed to make his way to shore holding on to a bit of wood. His name was Gudmund and the islands where he landed have since been called Gudmundareyjar (Gudmund's Islands).

Thorstein's daughter Gudrid, who was married to Thorkel Scarf, was to inherit her father's property after his death. The news of the drowning of Thorstein Surt and the others who were with him spread quickly. Thorkel lost no time in sending for Gudmund, the survivor. When he arrived Thorkel made a secret bargain with him to have Gudmund describe according to his instructions how those aboard ship had died. Gudmund agreed to this. Thorkel then asked him, in the presence of many other people, to tell them what had happened. According to Gudmund's story, Thorstein had drowned first, followed by his son-in-law Thorarin. At this point it was Hild, Thorarin's daughter, who would have inherited everything. The next to drown, said Gudmund, was the child, which meant that the property fell to her mother Osk. Osk was the last to die, and thus the property came into the hands of Thorkel Scarf, as Osk's sister, Gudrid, who inherited her sister's property, was his wife.

Thorkel and his followers spread this story, but Gudmund had earlier given a slightly different version of the events. Thorarin's kinsmen found the new version rather suspicious and said they were not convinced. They demanded that Thorkel split the property with them. Thorkel maintained that it was all his by right and offered to undergo an ordeal to prove it, according to the custom of the time.

The usual ordeal took the form of walking under an arch of raised turf. A long piece of sod was cut from a grassy field but the ends left uncut. It was raised up into an arch, under which the person carrying out the ordeal had to pass. Thorkel Scarf knew there was reason to doubt the truth of the later version of the drownings which he and Gudmund had reported. Heathen men were no less conscious of their responsibility when they underwent ordeals than are Christian men who perform them nowadays. A person managing to pass under the arch of turf without its collapsing was absolved of guilt.

Thorkel arranged for two men to pretend to start a dispute, for some reason or other, near the place where the trial was to be held. They were to knock against the arch with enough force that the onlookers could plainly see that they had caused it to collapse. The trial began, and at the moment when Thorkel passed under the arch these accomplices charged at each other with their weapons in the air, collided near the arch of turf and naturally caused it to collapse. Other men ran up to separate the combatants, which was an easy enough matter as they were hardly fighting in earnest. Thorkel Scarf then appealed to the onlookers for their verdict. All of his followers were quick to say that the ordeal would have been successful if these others had not spoilt things. Thorkel then took possession of all the property, but the farm at Hrappsstadir remained deserted.

19 The story now turns to Hoskuld. His situation was such that he enjoyed great respect and was an important chieftain. He was in charge of considerable wealth that belonged to his brother, Hrut Herjolfsson. More than one man pointed out that it would make a sizeable dint in Hoskuld's property if he had to pay out all of his mother's portion of the inheritance.

Hrut had become one of the followers of King Harald Gunnhildarson. He was held in high esteem by the king, mainly because he had proved his fighting prowess in dangerous situations. He was such a favourite with Gunnhild, the queen mother, that she maintained that none of the king's followers was his equal, either in word or deed. People might make comparisons of men, and praise men's excellence, but it was obvious to everyone that Queen Gunnhild considered it nothing but lack of judgement, if not envy, if anyone was compared to Hrut.

As Hrut knew that in Iceland there awaited him both well-born kinsmen and a share in great wealth, he wanted very much to go and seek both out. In parting the king presented him with a ship and said Hrut had proved a stalwart fellow.

Gunnhild accompanied Hrut to his ship and said, 'It's no secret that I regard you as an exceptional man; you are as capable as the best of our men, and far exceed them in intelligence.'

She then gave him a gold arm ring in farewell, hid her face in her shawl and walked stiffly and rapidly towards town, while Hrut boarded his ship and sailed out to sea.

He had a good journey and made land in Breidafjord. He sailed to the islands [at the mouth of Hvammsfjord], then into Breidasund, and landed at Kambsnes, where he laid a gangway from ship to shore. News of a ship's arrival, and the fact that Hrut Herjolfsson was at the helm, spread quickly. Hoskuld was little pleased by the news and did not go to meet and welcome him. Hrut had the ship drawn ashore and secured. He built a farmstead at Kambsnes, then approached Hoskuld to demand his mother's share of the inheritance. Hoskuld said he was not obliged to pay him anything, as his mother had not left Iceland empty-handed when she returned to Norway and married Herjolf. Hrut was far from happy at his reply, but rode off. All of Hrut's kinsmen, apart from Hoskuld, gave him a proper welcome.

Hrut lived at Kambsnes for three years and sought continually to press Hoskuld for his property at assemblies or other legal gatherings, where he put his case well. Most men said that Hrut was in the right, but Hoskuld maintained that Thorgerd had not obtained his consent to marry Herjolf, and that he was legally his mother's guardian. On this note they parted.

The following autumn Hoskuld accepted an invitation to visit Thord Goddi. Hrut learned of it and rode to Hoskuldsstadir with eleven followers. He took twenty head of cattle, leaving behind an equal number, and sent a messenger to Hoskuld to tell him where the missing cattle could be found. Hoskuld's farmhands lost no time in arming themselves and others nearby were summoned, until fifteen men had gathered. They rode after Hrut, each with as much speed as he could muster.

Hrut and his men did not notice the pursuers until they were only a short distance from the farm at Kambsnes. When they did, they dismounted, tethered their horses and went over to a gravelly stretch of land where Hrut said they would face their pursuers. He said that although he had made slow progress in regaining his property from Hoskuld he would not let it be said that he had fled from his lackeys. Hrut's companions said they would be facing superior numbers. Hrut replied that this was nothing to worry about and said that the more they were, the worse they would fare.

The men of Laxardal jumped down from their horses and prepared to do battle. Hrut told his men to forget the difference in numbers, and led the way against the pursuers. He had a helmet on his head, his sword raised in one hand and a shield in his other. No man fought better. Hrut was so aroused that few of his men could keep up with him. Both sides fought determinedly for a while, but after Hrut had killed two men in a single charge, the men of Laxardal realized that they were no match for him. They then surrendered, and Hrut said their lives should be spared. All of Hoskuld's farmhands who were still alive had been wounded by this time and four of them had been killed. Hrut returned home with substantial wounds but his companions were hardly hurt at all, as he had borne the brunt of the fighting. The site has been called Orrustudal (Battle valley) ever since. Hrut then had all the cattle butchered.

As for Hoskuld, upon hearing of the theft he collected his men together quickly and rode home. They arrived at nearly the same time as the farmhands returned – with a sorry tale to tell. Hoskuld was furious and swore that he did not intend to be robbed by Hrut of livestock and men again. He spent the day gathering supporters. His wife Jorunn approached him and asked what he planned to do.

'I haven't decided on any plan yet, but I hope to give people more to talk about than the death of my farmhands.'

Jorunn answered, 'Your intention is vile if it includes killing a man of your brother's stature. Many people feel that Hrut is only taking what is his by right, and that he should have taken the livestock sooner. His actions show that he does not intend to be written off as a bastard with no claim to property which is rightly his. Nor would he have set out on this errand, and placed himself in open conflict with you, if he did not have reason to expect that powerful men would back him up. I've been told that Hrut has secretly exchanged messages with Thord Bellower, which I find very ominous. Thord Goddi will be more than interested in supporting such a case where so much is at stake. You know only too well, Hoskuld, that since the split between Thord and Vigdis there's been no love lost between you and Thord Bellower and his kinsmen, though you managed to lessen their hostility towards you temporarily with gifts. And I think, Hoskuld,' said Jorunn, 'that they take offence at the way you and your son Olaf have been denying them their share.

'I think you'd better do right by your brother Hrut, for a hungry wolf is bound to wage a hard battle. Hrut will, I'm sure, be more than ready to accept an offer of settlement, as I'm told he is no fool. He must see that it would do honour to both of you.'

Listening to Jorunn's counsel, Hoskuld calmed down and saw the truth of her arguments. Mutual friends were then able to intervene and convey to Hrut Hoskuld's offer of settlement. Hrut responded positively, saying he was certainly willing to reach an agreement with Hoskuld; he had long since been ready to reach an agreement as brothers should, so long as Hoskuld granted him his rights. Hrut also said Hoskuld was entitled to compensation for the damage he had done him. The matters were discussed and an agreement reached between the two brothers, Hoskuld and Hrut. From that time onward the two got along as kinsmen should.

Hrut settled down to farm and became a powerful figure. He was not one to intervene often in other men's affairs, but when he did get involved he was determined to have his way. Hrut moved his farm site a short distance to the south to where the farm Hrutsstadir is located and lived there into his old age. He erected a temple in the hayfield nearby, the remains of which can still be seen. The site is called Trollaskeid (Trolls' path), and is now on the public road.

Hrut married and his wife was Unn, the daughter of Mord Gigja. She later divorced him and this became the beginning of a dispute between the people of Laxardal and of Fljotshlid. Hrut's second wife was Thorbjorg Armodsdottir. He was married to a third woman, whose name is not recorded. With his two later wives Hrut had sixteen sons and ten daughters. It is said that one summer Hrut attended the Althing accompanied by fourteen of his sons. Mention is made of the fact because it was considered an indication of his wealth and power. All of his sons were accomplished men.

20 By now Hoskuld was an elderly man and his sons full-grown. Thorleik built a farm at Kambsnes and Hoskuld turned over to him his share of the property. He then married Gjaflaug, the daughter of Arnbjorn, the son of Sleitu-Bjorn, and his wife Thorlaug Thordardottir from Hofdi. Gjaflaug was both a good-looking and a haughty woman, and was thought a fine match. Thorleik was anything but a peaceable man and was a great warrior. There was no love lost between Thorleik and his kinsman Hrut. Bard, Hoskuld's other son, lived at home with his father and the running of the farm was as much in his hands as Hoskuld's. There is little mention made of Hoskuld's daughters here, although they are known to have descendants. Olaf Hoskuldsson was also a young adult by this time and the most handsome man people had ever seen. He always dressed well and carried fine weapons. Melkorka, Olaf's mother, lived at Melkorkustadir, as was previously mentioned. Hoskuld became more and more reluctant to look after Melkorka's affairs, saying he felt it was just as much Olaf's responsibility

as his, and Olaf said he would offer her whatever help and advice he could.

Melkorka, however, felt humiliated by Hoskuld and made up her mind to repay him in kind. Thorbjorn Pock-marked had looked after most of the farming for Melkorka. Only a short time after she settled on the farm he had asked for her hand in marriage, but Melkorka had refused even to consider the offer. At this time there was a ship beached at Bordeyri in Hrutafjord. The skipper was a man called Orn, a follower of King Harald Gunnhildarson.

The next time Melkorka saw Olaf, she brought up the subject of his journeying abroad to seek out his high-born kinsmen, 'as everything I have told you is true, Myrkjartan is my father and he is king of the Irish. You could take the ship at Bordeyri.'

Olaf said, 'I have mentioned it to my father, and he was not in favour of the idea. And as far as my foster-father goes, his property consists mainly of land and livestock, and he has little in the form of Icelandic export goods.'

Melkorka answered: 'I've had my fill of people calling you the son of a slave-woman. If it's concern about trade goods that is preventing you from making the journey, then I would rather help you out by marrying Thorbjorn, if it means you'll make the journey. I'm sure he'll contribute whatever goods you feel you need for the journey if he gets me as his wife in the bargain.

'There is another advantage to this as well – it will give Hoskuld a double sting when he learns that you have left the country and I am married.'

Olaf said it was up to his mother to decide. Soon afterwards he spoke to Thorbjorn and asked him to provide him with a large quantity of export goods on loan.

Thorbjorn replied: 'Only on one condition, that I reach a marriage agreement with Melkorka. Then you can consider my property to be just as much yours as anything else you have at your disposal.'

Olaf told Thorbjorn he had himself a bargain. They discussed the details of the transaction, and agreed that it should remain a secret.

Hoskuld asked Olaf if he would accompany him to the Althing but Olaf replied that he was too occupied on the farm. He said he had to see about having a pasture walled off for his lambs down by the river Laxa. Hoskuld was pleased at Olaf's reply, and his apparent interest in the farm. No sooner had Hoskuld departed for the Althing than wedding feasting got under way at Lambastadir. Olaf set the conditions of the wedding agreement himself. He chose thirty hundreds of goods off the top, before the property was divided [between Thorbjorn and Melkorka], for which he was to make no payment. Bard Hoskuldsson attended the wedding and knew of their plans.

When the ceremonies were over, Olaf rode to the ship, met with Orn, the skipper, and arranged his passage. Before he left, his mother Melkorka handed Olaf a heavy gold arm ring, saying: 'This treasure my father gave me when I cut my first tooth, and he'll surely recognize it when he sees it again.'

She also gave him a knife and belt which he was to hand over to her nurse – 'who will not fail to know what these tokens mean'.

'I've now done all I can to help you,' Melkorka continued. 'I've also taught you to speak Irish, so that you'll be able to speak to people anywhere you make land in Ireland.'

They then parted. A favourable wind rose as Olaf reached the ship and they put out to sea at once.

21 Hoskuld returned from the Althing to be told the news. He was far from pleased, but as his own family were involved, he soon calmed down and took no action. Olaf and his shipmates had a good passage and made land in Norway.

Orn urged Olaf to go to pay his respects to King Harald, saying that men who had less to recommend them than Olaf had been handsomely received by the king. Olaf said he would take his advice. Olaf and Orn then proceeded to where the king sat and were well received; the king welcomed Olaf warmly as soon as he learned who his kinsmen were, and lost no time in offering him a place among his followers. Upon hearing he was Hrut's nephew, Gunnhild also took a great liking to him. Some people even said that she would have enjoyed Olaf's company regardless of who his kinsmen were. As the winter progressed, Olaf grew moody and Orn asked what was troubling him.

Olaf answered: 'I have to make the journey to the Western Isles. It's very important to me that you arrange it so that we make the voyage this summer.'

Orn told Olaf to forget the idea, saying he knew of no ship journeying westward.

As they were talking, Gunnhild came up and spoke: 'Now I hear something I have never heard before: the two of you disagreeing on anything.'

Olaf welcomed Gunnhild warmly but did not change the subject of their discussion. Orn left, and Olaf and Gunnhild continued the conversation. Olaf told her of his intentions and how important the journey was for him.

He said he knew for certain that King Myrkjartan was his grandfather.

To this Gunnhild replied: 'I will support your journey so that you can go as well equipped as you wish.'

Olaf thanked her for the offer. Gunnhild then ordered a ship to be made ready and manned, asking Olaf how many men he wished to have accompany him on his journey. Olaf asked for sixty men, and stressed the importance of choosing men who were more like warriors than merchants. She promised to see to this. Of Olaf's companions only Orn is named.

The company was well turned out. King Harald and Gunnhild accompanied Olaf to his ship and said they hoped their own good fortune would follow him along with their goodwill. King Harald added that this would not be difficult, as he had seen no young man more promising among the Icelanders of the time. King Harald then asked how old Olaf was.

Olaf replied: 'I am now eighteen years old.'

The king spoke: 'You will make the finest of men, as capable as you are and still barely more than a child. Come to us directly upon your return.'

Then the king and Gunnhild said farewell.

Olaf boarded his ship and they sailed out to sea. They had poor winds during the summer, the breezes light and blowing from the wrong direction, and spells of thick fog. They drifted long distances at sea. Most of the men on board soon lost their sense of direction. Eventually the fog lifted and a wind came up. The sail was hoisted and a discussion began on which direction to take to head to Ireland. There was no agreement among the men on the question: Orn was of one opinion, but most of the men were opposed and declared that Orn was wrong and that the majority should determine their course.

The question was put to Olaf, who said, 'Let the man of best judgement determine our course; the counsel of fools is the more misguided the more of them there are.'

The question was considered decided by Olaf's words, and from then on Orn decided on their course. They sailed night and day for several days, with little wind, until one night the men on watch leapt up and woke the others. They said they had seen land very close to the bow of the ship, and the sail was still up and only a light breeze blowing. The others jumped up at once and Orn told them to steer out to sea at once if they could.

'There's no point in us doing that,' Olaf said. 'I can see from the way the waves break there are skerries on all sides; reef the sail as quickly as you can. We'll discuss what course to take when it grows light and we can see what land this is.'

They cast the anchor, which struck bottom at once.

During the night there was considerable discussion as to where they might be, and when the day dawned they saw that it was Ireland.

Orn then spoke: 'I'm afraid we won't be well received. We're far from any port or merchant town where foreigners are assured of trading in peace, and now the tide has gone out and left us stranded here like a minnow. It's my guess that, according to Irish law, they'll lay claim to all the property we have on board; they call it a stranded ship when less than this has ebbed from the stern of the ship.'

Olaf said they would come to no harm. 'But I did see a group of men up on shore today, and the arrival of our ship is obviously news to the Irish. I checked the coastline carefully while the tide was out. There is a river flowing into the sea beside this point and water in the estuary even when the tide ebbs. If our ship is not damaged, I think we should put out our boat and draw the ship over there.'

The beach was clay where the ship lay at anchor, so that not a single plank was damaged. They moved the ship as Olaf suggested and dropped anchor there.

Later that day a large crowd of people came down to the beach. Two of them approached in a boat to ask who was in command of the ship. Olaf replied to them in Irish, as they had spoken in that tongue. When the Irish learned that they were Norse, they referred to their laws on ship strandings and said that if the ship's company handed over all the property on board they would be unharmed until the king had pronounced his judgement in their case. Olaf said that this was indeed the law if there was no interpreter among the traders.

'I warn you, we are men of peace but we don't intend to give up without a fight.'

Giving a war cry, the Irish charged into the sea, intending to wade out to the ship and draw it ashore with them aboard. The water was so shallow that it only came up to their armpits and just above the belts of the tallest of them. The pool where the ship was anchored was so deep, however, that they could not touch bottom. Olaf told his men to get their weapons out and form a line along the sides of the ship. They stood so close together that their shields formed an unbroken row, with a spear point extending from the lower end of each shield. Olaf took up position in the bow. He wore a coat of mail and on his head a helmet with golden plates. At his waist was a sword, its hilt inlaid with gold, and in his hand he held a spear with a hooked blade, also highly decorated. Before him he held a red shield, with the design of a lion in gold.

The sight of their readiness for battle struck fear into the hearts of the Irish, and they realized that the ship was not the easy prey they had imagined. They turned back and gathered in a group. Many were greatly upset, thinking this was obviously a vessel of war and likely to be followed by a number of others. They sent word to the king, who was visiting nearby. He came at once to the spot where the ship lay at anchor, accompanied by a group of followers. The distance between ship and shore was so narrow that it was possible to call from one to the other. The Irish had made several attacks, shooting arrows and casting spears, without any of Olaf's men coming to harm. Olaf stood in the bow attired as previously described, and people were greatly impressed by the imposing-looking leader of the ship.

Olaf's companions fell silent when they saw a group of horsemen approach, well armed and valiant-looking, as it now appeared they would have to face far superior forces.

When Olaf heard the words of concern expressed by his companions, however, he told them to pull themselves together – 'as our situation has taken a turn for the better. The Irish are now welcoming their king, Myrkjartan.'

The procession on shore then came near enough to exchange words with the men on board ship. The king asked who the skipper of the ship was. Olaf gave his name and asked in return who this valiant knight was with whom he spoke.

'My name is Myrkjartan,' he answered.

When Olaf asked, 'Are you then the king of the Irish?', he replied that he was.

Then the king asked for general news and Olaf provided suitable answers to all his questions, following which the king asked where they had sailed from and who they were. He enquired more carefully into Olaf's kin than before, as he realized that this man was both proud and careful to say no more than he was asked.

Olaf said, 'For your information we set sail from Norway, and the men on board are followers of King Harald Gunnhildarson. As to my own kin, my lord, my father who lives in Iceland is named Hoskuld, and is a man of a prominent family. As far as my mother's kinsmen are concerned, I expect you know more about them than I do; her name is Melkorka and I have been told truly that she is your own daughter, King. This was my reason for making such a lengthy journey, and it is of great importance to me to hear what reply you make to my words.'

Upon hearing this the king fell silent and went to speak to his followers. Learned men asked the king what truth there was in the words the man spoke. The king answered:

'This Olaf is obviously a man of high birth, whether or not he is our kinsman, and no one speaks better Irish.'

The king then got to his feet and spoke: 'My reply to your words is to grant protection to all of your companions on board. As to your kinship with us, we will have to discuss the question more fully before I can give you an answer.'

Gangways were then put out to the ship and Olaf went ashore, followed by his men. The Irish were impressed by their rugged appearance.

Olaf greeted the king courteously, removed his helmet and knelt before him, and the king welcomed him warmly. They began a discussion; Olaf repeated his story, speaking at length and with effect.

In conclusion he referred to the gold ring on his arm, which Melkorka had handed over to him at their parting in Iceland, 'saying that you, my lord, had given it to her when she cut her first tooth'.

The king took the ring in his hand and upon examining it, his face grew very red.

He then spoke: 'These tokens are irrefutable, and are even more convincing because you resemble your mother so much that you could be recognized by that alone. Such being the case, I do not hesitate to acknowledge you as my kinsman, Olaf, and may all who hear my words bear this witness. I therefore invite you, and all your men, to my court. What honour you receive there will depend upon the man you prove yourself to be when I put you to the test.'

The king obtained horses for them and appointed men to stand guard over their ship and cargo. The king then rode to Dublin and the news that the king was accompanied by his grandson, the son of his daughter who had been taken prisoner at the age of fifteen years, caused great stir. No one was more affected by the news than Melkorka's nurse. Despite being bedridden with old age and illness she rose and went, without the aid of her stick, to meet Olaf.

The king then told Olaf: 'The woman approaching was Melkorka's nurse and she will ask you for news of her.'

Olaf received her with open arms, set her upon his lap and told her that her former charge was living in comfort in Iceland. Then Olaf handed her the belt and knife, which the old woman recognized at once, and tears of joy came to her eyes.

She said her happiness was doubled by seeing this outstanding young son of Melkorka's – 'just like you'd expect from one of his kin'.

The old woman enjoyed good health for the rest of that winter.

The king seldom remained long in one place, as there was generally fighting somewhere in the British Isles. He spent the winter warding off both Vikings and other raiders. Olaf and his men fought with the king on his ship, and those they were pitted against found them hard to handle. The king soon came to seek the advice of Olaf and his men in all decisions, for he discovered him to be a clever and daring commander. As the winter drew to a close, the king called an assembly, which great numbers of people attended. The king addressed the assembly, beginning his speech with the following words:

'As you know, this past autumn a man came to us who proved to be the son of my daughter, and of good family on his father's side as well. Olaf has since shown himself to be highly accomplished and a man of such determination that we have no one in our kingdom to equal him. I wish Olaf to inherit the crown after my day, as he is better suited to rule than are my sons.'

Olaf thanked him for his offer with many well-chosen words and fair praise, but said he would not take the chance of having to deal with the reaction of Myrkjartan's sons after his death. He would rather, he said, enjoy a brief spell of honour than a long rule of shame. He said he intended to return to Norway as soon as the weather made it safe for ships to make the journey between the countries, and it would bring little joy to his mother should he fail to return. The king said it was up to Olaf to decide, and the assembly was then dissolved.

When Olaf was ready to sail, the king accompanied him to the ship and gave him a spear with gold inlay, a decorated sword and much other wealth. Olaf asked to take Melkorka's nurse with him, but the king said there was no need to do so, and so she remained. Olaf and his men boarded their ship and he and the king parted as great friends. Then Olaf and his men put to sea and had favourable winds until they made land in Norway, where news of Olaf's voyage spread widely. They beached their ship and Olaf obtained horses for himself and his companions to make the journey to King Harald.

22   When Olaf Hoskuldsson came to him, King Harald received him well, but Gunnhild better still. They invited him to stay with them, and pressed him to accept. Olaf agreed and both he and Orn became king's men. The king and Gunnhild showed Olaf more honour than any other foreigner had ever been shown. Olaf gave them a number of rare and precious objects which he had brought with him from Ireland. At Christmas the king gave Olaf a complete suit of clothes made from scarlet.*

Olaf remained with the king over the winter, but as spring passed he spoke privately to the king and asked his leave to journey to Iceland that summer.

'Many prominent kinsmen await me there,' he said.

'If I could decide,' the king answered, 'I would rather you settled here with me on whatever terms you choose.'

Olaf thanked the king for the honour he showed him but said he would prefer to go to Iceland, if the king did not oppose it.

Then the king answered, 'I'll not detain you against your wishes, Olaf. You will journey to Iceland this summer, as I can see your heart is set on doing so, but don't bother about making the preparations, for I will have that taken care of.'

On this note their conversation concluded.

King Harald had a ship set afloat that spring, a knorr, of good size and seaworthy. He had it loaded with timber and all necessary provisions and, when the ship was ready, he sent for Olaf and said, 'This ship is yours, Olaf. I won't have you sail from Norway this summer as another man's passenger.'

Olaf thanked the king profusely for his generosity. After completing his preparations to leave, he sailed his ship out to sea, taking leave of King Harald on the best of terms. Olaf was favoured by good winds that summer. His ship sailed south into Hrutafjord and landed at Bordeyri. News of the ship's arrival, and of its skipper, spread quickly. Hoskuld was very glad to learn of his son's return and set out at once northwards towards Hrutafjord, accompanied by several men. After a warm reunion, Hoskuld invited Olaf to come home and stay with them, and Olaf accepted. He had his ship beached

---

* Brightly dyed woollen material. The original *skarlat* is somewhat deceptive as the cloth could be red, but also dark brown, blue, grey or even white.

and his property sent south, then rode with eleven men to Hoskuldsstadir. Hoskuld gave his son a warm welcome, and his half-brothers also received him well, especially Bard.

Olaf became renowned as a result of his journey and the news that he was the grandson of Myrkjartan, king of the Irish. The story spread throughout Iceland, together with reports of the honour the powerful men whom he had visited had shown him. Olaf had also brought great wealth home.

He spent the winter at his father's farm. Melkorka soon came to meet her son and Olaf welcomed her warmly. She had much to ask him about Ireland, beginning with news of her father and other kinsmen. Olaf answered all her questions. She soon enquired whether her nurse was still alive, and Olaf replied, that yes, she was still living. Then Melkorka asked why he had not done her the favour of bringing the woman to Iceland.

To this Olaf replied: 'They did not want me, Mother, to bring your nurse with me to Iceland.'

'As you say,' Melkorka said, but it was evident that she was very disappointed.

Melkorka and Thorbjorn had a son called Lambi. He was a big, strong man, much like his father both in appearance and disposition.

The next spring following Olaf's return to Iceland, father and son discussed plans for his future.

'I suggest, Olaf,' said Hoskuld, 'seeking a wife for you and having you take over the farm at Goddastadir from your foster-father. It's still a good piece of property; you would take over the farm under my direction.'

Olaf replied: 'I haven't thought about it very much yet, nor do I know where I should find a woman it would do me honour to marry. As you can imagine, I won't be satisfied with anything but the best of matches. But I'm sure you wouldn't have brought the matter up, had you not already decided where it should come down.'

Hoskuld said, 'You're right about that. A man named Egil, the son of Skallagrim, lives at Borg in Borgarfjord. Egil has a daughter named Thorgerd whom I intend to seek as a wife for you, as there's no better match in all of Borgarfjord, or far beyond, for that matter. What's more it will strengthen your position to make an alliance with the Myrar family.'

Olaf replied: 'I'll take your advice in the matter, as it seems a good enough proposal – if it's accepted. But I warn you, father, that if we bring up the question only to be turned down, I'll be very annoyed.'

Hoskuld said, 'I'll take the risk of raising the question.'

Olaf said he would take his advice.

The time of the Althing approached and Hoskuld prepared to make the journey with a large number of followers, including his son Olaf. They set up their booth at the Althing. A great number of people were there, among them Egil Skallagrimsson. Everyone who saw Olaf remarked on how handsome and imposing a figure he was. He was well dressed and carried fine weapons.

23 One day, it is said, Olaf and Hoskuld paid a visit to Egil's booth. Egil received them warmly, for he and Hoskuld knew each other well. Hoskuld brought up the question of a match between Olaf and Egil's daughter Thorgerd, who was also attending the Althing. Egil responded positively to the idea, saying he had heard nothing but favourable reports of both father and son.

'I know, Hoskuld,' Egil said, 'that you're highly respected and a man of prominent family, while Olaf has become renowned for his journey abroad. It hardly comes as a surprise that such men, lacking neither good looks nor a good family, should set their sights high. But the question will have to be taken up with Thorgerd, because there's no man who could make Thorgerd his wife should she be set against it.'

Hoskuld said, 'I would like you, Egil, to discuss it with your daughter.'

Egil agreed and later spoke to Thorgerd privately.

'There's a man called Olaf, the son of Hoskuld,' Egil said, 'one of the most renowned in the country. His father has asked for your hand in marriage on his son's behalf. I have referred the question to you, and wait to hear what you say, but it seems to me that such a request deserves a good answer, as it's a good match.'

Thorgerd answered: 'I have heard you say, Father, that of all your children I was your favourite. It seems to me that can hardly be true if you intend to marry me to some slave-girl's son, however handsome and renowned he may be.'

Egil said, 'Your nose for news doesn't seem to have served you as well as usual in this instance; haven't you heard that he is the grandson of the Irish king, Myrkjartan? He's of even better family on his mother's side than his father's, which by itself would be more than good enough for us.'

Thorgerd was unconvinced, and the conversation ended in disagreement. The following day Egil went to Hoskuld's booth where he was well received. The two men spoke privately and Hoskuld asked for news of the marriage proposal. Egil said the prospects looked glum and related what had happened.

Hoskuld agreed that it did look difficult – 'but I still think you are doing the right thing'.

After Egil had left, Olaf, who had been elsewhere while they talked, asked for news of the marriage proposal. Hoskuld replied that Thorgerd seemed reluctant.

Olaf spoke: 'It's turned out just as I feared, father, and as I told you I am hardly pleased at being disgraced by a refusal. It was your idea to start this business; now I intend to carry it through to the proper end. It's true enough as they say, when one wolf hunts for another he may eat the prey. I'm going to pay Egil a visit.'

Hoskuld said it was up to him to decide.

Olaf was wearing the suit of scarlet which King Harald had given him, a gold-plated helmet on his head and the sword given to him by King Myrkjartan. Father and son set out for Egil's booth, with Hoskuld in the lead and Olaf following. Egil welcomed them warmly and Hoskuld sat down beside him, but Olaf remained standing and looked about the tent. He noticed a woman, seated on a cross-bench, who was both good-looking and well attired, and decided this must be Egil's daughter, Thorgerd.

Olaf approached the cross-bench and took a seat beside her. Thorgerd greeted him and asked who he was.

Olaf told her his own name and his father's, and added, 'You must think it bold of a slave-girl's son to dare to sit down beside you and strike up a conversation with you.'

Thorgerd replied, 'You must think you've done more dangerous things in your life than talk to women.'

The two of them then spent most of the day in conversation but no one else heard what they spoke about. Before they were finished, however, Hoskuld and Egil were called over, and discussion of the proposal of marriage began anew. Thorgerd agreed to abide by her father's decision and, as his consent was given readily, the two were betrothed then and there. The bride was to be brought to the wedding as an indication of respect for the people of Laxardal. It was agreed the wedding should be at Hoskuldsstadir when seven weeks of summer were remaining.

The families then parted, and Olaf and Hoskuld rode home to Hoskuldsstadir where the summer passed without event. Preparations commenced for the wedding, with nothing spared, for this was a wealthy family. The guests arrived at the appointed time. People from Borgarfjord came in great number, led by Egil and his son Thorstein, the bride and the leaders of the entire district. Hoskuld's own guests also attended in great number. The festival was outstanding and the visitors given handsome gifts at parting. Olaf gave the sword, Myrkjartan's Gift, to Egil, who made no attempt to conceal his great pleasure at the gift. Everything proceeded without event and afterwards people all returned to their homes.

24 Olaf and Thorgerd stayed at Hoskuldsstadir and cared greatly for each other. Everyone soon realized what a woman of strong character Thorgerd was: though she was not one to waste words, once she set her mind on something there was no swaying her – things had to go the way she wanted. Olaf and Thorgerd spent the winter months either at Hoskuldsstadir or with Olaf's foster-father, Thord Goddi. In the spring Olaf took over the farm at Goddastadir, and that summer Thord was taken ill and died. Olaf had him buried in a mound at the spot called Drafnarnes on the banks of the Laxa river. A stone wall near the site was called Haugsgard (Mound wall).

Olaf soon had no lack of supporters and became an important chieftain. Hoskuld in no way resented this, and even urged that Olaf be consulted in all affairs of importance. Olaf's farm was soon the most impressive in Laxardal. Among the members of his household were two brothers, both of whom were named An – one An the White, the other An the Black. A third servant was known as Beinir the Strong. They were good carpenters and capable men. Thorgerd and Olaf had a daughter named Thurid.

The lands which Hrapp had owned were deserted, as was previously written. Olaf thought this a likely piece of land, as it bordered on his own, and suggested to his father that they pay a visit to Thorkel Scarf to purchase the land at Hrappsstadir and other property connected to it. Their offer was readily accepted and the purchase concluded, as Thorkel felt that a bird in the hand was better than two in the bush. According to the terms of the bargain, Olaf was to pay three marks of silver for the lands, which was far below their worth. They included large stretches of prime pasture and plenty of other benefits, including salmon fishing and seal hunting, and large forests as well.

A short distance upriver from Hoskuldsstadir, on the north side of the Laxa, a grove had been cleared in the forest. Olaf's sheep could, more often than not, be found gathered in this clearing in both fair weather and foul.

One autumn Olaf had a house built in this same clearing, using wood from the forest as well as driftwood. The large and imposing house stood empty the first winter. The following summer Olaf moved his household there, after having rounded up his stock beforehand. This was no small herd, as no one in the Breidafjord district owned more livestock.

Olaf sent a request that his father stand outside where he could watch them go by on their way to the new farm and wish them good fortune, and Hoskuld agreed. Olaf then organized the procession: the men at the front drove the sheep which were most difficult to handle. Next came the milking ewes and cattle from the home pastures, followed by steers, calves and heifers, with the packhorses bringing up the rear. The members of the household were placed at close intervals to keep the livestock from straying off course. Those at the front had reached the new farm when Olaf himself rode out of the yard at Goddastadir, and the line stretched unbroken between them.

Hoskuld and his household stood outside on the farm.

He spoke words of congratulation, wishing his son Olaf fair tidings and good fortune in his new residence, 'and unless I guess wrongly things will turn out that way, and his name be long remembered'.

His wife Jorunn responded, saying 'with his wealth the slave-woman's son should be able to make a name for himself'.

The farmhands had just finished taking the packs off the horses when Olaf rode into the yard.

He addressed his household: 'You must be curious to know what the farm is to be called, and I know there has been a lot of speculation about it all winter. It will be called Hjardarholt (Herd wood).'

Everyone thought it a very good idea to take a name linked to the events which had occurred on the site. Olaf set about building up his farm at Hjardarholt, and the farm was soon an impressive one, lacking nothing. Olaf's own repute grew for a number of reasons: he himself was very popular, especially since he managed to resolve the disputes in which his advice was sought in such a manner that everyone was satisfied. His father did much to increase his honour, and his marriage alliance with the Myrar family was also to his credit. Olaf was thought to be the most outstanding of Hoskuld's sons.

During the first winter in Hjardarholt Olaf had a large number of resident servants and other farmhands. The farm chores were divided among the servants: some looked after the non-milking stock, others the milking cows. The cowshed was located in the forest some distance away from the farmhouse.

One evening the farmhand in charge of the non-milking cattle came to Olaf and asked him to assign the task to someone else and 'give me other duties'.

Olaf answered, 'I want you to look after your own duties.'

The man replied he would rather leave the farm.

'Then you must think something is seriously wrong,' Olaf said. 'I'll accompany you tonight when you tie the animals in their stalls, and if you've any cause for complaint, I won't blame you. Otherwise you'll pay for causing trouble.'

Olaf then took the spear known as the King's Gift in his hand and went out, the servant following him. Quite a lot of snow had fallen.

They reached the cowshed, which stood open, and Olaf told the servant to go inside, saying, 'I'll herd the animals inside for you and you tie them in their places.'

The servant went towards the door of the cowshed but suddenly came running back into Olaf's arms.

When Olaf asked what had frightened him so, the servant answered, 'Hrapp is standing there in the doorway, reaching out for me, and I've had my fill of wrestling with him.'

Olaf approached the door and prodded with his spear in Hrapp's direction. Hrapp gripped the spear just above the blade in both his hands and gave it a wrench, breaking the shaft. Olaf made a run at him, but Hrapp let himself sink back down to where he had come from, putting an end to their struggle. Olaf stood there with the spear shaft in his hand, for Hrapp had taken the blade.

Olaf and the servant tied the cattle in their places and returned to the farm where Olaf said the servant would not be punished for complaining. The following morning Olaf went out to where Hrapp had been buried and had him dug up. Hrapp's body was perfectly preserved and Olaf found his spear blade there. He then had a large bonfire prepared, and had Hrapp's body burned and his ashes taken out to sea. No one else was harmed by Hrapp's haunting after that.

25 The story now turns to Hoskuld's sons. Before he settled on his farm, Thorleik Hoskuldsson had been a successful merchant. He consorted with many men of noble birth abroad, and was considered a man of some note. He had also gone on Viking expeditions and earned himself a good reputation as a bold fighter. Bard Hoskuldsson had also been a merchant,

and was both liked and respected everywhere he went, for he treated others fairly and was easy-going about everything. Bard married a woman of Breidafjord named Astrid, who was of good family. Bard had a son named Thorarin and a daughter, Gudny, who was married to Hall, the son of Killer-Styr. They had a great number of descendants.

Hrut Herjolfsson gave his slave, Hrolf, his freedom, along with some livestock and a home-site on the border of his land and Hoskuld's. It lay so near the borderline, in fact, that Hrut and his men miscalculated and placed the freed slave on property that was actually Hoskuld's. He prospered and soon had a great deal of wealth.

Hoskuld was not pleased at Hrut settling his freed slave practically in his backyard and demanded that the man pay him for the land upon which he dwelt, 'as it is my property'.

Hrolf went and told this to Hrut, who said he should pay no attention to Hoskuld and refuse to pay him. 'I'm not at all sure,' he said, 'which of us actually owned that land.'

The freed slave returned home and continued his farming as before. Shortly afterwards Thorleik Hoskuldsson, acting on his father's bidding, went to Hrolf's farm with several men and killed him. Thorleik claimed for himself and his father all the wealth which the freed slave had acquired while dwelling there.

Hrut and his sons heard of this and were very angry. Many of his sons were now grown up and the family was an intimidating lot. Hrut tried prosecution to achieve compensation, but when men learned in law investigated the case, they gave Hrut scant hope of success. The main point was that Hrut had placed the freed slave on land belonging to Hoskuld without his permission and there his wealth had increased. Thorleik had killed a trespasser on land belonging to him and his father. Hrut was not happy with his lot, but so it was.

Afterwards Thorleik built a farm on the border of the lands owned by his father and Hrut, which was called Kambsnes, where he lived for some time, as has been mentioned. A son was born to Thorleik and his wife, sprinkled with water and given the name Bolli. He soon showed himself to be a promising child.

26 Hoskuld Dala-Kollsson fell ill in his old age and sent for his sons and other kinsmen.

When they arrived Hoskuld spoke to the brothers, Bard and Thorleik: 'An affliction has settled over me, although I've seldom been ill, and I expect this illness will put an end to me. Both of you know how things stand: as my legitimate sons you inherit all my property. I have a third son, who is illegitimate, and I ask you brothers to allow Olaf to be recognized so that each of you will inherit a third of my property.'

Bard was the first to answer and said that he would do as his father wished, 'as I expect Olaf to treat us fairly, the more so as he is much wealthier'.

Thorleik then said, 'I won't have Olaf acknowledged as heir. He has plenty of wealth already. You, Father, have given him many things and for some time now discriminated greatly between us brothers. I won't voluntarily give up my birthright.'

Hoskuld spoke: 'You can't wish to deprive me of my legal right to give my son twelve ounces for his inheritance, if only in recognition of Olaf's high birth on his mother's side.'

Thorleik consented to this. Hoskuld then took his gifts from King Hakon, a gold arm ring which weighed a mark and sword which was worth half a mark of gold, and gave them to his son Olaf, wishing him all his own good fortune and that of his kinsmen. Hoskuld added that despite his words he was not unaware that this fortune had already found its way to Olaf.

Olaf said he would take a chance on Thorleik's reaction and accepted the gifts. Thorleik was very angry, and felt that Hoskuld had tricked him.

Olaf answered: 'I don't intend to return the objects, Thorleik, as you consented to the gift in the presence of witnesses. I'll take my chances on keeping them.'

Bard said he would abide by his father's wishes. Hoskuld died soon afterwards and was greatly mourned, especially by his sons and all his kinsmen, in-laws and friends. His sons had a suitable mound built for his burial, but buried little wealth with him. Afterwards, the brothers discussed among themselves the holding of a memorial feast, a custom which had become fashionable at that time.

Olaf said, 'To my mind we won't be able to hold this feast right away, if we intend to make it grand enough to do us credit. It's late autumn already and not easy to collect the provisions we need. Many people, who have a long way to travel, will think making the journey in the autumn too difficult, and we can be sure that a lot of the people we want most to attend wouldn't come in fact. I suggest we announce the feast at the Althing next summer instead. I'll pay a third of the cost.'

The brothers agreed to this and Olaf returned home. Thorleik and Bard divided the inheritance between them. Bard took over their father's farm, as he had more supporters and was the more popular, while Thorleik received a larger share of the goods and livestock. Relations between Olaf and Bard were warm, but rather cool between Olaf and Thorleik. The winter passed and summer came and soon it was time for the Althing. When the Hoskuldssons got ready to attend the Althing it was evident that Olaf would take the lead. Upon arriving they set up their booth in fine style.

27   It is said that one day, as men were gathering at the Law Rock, Olaf got to his feet and called for attention.

He began by recalling his father's death: 'As many of his kinsmen and friends are here today, my brothers and I would like to invite all of you godis to a feast in honour of our father, Hoskuld, as most of you leading men were connected to him by marriage. I can also promise you that no man of influence will leave empty-handed. In addition, we invite farmers and any others who care to come, whether beggars or their betters, to attend this fortnight's feast at Hoskuldsstadir when ten weeks of summer remain.'

When Olaf had finished speaking, there was general approval of his speech and generosity. He returned to the booth and told his brothers of his plans, but they were not at all enthusiastic and felt he had gone too far. After the assembly the brothers returned home. The summer passed and they began preparations for the feast. Olaf contributed his third and more, and the feast was very sumptuous. Great quantities of supplies were needed, as large numbers of guests were expected. Most of the prominent people who had promised to come attended the feast at the appointed time. There were so many people that most reports put the figure at over a thousand guests. It was the second-largest feast ever held in Iceland, the largest being the memorial feast held by the Hjaltasons in memory of their father, which was attended by over fourteen hundred people.

The feast was grand in every respect and a great credit to the brothers, especially Olaf. For the parting presents, which were given to all the important men, he contributed a share equal to that of both his brothers.

When most of the guests had left, Olaf turned to his brother Thorleik and said, 'Brother, as you well know, we have shown each other little affection in the past. I wish we could do better in the future. I know you resented my accepting the gifts from our father on his deathbed and if you still feel yourself hard done by, I would like to make it up to you by fostering your son, as he who raises the child of another is always considered as the lesser of the two.'

Thorleik was pleased by the offer, and agreed that it did him great honour. Olaf then took over the upbringing of Thorleik's son Bolli, who was three years of age at the time. They parted on the best of terms, with Bolli returning home to Hjardarholt with Olaf. Thorgerd welcomed him warmly and Bolli grew up with them. They loved him no less than their own children.

28   Olaf and Thorgerd had a son. He was sprinkled with water and given the name Kjartan, after his grandfather Myrkjartan, and was almost the same age as Bolli. They had other children as well: their sons were Steinthor, Halldor and Helgi, and the youngest was Hoskuld. They had two daughters: Bergthora and Thorbjorg. All their children grew up into promising youngsters.

In Saurbaer, on the farm called Tunga, there lived a man called Bersi the Dueller. He came to Olaf and offered to foster his son Halldor. Olaf accepted the offer and Bersi took Halldor, who was a year old at the time, home with him. That same summer Bersi grew ill, and was bedridden for most of the summer. It is said that one day the household at Tunga were out haying and only the two of them, Halldor and Bersi, at home. Halldor lay in a cradle, which fell on one side and the youngster rolled out. Bersi couldn't get up to help him, and spoke the following verse:

1.   Both of us lie,
       flat on our backs,
       Halldor and I
       helpless and frail.
       Old age does this to me,
       but youth to you,
       you've hope of better,
       but I, none at all.

People soon returned home and picked Halldor up off the floor, and Bersi got better again. Halldor grew up at Tunga and was a large and robust man.

Kjartan Olafsson grew up with his parents at Hjardarholt. No fairer or more handsome man has ever been born in Iceland. He had a broad face and regular features, the most beautiful eyes and a fair complexion. His hair was thick and as shiny as silk, and fell in waves. He was a big, strong man, much like his grandfather, Egil, or Thorolf. No man cut a better figure than Kjartan, and people were always struck by his appearance when they saw him. He was a better fighter than most, skilled with his hands, and a top swimmer. He was superior to other men in all skills, and yet he was the humblest of men, and so popular that every child loved him. He also had a generous and cheerful disposition. Of all his children, Kjartan was Olaf's favourite.

His foster-brother, Bolli, grew into a large man. Next to Kjartan, he was the best at all skills and in other accomplishments. He was strong and handsome, a top fighter, with good manners and fond of fine clothes. The foster-brothers cared deeply for one another. Olaf stayed at home on his farm for many years after that.

29 It is said that one spring Olaf announced to Thorgerd that he intended to travel abroad, 'and I want you to look after our farm and family while I'm away'.

Thorgerd said she was not in favour of the idea, but Olaf said he intended to have his way. He bought a ship which was beached at Vadil and sailed abroad that summer. He made land in the Hordaland district. A short distance from shore lived a man known as Geirmund Thunder, a powerful and wealthy man and a great Viking. He was a troublemaker, who had settled down and become a follower of Earl Hakon the Powerful.

Geirmund went down to the ship and, on hearing his name, recognized Olaf from the stories he had heard of him. He invited Olaf to come and stay with him and bring as many men as he wished. Olaf accepted his offer and went to stay with him, taking five others with him. The rest of the crew were placed on various farms in Hordaland. Geirmund treated Olaf well. He had a large farmhouse and a large household; in the winter there was plenty of entertainment.

As spring approached, Olaf told Geirmund that the purpose of his voyage was to get building timber and that it was of great importance to him to get a prime selection of timber.

Geirmund replied: 'Earl Hakon owns the best forest around. I'm sure that if you seek his help, it'll be within your reach. Men who have less to recommend them than you, Olaf, have been handsomely received by the earl when they paid him a visit.'

In the spring Olaf prepared for his journey to Earl Hakon. He was warmly received by the earl, who invited him to stay with him as long as he wished.

Olaf told the earl the reasons for his voyage. 'I would like to request permission to cut lumber in your forest, my lord.'

The earl replied: 'It's an honour for me to fill your ship with wood from the forest, as it is not every day we receive guests like you from Iceland.'

In parting the earl gave Olaf an axe inlaid with gold, a prize weapon, and they parted the best of friends. Geirmund had secretly put others in charge of his lands and planned on going to Iceland that summer aboard Olaf's ship. He had kept this a secret from everybody, and before Olaf realized what was happening Geirmund had had all his wealth, which was no small sum, loaded aboard the ship.

Olaf said, 'You'd not be travelling aboard my ship if I'd known of your plans earlier, as I suspect it would be better if some people in Iceland never laid eyes upon you. But since you're here, with all your property, I can hardly run you off my ship like some stray dog.'

Geirmund said, 'I'm not about to turn back, despite your harsh words, and I'm not asking you for free passage.'

Both he and Olaf boarded the ship and sailed out to sea. They had favourable winds and made land in Breidafjord, setting the gangways ashore at the mouth of the Laxa river. Olaf had the timber unloaded and the ship drawn up into the boatshed which his father had had built. He invited Geirmund to stay at his farm.

That summer Olaf had a fire-hall built at Hjardarholt which was larger and grander than men had ever seen before. On the wood of the gables, and the rafters, ornamental tales were carved. It was so well crafted that it was thought more ornamental without the tapestries than with them.

Geirmund was a sullen man and made little effort to get along with most people. He usually wore a red woollen tunic with a grey fur cloak about his shoulders, and had a hat of bearskin on his head and a sword in his hand. His sword was a fine weapon, with a hilt of walrus ivory. It had no silver overlay, but the blade was sharp and without a spot of rust. He called the sword Leg-biter and never let it out of his sight.

Geirmund had only stayed with Olaf a short time when he began to fancy his daughter Thurid. He put a proposal of marriage to Olaf, who turned him down. Geirmund then approached Thorgerd and offered her money if she would support his suit. She accepted the money, which was no petty sum, and soon raised the subject with Olaf.

She said that in her opinion, their daughter could not wish for a better match – 'He's a great warrior, rich and generous with his money.'

To this Olaf replied, 'Have it your own way then, as you do in most things, but I would rather marry Thurid to someone else.'

Thorgerd went off highly satisfied with her efforts and told Geirmund of the results. He thanked her for interceding on his behalf and for her determination. When he approached Olaf a second time he received his consent. Geirmund was then engaged to Thurid, and their wedding was held later that winter at Hjardarholt. A great number of people attended the feast as the fire-hall was finished by that time. Among the guests was a poet, Ulf Uggason, who had composed a poem about Olaf Hoskuldsson and the tales carved on the wood of the fire-hall which he recited at the feast. It is called House Drapa and is a fine piece of verse. Olaf rewarded him well for the poem, and gave all the important people who attended the feast fine gifts, gaining considerable respect as a result.

30   There was little affection in the relations between Geirmund and Thurid, and the coolness was also mutual. Geirmund stayed at Olaf's farm for three years before declaring he wished to go abroad and leave behind Thurid and their daughter Groa, who was a year old, without any means of support. This pleased neither mother nor daughter and both of them complained to Olaf.

Olaf said, 'Why, Thorgerd, is your easterner not quite as generous now as he was that autumn when he asked you for your daughter's hand?'

They could not provoke Olaf into taking action, as he sought to resolve differences wherever possible and avoided trouble. He said that in any case the child should remain there until she was of an age to travel. In parting, Olaf made Geirmund a present of the merchant ship, completely outfitted. Geirmund thanked him well and said it was a most generous gift. He made ready and sailed from the mouth of the Laxa river on a light north-easterly breeze, but the wind died as they reached the islands. The ship lay at anchor off Oxney for a fortnight, without gaining a favourable wind for its departure.

During that time Olaf had to leave to oversee the collecting of driftwood on beaches he owned. After his departure Thurid summoned several servants and told them to accompany her. They were a party of ten, counting her infant daughter, whom she also took along. She had them launch a ferry which Olaf owned, and sail or row out to the mouth of Hvammsfjord. When they reached the islands, she told them to set out the boat which was on board the ferry. Thurid got into the boat along with two others, telling those who remained behind to look after the ferry until she returned. Taking the child in her arms, Thurid instructed the men to row across the current so that they could reach the ship. From the storage chest in the bow of the boat Thurid took an auger which she handed to one of her companions. She told him to make his way to the ship's boat and bore holes in it, so that it would be unusable if it were needed in a hurry. She then had them row her and the child ashore. By this time it was dawn. She walked up the gangway and on board the ship. Everyone aboard was asleep. Thurid made her way to Geirmund's leather sleeping sack where his sword Leg-biter hung. She placed the child in the sack, took the sword and made her way off the ship and back to her companions.

The child soon began to cry and woke Geirmund. He sat up and, recognizing his daughter, suspected who was behind all this. Jumping to his feet, he reached for his sword, only to find it gone, as might be expected. Running up on deck he saw Thurid and her companions rowing their boat away. Geirmund called out to his men to jump into the ship's boat and row after them. They did so, but hadn't gone far when they noticed the sea water flooding in and turned back to the ship.

Geirmund then called to Thurid to come back and return his sword Leg-biter – 'and take your daughter with you and whatever wealth you want'.

Thurid said, 'Do you mind the loss of your sword so much?'

Geirmund replied, 'I'd have to lose a great deal of money before I minded it as much as the loss of that sword.'

She said, 'Then you will never have it, as you have treated me dishonourably in more ways than one. This will be the last you'll see of me.'

Geirmund then spoke: 'That sword will bring you no luck.'

She replied that she would take that chance.

'Then I lay this curse upon it,' Geirmund said, 'that it will be the death of that man in your family who will most be missed and least deserve it.'

Thurid then returned to Hjardarholt. Olaf had returned and was not at all pleased at her escapade, but no action was taken. Thurid gave the sword Leg-biter to her kinsman Bolli, as she was no less fond of him than of her own brothers, and Bolli wore the sword for many years afterwards.

A favourable wind arose, and Geirmund and his men sailed out to sea, making land in Norway that autumn. One night they ran aground on rocks near Stad, and Geirmund and all aboard were drowned, bringing Geirmund's story to an end.

31 As written earlier, Olaf Hoskuldsson lived on his farm and enjoyed the respect of others.

A man named Gudmund Solmundarson lived at Asbjarnarnes in Vididal in north Iceland. Gudmund was a wealthy man. He asked for Thurid's hand in marriage and she was betrothed to him with a large dowry. Thurid was a shrewd, determined woman, quick to anger and demanding. They had four sons, named Hall, Bardi, Stein and Steingrim, and two daughters, Gudrun and Olof.

Olaf's daughter, Thorbjorg, was a good-looking, heavy-set woman. She was called Thorbjorg the Stout and was married to Asgeir Knattarson, a man of good family, in Vatnsfjord in the West Fjords. Their son Kjartan was the father of Thorvald, who was the father of Thord, who was the father of Snorri, who was the father of Thorvald. The people of Vatnsfjord trace their descent to them. Thorbjorg was married a second time, to Vermund Thorgrimsson. Their daughter Thorfinna was married to Thorstein Kuggason.

A third daughter, Bergthora, was married to Thorhall, a godi in Djupifjord in the West Fjords, who was the son of Oddi Yrarson. Their son was Kjartan, the father of Smid-Sturla, who fostered Thord Gilsson, the father of Sturla.

Olaf Peacock had many prime animals among his livestock. One of them was an ox, called Harri, which was dapple grey in colour and larger than other steers, with four horns. Two of them were large and well formed, but a third grew straight out and the fourth curved from his forehead down below his eyes. He used it as an icebreaker. He pawed the snow away to get at the grass like the horses.

During one long, hard winter which killed off great numbers of livestock Harri went from the farm at Hjardarholt to a place now called Harrastadir in the valley of Breidafjord. He ranged there all winter with sixteen steers and managed to find enough grass for all of them. In the spring he returned to the pastureland now known as Harrabol (Harri's Lair) at Hjardarholt. When he had reached the age of eighteen years the icebreaker fell from his forehead. Olaf had him slaughtered that autumn. The following night Olaf dreamed that a large, angry-looking woman approached him.

She spoke to him: 'Are you asleep?'

He replied that he was awake.

The woman said, 'You are asleep but you might just as well be awake. You have had my son killed and sent him to me disfigured, and for that I will make sure you see a son of yours covered with blood. I will also choose the one whom I know you will least want to part with.'

She then disappeared.

Olaf woke up with the image of the woman still before him. The dream made a strong impression on him and he told it to friends, but no one could interpret it for him to his satisfaction. He was most inclined to believe those who said that his dream was only a false indication of things to come.

32   A man named Osvif was the son of Helgi, the son of Ottar, the son of Bjorn the Easterner, the son of Ketil Flat-nose, the son of Bjorn Buna. His mother was Nidbjorg, the daughter of Kadlin, the daughter of Hrolf the Walker, the son of Ox-Thorir, who was a hersir of good family in Vik [in Norway]. He was called Ox-Thorir because he owned three islands with eighty oxen on each of them. He gained much renown by giving one of the islands, together with its oxen, to King Hakon.

Osvif was a very wise man. He lived at Laugar in Saelingsdal. The farm is located to the south of the Saelingsdalsa river, across from the Tunga farm. His wife was Thordis, the daughter of Thjodolf the Short. They had five sons, Ospak, Helgi, Vandrad, Torrad and Thorolf, all of them bold fighters.

They had a daughter named Gudrun. She was the most beautiful woman ever to have grown up in Iceland, and no less clever than she was good-looking. She took great care with her appearance, so much so that the adornments of other women were considered to be mere child's play in comparison. She was the shrewdest of women, highly articulate, and generous as well.

One member of Osvif's household, a woman named Thorhalla, called the Chatterbox, was distantly related to him. She had two sons named Odd and Stein, hardy men who shouldered their load and more on the farm. They were as talkative as their mother but unpopular, although they could always rely on the support of Osvif's sons.

The farmer at Tunga was Thorarin, the son of Thorir Saeling, and a successful farmer himself. Thorarin was a big man and strong. He had plenty of land but not enough livestock. Osvif had plenty of livestock and not enough land, and wanted to purchase land from Thorarin. They agreed that Osvif should purchase from Thorarin all the land on both sides of the valley extending from the Gnupuskord pass as far up as Stakkagil. This is good, fertile grassland and Osvif used it for a shieling. He had a fair number of servants and enjoyed great respect in the district.

West at Saurbaer, two brothers named Thorkel Pup and Knut lived with their brother-in-law on a farm called Hol. Their brother-in-law, Thord, was identified with his mother Ingunn and called Ingunnarson. His father was Glum Geirason. Thord was a fine, strapping figure of a man, highly capable, and often involved in lawsuits. Thord was married to the brothers' sister Aud, a woman who was neither good-looking nor exceptional in other ways, and Thord had little affection for her. He had married primarily for wealth, which Aud had brought him in quantity. The farm had prospered ever since Thord had joined up with the others.

33   A man called Gest Oddleifsson lived at Hagi on the Bardastrond coast of the West Fjords. He was an important chieftain and especially wise man, who could foretell many events of the future. Most of the foremost men of the country were on good terms with him and many sought his advice. He attended the Althing every summer and generally spent the night at Hol on his way.

On one occasion when Gest was on his way to the Althing and had stayed overnight at Hol, as usual, he was up and preparing to continue his journey early the next day, as he still had a long way before him. He intended to ride as far as the farm at Thykkvaskog that evening to his brother-in-law Armod, who was married to his sister Thorunn. They had two sons, Ornolf and Halldor.

He rode from Saurbaer and came to the hot springs Saelingsdalslaug, where he stopped awhile. Gudrun came down to the springs to greet her kinsman. Gest was pleased to see her and they struck up a conversation; their discussion was both shrewd and lengthy.

Later in the day, however, Gudrun said, 'I'd like to invite you, kinsman, to ride up to the farm, along with all your followers, and spend the night with us. It's my father's suggestion as well, but he's done me the honour of making me his messenger, and he also wanted to invite you to stop with us every time you journey through.'

Gest thanked her well, saying the offer was a generous one indeed, but said he would continue according to his original plan.

Gudrun said, 'I've had many dreams this winter, and four of them especially have caused me much concern. No one has yet been able to interpret them to my satisfaction, although I don't insist that they be favourably interpreted.'

Gest then replied, 'Tell me your dreams. I might be able to make something of them.'

Gudrun said, 'I seemed to be standing outdoors, by a stream, wearing a tall head-dress that I felt did not suit me well at all. I wanted to change the head-dress but many people advised against it. I refused to listen to them, tore the head-dress from my head and threw it into the stream. The dream ended there.'

She continued: 'In the beginning of the second dream I seemed to be standing by a lake. I seemed to have a silver ring on my arm which belonged to me and suited me especially well. I treasured it greatly and intended to keep it long and with great care. But the ring slid from my arm when I least expected it and fell into the lake and I never saw it again. I was filled with a sense of loss much greater than I should have felt at losing a mere object. After that I awoke.'

To this Gest replied only: 'No less remarkable is this dream.'

Gudrun continued on: 'In the third dream I seemed to have a gold ring on my arm; it was my own and seemed to make up for my loss. I expected to have the pleasure of owning this one longer than the previous one. All the same it wasn't as if it suited me so very much better, not if compared with how much more costly gold is than silver. Then I fell and reached out my hand to break my fall, but the gold ring struck a stone and broke in two, and I thought I saw blood seep from the pieces. My feelings afterwards were more like grief than regret. I realized that there had been a flaw in the ring, and upon examining the pieces I could see other flaws. All the same I had the impression that if I'd looked after it better the ring might still have been in one piece. The dream ended here.'

Gest answered: 'The source of your dreams is far from drying up.'

Once more Gudrun spoke: 'In my fourth dream I seemed to have a gold helmet on my head, set with many gems. This treasure was mine. But it did seem to me that it was too heavy for me to bear. I could hardly manage it and held my head bowed. I didn't blame the helmet for this, however, nor did I intend to get rid of it. But it fell suddenly from my head and into the waters of Hvammsfjord, after which I woke up. Now I have told you all the dreams.'

Gest replied: 'I can clearly see what the dreams mean, but you may find the fare lacking in variety, as I would interpret them all in a very similar way. You will have four husbands; I expect that the first man to whom you are married will not be a match to your liking. As you thought you bore a great head-dress, which you felt suited you poorly, you will care little for this man. And since you removed the head-dress and threw it into the water, this means that you will leave him. People say things have been cast to the tide when they refer to getting rid of possessions and getting nothing in return.'

Gest continued: 'In your second dream you thought you had a silver ring on your arm. This means you will be married to a second, fine man for whom you will care greatly and enjoy only a short time. It would not surprise me if he were drowned. There is no need to dwell any longer on this dream. In your third dream you thought you had a gold ring on your arm. This represents your third husband. He will not surpass his predecessor to the same extent that you felt that metal to be rarer and more precious. But if my guess is right, there will be a change in religion around that time and this husband of yours will have adopted the new religion, which seems to be much nobler. When the ring appeared to break in two, in part because of your own carelessness, and blood to seep from its parts, this signifies that this husband will be killed. It is then that you will see most clearly the faults of that marriage.'

Once more Gest spoke: 'It was in your fourth dream that you bore a gold helmet set with gems on your head, which was a heavy weight for you. This signifies that you will marry a fourth time and this husband will far surpass you. The helmet seemed to fall into the waters of Hvammsfjord, which indicates that this fourth husband will have an encounter with that same fjord on the final day of his life. I can make no more of this dream.'

Gudrun had grown blood-red while listening to her dreams being interpreted, but kept silent until Gest had finished.

Then she spoke: 'You would have made a prettier prediction if I had given you the material for it, and I thank you for interpreting the dreams for me. I will have plenty to think about if all of this comes to pass as you say.'

Gudrun then repeated her invitation to Gest to visit with them for the day, saying he and Osvif would have many interesting things to discuss.

He answered, 'I will ride onwards as I have planned, but give my greetings to your father and tell him that the time will come when the distance between our dwelling places will be shorter than at present. It will be easier for us to carry on a conversation then, if we are still allowed to talk.'

Gudrun then returned home, while Gest rode off. He met a servant of

Olaf's near a hayfield wall, who invited him to Hjardarholt on his master's bidding. Gest said he wished to see Olaf but would be staying the night at Thykkvaskog. The servant returned home at once and gave Olaf the message. Olaf had horses brought and rode to meet Gest along with several other men. They met near the Lja river. Olaf welcomed Gest and invited him and all his men to stay with them. Gest thanked him for the offer and said he would accompany him home and have a look at the farmhouse, but would stay the night with Armod. Gest made only a short visit, but was shown around much of the farm, which he admired, saying Olaf had obviously spared no expense.

Olaf followed him a short distance along his onward journey, down to the Laxa river. The two foster-brothers had been swimming in the river that day, a sport in which the Olafssons took the lead. Many other young men from nearby farms had joined them in swimming. As the group approached Kjartan and Bolli came running back from their swim and were almost fully dressed when Gest and Olaf came riding up. Gest looked at the two young men a moment and then told Olaf which was Bolli and which Kjartan. After that he pointed his spear at and identified each of the other Olafssons who were there. But although there were many other handsome young men who had come out of the water and sat on the riverbank near Kjartan and Bolli, Gest said that he could not see any resemblance to Olaf in any of them.

Olaf then said, 'The stories of your cleverness are hardly exaggerated if you can identify men whom you have never seen before. I want to ask you which of these young men will be the most outstanding.'

Gest replied, 'It will be much as your own affections predict, as Kjartan will be thought the most outstanding of them, as long as he lives.'

With that Gest prodded his horse and rode off.

A short while later his son Thord drew alongside him and asked, 'Why, Father, are there tears in your eyes?'

Gest answered, 'No need to mention it, but since you ask, I won't conceal it from you either, as you'll live to see it happen. I wouldn't be surprised if Bolli should one day stoop over Kjartan's corpse and in slaying him bring about his own death, a vision all the more saddening because of the excellence of these young men.'

They rode on to the Althing which passed without event.

34 A man named Thorvald, the son of Halldor the Godi of Garpsdal,
     lived at Garpsdal in Gilsfjord. He was a wealthy man but hardly a
hero. He asked for Gudrun Osvifsdottir's hand in marriage at the Althing
when she was fifteen years of age. His suit was not rejected but Osvif felt
the difference in their means would be evident in the marriage conditions.
Thorvald spoke indulgently, though, and maintained he was seeking a wife
and not a fortune. Gudrun was eventually betrothed to Thorvald according
to conditions which Osvif himself decided upon. He declared that Gudrun
should control their common finances once they were married and would
acquire the right to half of the estate, whether the marriage was a brief or
a lengthy one.

   Thorvald was also obliged to purchase whatever finery Gudrun required
in order that no other woman of equal wealth should own better, although
not to the point of ruining the farm. Having agreed to this, the men rode
home from the Althing. Gudrun was not asked for her opinion and, although
she was rather against the idea, nothing was done. The wedding was to be
held at Garpsdal at hay-time. Gudrun cared little for Thorvald and was
avid in demanding purchases of precious objects. There were no treasures
in all the West Fjords so costly that Gudrun felt she did not deserve them,
and vented her anger on Thorvald if he failed to buy them, however dear
they were.

   Thord Ingunnarson made a point of befriending Thorvald and Gudrun
and spent a great deal of time at their farm, until soon rumours of the growing
affection between Thord and Gudrun spread. When Gudrun subsequently
asked Thorvald to buy her a new treasure, he retorted that there was no
limit to her demands and slapped her in the face.

   To this Gudrun replied: 'Fine rosy colour in her cheeks is just what every
woman needs, if she is to look her best, and you have certainly given me
this to teach me not to displease you.'

   When Thord came to the farm that same evening, Gudrun told him of
her humiliation and asked how she should repay Thorvald.

   At this Thord smiled and replied, 'I know just the thing. Make him a
shirt with the neck so low-cut that it will give you grounds for divorcing
him.'*

   Gudrun did not oppose the idea and their conversation ended.

_____
* Wearing clothing considered suitable for the opposite sex was sufficient grounds for divorce,
and either men or women could advance such a claim.

That same spring Gudrun announced she was divorcing Thorvald and went home to Laugar. When their estate was divided Gudrun received half of all the property, which was larger than before. She had been married to Thorvald for two years. The same spring Ingunn sold her farm in Kroksfjord, which has since then been called Ingunnarstadir, and moved west to Skalmarnes. She had been married to Glum Geirason, as was previously mentioned.

At this time Hallstein the Godi lived at Hallsteinsnes on the western shore of Thorskafjord. Although he was a powerful man he was not especially popular.

35 A man named Kotkel had only recently immigrated to Iceland, along with his wife, Grima, and their sons Hallbjorn Slickstone-eye and Stigandi. They were from the Hebrides, all of them skilled in witchcraft and accomplished magicians. Hallstein had received them on their arrival and settled them at Urdir in Skalmarfjord, where their presence was anything but welcome.

That summer Gest attended the Althing, travelling by boat to Saurbaer as he was accustomed to do. He stayed the night at Hol where he borrowed horses for the journey as usual. Thord Ingunnarson accompanied him in this instance and came to Laugar in Saelingsdal. Gudrun Osvifsdottir was going to the Althing and Thord accompanied her.

One day, as they were riding across the Blaskogar heath in fine weather, Gudrun asked Thord 'whether the rumour is true, that your wife Aud is often dressed in breeches, with a codpiece and long leggings?'*

He replied that he had not noticed.

'You can't pay her much attention, in that case,' said Gudrun, 'if you haven't noticed such a thing, or what other reason is there then for her being called Breeches-Aud?'

Thord said, 'She can't have been called that for long.'

Gudrun replied, 'What is more important is how long the name will follow her.'

They arrived at the Althing soon after that, where the proceedings were without event. Thord spent most of his time at Gest's booth talking to Gudrun. One day he asked her what consequences it could have for a woman if she wore trousers like the men.

---

* All details of masculine clothing, cf. previous footnote, and thus grounds for divorce.

Gudrun answered: 'If women go about dressed as men, they invite the same treatment as do men who wear shirts cut so low that the nipples of their breasts can be seen – both are grounds for divorce.'

Thord then asked, 'Would you advise me to announce my divorce from Aud here at the Althing or at home before the local assembly? I'll have to collect a number of supporters because those whom I will offend by so doing will be determined on revenge.'

After only a moment, Gudrun replied, 'Tarry-long brings little home.'

Thord then jumped to his feet and made his way to the Law Rock. He named witnesses and announced he was divorcing Aud on the grounds that she had taken to wearing breeches with a codpiece like a masculine woman. Aud's brothers were not at all pleased but nothing was done. Thord rode home from the Althing with the Osvifssons.

When Aud learned the news she said,

2.   Kind of him to leave me so
       and let me be the last to know.

Thord rode west to Saurbaer with a party of eleven men to claim his share of the property, which was accomplished without difficulty since Thord was prepared to be generous about his wife's share. He drove a large herd of livestock back to Laugar and proceeded to ask for Gudrun's hand in marriage. Osvif agreed readily and Gudrun raised no objection, so they decided to hold the wedding feast at Laugar when ten weeks of summer remained. The feast was impressive and the marriage of Thord and Gudrun a happy one. Thorkel and Knut would have made an attempt to start a case against Thord but hadn't managed to convince others to help them do so.

The following summer Aud and other people from Hol were staying in the shieling with the milking ewes in Hvammsdal. The people of Laugar took their ewes to a shieling in Lambadal, which runs west up the mountain from the main valley of Saelingsdal. Aud asked the farmhand who looked after the ewes how often he expected to meet his counterpart from Laugar. The boy replied that this would probably happen frequently as there was only a single ridge separating the two valleys.

Aud then said, 'See if you can't run into the shepherd from Laugar today, then, and find out for me who is staying in their shieling and who is at home. Make sure you always speak of Thord in the friendliest of terms.'

The boy promised to do as she asked. When he returned that evening Aud asked what he had discovered.

The shepherd replied: 'I learned such news as will be pleasing to your ears, that there is a great distance separating the beds of Thord and Gudrun these days, since she is in the shieling while he is working feverishly at building a hall; only he and Osvif are at home.'

'You've done a fine job of spying,' Aud said. 'Have two horses saddled for me when the others go to bed.'

The shepherd did as she asked and shortly before sundown Aud mounted her horse, dressed in breeches, to be sure. The boy followed her on the second horse, but could hardly keep up with her flying pace. She rode southward over the Saelingsdal heath, not stopping until she reached the wall of the hayfield at Laugar. There she dismounted and told the shepherd to look after the horses while she proceeded to the house. She went up to the door, which was unlocked, into the fire-hall and found the bed closet where Thord lay sleeping. The door was closed but not latched. She entered the bed closet, where Thord slept on his back facing upwards. She woke Thord, but he only turned over on his side when he saw some man had come in. She drew her short-sword and struck him a great wound on his right arm which cut across both breasts. She struck with such force that the sword lodged in the wood of the bed. Aud then returned to her horse, sprang into the saddle and rode home. Roused by the attack, Thord tried to get to his feet, but was weakened by the wound and loss of blood. Osvif woke up at the disturbance and asked what was happening, and Thord replied that he had been wounded. While he dressed Thord's wound, Osvif asked if he knew who had attacked him. Thord replied that he suspected it was Aud, and Osvif offered to ride after her, as she would have brought few followers and deserved punishment. Thord told him not to think of doing so, as what Aud had done was only evening the score.

It was sunrise when Aud returned home, and her brothers asked where she had gone. Aud told them she had gone to Laugar and the news of her visit there. They were pleased but said Thord deserved worse. Thord was a long time recuperating from the wounds; the ones on his chest healed well but he never regained much use of his right arm.

The winter passed without event, but in the spring Thord's mother Ingunn came from her farm at Skalmarnes to visit him. Thord welcomed his mother warmly. She said she had come to him for help and protection, as Kotkel and his wife and sons were making her life miserable, stealing her livestock and practising sorcery under the protection of Hallstein the Godi. Thord responded at once and said he would not allow these thieves to get away with this even if Hallstein opposed him. He got ready to travel west immediately with Ingunn and nine others to accompany him. He took a ferry from Tjaldanes and they continued west to Skalmarnes.

Thord had all the property there which belonged to his mother loaded on the ferry and ordered men to herd the livestock overland. There were twelve of them aboard the boat, including Ingunn and one other woman. Thord rode to Kotkel's farm with nine men. Kotkel's two sons were not at home. Before witnesses, Thord charged Kotkel and his wife and sons with theft and sorcery, an offence punishable by full outlawry. They would have to answer the charges at the Althing. This accomplished he went back to the boat. Hallbjorn and Stigandi returned home just after Thord and the others had set sail, and were only a short distance from shore. Kotkel told his sons what had happened. The two brothers were furious and claimed none of their enemies had ever dared treat them like this. Kotkel then prepared a high platform for witchcraft which they all mounted. Then they chanted powerful incantations, which were sorcery. A great blizzard came up.

Thord Ingunnarson and his companions at sea felt how the force of the weather was directed at them and the ship was driven west beyond the headland at Skalmarnes. Thord struggled valiantly on board the ship. People on shore saw him throw everything overboard that could weigh the ship down except the travellers themselves. They expected that the ship would be able to make land after that, as they had passed the worst of the skerries, but all of a sudden a breaker rose where no one could ever recall having seen a skerry and rammed the ship so that it capsized at once. Thord and all his companions were drowned and the ship smashed into small pieces, the keel washing ashore on an island which has since been called Kjalarey (Keel Island). Thord's shield drifted ashore on an island called Skjaldarey (Shield Island). His body and the bodies of his companions drifted ashore directly afterwards and are buried in a mound at Haugsnes (Mound point).

36 The news of these events spread and was condemned; men capable of such sorcery as Kotkel and his family had performed were considered truly evil. Gudrun, who was pregnant and had only a short time left before she gave birth, was stricken with grief at Thord's death. She soon gave birth to a boy, who was sprinkled with water and named Thord.

At this time Snorri the Godi lived at Helgafell. He was Osvif's kinsman and friend and a source of great support to both him and Gudrun. When he visited them Gudrun told him of her dilemma and he promised to help her in the way he thought best. To give Gudrun some consolation he offered to foster her son, which she accepted; she agreed to follow his advice. The boy Thord was later given the nickname 'the Cat' and was the father of the poet Stuf.

Gest Oddleifsson then approached Hallstein and offered him a choice: Hallstein would either have to get rid of these sorcerers or else Gest would kill them, 'even though it's already too late'.

Hallstein was not long in choosing and told the family they would have to find another dwelling place at least as far away as the other side of the highlands of the Dalir heath, though they did not deserve to escape with their lives. Kotkel and his family then left, taking no possessions except a stud of four horses with them. The stallion was black, large and powerful and had proven its fighting prowess. Nothing is mentioned of their journey until they arrived at the farm of Thorleik Hoskuldsson at Kambsnes. He expressed an interest in purchasing the horses, which he could see were prime animals.

Kotkel answered, 'I'll give you the chance to own them: you provide me with a place to live near you and the horses are yours.'

Thorleik replied, 'I'll end up paying a high price for the horses if I do that – aren't you a wanted man in this district?'

Kotkel answered, 'The men of Laugar have told you that.'

Thorleik admitted this to be true.

Kotkel then spoke: 'The truth of our doings against Gudrun and her brothers is somewhat different from what you've been told. Accusations have been heaped on us of deeds we had no part in – accept the stallions in return for protecting us. If all the stories we hear of you are true, we won't be helpless prey for the dwellers of this district if we have your backing.'

Thorleik decided to accept the offer, as he was drawn both by the fine horses and Kotkel's cleverly convincing speech. He found the family a place to live at Leidolfsstadir in Laxardal, and supplied them with livestock, taking the horses into his charge in return.

When the men of Laugar learned of this, Osvif's sons wanted to attack Kotkel and his family at once.

Their father, however, said, 'We should take the advice of Snorri the Godi and leave this to others. It won't be long until their neighbours will have new complaints against them, and it will be Thorleik who'll suffer for it, which is so much the better. He'll soon have enemies where he once had supporters. But I won't try and dissuade you from doing whatever you like with Kotkel and his clan if three years pass without anyone driving them out of the district or putting an end to them once and for all.'

Gudrun and her brothers agreed to this.

Although Kotkel and his family were seldom seen working, they purchased neither hay nor food during the winter. They were anything but popular with the people of the district, but no one dared to raise a hand against them because of Thorleik.

37 One summer when Thorleik was attending the Althing, a large man entered his booth and greeted him. Thorleik returned the greeting and asked the man his name or origin. He said his name was Eldgrim and he lived in the Borgarfjord district on the farm called Eldgrimsstadir, located in the valley now called Grimsdal which runs westward up the mountain between the farms of Muli and Grisartunga.

Thorleik said, 'I've heard of you, and if the stories are true you're a man to be reckoned with.'

Eldgrim responded: 'My purpose in coming here is to purchase those fine horses which Kotkel made you a present of last summer.'

Thorleik answered, 'The horses are not for sale.'

Eldgrim said, 'I'm offering you an equal number of horses in exchange, plus a sizeable additional payment. Some people would say you'd be getting double the normal price.'

Thorleik answered, 'I'm not much of a horse-dealer, and you're not going to get those horses even if you offer me triple the price.'

Eldgrim said, 'People who told me you were arrogant and headstrong were obviously not lying. If I had my way you'd end up losing the horses and getting considerably less than I've been offering you.'

Thorleik grew very red in the face at his words, and replied, 'You'll need more than threats, Eldgrim, if you intend to take the horses from me by force.'

Eldgrim responded, 'You may think it unlikely that I should end up getting the better of you, but I'll go and take a look at the horses this summer, and we'll see which one of us ends up owning them after that.'

Thorleik answered, 'You can make good your threat any time, so long as you don't intend to outnumber me when you make your attack.'

The conversation ended on that note. People who overheard them said the two would end up with no more than they deserved. The Althing came to a close and everyone returned home without incident.

Early one morning a farmhand at Hrutsstadir returned from his morning chores and Hrut Herjolfsson asked him whether he had any news to tell.

The man replied that he had seen nothing except someone riding across the far side of the tidal flats towards where Thorleik's horses were grazing, 'then he dismounted and caught the horses'.

Hrut asked where the horses had been and the farmhand replied, 'They kept to their usual grazing area; they were in your meadow below the hayfield wall.'

Hrut answered, 'It's true that my kinsman Thorleik is not one to be choosy about his pasture, and I don't think those horses will have been herded off with his consent.'

With that Hrut sprang to his feet, dressed only in a shirt and linen breeches, pulled on a grey fur garment and took up a gold-inlaid halberd which King Harald had given him. He walked briskly out and saw a man driving several horses below the hayfield wall. He approached them and recognized the man as Eldgrim. When Hrut greeted him Eldgrim responded somewhat reluctantly, and Hrut then asked where he was taking the horses.

Eldgrim answered, 'I won't try to conceal from you, although I know you and Thorleik are close kin, that I intend to see to it that he won't get his hands on these horses again. I am only carrying out what I told him at the Althing that I intended to do, and I've not sought the horses by means of superior forces either.'

Hrut replied, 'There's hardly much prestige in driving the horses off while Thorleik is in bed asleep. If you really intend to keep your word, as the two of you agreed, you should face him before you ride off with his horses.'

Eldgrim said, 'Tell Thorleik if you wish; as you can see, I left home prepared to meet him,' and brandished the barbed spear which he held in his hand.

He was also wearing a helmet and coat of mail, with a sword at his waist and a shield at his side.

'I'm not about to make the journey to Kambsnes on my slow legs, but I don't intend to stand by while Thorleik is robbed, if I can do anything about it, even if he's no favourite relation of mine,' said Hrut.

'You don't mean you intend to take the horses from me?' asked Eldgrim.

'I'll offer you other horses instead, if you let these loose again, although they're no match for them,' said Hrut.

'Good of you to make the offer, Hrut,' Eldgrim replied, 'but now that I've got my hands on these horses of Thorleik's, neither bribes nor threats will make me let go of them again.'

Hrut then answered, 'Then I'm afraid your choice will turn out badly for both of us.'

Eldgrim was about to leave and prodded his horse, but when Hrut saw this he raised his halberd and struck Eldgrim between his shoulder blades. The mail-coat split asunder at the blow and the halberd cut right through the body. Eldgrim fell from his horse dead, as might be expected. Hrut buried the corpse at the spot called Eldgrimsholt (Eldgrim's rise), south of Kambsnes.

Afterwards Hrut rode to Kambsnes to tell Thorleik the news. Thorleik responded with anger and felt that he had been put to shame, while Hrut thought he had done him a real service. Thorleik said his actions were not only badly meant, they would also have serious consequences. Hrut said he could do as he chose, and the two parted on the worst of terms.

Hrut was over eighty when he killed Eldgrim, and gained a great deal of respect as a result of the deed. The fact that Hrut rose in esteem did not improve Thorleik's feelings towards him. Thorleik was convinced that he himself would have had the best of Eldgrim, since Hrut had made short work of him.

Thorleik then approached his tenants, Kotkel and Grima, to ask them to take some action to discredit Hrut. They agreed readily and promised to get right to work. Thorleik returned home and shortly afterwards Kotkel, Grima and their sons set out at night for Hrut's farm, where they began to practise strong magic rites. As the magic proceeded, the inhabitants of the farmhouse were puzzled by the sounds. The chants were sweet to the ear.

Only Hrut realized what the sounds meant and told his household that no one was to leave the house to see what was going on, 'but everyone is to remain awake, if he possibly can, and if we manage to do so no harm will come to us'.

Eventually, however, they all fell asleep. Hrut managed to keep awake the longest, but finally even he fell asleep. Hrut's son Kari was twelve years old at the time and the most promising of his children. He was a great favourite with his father. Kari slept lightly and uneasily, as the incantations were directed at him. Eventually he sprang to his feet and looked outside. He went outside into the magic and was struck dead immediately. The next morning Hrut awoke, along with the rest of his household, to find his son was missing. His dead body was found a short distance from the entrance to the house. It was a great blow to Hrut and he had a burial mound made for Kari.

He then paid a visit to Olaf Hoskuldsson to tell him what had happened. Olaf was furious at the news and said it showed great foolishness to have allowed such evildoers as Kotkel and his clan to settle so close by. He also said that Thorleik had repaid Hrut badly for his actions, and that things had doubtless turned out worse than Thorleik intended.

Olaf said that Kotkel and his sons should be put to death at once – 'even though it's already too late'.

Olaf and Hrut set out with fifteen others, but when Kotkel and his family saw riders approaching they fled towards the mountains. Hallbjorn Slickstone-eye was the first to be caught, and a sack was pulled over his head. Several men were left behind to guard him while the others went after Kotkel, Grima and Stigandi. Kotkel and Grima were taken on the ridge between Haukadal and Laxardal. They were stoned to death and their bodies placed in a shallow grave heaped with stones, the remains of which are still visible. It is called 'Sorcerers' Cairn'. Stigandi managed to make it through the pass and into Haukadal, where they lost sight of him. Hrut and his sons rowed out to sea with Hallbjorn. They removed the sack and tied a stone about his neck.

As they did so, Hallbjorn looked landwards with anything but a gentle gaze, saying, 'It was no lucky day for us, when my family approached Thorleik here on Kambsnes. I lay this curse that Thorleik will know little enjoyment here for the rest of his days, and that anyone who takes his place will know but ill fortune.' Events are thought to have proved how effective was his curse. They then drowned him and rowed back to shore.

Shortly afterwards Hrut went to Olaf and told him that he did not feel he had settled his affairs with Thorleik, and asked Olaf to lend him men to accompany him in a foray to Kambsnes.

Olaf replied, 'It's not right that you kinsmen should come to blows, even though Thorleik's actions have turned out very badly. I would rather try to negotiate a settlement between you. You have more than once had to wait to receive your due.'

Hrut answered, 'There's no question of that now; things will never be settled between us, and I don't want both of us to live here in Laxardal in the future.'

Olaf answered, 'It won't do you any good to attack Thorleik against my wishes; if you do you may find you've bitten off more than you can chew.'

Hrut then realized there was little he could do in this situation, and returned home very dissatisfied with the results. The following years passed without event.

38 To return to Stigandi, he became an outlaw and difficult to deal with. A man named Thord lived in Hundadal, a rich man but hardly exceptional. One summer the number of sheep rounded up in Hundadal was lower than normal. People noticed that a slave-woman who looked after the sheep in Hundadal had acquired many new possessions, and had often disappeared for hours at a time without anyone knowing of her whereabouts. Thord had her threatened to try to find out the truth.

When suitably frightened, the woman revealed that a man came to her, 'a large man, and handsome, he seemed to me'.

Thord then asked when she thought this man would return and she said she expected him to come soon.

Thord then approached Olaf and told him that it was very likely Stigandi was not far away and asked him to gather some men together and go after him. Olaf was quick to respond and went up to Hundadal, where the slave-woman was brought before him. Olaf asked where Stigandi's camp was, but she said she did not know. He then offered to buy her her freedom if she would deliver Stigandi into their hands, and she accepted his offer.

That day she watched over her sheep as usual and Stigandi came to her. She welcomed him warmly and offered to search his hair for lice. He lay down with his head in her lap and soon fell asleep. She then crawled out from under him and went to Olaf and his men to tell them how matters stood. They went to where Stigandi lay and were determined not to let him see anything he could put a curse on, as his brother had done, so they drew a sack over his head. Stigandi awoke and offered no resistance for there were many of them against him alone. There was a tear in the sack through which Stigandi could see the slope opposite. It was a fertile bit of land, green with grass, but suddenly it was as if a tornado struck it. The land was transformed and never again did grass grow there. It is now called 'The

Fire-Site'. Following this they stoned Stigandi to death and placed him in a shallow grave there. Olaf kept his promise to the slave-woman and gave her her freedom, and she returned to Hjardarholt with them.

Hallbjorn's Slickstone-eye's body washed up on the beach a short while after he was drowned. He was placed in a shallow grave at the spot called Knarrarnes, and haunted the area frequently.

A man called Thorkel the Bald lived at Thykkvaskog on a farm he had inherited from his father. He was a courageous man and extremely strong. One evening a cow was missing at Thykkvaskog and Thorkel and one of his farmhands went to look for her. It was after nightfall and there was a moon in the sky. Thorkel said they should split up and divide the area between them. When Thorkel was alone he thought he saw a cow on a rise before him. As he approached it turned out to be Slickstone-eye rather than a cow and they fought with one another. Hallbjorn had to give way and, just when Thorkel least expected it, he slipped out of his hands and let himself sink down into the ground. Thorkel returned home afterwards. His servant had already come home with the cow. After this Hallbjorn did no more harm.

By this time both Thorbjorn the Pock-marked and Melkorka were dead. They were buried in a mound in Laxardal and their son Lambi lived on their farm. He was a bold fighter and well off. He enjoyed more respect than his father had because of his mother's family, and the relations between him and Olaf were warm.

The winter following the killing of Kotkel and his family passed and the next spring the brothers Olaf and Thorleik met. Olaf asked whether Thorleik intended to continue farming at Kambsnes, and Thorleik replied that this was his intention.

Olaf said, 'I would like to ask you instead, kinsman, to change your plans and sail abroad. You will enjoy the respect of everyone wherever you go. But I'm afraid our kinsman Hrut cares little for your company, and I would rather not take the chance of having the two of you at such close quarters much longer. Hrut is a powerful man, and his sons are bold warriors and hotheads. For the sake of our family ties, I would rather avoid a clash between you two kinsmen.'

Thorleik replied, 'I'm not afraid of not being able to stand up to Hrut and his sons, and won't leave the country because of that. But if it makes a great difference to you, kinsman, and has put you into a difficult position, then I will do so at your request, and because I was more contented when

I was abroad. Nor do I fear that you will treat my son Bolli any less well though I am not nearby, and he is dearer to me than anyone else.'

Olaf answered, 'You're doing the right thing in agreeing to my request in this matter. And, as far as Bolli is concerned, I intend to continue as before, and treat him no less well than I do my own sons.'

Following this the brothers parted with great affection. Thorleik sold his property and used the proceeds to prepare for his journey abroad. He purchased a ship which was beached at Dagverdarnes, and when it was ready to sail went aboard accompanied by his wife and others of his family. They had a good passage and made land in Norway that autumn. From there he travelled south to Denmark, as he did not feel satisfied in Norway; his friends and relatives had died or been driven out of the country. From Denmark he travelled to Gotland. According to most people, Thorleik was not one to grow old gracefully, but was nevertheless respected as long as he lived. The story of Thorleik ends here.

39 Word spread of the dispute between Hrut and Thorleik, and most people in the dales of Breidafjord felt that Kotkel and his sons had dealt Hrut a heavy blow. Osvif reminded Gudrun and her brothers of his earlier words, and his advice that they avoid jeopardizing their own lives by taking on such fiends as Kotkel and his family.

Gudrun said, 'No one can be ill-advised, Father, who has the advantage of your advice.'

Olaf now enjoyed great respect on his farm. All of his sons lived at Hjardarholt, as did their kinsman and foster-brother, Bolli. Kjartan was the leader of Olaf's sons, and he and Bolli were very close. Kjartan never went anywhere without Bolli at his side.

Kjartan often went to the hot springs at Saelingsdal, and it usually happened that Gudrun was there as well. Kjartan enjoyed Gudrun's company, as she was both clever and good with words. Everyone said that, of all the young people of the time, Kjartan and Gudrun were best suited for one another. Olaf and Osvif were also good friends, and exchanged visits regularly, which did little to decrease the growing affection between the youngsters.

Olaf spoke to Kjartan one day, saying, 'I don't know why your visits to the springs at Laugar to spend time with Gudrun make me uneasy. It isn't because I don't appreciate how much superior to other women Gudrun is, as she is the only woman I consider a worthy match for you. But somehow

I have a feeling, although I won't make it a prediction, that our dealings with the Laugar family will not turn out well.'

Kjartan replied that he would do his utmost not to go against his father's wishes, but said he expected things would turn out better than Olaf anticipated. He continued his visits as before, with Bolli usually accompanying him. The year passed.

40 A man named Asgeir, who was called Scatter-brain, lived on the farmstead Asgeirsa in Vididal. His father, Audun Shaft, was the first of his family to make the journey to Iceland and had taken land and settled in Vididal. Another of Audun's sons was Thorgrim Grey-head who was the father of Asmund, the father of Grettir the Strong.

Asgeir had five children: one of his sons was Audun, the father of Asgeir, the father of Audun, the father of Egil who was married to Ulfheid, the daughter of Eyjolf the Lame. Their son was Eyjolf, who was killed at the Althing. Another of Asgeir's sons was Thorvald, whose daughter Dalla was married to Bishop Isleif and was the mother of Bishop Gizur. A third son was named Kalf. Asgeir's sons were all promising. At this time Kalf was sailing on trading voyages and had earned a good name for himself. Thurid, one of Asgeir's daughters, was married to Thorkel, the son of Thord Bellower, and their son was named Thorstein. His other daughter was named Hrefna. She was the finest-looking woman in the northern districts of Iceland and very well liked. Asgeir was a powerful figure.

Kjartan Olafsson set out on a journey to Borgarfjord, of which nothing is reported until he arrived at Borg. Thorstein Egilsson, his mother's brother, was farming at Borg at the time. Bolli accompanied Kjartan, as the affection between the two foster-brothers was such that both of them felt something was missing in the other's absence. Thorstein welcomed Kjartan warmly and said he hoped he would make his visit a long one, and Kjartan stayed at Borg for some time.

That summer a ship that was owned by Kalf Asgeirsson was beached at the mouth of the Gufua river. He had spent the winter with Thorstein Egilsson.

Kjartan confided to Thorstein that his main purpose in coming south to Borg had been to purchase a half-share in the ship from Kalf, 'as I want to journey abroad', and he asked Thorstein for his opinion of Kalf.

Thorstein replied that he considered Kalf to be a decent fellow, 'but it's a shame you long to go abroad and learn of foreign ways. Your journey will likely prove to be of importance in more ways than one. For your kinsmen a great deal depends upon how the journey turns out.'

Kjartan said that it would turn out well. He then purchased a half-share in the ship from Kalf and they reached an agreement to share the profits equally. They would set sail when Kjartan returned after the tenth week of summer. On departing from Borg, Kjartan was given fine gifts and he and Bolli rode home. When Olaf learned of the plans he felt that Kjartan had made a hasty decision, but said he would not fail to offer his support.

A short while later Kjartan rode to Laugar and told Gudrun of his proposed journey abroad.

Gudrun said, 'You were in a hurry to make this decision, Kjartan', and other words which made it clear to Kjartan that Gudrun was not at all pleased about it.

Kjartan said, 'Don't get angry about this and I'll make it up to you by doing anything you ask that would please you.'

Gudrun said, 'Make sure you mean that, because I'll hold you to it.'

Kjartan told her to go ahead and name whatever she wished, and Gudrun said, 'I want to go with you this summer, and by taking me you can make up for deciding this so hastily, for it's not Iceland that I love.'

'You can't do that,' Kjartan answered. 'Your brothers are inexperienced and your father is an old man. If you go abroad there'd be no one to look after things. Wait for me instead for three years.'

Gudrun said she would promise nothing of the sort, and they parted in disagreement. Kjartan returned home.

Olaf attended the Althing that summer, and Kjartan accompanied his father from Hjardarholt as far as the Nordurardal valley, where they parted ways. Kjartan rode to his ship, accompanied by his kinsman Bolli. There were ten Icelanders who went with Kjartan on his journey because they were so attached to him. With this group of followers Kjartan approached the ship, where Kalf Asgeirsson gave them a warm welcome. Kjartan and Bolli took with them goods of great value. They set about making their preparations, and as soon as a favourable wind arose they set sail from Borgarfjord out to the open sea.

They had a good crossing and made land in Norway north of Nidaros, at Agdenes, where they sought news of recent events from the people they met. They were told that there had been a change of rulers in the country, of the fall of Earl Hakon and the rise of King Olaf Tryggvason, who had managed to bring all of Norway under his rule. King Olaf decreed that the

Norwegians should adopt a new religion, and far from all of his subjects were prepared to agree to this.

Kjartan and his men docked their ship at Nidaros. There were a great number of prominent Icelanders in Norway at this time, and the three ships already docked there were all owned by Icelanders. Brand the Generous, the son of Vermund Thorgrimsson, owned one of them, Hallfred the Troublesome Poet a second and the third was owned by two brothers, Bjarni and Thorhall, who were the sons of Skeggi of Breida in Fljotshlid. All of them had intended to sail to Iceland that summer, but the king had forbidden all of the ships to put to sea because the owners refused to adopt the new religion which he had decreed. All the Icelanders welcomed Kjartan, especially Brand, as he and Kjartan were old acquaintances.

The Icelanders held counsel and agreed among themselves to refuse to adopt the new religion which the king had decreed. All of the men mentioned were party to the decision. Kjartan and his men then docked, unloaded their ship and saw to their goods. King Olaf, who was in town, learned of the arrival of the ship and that among those on board were a number of highly capable men.

One fine day that autumn, Kjartan and his men saw many people leaving the town to go swimming in the river Nid. Kjartan suggested to his men that they also go on a swimming outing, which they did. One of the swimmers was by far the best, and Kjartan asked Bolli if he wouldn't care to match himself against the local swimmer.

Bolli answered: 'I doubt that I'm good enough.'

'I don't know what's become of your sporting spirit,' Kjartan replied. 'I'll challenge him then.'

Bolli answered, 'Go ahead and do as you please.'

Kjartan then dived out into the river and swam over to the man who was such a strong swimmer, pushed him underwater and held him down for some time, before letting him come up again. The other had not been above water long before he grasped Kjartan and forced him underwater and held him under so long that Kjartan felt enough was enough. They both emerged once more, but neither spoke to the other. On the third try both of them went underwater and were under much longer. Kjartan was far from certain what the outcome would be and realized that he had never before been in such a tight situation. Finally both of them came up and swam ashore.

The local man then asked, 'Who is this man?'

Kjartan told him his name and the local man replied, 'You're a fair swimmer; are you as good at other skills?'

Kjartan answered, after a pause, 'It was said, in Iceland, that I was – not that it makes any difference now.'

The man spoke: 'It does make a difference who your opponent is; why haven't you asked me any questions?'

Kjartan replied, 'I don't care who you are.'

The man said, 'You're not only highly capable, but highly confident of yourself as well; but I intend to tell you my name, all the same, and who it is you have been swimming against. You have before you King Olaf Tryggvason.'

Kjartan made no answer but turned to leave without putting on his outer cloak. He was wearing an inner shirt of scarlet. By this time the king was practically fully dressed. He called out to Kjartan, asking him not to hurry off, and Kjartan turned back reluctantly. The king then removed a fine cloak from his own shoulders and gave it to Kjartan, saying it wouldn't do for him to return to his men without a cloak. Kjartan thanked the king for the gift, went back to his followers and showed them the cloak. They were not at all pleased, as they felt Kjartan had put himself in the king's debt, but nothing more occurred.

The weather was especially harsh that autumn, with long spells of heavy frost and cold.

The heathen men said it was hardly surprising that the weather should be bad – 'It's because of the new king and his new religion, that the gods have grown angry.'

All of the Icelanders spent the winter in the town, and Kjartan was the leader among them. When the weather improved a great number of people began arriving in town in answer to the summons of King Olaf. Some people in Nidaros had converted to Christianity, but the great majority were still opposed.

One day the king called a meeting at Oyr where he made a long and very eloquent speech to urge men to convert. The men of the Nidaros district had collected a small army and maintained they were prepared to do battle with the king rather than convert. The king told them to keep in mind that he had dealt with greater opponents than a bunch of local farmers from Nidaros. This was enough to strike fear into the hearts of the farmers and they all surrendered to him. A great number of people were baptized before the assembly was dissolved.

That same evening the king sent men to the quarters of the Icelanders to listen in on their conversations. Inside there was a great deal of noise.

Kjartan could be heard speaking to Bolli, 'How eager are you to adopt this religion that the king has decreed, kinsman?'

'I'm not eager at all,' Bolli answered, 'as this religion seems very weak to me.'

Kjartan asked, 'Didn't you think the king was threatening anyone who wasn't prepared to submit to his will?'

Bolli answered, 'I think the king left no doubt about his intentions to use force against them if need be.'

'No one is going to force me to do anything against my will,' said Kjartan, 'as long as I can stand on my own two feet and wield a weapon. Only a coward waits to be taken like a lamb from the fold or a fox from a trap. The other course looks better to me; if a man's got to die anyway, he might as well make a name for himself before it comes to that.'

Bolli asked, 'What is it you want to do?'

'I won't keep it from you,' Kjartan said. 'Burn down his quarters with the king inside.'

'I wouldn't call that a cowardly plan,' Bolli said, 'but something tells me little good will come of it. This king is not only favoured by destiny and fortune, he is also securely guarded both day and night.'

Kjartan replied that even courageous men lost their nerve now and again, to which Bolli answered, that he wasn't so sure who should be taunted about lack of courage. Many of their followers then told them to stop this pointless arguing. After listening to this, the king's spies left to report the entire exchange to the king.

The next morning the king called a meeting and summoned all the Icelanders. When they had assembled he stood up and thanked all those men who were his loyal friends and had converted to Christianity for answering his summons to the meeting. He ordered the Icelanders to come before him and asked whether they wished to be baptized. Not really, they replied.

He said they were choosing a course for themselves that would turn out badly for them – 'and which of you was it who expressed the wish to set fire to my quarters?'

At this Kjartan replied, 'You no doubt expect that the speaker of these words will not dare to admit to them, but he stands here before you.'

'I know you,' the king replied, 'and your daring, but you are not destined to stand over my dead body. You are guilty of enough in ignoring the advice of those who would teach you a better faith, without threatening to burn alive the king who attempts it. Since, however, I am not certain that you meant what you said, and you have honestly admitted to it, I will not have you put to death for the offence. Perhaps when you do convert you will keep your faith better than others – to the same extent you expressed more opposition to it than they did. I realize as well, that it will mean entire ship's crews will turn up for baptism the day that you decide of your own free will to convert. I think it very likely that your friends and kinsmen will pay heed to what you say when you return to Iceland, and if my guess is right, Kjartan, you will leave Norway under a better faith than you had when you arrived. Leave this meeting then in peace and proceed in safety, whatever course you choose; no one will force you to adopt Christianity for the time being, for God has said that he wishes no man to be forced to turn to him.'

There was general approval at the king's speech, especially among the Christians. The heathens, however, left it to Kjartan to answer as he saw fit.

Kjartan then spoke: 'We thank the king for promising us a fair peace. You tempt us most to adopt your faith by forgiving us our offences with gentle words, when our fate is completely in your hands. I do not intend to adopt the Christian faith here in Norway unless my regard for Thor remains just as low the next year after I return to Iceland.'

The king then said with a smile, 'From the way Kjartan behaves it is apparent that he puts more trust in his own strength and his weapons than in Thor and Odin.'

The meeting was then adjourned. Many men close to the king urged him to force Kjartan and his men to convert, and felt it unwise to have so many heathen men at such close quarters.

To this the king responded angrily, saying that to his mind many of the Christians did not conduct themselves as well as Kjartan or his men, 'and such men are worth waiting for'.

That winter the king had many useful works carried out. He had a church built and the town enlarged considerably. This church was completed by Christmas, and Kjartan suggested to his men that they go near enough to observe the services held by Christian men. Many of his men supported the idea, which they felt would prove amusing. The group included Kjartan and Bolli, along with Hallfred and many other Icelanders.

The king was urging listeners to convert. He spoke both eloquently and at length, and his speech met with general approval among the Christians.

When Kjartan and his men had returned to their quarters, they began discussing what they thought of the king during this festival which Christian men regarded as the second most important to their religion – 'since the king did say, in our hearing, that it was on this night that the prince was born in whom we are to believe, if we do the king's bidding'.

Kjartan said, 'The king gave me the impression from the first time I saw him that he was an exceptional man, and that impression has been confirmed every time that I have seen him in public since. But I have never been so impressed by him as I was today. It seems to me that our welfare depends upon our believing this God whom the king supports to be the one true God. I doubt that the king is now any more eager to have me convert than I am to be baptized. The only thing that keeps me from going to see him right away is how late in the day it is, as the king will be dining. We will need a whole day if all of our company are to be baptized.'

Bolli expressed his full agreement and said Kjartan should decide for them.

The king learned of the discussion between Kjartan and his men before his dinner was over, for he had an informer in each of the heathen men's quarters.

He was extremely pleased at the news and said, 'Kjartan has proved the truth of the saying, "Festivals are a time of fortune."'

Early that next morning, as the king was on his way to church, Kjartan approached him on the street with a large following. He greeted the king warmly and said he had a request to make of him.

The king replied just as warmly, and said he knew of his request, and 'I will grant it with pleasure.'

Kjartan said they should not waste time but fetch the holy water, and warned they would need plenty of it.

The king answered with a smile, 'Yes, Kjartan, and we wouldn't say you charged too high a price though it cost us more than that water.'

Kjartan and Bolli were then baptized along with all their crew and many others. It took place on the second day of Christmas, before morning service. Afterwards the king invited Kjartan, along with his kinsman Bolli, to his Christmas feast. According to most of the reports, Kjartan swore his allegiance to King Olaf the same day as he removed his white baptismal clothing, as did Bolli. Hallfred was not baptized that day, because he demanded that the king himself should bear witness to his baptism, which the king did two days later.

Kjartan and Bolli remained among the king's followers for the remainder of the winter. Both because of his family and his prowess, Kjartan was the king's favourite, and it is said that he was so popular that none of the king's men was jealous of him. It was also generally agreed that never had a man come from Iceland who could compare with Kjartan. Bolli was also a very capable man and was highly thought of by worthy men. The winter passed and as spring came everyone made ready for his journey, whatever direction that might take.

41 Kalf Asgeirsson approached Kjartan to ask him what his plans were for the summer.

'I had been thinking,' Kjartan answered, 'that we might sail to England, where there are good trade markets for Christians. But I want to discuss it with the king before I make a firm decision, because he did not seem much in favour of my journey when we spoke of it this spring.'

Kalf then left and Kjartan went to speak to the king, greeting him warmly. The king responded just as warmly and asked what he and his comrade had been speaking of. Kjartan told him of their plans and said that he had come to bid the king give him leave to make the journey.

The king replied, 'I will give you a choice, Kjartan: you can travel to Iceland this summer to convert the people there to Christianity, either by persuading them or by force. If you feel this journey to be too difficult, then I will not let you go elsewhere. I consider your talents should be put to better use by serving noble men than in making your fortune as a merchant.'

Kjartan chose to stay with the king rather than go on a missionary voyage to Iceland.

He said he did not wish to set himself up against his kinsmen. 'And I can well imagine that my father, and the other chieftains who are my close kin, will be less unwilling to do your bidding while I am here in your hands and enjoying your hospitality.'

The king said, 'You are making a wise and honourable choice.'

The king gave Kjartan a complete suit of newly made clothes of scarlet. They suited him very well, as people said that he and King Olaf were men of the same size when measured.

King Olaf sent his own royal cleric, a man named Thangbrand, to Iceland. His ship sailed into Alftafjord, where he spent the winter at Thvotta with Hall of Sida. He preached the Christian faith with both fair words and dire punishments. Thangbrand killed two men who most opposed his teachings.

Hall converted that spring and was baptized the Saturday before Easter along with all of his household. Gizur the White was also baptized, along with Hjalti Skeggjason and many other chieftains, but the great majority were opposed, and relations between the Christians and heathens soon grew dangerously tense. A number of chieftains made plans to kill Thangbrand and others who supported him. The hostilities eventually drove Thangbrand to Norway, where he made a report on his journey to King Olaf and added that the Icelanders would not adopt Christianity.

The king grew very angry at his words and said that many an Icelander would feel the consequences if they failed to come to their senses. At the Althing that same summer Hjalti Skeggjason was sentenced to outlawry for blasphemy. The case was prosecuted by Runolf Ulfsson, one of the country's leading men, who lived at Dal under the Eyjafjoll mountains. That summer Gizur sailed abroad, accompanied by Hjalti, made land in Norway and travelled directly to King Olaf and his followers. The king received them well, and praised their actions and invited them to become his men, which they accepted.

Sverting, the son of Runolf of Dal, had been in Norway that winter and had intended to sail for Iceland in the summer. His ship was loaded and moored at the dock awaiting favourable winds. The king forbade him to sail and said that no ship would sail for Iceland that summer. Sverting then went to the king and pleaded his case, asked for his leave to sail and said that it meant a great deal for him not to have to unload the cargo again.

The king answered him angrily, 'Fitting enough that the son of that sacrificing heathen stays where he least wants to be,' and Sverting remained.

The winter passed without event.

The following summer the king sent Gizur and Hjalti to Iceland as missionaries once more, but he kept four men behind as his hostages: Kjartan Olafsson, Halldor, the son of Gudmund the Powerful, Kolbein, the son of Thord Frey's Godi, and Sverting, the son of Runolf of Dal.

Bolli arranged passage for himself with Gizur and Hjalti and went to his kinsman Kjartan. 'I've made preparations to leave now. I'd wait for you over the winter, if there was much chance you'd be freer to travel then than now, but I'm fairly sure that the king is determined to keep you here. I also take for granted that you remember little that might entertain you in Iceland when you're conversing with the king's sister Ingibjorg.'

Ingibjorg was staying with the king at the time and was considered to be among the most beautiful women in Norway.

Kjartan replied, 'Don't go saying things like that, but do give my regards to our kinsmen and friends.'

42   After that Kjartan and Bolli parted. Gizur and Hjalti sailed from Norway and had a good voyage. They made land at the time of the assembly in the Westman Islands and went from there to the mainland, where they called a meeting and spoke to their kinsmen. Later they went to the Althing and urged men to convert to the new religion, both eloquently and at length, after which all the people of Iceland converted to Christianity.

Bolli rode home to Hjardarholt with his uncle Olaf who had welcomed him heartily. After he had been home for some time he rode to Laugar for a visit, and was given a good welcome. Gudrun asked in detail about his journey, and of Kjartan.

Bolli answered all her questions readily, and said there was little to report of his own travels, 'but as far as Kjartan is concerned, there's splendid news of his situation. He is King Olaf's man and none of the king's followers is in higher favour. But it wouldn't surprise me if we saw little of him here at home during the coming years.'

Gudrun asked if there was any reason for this other than the friendship between him and the king. Bolli told her of the stories about the friendship between Kjartan and Ingibjorg, the king's sister, and said in his opinion the king would rather marry Kjartan to Ingibjorg than let him leave, if he had his way.

Gudrun said that this was good news, 'as only the best of wives is a fair match for Kjartan', and ended the conversation.

She walked away blushing. Other people suspected that she hardly thought the news as good as she said.

Bolli stayed at home at Hjardarholt that summer and had earned himself a great deal of respect as a result of his journey. All of his kinsmen and acquaintances valued his strength and courage highly. Bolli had also made a large profit from his voyage. He often went to Laugar to visit Gudrun. Bolli once asked Gudrun what her answer would be if he asked her to marry him.

Gudrun replied quickly, 'There's no point in even discussing that, Bolli; I'll marry no man as long as I know Kjartan is still alive.'

Bolli answered, 'It's my guess that you'll have to sit here alone for a few years yet, if you wait for Kjartan. He could have asked me to give you a message, if he thought it important enough.'

They exchanged a few more words, then parted in disagreement, and Bolli returned home.

43 Some time afterwards Bolli was speaking to his uncle Olaf and said, 'Uncle, I've been thinking, now that I feel myself a full-grown man, that I should settle down and get married. I want to ask for your advice and assistance to accomplish this, as I know that most men here listen to what you have to say.'

Olaf answered, 'I'd think most women would consider you more than a fitting match. But you wouldn't have brought the question up if you hadn't already decided where it should come down.'

Bolli said, 'I won't have to go looking for a wife in distant districts as long as there are such fine women nearby. I want to ask for the hand of Gudrun Osvifsdottir; she is the most renowned of women.'

Olaf answered, 'That's a matter I want no part in. You know, Bolli, just as well as I do that the affection between Kjartan and Gudrun was spoken of everywhere. But if you consider this very important, then if you and Osvif reach an agreement I won't oppose it. Have you raised the question with Gudrun?'

Bolli said he had brought the question up on one occasion and she had been rather reluctant – 'but I expect that it will be first and foremost Osvif who will decide the question'.

Olaf said he would have to do as he wished.

Not long after this Bolli rode from Hjardarholt to Laugar, accompanied by eleven followers, among them Olaf's sons, Halldor and Steinthor. Osvif and his sons welcomed them. Bolli asked to speak to Osvif privately and brought up the question of marriage, asking for the hand of his daughter Gudrun.

Osvif replied, 'As you know, Bolli, Gudrun is a widow and as such she can answer for herself, but I will give it my support.'

Osvif then approached Gudrun and said that Bolli Thorleiksson had arrived, 'and has asked for your hand in marriage. You are to answer him. I can say without hesitation that if I were to decide, Bolli would not be turned down.'

Gudrun answered, 'You've been quick to decide this. Bolli brought the question up once with me and I tried to discourage him, and I still feel the same way.'

Osvif then said, 'If you refuse a man like Bolli many people will say that your answer shows more recklessness than foresight. But as long as I'm still alive, I intend to direct my children's actions in matters where I can see more clearly than they.'

Since Osvif opposed her so, Gudrun did not, for her part, refuse, although she was very reluctant in all respects. Osvif's sons were also very eager for her to make the match and felt it was an honour for them to have Bolli as their brother-in-law. The upshot of it was that they were betrothed and the date of the wedding set for the Winter Nights.

Bolli then rode home to Hjardarholt and told his foster-father Olaf of the arrangement. Olaf was not enthusiastic at the news. Bolli was at home until the time came for him to leave for the wedding. He invited his foster-father Olaf and, although Olaf was reluctant to attend, he agreed to it for Bolli's sake. The feast at Laugar was impressive and Bolli remained there after the wedding for the remainder of the winter. After they were married Gudrun showed little affection for Bolli.

When summer came and ships began to sail between the two countries, the news that Iceland was completely Christianized travelled to Norway. The news pleased King Olaf exceedingly and he gave his permission for all the men who had been his hostages to sail to Iceland or anywhere else they pleased.

Kjartan replied to the king, for he had been the spokesman for all the men who had been held hostages, 'We give you our thanks, and will be heading for Iceland this summer.'

The king answered, 'I don't intend to go back on my word, Kjartan, but I meant it more for the others than for you. In my view you have dwelt here more in amity than detention. I would rather you did not wish to go to Iceland, despite the fact that you have prominent kinsmen there, because I can offer you opportunities in Norway far beyond anything that awaits you in Iceland.'

To this Kjartan replied, 'May our Lord reward you for the honour you have shown me from the time I entered your service. But I expect you will grant me permission to leave no less than the others whom you have held here for some time.'

The king replied that so it would be, but said it would be difficult to find a man the equal of Kjartan outside of the ranks of the noblemen.

Kalf Asgeirsson had spent the winter in Norway after returning from England with their ship and trading goods. When Kjartan had received the king's leave to sail to Iceland he and Kalf began to make the ship ready.

When it was ready to sail, Kjartan paid a visit to the king's sister Ingibjorg. She received him warmly and made room for him to sit beside her and they conferred together. Kjartan told Ingibjorg that he had made his ship ready for the journey to Iceland.

To this she answered, 'I suspect, Kjartan, that you have done so more on your own initiative than because others urged you to leave Norway and return to Iceland.'

After that they had little to say to one another. Ingibjorg then reached for a nearby casket, from which she took a white head-dress, embroidered with golden threads, which she gave to Kjartan and said she hoped Gudrun Osvifsdottir would enjoy winding this about her head.

'You are to give it to her as a wedding present, as I want Icelandic women to know that the woman you have consorted with here in Norway is hardly the descendant of slaves.'

There was a covering of fine fabric around the head-dress. The gift was a great treasure.

'I won't come to see you off,' said Ingibjorg, 'but farewell and godspeed.' Kjartan then stood up and embraced Ingibjorg, and people say the truth is that both of them regretted having to part.

Kjartan then left to go to the king and tell him he was ready to leave. King Olaf and a large following accompanied Kjartan to his ship where it lay at anchor, with only a single gangway remaining between it and the shore.

The king then spoke: 'This sword, Kjartan, I wish to give you as a parting gift. May you carry it with you always, and I predict that no weapon will wound you while you bear it.'

The sword was very precious and highly decorated. Kjartan thanked the king graciously for all the honour and respect he had shown him while he had been in Norway.

The king said, 'Make sure, Kjartan, to keep your faith well.'

After saying this they parted as the warmest of friends, and Kjartan boarded his ship.

The king followed Kjartan with his gaze and said, 'Great is the worth of Kjartan and his kinsmen, but difficult it will be to alter that destiny which awaits them.'

44 Kjartan and Kalf set sail and had favourable winds and a speedy passage. They cast anchor at the mouth of the river Hvita in Borgarfjord. The news of Kjartan's arrival was quick to spread, and his father Olaf and other kinsmen were very glad to learn of it. Olaf rode south to Borgarfjord from the Dalir district at once and the meeting of father and son was a joyous one. Olaf invited Kjartan to come home with him and bring as many men as he wished. Kjartan gladly accepted and said that was the only place in Iceland he wanted to stay. Olaf and his men then returned home to Hjardarholt, while Kjartan stayed with the ship during the summer. He learned of Gudrun's marriage and showed no sign of response, although many people had been dreading his reaction.

Kjartan's brother-in-law Gudmund Solmundarson and his sister Thurid came to see them at the ship, and Kjartan welcomed them well. Asgeir Scatter-brain came to welcome home his son Kalf, accompanied by his daughter Hrefna, a lovely woman. Kjartan offered his sister Thurid the pick of the wares. Kalf said the same to Hrefna, opened up a large chest and told them to look over the contents.

That same day the winds grew strong and both Kjartan and Kalf had to hurry out to moor the ship better; when they returned to the booths, Kalf entered ahead of him. Thurid and Hrefna had gone through most of the contents of the chest. Hrefna snatched up the head-dress and began to unwind it, and both of them admiringly said what a beautiful object it was. Hrefna said she would like to try it on, and after Thurid advised her to go ahead, she did so.

Kalf noticed them and said she should not have done that, and told her to take it off at once: 'That's the only thing that's not both of ours to give.'

As he was saying this Kjartan entered. He had heard what they said and said at once that there was no harm done. Hrefna sat there still wearing the head-dress.

Kjartan looked her over closely and said, 'To my mind the head-dress suits you very well, Hrefna. I expect the best thing for me would be to own both the head-dress and the comely head it rests upon.'

Hrefna replied, 'People would expect you to take your time choosing a wife, and get the wife you choose.'

Kjartan said it mattered little what woman he married, but implied that he would not remain a suitor for long. Hrefna then removed the head-dress and handed it to Kjartan who put it away.

Gudmund and Thurid invited Kjartan to pay them a visit where they lived in north Iceland during the coming winter, and he promised to do so. Kalf Asgeirsson decided to head north with his father, so he and Kjartan each took their share of their common fund and parted the best of friends. Kjartan left the booths to ride to Dalir with eleven others, and everyone was pleased to see him when they arrived home at Hjardarholt. Kjartan had his property brought north from the ship in the autumn. They all spent the winter in Hjardarholt. Olaf and Osvif continued their usual custom of taking turns inviting each other to feasts in the autumn. This autumn Olaf and his family were to visit Laugar.

Gudrun now told Bolli that she felt not everything he had told her about Kjartan's return was true, but Bolli maintained he had told her what he knew as the truth. Although Gudrun hardly spoke of the matter, it was obvious that she was anything but happy, and most people assumed that she regretted having lost Kjartan, though she tried to conceal it.

Eventually the date of the feast at Laugar came. Olaf made ready for the journey and asked Kjartan to come along, but he said he intended to stay at home and look after the farm.

Olaf asked him to avoid hard feelings where kinsmen were concerned. 'Remember, Kjartan, that no one was as close to you as your foster-brother, Bolli. I want you to come and I'm sure you two will sort out your differences once you sit down together.'

Kjartan did as his father wished, and took out the suit of scarlet that King Olaf had given him in parting and other finery. He put on his sword, King's Gift, and on his head had a helmet with gold plating, and a shield with a red front and a gold cross marked on it. He also held a spear, the socket of which was inlaid with gold. All of his followers wore brightly coloured clothes. They made a party of more than twenty in all, who rode from Hjardarholt to Laugar, where a large number of people had already gathered.

45 Bolli and the Osvifssons went to meet Olaf and his party and welcomed them warmly. Bolli went up to Kjartan and welcomed him with a kiss, and Kjartan responded in like fashion. They then accompanied the party indoors. Bolli was in high spirits and Olaf was very pleased, although Kjartan seemed less enthused, and the feast was a success.

Bolli had a stud of horses regarded as the finest of animals. The stallion was large and handsome and had never been known to give way in a fight. It was white with red ears and forelock. Bolli said he wished to give the horse, along with three mares which were the same colour, to Kjartan, but Kjartan said he was no man for horses and refused to accept them.

Olaf asked him to accept the horses, saying 'They're a fine gift', but Kjartan absolutely refused.

They parted without warmth, and the people of Hjardarholt returned home. The winter proceeded without event. Kjartan was more withdrawn than usual; the others had scant pleasure conversing with him, and Olaf was concerned about the change in him.

After Christmas Kjartan made preparations to journey to the north of Iceland with eleven followers. They travelled as far as Vididal, to the farm at Asbjarnarnes, where Kjartan was given a warm welcome. The farm buildings there were very imposing. Hall, the son of Gudmund the Powerful, was then in his teens, and much resembled the men of Laxardal. It was said that a stauncher man was not to be found in all of the northern quarter. Hall gave Kjartan a very warm welcome, and organized games at Asbjarnarnes to which people from many parts of the surrounding region were invited. People came from Midfjord in the west, Vatnsnes and Vatnsdal and all the way from Langadal. A great number of people gathered, and everyone commented on how outstanding a man Kjartan was. Players were to be divided into teams under Hall's direction.

He invited Kjartan to take part. 'We hope you'll be gracious enough to join us, kinsman.'

Kjartan replied, 'I haven't had much practice at games recently, as in the service of King Olaf we had other things to keep us occupied, but I don't want to refuse your request in this instance.'

Kjartan then got ready to take part, and the men placed against him on the opposing team were those who were considered the strongest players. The game lasted all day, and no man could match Kjartan in strength or agility. In the evening, when the game was over, Hall Gudmundarson stood up and spoke: 'It is the wish of myself and my father that all of those people who have travelled a long distance should stay the night so that we may continue our entertainment tomorrow.'

His offer was well received and considered a handsome one indeed. Among the guests was Kalf Asgeirsson, and he and Kjartan enjoyed each other's company especially. Also there was his sister Hrefna, dressed in the finest of clothes. There were over a hundred people who stayed the night. The following day teams were formed again. This time Kjartan sat and watched the game.

His sister Thurid approached him and said, 'I've been told, brother, that you have been rather quiet this winter, and that people say it's because you regret the loss of Gudrun. They also say you and Bolli have little to do with each other, although the two of you were always inseparable friends. Do the right and fitting thing and try to put any malice behind you. Don't begrudge your foster-brother a good match. I think it would be best if you got married, as you yourself suggested last summer, even if Hrefna is not quite your equal, because in this country you won't find a woman who is. Her father, Asgeir, is a worthy man and of very good family, and has enough wealth to make the match an appealing prospect; his other daughter is already married to a powerful man. You yourself have told me what a capable man Kalf Asgeirsson is, and their situation is generally a fine one. I want you to have a talk with Hrefna. I'm sure you'll find her as clever as she is lovely.'

Kjartan concurred, saying that what she said made good sense, and it was arranged for him to meet Hrefna. They conferred together all that day. In the evening Thurid asked Kjartan what he thought of his conversation with Hrefna. He was very pleased and said that, as far as he could tell, she was the finest of women in all respects. The following morning messengers were sent to invite Asgeir to Asbjarnarnes, and discussions of a marriage settlement began, with Kjartan asking for the hand of Asgeir's daughter Hrefna in marriage. Asgeir responded positively to the proposal as he was no fool and realized what an honour the match was.

Kalf supported the proposal energetically, saying, 'I'll spare nothing to help bring it about.'

Hrefna, for her part, did not refuse but said her father should decide. Eventually an agreement was reached and witnessed. Kjartan would not hear of holding the wedding anywhere else but in Hjardarholt, and, as Asgeir and Kalf raised no objection, it was decided that the feast should take place there in the sixth week of summer. Kjartan then rode home bearing worthy parting gifts.

Olaf brightened at the news, for Kjartan was now in much better spirits than when he had left home. Kjartan fasted on dry foods alone during Lent, the first man known to have done so in Iceland. People found it so incredible that Kjartan could live for such a long time on such food, that they came from far and wide to witness it. In this, as in other ways, Kjartan's conduct surpassed that of other men. When Easter had passed, Kjartan and Olaf organized the wedding feast. Asgeir and Kalf rode down from the north at the appointed time, accompanied by Gudmund and Hall, and all together they made a party of sixty. Many other guests awaited them. The feast was a grand one and lasted a week.

Kjartan gave Hrefna the head-dress as a wedding present, and the gift was renowned throughout the country, as no Icelander was so cultured that he had seen, or so wealthy that he had possessed, such a treasure. According to reliable reports, there were eight ounces of gold woven into the head-dress.

Kjartan was in such high spirits at the wedding feast that he entertained everyone with his conversation and stories of his travels abroad. People were very impressed by how much he had to tell, after serving under that most worthy of rulers, King Olaf Tryggvason. When the feast came to an end Kjartan chose suitable gifts for Gudmund and Hall and the other men of distinction. Both Kjartan and Olaf gained much respect from the feast, and Kjartan and Hrefna's marriage was one of great affection.

46 Despite the ill-feelings between the younger members of their families, Olaf and Osvif remained good friends. Olaf held a feast two weeks before the beginning of winter and Osvif had organized a similar feast for the Winter Nights. Each of them invited the other to attend with as large a following as he felt did him the greatest honour.

It was Osvif's turn first to visit Olaf and he arrived at the appointed time in Hjardarholt. Among his company were Gudrun and Bolli and Osvif's sons. The following morning, as they walked towards the outer end of the hall, one of the women was discussing the women's seating plan. The discussion took place at just the moment when Gudrun had reached a point opposite the bed where Kjartan usually slept. Kjartan was dressing at that moment, and drew on a tunic of red scarlet.

To the woman who had mentioned the women's seating plan he called out – as no one was quicker to respond than he – 'As long as I'm alive, Hrefna will have the seat of honour and be treated in every way with the greatest respect.'

Previously it had always been Gudrun who had enjoyed the privilege of sitting in the seat of honour at Hjardarholt as elsewhere. Gudrun heard his words, looked at Kjartan and changed colour but said nothing.

The following day Gudrun asked Hrefna to put on the head-dress so everyone would be able to see one of the greatest treasures ever brought to Iceland.

Kjartan was not far off and, hearing Gudrun's words, was quicker to respond than Hrefna: 'She won't be wearing the head-dress at this feast, as it's more important to me that Hrefna should possess this treasure than to provide our guests at this time with a moment's diversion.'

Olaf's feast that autumn was to last a week. The following day Gudrun spoke to Hrefna privately and asked to see the head-dress, and Hrefna agreed. Later that day the two went to the outbuilding used for the storage of fine possessions. Hrefna opened a chest and took up a case made of costly woven material, out of which she took the head-dress and showed it to Gudrun. Gudrun unwound the head-dress and looked at it awhile, without either praising or criticizing it, until Hrefna took it and put it away. They then returned to their places in the hall for the evening's entertainment.

When the day came for the guests to depart, Kjartan was busy helping people who had come a long way to exchange their horses for fresh ones and assisting others in whatever way they needed. He was not carrying his sword, King's Gift, while he was doing this, despite the fact that he seldom let it out of his reach. When he finally returned to the place where he had left it, it was gone. Kjartan went directly to his father to tell him of its disappearance.

Olaf said, 'We must keep this as quiet as possible. I'll send men with each group which leaves to spy on their actions.'

This he did, sending An the White with Osvif's company to note whether anyone left the group or tarried on the way. They rode past Ljarskogar and the farm called Skogar and stopped at another farmstead called Skogar, where they dismounted. Thorolf Osvifsson and several other men left the farmhouse and disappeared into some bushes while the group stopped at Skogar.

An accompanied them when they continued their journey, riding as far as the Laxa river, where it runs out of Saelingsdal. There he said he would turn back, and Thorolf said it would not have done much harm if An had not come with them at all. The preceding night a light snow had fallen, so that it was possible to follow men's tracks. An rode back to Skogar, where he traced Thorolf's footsteps to a bog or marsh. Feeling around under the surface, he managed to grasp the hilt of a sword. He wanted to have other people witness what he did and rode to Saelingsdalstunga, to have the farmer Thorarin accompany him to recover the sword.

An presented the sword to Kjartan, who wrapped it in cloth and placed it in a chest. The spot where Thorolf and his companions had hidden King's Gift has been called Sverdskelda (Sword bog) ever since. The sheath was never recovered. Nothing was done about the theft but Kjartan valued the sword much less highly than before.

He was upset and did not want to let things go unanswered, but Olaf said, 'Don't let it disturb you. It's a poor trick they've played, but you've come to no real harm. Let's not give others something to laugh at by starting an argument with friends and kinsmen over a thing like this.'

Kjartan let himself be persuaded by Olaf's words and took no action.

Soon afterwards Olaf was preparing to make the journey to Laugar for the feast at the Winter Nights and asked Kjartan to come as well. Kjartan was reluctant to go but eventually agreed at his father's urging.

Hrefna was to go as well, and had planned to leave her head-dress behind, but her mother-in-law, Thorgerd, asked, 'When do you plan on using this treasure if it is to lie at home in a chest whenever you attend a feast?'

Hrefna answered, 'Many people say that I could well choose a place to visit where fewer people envy me than at Laugar.'

To this Thorgerd answered, 'I don't pay much heed to people who spread such gossip in the neighbourhood.'

As Thorgerd was so determined, Hrefna agreed to take the head-dress, and Kjartan did not oppose it when he saw it was what his mother wanted.

They set out soon afterwards and reached Laugar in the evening where they were given a hearty welcome. Thorgerd and Hrefna turned over their clothing to be put away but the following morning, when the women dressed and Hrefna looked for the head-dress where she had placed it, it had disappeared and was nowhere to be found although a search was made. Gudrun said it was most likely that she had either left the head-dress at home or failed to pack it carefully enough and lost it on the journey. Hrefna then told Kjartan that the head-dress had disappeared. He responded by saying that this time it would not be easy to keep an eye on their movements, told her to do nothing more for the moment and then told his father what had happened.

Olaf answered, 'As before, I want to ask you to take no action; try to ignore what has happened, and let me see what I can do privately. I will do everything I can to prevent a split between you and Bolli. Least said, soonest mended,' he added.

Kjartan replied, 'Of course you only want to do well by everyone here, but I'm not sure whether I'm prepared to let the people of Laugar ride roughshod over me.'

The day they were to leave Kjartan addressed his hosts and said, 'I warn you, Bolli, as my kinsman, to treat us more honourably in the future than you have up to now. This time I won't keep silent, because everyone already knows about the things which have disappeared here, and we suspect will have found their way into your possession. This autumn, when we hosted the feast at Hjardarholt, my sword was taken; I managed to recover it, but without the sheath. Once more property which could be described as valuable has disappeared. I want them both returned.'

Bolli answered, 'Neither of these things you accuse us of, Kjartan, are we guilty of, and least of all would I have expected you to accuse us of stealing.'

Kjartan said, 'In that case I imagine you might have offered those people here who were involved better advice, had you wanted to. You are going out of your way to insult us, and we've tried to ignore your enmity towards us for long enough. From now on, I warn you, I will suffer it no longer.'

Then Gudrun responded, saying, 'You're stirring up embers that would be better left to die out. And even if it were true someone here was involved in the disappearance of the head-dress, in my opinion they've done nothing but take what rightfully belonged to them. Believe what you like as to the whereabouts of the head-dress. I won't shed any tears if the result is that Hrefna will have little ornament from the head-dress from now on.'

After this exchange they parted rather stiffly, and the people of Hjardarholt rode homeward. The paying of visits ceased, but nothing else of event happened. Nothing more was ever heard of the head-dress, although people said Thorolf had burned it on his sister Gudrun's orders. Early in the winter Asgeir Scatter-brain died, and his sons took over his farm and wealth.

47 After Christmas that winter Kjartan collected a group of sixty men, without saying anything to his father of his plans. Olaf, for his part, showed little curiosity. Taking tents and provisions with him, Kjartan and his men set out for Laugar, where he told his men to dismount. He ordered some of them to watch the horses and others to set up the tents.

At this time it was fashionable to have outdoor privies some distance from the farmhouse, and such was the case at Laugar. Kjartan stationed men at each of the doors and prevented everyone from going outside so that they had to relieve themselves indoors for three whole days. Afterwards Kjartan rode home to Hjardarholt and all of his followers returned to their homes. Olaf expressed his displeasure at the journey, but Thorgerd said there was no need for any reproach, and the people of Laugar deserved the dishonour they had received, if not worse.

Hrefna then asked, 'Did you speak to any of the people at Laugar, Kjartan?'

He answered, 'Not really,' but added that he had exchanged a few words with Bolli.

Hrefna said, with a smile, 'I was told for a fact that you and Gudrun had a talk, and I also learned how she was dressed, that she had put on the head-dress and that it became her extremely well.'

At this Kjartan's colour rose, as Hrefna's bantering tone had obviously angered him.

'I was not aware of what you refer to, Hrefna,' Kjartan said, 'but Gudrun would not need the head-dress to look more becoming than any other woman.'

Hrefna said no more on the subject.

The men of Laugar were very upset and felt that Kjartan had done them a greater offence by these actions than if he had killed one or two of their men. Osvif's sons were the most infuriated, while Bolli tried to make little of it. Gudrun said little, but the few words she did let fall showed that it was not necessarily of less concern to her than to others. After this there was open enmity between the people of Laugar and those of Hjardarholt. Late in the winter Hrefna gave birth to a son who was named Asgeir.

Thorarin, the farmer at Tunga, declared that he wanted to sell his farm. He was in need of money, but he was also concerned at the growing hostilities in the district and was fond of both families. Bolli felt he needed a farm of his own, as the men of Laugar owned a great deal of livestock but little land. Acting on Osvif's advice, Bolli and Gudrun rode over to Tunga. They thought it highly fortunate to get this piece of land close by, and Osvif had told them not to let a small difference in price cause them to miss the opportunity.

They discussed the purchase with Thorarin and reached an agreement on the price and how payment was to be made, and the bargain with Gudrun and Bolli was concluded. There were no witnesses, however, because there were not enough people present to make it legal. Afterwards Gudrun and Bolli rode home.

When Kjartan Olafsson learned of this he rode off immediately with a party of eleven others and reached Tunga early in the morning. Thorarin welcomed him warmly and invited him to stay, and Kjartan replied that he would stop awhile but would return home that evening.

Thorarin asked what his business was and Kjartan answered, 'I came here to discuss with you the agreement you made with Bolli, because I'm opposed to your selling your land to Gudrun and Bolli.'

Thorarin said he could hardly do otherwise – 'the price Bolli offered me for the land was high and is to be paid in a short time'.

Kjartan said, 'You won't suffer financially by not selling the land to Bolli, for I'll buy it for the same price. Nor will it do you much good to refuse to do as I wish, for people will soon realize that I intend to determine the course of events in this district, and show more respect for the views of other people than those of the men of Laugar.'

Thorarin answered, 'The master's word is law in that case, but if I had my way the agreement I made with Bolli would stand unchanged.'

Kjartan replied, 'I wouldn't call it an agreement if it wasn't witnessed. Now either you agree to hand this land over to me on the same terms that you've already agreed to for the others, or keep the land for yourself.'

Thorarin chose to sell him the property, and the agreement was witnessed at once. After purchasing the land, Kjartan rode home.

The news was not long in spreading through all the valleys surrounding Breidafjord.

At Laugar they learned of it the same evening, and Gudrun said to Bolli, 'It looks to me, Bolli, as if Kjartan has given you a choice even less attractive than the one he gave Thorarin: either to turn over the district to him and gain little respect from it, or to show yourself less spineless when your paths cross in the future than you have up to now.'

Bolli made no answer, but walked away at once. Things remained quiet for the remainder of Lent.

On the third day of Easter Kjartan left Hjardarholt accompanied by An the Black. They arrived at Tunga the same day, where Kjartan wanted to have Thorarin make the journey to Saurbaer with him to agree to the debts he was to take over [as payment for his land], for Kjartan had considerable sums owed to him there. As Thorarin had gone to a nearby farm, Kjartan remained at Tunga awhile and waited for him to return. That day Thorhalla Chatterbox was at Tunga and asked Kjartan where he was headed.

He told her he was on the way to Saurbaer and she asked, 'What route will you follow?'

'Through Saelingsdal on the way there, but coming back I'll go through Svinadal,' Kjartan replied.

She asked how long he would stay, and Kjartan answered, 'I expect to return on Thursday.'

'Could you do me a service on the way?' Thorhalla then asked. 'A kinsman of mine, who lives to the west of Hvitadal in the Saurbaer district, has promised me half a mark of homespun cloth. Could I ask you to fetch it for me and bring it back with you?'

Kjartan promised he would do so.

Thorarin returned home then and joined them for the journey. They rode west over the Saelingsdal heath and reached the Hol farm in the evening. Kjartan was given a hearty welcome by the brothers and sister there, who were good friends of his. Thorhalla Chatterbox returned to Laugar that evening, and Osvif's sons asked for news of those she had met that day. She said she had met Kjartan Olafsson and they asked where he was going.

She told them what she knew, adding, 'and I've never seen him look so dashing. It's no wonder men like that feel themselves a cut above.' Thorhalla continued, saying, 'It was also clear that there were few things Kjartan would rather talk about than his purchase of Thorarin's farm.'

Gudrun answered, 'Kjartan can well afford to act as boldly as he likes, as experience has shown that no matter what offence he chooses to commit, no one dares to take him to task for it.'

Both Bolli and the Osvifssons heard their words. Ospak and his brothers gave little answer apart from a few scornful words about Kjartan as usual, but Bolli acted as if he had not heard, as was his custom. As a rule, if anyone criticized Kjartan, he kept silent or argued in his defence.

48 Kjartan spent the Wednesday following Easter at Hol, where there was plenty of entertainment and feasting. The following night An tossed and turned in his sleep, until others woke him.

They asked what he had been dreaming, and he replied, 'A horrible-looking woman approached me and tugged me sharply out of bed. She had a cleaver in one hand and a wooden meat tray in the other. Placing the cleaver on my chest, she slit me open right down the front, took out all my entrails and put in twigs instead. Then she went off.'

Kjartan and the others laughed at his story and said they would call him An Twig-belly from then on. They even grabbed him and said, teasingly, they wanted to see if they could feel the twigs in his stomach.

Aud said, however, that it was nothing to joke about, and suggested 'that Kjartan should either stay here a bit longer or, if he's determined to ride off straight away, take a few more men with him than he came with'.

Kjartan replied, 'You may value the words of An Twig-belly highly, since he sits here all day entertaining you with his stories, and think that his every dream is prophetic. But I intend to continue on my way as planned, dream or not.'

Kjartan got ready to leave early Thursday, along with Aud's brothers Thorkel Pup and Knut, at her insistence. Kjartan and his followers made a party of twelve altogether. As he had promised, he stopped in Hvitadal to pick up the homespun cloth for Thorhalla Chatterbox before heading southwards through Svinadal.

Meanwhile, at Laugar, Gudrun had risen early before the sun had come up and went to where her brothers slept. She roused Ospak, who was quick to awake, and then her other brothers. When Ospak recognized his sister he asked why she was up and about so early.

Gudrun said she wanted to know what their plans for the day were, and Ospak said he intended to remain at home, 'as there's not much farm work at the moment'.

Gudrun replied, 'With your temperament, you'd have made some farmer a good group of daughters, fit to do no one any good or any harm. After all the abuse and shame Kjartan has heaped upon you, you don't let it disturb your sleep while he goes riding by under your very noses, with only one other man to accompany him. Such men have no better memory than a pig. There's not much chance you'll ever dare to make a move against Kjartan at home if you won't even stand up to him now, when he only has one or two others to back him up. The lot of you just sit here at home, making much of yourselves, and one could only wish there were fewer of you.'

Ospak said she was anything but spare of words, but it was hard to protest against the truth of what she said. He sprang to his feet at once and got dressed and the other brothers followed him. They made preparations to ambush Kjartan. Gudrun asked Bolli to go with them, but he replied that it was not right for him to attack his kinsman and reminded her of how lovingly Olaf had raised him.

Gudrun replied, 'What you say is true enough, but you're not fortunate enough to be in a position where you can please everyone, and if you refuse to go along it will be the end of our life together.'

At Gudrun's urging Bolli's resentment of Kjartan and his offences grew, and he quickly gathered up his weapons. They were nine in number: Osvif's five sons, Ospak, Helgi, Vandrad, Torrad and Thorolf, Bolli was the sixth, the seventh was Gudlaug, Osvif's nephew and a promising young man. Odd and Stein, the sons of Thorhalla Chatterbox, completed the party. They rode to Svinadal and stopped by the ravine called Hafragil, where they tethered their horses and sat down to wait. Bolli was silent all day and lay up near the top of the ravine.

When Kjartan and his party had passed Mjosund and entered the part of the valley where it widens out, he told Thorkel and his men they should turn back. Thorkel said he would follow them all the way to the mouth of the valley. When they had passed the shielings called Nordursel, Kjartan told the brothers they should not ride any further: 'I won't have that thief, Thorolf, laughing at me for not daring to go my way with only a few men.'

Thorkel replied, 'We'll do as you tell us and go no further, but we'll regret it if we aren't there to help you today if you need it.'

Kjartan then said, 'I'm sure my kinsman Bolli won't be out to kill me, and if the Osvifssons are planning on ambushing me the outcome is anything but a foregone conclusion, even if I'm a bit outnumbered.'

The brothers then headed back.

49   Kjartan continued south through the valley along with An the Black and Thorarin. At that time a man called Thorkel lived on the Hafra-tindar farm in Svinadal which is now deserted. He had gone to see to his horses that day, taking his shepherd along with him. They could see both the men of Laugar lying in wait and Kjartan as he rode down the valley with his two companions. The boy suggested they change their course and ride towards Kjartan, saying it would be very fortunate if they could prevent such a disaster as was now looming on the horizon.

Thorkel said to him, 'Do shut up! Do you think, you fool, that you could save the life of one doomed to die? To tell you the truth, I won't be sorry to see them do whatever damage they please to one another. We're better off finding a spot where we're in no danger ourselves, but have the best view of their meeting so we can enjoy the sport. Everyone says that Kjartan is the best fighter there is; well, I expect he'll need all the fighting prowess he can muster, as we can see they are considerably outnumbered.'

They did as Thorkel wished.

Kjartan and his party were now approaching the ravine Hafragil. By this time the Osvifssons had begun to suspect that Bolli had taken up a position where anyone approaching from the north could see him. They conferred together and felt that Bolli might be going to betray them, so they went up to him on the slope and, pretending it was all in jest, began to wrestle with him, took hold of his feet and drew him further down the slope.

Kjartan and his followers, however, were riding at a good speed and approached quickly. They caught sight of the ambushers when they reached the ravine and recognized them. Kjartan jumped down from his horse immediately and turned towards the Osvifssons. There was a very large rock where Kjartan said they should stand to meet the attack. Before they met, Kjartan threw his spear and struck Thorolf's shield above the handle, forcing it back against him. The point of the spear went through the shield and into Thorolf's arm above the elbow where it severed the large muscle. Thorolf dropped his shield and his arm was of no use to him that day.

Next Kjartan drew his sword – but he was not bearing the one called King's Gift. The two sons of Thorhalla Chatterbox grappled with Thorarin, as this was the role which had been assigned to them. Their struggle was a hard one, for Thorarin was very strong, but the brothers were sturdy men as well. It was difficult to say who would come out on top.

The Osvifssons and Gudlaug attacked Kjartan. There were six of them against Kjartan and An. An defended himself valiantly and tried his best to protect Kjartan. Bolli stood back and watched, holding his sword Leg-biter. Kjartan struck powerful blows, which proved to be more than his sword could bear, and more often than once he had to straighten it by standing on it. The Osvifssons and An had all been wounded, but Kjartan was still untouched. Kjartan fought so fiercely that the Osvifssons had to fall back under the force of his onslaught and instead turned on An. After having fought for some time with his entrails exposed, An finally fell.

At the same moment Kjartan severed Gudlaug's leg above the knee, a wound which proved fatal. Four of the Osvifssons then charged at Kjartan, but he defended himself so valiantly that he did not give way under their attack at all.

Then Kjartan called out, 'Why did you leave home, kinsman Bolli, if you intended only to stand and watch? You're going to have to decide whose side you're on and then see what Leg-biter can do.'

Bolli acted as if he had not heard.

When Ospak saw that they would not be able to overcome Kjartan, he began to urge Bolli in every way he knew to join in, saying that Bolli could not wish it to be said of him afterwards that he had promised to help them in the attack and then failed to do so. 'Kjartan has proved hard enough to handle, even when we'd done much less than this to offend him, and if he should manage to escape now, a harsh punishment will await you, Bolli, no less than us.'

At this Bolli drew the sword Leg-biter and turned towards Kjartan.

Kjartan then said to him, 'An evil deed this is, that you're about to do, kinsman, so much is certain. But I'd rather receive my death at your hands than cause yours.'

With that Kjartan threw down his weapons and refused to defend himself further. He was only very slightly injured, although exhausted from fighting. Bolli made no response to Kjartan's words, but dealt him a death blow, then took up his body and held him in his arms when he died. Bolli regretted the deed immediately and declared himself the slayer.

Bolli told the Osvifssons to return home but himself remained there with Thorarin by the bodies. When they arrived at Laugar they told the news to Gudrun, who was very pleased. Thorolf's wounded arm was bandaged but took a long time healing and was always a handicap to him.

After Kjartan's body was taken to the farm at Tunga, Bolli rode back to Laugar. Gudrun went out to meet him, and asked how late in the day it was.

Bolli replied that it was almost mid-afternoon, and Gudrun said, 'A poor match they make, our morning's work – I have spun twelve ells of yarn while you have slain Kjartan.'

Bolli replied, 'I'll not soon forget this misfortune, even without you to remind me of it.'

Gudrun then said, 'I wouldn't consider it misfortune. I think you were held in much greater esteem the winter Kjartan was still in Norway than now, after he returned to Iceland and has walked all over you. And last but most important, to my mind, is the thought that Hrefna won't go to bed with a smile on her face this evening.'

At this Bolli was furious and replied, 'I wonder whether she'll pale at the news any more than you, and I suspect that you would be much less upset if it were me lying there slain and Kjartan who lived to tell the tale.'

Gudrun then realized how angry Bolli was and said, 'Don't say things like that. I'm very grateful for what you have done. Now I know that you won't go against my will.'

The Osvifssons then went into hiding in an underground shelter which had been secretly prepared for them, and Thorhalla Chatterbox's sons were sent to Helgafell to tell the news to Snorri the Godi. They were also to ask him to send them assistance quickly for support against Olaf and others seeking recourse for Kjartan's slaying.

A surprising event occurred at Saelingsdalstunga the night after the battle. An, whom everyone had thought to be dead, suddenly sat upright.

The people keeping watch over the bodies were very frightened and thought this a wondrous event, but An spoke to them, saying, 'Fear not, I tell you, in God's name. I was alive and in my right mind up until the moment when I lost consciousness. Then I dreamed this same woman came to me as before, and now she removed the twigs from my stomach and replaced my entrails, after which I became whole again.'

The wounds he had received were then bandaged and healed well, but he was ever afterwards known as An Twig-belly.

For Olaf Hoskuldsson the news of Kjartan's killing was a heavy blow, although he took it with dignity.

His sons wanted to attack and kill Bolli immediately, but Olaf replied, 'That's the last thing I want. It's no compensation for my son though Bolli be slain, and though I loved Kjartan more dearly than any other person, I can't agree to Bolli being harmed. I can give you something worthwhile to do; you should go after those two sons of Thorhalla's who were sent to Helgafell to gather forces against us. Anything you do to punish them will please me.'

The Olafssons lost no time in setting out. First, taking a ferry that belonged to Olaf, they rowed towards the mouth of Hvammsfjord. They were a party of seven, and made speedy progress. The light wind that blew was in their favour and they used their oars as well as the sail until they came to Skorey Island. They stopped there for a while to ask about the movements of people of the district. A short time later they saw a boat being rowed down from the north of the fjord and recognized the men aboard as Thorhalla's sons. Halldor and his men set out to attack them at once and met with little resistance. After boarding the ship, the Olafssons seized Stein and his brother, killed them and threw their bodies overboard. They then returned home and their journey was thought to have been very effectively carried out.

50   Olaf went out to meet Kjartan's body as it was borne home. He sent messengers south to Borg to tell Thorstein Egilsson the news and ask him for support in prosecuting the slayers. In case powerful men were to throw their weight behind the Osvifssons, he said, he wanted to make sure he would still be able to determine the course of events. He sent similar messages north to his son-in-law Gudmund in Vididal and to the Asgeirssons, and told them that he had declared all of the men guilty of the slaying who

had taken part in the assault, with the exception of Ospak Osvifsson. Ospak had previously been outlawed for seducing a woman named Aldis, the daughter of Ljot the Dueller of Ingjaldssand. Their son Ulf later became a steward among King Harald Sigurdarson's followers. His wife was Jorunn Thorbergsdottir, and their son Jon was the father of Erlend the Torpid, who was the father of Archbishop Eystein.

Olaf had declared his intent to prosecute the case at the Thorsnes Assembly. He had Kjartan's body brought home and a tent raised over it, as no church had been built in Dalir district at this time. When Olaf learned that Thorstein had responded to his message at once and collected a large number of men, as had the men of Vididal, he sent word asking his neighbours throughout the Dalir for their support.

Many men gathered in answer to his call and Olaf sent them all to Laugar, saying, 'I want you to show Bolli no less support, should he need it, than you would offer me, because if my guess is right the men from the other districts, who will soon be upon us, will feel they need to wreak their vengeance on him.'

Soon after things had been arranged in this manner, Thorstein and his company arrived, followed by the men of Vididal, all in a state of fury. Hall Gudmundarson and Kalf Asgeirsson were the most adamant in demanding that they attack Bolli and search out the Osvifssons until they were found, saying they could hardly have left the district. But when Olaf spoke determinedly against it, a message of conciliation was sent. Bolli agreed readily, and said Olaf should decide the terms for him. Osvif saw no possibility of protesting, as no support had come from Snorri. At a conciliation meeting held at Ljarskogar the judgement was awarded entirely to Olaf. He was to name whatever compensation he chose for Kjartan's slaying, either fines or outlawry. The conciliation meeting was then dissolved. Bolli did not attend, on Olaf's advice. The sentences were to be pronounced at the Thorsnes Assembly. Both the Myrar people and those from Vididal then rode back to Hjardarholt. Thorstein Kuggason offered to foster Kjartan's son Asgeir, as consolation for Hrefna, who returned north with her brothers. She was wracked with grief, but maintained a dignified and courteous manner, conversing cheerfully with everyone. Hrefna did not marry again after Kjartan's death. After returning north she lived only a short while, and it was generally said that she had been shattered by her grief.

51 Kjartan's body had remained a week at Hjardarholt. As Thorstein Egilsson had had a church built at Borg, he took the body home with him, and Kjartan was buried at Borg in the graveyard of the newly consecrated church, still in its white drapings.

The time soon came for the Thorsnes Assembly. The case against the Osvifssons was presented and all of them sentenced to outlawry. Atonement was made so that they might be transported from the country, but they were not allowed to return as long as any of the Olafssons or Asgeir Kjartansson were alive. No compensation was to be paid for Osvif's nephew Gudlaug for having taken part in the ambush and attack upon Kjartan, nor was Thorolf to receive any redress for the bloody wounds inflicted on him. Olaf refused to have Bolli outlawed and pronounced a fine as his compensation. His sons, especially Halldor and Steinthor, protested angrily at this, and said they would find it difficult to dwell in the same district as Bolli in the future. Olaf said that as long as he were alive no difficulties would arise.

A ship beached at Bjarnarhofn belonged to a man called Audun Halter-dog. He was attending the assembly and spoke out, saying, 'It could turn out that these men will be treated as much as outlaws in Norway if Kjartan's friends there are still alive.'

Osvif then replied, 'You, Halter-pup, will not prove much of a prophet, as my sons will gain the respect of worthy men, while you'll be wrestling with the trolls before this summer is out, Halter-dog.'

Audun Halter-dog sailed abroad that summer and his ship was wrecked near the Faroe Islands. Everyone aboard was drowned and people said that Osvif's prophecy had certainly been proven true.

The Osvifssons journeyed abroad that summer and none of them ever returned to Iceland. With the case thus concluded, it was Olaf who gained in stature as a result of having ensured that those who deserved the most severe punishment, the Osvifssons, paid the price, while sparing Bolli because of his close family ties. Olaf thanked his supporters warmly for their assistance. At Olaf's suggestion Bolli purchased the farm at Tunga. Olaf is said to have lived another three years after Kjartan's slaying. After his death, his sons divided up the property, with Halldor taking over the farm at Hjardarholt. Thorgerd, their mother, lived with Halldor and was filled with hatred towards Bolli, feeling she had been sorely repaid for raising him.

52   The following spring Gudrun and Bolli set up house at Saelings-dalstunga, which soon became an impressive farm. A son born to them was named Thorleik. Even as a young lad he was very handsome and precocious.

Halldor Olafsson lived at Hjardarholt, as was mentioned earlier, and acted as leader for his brothers in most matters. The spring Kjartan was slain Thorgerd Egilsdottir sent a young lad related to her to work as a servant for Thorkel of Hafratindar. The boy looked after the sheep during the summer. Like others, he was very grieved at the loss of Kjartan, but he could never mention his name in the presence of Thorkel, who generally spoke scornfully of Kjartan, saying he was cowardly and lacked daring. He often imitated Kjartan's reaction at being dealt his wound. The boy was greatly upset by this and went to Hjardarholt to report it to Halldor and Thorgerd and ask them to take him in.

Thorgerd told him he should remain in the position until the winter came, but the boy said he could not hold out any longer, 'and you wouldn't ask me to if you knew how much it tortures me'.

At that Thorgerd sympathized with him and said that, for her part, she could offer him a place.

Halldor said, 'Don't pay any attention to the boy; he's of no consequence.'

To this Thorgerd replied, 'The boy may be of little consequence, but Thorkel's behaviour has been nothing but despicable. He knew of the men of Laugar waiting there to ambush Kjartan and wouldn't warn him, but instead enjoyed himself watching their encounter and now adds insult to injury. There's little chance of you brothers ever doing much to get revenge against a more powerful opponent if you can't even deal with a miserable swine of the likes of Thorkel.'

Halldor had little to say in reply but told his mother to do as she liked regarding the boy's position.

A few days later Halldor left Hjardarholt accompanied by several men and went to Hafratindar where he attacked Thorkel in his farmhouse. When Thorkel was brought outside to be killed, his behaviour was anything but courageous. Halldor prevented the men from taking anything and returned home afterwards. Thorgerd expressed her pleasure at his actions, feeling that this action was better than none at all.

The summer passed without event, despite the strained relations between Bolli and the Olafssons. The brothers showed Bolli nothing but hatred, while he attempted to avoid coming into conflict with the Olafssons and their relatives in every way he could without sacrificing his own honour, for he had no lack of ambition himself. Bolli kept a large number of servants and lived in style, for he did not lack wealth.

Steinthor Olafsson farmed at Donustadir in Laxardal. His wife was Thurid Asgeirsdottir, who had earlier been married to Thorkel Kuggi. Their son Steinthor was called Groslappi (Groa's Layabout).

53 Late in the winter following the death of Olaf Hoskuldsson, Thorgerd Egilsdottir sent word to her son Steinthor, asking him to pay her a visit. When he answered her summons, his mother told him she wished to travel to Saurbaer to visit her friend Aud. She told Halldor to accompany them as well. They made a party of five, with Halldor escorting his mother. They rode along until they were passing the farm at Saelingsdalstunga.

Thorgerd turned her horse towards the farm and asked, 'What is the name of this farm?'

Halldor replied, 'You're hardly asking for an answer you don't already know, Mother; the farm is called Tunga.'

'Who is it lives here?' she asked.

He answered, 'You also know that only too well, Mother.'

She answered with a snort. 'What I do know,' she said, 'is that here lives Bolli, your brother's slayer, and not a shred of resemblance do you bear to your great ancestors since you won't avenge a brother the likes of Kjartan. Never would your grandfather Egil have acted like this, and it grieves me to have such spineless sons. You would have made your father better daughters, to be married off, than sons. It shows the truth of the saying, Halldor, that "every kin has its coward". I see only too well now that fathering such sons was Olaf's great failing. I address my words to you, Halldor,' she said, 'because you've taken the lead among your brothers. We will turn back now; I made the journey mainly to remind you of what you seem to have forgotten.'

Halldor then answered, 'You're the last person we could blame, Mother, if it did slip from our minds.'

Halldor had little else to say, although his hatred for Bolli swelled.

The winter passed and the summer came. When the time of the Althing approached, Halldor declared he and his brothers would attend. They rode together in a large company and set up their booth at Olaf's site. The Althing was uneventful. Also attending were the northerners from Vididal, the sons of Gudmund Solmundarson. Bardi Gudmundarson was eighteen at the time and a big, strapping man. The Olafssons invited him to come back to Hjardarholt and urged him to accept. His brother Hall was not in the country at the time, and Bardi was more than willing to accept their invitation, as the kinsmen were good friends. After the Althing Bardi rode westward with the Olafssons to Hjardarholt, where he stayed for the remainder of the summer.

54 Halldor soon confided to Bardi that the brothers were planning an attack on Bolli, adding that he could no longer stand merely to listen to his mother's taunts – 'I won't try to hide the fact, kinsman Bardi, that it was not least because we hoped for your help and support that we invited you to come home with us.'

Bardi replied, 'It will bring you no credit if you renege on a settlement made with your own kinsman. Besides that, Bolli will be no easy mark; he always has a large number of men about him, and is himself the best of fighters. Nor does he lack clever advice, both from Gudrun and Osvif. All in all it looks like anything but an easy task to me.'

Halldor said, 'We scarcely need anyone to make things more difficult for us. I wouldn't have brought the matter up if we weren't already determined to seek our revenge on Bolli. And I don't expect you, kinsman, to back out on making this trip with us.'

Bardi replied, 'I know you'd think it unsuitable for me to refuse, and if I can't manage to convince you otherwise, I won't let you down.'

'You make me a good answer,' Halldor said, 'just as I'd expect of you.'

When Bardi said that they would have to plan the attack wisely, Halldor said he had learned that Bolli had sent most of his servants off, some north to a ship in Hrutafjord and others down to Strond – 'I'm also told that Bolli himself is at the shieling up in Saelingsdal with only some servants who are making hay there. It looks to me as if there'll be no better time to confront him.'

Halldor and Bardi agreed on this.

A man named Thorstein the Black lived in Hundadal in the Dalir district of Breidafjord. He was both wealthy and wise and had long been a friend of Olaf's. Thorstein's sister Solveig was married to a man called Helgi, the son of Hardbein. Helgi was a big, strong man who had sailed on many merchant voyages. He had only recently settled in Iceland and was staying on his brother-in-law Thorstein's farm. Halldor sent word to Thorstein and

Helgi, and when they arrived in Hjardarholt he told them of his plans and preparations and asked them to come along.

Thorstein was not in favour of the plan. 'It's a terrible loss if you kinsmen continue killing one another off. There are now few men the equal of Bolli in your family.'

Thorstein's words were to no avail. Halldor sent word to Lambi, his father's half-brother, and told him of his plans when he arrived. Lambi supported the project enthusiastically. Thorgerd, mistress of the house, was another who never flagged in encouraging them to make the journey. Kjartan would never be properly revenged to her mind, she said, until Bolli paid with his life.

Soon afterwards they made ready for the journey. The four Olafssons, Halldor, Steinthor, Helgi and Hoskuld, were accompanied by Bardi, Gudmund's son, Lambi was the sixth, Thorstein the seventh, Helgi his brother-in-law the eighth, and An Twig-belly made up the ninth. Thorgerd also got ready to accompany them.

When they protested, saying this was no errand for a woman, she replied that she intended to go along, saying, 'No one knows better than I do that it is likely my sons will require some urging yet.' They replied that she would have to decide for herself.

55   The nine of them then set out from Hjardarholt, with Thorgerd making it a party of ten. Following the shore, they reached Ljarskogar early in the night, but did not slow their pace until they arrived in Saelingsdal shortly after dawn. In those days the valley was thickly wooded. As Halldor had been told, Bolli was in the shieling. The buildings stood down by the river, on the spot now known as Bollatoftir (Bolli's ruins). There is a large hill which extends back from the shieling up to the ravine Stakkagil. Between this hill and the mountain slopes there is a large meadow, called Barm, where Bolli's farmhands were haying.

Halldor and his followers approached Oxnagrof, across the plain Ranarvellir and above Hamarengi, which was opposite the shieling. They knew that there were many people staying at the shieling, so they dismounted and planned to wait there until they had left to pursue their day's tasks.

Bolli's shepherd had gone out to see to the flocks up on the mountain early that morning. He caught sight of the men in the wood and their tethered horses, and suspected that anyone who moved so secretly could hardly be on a peaceful errand. He headed straight back to the shieling to tell Bolli of the men's arrival. Halldor, who was a man of keen sight, saw him running down the hillside towards the shieling.

He told his companions that this would be Bolli's shepherd, 'who will have seen our movements. We'll have to cut him off so he won't be able to give them a warning at the shieling.'

They did as he suggested. An Twig-belly was the first to catch up with the boy. He lifted him up into the air and then threw him forcefully to the ground, breaking his spine when he fell. They then rode up to the two buildings of the dairy, a sleeping cabin and a storehouse. Bolli had been up early that morning to give instructions for the day's work, then had gone back to bed after the farmhands had set off. The two of them, Gudrun and Bolli, were alone in the sleeping cabin. They awoke at the noise of the men dismounting and heard them discussing who should be the first to enter the building and attack Bolli. Bolli recognized the voices of Halldor and several of his companions and told Gudrun to leave the cabin. The encounter at hand, he said, could only prove to be poor entertainment for her.

Gudrun replied that she felt she could look upon whatever happened, and said she would not prove any hindrance to Bolli though she remained near him. Bolli said he intended to have his way this time, and Gudrun left the building. She walked down the slope to a small stream and began to wash some linen. When Bolli was alone in the cabin he collected his weapons, placed his helmet on his head and picked up his shield and sword Leg-biter. He had no coat of mail.

Halldor and the others discussed how to go about the attack, as no one was eager to be the first to enter the cabin.

An Twig-belly then spoke: 'Others in this company may be closer kin to Kjartan, but in none of your minds do the events of Kjartan's death stand out as clearly. I remember thinking, as I was carried home to Tunga and assumed to be dead, and Kjartan was slain, how gladly I would strike back at Bolli if I got the chance. So I'll be the first one to enter.'

To this Thorstein the Black answered, 'Those are courageous words, but discretion is the better part of valour. Bolli is not simply going to stand still when attacked. Despite the fact that he has few men to back him up, you can expect him to put up a good defence. Bolli is not only strong and an excellent fighter, he also has a sword that never fails him.'

An Twig-belly then entered the cabin in a quick rush, holding his shield over his head with the narrow end foremost. Bolli struck him a blow with Leg-biter, cutting off the tail of the shield and splitting An right down to his shoulders and killing him immediately. Lambi followed on An's heels, with his sword drawn and a shield before him. At that moment Bolli jerked Leg-biter loose from An's wound, and as he did so his shield slipped to one side. Lambi used the moment to strike him in the thigh, giving him a bad wound. Bolli responded with a blow at Lambi's shoulder. The sword cut down his side and put him out of action. He never regained the full use of his arm. At this same instant Helgi Hardbeinsson entered, bearing a spear whose blade was a full ell in length, with iron wound around the shaft. When Bolli saw this, he threw down his sword, took his shield in both hands and went towards the doorway to meet Helgi. Helgi lunged at Bolli, and the spear pierced both the shield and Bolli himself. Bolli leaned against the wall of the cabin. Halldor and his brothers then came rushing in, followed by Thorgerd. Bolli spoke: 'Now's the time, brothers, to come a bit closer than you have done,' and added that he expected that his defence would soon be over. It was Thorgerd who answered, and urged them not to hesitate to finish Bolli off and to put some space between trunk and head.

Bolli was still leaning against the wall of the cabin, holding his cloak tightly to contain his entrails. Steinthor Olafsson rushed at him and struck him a blow on the neck just above the shoulders with a great axe, severing his head cleanly.

Thorgerd said, 'May your hands always serve you so well,' and said Gudrun would be busy awhile combing Bolli's bloody locks.

They then left the cabin.

Gudrun then walked away from the stream and came up towards Halldor and his party, and asked for news of their encounter with Bolli. They told her what had happened. Gudrun was wearing a long tunic, a close-fitting woven bodice and a mantle on her head. She had bound a shawl about her that was decorated in black stitching with fringes at the ends. Helgi Hardbeinsson walked over to Gudrun and used the end of her shawl to dry the blood off the spear with which he had pierced Bolli. Gudrun looked at him and merely smiled.

Halldor said to him, 'That was a vile thing to do, and merciless of you.'

Helgi told him to spare his sympathy, 'as something tells me that my own death lies under the end of that shawl'.

Gudrun followed them a short way and talked to them as they untied their horses and rode off, then turned back.

56   Halldor's companions remarked that Gudrun had seemed to care but little that Bolli had been slain, since she followed them on their way and even spoke to them as if they had done nothing at all to offend her.

Halldor answered them, saying, 'I suspect that it was not because Bolli's killing meant little to her that she saw us off, but rather that she was intent on finding out exactly who had taken part in the attack. It's no exaggeration when people say that Gudrun is a woman of exceptionally strong character. Besides, it's only natural that she should greatly regret losing Bolli, because there's no denying that a man of Bolli's stature is a severe loss, despite the fact that we kinsmen were not destined to get along together.'

After this they rode back to Hjardarholt.

The news of these events soon spread and created plenty of comment. Bolli was mourned widely. Gudrun sent men to Snorri the Godi immediately, because she and Osvif felt they could place all their trust in Snorri. Snorri lost no time in answering Gudrun's summons and arrived at Tunga with a party of sixty men.

Gudrun was very glad to see him, but when he offered to seek a reconciliation she was anything but eager to accept payment for Bolli's killing on behalf of her son Thorleik. 'The best help you could offer me, Snorri,' Gudrun said, 'would be to exchange residences with me, so that I won't have the Hjardarholt clan in the next field to me.'

At this time Snorri was involved in extensive disputes with his own neighbours, the people of Eyrar.

He replied that he would make the change for Gudrun's sake, 'but you'll have to remain at Tunga for a year yet'.

Snorri then prepared to leave and Gudrun gave him worthy gifts at parting. He returned home and the year followed without event. Gudrun gave birth to a child the winter after Bolli's death, a boy, who was named Bolli. Even as a young child he was large and handsome and Gudrun loved him deeply. The winter passed and spring arrived, and the time came for the exchange of lands which had been agreed upon between Gudrun and Snorri. Snorri settled down at Tunga and lived there for the remainder of his life, while Gudrun and Osvif moved to Helgafell, where they built up a substantial farm. Gudrun's sons, Thorleik and Bolli, grew up there. Thorleik was four years of age when his father Bolli was slain.

57   There was a man named Thorgils who was identified with his mother
        and known as Halla's son (Holluson), because she had outlived his
father. His father Snorri was the son of Alf from Dalir, while his mother
Halla was the daughter of Gest Oddleifsson. Thorgils's farm Tunga was in
Hordadal. He was a large, handsome man, very haughty, and not at all fair
in his dealings. There was no love lost between him and Snorri the Godi,
who considered Thorgils to be an interfering fellow who liked to make his
presence felt.

Thorgils often travelled to the district to the west on one pretext or
another. He was a frequent visitor at Helgafell and offered Gudrun his
assistance. She answered him politely enough but refrained from giving any
definite answer. Thorgils offered to have her son, Thorleik, come and stay
with him, and the boy was at Tunga for quite some time, where he learned
law from Thorgils, who was clever at the law.

Thorkel Eyjolfsson, a renowned man of prominent family and a great
friend of Snorri the Godi, was sailing at this time on merchant voyages.
When in Iceland he generally stayed with his kinsman, Thorstein Kuggason.
Once, when Thorkel's ship was beached at Vadil on the coast of Bardastrond,
the son of Eid of As was slain by the sons of Helga of Kropp. The killer
himself was named Grim and his brother Njal. Njal was drowned soon
afterwards in the Hvita river, while Grim was sentenced to full outlawry
for the killing and fled to the mountains after being outlawed. He was a big,
strong man. Eid was an old man when this occurred and no action was taken
against the outlaw and many people criticized Thorkel Eyjolfsson for not
acting in the case.

The following spring, when Thorkel had made ready to sail, he went south
to Breidafjord, where he got himself a horse and rode alone all the way to his
kinsman Eid at As without slowing his pace. Eid welcomed him with great
pleasure. Thorkel told him that the reason for his coming was to seek out the
outlaw Grim, and asked Eid if he had any idea where his lair might be.

'I'm not sure I like this idea,' Eid answered. 'It seems to me you're taking
quite a chance on the outcome in confronting a fiend like Grim. If you must
go, at least take some other men with you, so you will control the course
of events.'

'There's little prestige to be gained from it,' said Thorkel, 'if a whole
group attacks a single man, but I would like you to lend me your sword
Skofnung. With it, I'm sure I'll manage to deal with a single man, no matter
how capable a fighter he is.'

'Please yourself, then,' Eid said, 'but I wouldn't be surprised if you ended up regretting your stubbornness sooner or later. And since you feel you are doing this for my sake, I won't refuse your request, as I think Skofnung will be in good hands with you. But the sword can only be used under certain conditions: the sun must not be allowed to shine on its hilt, nor may it be drawn in the presence of women. Any wound it inflicts will not heal unless rubbed with the healing stone which accompanies it.' Thorkel promised to follow these instructions carefully and took the sword, asking Eid to show him where Grim had his lair. Eid said it was most likely that he hid east of As, on the Tvidaegra heath by the Fiskivotn lakes. Thorkel then rode northwards up into the highlands following the trail Eid had pointed out to him. After travelling a long distance he saw a hut by a large lake and headed towards it.

58 As Thorkel approached the hut he caught sight of a man wearing a fur cloak who sat fishing near the mouth of a stream emptying into the lake. Thorkel dismounted and tethered his horse by the wall of the hut, then headed towards the lake where the man sat fishing.

Grim saw the shadow of a man on the water and sprang to his feet. By that time Thorkel was right beside him and struck a blow at him. The blow landed on his arm just above his wrist, but the wound was not deep. Grim took hold of Thorkel and as they wrestled with one another the difference in strength soon became apparent, with Thorkel falling to the ground and Grim on top of him.

Grim then asked who he was, but Thorkel replied that it was none of his concern.

Grim said, 'Things have turned out differently than you expected, and now it's your life which seems to be in my hands.'

Thorkel replied that he wouldn't ask to be spared. 'Things have turned out unluckily for me.'

Grim replied that he had caused enough misfortune already, even if this deed were to go undone. 'Fate has other things in store for you than to die at this meeting of ours, so I'll spare your life. You can reward me in whatever way you wish.'

They both then got to their feet and walked back to the hut. Thorkel saw that Grim was weakened by the loss of blood and took Skofnung's healing stone, rubbed it on the wound and bound the stone against it. All the pain and swelling disappeared from the wound immediately. Both of them spent the night there, and the next morning Thorkel prepared to leave and asked Grim if he wished to come along. When Grim accepted, Thorkel rode westward, without returning first to Eid. They did not stop until they reached Saelingsdalstunga, where Snorri the Godi gave him a warm welcome.

Thorkel told him that his journey had turned out badly, but Snorri said things had gone well, 'and to my mind Grim has a lucky look about him. I want you to treat him generously. And if you take my advice, my friend, you'll put an end to your voyaging, settle down and get married and become the leader that a man of such good family should.'

Thorkel replied, 'Your counsels have served me well often enough', and asked whether Snorri had given thought to what woman he should propose to.

Snorri answered, 'You should propose to the woman who is the finest possible match and that is Gudrun Osvifsdottir.'

Thorkel said there was no denying the match was a worthy one, 'but it's her single-mindedness and fanaticism that cause me concern; she will presumably be intent on seeking revenge for Bolli, her husband. Thorgils Holluson seems to be involved in this with her and I'm not sure that he would like this. Not that I don't find the prospect of Gudrun appealing.'

Snorri replied, 'I'll see to it that you won't be in any danger from Thorgils, and I expect we'll see developments in the matter of Bolli's revenge before the end of the coming winter.'

Thorkel answered, 'You may be speaking more than just empty words when you say that, but I can't see that there's any more likelihood of Bolli's being avenged now than before, unless some of the leading men are ready to lend a hand in it.'

Snorri said, 'I think you should sail abroad once more this summer, and we'll see what happens.'

Thorkel agreed to this and on this note they parted company.

Thorkel travelled west across Breidafjord to his ship. He took Grim along with him on his voyage abroad. They had good winds that summer and made land in the south of Norway.

Thorkel then spoke to Grim: 'You know well enough the events and circumstances of our acquaintance, so that there is no need for me to speak of it. But I would like it to end with less hostility than we once showed each other. You have proved a staunch fellow, and I would like to part with you as if I had never borne any ill will towards you. Money enough will you have to enable you to join a company of courageous men. But you should avoid dwelling in the north of this country, as many of Eid's kinsmen sail on merchant voyages and they will bear you ill will.'

Grim thanked him for his words and said he had been offered more than he could ask for. Thorkel gave Grim plenty of trading goods at parting, and many men called his act a very generous one. After this Grim went east to the Vik region where he settled and was considered a valiant man. This is the last that is said of Grim.

Thorkel spent the winter in Norway and was regarded as a man of importance. He was both very wealthy and boldly ambitious. This scene will now be left for a while, and the thread taken up again once more in Iceland, with news of the events taking place while Thorkel was abroad.

59 At hay-time Gudrun Osvifsdottir left home and rode to the Dalir district and to Thykkvaskog. At the time Thorleik either stayed at the farm at Thykkvaskog with the Armodssons, Halldor and Ornolf, or at Tunga with Thorgils. That same night Gudrun sent word to Snorri the Godi that she wished to meet with him straight away the following day. Snorri responded at once and taking a companion with him rode off directly until he came to the Haukadalsa river. There is a cliff on the north bank of the river known as Hofdi, on the land belonging to the Laekjarskog farm. Gudrun had said they should meet there. They arrived at much the same time. Only one person followed Gudrun as well, Bolli Bollason. He was twelve years old at the time, but had the strength and wit of a full-grown man, and many a man would never be more mature though fully grown. He also bore Leg-biter.

Snorri and Gudrun spoke to each other privately, while Bolli and Snorri's companion sat at the top of the cliff to keep watch for people travelling in the district. When Snorri and Gudrun had exchanged the usual news, Snorri asked what Gudrun's purpose was – what had happened recently to bring about this sudden summons?

Gudrun replied, 'Nothing could be fresher in my mind than the event which I intend to refer to although it occurred twelve years ago. It is Bolli's revenge I intend to discuss, and it cannot come as a surprise to you, as I have reminded you of it now and again. And I remind you as well that you promised me your assistance, if I waited patiently. By now I have lost all hope of you giving your attention to our case, and I have waited as long as my patience admits. I want to ask your advice in deciding where to take revenge.'

Snorri asked what she had in mind, and Gudrun answered, 'That not all the Olafssons will remain unscathed.'

Snorri said he would forbid any action against those men who were of highest standing in the district, 'as their close kinsmen will take no small revenge and it is important to put an end to this feud'.

Gudrun said, 'Then Lambi should be attacked and killed, and that will get rid of the most malicious of them.'

Snorri answered, 'Lambi is certainly guilty enough to be killed, but I don't feel it would avenge Bolli to have Lambi killed, nor will you get the difference in compensation that Bolli's death deserves if those killings are equalled out.'

Gudrun spoke: 'It may well be that we won't be able to take an equal toll of the men of Laxardal, but someone is going to pay the price, whatever dale he dwells in. Let's turn then to Thorstein the Black; no one has played a less honourable part in this affair than he.'

Snorri spoke: 'You have no more complaint against Thorstein than any of the others who went along on the attack but inflicted no wound on Bolli. But you pass over completely men who to my mind are more worthy of taking revenge upon, and actually dealt Bolli his death-blow, such as Helgi Hardbeinsson.'

Gudrun said, 'That is true enough, but I am not content to let off all the others against whom I've nurtured such hostility.'

Snorri answered, 'I see a good plan. Lambi and Thorstein will assist your sons in the attack, as a fair way of settling their debt to you. If they refuse, I won't attempt to protect them or deter you from punishing them in any way you wish.'

Gudrun asked, 'How do we go about getting these men you have named to take part?'

Snorri replied, 'Those who head the attack will have to look after that.'

Gudrun said, 'I should like you to suggest who is to lead and direct the attack.'

Snorri smiled at this and said, 'You have already picked the man for the job.'

Gudrun replied, 'By that you mean Thorgils?'

Snorri said that indeed he did. Gudrun replied, 'I have spoken of this to Thorgils, but the subject is as good as closed. He set the one condition that I could not consider: he would not refuse to avenge Bolli, if I would agree to marry him. Of that there is no hope at all, and so I will not ask him to make the journey.'

Snorri spoke: 'I will tell you a way to go about it, because I would not mind Thorgils making this journey. He will, naturally, be promised a match, but with the catch that you should otherwise marry no other man in the country. That promise you can keep, as Thorkel Eyjolfsson is not in this country at the moment, and it is he whom I intend you to marry.'

Gudrun replied, 'Surely he will see the catch.'

Snorri replied, 'He surely will not. Thorgils is a man more given to acting than thinking. Make the agreement with him in the presence of only a few witnesses; have Halldor, his foster-brother, present but not Ornolf, who is cleverer, and I'll take the blame if it doesn't work.'

Snorri and Gudrun then brought their conversation to an end and said their farewells to one another. Snorri rode home and Gudrun to Thykkvaskog. The following morning Gudrun left Thykkvaskog in the company of her sons, and as they travelled westward along the Skogarstrond shore they noticed men following them. As these men were riding hard, they soon caught up and proved to be Thorgils Holluson and followers. They greeted each other warmly and rode on together to Helgafell that day.

60   Several nights after returning home, Gudrun asked her sons to come and speak to her in her leek garden. When they arrived they saw spread out garments of linen, a shirt and breeches much stained with blood.

Gudrun then spoke: 'These very clothes which you see here reproach you for not avenging your father. I have few words to add, for it is hardly likely that you would let the urging of words direct you if unmoved by such displays and reminders.'

Both brothers were greatly shaken by Gudrun's words, but answered that they had been too young to seek revenge and had lacked someone to lead them. They had neither been able to plan their own actions nor those of others, 'though we well remember what we have lost'.

Gudrun said she suspected that they gave more thought to horse-fights or games. After this the brothers left, but they could not sleep that night. Thorgils noticed this and asked what was troubling them. They told him everything of the conversation with their mother, adding that they could no longer bear their grief and her reproaches.

'We wish to seek revenge,' said Bolli. 'We brothers are mature enough now that people will begin to count it against us if we fail to take action.'

The following day Gudrun and Thorgils were talking privately together.

Gudrun began by saying, 'It looks to me, Thorgils, as if my sons have had their fill of inaction, and will be looking to avenge their father. Things have had to wait until now mostly because I felt Thorleik and Bolli were too young to go about slaying men. There was certainly more than enough cause to have retaliated earlier.'

Thorgils answered, 'You have no reason to discuss this matter with me, since you have absolutely refused to marry me; I'm still of the same mind, however, as before when we discussed this. I don't think it too tall an order to knock off one or both of the men who played a major part in Bolli's killing if I can get you to marry me.'

Gudrun spoke: 'It seems that Thorleik feels no one is better suited as the leader for any difficult undertaking. But I will not conceal from you that the lads intend to attack the berserk Helgi Hardbeinsson, who lives on his farm up in Skorradal, and is completely off his guard.'

Thorgils spoke: 'It makes no difference to me whether his name is Helgi or anything else. I don't feel it beyond me to take on Helgi or any other man. I've said my last word on it; you promise before witnesses to marry me if I manage to help your sons get their revenge.'

Gudrun replied that she would keep any promise she gave, though it were made before but a few witnesses, and said they should agree on this bargain. She asked that Thorgils's foster-brother Halldor be summoned and then her sons.

Thorgils asked that Ornolf be present as well, but Gudrun said there was no need for that – 'I am more suspicious of Ornolf's loyalty towards you than I expect you are.'

Thorgils said she should have her way.

The brothers then approached Gudrun and Thorgils, who were talking to Halldor as they came.

Gudrun explained the situation to them, that 'Thorgils has promised to offer his leadership on a journey to attack Helgi Hardbeinsson, along with my sons, to avenge Bolli. Thorgils made it a condition for the journey that I agree to marry him. Now I declare in your presence as witnesses, that I promise Thorgils to marry no other man in this country than him; nor do I intend to marry abroad.'

Thorgils was satisfied that the promise was binding enough and saw nothing questionable about it. They then brought the conversation to an end. It was now settled that Thorgils would lead the attack. He made preparations to set out from Helgafell, accompanied by Gudrun's sons. They rode eastward to the Dalir district, stopping first at Thorgils's Tunga farm.

61   The next Lord's Day the local Autumn Meeting was held, which Thorgils attended with his party. Snorri the Godi did not attend the assembly, but a large crowd was there.

During the day Thorgils managed to speak to Thorstein the Black, saying, 'Since, as you know, you went along with the Olafssons when Bolli was slain, you owe his sons some unpaid compensation. And although it's a long time since the events took place, I don't imagine they have forgotten those men who took part. In the opinion of the two brothers, it would hardly be to their honour to seek revenge on the Olafssons, for the sake of kinship. So they now intend to attack Helgi Hardbeinsson, as it was he who dealt Bolli his death blow. We want to ask you, Thorstein, to accompany them on their journey, and in so doing buy your own settlement.'

Thorstein answered, 'It does me little honour to plot an attack on my brother-in-law Helgi; I would much rather give money to buy peace, and I'll make it enough to serve as an honourable settlement.'

Thorgils answered, 'I scarcely expect the brothers are doing this for the sake of money. Make no mistake, Thorstein, you have two choices before you: either you make the journey or face harsh punishment when it's dealt out. I also want you to accept this offer, despite your obligations to Helgi. Each man must look out for himself in a tight situation.'

Thorstein said, 'Will you be making such an offer to others, with whom Bolli's sons have a score to settle?'

Thorgils answered: 'It's the same choice Lambi will have to make.'

Thorstein said he thought it better if he were not the only one involved.

After that Thorgils sent word to Lambi to meet with him, and invited Thorstein to be present at their conversation.

He said, 'I intend to speak to you, Lambi, about the same matter which I have already raised with Thorstein. What honour are you ready to do Bolli's sons for the grievance they have against you? I have been told truthfully enough that you wounded Bolli, and, in addition, you share a major portion of the guilt for having strongly urged that he be killed. You were admittedly among those with the most cause for offence, next to the Olafssons.'

Lambi asked what would be demanded of him. Thorgils answered that he would be offered the same choice as Thorstein, to accompany the brothers on an attack or face punishment.

Lambi replied, 'This is a poor and ignoble way of buying one's peace. I'm not willing to make this journey.'

Thorstein then said, 'It's not so simple a question, Lambi, that you should refuse so quickly. Important and powerful men are involved, who feel they have received less than their due for a long time. I am told that Bolli's sons are promising young men, bursting with pride and eagerness, and with cause enough to seek revenge. We can only expect to have to make them some redress after such a deed. People will place most of the censure on me, in any case, because of my connections to Helgi. And like most others I am ready to do most anything to save my own skin. Each pressing problem that arises demands its own solution.'

Lambi spoke: 'It's clear which way you're leaning, Thorstein. I suppose it's just as well to let you decide, if you're so determined about it; we're old partners in troublemaking. But I want to make it a condition, if I agree to this, that my kinsmen, the Olafssons, will be left alone and in peace, if revenge against Helgi is successful.'

Thorgils agreed to this on behalf of the brothers.

Thus it was decided that Thorstein and Lambi would accompany Thorgils in the attack. They agreed to meet early in the day at Tunga in Hordadal three days later. After this they parted and Thorgils returned to his farm at Tunga that evening. The appointed time for the men intending to make the journey to meet with Thorgils came. Before sunrise on the third morning Thorstein and Lambi arrived at Tunga. Thorgils gave them a warm welcome.

62 Thorgils now made ready to set out and the party of ten rode off up Hordadal, with Thorgils Holluson leading the group. Others making the journey included Bolli's sons, Thorleik and Bolli. The fourth man was their half-brother Thord the Cat, Thorstein the Black was the fifth, Lambi the sixth, Halldor and Ornolf the seventh and eighth, Svein and Hunbogi, both sons of Alf from Dalir, were the ninth and tenth. All of them looked like fighters to be reckoned with. They set out on their way, up the Sopandaskard pass and over Langavatnsdal, then cut straight across the Borgarfjord district. They crossed the river Nordura at Eyjarvad ford, and the Hvita river at the Bakkavad ford, just above Baer. They rode through Reykjadal and over the ridge to Skorradal where they followed the woods

to the vicinity of the farm at Vatnshorn. There they dismounted; it was late in the evening.

The farmhouse at Vatnshorn stands a short distance from the water's edge on the south side of the river.

Thorgils told his companions they would spend the night there. 'I intend to go up to the farm and look around, and try to learn whether Helgi is at home. I am told that he usually keeps few servants, but is always very much on his guard and sleeps in a sturdily built bed closet.'

His companions said Thorgils should decide their course.

Thorgils then had a change of clothes, removing his black cloak and pulling on a hooded cowl of grey homespun. He went up to the farm and when he had almost reached the hayfield wall he saw a man approaching.

When they met, Thorgils asked, 'You may think my question an ignorant one, comrade, but what district is this I'm in, and what is the name of that farm or the farmer who lives there?'

The man replied, 'You must be very foolish and ignorant indeed, if you haven't heard of Helgi Hardbeinsson, such a great warrior and important man as he is.'

Thorgils then asked what sort of welcome Helgi gave strangers who knocked at his door, especially those in much need of assistance.

The man replied, 'I can in truth give you a good answer there, as Helgi is the most generous of men, both in taking men in as in other dealings.'

'Would he be at home now?' asked Thorgils. 'I was hoping to ask him to take me in.'

The other man asked what his problem was and Thorgils replied, 'I was made an outlaw this summer at the Althing. I wanted to seek the protection of someone who had enough power to offer it. In return I can offer him my service and support. Now, take me to the farm to meet Helgi.'

'I can easily enough,' he said, 'take you home, and you'll be allowed to stay the night. But you won't meet Helgi, because he's not at home.'

Thorgils then asked where he was.

The man answered, 'Helgi is at his shieling, in the place called Sarp.'

Thorgils asked where that was, and who were there with him. He replied that Helgi's son, Hardbein, was there and two other men Helgi had taken in who were also outlaws.

Thorgils asked him to show him the straightest route to the shieling, 'as I want to meet with Helgi right away, wherever he can be found, and put my request to him'.

The servant then showed him the way and they parted after that.

Thorgils returned to the wood to his companions and told them what he had learned of Helgi's circumstances. 'We'll stay here overnight and wait until morning to make our way to the shieling.'

They did as he proposed. In the morning Thorgils and his men rode on up through the wood until they were only a short way from the shieling. Thorgils then told them to dismount and eat their breakfast, which they did, stopping there awhile.

63 Now to news of the shieling, where Helgi and those men previously mentioned were staying. In the morning Helgi spoke to his shepherd, telling him to look around in the woods near the shieling and see if there were any men about or anything else worthy of reporting. 'My dreams last night were troubled.'

The boy did as Helgi said. He disappeared awhile and when he returned Helgi asked him what he had seen.

He answered: 'I have seen something which I think is newsworthy enough.'

Helgi asked what this was. He said he had seen no small number of men, 'and they look like men from another district to me'.

Helgi said, 'Where were they when you saw them, and what were they doing? Did you notice their appearance, or how they were dressed?'

He answered, 'I was not so stricken with fear that I didn't observe things like that, because I knew you would ask about them.'

He added that they were only a short distance away from the shieling and were eating breakfast. Helgi asked whether they sat in a circle or in a row. The boy replied that they sat in a circle on their saddles.

Helgi said, 'Tell me what they looked like. I want to see if I can guess from their descriptions, what men these are.'

The boy said, 'One of the men sat on a saddle of coloured leather and wore a black cloak. He was a large man of manly build, balding at the temples and with very prominent teeth.'

Helgi said, 'I recognize that man clearly from your words; you have seen Thorgils Holluson from Hordadal. What can that fighter want with us?'

The boy spoke: 'Next to him sat a man in a gilded saddle; he was wearing a tunic of red scarlet and a gold ring on his hand. About his head was fastened a band of gold-embroidered cloth. This man had fair hair, falling in waves down to his shoulders. He was also fair-complexioned, with a bent nose, somewhat turned up at the end, handsome eyes, blue and piercing and restless, a wide forehead and full cheeks. His hair hung down in the front and was clipped at the eyebrows, and he was well built at the shoulders and broad across the chest. His hands were well formed, his arms strong, and his entire bearing refined. I must say in conclusion that no other man have I seen so valiant-looking in all respects. He was also a youthful man, with hardly a hair on his face yet. He seemed to me as if he were burdened with sorrow.'

Helgi then answered, 'You've observed this man carefully and he appears to be a man of great worth. I doubt that I have ever seen him, but I imagine it will be Bolli Bollason, because I am told he is a very promising young man.'

The boy then said, 'Another man sat on an enamelled saddle, wearing a yellow-green tunic and a large ring on his hand. He was a most handsome youngster, with brown hair which suited him well and everything about him was very refined.'

Helgi answered, 'I think I know who this man you have described is. This will be Thorleik Bollason. You're a clever lad, with a keen eye.'

The boy said, 'Next to him sat a young man in a black tunic and black breeches girded at the waist. He had a straight face and pleasing features, with light hair, slender and refined.'

Helgi answered, 'I recognize this man and have likely seen him before; he will have been fairly young in age. This is Thord Thordarson, Snorri the Godi's foster-son. A well-mannered group they have here, these men of the West. Any more?'

The boy then said, 'Next was a man in a Scottish saddle, with a greying beard and bushy brows. His hair was black and curly, and he was not very good-looking, although he had the look of a fighter all right. Over his shoulders he wore a grey gathered cape.'

Helgi said, 'I can see clearly who this man is. This is Lambi Thorbjarnarson from Laxardal. I don't know what he is doing accompanying the two brothers.'

The boy said, 'Next was a man sitting on a stand-up saddle with a black outer garment and a silver ring on his hand. A farmer by the look of him, he was no longer young, with dark brown and very curly hair and a scar on his face.'

'Your tale is taking a turn for the worse,' said Helgi. 'This man you have seen must be my brother-in-law Thorstein the Black, and I find it very surprising that he should have come along on such a journey. I wouldn't pay him a visit like this. But were there any more of them?'

The boy answered, 'Next there were two men of similar appearance and about middle age. They were both of them powerful men, with red hair and freckled faces, but handsome all the same.'

Helgi said, 'I know well who these men are. These are the Armodssons, Halldor and Ornolf, Thorgils's foster-brothers. You have given a thorough report – are these all of the men you saw?'

The boy answered, 'There's little more left to tell. The next man looked away from the group. He wore a plated coat of mail and a steel helmet with a brim as wide as the width of your hand. He held a gleaming axe over his shoulder, the blade of which was an ell in length. This man was dark, with black eyes and the appearance of a Viking.'

Helgi answered: 'This man I recognize clearly from your report. It was Hunbogi the Strong you saw, the son of Alf from Dalir. I can't quite see their intentions but they have certainly a choice selection of men for their journey.'

The boy spoke: 'Yet another man sat next to this strong-looking one; he had dark brown hair, a round and ruddy face and heavy brows, just over medium height.'

Helgi spoke: 'You need not say more; it will have been Svein, the son of Alf from Dalir and brother of Hunbogi. We had better be prepared for these men, as it's my guess that they will intend to pay me a visit before they leave the district; some of them making the journey would have thought it more fitting had our paths crossed earlier. Those women who are here in the shieling will throw on some men's clothes, take the horses close to the shieling and ride as fast as they can to the main house. Those men awaiting nearby may not be able to tell whether it is men or women who go riding off. We need only gain a little time to seek more help, and then we'll see whose position is the better.'

All four women rode off together.

Thorgils suspected that their presence may have been reported and told his men to mount their horses and ride up to the shieling at once, which they did. But before they could mount a man rode up to them in plain view. He was short in stature and brisk in his movements. His eyes darted about in a strange manner, and his horse was a strong one. This man greeted Thorgils like an old acquaintance. Thorgils asked him his name and who his kinsmen were, and where he had come from.

The man said his name was Hrapp and his mother's family hailed from Breidafjord, 'where I have been raised. I am named for Killer-Hrapp, and

the name fits, for I am no man of peace, although I am small in size. My
father's people are from the south of Iceland, and I have spent the last few
winters there. It's a lucky chance I happened upon you here, Thorgils, as I
was going to seek you out, even if I'd had to go to more trouble to do so.
I'm in some difficulty; I've quarrelled with my master, as his treatment of
me left much to be desired. As my name indicates, I'm not one to put up
with such insults, so I tried to kill him, although with little or no success, I
think. I didn't wait to find out, as I felt I was better off astride this horse I
took from the farmer.' Hrapp spoke at length, but asked few questions. He
soon became aware of their intention to attack Helgi, however, which he
supported eagerly, saying no one should look for him in the back ranks of
the attackers.

64   After mounting their horses, Thorgils and his men set out at good
speed and soon left the wood behind. They saw four riders leave the
shieling, urging their horses on quickly.

Some of Thorgils's companions said they should give chase at once, but
Thorleik Bollason replied, 'Let's go up to the shieling first and see what
men are there. I think these riders are hardly Helgi and his companions –
they look to me only to be women.'

More of the men opposed him than agreed, but Thorgils said that they
should follow Thorleik's advice, for he knew him to be the most keen-sighted
of men. They then approached the shieling.

Hrapp charged onward ahead of them, brandishing a puny spear he held
in his hand, lunging forward with it and saying it was high time to show
what they could do. Before Helgi and his men knew what was happening,
Thorgils and his party attacked the shieling. Helgi and his men shut the
door and took up their weapons. Hrapp ran up to the shieling straight away
and asked whether Reynard was at home.

Helgi answered, 'You will find the fox here inside fierce enough, since
he dares to bite so near his lair.'

As he said this, Helgi thrust his spear from the shieling window right
through Hrapp, who fell to earth dead.

Thorgils told his men to approach with caution and protect themselves
from injury. 'We should have more than enough strength to take the shieling
and Helgi there inside it, as I think there are few men with him.'

The shieling was built with a single roof beam, which reached from one
gable to the other and protruded at the ends, with a thatch of turf only a

year old which had not yet fully taken root. Thorgils told several men to take each end of the roof beam and put enough pressure on it to break it or loosen the rafters from it. Others were to watch the doors, in case they should attempt to come out. Helgi and his companions in the shieling were five in number, including his son Hardbein, who was twelve years old, his shepherd and two other men, named Thorgils and Eyjolf, who were outlaws and had sought his protection that summer. Thorstein the Black stood at the door of the shieling along with Svein, the son of Alf from Dalir, while their companions set to work in two groups tearing the roof off the shieling. Hunbogi the Strong took hold of one end of the roof beam along with the Armodssons; Thorgils and Lambi and Gudrun's sons took the other. When they lifted the beam upwards sharply it split apart in the middle. At that moment Hardbein thrust his halberd out through a gap where the door had been broken. The point struck Thorstein's steel helmet and pierced his forehead, causing a bad wound. At this Thorstein said, as was true enough, that there must be men inside.

Helgi then charged out through the door so forcefully that those men standing next to it fell back. Thorgils was standing close by and struck at him with his sword, landing a blow on his shoulder that left a large wound.

Helgi turned towards him with a wood-axe in his hand, saying, 'This old fellow still dares to face others.'

He threw the axe at Thorgils, striking him on the foot and giving him a severe wound. When Bolli saw this he charged at Helgi with Leg-biter in his hand and thrust it through Helgi, dealing him his death wound. At once Helgi's companions and Hardbein rushed out of the shieling. Thorleik Bollason turned to face Eyjolf, who was a strong man. Thorleik struck him a blow with his sword on the thigh just above the knee which cut off his leg, and he fell to the ground dead. Hunbogi the Strong charged at Thorgils and swung his axe at him, striking him on the spine and splitting him in two in the middle. Thord the Cat was standing nearby when Hardbein ran out of the shieling and wanted to charge at him.

When he saw this, Bolli ran up and told him not to harm Hardbein, saying, 'No base deeds are to be done here; Hardbein is to be spared.'

Helgi had another son called Skorri. He was being brought up on the farm called England in southern Reykjadal.

65 After these events Thorgils and his men rode over the ridge into Reykjadal to declare responsibility for the killings. They then took the same route back as they had come, not slowing their pace until they had come to Hordadal. There they related what had happened on their journey. The foray became renowned and the slaying of a fighter the likes of Helgi was thought a deed of great note. Thorgils thanked the men warmly for making the journey, as did both of Bolli's sons. The men who had accompanied Thorgils then went their separate ways. Lambi rode northward to Laxardal, stopping on his way at Hjardarholt, where he told his kinsmen the details of the events which had taken place in Skorradal. They were greatly upset by his part in it and criticized him angrily. His actions, they maintained, showed him to be more the descendant of Thorbjorn the Pock-marked than Myrkjartan, king of the Irish. Lambi grew very angry at their words and said their scolding him showed their own lack of manners, 'as I have managed to have all of you spared from certain death'. They exchanged few more words, with both sides even more displeased than before, and Lambi rode home to his farm.

Thorgils Holluson then rode to Helgafell, accompanied by Gudrun's sons and his foster-brothers, Halldor and Ornolf. When they arrived late in the evening everyone had gone to his bed. Gudrun got up at once and told the servants to get up and wait upon them. She went into the main room to greet Thorgils and all his party and hear their news. Thorgils responded to Gudrun's greeting after removing his cloak and weapons and sat leaning against the posts of the wall. He was dressed in a reddish brown tunic with a wide belt of silver. Gudrun sat down on the bench beside him and Thorgils spoke this verse:

3. Home to Helgi we rode,
   gorged ravens on blood;
   reddened shining shields' oak,   *shields' oak*: weapons
   when we went with Thorleik.
   There we felled three
   skilful helmet-trees   *helmet-trees*: warriors, men
   of rare renown.
   Bolli's vengeance is done.

Gudrun asked more closely about the events occurring on their journey. Thorgils answered whatever she asked. Gudrun said their journey had turned out splendidly and thanked them all. After that they were waited

upon and when they had had their fill they were shown to their beds, where
they slept until the night was past.

The following day Thorgils spoke to Gudrun alone, saying, 'The situation
is, as you know, Gudrun, that I have carried out this foray as you asked me
to. I feel I have done my part completely and I hope it has been worth my
while. You will remember what you have promised me in return, and I feel
that I am now entitled to collect my bargain.'

Gudrun then spoke: 'Hardly has the time which has passed since we
spoke of this been so long as to make me forget it. I have no intention of
doing otherwise than fulfilling the bargain we agreed upon completely. Do
you remember what it was that we agreed upon?'

Thorgils said she must remember that.

Gudrun answered, 'I think I promised you I would marry no other man
in the country except you; do you have any objection to make to that?'

Thorgils said she remembered correctly.

'It is well that we both are agreed on this. I will not conceal from you
any longer that I do not intend you to be so fortunate as to have me for
your wife. I keep every word of my promise to you though I marry Thorkel
Eyjolfsson, for he is at present not in this country.'

Thorgils then spoke, becoming very flushed as he did so. 'Clearly do I
see, where the current came from that sent this wave; they have generally
been cold, the counsels that Snorri the Godi has sent my way.'

Thorgils broke off the conversation, sprang to his feet in fury, went to
his companions and told them he wished to leave at once. Thorleik was
displeased at the way Thorgils had been offended, but Bolli supported his
mother's wishes. Gudrun offered to give Thorgils handsome gifts to soften
his anger, but Thorleik said that this would be to no avail.

'Thorgils is too proud a man to bow down for a few trinkets.'

Gudrun said he would then have to return home and console himself.
On this note Thorgils made his departure from Helgafell along with his
foster-brothers. He returned home to Tunga highly displeased with his lot.

66 Osvif was taken ill and died that winter. His passing was thought a
great loss, for he had been among the wisest of men. Osvif was buried
at Helgafell, where Gudrun had had a church built.

Gest Oddleifsson became ill that same winter and as his condition
worsened, he summoned his son Thord the Short and spoke to him, saying,
'If my suspicions are correct, this illness will make an end of our life together.

I wish to have my body taken to Helgafell, as it will be the most prominent seat in the district. I have also often seen brightness there.'

Gest died soon afterwards.

The winter had been a cold one, and there was a thick layer of ice along the shore and far out into the bay of Breidafjord, preventing ships from setting out from the Bardastrond shore. On the second night Gest's body had lain at Hagi, a storm blew up with winds so strong that the ice was driven from the shore. The following day the weather was mild and calm. Thord laid Gest's body in a boat and that day they headed south across the bay of Breidafjord, reaching Helgafell in the evening. Thord was well received and stayed the night there. Gest's body was buried the following morning in the same grave as Osvif. The prediction made by Gest now came true, as the distance between the two was now much shorter than when one lived at Bardastrond and the other in Saelingsdal. Thord the Short returned home after concluding his errand. The following night a wild storm raged, driving all the ice back to the shore. It remained thus for most of the winter, preventing all journeys by boat. That the chance to transport Gest's body had arisen was thought to be a great omen, as all travelling was impossible both before and afterwards.

67 A man named Thorarin lived in Langadal. He held a godord, but was a man of no influence. His son Audgisl was a man quick to act. Thorgils Holluson had dispossessed them of their godord and they considered this a grievous insult. Audgisl approached Snorri, told him of the ill-treatment which they had suffered and asked for his support.

Snorri replied positively, but made light of it all saying, 'So Halla's layabout is getting ambitious and pushing people around, is he? When is Thorgils going to run into someone who won't let him have his way in everything? It's true enough that he's a tough, strong fellow but other men of the sort have been done away with before now.'

When Audgisl departed Snorri made him a present of an inlaid axe.

That spring Thorgils Holluson and Thorstein the Black journeyed south to Borgarfjord and offered Helgi's sons and kinsmen compensation for his slaying. A settlement was reached in the matter which gave them honourable recompense. Thorstein paid two-thirds of the compensation for the killing, and Thorgils was to pay one-third, with payment to be made at the Althing. Thorgils rode to the Althing that summer, and as he and his party reached the lava field at Thingvellir they saw a woman coming towards them of very great size. Thorgils rode towards her, but she turned aside, speaking this verse:

4.   Let them take pains,
    these men of note,
    to protect themselves
    from Snorri's plots;
    none will escape,
    so wily is Snorri.

She then proceeded on her way.

Thorgils said, 'Seldom did you, when the future looked bright for me, leave the site of the Althing as I arrived.'

Thorgils then rode on to the Althing and to the site of his booth, and the first days of the session passed without incident until a portent occurred one day during the Althing. Clothing had been hung out to dry. A black, hooded cloak belonging to Thorgils had been spread out on the wall of the booth. People heard the cloak speak this verse:

5.   Wet on the wall it hangs
    yet knows of wiles, this hood;
    it will not dry again,
    I do not hide that it knows of two.

This was thought a great wonder. The following day Thorgils crossed over to the west side of the river where he was to pay his compensation to Helgi's sons. Accompanied by his foster-brother Halldor and several other men, he sat down on the rock above the booth sites. Helgi's sons came to meet them. Thorgils had begun counting out the silver when Audgisl Thorarinsson passed by, and, just as Thorgils said ten, Audgisl swung at him; everyone thought they could hear his head say eleven as it flew off his body.

Audgisl ran off immediately to the booth of the men of Vatnsfjord, but Halldor ran after him and dealt him his death blow in the entrance way. News of these events, and that Thorgils Holluson had been slain, soon came to Snorri the Godi's booth.

Snorri said, 'You can't have understood; Thorgils will have done the slaying.'

The man replied, 'Still, it was his head that flew off his body.'

'Then perhaps the news is true,' said Snorri.

A settlement was reached regarding the slaying, as is related in the saga of Thorgils Holluson.

68 The same summer that Thorgils Holluson was slain a ship owned by Thorkel Eyjolfsson arrived in Bjarnarhofn. By that time he was a man of such wealth, that he owned two knorrs making voyages to Iceland. The other sailed into Hrutafjord and landed at Bordeyri. Both of them were laden with timber. When Snorri learned of Thorkel's arrival he rode to his ship at once. Thorkel welcomed him warmly. He also had a good supply of drink aboard his ship and it was served up generously. They had much to talk of. Snorri asked for news from Norway and Thorkel spoke both at length and in detail.

In return, Snorri told him of the events which had occurred while he had been abroad. 'Now seems to me a suitable time,' Snorri said, 'to do as I advised you before you sailed abroad: make an end to your sailing, settle down and take yourself the wife that we spoke of then.'

Thorkel answered, 'I understand what you're about, and I'm of the same mind now as I was when we spoke then. Far be it from me to pass up the chance of such a worthy match if it can be arranged.'

Snorri spoke: 'I am more than ready and willing to support this proposal on your behalf. Both of the difficult obstacles which you felt prevented your marrying Gudrun have now been removed. Bolli has been avenged and Thorgils done away with.'

Thorkel spoke: 'Your counsels run deep, Snorri, and I'll certainly follow this course.'

Snorri stayed on board the ship for several nights, after which they took a ten-oared boat floating alongside the merchant vessel, made their preparations and set out for Helgafell, a party of twenty-five in number.

Gudrun received Snorri especially warmly and they were waited on amply.

When they had spent the night there, Snorri asked to speak privately with Gudrun and said, 'The situation is this. I made this journey on behalf of my friend Thorkel Eyjolfsson. He has come here, as you can see, and for the purpose of asking for your hand in marriage. Thorkel is a worthy man; you know all about his family and his deeds, and he has no lack of wealth. To my mind he's the man most likely to have the makings of a leader in him here, if he has a mind to become one. Thorkel is held in high esteem out here in Iceland, but in much higher repute when he is in Norway among noblemen.'

Gudrun then answered, 'My sons, Thorleik and Bolli, will have the deciding say in this matter, but you are the third man to whom I look most for counsel, Snorri, when I feel the outcome to be important, as for many years now you have proved a good adviser to me.'

Snorri said he thought it very clear that Thorkel should not be rejected. He then had Gudrun's sons summoned and raised the question with them, explaining how much a match with Thorkel would strengthen their position, both because of his money and guidance, putting his case very convincingly.

Bolli answered, 'My mother will know what is best and I agree to her wishes, but we certainly feel the fact that you support this proposal, Snorri, lends it considerable weight, for you have done much to our great benefit.'

Gudrun then spoke: 'We should make every effort to follow Snorri's guidance in this matter, because your counsel has been good counsel to us.'

Snorri's every word was an encouragement, and the match between Thorkel and Gudrun was thus decided.

Snorri offered to hold the wedding feast, which suited Thorkel well – 'I have no lack of supplies to provide whatever you please.'

Gudrun then spoke: 'It is my wish that this feast be held here at Helgafell. I am not concerned about the cost involved, and I will ask neither Thorkel nor anyone else to take a hand in it.'

'You have shown more than once, Gudrun,' Snorri said, 'that you are the most determined of women.'

It was decided that the wedding should be held at Helgafell, when seven weeks remained of summer. Both Snorri and Thorkel then departed, Snorri to return home and Thorkel to his ship. He divided his time that summer between his ship and visiting Snorri at Tunga.

The time of the feast approached. Gudrun had made extensive preparations and laid in great stores of provisions. Snorri the Godi accompanied Thorkel to the wedding feast and their party numbered almost sixty people. It was a select group, as almost all of them wore fine, coloured clothing. Gudrun had invited well over a hundred guests herself. The brothers Bolli and Thorleik went out to receive Snorri and his party, accompanied by their mother's guests. Snorri and his followers were given a good welcome; they were relieved of their horses and their outer garments and led into the main room. Thorkel and Snorri were given the positions of highest honour on one upper bench, while Gudrun's guests occupied the opposite one.

69 That autumn Gunnar, who was called Thidrandabani (Slayer of Thidrandi), had been sent to Gudrun for shelter and protection; she had accepted him into her household and concealed his true name. Gunnar had been outlawed for slaying Thidrandi Geitisson of Krossavik, as is related in the saga of the People of Njardvik. He took great pains to conceal himself, as there were many powerful men who sought recourse in the case. The first evening of the feast, when people went to wash, a large man stood by the water, broad-shouldered and deep-chested, wearing a hat on his head. When Thorkel asked who he was, he answered with the first thing that came into his head.

Thorkel answered, 'You won't be telling the truth. You are more like the descriptions of Gunnar Thidrandabani, and if you are as much of a warrior as people say, you can't wish to conceal your name.'

Gunnar answered, 'Since you press the point so forcefully, I suppose I need not conceal it from you. You have spotted your man fairly enough – what do you have in mind for me?'

Thorkel said he intended to make that known soon enough, and ordered his men to seize him.

Gudrun sat in the centre of the cross-bench with the other women, all with linen veils on their heads. When she realized what was happening she stood up from the bridal bench and urged her followers to assist Gunnar. She also told them to spare no one who brought on violence. Gudrun had a much larger following and things appeared to be headed in a direction other than that intended.

Snorri interceded between them and told them to calm the storm – 'You, Thorkel, should obviously not pursue this matter so forcefully. You must see just how determined a woman Gudrun is, as she dares to overrule us both.'

Thorkel protested, saying that he had promised his namesake, Thorkel Geitisson, 'who is a great friend of mine', to kill Gunnar if he made his way to the west of Iceland.

Snorri said, 'You're under a greater obligation to do my bidding, and it's absolutely necessary for your own sake – you'll never get another woman the likes of Gudrun for your wife, though you search far and wide.'

At Snorri's urging, and since he could see for himself that Snorri spoke the truth, Thorkel calmed down, while Gunnar was escorted away that evening. The feast proceeded well, and was highly impressive. At its conclusion people prepared to depart. Thorkel had rich gifts to give Snorri at parting, and for all the other worthy guests. Snorri invited Bolli Bollason to come and stay with him whenever and for as long as he wished. Bolli accepted his offer and rode back to Tunga with him.

Thorkel settled in at Helgafell and took over the running of the farm. It soon became obvious that he was no less adept at this than at merchant voyages. He had the hall torn down that autumn, and the rafters were raised over a new one, large and impressive, by the next winter. Gudrun and Thorkel grew to love one another very deeply. The winter passed and the following spring Gudrun asked him what he wished to do about Gunnar.

Thorkel said she should decide that. 'You have taken such strong measures that you won't be satisfied unless he is given decent treatment at parting.'

Gudrun said that he had drawn the right conclusion on that point. 'I want you,' she said, 'to give him your ship and with it anything that he cannot do without.'

Thorkel answered with a smile, 'You're not one to think on a small scale, Gudrun. A petty husband would never suit you; nor would he be a match for a spirit like yours. It will be as you wish.'

When the arrangements were made, Gunnar accepted the gift with great thanks: 'Never will my reach extend far enough to repay you all the honour that the two of you have shown me.'

Gunnar then sailed abroad, making land in Norway whence he proceeded to his own estate. He was very wealthy, and a truly worthy and trusty man.

70 Thorkel Eyjolfsson became a prominent chieftain, and did much to make himself popular and respected. His was the leading voice in the district and he often took part in lawsuits. No mention is made of his legal disputes here, however. Next to Snorri, Thorkel was the most powerful man in Breidafjord, until his own death. Thorkel looked after his farm well; he rebuilt all the buildings at Helgafell, making them large and sturdy. He also marked out the foundations for a church and declared his intention to go abroad to obtain the timber for it. Thorkel and Gudrun had a son called Gellir. From a young age he was extremely promising. Bolli Bollason divided his time between Tunga and Helgafell, and Snorri treated him exceedingly well. His brother Thorleik lived at Helgafell. The two brothers were large and capable men, with Bolli the more outstanding of the two. Thorkel treated his stepchildren well.

Of all her children, it was Bolli whom Gudrun loved the most. He was now sixteen years of age and Thorleik twenty.

Thorleik then spoke to his stepfather Thorkel and his mother of his wish to travel abroad. 'I am bored by sitting at home like the women do. I want to ask you to provide me with the means to journey abroad.'

Thorkel answered, 'To my mind, I've seldom opposed the wishes of you brothers since our family bonds were tied. And I can understand only too well your longing to go abroad and learn foreign ways, since I expect you will be considered a stalwart fellow among capable men everywhere.'

Thorleik said he did not wish to take a great amount of wealth, 'because it's far from certain that I would be able to handle it properly; I'm young and inexperienced in many ways'.

Thorkel told him to take what he wished.

Thorkel then purchased a share in a ship, which had been beached at Dagverdarnes, for Thorleik. He accompanied Thorleik to his ship and made sure he was well equipped in every respect. Thorleik sailed abroad that summer and his ship made land in Norway. At that time King Olaf the Saint ruled in Norway. Thorleik made his way directly to King Olaf. The king received him well and recognized his lineage. He invited him to join him and Thorleik accepted. He spent the winter with the king and became his follower. The king thought highly of him. Thorleik was considered the most courageous of men and spent a number of years with the king.

The story now returns to Bolli Bollason. In the spring when he turned eighteen he told Thorkel, his stepfather, and his mother that he wished to be given his share of his father's inheritance. Gudrun asked what he was planning that made him ask them to make over the money.

Bolli answered, 'I want to have a request of marriage made on my behalf, and I want you, Thorkel,' he said, 'as my stepfather to do the asking, so that it will be successful.'

Thorkel asked what woman he intended to seek and Bolli answered, 'The woman is named Thordis, and she is the daughter of Snorri the Godi. She is the woman I have my mind set on marrying, and I won't be marrying in the near future if I don't make this match. It means a great deal to me that this should succeed.'

Thorkel answered, 'You're entitled to my support in this, stepson, if you think it will make a difference. I expect Snorri will be more than willing to give his consent, as he will see well enough that in your case he'll be making a fine match.'

Gudrun spoke: 'I can say at once, Thorkel, that I wish nothing to be spared in order that Bolli obtain the wife he wishes. Both because he is dearest to me and because he has always been the one among my children most loyal in doing as I wished.'

Thorkel said he intended to see to it that Bolli received proper treatment at parting, 'and he deserves it for more than one reason, especially since I expect he will prove the best of men'.

Shortly after that Thorkel and Bolli, together with a large number of followers, set out on a journey to Tunga. Snorri welcomed them well and warmly, and showed them the greatest hospitality. Thordis Snorradottir lived at home with her father. She was both fine looking and a woman to be taken seriously. When they had been at Tunga several nights, Thorkel brought up the question of a family alliance with Snorri on Bolli's behalf by proposing his marriage to Snorri's daughter, Thordis.

Snorri answered, 'You have made a worthwhile proposal, as I would have expected of you. I want to answer it well, because I think Bolli is the most promising of men, and any woman married to him is well married, to my mind. But it will depend mainly on how Thordis feels about it, because she will only be betrothed to a man of her liking.'

When the question was put to Thordis she replied that she would abide by her father's guidance. She would rather, she said, marry Bolli, a local man, than a stranger from far away. When Snorri realized that she was not opposed to a marriage with Bolli, he then agreed to the proposal and the two were betrothed. Snorri was to hold the wedding feast, which was to be at midsummer. This done, Bolli and Thorkel rode home to Helgafell where Bolli remained until the date of the wedding arrived.

Bolli and Thorkel then made their preparations for the journey, along with the others who were to attend. It was both a large and imposing group who rode to Tunga where they were given a fine welcome. There was a great number of guests and the wedding feast was highly impressive. After the conclusion of the feasting, as people were preparing to depart, Snorri gave both Thorkel and Gudrun worthy gifts, and did the same for his other friends and kinsmen. Everyone who had attended the feast then returned home. Bolli stayed at Tunga, and he and Thordis soon came to love one another dearly. Snorri was also determined to do well by Bolli and treated him in all respects better than he treated his own children. Bolli responded well to his kindness and spent the next year in comfort at Tunga.

The following summer an ocean-going vessel sailed into the Hvita river. Thorleik Bollason owned a half-share in the ship and Norwegians the other half. When Bolli learned of the arrival of his brother, he rode immediately south to Borgarfjord to the ship. The brothers were very glad to see each other, and Bolli spent several nights there. They then rode west to Helgafell. Both Thorkel and Gudrun gave them the warmest of welcomes, and invited Thorleik to spend the winter with them, which he accepted. Thorleik stayed at Helgafell awhile, then returned south to the Hvita river to have his ship beached and the goods transported westward. Thorleik had got on well in the world, earning both wealth and respect, as he had become the follower of that most noble of men, King Olaf. He spent that winter at Helgafell and Bolli at Tunga.

71   That winter the brothers met regularly, spending their time talking privately to one another and showing little interest in games or other entertainment. Once, when Thorleik visited Tunga, the two brothers spent days talking. Snorri felt that they were certain to be planning some major venture, and eventually he approached them while they were talking. They greeted him well and immediately broke off their conversation.

He responded well to their greetings and said, 'What are you planning that makes you forget about eating and sleeping meanwhile?'

Bolli answered, 'You would hardly call it planning, for there is little point in what we are discussing.'

Snorri realized that they wished to conceal from him whatever it was that occupied their thoughts, but suspected that what they spoke most about would cause major problems if it materialized.

Snorri spoke to them, saying, 'I suspect all the same that you wouldn't spend so much time speaking of nonsense or jesting, and I can understand that well enough. But I ask you now to tell me about it without concealing anything from me; the three of us will be no less capable of making plans, as I will not oppose anything that will be to your greater honour.'

Thorleik was pleased by Snorri's response. He said briefly that the brothers had been planning to attack the Olafssons, and mete them out a harsh punishment. He said they felt that in their present position they lacked nothing to enable them to even scores with the Olafssons, since Thorleik had become the follower of King Olaf and Bolli the son-in-law of a godi of Snorri's stature.

Snorri answered, 'Bolli's killing has been avenged fully enough with the vengeance on Helgi Hardbeinsson. More than enough hostility has already resulted without pursuing the question further.'

Bolli then said, 'How does it happen, Snorri, that you aren't as ready to offer your support as you professed to be just a short while ago? Thorleik wouldn't have told you of the plan if he had asked me about telling you first. And regarding your contention that Bolli was avenged with the killing of Helgi, everyone knows that compensation was paid for Helgi's killing, whereas my father remains unredressed.'

When Snorri saw that he would not be able to change their minds, he offered to seek a settlement with the Olafssons to avoid any killing and the brothers agreed to this.

Snorri then rode with several men to Hjardarholt where Halldor received him well and asked him to stay the night with them.

Snorri said he would be returning that same evening, 'but I have something I must discuss with you'.

The two of them then conferred and Snorri explained the purpose of his visit, saying he had learned that Bolli and Thorleik were no longer content to have received no compensation from the Olafssons for their father, 'but I wanted to seek a settlement and see if it weren't possible to bring the ill fortunes of your family kinsmen to an end.'

Halldor did not reject the possibility, and answered, 'I know well enough that Thorgils Holluson and the brothers intended to attack me or my brothers before you turned their vengeance aside, with the result that they decided to kill Helgi Hardbeinsson. You have for your part acted well in that instance, whatever your earlier involvement in the dealings between us kinsmen.'

Snorri spoke: 'To my mind it's very important to achieve my purpose in coming here, and to accomplish what I have in mind, to reconcile you and these kinsmen of yours properly, because I know the natures of these men you are dealing with; they will abide well and fully by any settlement which they conclude.'

Halldor answered, 'I will agree, if it is the wish of my brothers as well, to pay such compensation for the slaying of Bolli as is awarded by the men selected as arbitrators. But this must exclude all outlawry, together with my godord and farm property. This also applies to the farms where my brothers dwell; I wish them to be excluded from any award of compensation.'

Snorri said, 'This is an honourable and generous offer. The brothers will accept it if they pay any heed to my advice.'

Snorri then returned home and told the brothers the outcome of his journey, adding that he would offer them no further support if they failed to agree to this.

Bolli said that he should decide for them, 'and I want you to arbitrate on our behalf'.

Snorri then sent word to Halldor that a settlement had been arranged and asked him to choose someone to serve as his counterpart in deciding the terms. Halldor chose Steinthor Thorlaksson from Eyri to act on his behalf. The settlement was to be decided at Drangar on the Skogarstrond shore when four weeks of the summer had passed. Thorleik Bollason returned to Helgafell and the winter passed without event. When the time set for the meeting approached, Snorri accompanied the Bollasons to the site; they made a party of fifteen, the same number as Steinthor and his party. Snorri and Steinthor discussed the matter and reached agreement. They then decided on the compensation, but it is not reported here how high was the figure they set, only that it was paid as stipulated and the men honoured the settlement. Payment took place at the Thorsnes Assembly. Halldor gave Bolli a handsome sword and Steinthor Olafsson gave Thorleik a shield, both of which were fine weapons. Following this the assembly was dissolved, and both parties were felt to have risen in esteem as a result.

72 Following their reconciliation with the Olafssons, and after a year had passed since Thorleik returned from abroad, Bolli declared that he intended to sail abroad.

Snorri tried to discourage him, saying, 'It seems to me you are risking a lot on the outcome. If you feel you want more responsibility than you now have, then I will provide you with a farm of your own and obtain a godord for you, and help you rise in importance in every way. I expect it will be easy enough, as most people are well inclined towards you.'

Bolli answered, 'For a long time now I have wanted to make a journey south; a man is considered ignorant if he has explored no more than the shores of Iceland.'

When Snorri saw that Bolli had his mind so set on this that there was no point trying to dissuade him, he offered Bolli as much wealth as he wished for the journey.

Bolli agreed to take a great deal of wealth, 'as I want charity from no man, either here or abroad'.

Bolli then rode south to Borgarfjord to the Hvita river, where he purchased a half-share in Thorleik's ship from the men who owned it. The two brothers then owned the ship together. Bolli then rode home again.

Bolli and Thordis had a daughter named Herdis, whom Gudrun offered to foster. She was one year old when she went to Helgafell. Thordis also stayed there much of the time and Gudrun treated her very well.

73   The two brothers then proceeded to their ship. Bolli took a great deal of wealth abroad with him. They made the ship ready and after everything was prepared they set sail out to sea. It was some time before they got favourable winds, and their passage was a lengthy one. They made land in Norway in the autumn and made land in the north at Nidaros. King Olaf was in the east of the country, in Vik, with his followers, where he had collected provisions for the winter. When the brothers learned that the king would not be coming north to Nidaros that autumn, Thorleik said he wanted to head to the east of the country to seek out the king.

Bolli answered, 'I'm not excited at the prospect of tramping around from one town to another in the autumn; it seems like nothing but bondage and servitude. I want to spend the winter here in town. I'm told the king will be coming north in the spring, and if he doesn't I won't deter you from taking us to meet him then.'

They did as Bolli wished, unloading their ship and settling down in the town for the winter. It was soon apparent that Bolli was a man of ambition, who intended to be a leader among men. This he managed to do, not the least through his generosity. He was soon held in high esteem in Norway. That winter in Nidaros Bolli kept a company of men, and was recognized at once whenever he went drinking, as his men were better armed and dressed than other townspeople. He alone paid for the drinks of all his company when they went drinking. This was typical of his generosity and grand style. The brothers spent the winter in the town.

King Olaf spent that winter in Sarpsborg in the east of his kingdom, and according to news of him, the king was not expected to head northwards. Early in the spring the brothers made ready their ship and sailed eastward following the coast. Their journey went well and when they arrived in Sarpsborg they proceeded directly to meet King Olaf. He gave his follower Thorleik and his companions a good welcome, and then asked him who this impressive-looking man was who accompanied him.

Thorleik replied, 'This is my brother, who is named Bolli.'

'He certainly looks to be a most outstanding man,' said the king.

The king then offered to have both of the brothers to stay with him, and they accepted gratefully, remaining with him that spring. The king treated Thorleik as well as before, but held Bolli in much higher regard, as the king felt him to be among the most exceptional of men.

As the spring advanced the brothers discussed their travelling plans, and Thorleik asked Bolli whether he wished to sail for Iceland that summer, 'or do you wish to remain in Norway longer?'

Bolli answered: 'I intend to do neither, and to tell you the truth when I left Iceland I had intended that people would not hear of me settling down next door. I want you, brother, to take over our ship.'

Thorleik was saddened at the prospect of their parting, 'but you will have your way in this as everything else, Bolli'.

When they told these same plans to the king, he answered, 'Do you not wish to dwell here with us any longer, Bolli? I would prefer you to stay here with me for a while, and I will offer you the same title that I have conferred upon your brother Thorleik.'

To this Bolli answered: 'More than willing enough am I, my lord, to enter your service, but I intend first to travel to the destination which I originally set out for and where I have long wished to go. Should I manage to return I will gladly accept this offer of yours.'

'You will decide your course yourself, Bolli, as you Icelanders usually intend to have your own way in most things. But I have to say that I regard you, Bolli, as the most remarkable man to have come from Iceland during my day.'

Once Bolli had received the king's leave, he made ready for his journey and boarded a cog heading south to Denmark. He took a great deal of wealth with him and was accompanied by several of his companions. He and King Olaf parted the best of friends, and the king gave Bolli worthy farewell gifts. Thorleik remained behind with King Olaf, while Bolli proceeded south to Denmark. He spent the winter there and was shown great honour by powerful men. He conducted himself there in a style no less luxurious than he had in Norway. After a year in Denmark, Bolli began his journey through foreign countries, not stopping until he reached Constantinople. After a short time there he entered the company of the Varangian guard, and we know no reports of northerners having entered the service of the Byzantine emperor before Bolli Bollason. He spent many years in Constantinople, where he was regarded as the most valiant of fighters in any perilous situation, where he was among the foremost of them. The Varangians thought highly of Bolli during his stay in Constantinople.

74 The story now returns to Thorkel Eyjolfsson, who had become a leader of prominence in Iceland. Gellir, son of Thorkel and Gudrun, grew up at home and was from an early age a very manly and well-liked lad.

It is said that Thorkel once told Gudrun of a dream he had: 'I dreamt,' he said, 'that I had such a long beard that it spread over all of Breidafjord.'

Thorkel asked her to interpret the dream.

Gudrun asked, 'What do you think the dream means?'

'It seems to me obvious that it means my domain will extend over the whole of Breidafjord.'

'That may well be the case,' said Gudrun, 'but I am inclined to expect that it means that you will be dipping your beard into Breidafjord.'

That same summer Thorkel had his ship launched and made preparations to sail to Norway. His son Gellir was twelve years old at the time and sailed abroad with his father. Thorkel declared that he intended to obtain timber for his church and put out to sea as soon as everything was ready. He had light winds and the passage was anything but brief. They made land in the north of Norway. King Olaf was in Nidaros at the time, and Thorkel made his way directly to the king, taking his son Gellir along with him. They were well received and Thorkel was held in such high regard by the king during the winter that it was widely said that the gifts the king gave him were worth no less than five score marks of refined silver. At Christmas the king gave Gellir a wonderfully crafted cloak that was truly a treasure. That same winter King Olaf had a church built of wood in the town. It was large and very impressive, and care taken with its every aspect. The following spring the timber which the king had given Thorkel was loaded aboard ship. The timber was both of fine quality and in great quantity, for Thorkel spared no pains with its selection.

One morning when the king had risen early and was accompanied by only a few men, he saw a man up on the church which was then under construction. He was very surprised at this, for the morning had not yet advanced to the time when his carpenters were accustomed to rise. The king recognized the man: it was Thorkel Eyjolfsson, who was measuring all the largest beams, the cross-ties, joists and supports.

The king went over to him immediately and said, 'What are you up to, Thorkel? Do you plan to cut timber for your church in Iceland on this model?'

Thorkel answered, 'Right you are, my lord.'

Then King Olaf spoke: 'Chop two ells off the length of each beam and your church will still be the greatest in Iceland.'

Thorkel answered, 'Keep your timber then, if you fear you have given of it too generously, or regret making the offer, but I'll not chop so much as an ell's length off it. I lack neither the energy nor the means to obtain my timber elsewhere.'

The king then said, in a pacifying tone, 'You are a man of great worth, and of no small ambition. Of course it's absurd for a farmer's son to compete with us. But it is not true that I begrudge you the timber. If you should manage to build a church with it, it will never be so large as to contain your own conceit. But unless I am mistaken, people will have little use of this timber, and even less so will you be able to build any structure with it.'

With that their conversation came to an end. The king walked away and it was clear that he disliked Thorkel's disregard for his advice. The king let the matter drop, however, and he and Thorkel parted as the best of friends. Thorkel boarded his ship and sailed out to sea. They had favourable winds and a brief passage.

Thorkel's ship made land in Hrutafjord, and he rode promptly to Helgafell. Everyone was very glad to see him and he gained a great deal of honour from his journey. He had his ship beached and secured for the winter and the timber set in secure storage, as he would be too busy that autumn to have it transported westward. Thorkel spent that winter at home on his farm. He held a Christmas feast at Helgafell attended by a great number of people. Everything he did that winter was done extravagantly, with no opposition from Gudrun, who said that wealth was well spent if people gained esteem as the result, and anything Gudrun needed in order to have things in grand style was made available. That winter Thorkel gave as gifts to his friends many valuable objects he had brought with him from abroad.

75 After Christmas Thorkel prepared to set out for the journey north to Hrutafjord to transport his timber home. He rode first up into the Dalir district, then to his kinsman Thorstein at Ljarskogar to borrow both men and horses. He then went north to Hrutafjord where he stayed a while and planned his journey. He collected horses from the farms along the fjord, as he hoped to make only a single trip if this were possible. This was not accomplished quickly, and Thorkel was kept busy past the beginning of Lent before he could set out. He had the wood drawn southward by more than twenty horses to Ljaeyri, where he intended to load it aboard a ship

for the rest of the journey to Helgafell. Thorstein owned a large ferry which Thorkel intended to use for his homeward journey.

Thorkel stayed at Ljarskogar during Lent, as he and his kinsman Thorstein were close friends.

Thorstein suggested to Thorkel that he make a journey with him to Hjardarholt – 'I want to ask Halldor to sell me land, as he has little livestock left after paying the Bollasons compensation for their father, and it's his land that I want to obtain the most.'

Thorkel said he would oblige him, and they set out with a party that numbered over twenty men.

When they arrived at Hjardarholt, Halldor received them well and kept up a lively conversation. Only a few members of the household were at home, as Halldor had sent many of them north to Steingrimsfjord, where a whale had stranded, and he was entitled to a share. Beinir the Strong was at home, the only one still alive of those who had served Olaf, Halldor's father.

When he saw Thorstein and his men approaching, Halldor said to Beinir, 'I know well enough what brings those kinsmen here. They are going to ask me to sell them my land, and if they do so they will ask to speak to me privately. I expect they will sit down, one of them on each side of me, and if they show me any hostility, you will attack Thorstein the moment I turn on Thorkel. You have shown my family many years of loyalty. I have also sent men to seek help from neighbouring farms. I hope they will arrive at much the same moment as we make an end of the conversation.'

Later that day Thorstein suggested to Halldor that they speak privately, 'as we have something to discuss with you, Halldor'.

Halldor said that was fine with him and Thorstein told his companions that they need not follow them. Beinir went along with them, nevertheless, as he thought things were turning out much as Halldor had predicted. They walked a long way out into the hayfield. Halldor wore a cloak fastened with a long clasp, as was common at that time. He sat down in the field, with a kinsman on either side of him, sitting practically on his cloak. Beinir stood behind them with a large axe in his hand.

Thorstein then said, 'My purpose in coming here was to purchase your land from you. I bring this up now while my kinsman Thorkel is here. I thought it should suit both of us, because I'm told you have insufficient livestock and good land is going to waste. I offer you in return a suitable farm, as well as whatever sum we both agree upon to make up the difference.'

Halldor did not reject the idea, and they began discussing possible details of the bargain. Once Halldor had shown some interest, Thorkel became very involved in the discussion and wanted to get them to agree on a bargain. Halldor then began to retreat, at which they pressed their suit more forcefully, and eventually the more they pressed the more he withdrew.

Thorkel then said, 'Don't you realize where this is heading, Thorstein? He's just been leading us on all day. We've been sitting here letting him mock and delude us. If you intend to have anything come of this attempt at purchasing land, we're going to have to spare no pains.'

Thorstein said that he wanted to know clearly how things stood, and told Halldor to make it clear whether or not he was willing to sell him the land.

Halldor answered, 'I think I can state plainly the fact that you will be returning home empty-handed this evening.'

Thorstein then said, 'And I think I need not wait to tell you what I have planned, and that is to offer you two possibilities to choose from, as I think we'll have our way by force of numbers. The first choice is to agree to this purchase of your own accord, and enjoy our friendship in return; the second and clearly poorer choice is to be forced to shake my hand and thus agree to the sale of the Hjardarholt land.'

No sooner had Thorstein spoken this than Halldor sprang to his feet, so abruptly that the clasp was torn from his cloak, and said, 'Something else will happen before I utter words that I have no wish to speak.'

'And what might that be?' Thorstein asked.

'A wood-axe, wielded by the worst of men, will be wedged in your skull, and put an end to your high-handedness and bullying.'

Thorkel answered, 'This is an evil prophecy, and we hardly expect it to be fulfilled. I'd say that you've done enough now, Halldor, to deserve to hand over your land without any payment for it.'

To this Halldor replied, 'And you'll have the bladderwrack of Breidafjord in your arms before I'll be forced to sell my land.'

After that Halldor returned home to the farm, just as the men for whom he had sent came rushing up.

Thorstein was enraged and wanted to attack Halldor at once, but Thorkel asked him not to, saying, 'It would be a serious offence at this time, but when Lent is over I won't try to prevent any settling of differences.'

Halldor replied that he would be ready for them anytime.

After this they rode off and talked a great deal about the events of their journey. Thorstein said it was true enough that this excursion had turned out very badly, 'and why did you, Thorkel, hesitate to attack Halldor and do him some damage?'

Thorkel answered, 'Did you not see Beinir standing over you with his axe aloft? It would have been a fatal move; he would have brought his axe down on your head the moment I appeared likely to make a move.'

They then rode home to Ljarskogar. Lent passed and Easter week approached.

76 Early on the morning of Maundy Thursday Thorkel made preparations to leave.

Thorstein tried hard to dissuade him, saying, 'It looks like unfavourable weather is brewing.'

Thorkel said the weather would serve him fine, 'and don't attempt to advise me against it, kinsman, for I intend to be home before Easter'.

Thorkel had the ferry set afloat and loaded. Thorstein immediately unloaded again all that Thorkel and his companions loaded on board – until Thorkel spoke: 'Now stop delaying our journey, kinsman; you won't have your way this time.'

Thorstein answered, 'The one of us who decides, then, will be the worse for it; this will be a journey of great event.'

Thorkel wished him farewell until they met again, and Thorstein returned home very sadly. He went into the main room and asked for something to rest his head upon, and the servant woman saw the tears streaming from his eyes on to the cushion.

A short while later the roar of a great wind could be heard in the room, and Thorstein spoke: 'There you can hear the roaring of my kinsman Thorkel's killer.'

The story now returns to Thorkel and his journey. As the party of ten sailed the length of Breidafjord that day, the wind began to rise and turned into a great storm before it subsided again. They pressed on determinedly, as they were the hardiest of men. Thorkel had his sword Skofnung with him, in a chest. They sailed onwards until they reached Bjarnarey – with people watching their crossing from both shores – but when they had reached the island, a gust of wind filled the sail and capsized the boat. Thorkel was drowned there along with all the men who were with him. The timber was washed ashore on islands all around: the corner posts on an island which has been called Stafey (Pillar Island) ever since. Skofnung had lodged in the inner timbers of the ferry itself and washed ashore on Skofnungsey (Skofnung's Island).

In the evening of the same day that Thorkel and his men were drowned Gudrun went to the church at Helgafell after the household had gone to bed. As she passed through the gate of the churchyard, she saw a ghost standing before her.

It bent down towards her and spoke: 'News of great moment, Gudrun,' it said, and Gudrun answered, 'Then keep silent about it, you wretch.'

Gudrun went towards the church as she had intended, and when she had reached the church she thought she saw that Thorkel and his companions had arrived home and stood outside the church. She saw the seawater dripping from their clothing. Gudrun did not speak to them but entered the church and stayed there as long as she cared to. She then returned to the main room, thinking that Thorkel and his companions would have gone there. When she reached the house there was no one there. Gudrun was then very shaken by all these occurrences.

On Good Friday Gudrun sent men to check on Thorkel's journey, some in along Skogarstrond and others out to the islands. By that time the timber had drifted ashore on many islands and on both sides of the bay. On the Saturday before Easter Sunday the news reached them, and was thought momentous, as Thorkel was a great chieftain. Thorkel had completed the eighth year of his fifth decade when he died, and it was four years before the fall of King Olaf the Saint. Gudrun was greatly stricken by Thorkel's death, but bore her grief with dignity. Only a little of the timber for the church was recovered. Gellir was fourteen years old at the time. He took over the running of the farm, together with his mother, along with Thorkel's duties as godi. It was soon clear that he had the makings of a leader of men.

Gudrun became very religious. She was the first Icelandic woman to learn the Psalter, and spent long periods in the church praying at night. Herdis Bolladottir usually went with her to her nightly prayers, and Gudrun loved Herdis dearly. It is said that one night young Herdis dreamed that a woman approached her. She wore a woven cape and a folded head-dress, and her expression was far from kindly.

She said to Herdis, 'Tell your grandmother that I care little for her company; she tosses and turns on top of me each night and pours over me tears so hot that I burn all over. I am telling you this because I prefer your company, although you have a strange air about you. All the same I could get along with you, if the distress caused me by Gudrun were not so great.'

Herdis then awoke and told Gudrun her dream. Gudrun thought it was a revelation and the following morning she had the floorboards in the church removed at the spot where she was accustomed to kneel in prayer and the ground below dug up. There they found bones, which were blackened and horrible, along with a chest pendant and a large magician's staff. People then decided that a prophetess must have been buried there. The bones were moved to a remote place little frequented by men.

77 Four winters after the drowning of Thorkel Eyjolfsson, a ship owned by Bolli Bollason sailed into Eyjafjord. Most of the crew were Norwegians. Bolli had brought with him a great deal of wealth from abroad and many treasures given him by princes. He had become such a fine dresser by the time he returned from his journey abroad that he wore only clothes of scarlet or silk brocade and all his weapons were decorated with gold. He became known as Bolli the Elegant. He declared to his crew that he intended to go westward to visit his own district and left the ship and its cargo in their hands. He took eleven men with him, and all of them were dressed in clothes of scarlet and mounted on gilded saddles. They were all comely men, but Bolli was in a class by himself. He wore a suit of silk brocade given to him by the emperor of Byzantium, with a cloak of red scarlet outermost. About his waist he had girded the sword Leg-biter, now inlaid with gold at the top and shank, and gold bands wound about its hilt. On his head he wore a gilded helmet and he held a red shield at his side with the figure of a knight drawn on it in gold. He had a lance in his hand, as is common in foreign parts. Wherever the group stopped for the night, the women could do nothing but gaze at Bolli and the finery which he and his companions bore.

In such style did Bolli ride westward, until he and his companions reached Helgafell, where Gudrun was delighted to receive her son. Bolli did not stay there long before riding to Saelingsdalstunga to his father-in-law, Snorri, and his wife Thordis. Their reunion was a joyous one. Snorri invited Bolli to stay there with as many of his companions as he wished and Bolli accepted. He and the men who had ridden south with him stayed with Snorri that winter. Bolli became renowned for this journey abroad. Snorri made no less effort to treat Bolli with great affection now than when he had stayed with him in former times.

78   After Bolli had been a year in Iceland Snorri the Godi was taken ill.
      His illness advanced only slowly and Snorri lay abed for a lengthy time.
When his illness had worsened he summoned his kinsmen and dependants.

He then addressed Bolli, 'It is my wish that you take over my farm and godord after me, as I wish to show you no less honour and affection than my own sons. The son of mine whom I expect to be foremost among them, Halldor, is not in this country now.'

Snorri then died, aged threescore years and seven, one year after the fall of King Olaf the Saint, according to the priest Ari the Learned. Snorri was buried at Tunga and Bolli and Thordis took over the farm at Tunga, as Snorri had requested. Snorri's sons were not displeased, and Bolli became a highly capable and popular man.

Herdis Bolladottir grew up at Helgafell and was the loveliest of women. Orm, the son of Hermund Illugason, asked for and received her hand in marriage. Their son Kodran married Gudrun Sigmundardottir, and Kodran's son Hermund married Ulfheid, the daughter of Runolf, the son of Bishop Ketil. Their sons were Ketil, who became the abbot at Helgafell, Hrein, Kodran and Styrmir. Thorvor, the daughter of Herdis and Orm, was married to Skeggi Brandsson and their descendants are the people of Skogar.

Bolli and Thordis had a son named Ospak, whose daughter Gudrun was married to Thorarin Brandsson. Their son Brand endowed the church at Husafell. His son Sighvat became a priest and lived there for a long time.

Gellir Thorkelsson married Valgerd, the daughter of Thorgils Arason of Reykjanes. Gellir journeyed abroad and served with King Magnus the Good, receiving from him twelve ounces of gold and a great deal of additional wealth. Gellir's sons were named Thorgils and Thorkel, and Ari the Learned was the son of Thorgils. Ari's son was named Thorgils and his son was Ari the Strong.

Gudrun was now well advanced in years and burdened with her grief, as was related earlier. She was the first woman in Iceland to become a nun and anchoress. It was also widely said that Gudrun was the most noble among women of her rank in this country.

It is said that once when Bolli was visiting Helgafell, he sat with his mother, because Gudrun was always pleased when he came to see her, talking of many things for a long time.

Then Bolli spoke: 'Will you tell me something, Mother, that I'm curious to know? Which man did you love the most?'

Gudrun answered: 'Thorkel was the most powerful of men and most outstanding chieftain, but none of them was more valiant and accomplished than Bolli. Thord Ingunnarson was the wisest of these men and the most skilled in law. Of Thorvald I make no mention.'

Bolli then spoke: 'I understand clearly enough what you say of the qualities of each of your husbands, but you have yet to answer whom you loved the most. You've no need to conceal it any longer.'

Gudrun answered, 'You press me hard on this point, my son,' she said. 'If I wished to say this to anyone, you would be the one I would choose.'

Bolli asked her to do so.

Gudrun then spoke: 'Though I treated him worst, I loved him best.'

'That I believe,' said Bolli, 'you say in all sincerity', and thanked her for satisfying his curiosity.

Gudrun lived to a great age and is said to have lost her sight. She died at Helgafell and is buried there.

Gellir Thorkelsson lived at Helgafell into his old age and many remarkable stories are told of him. He figures in many sagas, although he is mentioned but little here. He had a very fine church built at Helgafell, as is stated explicitly by Arnor the Earl's Poet in the memorial poem he composed about Gellir. When Gellir had reached an advanced age he made preparations for a journey abroad. He went first to Norway, but stayed there only briefly before leaving to travel south to Rome on a pilgrimage to St Peter the Apostle. His journey was a lengthy one; he returned northwards as far as Denmark where he was taken ill and, after a lengthy illness, received the last rites. He then died and is buried in Roskilde. Gellir had taken Skofnung abroad with him, and the sword was never recovered after that. It had been taken from the burial mound of Hrolf Kraki. When news of Gellir's death reached Iceland, his son Thorkel took over his father's estate at Helgafell. Thorgils, another of Gellir's sons, had drowned in Breidafjord at an early age, along with all those who were with him aboard ship. Thorkel Gellisson was a practical and worthy man and was said to be among the most knowledgeable of men.

Here ends the saga.

Translated by KENEVA KUNZ

BOLLI BOLLASON'S TALE

Bolla þáttur Bollasonar*

I   At the same time as Bolli Bollason lived at Tunga, as was spoken of earlier, a man called Arnor Crone's-nose, the son of Bjarni Thordarson of Hofdi, lived on the farm Miklabaer in Skagafjord.

Another man, named Thord, lived with his wife Gudrun at Marbaeli. They were fine, upstanding farmers with wealth in plenty. Their son Olaf was still a boy at the time and a most promising young man. Gudrun, Thord's wife, was a near relative of Bolli Bollason, as her mother was his aunt. Gudrun's son Olaf was named after Olaf Peacock of Hjardarholt.

At Hof in Hjaltadal lived Thord and Thorvald Hjaltason, two prominent leaders.

A man called Thorolf Stuck-up lived at Thufur. He had an unfriendly nature and was often uncontrollable when angry. He owned a very aggressive grey bull. Thord of Marbaeli had sailed on merchant voyages with Arnor. Thorolf Stuck-up was married to a kinswoman of Arnor's and was one of the thingmen of the Hjaltasons. He was on hostile terms with his neighbours and was used to making trouble, of which the people of Marbaeli bore the brunt. After he was driven home from the summer pastures, Thorolf's bull caused a great deal of trouble. He wounded farm animals and could not be chased off with stones. He also damaged stacks of hay and did much other mischief.

Thord of Marbaeli went to Thorolf and asked him to see to it that the bull did not wander around loose.

'We don't want to have to put up with his rampages.'

Thorolf said he did not intend to stand guard over his livestock, and Thord returned home with this reply.

Not long afterwards Thord noticed that the bull was tearing apart stacks

---

* From *Möðruvallabók*. Translated from *Íslendinga sögur*.

of peat. He ran over to the spot with a spear in his hand, and when the bull caught sight of him it began moving towards him with such heavy steps that it sank into the ground almost over its hooves. Thord lunged at it with his spear and the bull fell to the earth dead. Thord then went to Thorolf to tell him the bull was dead.

'The deed does you little honour,' Thorolf replied, 'and I should like to treat you to something just as unpleasant.'

Thorolf was furious and his every word bore menace.

Soon Thord had to leave his farm. His son Olaf, then seven or eight years of age, went off some distance from the farmhouse to build himself a play house, as children often do. There Thorolf came upon him and pierced him with his spear. He then returned home and told his wife of it.

She replied, 'This is a vile and unmanly deed and you'll reap an ill reward.'

Since his wife responded so negatively, Thorolf rode off and did not slow his pace until he came to Arnor at Miklabaer.

They exchanged news and Thorolf told him of the slaying of Olaf, saying, 'I look to you for support because of our family connections.'

'You'll go looking blindly for that in this case,' Arnor said, 'as I do not value my connections with you more highly than my own honour. No protection can you expect from me.'

Thorolf then went to Hof in Hjaltadal, where he sought out the Hjaltasons. He told them of his situation and that 'I look to the two of you for support.'

Thord answered, 'This is a base deed, and I will give you no protection in this matter.'

Thorvald had nothing to say, and Thorolf got nothing from them in this instance. He rode off and farther up into Hjaltadal to Reykir where he bathed in the hot spring. That evening he rode down the valley again and as he neared the fence around the farmhouse at Hof he spoke to himself, as if to someone standing there, who greeted him and asked who he was.

'My name is Thorolf,' he said.

'Where are you headed and what is your problem?' asked the unseen man.

Thorolf told him of all that had happened – 'I asked the Hjaltasons for protection,' he said, 'as I'm in need of help.'

The man who was supposed to be there with him answered, 'They have now left the place where they held the wake attended by so many people that there were twelve hundred at table; such leaders have surely fallen in stature if they won't now offer a single man protection.'

Thorvald was standing outside and heard the conversation.

He came over and took hold of the reins of Thorolf's horse and told him to dismount, 'though it is hardly likely to bring much honour to help a man as feckless as you'.

2   The story now turns to Thord who returned home to learn of the slaying of his son, for whom he grieved deeply.

His wife Gudrun said, 'You had better declare Thorolf responsible for slaying the lad, and I will ride south to Tunga to my kinsman Bolli to see what help he is willing to offer us to gain redress.'

This they did. Gudrun was given a good welcome when she arrived at Tunga. She told Bolli of the slaying of her son Olaf and asked him to take over the prosecution of the case.

He answered, 'It doesn't look to me as if it will be easy to obtain honourable redress from those Northerners. What's more, I have also learned that this man is now keeping himself where it will not be easy to search him out.'

Bolli did, however, eventually agree to take on the case, and Gudrun returned north. When she arrived home she told her husband Thord how things stood and for some time nothing more happened.

After Christmas a meeting was to be held in Skagafjord at the Thvera farm, to which Thorvald had summoned Starri of Guddalir, a friend of the Hjaltason brothers. Thorvald and his followers set out for the meeting, and as they passed Urdskriduholar a man came running down the slope towards them. It proved to be Thorolf, who joined Thorvald and his men.

When they had only a short distance remaining to Thvera, Thorvald spoke to Thorolf: 'Take three marks of silver with you and wait here above the Thvera farmhouse. It will be a sign to you, when I turn the inside of my shield towards you, that it is safe for you to approach. The shield is white on the inside.'

When Thorvald arrived at the meeting he met Starri and they conferred together.

Thorvald spoke: 'The situation is this: I want you to accept Thorolf Stuck-up for safekeeping and support. In return you will have three marks of silver and my friendship.'

'The man you speak of,' answered Starri, 'is neither popular in my eyes nor likely to bring much luck. But for the sake of our friendship I will take him in.'

'You act well, in that case,' said Thorvald.

He then turned his shield so that the inside faced away from him. When Thorolf saw this he came forward, and Starri took him under his protection. Starri had an underground shelter at Guddalir because he often sheltered outlaws. He himself had also been charged with offences left unsettled.

3   Bolli Bollason prepared to prosecute the slaying of Olaf. He made preparations for the journey and set out north to Skagafjord, accompanied by thirty men. He was warmly received when he arrived at Miklabaer.

He explained the reason for his journey, saying, 'I intend to bring the case against Thorolf before the Hegranes Assembly, and I would like you to assist me.'

Arnor answered, 'I don't think, Bolli, that you're headed for fair sailing, if you intend to prosecute a case here in the north against men as unjust as the ones involved here. They will defend the case by any means, whether just or not. But your case is certainly a pressing one, so we'll do what we can as well to see it successfully concluded.'

Arnor collected a large number of men and accompanied Bolli to the assembly. The brothers also attended the assembly with a large number of followers. They had learned of Bolli's journey and intended to defend the case. When people had assembled Bolli presented the charges against Thorolf. When it was the turn of the defence, Thorvald and Starri came forward with their followings, intending to block Bolli's prosecution by force of arms and numbers.

Upon seeing this, Arnor led his followers between them, saying, 'It is clear that so many good men should not be involved in the dispute as now appears likely, so that people fail to obtain justice in their cases. It is misguided to support Thorolf in this case, and you, Thorvald, will have scant backing if it comes to a show of force.'

Thorvald and Starri now saw that the case would be concluded, since they lacked the numbers to match Arnor and his men, so they withdrew. Bolli had Thorolf outlawed there at the Hegranes Assembly for the slaying of his kinsman Olaf and then returned home. He and Arnor parted the warmest of friends. Bolli remained on his farm awhile.

4   A man named Thorgrim owned a ship which had been drawn ashore in Hrutafjord. Starri and Thorvald went to pay him a call.

Starri spoke to the captain: 'I have a man here whom I want you to transport abroad. You will have three marks of silver and my friendship as well.'

Thorgrim said, 'It looks to me as though it will prove a problem to do so, but since you urge me to, I will take him on. He doesn't look to me like a man to bring much luck, though.' Thorolf then joined the merchants while Starri returned home.

To turn now to Bolli, who had been considering what to do about Thorolf, he felt he would hardly have followed the case to a proper end if Thorolf were to escape. He then learned that passage had been obtained for Thorolf aboard a ship. At that he made preparations to set out, placed his helmet on his head and his shield at his side. He held a spear in one hand and buckled on the sword Leg-biter. He rode north to Hrutafjord and arrived just as the merchants were completing preparations for their voyage. Soon a wind came up. As Bolli rode up to the entrance of the camp, Thorolf came out carrying his bedroll. Bolli drew Leg-biter and struck a blow right through him. Thorolf fell backwards into the camp and Bolli jumped on to the back of his horse. The merchants ran out and towards him.

Bolli spoke to them: 'You would be best advised to leave things as they are, since it will prove too great a task for you to bring me down, and I'm likely to trim off one or two of you before I'm done in.'

Thorgrim answered, 'I expect that's true.'

They took no action, and Bolli returned home. He earned himself a great deal of honour by this, as men thought it quite an accomplishment to have the man outlawed in another district and then venture alone into the hands of his enemies and kill him there.

5   That summer at the Althing Bolli met with Gudmund the Powerful, and the two conversed together at length.

Gudmund said, 'I want to say, Bolli, that it's men like you that I want to count among my friends. I invite you to come north for a fortnight's feast, and will be disappointed if you fail to accept.'

Bolli answered that he would certainly accept this honour from a man such as him and promised to make the journey. There were others who made him offers of friendship as well. Arnor Crone's-nose invited him to a feast at Miklabaer. A man named Thorstein who lived at Hals, the son of

Hellu-Narfi, invited Bolli to stay with them on his way south again, as did Thord of Marbaeli. When the Althing ended Bolli rode home.

That summer a ship made land at Dagverdarnes and was drawn ashore there. Bolli lodged twelve of the merchant crew at Tunga over the winter and provided for them generously. They all remained there until Christmas had passed. Bolli then intended to make his promised visits to the north, had horses shod and made preparations for the journey. They were a party of eighteen, with all of the merchant sailors bearing arms. Bolli was wearing a black cape with his splendid spear, King's Gift, in his hand. They rode northward until they reached Marbaeli, where Thord gave them a good welcome. They spent three nights there in festive hospitality. Then they rode to Miklabaer, where Arnor received them warmly. The festivities there were superb.

Arnor then spoke: 'You have done well, Bolli, in paying me this visit. In doing so, I feel you have declared your great comradeship for me. And no better gifts will remain here with me than the ones you accept at parting. My friendship is also yours for the asking. But I suspect not everyone in this district feels well inclined towards you. Some of them, especially the Hjaltasons, feel they have been robbed of their honour. I intend to follow you north as far as the Heljardal heath when you leave here.'

Bolli answered, 'I wish to thank you, Arnor my host, for all the honour you have shown me, and it will certainly improve our company if you ride along with us. We plan on proceeding peacefully through this district, but if anyone should make any attempt to attack us, we may well repay them in kind for their trouble.'

Arnor then got ready to accompany them, and they set out on their way.

6 To return to Thorvald, he spoke to his brother Thord: 'You likely know that Bolli is now here in the district making visits. There are eighteen of them altogether in his party at Arnor's, and they will be heading north over Heljardal heath.'

'I know that,' Thord replied.

Thorvald said, 'The idea of Bolli passing by under our noses, without our making any attempt to confront him, irks me. I don't know of anyone who has done more to diminish my honour than he has.'

Thord said, 'You're a great one for getting more involved in things than I care to. This is one road to be left untravelled, if I am the one to decide.

I think it's far from certain that Bolli won't know how to answer any attack you make.'

'You won't talk me out of it,' Thorvald replied, 'but you must decide your own course.'

Thord said, 'You won't see me sitting at home, brother, if you set out. And I'll give you the credit for any honour we reap from the journey, or any other consequences.'

Thorvald began collecting men for the journey and formed a party of eighteen. They set out towards the route of Bolli and his party where they intended to wait in ambush.

Arnor and Bolli rode their way with their companions.

When they were only a short distance from the Hjaltasons, Bolli said to Arnor, 'Isn't it best if you turn back now? You have given us a more than fitting escort, and the Hjaltasons won't try any treachery with me.'

Arnor said, 'I won't turn back, because something tells me Thorvald is intending to seek you out. What is it I see moving there? Aren't those shields shining? That will be the Hjaltasons, and we will see to it that they will get no honour from this journey as it can be taken as a plot against your life.'

Thorvald and his brother and their men now saw that Bolli and his party were anything but fewer than they themselves were and realized that any show of aggression on their behalf would put them in a bad position. Their best course appeared to be to turn back, since they were not able to carry out their intentions.

Thord then spoke, 'Things have now turned out as I feared, that this journey would make a mockery of us and we'd have done better to sit at home. We have shown our hostility to men and accomplished nothing.'

Bolli and his companions continued on their way. Arnor accompanied them up on to the heath and did not leave them until the route began to slope downwards to the north. He then returned home, while they continued down through Svarfadardal until they reached the farm called Skeid. There lived a man named Helgi, who was ill-tempered and not of good family, though wealthy enough. His wife Sigrid, who was a kinswoman of Thorstein Hellu-Narfason, was the more outstanding of the two.

Bolli and his party noticed a store of hay nearby. They dismounted and began to take hay to give their horses, taking rather little, and Bolli restrained them even more.

'I don't know,' he said, 'what sort of nature this farmer has.'

They took handfuls of hay and let the horses eat them.

One of the farm workers came out of the house, and then returned indoors and said, 'There are men at your haystack, master, trying the hay.'

Sigrid, the farmer's wife, said, 'The only ones who would do that are men on whom one shouldn't spare the hay.'

Helgi sprang to his feet and said furiously he would never let her allow others to steal his hay. He ran out immediately as if he were crazed and came up to where the men had paused in their journey. Bolli got to his feet when he saw the man approach, supporting himself with his spear, King's Gift.

When Helgi reached him, he spoke: 'Who are these thieves that harass me so, stealing what is mine and tearing apart my haystack for their mounts?'

Bolli told him his name.

Helgi replied, 'That's an unsuitable name and you must be an unjust man.'

'That may well be true,' said Bolli, 'but you will have your justice.'

Bolli then drove the horses away from the hay, and told his men they would stay no longer.

Helgi said, 'I declare that what you have taken has been stolen from me and you have committed an offence liable to outlawry.'

'You will want us, farmer,' said Bolli, 'to make you compensation so that you will not prosecute us. I will pay you double the price of your hay.'

'That's nowhere near enough,' he answered. 'My demands will become more rather than less when our ways part.'

'Are there any objects of ours, farmer, that you would accept as compensation?' Bolli said.

'I think there might be a possibility,' Helgi answered, 'that I would have that gold-inlaid spear which you hold in your hand.'

'I'm not sure,' Bolli said, 'whether I care to give it up. I had other plans for it. And you can hardly ask me to hand over my weapon to you. Take instead as much money as you feel does you honour.'

'There's no chance of that,' Helgi said, 'and it's best that you be made to answer properly for what you have done.'

Helgi then pronounced his summons and charged Bolli with theft and made it liable to outlawry. Bolli stood there listening with a slight smile.

When Helgi had finished his accusation, he asked, 'When did you leave home?'

Bolli told him and the farmer then said, 'In that case I consider you to have lived on others for more than a fortnight.'

Helgi then pronounced another summons, charging Bolli with vagrancy. When he had finished, Bolli said, 'You're making much of this, Helgi, and I'd better make a move against you.'

Bolli then pronounced a summons, charging Helgi with slander, and another summons accusing him of trying to get hold of his property by treachery. His companions said they should kill this rogue, but Bolli said they should not. Bolli made the offences liable to outlawry.

After concluding the summons he said, 'You will take this knife and belt from me to Helgi's wife, as I'm told she spoke up for us.'

Bolli and his men then rode off, leaving Helgi behind. They came to Thorstein's farm at Hals where they were given a fine welcome and a goodly feast awaited them.

7 Helgi, on the other hand, returned to the farmhouse at Skeid and told his wife of the dealings between him and Bolli.

'I have no idea,' he said, 'what I should do to deal with a man like Bolli, as I'm no man of law. And I don't have many who will support me in the case.'

Sigrid his wife said, 'It's a proper fool you've made of yourself. You have been dealing with the noblest of men and you made a spectacle of yourself. You'll end up as you deserve, losing all your wealth and your life as well.'

Helgi listened to her words, which he found rather hard to take, but he suspected they would prove true, as he was a cowardly wretch, despite his bad temper and foolishness. He saw no way out of the impasse he had talked himself into and became more than a little cowed by it all.

Sigrid had a horse sought and rode to seek out her kinsman Thorstein Narfason. Bolli and his men had arrived by then. She asked to speak to Thorstein privately and told him how the situation stood.

'This has turned out very badly,' Thorstein replied.

She told him as well how handsome Bolli's offers had been, and how stupidly Helgi had acted. She asked Thorstein to use all his influence to see to it that things were straightened out. Afterwards she returned home, and Thorstein went to speak to Bolli.

'What's this I hear, my friend?' he said. 'Has Helgi of Skeid been provoking you unjustly? I want to ask you to drop the charges and dismiss the incident, at my request, as the words of simpletons are not worthy of notice.'

Bolli answered, 'It's true enough that this is nothing of worth. Nor do I intend to let it upset me.'

'Then I want to ask you,' said Thorstein, 'to drop the charges against him for my sake, and accept my friendship in return.'

'There's no threat of disaster right away,' Bolli said. 'I intend to take things calmly and we'll wait until spring.'

Thorstein spoke: 'Then I will show you how important it is to me to have my way in this. I will give you the best horse here in the district, and his herd, twelve altogether.'

Bolli answered, 'It's a fine offer, but you don't have to go to such lengths. I wasn't upset by it, nor will it be upsetting when the judgement comes.'

'The truth is,' said Thorstein, 'I want to offer you self-judgement in the case.'

Bolli answered, 'I expect the truth to be that there is no use making the offer, because I do not wish to accept a settlement in the case.'

'Then you're choosing the course that will prove bad for all of us,' said Thorstein. 'Although Helgi is hardly a worthy man, I am related to him by marriage. I won't deliver him into your hands to be killed since you refuse to pay heed to my words. And as far as the charges that Helgi brought against you, I can hardly see that they will do you honour by being presented at the assembly.'

Thorstein and Bolli then parted rather coldly. Bolli rode off with his companions, and there is no mention of him receiving parting gifts.

8   Bolli and his companions arrived at the farm of Gudmund the Powerful at Modruvellir. He came out to meet them and welcomed them warmly and was in the best of spirits. They remained there a fortnight and enjoyed festive hospitality.

Gudmund then said to Bolli, 'Is there any truth to the rumour that you and Thorstein have had a disagreement?'

Bolli said there was little truth in it and changed the subject.

Gudmund said, 'What route do you intend to take homeward?'

'The same one,' answered Bolli.

Gudmund said, 'I would advise you against it, as I'm told that you and Thorstein parted rather stiffly. Stay here with me instead and ride south in the spring, and let things run their course then.'

Bolli said he did not intend to alter his travel plans because of their threats.

'While that fool Helgi was carrying on so stupidly, speaking one slanderous charge after another, and hoping to take my spear King's Gift off me for a mere tuft of hay, I thought to myself that I would see to it that he got what he deserved for those words. I have other plans for my spear and intend to give it to you, along with the gold arm ring that the emperor gave me. I feel that the treasures are better off in your hands than in Helgi's clutches.'

Gudmund thanked him for the gifts, and said, 'The gifts you receive in return are much less worthy than they should be.'

Gudmund gave Bolli a shield decorated with gold, a gold arm ring and a cape made of the costliest material and embroidered with gold threads wherever this could add to its beauty. All of the gifts were very fine.

Gudmund then said, 'I think you're doing the wrong thing, Bolli, choosing to ride through Svarfadardal.'

Bolli replied that no harm would come of it. They then rode off, with Bolli and Gudmund parting the best of friends, and he and his party rode north along Galmarstrond.

That evening they came to the farm known as Krossar, where a man named Ottar lived. He was standing outside, a bald man wearing an outer jacket of skin. Ottar greeted them well and invited them to stay the night, and they accepted. They were waited upon well and the farmer was in the best of spirits. They spent the night there.

When Bolli and his party were ready to leave the next morning, Ottar said, 'You have done me an honour, Bolli, in visiting my farm. I would also like to do you a small favour, give you a gold arm ring, and would be grateful if you accept it. Here is also a ring to accompany it.'

Bolli accepted the gifts and thanked the farmer. Then Ottar mounted his horse and rode ahead to show them the way, as there had been a light fall of snow during the night. They continued on their way up to Svarfadardal.

They had not ridden far when Ottar turned back to them and said to Bolli, 'I want to show you how much I desire your friendship. Here is another arm ring of gold which I wish to give you. I would like to be of help to you in any way I can, as you are going to need it.'

Bolli said the farmer was treating him far too generously, 'but I will accept the ring all the same'.

'You're doing the right thing,' said the farmer.

9 To return to Thorstein of Hals. When he expected Bolli to be returning southward again, he collected a party of men and intended to lie in ambush for Bolli, wishing to alter the situation between him and Helgi. Thorstein and his men, who made up a party of thirty, rode out to the river Svarfadardalsa where they took up position.

A man named Ljot lived at Vellir in Svarfadardal. He was a prominent chieftain, a popular man and much involved in lawsuits. For everyday pursuits he wore a dark brown tunic and carried a light pole axe, while if he were preparing for a fight he had a black tunic and a broad-bladed axe, with which he appeared more than a little intimidating.

Bolli and his men rode westward in Svarfadardal. Ottar followed them past the Hals farm and out to the river. There Thorstein and his men were waiting for them, and when Ottar saw the ambush he responded abruptly, turned his horse and rode off to one side at top speed. Bolli and his party rode on boldly, and when Thorstein and his men saw this they sprang forward. They were on opposite sides of the river. The ice had broken up along its banks, but there was still a frozen patch down the middle. Thorstein and his men ran out on to the ice.

Helgi of Skeid was also there and urged the men on energetically, saying it was time to see whether Bolli's ambition and eagerness would be enough to carry the day, or whether there were any men of the north there who would dare to take him on.

'There's no reason to hesitate in killing all of them. It will also,' said Helgi, 'deter others from attacking us.'

Bolli heard Helgi's words and saw where he had advanced out on the ice. He threw his spear at Helgi and it struck him in the middle of his body, driving him backwards into the river. The spear struck the bank on the opposite side where it stuck fast, with Helgi hanging from it down into the water. A hard battle then began. Bolli pressed forward so boldly that men nearby were forced to give way. Thorstein then came forward against Bolli, and when they came together Bolli struck Thorstein a blow on the shoulder, giving him a severe wound. Thorstein received another wound on the leg. The struggle was a fierce one. Bolli himself had been wounded but not severely.

The story now turns to Ottar.

He rode up to Vellir, to Ljot, and when they met Ottar spoke: 'No cause to sit about, Ljot,' he said, 'what's at stake is to prove yourself a man of honour.'

'What would that involve, Ottar?'

'I expect them to be fighting here down at the river, Thorstein of Hals and Bolli, and it would be a most fortunate thing to put a stop to their hostilities.'

Ljot said, 'You've proved your worth more often than once.'

He reacted quickly and he and several others hurried back with Ottar.

When they reached the river, Bolli and the others were fighting furiously. Three of Thorstein's men had been killed. Ljot and his men quickly ran between the fighters and held them back from attacking each other.

Then Ljot spoke: 'You are to separate at once,' he said; 'more than enough harm has been done. I intend to decide the terms of a settlement between you in this case, and if either of you refuses, he will be attacked.'

Ljot's decisive action caused them to cease their fighting, and both sides agreed that he should decide the terms of settlement in the dispute between them. They then went their separate ways, Thorstein returned home and Ljot invited Bolli and his men home to his farm, which they accepted. Bolli and his men rode up to Ljot's farm Vellir.

The site where they had fought is known as Hestanes. Ottar did not take his leave of Bolli and his party until they had reached Ljot's farm. Bolli gave him generous gifts at their parting and thanked him warmly for his assistance. He also promised Ottar his friendship. Ottar returned home to his farm at Krossar.

10   After the fight at Hestanes, Bolli and all his men had returned home with Ljot to Vellir, where Ljot bandaged their wounds. They healed quickly because they were well looked after. When they had recovered from their wounds, Ljot called together a large assembly. He and Bolli rode to the assembly, as did Thorstein of Hals, along with his companions.

When the assembly had convened, Ljot spoke: 'No longer will I postpone the announcement of the settlement I have arrived at in the dispute between Thorstein of Hals and Bolli. To begin with, Helgi is deemed to have fallen without right to compensation because of his slanderous remarks and behaviour towards Bolli. The wounds received by Thorstein and Bolli will balance each other out. But for those three of Thorstein's men who were slain Bolli will pay compensation. And for his attempt on Bolli's life, Thorstein will pay him the value of fifteen hundred three-ell lengths of homespun. When this is concluded they will be fully reconciled.'

After this the assembly was dissolved. Bolli told Ljot that he intended to head homeward and thanked him well for all his assistance. They exchanged fine gifts and parted as good friends. Bolli took custody of the livestock and property at Skeid on Sigrid's behalf, as she wished to accompany him westward. They rode on together until they came to Miklabaer and met Arnor. He welcomed them warmly. They stayed there awhile and Bolli told Arnor everything of his dealings with the men of Svarfadardal.

Arnor said, 'You have been very lucky in this journey, and in your dealings with a man like Thorstein. It can be truly said that few if any chieftains from other districts will have gained more honour here in the north, especially considering how many men bore grudges against you beforehand.'

Bolli then left Miklabaer and headed southward with his companions. He and Arnor pledged each other friendship anew at parting. When Bolli returned home to Tunga his wife, Thordis, was relieved to see him. She had already heard some news of their skirmishes with the Northerners and thought they were at great risk as to the outcome. Bolli now lived quietly on his farm and enjoyed great respect.

This journey of Bolli's became the subject of new stories in all districts. Everyone felt that hardly any journey had been made to equal it. He gained in respect from this and many other things. Bolli found a worthy match for Sigrid and treated her generously.

We have heard no more of the story than this.

Translated by KENEVA KUNZ

THE SAGA OF HRAFNKEL FREY'S GODI

Hrafnkels saga Freysgoða

Time of action: 925–950
Time of writing: 1280–1350

The *Saga of Hrafnkel Frey's Godi*, succinct, direct and supremely realistic, is widely considered to capture the essence of the classical saga. Set in the first half of the tenth century in East Iceland, but with important episodes in the West Fjords and at the Althing, it appears on the surface to be a straightforward and simple story. It tells how Hrafnkel, a worshipper of the god Frey, forbids a shepherd to ride one of his stallions and then kills him for breaking this rule. Hrafnkel is punished for this overbearing behaviour when Sam, a kinsman of the shepherd, uses skill at law and the support of two powerful brothers to have him sentenced at the Althing, confiscate his property and take over his godord. Eventually Hrafnkel takes vengeance and regains his position of power. The pace of the narrative is brisk and confident, and the main characters are few and clearly contrasted, in a firmly male political world.

Perhaps precisely because of its realism and apparent simplicity, the *Saga of Hrafnkel Frey's Godi* has invited a wealth of interpretations. It has been seen as a moral tale of 'pride coming before a fall', both as a Christian parable and as an exposition of the heathen code of moderation found in the eddic poem *The Sayings of the High One*. At one level it can be read as an exhortation to tolerance, at another as a reworking in the pioneer community of the notion of the forbidden fruit. Yet another viewpoint is that the saga is political in character, a study of the nature and characteristics of power and authority: What are the qualities needed in a leader of men, how should he behave towards men of similar social standing and those from lower walks of life? Should the laws of the community encroach on the chieftain's private domain? Such questions, of course, are invited by episodes in more complex sagas, but the *Saga of Hrafnkel Frey's Godi* is unrivalled for its presentation of them in a perfectly rounded plot and economically constructed self-contained world.

Scholars have disagreed about the historical basis of this saga, regarding it first as a more or less factual account of real events and later as a purely fictional moral tale loosely grounded in oral tradition. Most recently, the historical idea has been reasserted in the light of new information from the field of archaeology and the renewed interest in applying the theories of oral tradition.

The saga has traditionally been dated to the 13th century, but there are strong arguments for considering it to have been written somewhat later. With one exception (AM 162 I fol., a vellum fragment dated 1500) the *Saga of Hrafnkel Frey's Godi* is only found in younger paper manuscripts. The saga is preserved in more than one version; it is translated here by Terry Gunnell from the text in *Íslendinga sögur II* (Reykjavík 1987), which is based on the main text (AM 551 c 4to) used by Peter Springborg (of the Arnamagnæan Institute in Copenhagen) in his forthcoming scholarly edition.

I   It was in the days of King Harald Fair-hair, son of Halfdan the Black, son of Gudrod the Hunting King, son of Halfdan the Mild and Meal-stingy, son of Eystein Fart, son of Olaf Wood-carver, King of the Swedes, that a man named Hallfred brought his ship to Breiddal in Iceland, below the district of Fljotsdal. On the ship were his wife and his son, who was named Hrafnkel. He was then fifteen years of age, promising and able.

Hallfred built a farm. During the winter, a foreign slave-woman named Arnthrud died there, and that is why it has since been called Arnthrudarstadir (Arnthrud's place). In the spring, Hallfred moved his farm north across the heath, and built a new home at a place called Geitdal (Goat valley).

Then one night he dreamed that a man came to him and said, 'There you lie, Hallfred, and rather carelessly too. Move your farm away, west across Lagarfljot river. That is where your luck is.'

After that he woke up, and moved his farm across the Ranga river in Tunga, to a place that has since been called Hallfredsstadir (Hallfred's place) where he lived until his old age. But he left a boar and a he-goat behind him, and on the same day that Hallfred left, a landslide came down on the buildings. The animals were lost, and that is why the place has since been called Geitdal.

2   Hrafnkel made a habit of riding on the moors during the summer. At that time, Jokulsdal had been settled up as far as the bridges over the Jokulsa river. Hrafnkel rode up through the Fljotsdal district, and saw an uninhabited valley that branched off Jokulsdal. To Hrafnkel's mind, this valley was more habitable than any other valley he had ever seen.

When Hrafnkel got home, he asked his father to divide the property, and said that he wanted to build his own farmstead. His father granted him this. He then built himself a farm in the valley, and called it Adalbol. Hrafnkel married Oddbjorg Skjoldolfsdottir from Laxardal. They had two sons. The elder was named Thorir, and the younger Asbjorn.

When Hrafnkel had taken the land at Adalbol, he held great sacrifices, and had a great temple built. Hrafnkel loved no other god more than Frey, and he dedicated half of all his best livestock to him. Hrafnkel settled the entire valley and gave people land, but he wanted to be their superior, and took the godord over them. Owing to this, his name was extended, and he was called Frey's Godi. He was unfair towards other people, but was well accomplished. He forced the people of Jokulsdal to become his thingmen, and was mild and gentle with his own people, but stiff and stubborn with the people of Jokulsdal who never received any justice from him. Hrafnkel was often involved in single combats and never paid anyone reparation. No one received any compensation from him, whatever he did.

Fljotsdal heath is difficult to cross, and very rocky and wet, but father and son often rode over to visit each other because they had a good relationship. Hallfred felt that the route was hard going, and searched for another route for himself above the fells in the Fljotsdal district. There he found a drier, longer route which is called Hallfredargata (Hallfred's track). This route is only travelled by those who know the Fljotsdal district well.

3   There was a man named Bjarni who lived on the farm at Laugarhus. That is near Hrafnkelsdal. He was married and had two sons with his wife, one named Sam, and the other Eyvind, both good-looking and promising men. Eyvind lived at home with his father, but Sam was married and lived at the northern end of the valley on a farm named Leikskalar, and he owned plenty of livestock. Sam was a very argumentative man, and clever with the law. Eyvind became a merchant. He went abroad to Norway, and was there for the winter. From there he went to other countries, and stopped in Constantinople where he gained great honour from the King of the Greeks. He stayed there for a while.

Hrafnkel had one animal in his possession that he valued more than others. It was a dun stallion with a dark mane and tail and a dark stripe down its back, which he named Freyfaxi. He dedicated half of this horse to his friend, Frey. He had such love for this stallion that he made an oath to bring about the death of any man who rode it without his permission.

4   There was a man named Thorbjorn. He was Bjarni's brother and lived
    on a farm called Hol, opposite Adalbol to the east. Thorbjorn had few
livestock, but many dependants. His eldest son was named Einar. He was
big and well accomplished.

One spring, Thorbjorn told Einar that he should look for service somewhere, 'because I need no more labour than the rest of this household can
provide, and you will have a good chance of getting service because you
are well accomplished. This dismissal isn't brought about by any lack of
love, for you are the child that is most dear to me. It is brought about by
my own lack of means and poverty. My other children will also become
labourers, but you will get a better position than they will.'

Einar answered, 'You've told me about this too late, because now all of
the best positions have been taken. I don't like having to choose from what's
left.'

One day, Einar took his horse and rode over to Adalbol. Hrafnkel was
sitting in the main room. He greeted him warmly, and with pleasure. Einar
asked for service with Hrafnkel.

He answered, 'Why are you asking for this so late? I would have taken
you on first, but now I have taken on all my servants except for the only
job that you wouldn't want.'

Einar asked what that might be. Hrafnkel said that he had not taken on
anybody to herd the sheep, but that he had great need of such a person.
Einar stated that he did not care what work he did, whether it was this job
or another, but said that he needed provision for a year.

'I will give you a quick choice,' said Hrafnkel. 'You will herd fifty ewes
back to the shieling each night, and gather all the wood for the summer.
This you will do in return for your keep for a year. But I want to make one
thing clear to you, as I have done with all my other herdsmen. Freyfaxi
roams near the bottom of the valley with his herd. You are to take care of
him during both summer and winter. But I warn you against one thing. I
never want you to mount him, whatever need you may be in, because, as I
have most seriously sworn, I will bring about the death of any man who
rides him. Ten or twelve horses follow him. You are welcome to use any
of these that you wish, be it day or night. Now do as I say, because there is
an old saying that "he who gives warning is not at fault". Now you know
what I have stated.'

Einar said that he would not be so ill-fated as to have to use the one
horse he was forbidden to ride if there were many others available.

5 Einar then went home to fetch his clothes, and moved over to Adalbol. The sheep were then driven up to a shieling near the head of Hrafnkelsdal, a place called Grjotteigssel. Einar did so well during the summer that no sheep were lost before midsummer, but then one night almost thirty ewes were found to be missing. Einar searched all the pastures, but found nothing. They were missing for almost a week.

Early one morning Einar went out, and the mist from the south and the drizzle had cleared. He took a staff in his hand, a bridle and a saddle-cloth. He went over the river Grjotteigsa which flowed in front of the shieling. There, lying on the gravel flats beside the river, were the sheep that had been at home during the evening. He drove them back to the shieling, and went to look for the other sheep that had gone missing earlier. He then saw the horses on the gravel flats, and thought of catching a horse to ride, believing that he would travel faster if he rode rather than walked. When he reached the horses, he chased them. Those which had never used to run away from people now all shied away from him; except for Freyfaxi alone. The stallion stood so still that it was as if he was rooted to the ground.

Einar knew that the morning was getting on, and did not think that Hrafnkel would find out if he rode the stallion. Then he took the stallion, bridled him, placed the saddle-cloth beneath himself on the horse and rode up by Grjotagil, up to the glaciers, and west alongside the glaciers to where the Jokulsa river flows out from beneath them, and then down beside the river to the Reykjasel shieling. He asked all the shepherds at the shielings whether anyone had seen the sheep, but no one had seen a thing. Einar rode Freyfaxi from the last part of the night until early next evening. The stallion carried him fast and far, because he was a good horse.

Einar decided that it was time to head back and herd together the sheep that were at home, even if he did not find the others. He then rode east over the ridges towards Hrafnkelsdal. When he came down to Grjotteig, though, he heard the sound of bleating near the end of the ravine he had ridden past earlier. He turned towards this place, and saw thirty ewes coming towards him, the same sheep that he had been missing for the previous week. He drove the sheep home, released the stallion beside the herd and walked back to the shieling.

The stallion was so soaked in sweat that it was dripping off every hair. He was splattered with mud and terribly exhausted. He rolled over some seven times, and after that gave a great neigh. He then set off down the track at great speed. Einar went after him, hoping to head the stallion off, catch him, and bring him back to the horses, but he was so shy that Einar could not get anywhere near him.

The stallion galloped down the valley, and did not stop until he came to Adalbol. Hrafnkel was eating. When the stallion reached the door, he neighed loudly. Hrafnkel told one of the women who was serving at the table that she should go out, 'because a horse neighed, and it sounded to me like the neigh of Freyfaxi'.

She went to the door and saw Freyfaxi in a very dirty state. She told Hrafnkel that Freyfaxi was outside the door, looking thoroughly filthy.

'What should the champion want that he should have come back home?' said Hrafnkel. 'This does not mean anything good.'

He then went out and saw Freyfaxi, and said, 'I don't like the way you've been treated, my foster-son. But you had your wits about you when you told me of this. It will be avenged. Go to your herd.'

Freyfaxi went up the valley to his horses. Hrafnkel went to his bed that evening and slept through the night.

In the morning, he had a horse taken and saddled for him, and rode up to the shieling. He rode wearing black clothes. He had an axe in his hand, but no other weapons. Einar had just finished herding the sheep into the pen. He was lying on the wall of the pen, counting the sheep, and the women were milking. They greeted Hrafnkel. He asked how things had been going for Einar.

Einar answered, 'Things haven't been going well for me. Thirty ewes were missing for nearly a week, but they've now been found.'

Hrafnkel said that that was of no real importance. 'Hasn't anything worse happened? It hasn't often occurred that sheep have been missing. But did you ride Freyfaxi yesterday?'

Einar said he could not argue with that at all.

Hrafnkel responded, 'Why did you ride the horse that you were forbidden to ride when there were plenty of others that you had permission to take? I would have forgiven you this one time if I had not sworn such a serious oath, and you have owned up well. But we have the belief that nothing goes well for people when the words of an oath come down on them.'

Then he leapt off his horse and swung his axe at Einar. He met his death immediately. After he had completed that, Hrafnkel rode home to Adalbol and announced the news. He then sent another man out to herd at the shieling. He had Einar taken to a ledge west of the shieling, and raised a cairn beside his shallow grave. This is called Einarsvardi (Einar's cairn). From the shieling, this site is used to reckon the time of early evening.

6   Over at Hol, Thorbjorn heard about the slaying of his son Einar. He took this news badly. Then he fetched his horse and rode to Adalbol and demanded compensation from Hrafnkel for the killing of his son. Hrafnkel said he had killed more men than just this one.

'You are not unaware that I never pay anyone reparations. People have to put up with that. All the same, I will admit that I regard this deed as one of the worst acts I have committed. You have been a neighbour of mine for a long time. I have liked you, and the feeling has been mutual. No great matter would have come up between Einar and myself if he had not ridden the horse. But we often have cause to regret having said too much, and we would more rarely have cause for regret if we spoke less rather than more. I will now show you that I regard this deed as worse than any other acts I have committed. I will supply your farm with dairy cows in the summer, and slaughtered meat in the autumn. I will do this for you every season for as long as you wish to live here. I will set up your sons and daughters elsewhere under my guardianship, and strengthen their position so that they come into improved circumstances. And from now on, anything that you know to be in my homestead, and need to have, then you must tell me and you will never want for these things again. You will live on your farm for as long as you wish, and then come here when you grow weary of that. I will then take care of you until your dying day. Let us now settle on this. I expect that most people will remark that this man was truly expensive.'

'I don't want that offer,' said Thorbjorn.

'What do you want then?' said Hrafnkel.

'I want us to choose others to arbitrate a settlement between us.'

Hrafnkel answered, 'You regard yourself as my equal then, and we will never come to an agreement on that basis.'

Then Thorbjorn rode off, down through Hrafnkelsdal. He came to Laugarhus and met his brother Bjarni. He told him the news and asked him to take a share in seeking redress in this matter.

Bjarni said that he would not be dealing with an equal in the case of Hrafnkel: 'Even if we had some money to dispose of, we mustn't get involved in a dispute with Hrafnkel. It's true that "it's a wise man who knows himself". Hrafnkel has complicated many law cases with stronger men than ourselves. I think you're stupid to have turned down such a good deal. I don't want any part in this.'

Thorbjorn uttered a number of cutting words to his brother, and said that the greater the stakes were, the less courageous his heart was. He then rode off, and they parted with little warmth.

He did not stop until he came down to Leikskalar, where he knocked at the door. Someone answered it, and Thorbjorn asked Sam to come outside. Sam greeted his uncle warmly, and with pleasure, and invited him to stay. Thorbjorn took that somewhat coolly. Sam sensed Thorbjorn's unhappiness and asked him for the news, and Thorbjorn told him about the slaying of his son Einar.

Sam responded, 'It's no great news that Hrafnkel kills people. He's pretty handy with a wood-axe.'

Thorbjorn asked whether Sam would offer him some support: 'This matter is such that, even though I am the closest relative, the blow has landed not so very far away from yourself.'

'Have you spoken to Hrafnkel about the question of your redress?' asked Sam.

Thorbjorn told him the truth about how things had gone between him and Hrafnkel.

'I'm not aware,' said Sam, 'that Hrafnkel has ever offered anybody such redress as he has offered you. Now I would like to ride back up to Adalbol with you. We'll approach Hrafnkel very humbly and see if he is still prepared to keep to the same offer. In one way or another, he will act well.'

'There are two things: Hrafnkel will now be unwilling, and I myself have no more mind to accept now than I had when I rode away from there.'

'I believe it will be a heavy matter to get involved in a legal dispute with Hrafnkel.'

Thorbjorn responded, 'The reason you young people never amount to anything is that you keep making such a huge fuss about everything. I doubt if there is any man who has such worthless relations as I have. I don't think much of people like you, who make out that they are clever with the law, and eagerly take on small cases, but don't want to accept a case like this which is so immediate. You will suffer reproach for this, and that is quite fitting since you are the loudest member of our family. Now I can see how this case is likely to go.'

Sam responded, 'What benefit are you likely to gain if I take on this case, and we both end up getting humiliated?'

Thorbjorn answered, 'It will still be a great consolation to me if you take on this case. We'll just have to see what bargain comes out of this,' he said.

Sam responded, 'I go into conflict with Hrafnkel unwillingly. I do this mainly for the sake of my relationship with you. But you ought to know that I think I'm helping a fool.'

Then Sam reached out his hand, and took over the case from Thorbjorn.

7   Sam had his horse fetched for him, and rode up the valley. He rode to a farm where he gathered some people together and declared Hrafnkel responsible for the killing. Hrafnkel heard about this and found it ridiculous that Sam had taken on a case against him. He did not make any move for the moment.

That summer passed and the following winter. But in the spring, when the Summons Days arrived, Sam rode from his home up to Adalbol and gave Hrafnkel a summons for the murder of Einar. After that Sam rode down the valley and summoned neighbours to ride to the Althing with him. He then stayed at home until people started preparing to leave for the meeting.

Hrafnkel then sent people down the valley and summoned men. He got seventy men from his Thing district. With this company, he rode east over Fljotsdal heath, past the end of the lake, directly across the ridge into the Skridudal valley, and then up Skridudal and south over Ox heath to Berufjord. They then took the usual thingman route to Sida. Going south from Fljotsdal, it is a seventeen-day journey to Thingvellir.

After Hrafnkel had ridden out of the district, Sam started looking for followers. Apart from the men he had summoned, those that he found most prepared to go were unattached men. Sam gave them weapons, clothes and provisions. He took another route out of the valley. He went north to the bridges, crossed the bridge and Modrudal heath, and arrived in Modrudal where they stayed for one night. They then rode to Herdibreidstunga, above Blafjoll into Kroksdal, and from there south to Sand. They came down into Sandafell, and from there went on to Thingvellir. Hrafnkel still had not arrived. He came later because he had taken a longer route.

Sam set up a temporary booth for his men, nowhere near the place where the people of the East Fjords usually camped. Sometime later Hrafnkel arrived at the Althing. He set up his booth in his usual place and heard that Sam was already there at the Thing. He found this ludicrous.

This Thing was particularly well attended. Most of the chieftains in Iceland were there. Sam sought out all of the chieftains and asked for their help and support, but they all gave the same reply. None of them felt that they owed Sam anything to make it worth their while entering into a dispute with Hrafnkel, and risking their honour. They said that most of the Thing disputes that people had entered into with Hrafnkel had ended in the same way: he had routed everyone in the legal cases they had taken up with him.

Sam went back to his booth. He and his uncle were in a heavy mood and feared that this matter would go in such a way that they would gain nothing from it but shame, dishonour and ridicule. The two kinsmen were so troubled that they could neither sleep nor eat. All the chieftains had refused to offer them support, even those people that they had expected would provide them with assistance.

8 Early one morning, old Thorbjorn woke up. He awakened Sam and asked him to get up straight away, and not go back to sleep. Sam got up and put his clothes on. They went out, and down to the Oxara river, below the bridge. There they washed themselves.

Thorbjorn said to Sam, 'I suggest that you have them collect our horses and that we get ready to go home. It is now obvious that we will get nothing other than ridicule.'

Sam answered, 'That's very good! All you wanted to do was have a dispute with Hrafnkel. You didn't want to take the alternative which many others would have gladly accepted if they had to seek redress for a close relation. You questioned the courage of those of us who didn't wish to enter into this matter with you. Now I will never give up until I see that there is no hope that I can do anything.'

When this speech ended, Thorbjorn was so moved that he burst into tears.

Then, on the west side of the river, some distance further down from where they were sitting, they saw five men walking together from a booth. The man in front was tall, but not particularly strongly built. He was wearing a leaf-green tunic and carrying an ornamented sword in his hand. He was a man with regular features, a ruddy face and an air of distinction, with light chestnut hair and good eyes. This man was easily recognizable because he had a light streak in his hair on the left side.

Sam said that they should get up, and cross over to the west side of the river to meet the men. They walked down beside the river, and the man in front greeted them first and asked them who they were. They introduced themselves.

Sam asked these men for their names. The man in front was named Thorkel, and he said he was the son of Thjostar. Sam asked him about his family background, and where he lived. He said both he and his family came from the West Fjords, and that his home was in Thorskafjord. Sam asked if he was a godi. He said that was far from the case.

'Are you a farmer then?' said Sam.

He said that he was not.

Sam said, 'What sort of person are you then?'

He answered, 'I'm unattached. I came home the year before last. I'd been abroad for six years, and been to Constantinople. I am a sworn follower of the Greek Emperor but am now staying with my brother whose name is Thorgeir.'

'Is he a godi?' asked Sam.

'Certainly. He's the godi for Thorskafjord and a number of other places in the West Fjords.'

'Is he here at the Althing?'

'Certainly he's here.'

'How many men has he got with him?'

'Seventy men,' said Thorkel.

'Have you any other brothers?' said Sam.

'There's a third.'

'Who is that?' said Sam.

'His name is Thormod,' said Thorkel, 'and he lives in Gardar in Alftanes. He is married to Thordis, the daughter of Thorolf Skallagrimsson of Borg.'

'Will you give us some support?' asked Sam.

'What kind of support do you need?' said Thorkel.

'The support and the might of chieftains,' said Sam, 'because we are involved in a lawsuit with Hrafnkel the Godi about the slaying of Einar Thorbjarnarson, and we can trust in our pleading of the case if we have your assistance.'

Thorkel responded, 'As I said, I am no godi.'

'Why were you passed over, when you are the son of a chieftain just like your brothers?'

Thorkel said, 'I didn't say that I didn't own it. I passed my position of authority over to my brother before I went abroad. Since then I have not taken it back, because I think it is in good hands as long as he takes care of it. You go and speak to him. Ask him for help. He has a firm temperament, is a good comrade and is in all ways a well-accomplished, ambitious young man. Such people are most likely to offer you support.'

Sam said, 'We won't get anything from him unless you plead with him alongside us.'

Thorkel said, 'I promise to stand with you rather than against you because I think it's necessary to bring a suit after the slaying of a close relative. Now you go off to the booth, and walk inside. Everybody will be asleep. You will see two leather sleeping sacks placed across the floor at the far end of the booth. I just got out of one of them, but my brother Thorgeir is sleeping in the other. He has had an enormous boil on his foot ever since he came to the Thing, and so he hasn't slept much at night. But the boil burst early this morning, and the core of the boil came out. He has been sleeping ever since, and has got his foot stretched out from under the sack on to the foot-board at the end of the bed because of the inflammation in his foot. Have the old man lead you as you go into the booth. He looks rather decrepit to me, both in terms of sight and age. And then, man,' said Thorkel, 'when you reach the sleeping sack, you should stumble badly, fall on to the foot-board, grab the toe that is bandaged, jerk it towards you and see how he reacts.'

Sam said, 'You may be giving us good advice, but this does not feel like the advisable thing to do.'

Thorkel responded, 'You are going to have to do one thing or the other: either you accept what I propose, or you don't come to me for advice.'

Sam said that it would be as he advised.

Thorkel said, 'I will come along later, because I am waiting for my men.'

9   Sam and Thorbjorn set off, and came into the booth. Everyone in there was sleeping. They saw immediately where Thorgeir was lying. Old Thorbjorn went first, stumbling badly. When he came towards the leather sleeping sack, he fell on to the foot-board, grabbed at the sick toe and jerked it towards himself. This woke Thorgeir. He sprang up in the sack and demanded to know who was going around so clumsily that they trampled on the feet of people who were already unwell.

Sam and Thorbjorn were speechless, but then Thorkel rushed into the booth and said to Thorgeir, his brother, 'Don't be so fast and furious about this, kinsman. It won't do you any harm. For many people, things go worse than they intend, and many, when they have a lot on their minds, just don't manage to be careful enough. Your excuse, kinsman, is that your foot is sore and has been very painful. You're the one who has felt it most. Now it may well be that the old man is in no less pain at the death of his son, but he can't get any compensation, and lacks the wherewithal himself. He'll be the one who feels it most, and it can be expected that a man who has a lot on his mind will not always be careful enough.'

Thorgeir answered, 'I don't see how he can blame me for that. I didn't kill his son, so he shouldn't be taking it out on me.'

'He didn't mean to take it out on you,' said Thorkel. 'He came towards you harder than he intended, and has paid the price for his weak-sightedness, just when he was hoping for a little support from you. It is noble to extend generosity to an old man in need. For him it is not greed, but necessity that makes him bring a suit for the killing of his son. All the other chieftains pare refusing to give their support, which shows just how ignoble they are.'

Thorgeir said, 'Whom are these men accusing?'

Thorkel answered, 'Hrafnkel the Godi killed Thorbjorn's son without cause. He commits one evil deed after another, but refuses to give any man just recompense.'

Thorgeir responded, 'I will act just like the others, because I know there isn't a thing that I owe these men to make me wish to enter into a dispute with Hrafnkel. It seems to me that every summer he treats those who have cases against him in the same way. Most of those people gain little honour, if any, by the time things have been concluded. It goes the same way for everyone. I expect that's why most people act unwilling towards somebody whom they are not drawn to through any necessity.'

Thorkel responded, 'It may be that I'd act in the same way if I were a chieftain, and that I wouldn't like the idea of entering a dispute with Hrafnkel. But I don't think so, because I prefer competing with someone who has routed everyone else. And, to my mind, my honour, like that of any chieftain who can get the better of Hrafnkel in any way, will grow rather than diminish, even if things go the same way for me as they have for others, because I can take what has happened to many before me. Who dares wins.'

'I see how you are inclined,' said Thorgeir, 'and that you want to help these men. I will now pass over to you our godord and our position of authority. You will have it as long as I have now had it, and after that we will both share it equally between us, so you can help those that you wish.'

'It strikes me,' said Thorkel, 'that the longer our godord is in your hands, the better. There is nobody I'd care to have it more than you, because in many ways you're the most accomplished of us brothers, while at this time I am undecided about what I want to do with myself. You know, kinsman, that I haven't really taken part in anything since I came back to Iceland. I can now see how much my advice is worth. I have now spoken all the words I mean to utter for the time being. It may be that Thorkel Streak will find a place where his words are more appreciated.'

Thorgeir responded, 'I see where things are heading, kinsman. You are displeased, and I can't stand knowing that. We'll assist these men whatever comes of it, if that's what you want.'

Thorkel said, 'I only ask for what seems to me were best granted.'

'What do these men think they are capable of doing to ensure that their case goes through?' asked Thorgeir.

'As I said,' said Sam, 'we need the backing of chieftains, but I will be in charge of presenting the case.'

Thorgeir said that made it easy to help him: 'Now it's a matter of preparing as correct a case as possible. But I think that Thorkel would like you to visit him before the court convenes. Your persistence will then reward you with consolation, or disgrace, or yet more anguish and torment. Now go home, and be cheerful, because you are going to need to be so if you mean to enter a dispute with Hrafnkel. Keep your heads high for a while, but don't tell anyone that we have promised to give you assistance.'

They then walked home to their booth and both were in very high spirits. Their men were amazed at this sudden change in mood, because they had been so depressed when they went out.

10 They stayed there until the court convened. Then Sam summoned his men and went up to the Law Rock where the court was set. Sam went boldly up to the court, and immediately began calling forth witnesses, prosecuting his case against Hrafnkel the Godi in full accordance with the true law of the land, in a faultless and powerful presentation. After this, the Thjostarssons arrived with a large force of men. Everyone present from the west of the country joined them, which showed how popular the Thjostarssons were.

Sam prosecuted his case at the court until Hrafnkel was invited to come and make his defence, unless somebody else was present who wished to make a legal defence on his behalf in accordance with the true law of the country. There had been much applause for Sam's case, so nobody said that they wished to do this.

People ran to Hrafnkel's booth and told him what was happening. He reacted immediately, summoned his men and set off for the court. He did not think there would be much defence. He intended to discourage small fry from prosecuting cases against him, and was going to break up the court, and drive Sam off the case. But this turned out to be impossible. There was such a crowd in the way that Hrafnkel could not get anywhere near. He was forced back by the sheer weight of numbers so he did not manage to hear the case of those who were prosecuting him. It was therefore difficult for him to present any legal defence for himself.

Sam prosecuted his case to the full extent of the law, until Hrafnkel was finally sentenced to greater outlawry at this Thing meeting.

Hrafnkel went to his booth, had his horses fetched and rode off from the Thing, greatly displeased at the way things had ended because this had never happened to him before. He rode east across Lyngdal heath, and then east to Sida, and did not stop until he came home to Hrafnkelsdal. He then settled back down at Adalbol, and acted as if nothing had happened.

Sam stayed at the Thing and strode about very haughtily. Many people were pleased, even though Hrafnkel had ended up being humiliated. They remembered that Hrafnkel had treated many people unfairly.

Sam waited until the Thing was dissolved, and people started preparing to go home. He thanked the brothers for their support. Thorgeir asked Sam with a laugh how he felt things had gone. Sam said he was pleased.

Thorgeir said, 'Do you think you're any better off now than before?'

Sam answered, 'I think Hrafnkel has suffered such dishonour that he will be ridiculed for a long time to come. There are also many possessions involved.'

Thorgeir said, 'No man is a full outlaw as long as the confiscation court has not been held, and that has to take place at his home. It must be done fourteen days after Weapon Taking.'

Weapon Taking is when a Thing is dismissed and the people all ride home again.

'But I expect,' said Thorgeir, 'that Hrafnkel has now reached home, and that he means to stay on in Adalbol. I expect that he means to keep his position of authority from you. And you probably intend to ride home and settle back down on your farm as best you can, if you manage to settle at all. I expect that you have succeeded in so far as you can call him an outlaw. But I also expect that he will be wielding the same terror over other people that he did before. The only difference is that now you find yourself set even lower.'

'That won't ever bother me,' said Sam.

'You're a courageous man,' said Thorgeir, 'but I don't think my kinsman Thorkel means to leave you in the lurch. He means to help you until this business between you and Hrafnkel has come to an end, so that you can live in peace. Indeed, we feel duty-bound to accompany you to the East Fjords this one time since we have been most involved until this point. Do you know any route to the East Fjords that is not commonly used?'

Sam said that he would take the same route that he had taken from the east.

Sam was very pleased about this. Thorgeir chose his party, and had a following of forty men. This party was well equipped with weapons and horses.

They then set off, and all rode along the same route until they arrived in Jokulsdal in the last part of the night, and crossed the bridge over the river. This was the morning that the confiscation court was supposed to be carried out.

Then Thorgeir asked how they could best take Hrafnkel by surprise. Sam said that he knew a way of doing this. He immediately turned off the track and went up on to the mountainside and along the ridge between Hrafnkelsdal and Jokulsdal until they came out below the mountain that stands above Adalbol. There were some grassy gullies running up on to the heath there, and a steep slope going down the mountainside into the valley. There below stood the farm.

Sam dismounted there and said, 'It is my advice that you dismount and let our horses go free. Have twenty men watch the horses. We'll take sixty men and run down to the farm as fast as possible. We'll go faster if we don't take the horses, because it's very steep. I don't expect there will be many people awake.'

They did as Sam advised. That place has since been called Hrossageilar (Horse gullies).

II   They dashed down towards the farm, and reached it quickly just after rising time. People were not yet up. They rammed a log against the door and ran in. Hrafnkel was lying in his bed. They took him from there along with all those men on the farm who were capable of bearing weapons. The women and children were herded into another building.

There was a storehouse standing in the meadow, and running between the storehouse and the wall of the farmhouse was a beam that was used for drying clothes. They led Hrafnkel and his men over to this. He made many pleas for himself and his men, but when he saw that no notice was paid to this, he begged for the lives of his men, 'since they have done you no wrong, while killing me will bring you no dishonour. I will make no protest against that. But I will protest against being humiliated. There is little honour for you in that.'

Thorkel said, 'We've heard that you've been rather deaf to the pleading of your enemies, and it is right that you should suffer the same treatment today.'

They took Hrafnkel and his men, and bound their hands behind their backs. After that, they broke open the storehouse and took a rope down from some hooks. They then took their knives, pierced holes through the men's heels behind the tendons and dragged the rope through these holes.

They threw the rope over the beam, and strung the eight of them up together.

Then Thorgeir said, 'So this is your present situation, and it seems quite fitting, Hrafnkel. You might have thought it unlikely that you would ever receive such shame as this from any man. What do you want to do, Thorkel? Sit here with Hrafnkel and keep a watch on them, or go with Sam to a safe place an arrow-shot away from the farm, and then carry out the confiscation court on some rocky knoll where there is neither a ploughed field nor a meadow?'

This was supposed to be performed when the sun was directly in the south.*

Thorkel said, 'I will stay here with Hrafnkel. That seems less work.'

Thorgeir and Sam then went and carried out the confiscation court. After that, they walked home. They took Hrafnkel and his men down and laid them in the hayfield. The blood had run into their eyes.

Then Thorgeir told Sam that he could do what he liked with Hrafnkel, 'because I don't think you'll have any problem with him now. It's clear that Hrafnkel never expected to fall into your hands.'

Sam answered, 'I will give Hrafnkel two choices: the first is that he be led away along with those men that I choose, and be put to death. But since he has so many dependants to look after, I want to grant him the possibility of taking care of them. If he wishes to have his life, he must leave Adalbol with his close relations and only those goods that I allot for him. I will take over his present place of abode and his position of authority. Neither you nor your heirs will ever lay claim to it again. You must come no closer than the eastern side of Fljotsdal heath. We can shake hands on this if you wish to accept.'

Hrafnkel said, 'Many would prefer a quick death to such humiliation, but I will be like so many others and choose life if it is an alternative. I do this mainly because of my sons. They will have little chance of ever amounting to anything if I die.'

Hrafnkel was then released and he granted Sam self-judgement. Sam apportioned to Hrafnkel those goods that he thought fit. That day, Hrafnkel moved all of his people and the goods he had been allowed away from Adalbol.

---

* The idea that the confiscation court should take place at a particular time of the day, in a sacred area an 'arrow-shot' away from the farm, outside the limits of cultivated land, must go back to early pagan belief and custom.

Thorkel said to Sam, 'I don't know why you are doing this. You yourself will most regret having given Hrafnkel his life.'

Sam said that that was how it would have to be.

Hrafnkel moved his farm east over Fljotsdal heath, and across Fljotsdal to the east of Lagarfljot river. Near the end of the lake, there was a small farm which was called Lokhilla. Hrafnkel bought this farm on credit, because he had no more than what he needed for provisions. People talked much about how his arrogance had been deflated, and many remembered the old proverb, 'brief is the life of excess'.

It was a wide area of forested countryside, but the buildings were very poor and that is why he bought it at a low price. Hrafnkel was not so worried about the cost, though. He felled the forestland because it was so wide, and built a grand farm which has since been called Hrafnkelsstadir (Hrafnkel's place). It has always been regarded as a good farm since that time. Hrafnkel lived there in great hardship for the first seasons, but he gained a great yield from fishermen. Hrafnkel worked very hard himself when the farm was being constructed. He reared calves and goat kids over the winter during that first season. He did well that first winter. Almost everything that he was responsible for survived. It might be said that by the spring there were two heads on each animal.

That summer a great run of trout entered Lagarfljot. Such things greatly improved living conditions for the people in the district, and this continued every summer.

12   Sam set up his farm at Adalbol after Hrafnkel had left, and held a splendid feast. He invited all of those who had been Hrafnkel's thingmen, and offered to be their leader in place of Hrafnkel. People accepted this, but there were mixed feelings about it.

The chieftains, the Thjostarssons, advised him to be kind and generous to his thingmen, and a useful supporter for anybody who needed him: 'Then they won't be real men if they don't follow you whenever you have need of any of them. We advise you to do this so that you will have success in everything, because you seem to us to be a brave man. Now take care, and keep your eyes open because you must always watch out for the wicked.'

During the day, the Thjostarssons sent for Freyfaxi and his herd, saying they wanted to see these wonderful animals that so many tales had been told about, 'because you won't find any better animals of this kind than these horses'.

The horses were led home, and the brothers looked them over.

Thorgeir said, 'These mares look ideal for farming people. I recommend that they be put to work for people for as long as possible, until the winter or age start troubling them. But this stallion doesn't seem any better to me than any other horses. If anything, he is worse since he's been the cause of so much trouble. I don't want him to be the cause of any more slayings than those which have already taken place. It would be most fitting that he who owns him should take him.'

They now led the stallion down through the meadows, and along beside the river. Below the farm, there are some high cliffs and a waterfall. There is a deep pool in the river there. They led the stallion out on to the cliff. The men from the West Fjords pulled a leather sack over the head of the horse, and took some stout poles and set them against his flanks. They then tied a stone around his neck, leaned hard against the poles and pushed him forward and off the cliff, so that he was destroyed. This place has since been called Freyfaxahamar (Freyfaxi's cliff).

Standing above them were the temple buildings that had belonged to Hrafnkel. Thorgeir wanted to burn them. He had them stripped, and after that set fire to the temple building, burning everything up. They then went back to the farm. The guests prepared to leave and Sam gave fine gifts to everyone.

The brothers were ready to leave. Sam chose some excellent treasures for them, and they promised each other complete friendship. They parted as warm friends, and rode along the usual route west to the fjords. They came home to Thorskafjord with respect.

Sam sent Thorbjorn down to Leikskalar where he was supposed to live. Sam's wife came to live with him at Adalbol, and they stayed there for the time being. Both sides now lived peacefully.

13   East in Fljotsdal, Hrafnkel heard about the activities of the Thjostarssons, how they had first destroyed Freyfaxi, and then burned the temple building and the images of the gods in Hrafnkelsdal. He then said that he considered it vanity to believe in gods and said that from that time onwards he would never believe in them. He kept his word, and after this never made any more sacrifices.

Hrafnkel stayed in Hrafnkelsstadir, and raked in riches. He soon won great respect in the district. Everybody was glad to stand or sit, just as he wished.

At that time, the traffic of ships from Norway to Iceland was at its height. Most of the land in the district was settled during Hrafnkel's day. Nobody was allowed the freedom to stay there unless Hrafnkel granted them permission. Everyone had to promise him their support. He promised them his help and support in return, and took control of all the land east of Lagarfljot. This assembly district soon became much greater and more populous than the one he had had before, stretching out to Selfljot, all the way up Skridudal, and all the way along Lagarfljot. A great change had suddenly taken place in that the man was much more popular than before. He had the same temperament as regards his helpfulness and generosity, but was now a more gentle man than before, more restrained in all ways.

Sam and Hrafnkel often met at public gatherings, but they never mentioned their dealings with each other.

14 Sam lived on in this position of respect for six years. He was popular among his thingmen because he was peaceful and restrained, and good at providing solutions. He remembered what the brothers had advised him.

It is told that one summer a ship came in from the sea into Reydarfjord, and the skipper was Eyvind Bjarnason. He had been abroad for six years. Eyvind had developed greatly in character and had become the bravest of men. He was soon given the news of what had happened, but he showed little outward reaction to it because he was a man who kept himself to himself.

When Sam heard about this, he rode to the ship. The brothers had a very joyful meeting, and Sam invited Eyvind to come west to him. Eyvind gladly accepted this offer. He asked Sam to ride home first and send some horses to fetch his goods. He drew his ship up on land and set it in order. Sam now did as he had been told. He went home, had horses collected and sent his men to meet Eyvind.

When Eyvind had packed his goods, he prepared for his journey to Hrafnkelsdal. He loaded the pack-horses and went up Reydarfjord. There were five of them. The sixth was Eyvind's servant boy. He was Icelandic by birth, and closely related to Sam and Eyvind. Eyvind had taken this boy out of poverty when he was living at home. He had taken the boy abroad with him, and treated him as he did himself. This act of Eyvind's was much talked about, and it was generally rumoured that he had done other such things.

They rode up on to Thorsdal heath, driving sixteen pack-horses ahead of them. Two of Sam's servants were there, and four traders. They were all dressed in colourful clothes, and rode carrying beautiful shields. They rode across Skridudal and over the ridge into Fljotsdal, to a place called Bolungarvellir, and then down to the Gilsareyri flats. They run along the east side of the lake between Hallormsstadir and Hrafnkelsstadir. They rode up beside Lagarfljot below the meadow at Hrafnkelsstadir, and then round the end of the lake and over the Jokulsa river at a place named Skalavad. It was midway between rising time and breakfast time.

A woman was by the lake washing her linen. She saw some people riding. The servant woman bundled together the linen, ran home, threw it down beside a wood pile and ran in. Hrafnkel had not got up, and some friends of his were still lying in the farmhouse, but the farm labourers had all gone off to work. It was hay time.

The woman started speaking as she came in: 'It's true what they said in the old days that "the older you get, the wetter you become". The respect a man receives early in life isn't worth much if he later loses it through dishonour and hasn't got the self-confidence to go off and rescue his rights. And it's a particularly big surprise in those men who have been made out to be courageous. Now those people who grew up with their fathers, their lives are different. You think nothing of them compared with yourselves, but then they grow up and they go from country to country and are thought of as being terribly important wherever they travel. And then they come back home and they're thought of as being greater than chieftains. Eyvind Bjarnason, who just rode over the river at Skalavad with a shield so beautiful that it shone, is so accomplished that he'd make a worthy object for revenge.'

The servant woman went on relentlessly.

Hrafnkel got up and answered her: 'It may be that much of what you say is true, even if you mean no good by it. You deserve to suffer more hardship for it. Go quickly south to Vidivellir and fetch Sighvat and Snorri, Hallstein's sons. Ask them to come immediately with all the men that are still with them and are capable of bearing weapons.'

He sent another servant woman to Hrolfsstadir to fetch Thord and Halli, Hrolf's sons, and those people there who were capable of bearing weapons. These were both worthy and able men. Hrafnkel also sent for his servants. When they arrived, there was a total of eighteen men. They armed themselves boldly, and rode over the river where the others had gone.

Eyvind and the others had reached the heath when Hrafnkel and his men were crossing the valley. Eyvind rode west until he reached the middle of the heath. That place is called Bersagotur (Bersi's tracks). There is an open bog there, and it is like riding through mud, which sometimes reaches up to the horse's knees or the middle of its legs, sometimes even its belly, but under that it is as hard as rock, so no one should expect that it will get any deeper. There is a big lava field to the west. They rode west over the rocky ground.

When they came on to the lava, the lad looked back and spoke to Eyvind: 'There are some men riding after us,' he said, 'no less than eighteen or twenty of them. There is a big man in black clothes riding on horseback, and it looks to me like Hrafnkel, although it is a long time since I have seen him.'

Eyvind answered, 'What has that got to do with us? I know of no cause to be frightened of Hrafnkel out riding. I have done him no harm. He must have some reason to meet his friends in the valleys to the west.'

The lad answered, 'It strikes me that he wants to meet you.'

'I don't know of anything that has come up between him and my brother Sam since they came to terms,' said Eyvind.

The lad responded, 'I'd like you to ride ahead, west to the valley. You'll be safe then. I know Hrafnkel's temperament. He'll do us no harm if he doesn't catch you. Everything is taken care of if you are. Then there will be no tethered prey for them, and whatever happens to us, all will be well.'

Eyvind said that he would not ride ahead, 'because I don't know who these people are. Many people would think it ridiculous if I ran away without having any proof.'

They now rode west out of the lava field. Ahead of them was another bog called Uxamyri, which is very grassy. It has many wet patches so it is almost impassable for those who do not know it. Both bogs take equally long to cross, but this one is worse because it is wetter, and people often have to unload horses. That was why old Hallfred had made the track farther up, even though it was longer, because he found it difficult crossing here with these two bogs. Eyvind now rode west into the bog with his men. They got badly bogged down, and were much delayed. The others, who were riding unhindered, were travelling much faster, and they now rode into the bog too. When Eyvind and the others reached the western side, they recognized that it was Hrafnkel who was in pursuit, along with both of his sons. They also recognized many other men.

They begged Eyvind to ride ahead: 'All the obstacles are now behind us, and you can ride west, down from the heath, quickly. As long as the bog is between us, you can still reach Adalbol. You'll be safe there.'

Eyvind answered, 'I will not ride away from men that I have done no wrong to.'

They now rode west out of the bog, and up on to the ridge. West of the ridge, there is a good, grassy valley, and as you come out of that valley to the west, there is another ridge before you come down into Hrafnkelsdal. They now rode up on to the eastern ridge. There are some peaks on this ridge, and on the outer edge of one of these, there is a knoll with lyme grass on top. It is much eroded, and has steep sides. There are good pastures there, and a bog. Eyvind rode off the track, and south into the gullies running to the east of the knoll. There he dismounted, and asked his men to let the horses graze.

'We'll soon discover what our lot will be; whether these men will turn to meet us or whether they have some other business west of the heath.'

Hrafnkel and his men were now very close behind. Eyvind hobbled his horse. After that they went up on to the knoll, and carried up some rocks from the sides. Hrafnkel turned off the track, south towards the knoll. He did not say a word to Eyvind, but went straight on to the attack. Eyvind defended himself well and bravely.

Eyvind's servant boy did not think he was strong enough to fight, so he took his horse and rode west over the ridge to Adalbol, and told Sam about the game that was afoot. Sam reacted immediately and sent men off to the next farms. That made a total of twenty men altogether. This party was well equipped. Sam rode east on to the heath to the place where the fight had taken place.

By that time, the exchange was over and done with. Hrafnkel was riding east over the heath, away from the site of the conflict. Eyvind was lying dead along with all his men. The first thing Sam did was search for signs of life in his brother. It had been a thorough job. They had all lost their lives. Twelve of Hrafnkel's men had also fallen, but six were riding away.

Sam did not stay there long, and told his men to ride after them immediately: 'Their horses are exhausted, but all of ours are rested. It will be a close thing whether we catch them up or not before they come down off the heath.'

By that time, Hrafnkel had come east over Uxamyri.

Both groups rode on, and when they got to the eastern side of the bog, Sam's men entered the lava field. By that time, Hrafnkel had reached the eastern side of the rocky ground, so the lava was now between them. While Sam was crossing the rocky ground, Hrafnkel got far ahead. Sam and his men rode on together until they reached the edge of the heath. Sam then saw that Hrafnkel had got far down the slopes, and realized that he would reach his own district ahead of them.

He told his men that they would not ride any farther, 'because it will now be easy for Hrafnkel to gather reinforcements, so that he will soon have us in his hands'.

Having said this, Sam turned back. He came to where Eyvind lay, started work, and built a mound over him and his fellows who had fallen. These places are called Eyvindartorfa (Eyvind's knoll) and Eyvindarfjoll (Eyvind's peaks) and Eyvindardal (Eyvind's valley).

Sam had the horses collected, loaded up the pack-horses and drove them home to Adalbol. When he came home, he sent men throughout Hrafnkelsdal in the evening, saying that all of his thingmen should come to him before breakfast, because he intended to go east over the heath: 'My trip will turn out as it may.'

That night, when Sam went to bed, a great number of men had already arrived.

15   Hrafnkel rode home that night to Hrafnkelsstadir, and gave the news. He ate some food, and after that he collected men until he had seventy, and with that force, he rode west across the heath and made a surprise attack. He took Sam in his bed, led him out and gave him two choices.

Hrafnkel said, 'So this is your present situation, Sam. A short while ago you might have thought it unlikely that I would have your life in my hands. I will be no worse a comrade than you were to me: I will offer you life if you wish, just as you did with me, or you can be killed. The other condition is that I alone will divide and choose things.'

Sam said that he would rather choose to live, but thought that both alternatives were hard.

Hrafnkel said that he could expect that, 'because we have a debt to pay. I would treat you much better if you deserved it. You will leave Adalbol, and go back down to Leikskalar and live there on your farm. You will take with you those riches that Eyvind brought. You will take no other goods away unless people can confirm that you brought them here with you. I want to take back my godord and my position of authority, my farm and place of abode, and all the other possessions that I owned. I see that there has been quite an increase here recently in terms of wealth. You will not reap the benefit of that because I mean to take it. You will receive no compensation for your brother Eyvind, because you brought a very bold suit for the slaying of that other relation of yours. You have received quite sufficient compensation for your cousin Einar, since you have had both power and possessions for this time. I don't regard the killing of Eyvind and that of his men as being worth any more than the injury done to myself and those injuries done to my men. You can stay at Leikskalar as long as your pride does not lead to your downfall. You will remain my underling as long as we are both alive. You can also expect to find yourself lower set than before.'

Then Sam went away, down to Leikskalar with his close relations, and settled back down on his farm there.

16   Hrafnkel then took over the farm at Adalbol with his people. There were both wealth and abundance for the taking. He placed his son Thorir at Hrafnkelsstadir, along with a housekeeper. He now held the godords for all the local districts. His son Asbjorn went west to Adalbol with his father because he was the younger.

Sam stayed at Leikskalar that winter. He was quiet and kept himself to himself. Many people felt that he was far from happy about his lot.

Later that winter, when the days started to grow longer, Sam had a horse shod, and got himself a groom. He took three horses, one of them for clothes, and rode over the bridge. From there, he went across Modrudal heath, and crossed the Jokulsa river up in the mountains, riding on to Myvatn lake, over Fljot heath and through the Ljosavatn pass. He did not stop until he came west to Thorskafjord. He was well received there. Thorkel had just returned from a voyage. He had been abroad for four years.

Sam was there for a week, resting himself. After that he told them about his dealings with Hrafnkel, and asked the brothers for assistance and support as before.

This time Thorgeir spoke more on behalf of the two of them, saying that they had already done a great deal, that he was a long way off and that there was a great distance between them, 'since you are living in the east of the country, and we in the west. We thought we placed everything pretty firmly in your hands before we left, so that it would be possible for you to keep things as they were. It has followed my intuition that if you granted Hrafnkel his life you would come to regret it most. We urged you to execute Hrafnkel; we thought that most advisable for you, but you wanted to have your own way. The difference in wisdom between the two of you is obvious, since he left you in peace, and did not make a move until he got the chance to kill the person that he thought was wiser than you. We can't have anything to do with this lucklessness of yours. We don't have such a great desire to get involved in disputes with Hrafnkel that we feel like risking our honour any more. The main reason, though, is that we think there is too much distance between us for us to visit the East Fjords. But we would like to invite you and your dependants to come and live here under our protection if you think it less galling here than in the vicinity of Hrafnkel.'

Sam said that he did not feel like going to all the work of moving everything from the East Fjords, and thought they could only help him in the way that he had asked. He said he wanted to get ready to go back home and asked them to exchange horses with him. That was done immediately.

The brothers wanted to give Sam fine gifts but he would not accept any of them. He said they were small-minded men. After that, Sam rode home. None of them was totally happy about all this. Sam settled back down on his farm, and lived there into his old age. He never improved his position nor got any redress from Hrafnkel as long as he lived.

Hrafnkel stayed on at his farm and kept his honour for many years. He did not live to be an old man, because he died of an illness. His burial mound is in Hrafnkelsdal just outside Adalbol.

His sons took over his lands and position of authority. They met and divided the property between them, but held the position of authority together. Thorir got Hrafnkelsstadir and set up a farm there, while Asbjorn took over Adalbol and the valuables.

Translated by TERRY GUNNELL

THE SAGA OF THE CONFEDERATES

Bandamanna saga

Time of action: 1040–60
Time of writing: 1270–1300

The Saga of the Confederates takes place after the actual 'Saga Age', around the mid-eleventh century, and is set in Midfjord, north Iceland, and at the Althing. In contrast with the tendency of most saga plots to branch out into sequences of episodes, *The Saga of the Confederates* quickly establishes the background to the main confrontation and focuses on a single event. Furthermore, this conflict takes the form of a battle of words and money, not of weapons, in an unusually explicit criticism of the chieftain class. In his *Epic and Romance*, W. P. Ker pointed out another contrast with tradition when he identified *The Saga of the Confederates* as 'the one intentionally comic history . . . in which what may be called the form or spirit or idea of the heroic Saga is brought within one's comprehension by means of contrast and parody'.

It tells the story of the 'self-made man' Odd Ofeigsson, who, after a disagreement with his father Ofeig, leaves home to acquire wealth from trading and fishing. Odd returns and buys himself land in Midfjord, near to his father's home. According to the saga, at that time it was very common to set up new godords or to purchase them, and Odd buys himself one in order to enter the ranks of the chieftains. Odd then goes on a trading journey abroad, and hands over his godord and the running of his farm to the villainous Ospak. On his return he faces his first involvement in public affairs, when he is obliged to bring a case against Ospak for the slaying of his friend and advisor Vali. When the nouveau riche Odd loses the case on a procedural flaw, the greatest chieftains in Iceland – the confederates of the title, who are carefully chosen as representatives of the old ruling class from all around the country – try to capitalize on his legal error and seize his wealth. When all hope seems lost, his father Ofeig reappears on the scene as the only man wise and shrewd enough to be able to help Odd. Ofeig then uses money, influence and eloquence to beat the chieftains at their own game and secure a 'happy ending' with the reconciliation of father and son.

With its psychological insight, keen sense of intrigue and Jonsonian manipulation of its characters' ignorance, vanity and avarice, *The Saga of the Confederates* is an extremely well-written and structured satire with exceptional dramatic qualities, reinforced by the unusually high amount of direct speech.

In *The Saga of the Confederates*, the chieftains have lost sight of the noble goals of truth and justice on which the settlers founded their society. Instead of cementing the community together, the law itself has turned into an instrument wielded by the rich and powerful; trickery and deceit have become survival skills, and the end justifies any means. In its satirical approach and its resolution of events, the saga can be read as a social or political allegory addressing the question of how to renew the chieftain class, which was a genuine problem at the time it was written towards the end of the thirteenth century.

Two versions of the saga are extant, the main differences between them being in length and style. The older and more detailed version (in *Möðruvalla-bók*, AM 132 fol., dated 1330–70) is now considered closer to the original. *The Saga of the Confederates* is translated here by Ruth C. Ellison from Hallvard Magerøy's edition (London, Oslo 1981) which is mainly based on this text.

I   There was a man named Ofeig who lived to the west, in Midfjord, at a farm called Reykir. He was the son of Skidi, and his mother's name was Gunnlaug; her mother was Jarngerd, daughter of Ofeig Jarngerdarson from Skord in the north. Ofeig was a married man; his wife was named Thorgerd, Vali's daughter, a woman of good family and very strong character. Ofeig was a very wise man and a shrewd adviser. He was a man of distinction in every respect, but was not well off financially, because he had extensive lands but not much cash. Although it was quite a struggle to supply the needs of his household, he denied no one hospitality. He was a thingman of Styrmir from Asgeirsa, who was considered the most important chieftain there in the west at that time. Ofeig and his wife had a son named Odd, who was a good-looking man and showed ability from an early age, but he got little affection from his father; he was disinclined to work.

A man named Vali grew up in Ofeig's home, a handsome and popular man. Odd grew up in his father's house until he was twelve. Ofeig treated Odd coldly most of the time and cared little for him, but the opinion spread that nobody in the district had more ability than Odd.

One day Odd went to talk to his father and asked him to fund him: 'I want to leave here. It's this way,' he said, 'you give me little status, and I'm of no use to your household.'

Ofeig answered, 'I'll give you no less than you have earned, and I'll do it right away, and then you'll see what support that gives you.'

Odd said that he would not be able to support himself very far on that, and they broke off the conversation.

The next day Odd helped himself to a fishing line and all the tackle from the wall and twelve ells of homespun cloth, and went away without saying goodbye to anyone. He went north to Vatnsnes and there joined a group of fishermen, borrowing or hiring from them what equipment he most needed, and because they knew he was from a good family and he himself was well liked, they took the risk of lending to him. So he bought everything on credit, and for the rest of that year he worked with them in the fishery, and it is said that the group Odd was with had the best catches. He stayed there three winters and three summers, and by then he had repaid everyone what he owed and had still built up a good trading capital for himself. He never visited his father and they both behaved as if there were no bond between them, but Odd was popular with his business partners.

At this point he got involved in cargo trips north to Strandir and bought a share in a ferry; he made money at this too. Now he quickly earned so much that he became sole owner of the ferry, and kept up this trade between Midfjord and Strandir for several summers. He was beginning by now to be a rich man. Then he grew tired of this occupation too, bought a share in an ocean-going ship and went abroad, spending some time in trading voyages. In this too he succeeded ably, profiting both in money and in reputation. He kept up this business until he owned the whole knorr and most of the cargo; he went on trading, becoming very prosperous and famous. When he was abroad he often stayed with men of rank and other leading people, and was highly regarded wherever he went. Now he became so wealthy that he owned two knorrs; it is said that no other trader sailing at that time was as rich as Odd. He was also a luckier sailor than others, never making land in Iceland further north than Eyjafjord or west of Hrutafjord.*

2   It is reported that one summer Odd brought his ship into Hrutafjord at Bordeyri, intending to spend the winter in Iceland. Then he was urged by his friends to settle down here and he did as they asked, buying land in Midfjord at a place called Mel. There he started farming on a large scale and living in grand style, and it is said that this enterprise was thought no less impressive than his former voyages, so that now Odd had no equal in the north of the country. He was more generous with his money than most and good at helping out people who needed it in his neighbourhood, but he never gave his own father any assistance.

He laid up his ship in Hrutafjord. It is said that not only was there no one else in Iceland as rich as Odd, but he was as wealthy as the three next richest men put together. He was well off in every respect, in gold and silver, lands and livestock. His kinsman Vali was always with him, whether at home or abroad. Now Odd settled down on his farm with all the prestige described.

---

* I.e. he never made land near the home of his father in Midfjord.

There was a man named Glum, who lived at Skridinsenni; that is between Bitra and Kollafjord. He had a wife named Thordis, daughter of Asmund Grey-locks, the father of Grettir Asmundarson. Their son was named Ospak. He was a big, strong man, overbearing and very assertive, who started young in the cargo business between Strandir and the north country, an able man who grew immensely strong. One summer he put into Midfjord to sell his goods. He borrowed a horse one day and rode up to Mel to meet Odd. They exchanged greetings and general news.

Ospak said, 'It's like this, Odd: people speak well of your circumstances and praise you highly, and all your employees think themselves well placed. Now I hope that it would turn out like that for me too; I'd like to join your household.'

Odd answered, 'You don't have a very good reputation and you're not well liked; you're reckoned to be a tricky customer, like the rest of your family.'

Ospak answered, 'Trust your own experience rather than hearsay, because reputation rarely flatters. I'm not asking you to make a gift of it – I'd like you to house me, but I would feed myself, and then see how you feel about it.'

Odd replied, 'You and your kinsmen are big men and difficult to cope with if it suits you to turn against anyone, but since you challenge me to take you in, we may as well chance it for one winter.'

Ospak accepted with thanks, moved to Mel that autumn with his belongings and quickly proved loyal to Odd, busying himself about the farm and doing the work of two men. Odd was very pleased with him. That winter passed, and when spring came Odd invited him to be fully part of his household, saying he thought that would be best. Ospak was very willing; he took charge of the farm and it prospered greatly. People were very impressed with how this man was turning out, and he was also personally popular. The farm was flourishing, and Odd seemed to be established more admirably than anyone. People thought only one thing detracted from his complete distinction, that he lacked a godord. At that time it was very common to set up new godords or to purchase them, and Odd now did so. Thingmen quickly flocked to him, all eager to join him, and for a time everything was peaceful.

3   Odd was well pleased with Ospak and gave him a free hand with the estate. He was both skilful and hardworking and an asset to the farm. Another winter passed, and Odd was even more pleased with Ospak, because he was undertaking more tasks. In the autumn he rounded up the sheep

from the hills and did so very successfully, with not a single sheep missing.

Now the next winter passed and spring came. Then Odd announced that he intended to go abroad that summer, and said that his kinsman Vali should take over the running of the farm.

Vali answered, 'The fact is, kinsman, that I'm not used to that, and I'd rather take care of our money and trade goods.' Then Odd turned to Ospak and asked him to take over the farm.

Ospak answered, 'That's too much for me, though things go well enough while you are on the spot.' Odd pressed him, but Ospak made excuses, although he was really very keen for the job, and in the end he allowed Odd to have his way, as long as Odd promised him his help and support. Odd said he was to manage his property for his own advancement and popularity, and said that he had proved by experience that there was no one else who could or would take better care of his possessions. Ospak said it should be as he pleased, and they broke off their conversation.

Now Odd prepared his ship and had his cargo loaded. The news of this spread and was much talked about. It did not take Odd long to get ready. Vali was to travel with him, and when everything was ready, people saw Odd on his way to his ship. Ospak went with him further than most, because they had much to discuss.

When they were only a short way from the ship Odd said, 'Now there is just one thing which has not been settled.'

'What's that?' said Ospak.

'Nothing has been arranged about my godord,' said Odd, 'and I'd like you to take it over.'

'There's no sense in that,' said Ospak, 'I'm not up to the job. I've already taken on more than I'm likely to cope with or tackle well. There is nobody as suitable for the godord as your father; he's an expert in law and very wise.'

Odd said he would not entrust it to him – 'I want you to take it on.'

Ospak made excuses, but was very keen to do it. Odd said he would get angry if he did not accept, and when they parted Ospak took over the godord. Odd now went abroad and had a successful voyage, as he usually did. Ospak went home, and this matter was much discussed; Odd was thought to have put a lot of power into this man's hands.

Ospak rode to the Althing in the summer with a group of supporters, and succeeded ably. He knew how to discharge successfully all the duties the law required of him, and he rode away from the Althing with honour. He supported his thingmen enthusiastically, so that they held their own in everything and were not imposed on at all, and he was generous and helpful to all his neighbours. In no way did the splendour and hospitality of the estate seem less than before; there was no lapse in management, and the household affairs flourished. Now the summer passed. Ospak rode to the Autumn Meeting and protected it by law, and as autumn drew on he went into the hills at round-up time and made a good job of gathering the sheep; it was pursued with energy, and not a single sheep went missing, either of his own or Odd's.

4   During the autumn Ospak happened to come north into Vididal to Svolustadir, where a woman named Svala lived. He was offered hospitality there. Svala, who was a good-looking young woman, talked to Ospak and asked him to manage her affairs.

'I've heard that you're a good farm manager,' she said.

He responded positively, and they talked about many things. Each was attracted to the other and they exchanged warm glances. Their discussion ended with him asking who was responsible for finding her a husband.

'No one of any importance is more closely related to me,' she said, 'than Thorarin the Wise, the Godi of Langadal.'

Ospak then rode to visit Thorarin, who welcomed him without enthusiasm. He explained his errand and asked for Svala's hand.

Thorarin answered, 'I don't find you a desirable in-law; your doings are much talked about. I can see that it's necessary to deal unambiguously with people such as you: either I'll have to confiscate her farm and move her in here, or the two of you will do as you please. Now I'll have nothing to do with this, and I declare it to be no affair of mine.'

After that Ospak went back to Svolustadir and told Svala how things stood. Then they settled their marriage themselves, with Svala declaring her own betrothal; she moved with him to Mel, but they kept the farm at Svolustadir and employed people to run it. Ospak now kept house at Mel in grand style, but people nonetheless found him very overbearing.

Now another winter passed, and in the summer Odd made land in Hrutafjord, having yet again done well in terms of both money and reputation. He came home to Mel and looked over his property; he thought it well cared for, and approved of it. As summer passed, one day Odd raised the matter with Ospak that it would be proper for him to take back his godord.

'Of course,' said Ospak. 'That was the thing I was least willing and fit to deal with. I'm quite ready to hand it over, but I think such transfers are most usually made either at autumn assemblies or at Things.'

Odd answered, 'That's fine by me.'

Summer passed until time for the Autumn Meeting. When Odd woke up on the assembly morning, he looked about him and saw few people in the hall. He had slept long and deep. He leapt out of bed and realized that all the men had left the hall. He thought this was strange, but said little; he got dressed and rode to the assembly, taking several men with him. When they arrived there was a crowd of people there, but they were nearly ready to leave, and the assembly had been protected by law. Odd was taken aback, and thought this behaviour strange.

Everyone went home, and some days passed. Then one day when Odd was sitting at table with Ospak opposite him, without any warning Odd leapt up from the table, threatening Ospak with a raised axe, and ordered him to hand over the godord now.

Ospak answered, 'There's no need to pursue the matter with such vigour – you can have your godord whenever you want. I had no idea you were serious about taking it over.'

Then he stretched out his hand to Odd and transferred the godord to him.

Things were now quiet for a time, but there was no love lost between Odd and Ospak. Ospak was savage tempered, and people suspected that he must have been intending to keep the godord for himself and not give it back to Odd, if it had not been forced from him in a way he could not escape. Now his management of the farm came to nothing; Odd gave him no orders, and they never exchanged a word. One day Ospak got ready to leave. Odd pretended not to notice, and they parted without either of them saying goodbye. Ospak now went to his farm at Svolustadir. Odd behaved as if nothing had happened, and things were quiet for a time.

It is reported that when men went to the hills in the autumn, there was a striking difference in Odd's success in collecting his sheep compared with previous years. In the autumn round-up he was forty wethers short, all the best of his stock; they were searched for far and wide in the hills and mountains but could not be found. People thought this strange, because Odd was reckoned to be luckier with his livestock than other men. So much effort was put into the hunt that the sheep were searched for both locally and in other districts, but without success. In the end this tailed off, but there was still a lot of discussion as to what could be behind it.

Odd was not cheerful that winter. His kinsman Vali asked him why he was so gloomy.

'Does the disappearance of the wethers prey on you so much? You're not a very high-minded man if such a thing can get you down.'

Odd replied, 'It's not the loss of the wethers which bothers me so much as not knowing who stole them.'

'Are you sure that's what has happened to them?' said Vali.

'Whom do you most suspect?' Odd said. 'There's no hiding the fact that I think Ospak is the thief.'

Vali answered, 'Your friendship has gone downhill since the time when you put him in charge of all your property.'

Odd said that that had been a very stupid thing to do, and it had turned out better than might have been expected.

Vali said, 'Many people said at the time that it was strange. Now I don't want you to rush into making a serious accusation against him; if it is thought ill-founded, there's a danger to your reputation. Now we two will do a deal,' said Vali, 'that you will leave it to me to decide how to go about this, and I will find out the truth for certain.' They agreed on this.

Vali now got ready for a journey and rode on a trading trip north to Vatnsdal and Langadal, selling his merchandise. He was a popular man, helpful with advice. He went on his way until he came to Svolustadir, where he was warmly received. Ospak was in very cheerful mood. Next morning, when Vali prepared to leave, Ospak saw him off from the farm, asking for all the news of Odd. Vali said he was doing well.

Ospak spoke approvingly of Odd and praised his magnificent life-style: 'But didn't he suffer some losses last autumn?'

Vali said that was true.

'What are people's guesses about the disappearance of his wethers? Odd has been so lucky with his livestock up to now.'

Vali replied, 'Opinions vary, but some people think it was no accident.'

'Unthinkable!' said Ospak. 'Few men would be capable of such a thing.'

'Just so,' said Vali.

Ospak said, 'Has Odd himself any views?'

Vali said, 'He doesn't talk about it much, but there's plenty of speculation from other people about what was behind it.'

'That's to be expected,' said Ospak.

'It's like this,' said Vali, 'since we're speaking of the matter: some people want to suggest that you might very probably be responsible. They put two and two together about your cold parting from Odd and the disappearance of the sheep not long after.'

Ospak answered, 'I never expected to hear you say such a thing, and if we weren't such good friends I would make you pay bitterly for that.'

Vali replied, 'There's no point in trying to deny this, or in getting so worked up about it. It won't clear you of the charge; I've been looking over the state of your supplies, and I can see that you have much more than you would be likely to come by honestly.'

'That will not prove true,' Ospak answered, 'and I don't know what my enemies can be saying, if this is how my friends are talking.'

Vali replied, 'I'm not saying this out of enmity towards you, and you are the only one hearing it. Now if you do as I want and come clean with me, you'll get off lightly, because I have a plan. I have been selling my goods all over the countryside: I'll say that you bought them all and used them to buy meat and other things. Nobody will disbelieve it. In this way I can contrive that you get out of this without dishonour, if you follow my advice.'

Ospak said he was not confessing anything.

'Then it will be the worse for you,' said Vali, 'and it will be your own fault.' Then they parted, and Vali went home.

Odd asked what he had discovered about the disappearance of the sheep, but Vali had little to say.

Odd said, 'There's no point in denying that Ospak is the thief, because you would be quick to clear him if you could.'

The rest of the winter was uneventful, but in the spring when the Summons Days came, Odd set out with twenty men.

When they got near the farm at Svolustadir, Vali said to Odd, 'Now you let your horses graze, and I'll ride up to the house and meet Ospak and see if he is willing to come to terms. Then the case will not need to go further.'

They did as he said.

Vali rode up to the house. There was nobody outside, but the door was open, so Vali went in. The house was dark. Without any warning, someone leapt from the benches and struck Vali between the shoulders so that he fell at once. It was Ospak.

Vali said, 'Run for it, you miserable wretch. Odd is almost at the farm and he means to kill you. Send your wife to tell Odd that we have come to terms and you have confessed to the charge, but that I have ridden north to the valleys about my business affairs.'

Then Ospak said, 'This act has turned out very badly; I meant this for Odd, not for you.'

Svala now went to meet Odd and told him that Ospak and Vali had come to terms: 'Vali said that you should go home.'

Odd believed her and rode home, but Vali died, and his body was taken to Mel. Odd thought this terrible news. He received dishonour from the affair, which was considered to have turned out disastrously for him. Ospak now disappeared, so that no one knew what had become of him.

5 To return to Odd, he prepared to take this case to the Althing by summoning a panel of neighbours from his home district. Now it happened that one of the panel died, and Odd summoned another man in his place. Then men went to the Althing, and nothing happened until the courts were in session. When the courts sat, Odd began an action for manslaughter, and it went smoothly for him until the defence was invited to speak.

A short distance from the court two chieftains, Styrmir and Thorarin, were sitting with their supporters.

Then Styrmir said to Thorarin, 'The defence has just been invited on the manslaughter charge; do you want to offer any defence in this case?'

Thorarin answered, 'I'll have nothing to do with it. Odd seems to me more than justified in bringing a suit following the killing of such a man as Vali, and I regard the accused as a thoroughly bad lot.'

'Yes,' said Styrmir, 'the fellow is certainly bad, but you do have some duty towards him.'*

'I couldn't care less,' said Thorarin. Styrmir said, 'But you have to look at the fact that he is going to be your problem, and will be a worse and more complicated one if he's outlawed. I think it is worth considering what steps we can take in the case, because we can both see a legal defence.'

'I spotted that long ago,' said Thorarin, 'but I don't think it a good idea to hinder this case.'

Styrmir said, 'But this affects you most, and people will say that you have acted feebly if the case goes through when there is an unanswerable legal defence. The fact of the matter is that it would also do Odd good to realize that he's not the only person of consequence around. He tramples over all of us and our thingmen, so that he gets all the attention. It will do him no harm to discover just how skilled in law he really is.'

Thorarin answered, 'Have it your own way, and I'll back you up, but no good is likely to come of it, and it will end badly.'

'We can't let that influence us,' said Styrmir, jumping up and going over to the court.

He asked what case was in progress, and was told.

---

* Thorarin's 'duty' towards Ospak arises from his kinship with Ospak's wife Svala, even though he had refused to countenance the marriage.

Styrmir said, 'The situation is, Odd, that there is a legal defence against your charge. You have prepared the case incorrectly, in summoning a tenth panel-member at home. That is a legal error: you should have done that at the Althing and not in your home district. Now you can either leave the court as the case stands, or we will move this defence.'

Odd was dumbstruck and thought the matter over. He realized it was true, left the court with his supporters and went back to his booth. When he reached the passage between the booths, there was a man coming towards him. He was an elderly man in a black-sleeved cape; it was threadbare and had only one sleeve, hanging down the back. He had a metal-pointed staff in his hand. He wore his hood low over his face, peering sharply out from under it. He walked with a stoop, jabbing his stick down for support. It was old Ofeig, his father.

'You're leaving the court early,' said Ofeig. 'You can boast more than one talent, when everything goes so promptly and decisively for you – or hasn't Ospak been outlawed?'

'No,' said Odd, 'he has not been outlawed.'

Ofeig said, 'It's not acting like a great man to make fun of me when I'm old. Why would he not be outlawed? Wasn't he guilty of the crime?'

'Of course he was guilty,' said Odd.

'What is it then?' said Ofeig. 'I thought the charge ought to stick – or did he not kill Vali?'

'No one's denying that,' said Odd.

'Then why isn't he outlawed?' said Ofeig.

Odd answered, 'A defence was found in the case and it collapsed.'

Ofeig said, 'How can there be a defence in a case brought by such a rich man?'

'They said it was wrongly prepared in the first place,' said Odd.

'That can't be so, when you were the prosecutor,' said Ofeig, 'though perhaps you are better at moneymaking and voyages than the perfect management of lawsuits. But I still think you are not telling me the truth.'

'I don't give a damn whether you believe me or not,' Odd replied.

'That may well be,' said Ofeig, 'but I knew before you set out from home that the case had been wrongly prepared, but you thought yourself all-sufficient and wouldn't ask anyone's advice. Now you will still be self-sufficient in the matter, I suppose. It's bound to turn out well for you, but it is a demanding situation for the likes of you, who look down on everyone else.'

Odd answered, 'It's more than plain that there will be no help from you.'

Ofeig said, 'The only hope in your situation is for you to make use of my help. How reluctant would you be to pay out if someone rectified your case?'

'I would spare no money,' Odd replied, 'if someone would take over the case.'

'Then hand over a reasonably plump purse to this old man,' said Ofeig, 'because many eyes squint when there's money around.'

Odd gave him a heavy purse. Then Ofeig asked, 'Was the defence formally made or not?'

'We walked out of the court first,' said Odd.

Ofeig answered, 'The only useful step you made was taken in ignorance.' Then they parted, and Odd went back to his booth.

6   Now to go back to old Ofeig: he went up to the upper fields of the Thing site and to the courts. He came to the court for the North Quarter and asked how people's cases were going. He was told that some had been judged and some were ready for summing up.

'What about the case of my son Odd? Has that been dealt with?'

'As much as it ever will be,' they said.

Ofeig asked, 'Has Ospak been outlawed?'

'No,' they said, 'he hasn't.'

'For what reason?' asked Ofeig.

'A legal defence was found,' they said, 'that the case had been wrongly prepared.'

'Ah yes,' said Ofeig. 'Will you permit me to enter the court?'

They agreed, so he went into the judgement circle and sat down.

'Has the case of my son Odd been judged?' said Ofeig.

'As much as it ever will be,' they said.

'For what reason?' asked Ofeig. 'Was Ospak falsely accused? Didn't he kill Vali, an innocent man? Was the impediment that the case was not important?'

They said, 'A legal defence was established and the case collapsed.'

'What sort of defence was it?' asked Ofeig.

They told him.

'Quite so,' he said. 'Did there seem to you any kind of justice in paying attention to such a triviality instead of condemning a thoroughly bad man, a thief and a murderer? Isn't it a serious responsibility to acquit someone who deserves death and thus judge in contradiction to justice?'

They said that they thought it unjust, but that it was required of them by law.

'Maybe so,' said Ofeig. 'Did you swear the oath?'

'Of course,' they said.

'You must have done,' he said. 'And what form of words did you use? Wasn't it on these lines, that you would judge as truthfully and fairly and lawfully as you knew how? You must have said that.'

They agreed that he was right.

'But what could be truer or fairer,' said Ofeig then, 'than to condemn a thoroughly bad man to outlawry, to be killed with impunity and denied all help, when he has been clearly proved guilty of theft and of killing an innocent man, namely Vali? As to the third point in the oath, that may be bending things a bit. But think seriously for yourselves what is more important, the two terms touching truth and fairness or the one referring to the law? Then you'll see things as they are, because you must be able to see that it is a heavier responsibility to acquit someone who deserves death, when you have sworn an oath to judge as fairly as you knew how. One might consider that this responsibility will fall heavily on you, and you can't wriggle out of it.'

From time to time Ofeig let the purse slip down below his cape and then pulled it up again.

When he saw that they were following the purse with their eyes, he said to them, 'You'd be better advised to judge fairly and truly, as you have sworn, and so get in return the thanks and gratitude of all prudent and right-thinking men.'

Then he took the purse and emptied it out and counted the silver in front of them.

'Now I want to show you a token of friendship,' he said, 'though I can see more in this for you than for me. I'm doing this because some of you are my friends and some are related to me, though not so closely but that each should look to his own advantage. I intend to give an ounce of silver to every judge sitting in this court and half a mark to the one who sums up in the case, and then you will both have the money and rid yourselves of the responsibility and, most important of all, avoid breaking your sworn word.'

They considered the matter and found his arguments plausible, and thought they had been in danger of breaking their oaths, so they chose to accept Ofeig's offer. Then they sent at once for Odd, and he came, but Styrmir and Thorarin had gone back to their booths by then. Now the case was immediately resumed, and Ospak was sentenced to outlawry; and then witnesses were named to testify that sentence had been delivered. At this juncture people went home to their booths.

News of this did not spread that night, but next morning Odd stood up at the Law Rock and announced loudly: 'A man named Ospak was declared an outlaw last night in the North Quarter Court for the killing of Vali. This is the outlaw's description: he is a big, manly-looking man, with brown hair and strongly marked cheekbones. He has dark eyebrows, big hands and thick legs. His whole build is uncommonly big and he has a thoroughly criminal appearance.'

People were taken very much by surprise, for many had had no news of this beforehand. Odd was thought to have pressed his case with determination and to be lucky in the outcome, seeing the turn it had taken.

7 It is said that Styrmir and Thorarin had a talk together.

Styrmir said, 'We've been badly shamed and humiliated by this case.'

Thorarin said it was to be expected, 'And crafty men must have manipulated it.'

'Yes,' said Styrmir. 'Can you see any way of putting it right?'

'I don't know that we can do it quickly,' said Thorarin.

'What's the best way?' asked Styrmir.

Thorarin answered, 'If those who bribed the judges were prosecuted, the charge would stick.'

'That's a pleasant prospect, if we can get our own back,' said Styrmir.

Then they walked away and back to their booths. Now they called together their friends and relations for a meeting. One of these was Hermund Illugason, the second Gellir Thorkelsson, the third Egil Skulason, the fourth Jarnskeggi Einarsson, the fifth Beard-Broddi Bjarnason and the sixth Thorgeir Halldoruson, plus Styrmir and Thorarin. These eight men now conferred together. Styrmir and Thorarin explained the situation and how the case then stood, and also how much of Odd's wealth was up for grabs and that they would all get very rich out of it.

Then they all made a firm agreement to support one another in the case, so as either to get Odd outlawed or to win self-judgement against him. Then they swore a formal covenant, reckoning that this could not be broken and that no one would have the confidence or skill to challenge them. With this settled, they parted.

People rode home from the Althing, and at first the plot was kept secret. Odd was very pleased with his journey to the Althing, and his relationship with his father was better than it had been. Nothing much happened that winter.

In the spring Odd and his father met at the warm baths, and Ofeig asked the news. Odd said he had none and asked in his turn. Ofeig told him that Styrmir and Thorarin had gathered supporters and intended to ride to Mel to summons him. Odd asked what the charge was, and Ofeig told him all their plans.

Odd replied, 'This doesn't look too serious to me.'

'Maybe it won't be too much for you,' said Ofeig.

Time passed, and at the Summons Days Styrmir and Thorarin arrived at Mel with a large following. Odd too was well supported. They stated their case and summonsed Odd to the Althing for having caused money to be unlawfully brought into court. Nothing else happened there, and they rode away with their supporters.

It happened again that Odd and his father met and talked.

Ofeig asked whether he still thought it an unimportant matter.

Odd replied, 'The case doesn't look serious to me.'

'That's not how it looks to me,' said Ofeig. 'How clearly do you understand the situation?'

Odd said he knew what had happened so far.

Ofeig answered, 'It seems to me that there will be more to follow, because six others of the most important chieftains have come into the case with them.'

'They must think they need a lot of help,' said Odd.

Ofeig asked, 'What do you plan to do now?'

Odd answered, 'What else but to ride to the Althing and muster support?'

'That doesn't seem to me a good idea as matters stand,' replied Ofeig. 'It's not good to have your reputation dependent on too many people's help.'

'What do you suggest then?' asked Odd.

Ofeig said, 'I suggest that you should fit out your ship during the Althing and be ready to leave with all your movable property by the time men ride away from the Althing. And which money do you think will be in better hands, what they will confiscate from you, or what I hold?'

'I think it the lesser of two evils that you should have it.'

So Odd handed his father a bulging moneybag full of silver, and with this they parted.

Odd fitted out his ship and hired a crew, and these arrangements were made quietly so that few got to know about them. The time for the Althing drew near.

8   Now the chieftains rode to the Althing, taking a very large following with them. Old Ofeig was in Styrmir's party. The confederates, Egil, Gellir, Styrmir, Hermund and Thorarin, had agreed to meet on Blaskogar heath; from there they all rode south to Thingvellir together. Beard-Broddi and Thorgeir Halldoruson from Laugardal rode from the east and Jarnskeggi from the north, and they met at Reydarmuli. Now all the parties rode down to the fields and so to the area of the Althing.

The chief topic of conversation there was the case against Odd. It seemed certain to everyone that nobody would be found to defend him, since they thought few would dare, and in any case it would get them nowhere, seeing what important men were on the other side. The confederates too were confident of success and swaggered a lot, and no one said a word against them. Odd had not asked anyone to defend his cause; he began preparing his ship in Hrutafjord as soon as men left for the Althing.

One day old Ofeig walked away from his booth with a lot on his mind. He could see no one likely to help him and thought he had a great deal to contend with, for he could scarcely see how he could cope on his own against such powerful men, when there was no legal defence to be made in the case. He walked bent at the knees, wandering and stumbling between the booths for a long time, until he came at length to the booth of Egil Skulason. There were some men there who had come to talk to Egil, so Ofeig went past the booth-door and waited there until the men left. Egil showed them out, and when he was going back indoors Ofeig stepped in front of him and greeted him. Egil looked at him and asked who he was.

'Ofeig is my name,' he said.

Egil said, 'Are you Odd's father?'

He said he was.

'Then you will be wanting to talk to me about his case, but it's no use discussing it with me; things have gone much too far for me to be able to do anything. Anyway, there are others more responsible for the case than I am, namely Styrmir and Thorarin. It's chiefly their concern, though the rest of us support them.'

Ofeig answered with a verse:

1. Before, I could speak
   of my son with pride,
   though I never came
   in Odd's company.
   Little heed to laws
   the loud-mouth paid,
   though money he has
   more than enough.

Then he added another:

2. An old stay-at-home
   finds satisfaction
   in talking chiefly
   with intelligent men.
   You won't refuse
   to confer with me,
   because worthy men
   call you wise.

'I'll find something more entertaining to talk about than Odd's affairs,' Ofeig went on. 'Time was when they were rather better than now. You won't refuse me a chat; it's an old man's chief pleasure to pass the time by talking with people like you.'

Egil replied, 'I won't refuse you a talk.'

They walked off together and sat down.

Then Ofeig began, 'Are you a good farmer, Egil?'

He said he was.

'Do you farm at Borg?'

'That's right,' said Egil.

Ofeig said, 'I've been told good and agreeable things about you; they say that you begrudge food to nobody and live in lavish style. We're not unalike: we are both men of good family and generous with what we have, but find ourselves in financial difficulties; and I'm told that you like to help your friends.'

Egil answered, 'I would like to think I was as well spoken of as you, because I know that you are of good family and also wise.'

Ofeig said, 'There is one difference between us: you're an important leader and fear nothing, whatever happens, and never fail to defend your rights against anyone at all, but I am a nobody. But still we are alike in temperament, and it is a great pity that men like us, who are so high-minded, should be short of money.'

'That may soon change,' said Egil, 'and then I'll be better off.'

'How so?' asked Ofeig.

'It seems to me,' said Egil, 'that if Odd's money comes our way, we won't go short of much, considering the great tales we have heard of his wealth.'

Ofeig answered, 'They won't have been exaggerated, even if he was said to be the richest man in Iceland. But you must be curious to know how large your share will be, seeing that you need the money so badly.'

'That's true,' said Egil. 'You're a good fellow and intelligent with it. You must know precisely how rich Odd is.'

He replied, 'I don't suppose anyone knows more about it than I do, and I can tell you that he is richer than anybody has ever said. But I have already been calculating what your share will come to.'

And then he spoke this verse:

3.	Injustice, I grant you, has engaged
	eight gold-greedy men.
	These gods of wealth
	make words worthless.
	You battle-windswept warriors,
	I wish you'd suffer
	loss of giant's laughter
	and good fame both.

gods of wealth: (noble) men

giant's laughter: gold

'What's that?' said Egil. 'That's not likely to happen, but you are a good poet.'

Ofeig said, 'I won't hold back from you just what a fortune you will come in for: a one-sixteenth share of the Mel lands.'

'What's this I hear?' said Egil. 'Then the fortune can't be as great as I thought. How can this be?'

Ofeig answered, 'No, the fortune is there all right, but I think this is pretty well exactly what you will get of it. Haven't you agreed that you and your allies should have half of Odd's fortune and the men of his quarter the other half? I reckon from that, that if there are eight of you confederates, you will each get a one-sixteenth share of the Mel lands, for these must be the terms you planned and agreed. Even though you entered on this business for the most scandalous reasons ever heard of, you must have had this kind of agreement. But did you really expect my son Odd to sit still and wait for you to ride north and attack him? Oh no,' said Ofeig, 'Odd is not going to be short of a plan to outwit you, for well supplied as he is with wealth, he is no less blessed with intelligence and resourcefulness, when he finds he needs it. And though you may name him outlaw, I suspect that his knorr will glide no less smoothly with him across the Iceland Sea for that. Anyway, you can't call it outlawry when it arises from such an unjust charge, which will rebound on the men who brought it. I expect Odd will be at sea by now with all his possessions except the lands at Mel – that's all he means you to get. He had heard too that it would be only a short walk from the sea to Borg, should he happen to put in to Borgarfjord. This case is going to end as it began, with you all being shamed and disgraced and condemned by everybody – which is only what you deserve.'

'That's plain as daylight,' said Egil, 'and now the matter is getting tricky. It's obvious that Odd wasn't going to sit around doing nothing, and I for one don't blame him. There are some people involved in this case whom I wouldn't mind seeing humiliated, like Styrmir or Thorarin or Hermund, and they have been pressing it hardest.'

'It will all turn out for the best,' Ofeig said. 'They will get their deserts and be widely condemned for this affair. But I think it would be a shame if you didn't come out of this well, because I like you better than any of your confederates.'

As he spoke he let a well-rounded moneybag drop into sight below his cape. Egil spotted it at once, and when Ofeig saw that, he quickly pulled the bag back up out of sight.

'As I was saying, Egil,' he said, 'I think things will turn out pretty much as I've told you. Now I'd like to offer you a token of my respect.'

Then he pulled out the moneybag and emptied the silver out into the lap of Egil's cloak; it came to two hundreds of the finest silver obtainable.

'This is for you as a little token of my regard – if you don't oppose me in this business.'

'You're no average rogue!' replied Egil. 'You can't expect me to be willing to break my oath.'

Ofeig said, 'You and your allies are certainly not what you make yourselves out to be: you want to be called chieftains, but as soon as you land in any difficulty, you have no idea how to get out with advantage. Now you mustn't let that happen to you, for I will hit on a way for you to keep your oath.'

'What way?' said Egil.

Ofeig said, 'Haven't you agreed that you will press for either outlawry or self-judgement?'

Egil confirmed it.

'It may well be,' said Ofeig, 'that we, Odd's kinsmen, are granted the privilege of deciding which it will be. Now it might also chance that you, Egil, were asked to pronounce the settlement, and in that case I'd like you to arrange it.'

'You're quite right,' said Egil. 'What a sly and intelligent old fellow you are! But I'm still not prepared to do this for you, because I have neither the strength nor the manpower to stand alone against all these chieftains, since anyone who opposes them is bound to face their enmity.'

Ofeig said, 'How about if someone else joined you in the matter?'

'That would be more like it,' said Egil.

Ofeig asked, 'Which of the confederates would you soonest have, supposing me to have the pick of all of them?'

'There are two possibilities,' said Egil. 'Hermund lives closest to me, but we are on bad terms; the other is Gellir, and I would prefer him.'

'It's a lot to ask of me,' said Ofeig, 'because I would like to see them all come badly out of this case – except you, of course. But Gellir will have the wit to see which is the better choice, getting money and honour, or losing money and being shamed. So you are willing to undertake this and reduce the settlement, if the matter is referred to your judgement?'

'That's my firm intention,' said Egil.

'Then let this be a definite agreement between us,' said Ofeig, 'and I'll get back to you in a short time.'

9   Now they parted, and Ofeig went away. He wandered shuffling among the booths, but he was not as dejected in mind as he was tottering on his feet, nor so haphazard in his plans as he was feeble in his gait. In the end he came to the booth of Gellir Thorkelsson and had him called outside. He came out and, being an unpretentious man, greeted Ofeig first and asked what he wanted.

'I just wandered over this way,' answered Ofeig.

Gellir said, 'You'll be wanting to talk about Odd's case.'

'I don't want to talk about that,' said Ofeig. 'I've washed my hands of it, and I'm looking for other entertainment.'

Gellir said, 'Then what do you want to talk about?'

Ofeig said, 'I'm told that you are a wise man, and I enjoy talking to such people.'

Then they sat down and began talking together.

Ofeig asked, 'What young men are there in your west country who seem to you likely to become important chieftains?'

Gellir said there were plenty to choose from, and mentioned the sons of Snorri the Godi and the men of Eyri.

'That's what I've been told,' said Ofeig, 'but now I am indeed well placed to get news, since I'm talking to a man who is both truthful and obliging. But which of the women there in the west are the best matches?'

Gellir named the daughters of Snorri the Godi and those of Steinthor of Eyri.

'That's what I've been told,' said Ofeig. 'But how's this, haven't you some daughters too?'

Gellir said he had indeed.

'Then why didn't you mention them?' said Ofeig. 'To judge from probability, none can be prettier than your daughters. They're not married, are they?'

'No,' said Gellir.

'Why not?' asked Ofeig.

Gellir said, 'Because no suitors have come forward who are both rich enough and well established, of powerful family and good personal qualities. I may not be wealthy myself, but I am still choosy about sons-in-law, for the sake of my ancestry and reputation. But I mustn't let you ask all the questions. What men up there in the north are promising as chieftains?'

Ofeig replied, 'There are plenty to choose from. I reckon Einar the first, the son of Jarnskeggi, and then Hall Styrmisson. Some people say too that my son Odd is a promising man – and that brings me to the message he asked me to give you, that he would like to become your son-in-law and marry your daughter Ragnheid.'

'Yes, well,' said Gellir, 'there was a time when my answer would have been favourable, but as things stand I think we'll have to put the matter off.'

'On what grounds?' said Ofeig.

Gellir said, 'There seems to be a cloud over the prospects of your son Odd as things are now.'

Ofeig replied, 'I can tell you as a fact that you will never find her a better husband than him, because everyone agrees that Odd is the most accomplished man around, and he certainly lacks neither money nor good family. But you are much in need of money, and you might find him a source of strength to you, because he is a man generous to his friends.'

'That would be worth thinking about,' said Gellir, 'if this lawsuit were not impending.'

Ofeig answered, 'Don't mention that silly nonsense. There's nothing in it but folly and the dishonour of the people pressing it.'

'It's likely to turn out quite otherwise,' replied Gellir, 'so I'm not willing to agree to your proposal. But if this problem could be solved, I'd be glad to accept.'

Ofeig answered, 'It may be, Gellir, that you are all about to make a fortune here, but I can tell you what your share of it will amount to, because I know precisely. At very best, you confederates will get half the Mel lands between you. Your share won't be much good to you though: you'll get little of the money and lose your honour and integrity, when you have been known before as one of the most decent men in the country.'

Gellir asked how this might be.

Ofeig replied, 'I think it most likely that Odd is now at sea with all his possessions except the lands at Mel. You can't have expected him to sit there helplessly while you divide up his property and share it between you. No,' said Ofeig, 'on the contrary, he said that if he came to Breidafjord he would find his way to your farm, and then he could take his pick of a wife from your family, and he said he would have enough firewood with him to burn down your house if he wanted. So too if he came to Borgarfjord, he had heard that it was only a short walk from the sea to Borg. He mentioned as well that if he came to Eyjafjord, he might find Jarnskeggi's farm, and in the same way, if he came to the East Fjords, he would find where Beard-Broddi lived. Now it doesn't matter to him if he never comes back to Iceland, but you will all have got what you deserve from this, namely shame and disgrace. I think it a pity that such a good chieftain as you have been should come by such a bad fate, and I would gladly spare you this.'

'You must be right,' replied Gellir, 'and I don't much mind if some trick is tried to escape the confiscation. I let myself be talked into this by my friends, rather than being set on it myself.'

Ofeig said, 'You'll see, as soon as you are under less pressure, that it would be a more honourable role to marry your daughter to my son Odd, as I said in the first place. Take a look at the money he has sent you! He said that he would provide her dowry himself, since he knew you were hard up, and this is two hundreds of a silver that can hardly be matched. Consider who else could make you such an offer, marrying your daughter to such a husband, who will provide her dowry himself. You will probably never go short again, and your daughter will have fallen into the lap of luxury.'

Gellir answered, 'This is such a splendid offer that it is hard to put a valuation on it, but on no account will I betray those who put their trust in me, even though I see that nothing is to be had from this case but ridicule and scorn.'

'How wise you chieftains are!' replied Ofeig. 'Who said anything about betraying those who trust you, or breaking your oath? On the other hand, it could happen that the settlement is put into your hands, and then you could reduce the amount and still keep your oath.'

'That's true,' said Gellir. 'What a crafty old man you are, and so cunning! But I can't take on the whole lot of them on my own.'

Ofeig said, 'How would it be if I could get another man in on it? Would you help me out then?'

'I'm willing,' said Gellir, 'if you can bring it about that I decide the terms.'

Ofeig asked, 'Who would you choose to have with you?'

Gellir answered, 'I'll choose Egil; he lives nearest me.'

'I never heard anything like it!' said Ofeig. 'You pick the worst of the whole bunch. It goes against the grain for me to offer him a share in the honour, and I don't know whether I can bring myself to do it.'

'That's up to you,' said Gellir.

Ofeig said, 'If I persuade him to join you, will you take the matter on? He'll be shrewd enough to see that it's better to gain some honour than none at all.'

'Since I stand to gain so much from it,' said Gellir, 'I think I'll take the risk.'

Then Ofeig said, 'Actually, Egil and I have already talked it over, and the matter doesn't look too difficult to him, so he's committed. Now I'll advise you how to handle this. You confederates and your supporters are all going about as one party, so no one will be suspicious if you and Egil get talking as much as you want while you are going to evensong.'

Gellir accepted the money, and the matter was settled between them. Then Ofeig went away and back to Egil's booth, walking neither slowly nor uncertainly, nor yet with a stoop. He told Egil how things had gone, and he was delighted. Later in the evening, when people went to evensong, Egil and Gellir had a talk and agreed the matter between them, without anyone having any suspicion.

10 Now it is said that the next day men gathered in large numbers at the Law Rock. Egil and Gellir mustered their friends about them, and Ofeig helped Styrmir and Thorarin to gather their supporters.

When everyone who was expected had arrived at the Law Rock, Ofeig called for silence and said, 'I have stayed out of the case against my son Odd up to now, even though it was begun in such a scandalous fashion that no one can think of a parallel, is continuing like that and looks like ending in the same way. I know that all the men who have been pursuing the case are now present, and I'd like to call on Hermund first: I want to ask whether there is any possibility of a settlement out of court.'

Hermund answered, 'We will be satisfied with nothing less than self-judgement.'

Ofeig said, 'You'd be hard put to it to find a precedent for one man conceding self-judgement to eight opponents in a single lawsuit, though there are examples enough of a one-to-one agreement. But even though this case has been prosecuted with more shocking irregularity than any other, I am willing to concede that two of your party should act as arbitrators.'

'Naturally we'll agree to that,' replied Hermund, 'and we don't mind which two they are.'

'Then you'll grant me the petty privilege,' said Ofeig, 'of selecting from among you confederates the two I want.'

'Yes, certainly,' said Hermund.

Then Thorarin said, 'Mind you don't agree today to what you'll regret tomorrow.'

'I'm not going back on my word,' said Hermund.

Then Ofeig sought guarantors, and they were easy to find, because the money looked to be easily recoverable. They shook hands on the pledge that the guarantors would pay over whatever sum was awarded by the men Ofeig picked, and the confederates pledged themselves to drop the outlawry suit. Now it was agreed that the confederates and their supporters should move up to the fields; the parties of Gellir and Egil stuck close together. They sat down in a circle at a certain place, but Ofeig went into the ring, looked around him and put back the hood of his cape. He straightened up and stroked his arms. Then his eyes sparkled as he spoke:

'There you sit, Styrmir, and people will think it strange if I don't choose you for a case which concerns me, since I am one of your thingmen and have a right to expect support from you. You've accepted plenty of good gifts from me too – and all of them ill rewarded. It seems to me that you have been first of anybody to show enmity to my son Odd in this matter and the most responsible for getting the case prosecuted. So I'll count you out.

'There you sit, Thorarin,' said Ofeig. 'There's no question of your lacking the intelligence to judge this case, but your contribution to this matter has been to damage Odd, and you were the first person to join Styrmir in prosecuting the case. So I won't choose you.

'There you sit, Hermund, an important chieftain, and I think it could be a good idea to refer the case to you. But nobody has got so worked up about the case since it all started, and it's plain that you want to make this dirty business public. Nothing but dishonour and avarice has drawn you into it, since you are not short of money yourself, and therefore I count you out.

'There you sit, Jarnskeggi. You don't lack the pride to judge this case, and it wouldn't displease you to have it referred to you. Indeed, your pride is so great that you had a banner carried before you at the Vodla Assembly, as if before a king; yet you will not be king over this lawsuit, and I count you out.'

Then Ofeig looked around and said, 'There you sit, Beard-Broddi. Is it true that when you were with King Harald Sigurdarson he said that, of all the men in Iceland, he thought you best fitted to be a king?'

Broddi answered, 'The king often spoke graciously to me, but it's not certain that he meant everything he said.'

'You can king it over other things than this lawsuit,' said Ofeig, 'and I count you out.

'There you sit, Gellir,' Ofeig went on, 'and nothing but avarice has drawn you into this case. Still, you have some excuse, since you're short of money and have large responsibilities. Now, although I think you all deserve a bad outcome from this case, I don't know but that someone will have to get some credit from it. There are few of you left now, and I don't care to pick any of those I've already turned down, so I'll choose you, Gellir, because you have never before been known for injustice.

'There you sit, Thorgeir Halldoruson,' said Ofeig, 'and it's common knowledge that no case of any importance has ever been referred to you, because you don't know how to judge cases and have no more brains for it than an ox or an ass. So I count you out.'

Then Ofeig looked around him and spoke this verse:

4. It's ill for men
    to endure old age;
    it snatches from them
    sight and sense.
    I'd the option just now
    of able judges:
    now the one thing left
    is the wolf's tail.   *wolf's tail*: i.e. worst choice

'I've ended up the same way as the wolves – they devoured one another, and didn't notice it until they got down to the tail. I had the choice of many chieftains, and now the only one left is a man from whom everyone expects the worst. He is known to be guilty of more injustice than any of the others, and he doesn't care what he does for money as long as he gets more than he had before. But he has an excuse for being unscrupulous in this case, when so many others have got tangled in it who previously had a reputation for fairness, but have abandoned honour and integrity in exchange for injustice and greed. Now it would never occur to anyone that I would choose a man of whom everyone expects the worst, when there isn't a craftier man to be found in your party, but that's what it comes down to, since all the others have been counted out.'

Egil grinned and said, 'It's not the first time I've ended up with an honour which other people didn't want me to have. What we must do now, Gellir, is stand up and withdraw to discuss the case.'

This they did: they walked away from there and sat down.

Then Gellir said, 'What will we say about this?'

Egil said, 'It's my advice that we impose a small fine, and I don't see what else can be done. But we're not going to win much popularity by this.'

'Wouldn't it be quite sufficient if we settled for thirteen ounces of scrap silver?' said Gellir. 'Seeing that the whole charge was based on a great injustice, the worse they like it, the better. But I'm not keen to announce the settlement, because I expect it to be badly received.'

'Choose which you'd rather do,' said Egil. 'Either announce the settlement or field the criticism.'

'I prefer to make the announcement,' said Gellir.

Then they went back to the confederates.

Hermund said, 'Let's rise and listen to this disgraceful business.'

Then Gellir spoke: 'We two won't be any wiser for putting it off, and it will all come to the same thing in the end. Egil and I have decided to award to us, the confederates, thirteen ounces of silver.'

'Did I hear that right?' said Hermund. 'Did you say a hundred and thirty ounces of silver?'

Egil answered, 'Come now, Hermund, you can't have been sitting on your ear when you were standing up. Thirteen ounces was what we said, and of such silver as no one would accept who wasn't wretchedly poor: it's to be paid in broken brooches and bits of rings and all the poorest stuff that can be found, to please you least.'

Then Hermund said, 'You've cheated us, Egil!'

'Oh really,' said Egil. 'You think you've been cheated?'

'Yes, I think myself cheated, and it's you who've cheated me.'

Egil answered, 'I'm glad I have managed to cheat a man who trusts no one, not even himself. I can prove what I say of you: you went and hid your treasure during such a thick fog that you thought you could never find it again if it crossed your mind to look for it.'

'That's another of your lies, Egil,' answered Hermund, 'like the one you told last winter, when you came home after I had invited you from your wretched hovel to spend Christmas with me. You were glad of the invitation, as one might expect, but when Christmas was over you got depressed, of course, about going home to starvation rations. I realized that, and invited you to stay on, with one companion, and you accepted gladly. But in the spring, after Easter, when you got back to Borg, you said that thirty of my horses, which were wintering outside, had died – and that we'd eaten them all.'

Egil replied, 'I don't think it's possible to exaggerate the poor state of your livestock, but I think that few or none of them got eaten. But everyone knows that I and my household never go short of food, even if my financial state is not always easy, but the conditions at your home don't bear speaking of.'

'I would like to think,' said Hermund, 'that we will not both be alive to attend next year's Althing.'

'Now I'm going to say words which I never expected to speak,' said Egil. 'Namely, "may your words be fortunate!" – because it's been prophesied of me that I will die of old age, but I think the sooner the trolls take you, the better.'

Then Styrmir spoke: 'Whoever speaks worst of you, Egil, is nearest the truth, if he calls you underhanded.'

'Now things are going nicely,' said Egil, 'and I'm the better pleased the more you insult me and back your insults with proof, because I'm told that when you were all amusing yourselves over your ale by choosing men to compare yourselves with, you claimed me as your equal. Now it's true, of course,' he continued, 'that you have some nasty vices, which others may not know about but you most certainly do. But there's one difference between us – when each of us promises to back other people, I do all I can and spare no effort, but the moment black-handled axes are raised, you take to your heels. And it's true that I generally have difficulty making ends meet, but I turn no one away hungry, while you are miserly with food. As a token of that, you own a bowl called "Food in plenty", but no visitor to your farm has ever seen what's in it – only you know. Now it's no disgrace to me if my household have to tighten their belts when there's nothing in the larder, but it is shameful for someone to starve his household when there's no shortage. You can guess who I mean!'

Now Styrmir was silenced, but Thorarin stood up.

Then Egil said, 'Shut up and sit down, Thorarin. Don't say a word, or I'll accuse you of such shameful things that it would be better for you to keep silent. I don't find it funny, though your servants laugh about it, when you sit with your legs tight, rubbing your thighs together.'

Thorarin answered, 'Wisdom is welcome, wherever it comes from.'

Then he sat down and kept quiet.

Then Thorgeir said, 'Everyone can see that this settlement is pointless and silly, awarding no more than thirteen ounces of silver in a case on this scale.'

'But I thought,' said Egil, 'that you at least would see the point of this settlement, and so you will if you think it over. Then you'll remember how, at the Ranga Assembly, some poor smallholder raised thirteen lumps on your skull, and you accepted thirteen ewes with their lambs in compensation. I thought this would be a good reminder for you.'

Thorgeir fell silent. Neither Beard-Broddi nor Jarnskeggi wanted to bandy words with Egil.

Then Ofeig spoke up: 'Now I want to recite you a verse, so that more people will remember this Althing and the outcome of this case:

5. Many a metal-tree   *metal-tree*: warrior
    of much less has boasted:

I record it in the pledge
that appeased dwarf and giant.
In rings I'm not rich, but –
I revel in telling it –
I hoodwinked those heroes,
hurling dust in their eyes.

pledge: poetry, the mead that reconciled Am (a giant) and Austri (a dwarf)

Egil answered, 'Well might you pat yourself on the back! No one man can ever have taken the wind out of the sails of so many chieftains.'

After this people went back to their booths.

Gellir said to Egil, 'I want us both to stick together, with all our men.'

This they did. There was a great deal of hostility during the remainder of the Althing and the confederates were very unhappy with the outcome of the case. None of them would touch the money awarded, and it got scattered all over the upper fields. Then people rode home from the Althing.

11   Odd was all ready to put to sea, when he and his father met, and Ofeig told Odd that he had conceded the confederates self-judgement.

'You miserable creature, you abandoned the case!' said Odd.

'The full story has not been told yet, kinsman,' replied Ofeig, and related the whole course of events, with the fact that a wife was betrothed to him.

Then Odd thanked him for all his help, saying that he had pursued matters far beyond anything that had occurred to Odd as possible, and he should never go short of money again.

'Now you must sail as you planned,' said Ofeig, 'and your wedding will take place at Mel six weeks before winter begins.'

After that, father and son parted on the best of terms.

Odd put to sea, and got a favourable wind north as far as Thorgeirsfjord, where there were merchants lying at anchor. Then the breeze failed and the ship lay there becalmed for several days. Odd grew impatient waiting for a wind, so he climbed a certain high hill and saw that out beyond the fjord the weather was quite different. He went back aboard his knorr and ordered his men to put out of the fjord under oars.

The Norwegian merchants mocked them and said that it would be a long row to Norway.

Odd said, 'Who knows whether you'll still be waiting when we get back?'

When they got clear of the fjord, they picked up a favourable wind, and did not lower their sail until they reached the Orkneys. There Odd purchased malt and grain, and spent a short while there preparing his ship. Just when he was ready, an easterly wind rose, and they set sail before it. They made an excellent voyage, and put in to Thorgeirsfjord to find the merchants still there. Odd sailed on west along the coast and put in at Midfjord, having been away seven weeks.

Then preparations were made for the wedding feast, and good provisions were in plentiful supply. A great crowd of guests came, including Gellir and Egil and many other important men. The feast went off well and indeed magnificently, and people thought they had never attended a better wedding in Iceland. When the party was finally over, the guests were seen off with splendid presents, the costliest falling to Gellir's share.

Gellir said to Odd, 'I hope you are going to be generous to Egil. He deserves it.'

'It seems to me,' said Odd, 'that my father has been pretty generous to him already.'

'You can improve on it though,' said Gellir.

Then he rode away with his supporters.

When Egil left, Odd saw him on his way and thanked him for his help: 'I can never do as much for you as you deserve, but yesterday I had sixty wethers and two oxen driven south to Borg, and they'll be waiting for you when you get home. And I'll never be ungenerous to you as long as we both live.'

Egil was very pleased at this, and they pledged friendship. Then they parted and Egil went home to Borg.

12   That same autumn Hermund gathered his forces and went out to the Hvamm Assembly, intending to go on to Borg and burn Egil in his house. When they came level with Valfell, they heard a sound like a bowstring twanging up on the hillside, and at the same moment Hermund felt a sickness and a stabbing pain in his armpit, so they had to turn back from their expedition. Hermund's sickness increased, and when they had come by Thorgautsstadir, they had to lift him from his horse. They sent to Sidumuli for a priest, but when he came, Hermund could not speak, so the priest stayed by him.

One time when the priest bent over Hermund, his lips moved, and he mumbled, 'Two hundreds in the gully, two hundreds in the gully.'*

---

* The implication is that Hermund has buried two hundreds of silver in the gully, so that Egil's insult to him (p. 490) was at least partly true.

Then he breathed his last, and his life ended just as reported here.

Odd now lived on his farm in lordly style and was well content with his wife.

All this time nothing had been heard of Ospak. A man named Mar Hildisson married Svala and moved into the farm at Svolustadir. He had a brother called Bjalfi, half imbecile and extremely strong.

There was a man named Bergthor, living at Bodvarsholar; he had summed up the case when Ospak was outlawed. It happened one evening at Bodvarsholar when people were sitting by the fire, that someone came and banged on the door and asked the farmer to come out. The farmer realized it was Ospak who had arrived, and he refused to go out. Ospak kept taunting him to come out, but he was not to be moved and he forbade his men to go out either, and so they parted. But in the morning when the women came in to the cowshed, nine cows had been mortally injured. This news spread widely.

Some time later it happened at Svolustadir that someone walked into the room where Mar was sleeping. It was early morning. The man went across to the bed and thrust at Mar with a short sword, right into his belly. It was Ospak, and he spoke a verse:

6.   Sharp from the sheath
       my short sword I drew
       and stabbed it into
       the stomach of Mar.
       I hate the thought
       that Hildir's heir
       should share the embrace
       of shapely Svala.

As he turned to the door, Bjalfi jumped to his feet and drove a wood-working knife into him. Ospak walked to the farm called Borgarhol and declared the killing, and then went away, and nothing was heard of him for some time. The news of Mar's killing spread and was widely condemned.

The next item of news was that the best five stud horses which Odd owned were all found dead, and people held Ospak to blame for that.

Now for a long time nothing was heard of Ospak. Then in the autumn, when some men went to round up wethers, they found a cave in some crags, and in it a dead man. Beside him stood a basin full of blood, and it was as black as pitch. It was Ospak, and people reckoned that the wound Bjalfi dealt him must have weakened him, so that he then died for lack of food and help. That was the end of him. It is not reported that any case was ever brought over the killings of Mar and Ospak.

Odd lived at Mel until old age and was thought a most outstanding man. Many important men in Midfjord are descended from him, including Snorri Kalfsson. The friendship and good family feeling between Odd and his father lasted the rest of their lives. And there this saga ends.

Translated by RUTH C. ELLISON

GISLI SURSSON'S SAGA

Gísla saga Súrssonar

Time of action: 940–80
Time of writing: 1270–1320

Gisli Sursson's Saga is a classic outlaw saga, and dwells with exceptional insight on the inner torment of its central character. Unlike many sagas with a vengeance theme, it is not ultimately a vindication of the family as a social unit, but rather maps the dissolution of a family through tragic conflicts and complex divided loyalties: Gisli is exiled when he takes revenge for the killing of his wife's brother, by killing his sister's husband.

Thorbjorn Sur, his sons Gisli, Thorkel and Ari and his daughter, Thordis, leave Norway for Iceland largely because Gisli kills several of Thordis's suitors, introducing a hint of ambiguity about sexual relationships which is never dispelled. The action switches to west Iceland where, after Thorbjorn's death, Gisli and Thorkel and their wives Aud and Asgerd farm together at Hol, next to Thordis and her husband, Thorgrim the Godi, at Saebol. Thorkel moves to Saebol when he overhears his wife and Aud talking – it appears that Asgerd has had an affair with Aud's brother Vestein, and also that Aud was involved with Thorgrim before marrying Gisli. Soon afterwards, Vestein is slain at night, and although the saga writer leaves the killer's identity as one of the great mysteries of Icelandic literature, this seems to be the work of Thorgrim and Thorkel. Gisli avenges him by killing Thorgrim, who is lying in bed by Thordis's side; she promptly marries her dead husband's brother, Bork. Finally, the scene moves to the remote West Fjords of Dyrafjord and Geirthjofsfjord where Gisli, outlawed for the killing, evades his pursuers until providence has the final word.

Heathen ritual plays a crucial role in the development of the story. The neighbours Gisli, Vestein, Thorkel and Thorgrim prepare a ceremony to take the traditional blood oath of sworn brotherhood, but end up quarrelling

Main Characters in Gisli Sursson's Saga

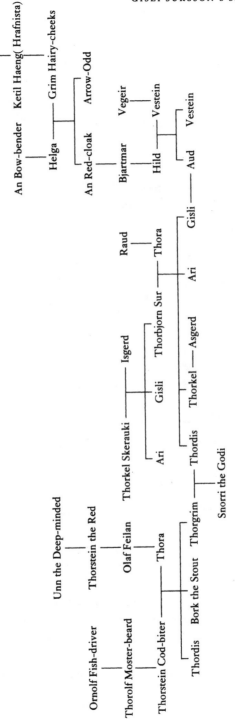

instead, as if the constant presence of another heathen notion – fate – has somehow gained the upper hand in this scene. Then, before the identity of Thorgrim the Godi's killer is known, the sorcerer Thorgrim Nef lays a heathen curse on him – like Grettir the Strong, Gisli can apparently only be overcome by the evil arts. Like Grettir, too, Gisli divides his outlawry between heroic escapes and comic outwitting of his adversaries, in almost slapstick interludes which heighten the drama and tragedy. And the two outlaws share a fear of the dark: Gisli's sleep is plagued by the good and bad dream-women of his verses, who seem to bode Christian hope and heathen despair in the dark night of his soul. Inevitably, Gisli dies in a heroic stand against insuperable odds – human odds, but also those of fate itself.

The saga has a skilfully devised binary structure, with numerous opposites that overlap and interact. For example, the short preamble in Norway presents a miniature of the main story which takes place in Iceland; two brothers and two brothers-in-law are killed; two farms, Hol and Saebol, are the centre of the action in Haukadal; two dream-women rob Gisli of his sleep; and two women are the main shapers of his fate. Gisli's wife, Aud, who devotes her life to preserving and comforting her husband, has her opposite in Gisli's sister, the hard-hearted Thordis who urges men to take vengeance and to win honour at any cost. Thordis even goes so far as to strike a blow at Gisli's killer, and divorces her second husband for his involvement, even though the pursuit of her brother was largely brought on at her instigation. Together with the two dream-women, Gisli's sister and wife create a powerful and varied female profile in what is essentially the story of a typical male hero's resourceful but vain battle against misfortune.

Gisli is a split personality in several ways, torn between his dream-women, unable to reconcile the roles of husband and outlaw, proving his nobility of character by living in a den like a beast. He is firmly committed to the ancient heroic values, a fearless and ruthless fighter who without compunction sacrifices his personal happiness on the altar of honour and the code of vengeance. Nonetheless, the heroic element is only one part of his makeup, since he is also an industrious worker and accomplished craftsman with all the qualities of the model pioneer farmer, and a fine actor too, a master of disguise when his life is at stake and he needs to dissemble. At times in his outlawry he is slightly coloured by the medieval trickster figure, in comic interludes which temporarily divert from the tragedy but ultimately serve to intensify it.

Although it is only preserved whole in later manuscripts, *Gisli Sursson's Saga* is thought to have been written in the late thirteenth or early fourteenth century. Two versions are extant, of which the shorter is translated here by Martin S. Regal from *Íslendinga sögur II* (Reykjavík 1987).

I   This story begins at the time when King Hakon, foster-son of King Athelstan of England, ruled Norway and was near the end of his days.

There was a man named Thorkel, known as Skerauki, who lived in Surnadal and held the title of hersir. He had a wife named Isgerd and they had three sons. Ari was eldest, then came Gisli,* and finally Thorbjorn. All three were brought up at home. There was a man named Isi, who lived in the fjord of Fibule in North More with his wife, Ingigerd, and his daughter, Ingibjorg. Ari, son of Thorkel from Surnadal, asked for Ingibjorg's hand and she was given to him with a large dowry. A slave named Kol went with her.

There was a man named Bjorn the Black, a berserk. He went around the country challenging men to fight with him if they refused to yield or accede to his demands. One winter, he arrived at Surnadal while Thorkel's son Ari was taking care of the farm. Bjorn gave Ari a choice: either he fight him on the island of Stokkaholm in Surnadal or hand over his wife, Ingibjorg. Without hesitation, Ari decided that he would fight Bjorn rather than bring shame on himself or his wife. The duel was to take place three days later.

The time appointed for the duel arrived, and they fought – the result being that Ari fell and lost his life. Bjorn assumed he had won both the land and the woman, but Ari's brother Gisli said that he would rather die than allow this to happen. He was determined to fight Bjorn.

Then Ingibjorg spoke, 'I did not marry Ari because I preferred him to you. Kol, my slave, has a sword called Grasida (Grey-blade). You must ask him to lend it to you since whoever fights with it is assured of victory.'

Gisli asked the slave for the sword and Kol lent it to him, but with great reluctance.

Gisli prepared himself for the duel. They fought and Bjorn was slain.

---

* Gisli, son of Thorkel, is the uncle of the eponymous hero of the saga. Gisli Sursson himself is not introduced until Chapter 2.

Gisli felt he had won a great victory, and it is said that he asked for Ingibjorg's hand because he did not want the family to lose a good woman. So he married her, took over her property and became a powerful figure. Thereafter Gisli's father died, and Gisli inherited all his wealth. Gisli saw to it that all the men who had come with Bjorn were put to death.

Kol demanded that his sword be returned. Gisli, unwilling to part with it, offered him money instead. Kol wanted nothing but the sword, but it was not returned. Greatly displeased with this, the slave attacked Gisli and wounded him badly. In response, Gisli dealt Kol such a blow to the head with Grasida that the blade broke as it smashed through his skull. Thus both men met their death.

2   Thorbjorn then inherited all the wealth that previously belonged to his father and two brothers, and continued to live at Stokkar in Surnadal. He asked for the hand of a woman named Thora, the daughter of Raud from Fridarey, and his request was granted. The couple were well suited and soon began to have children. The eldest was a daughter named Thordis. The eldest of their sons was named Thorkel, then came Gisli and the youngest was named Ari. They were regarded in the district as the finest men of their generation. Ari was taken in as a foster-son by Styrkar, his mother's brother. Thorkel and Gisli were brought up at home.

There was a young man named Bard who lived in Surnadal, who had recently inherited his father's wealth. Another young man named Kolbjorn lived at Hella in Surnadal. He, too, had newly inherited his father's property.

There was a rumour abroad that Bard had seduced Thordis, Thorbjorn's daughter, a good-looking and intelligent girl. Thorbjorn took this badly and said that there would be trouble if his son Ari were living at home. Bard remarked that he took no heed of the words of idle men – 'I will continue as before,' he said.

Thorkel was a close friend of Bard's and party to this liaison. Gisli, however, was as deeply offended as his father by the way people were talking.

It is said that Gisli went along with Thorkel and Bard one time to Bard's farm at Granaskeid. When they were halfway there, with no warning whatsoever, Gisli dealt Bard his death blow. Thorkel was angry and told Gisli that he had done great wrong. Gisli told his brother to calm down and jested with him.

'We'll swap swords,' he said, 'then you'll have the one with the better bite.'

Thorkel composed himself and sat down beside Bard's body. Gisli rode off home to tell his father, who was greatly pleased by the news. There was never the same warmth between the two brothers after this. Thorkel refused the exchange of weapons and, having no desire to stay at home, he went to stay with a close relative of Bard's, called Skeggi the Dueller, who lived on the island of Saxo. He strongly urged Skeggi the Dueller to avenge his kinsman's death and take Thordis as his wife.

Twenty men set off for Stokkar and when they reached the farm, Skeggi the Dueller suggested to Thorbjorn that their families be united. 'I'll marry your daughter, Thordis,' he said.

But Thorbjorn did not want the man to marry his daughter. Thordis, it was said, had since become friendly with Kolbjorn. Suspecting this was the real reason his proposal had been rejected, Skeggi went to meet Kolbjorn and challenged him to a duel on the island of Saxo. Kolbjorn agreed to take up the challenge, saying that he would not be worthy of Thordis if he dared not fight Skeggi. Thorkel and Skeggi returned to Saxo and stayed there until the fight was due to be fought. Twenty other men went with them.

After three nights had passed, Gisli went to meet Kolbjorn and asked him if he was ready for the duel. Kolbjorn answered him by asking whether this was really the way to achieve what he wanted.

'What kind of talk is that?' said Gisli.

'I don't think I'll fight Skeggi to win Thordis,' said Kolbjorn.

Gisli told Kolbjorn he was the greatest scoundrel living – 'And though it shame you forever,' he said, 'I will go instead.'

Gisli went to the island of Saxo with eleven men. Skeggi had already arrived at the spot where the duel was to be fought. He announced the rules and marked out where Kolbjorn was to stand, but he could not see his opponent nor anyone to replace him.

There was a man named Ref, who worked for Skeggi as a carpenter. Skeggi asked him to make wooden effigies in the likenesses of Gisli and Kolbjorn.

'And one will stand behind the other,' he said, 'and these figures of scorn*** will remain like that forever to mock them.'

Gisli, who was in the woods, heard this and answered, 'Find some better employment for your farmhands. Here is a man who dares to fight you.'

They took up their duelling positions and began to fight, each of them bearing a shield. Skeggi had a sword called Gunnlogi (War-flame) that rang loud in the air as it struck out at Gisli. Then Skeggi said,

---

* Both the wording of the original and the positioning of the two effigies make it clear that a sexual insult is intended.

1. War-flame sang
   Saxo is amused.

Gisli struck back with his halberd which sliced through the lower end of Skeggi's shield and cut off his leg. Then Gisli spoke:

2. Spear swept
   I struck at Skeggi.

Skeggi bought his way out of the duel, and from that time he walked with a wooden leg. Thorkel went home with his brother Gisli. The two of them were now on very good terms, and Gisli's reputation was thought to have increased considerably as a result of this affair.

3   Two brothers are mentioned in the story: Einar and Arni, the sons of Skeggi from Saxo. They lived at Flyndrenes, north of Trondheim. The following spring, Einar and Arni gathered together a large party of men and went to see Kolbjorn in Surnadal. They offered him a choice – either he go with them and burn Thorbjorn and his sons to death in their house or they kill him on the spot. He chose to go with them.

Sixty of them left for Stokkar by night and set fire to the houses there. Thorbjorn, his sons and Thordis were all asleep in an outbuilding. In the same outbuilding were two barrels of whey. Gisli, his father and his brother took two goat hides, dipped them in the whey to fight the fire and managed to douse it three times. Then they broke down a wall, and ten of them succeeded in escaping to the mountainside, using the smoke as cover. They were now such a distance from the farm as to be out of range of the dogs' barking.* Twelve people were burned to death in the fire. The attackers believed they had killed everyone.

Those who went with Gisli journeyed until they reached Styrkar's farm on Fridarey. There they gathered a force of forty men, went to Kolbjorn's farm and, without warning, set fire to his house. Kolbjorn was burned to death with eleven other men. Then they sold up their lands, bought a ship and left with all their belongings. There were sixty of them on board.† They arrived at a group of islands called the Asen and laid over there before setting out to sea.

They left the Asen Islands in two boats, forty men in all, and sailed north to Flyndrenes. At the same time, Skeggi's two sons were on their way to

---

* The Icelandic suggests that they could not hear the dogs which means they were safe.
† These are the figures given in the original.

collect land rent with a group of seven men. Gisli's party confronted them and killed them all. Gisli slew three men and Thorkel two. From there they went to the farm and took a great deal of goods and livestock. Skeggi the Dueller was there at his sons' farm. This time Gisli cut off his head.

4   After this, they went back to their ship and set out to sea. They sailed for more than sixty days and nights, finally reaching the mouth of the Haukadalsa river on the south side of Dyrafjord in the west of Iceland.

Two men are mentioned, both named Thorkel, who lived on opposite sides of the fjord. One of them, Thorkel Eiriksson, lived at Saurar in Keldudal on the south side, and the other, known as Thorkel the Wealthy, lived on the north side at Alvidra. Thorkel Eiriksson was the first man of standing to go down to the ship to greet Thorbjorn Sur (Whey),* who was called that since the time he used whey to escape being burned to death. None of the lands on either side of the fjord were settled at the time, so Thorbjorn Sur bought some land at Saebol in Haukadal on the south side. Gisli built a farm there at which they lived from that time on.

There was a man named Bjartmar who lived at the head of Arnarfjord. His wife, Thurid, was the daughter of Hrafn from Ketilseyri in Dyrafjord, and Hrafn was the son of Dyri who first settled the fjord. Bjartmar and Thurid had several children. The eldest was a girl named Hild, and their sons were named Helgi, Sigurd and Vestgeir.

There was a Norwegian named Vestein, who arrived at the time of the settlement. He lodged at Bjartmar's farm. Vestein took Bjartmar's daughter, Hild, as his wife, and it was not long before they had two children, a daughter named Aud and a son named Vestein.

Vestein the Norwegian was the son of Vegeir, the brother of Vebjorn the Champion of Sognefjord. Bjartmar was the son of An Red-cloak, son of Grim Hairy-cheeks, brother of Arrow-Odd, son of Ketil Haeng, son of Hallbjorn Half-troll. An Red-cloak's mother was Helga, the daughter of An Bow-bender.

Vestein Vesteinsson eventually became a skilled seafarer, though at this point in the story he lived on a farm in Onundarfjord below Hest mountain. He had a wife, Gunnhild, and two sons, Berg and Helgi.

Soon after, Thorbjorn Sur passed away, followed by his wife, Thora. Gisli and his brother Thorkel took over the farm. Thorbjorn and Thora were laid to rest in a burial mound.

* Gisli is referred to, not as Thorbjornsson (i.e. son of Thorbjorn), but Sursson after his father's nickname.

5   There was a man named Thorbjorn, nicknamed Selagnup (Seals' Peak).
    He lived at Kvigandafell in Talknafjord. He was married to a woman
called Thordis and had a daughter named Asgerd. Thorkel, the son of
Thorbjorn Sur, asked for Asgerd's hand and she became his wife. Gisli asked
for the hand of Aud, Vestein's sister, and married her. The two brothers
lived together in Haukadal.

One spring, Thorkel the Wealthy travelled to the Thorsnes Assembly,
and Thorbjorn Sur's two sons accompanied him. At that time, Thorstein
Cod-biter, the son of Thorolf Moster-beard, was living at Thorsnes with
his wife, Thora, the daughter of Olaf Thorsteinsson, and their children,
Thordis, Thorgrim and Bork the Stout. Thorkel settled his business at the
assembly, and when it was over, Thorstein invited him, along with Gisli
and Thorkel, to his home. When they left, he gave them good gifts, and
they responded by inviting Thorstein's sons to their assembly in the west
the following spring.

Thorkel the Wealthy and the brothers Gisli and Thorkel returned home.
The following spring, Thorstein's sons went to the Hvolseyri Assembly
along with a party of ten men. On their arrival they met up with Thorbjorn
Sur's sons, who invited them home when the assembly was over. They had
already accepted an invitation to the home of Thorkel the Wealthy, but
after they visited him they went off to Gisli and Thorkel's farm and enjoyed
an excellent feast there.

Thorgrim, the son of Thorstein, found Thordis, the sister of Gisli and
Thorkel, very attractive and asked for her hand in marriage. She was
betrothed to him and the wedding followed soon in the wake of the betrothal.
Thordis had the farm at Saebol as her dowry, and Thorgrim moved west
to live there with her. Bork, however, remained at Thorsnes with his sister's
sons, Outlaw-Stein and Thorodd.

Thorgrim now lived at Saebol, and Gisli and Thorkel moved to Hol
where they built a good farmhouse. The two farms, Hol and Saebol, lay
side by side, divided by a hayfield wall, and both parties lived on friendly
terms. Thorgrim had a godord and afforded both brothers considerable
support.

One spring, they left for the Spring Assembly with forty men, all of them
wearing coloured clothes.* Vestein, Gisli's brother-in-law, joined up with
them and so did the men from Surnadal.

---

* The fact that they had dyed or coloured clothes was a sign of their prosperity.

6   There was a man named Gest, son of Oddleif. He arrived at the
    assembly and shared a booth with Thorkel the Wealthy. The men
from Surnadal were sitting in the Haukadal booth drinking, while the others
were at court because there were lawsuits to be heard.

A man came into the Haukadal booth, a noisy fellow named Arnor, and
spoke to them: 'You Haukadal people don't seem to want to do anything
other than drink while your thingmen are dealing with important matters.
That's what everyone thinks, though I'm the only one to say so.'

Then Gisli said, 'Then we will go to court. It could well be that the others
are saying the same.'

So they all walked over to the court where Thorgrim asked if any of
them needed his support.

'Having pledged our support, we will do all in our power to help you, as
long as we are standing,' he told them.

Then Thorkel the Wealthy answered, 'The matters that men are concerned with at present are of little importance, but we will let you know if
we need your support.'

People began to talk about how much finery the group possessed, how
imposing they were and how well they spoke.

Then Thorkel said to Gest, 'How long do you expect the ardour and
arrogance of these people from Haukadal to last?'

Gest answered, 'Three summers from now, the men in that party will no
longer see eye to eye.'

Now Arnor was present while they were talking, and he rushed into the
Haukadal booth and told them what had been said.

Gisli answered, 'I am sure this report is correct, but let us make certain
that his prediction does not come true. And I see a good way to avert it.
We four will make our bond of friendship even stronger than before by
pledging our sworn brotherhood.'

This seemed good counsel to them, so they walked out to Eyrarhvolsoddi
and scored out a long strip of turf, making sure that both ends were still
attached to the ground. Then they propped up the arch of raised turf with
a damascened spear so long-shafted that a man could stretch out his arm
and touch the rivets. All four of them had to go under it, Thorgrim, Gisli,
Thorkel and Vestein. Then they drew blood and let it drip down on to the
soil beneath the turf strip and stirred it together – the soil and the blood.
Then they all fell to their knees and swore an oath that each would avenge
the other as if they were brothers, and they called on all the gods as their
witnesses.

But as they all clasped hands, Thorgrim said, 'I will have enough trouble to deal with if I so bind myself to Thorkel and Gisli, my brothers-in-law, but I bear no obligation to Vestein' – and he quickly withdrew his hand.

'Then others may do the same,' said Gisli, and he withdrew his hand, too. 'I will not burden myself with ties to a man who refuses to bind himself to Vestein, my brother-in-law.'

They were all deeply affected by this. Then Gisli said to Thorkel, his brother, 'This is what I thought would happen. What has taken place here will come to nothing. I suspect fate will take its course now.'

After this, everyone went home from the assembly.

7   That summer, a ship arrived in Dyrafjord owned by two brothers from Norway. One was named Thorir and the other Thorarin, and they were from Oslo Fjord. Thorgrim rode out to the ship and bought four hundreds of timber, paying part of the sum immediately and leaving the balance until later. Then the traders put up ship in the Sandar estuary and found a place to lodge.

There was a man named Odd, the son of Orlyg, who lived at Eyri in Skutilsfjord. Thorgrim lodged the skipper and the helmsman at his house, then he sent his son, Thorodd, to stack and count the timber because he wanted it brought to his house soon. Thorodd went and took the timber and stacked it, and found that it was far from being the bargain his father had described. Then he spoke harshly to the Norwegians, which they could not tolerate, and they set about him and killed him.

After this, the Norwegians left their ship and travelled about Dyrafjord, where they obtained some horses, and then headed off towards their lodgings. They travelled all day and night, eventually arriving at a valley that leads up out of Skutilsfjord. They ate breakfast there and then went to sleep.

When Thorgrim heard the news, he set out from home without delay, had someone ferry him across the fjord and then pursued the Norwegians alone. He arrived at the spot where they were sleeping and woke Thorarin by prodding at him with the shaft of his spear. Thorarin jumped up and, recognizing his assailant, was about to grab his sword, but Thorgrim thrust out with his spear and killed him. Then Thorir awoke, ready to avenge his brother, but Thorgrim speared him clean through. The place is now called Dagverdardal (Breakfast dale) and Austmannafall (Eastman's fall). This done, Thorgrim returned home and became renowned as a result of this expedition.

Thorgrim remained at his farm for the winter, and when spring arrived, he and his brother-in-law, Thorkel, fitted out the ship that had belonged to the Norwegians. The two men from Oslo Fjord had been great trouble-makers in Norway and they had not been safe there. With the ship fully ready, Thorgrim and Thorkel set sail. That summer, Vestein and Gisli also set off from Skeljavik in Steingrimsfjord. Thus both ships were at sea. Onund from Medaldal was left in charge of Thorkel and Gisli's farm, while Outlaw-Stein and Thordis took care of the farm at Saebol.

All this took place when Harald Grey-cloak ruled Norway. Thorgrim and Thorkel came ashore in the north of that country and soon afterwards arrived at the court, where they presented themselves to the king and greeted him warmly. The king gave them a friendly welcome, and they pledged themselves as his followers. They became wealthy and well established.

Gisli and Vestein had been at sea for more than fifty days and nights when they eventually ran ashore at Hordaland. It was early winter, in the dead of night, and a great blizzard was blowing. Their ship was wrecked, but the crew escaped drowning and the goods were salvaged.

8   There was a man named Beard-Bjalfi, who owned a trading ship and was about to set out south for Denmark. Gisli and Vestein asked him if they could buy a half share in the ship. He replied that he had heard that they were decent men and agreed to the deal. They responded at once by giving him gifts worth more than the price of their share.

They sailed south to Denmark and arrived at a place called Viborg, staying the winter there with a man named Sigurhadd. There were three of them, Vestein, Gisli and Bjalfi, and they were all good friends and gave each other gifts. Early in the spring, Bjalfi prepared his ship to sail for Iceland.

There was a man named Sigurd, a trading partner of Vestein's and a Norwegian by birth, who at that time was living out west in England. He sent word to Vestein, saying that he wanted to break up their partnership, claiming that he no longer needed Vestein's money. Vestein asked Gisli's leave to go and meet the man.

'Then you must promise me,' said Gisli, 'if you return safely, you will never leave Iceland again without my consent.'

Vestein agreed to these terms.

One morning Gisli arose early and went out to the smithy. He was a very skilled craftsman and a man of many talents. He made a coin, worth no less than an ounce of silver, and riveted it together with twenty studs, ten on each half, so that the coin appeared whole even though it could be separated into two halves.

It is said that he pulled the coin apart and gave one half to Vestein, asking him to keep it as a token.

'We will only have these sent to each other if our lives are in danger,' said Gisli. 'And something tells me that we will need to send them, even though we may never meet each other again.'

Vestein then went west to England. Gisli and Bjalfi made for Norway, and in the summer they sailed to Iceland. They became wealthy and well-respected men and eventually parted on good terms, Bjalfi buying Gisli's share of the ship.

Then Gisli went west to Dyrafjord on a cargo vessel with eleven men.

9 Thorkel and Thorgrim made their ship ready in another place and they arrived at the Haukadal estuary in Dyrafjord later on the same day that Gisli had sailed in on board the cargo vessel. They met up soon afterwards and greeted each other warmly, then each of them went off to his own home. Thorgrim and Thorkel had also become wealthy.

Thorkel bore himself aloof and did not work on the farm. Gisli, on the contrary, worked day and night.

One day when the weather was fine, Gisli sent all his men out haymaking – except Thorkel. He was the only man left at the farmhouse, and he laid himself out in the fire-room after having finished his breakfast. The fire-room was a hundred feet long and sixty feet wide, and on its south side was the women's area, where Aud and Asgerd sat sewing. When Thorkel woke up he went over to the women's area because he heard voices coming from it, and he lay down close by.

Asgerd was speaking: 'Aud, could you please cut out a shirt for my husband, Thorkel?'

'I'm no better than you at such things,' said Aud, 'and, besides, you would not have asked for my help if you had been cutting out a shirt for my brother, Vestein.'

'That's a separate issue,' said Asgerd, 'and, to my mind, will remain so for some time.'

'I've known what was going on for quite a while,' said Aud, 'and we will not say any more about it.'

'I cannot see anything wrong with my liking Vestein,' said Asgerd. 'What's more, I've heard tell that you and Thorgrim saw a lot of each other before you married Gisli.'

'There was no shame in that,' said Aud. 'I was never unfaithful to Gisli and have therefore brought no disgrace upon him. We will stop talking about this now.'

But Thorkel heard every word they spoke, and when they stopped, he said:

3.   Hear a great wonder,
      hear of peace broken,
      hear of a great matter,
      hear of a death
      – one man's or more.

And after this he went inside.

Then Aud spoke: 'Women's gossip often leads to trouble, and here it may turn out to be the worst kind of trouble. We must seek counsel.'

'I've thought of a plan,' said Asgerd, 'that I think will work for me. But I do not see what you can do.'

'What is it?' asked Aud.

'I'll put my arms around Thorkel's neck when we are in bed and say it's a lie. Then he'll forgive me.'

'That will not be enough to prevent harm coming from this,' said Aud.

'What will you do?' asked Asgerd.

'Tell my husband, Gisli, everything I have left unsaid as well as all that to which I cannot find a solution.'

That evening Gisli came home from the haymaking. Usually, Thorkel would have thanked his brother for doing this work, but now he was silent and did not utter a word. Gisli asked him if he was feeling unwell.

'I am not sick,' said Thorkel, 'but this is worse than sickness.'

'Have I done anything to upset you?' said Gisli.

'No, not a thing,' said Thorkel, 'but you will find out eventually what this is about.'

And then each of them went about his business, and there was no more talk of the matter at that time.

Thorkel ate very little that evening and was the first to retire to bed.

Once he was there, Asgerd came to him, lifted the blanket and was about to lie down when Thorkel said, 'I will not have you lying here tonight, nor for a very long time to come.'

Asgerd replied, 'Why this sudden change? What is the reason for this?'

'We both know what's behind this,' said Thorkel, 'though I have been kept in the dark about it for a long time. It will not help your reputation if I speak more plainly.'

'You think what you will,' answered Asgerd, 'but I am not going to argue with you about whether I may sleep in this bed or not. You have a choice – either you take me in and act as if nothing has happened or I will call witnesses this minute, divorce you and have my father reclaim my bride-price and my dowry. Then you wouldn't have to worry about my taking up room in your bed ever again.'

Thorkel was quiet for a while, then he said, 'I advise you to do as you wish. I will not stop you from sleeping here all night.'

She soon made clear what she wanted to do, and they had not been lying together for too long before they made up as if nothing had happened.

Aud got into bed with Gisli and told him what she and Asgerd had been talking about. She asked him not to be angry with her, but to see if he could think of a reasonable plan.

'I see no plan that will work,' he said, 'but I will not be angry with you for this. Fate must find someone to speak through. Whatever is meant to happen will happen.'

10 The year wore on and the Moving Days came round again. Thorkel asked his brother Gisli to have a talk.

'It's like this, brother,' he said. 'I have a few changes in mind that I'm disposed to carry out, and they are along these lines – I want to divide up our wealth and start farming with Thorgrim, my brother-in-law.'

Gisli answered him, 'What brothers own jointly is best seen together. I would appreciate having things remain as they are and that we make no division.'

'We cannot go on like this any longer,' said Thorkel, 'jointly owning the farm. It will lead to great loss. You have always dealt with the work and the responsibility of the farm alone, and nothing comes of anything I take a hand in.'

'Don't concern yourself with this,' said Gisli, 'while I make no complaint. We have been on both good and bad terms with each other.'

'That's not what's behind it,' said Thorkel. 'The wealth must be divided, and since I demand this division, you may have the farm and the land and I will take the movable goods.'

'If there is no other way than to separate, then do whatever you wish. I do not mind whether I do the dividing or the choosing.'

So it ended with Gisli dealing with the division. Thorkel chose the goods while Gisli had the land. They also divided the dependants – two children, a boy named Geirmund and a girl named Gudrid. The girl went with Gisli and the boy with Thorkel.

Thorkel went to his brother-in-law and lived with him, while Gisli was left with the farm which he felt was none the worse for the loss.

Summer drew to a close and the Winter Nights began. In those days it was the custom to celebrate the coming of winter by holding feasts and a Winter Nights' sacrifice. Gisli no longer sacrificed after he left Viborg, but he still held feasts and showed the same magnanimity as before. Then, as the aforementioned time approached, he made everything ready for a magnificent feast and invited both Thorkels – that is, Thorkel Eiriksson and Thorkel the Wealthy – as well as the sons of Bjartmar, who were Aud's uncles, and many other friends and acquaintances.

On the day the guests arrived, Aud said, 'If the truth be told, there is one person missing who I wish was here.'

'Who is that?' asked Gisli.

'Vestein, my brother. I wish he were here to enjoy this feast with us.'

'That's not how I feel,' said Gisli. 'I would gladly pay a great deal for him not to come here now.'

And that ended their conversation.

II   There was a man named Thorgrim, who was known as Thorgrim Nef (Nose). He lived at Nefsstadir on the east side of the Haukadalsa river and was versed in all manner of spells and magic – the worst kind of sorcerer imaginable. Thorgrim and Thorkel invited him home because they were also holding a feast. Thorgrim Nef was a very skilled blacksmith, and it is told that both Thorgrim and Thorkel went to the smithy and locked themselves in. Then they took the fragments of Grasida,* of which Thorkel had taken possession when he split up with his brother Gisli, and Thorgrim Nef made a spearhead out of them. By evening the spearhead was completely finished. The blade was damascened, and the shaft measured about a hand in length.

This matter must rest here for a while.

The story goes on to say that Onund from Medaldal came to Gisli's feast and took him aside to tell him that Vestein had returned to Iceland and 'is to be expected here'.

Gisli reacted quickly and summoned two of his farmhands, Hallvard and Havard, whom he told to go north to Onundarfjord to meet Vestein.

'Give him my greetings,' said Gisli, 'and tell him to stay where he is and wait until I come to visit him. He must not come to the feast at Haukadal.'

* See Chapter I.

He then handed them a small kerchief which contained the half-coin token, in case Vestein did not believe their story.

They left and took the boat from Haukadal. Then they rowed to Laekjaros and went ashore to see Bersi, a farmer who lived at Bersastadir. They informed him that Gisli had requested that he lend them two of his horses, which were known as Bandvettir (Tied-together) – the fastest horses in the fjords. He lent them the horses and they rode until they reached Mosvellir, and from there towards Hest.

Now Vestein rode out from home, and it turned out that as he rode below the sandbank at Mosvellir, the two brothers, Hallvard and Havard, rode above it. Thus he and they missed each other in passing.

12 There was a man named Thorvard who lived at Holt. His farmhands had been arguing about some task and had struck each other with scythes, so that both were wounded. Vestein came by and had them settle their differences so that they were both satisfied. Then he rode on to Dyrafjord with his two Norwegian companions.

Hallvard and Havard reached Hest and learned where Vestein was actually heading. They rode after him as fast as they could and when they reached Mosvellir, they could see men riding down in the valley but there was a hill between them. They rode into Bjarnadal and when they reached Arnkelsbrekka both their horses gave out. They took to their feet and began to shout. Vestein and his companions had reached the Gemlufall heath before they heard the men shouting, but they waited there for Hallvard and Havard who conveyed Gisli's message and presented him with the coin which Gisli had sent him.

Vestein took a coin from the purse which hung from his belt and turned very red in the face.

'What you say is true,' he said. 'I would have turned back if you had met me sooner, but now all waters flow towards Dyrafjord and that is where I will ride. Indeed, I am eager to do so. The Norwegians will turn back, but you two will go by boat,' said Vestein, 'and tell Gisli and my sister that I am on my way to them.'

They went home and told Gisli what had happened, and he answered: 'Then this is the way it has to be.'

Vestein went to see his kinswoman, Luta, at Gemlufall and she had him ferried across the fjord.

'Vestein,' she said to him, 'be on your guard. You will have need to be.'

He was ferried across to Thingeyri. A man called Thorvald Gneisti

(Spark) lived there. Vestein went to his house and Thorvald lent him his horse. Then he rode out with his own saddle gear and had bells on his bridle. Thorvald accompanied him as far as Sandar estuary and offered to go with him all the way to Gisli's. Vestein told him that was not necessary.

'Much has changed in Haukadal,' said Thorvald. 'Be on your guard.'

Then they parted.

Vestein rode onward until he reached Haukadal. There was not a cloud in the sky and the moon shone. At Thorgrim and Thorkel's farm, Geirmund and a woman named Rannveig were bringing in the cattle. Rannveig put them in stalls after Geirmund drove them inside to her. At that moment, Vestein rode by and met Geirmund.

Geirmund spoke, 'Don't stop here at Saebol. Go on to Gisli's. And be on your guard.'

Rannveig came out of the byre, looked at the man closely and thought she recognized him. And when all the cattle were inside, she and Geirmund began to argue about who the man was as they made their way to the farmhouse. Thorgrim was sitting by the fire with the others, and he asked what they were quarrelling about and whether they had seen or met anyone.

'I thought I saw Vestein stop by,' said Rannveig. 'He was wearing a black cloak, held a spear in his hand and had bells on his bridle.'

'And what do you say, Geirmund?' asked Thorgrim.

'I couldn't see very well, but I think he was one of Onund's farmhands from Medaldal, wearing Gisli's cloak. He had Onund's saddle gear and carried a fishing spear with something dangling from it.'

'Now one of you is lying,' said Thorgrim. 'Rannveig, you go over to Hol and find out what's going on.'

Rannveig went there, and arrived at the door just as the men had started drinking. Gisli was standing in the doorway. He greeted her and invited her inside. She told him that she had to get back home, but 'I would like to meet the young girl, Gudrid.'

Gisli called to the girl, but there was no response.

'Where is your wife, Aud?' asked Rannveig.

'She is here,' said Gisli.

Aud came out and asked what Rannveig wanted. Rannveig said that it was only a trivial matter, but got no further. Gisli told her either to come inside or go home. She left and looked even more foolish than before – if that were possible – and she had no news to tell.

The following morning Vestein had the two bags of goods brought to him which the brothers, Hallvard and Havard, had brought back with them.

He took out a tapestry sixty ells long and a head-dress made from a piece of cloth some twenty ells long with three gold strands woven along its length, and three finger bowls worked with gold. He brought these out as gifts for his sister, for Gisli and for his sworn brother, Thorkel – should he want to accept them. Gisli went with Thorkel the Wealthy and Thorkel Eiriksson to Saebol to tell his brother that Vestein had come and that he had brought gifts for both of them. Gisli showed him the gifts and asked his brother to choose what he wanted.

Thorkel answered, 'It would be better if you took them all. I don't want to accept these gifts – I cannot see how they will be repaid.'

And he was determined not to accept them. Gisli went home and felt that everything was pointing in one direction.

13   Then something unusual happened at Hol. Gisli slept unsoundly for two successive nights and people asked him what he had dreamed. He did not want to tell them. On the third night, after everyone was fast asleep in bed, such a heavy gust of wind hit the house that it took off all the roofing on one side. At the same time, the heavens opened and rain fell like never before. Naturally, it poured into the house where the roof had split.

Gisli sprang to his feet and rallied his men to cover the hay. There was a slave at Gisli's house named Thord, known as the Coward. He stayed home while Gisli and almost all his men went out to attend to the haystacks. Vestein offered to go with them but Gisli did not want him to. And then, when the house began to leak badly, Vestein and Aud moved their beds lengthways down the room. Everyone else except these two had deserted the house.

Just before daybreak, someone entered the house without a sound and walked over to where Vestein was lying. He was already awake but before he knew what was happening, a spear was thrust at him and went right through his breast.

As Vestein took the blow, he spoke: 'Struck there,' he said.

Then the man left. Vestein tried to stand up, but as he did so he fell down beside the bedpost, dead. Aud awoke and called out to Thord the Coward and asked him to remove the weapon from the wound. At that time, whoever drew a weapon from a death wound was obliged to take revenge, and when a weapon was thus left in the fatal wound it was called secret manslaughter rather than murder. Thord was so frightened of corpses that he dared not come near the body.

Then Gisli came in, saw what was happening and told Thord to calm down. He took the spear from the wound himself and threw it, still covered in blood, into a trunk so that no one might see it, then sat down on the edge of the bed. Then he had Vestein's body made ready for burial according to the custom in those days. Vestein's death was a great sorrow both to Gisli and the others.

Then Gisli said to his foster-daughter, Gudrid, 'Go to Saebol and find out what they are up to there. I'm sending you because I trust you best in this as in other matters. Make sure you tell me what they are doing.'

Gudrid left and arrived at Saebol. Both the Thorgrims and Thorkel had arisen and sat fully armed. When she came in no one hurried to greet her. Indeed, most of them said nothing at all. Thorgrim, though, asked her what news she brought and she told them of Vestein's death, or murder.

Thorkel answered, 'There was a time when we would have regarded that as news indeed.'

'A man has died,' said Thorgrim, 'to whom we must all pay our respects by honouring his funeral and by making a burial mound for him. There's no denying that this is a great loss. Tell Gisli we will come there today.'

She went home and told Gisli that Thorgrim sat fully armed with helmet and sword, that Thorgrim Nef had a wood-axe in his hand and that Thorkel had a sword which was drawn a hand's breadth – 'all the men there were risen from their beds, some of them were armed'.

'That was to be expected,' said Gisli.

14 Gisli and all his men prepared to build a mound for Vestein in the sandbank that stood on the far side of Seftjorn pond below Saebol.

And while Gisli was on his way there, Thorgrim set out for the burial place with a large group of men.

When they had decked out Vestein's body according to the ways of the time, Thorgrim went to Gisli and said, 'It is a custom to tie Hel-shoes* to the men that they may wear them on their journey to Valhalla, and I will do that for Vestein.'

And when he had done this, he said, 'If these come loose then I don't know how to bind Hel-shoes.'

After this they sat down beside the mound and talked together. They

* Shoes tied to the feet of a dead man. See note on p 222.

thought it highly unlikely that anyone would know who committed the crime.

Thorkel asked Gisli, 'How is Aud taking her brother's death? Does she weep much?'

'It seems you know quite well,' said Gisli. 'She shows little and suffers greatly.' Then he said, 'I dreamed a dream the night before last and last night too, and though my dreams indicate who did the slaying, I will not say. I dreamed the first night that a viper wriggled out from a certain farm and stung Vestein to death, and, on the second night, I dreamed that a wolf ran out from the same farm and bit Vestein to death. I have not told either dream until now because I did not want them to come true.'

And he spoke a verse:

4.   Better, I believed,
      to remember Vestein
      gladdened with mead
      where we sat drinking
      in Sigurhadd's hall,
      and none came between us,
      than to wake a third time
      from so dark a dream.

Then Thorkel asked, 'How is Aud taking her brother's death? Does she weep much?'

'You keep asking this, brother,' said Gisli. 'You are very curious to know.' Gisli spoke this verse:

5.   In secret, bowed beneath
      the cover of her bonnet,
      she, gold of goddess given,   *gold of goddess given*: woman
      lacks solace of sound sleep.
      From both kindly eyes
      and down her cheeks
      flows the dew of distress   *dew of distress*: tears
      for a brother lost forever.

And again he spoke a verse:

6.   Like a stream fast flowing,
      sorrow, the death of laughter,
      through the brow's white woods,   *brow's white woods*: eyelashes
      forces tears down into her lap.
      The snake-lair's goddess,   *snake-lair*: bed of gold; its *goddess*:
      her weeping eyes swollen   woman
      with bitter fruit, looks to me,
      Odin's craftsman, for consolation.   *Odin's craftsman*: poet

After that, the two brothers went home together.

Then Thorkel said, 'These are sad tidings and you will bear them with greater grief than we, but each man has to look out for himself, and I hope you don't let this affect you so much that people begin to suspect anything. I would like to have the games begin again and things to be as good as they have ever been between us.'

'That is well spoken, and I will gladly comply,' said Gisli, 'but on one condition – if anything takes place in your life that pains you as badly as this pains me, you must promise to behave in the same manner as you now ask of me.'

Thorkel agreed to this. Then they went home and Vestein's funeral feast was held. When it was over, everyone went back to his own home and all was quiet again.

15   The games now started up as if nothing had happened. Gisli and his brother-in-law, Thorgrim, usually played against each other. There was some disagreement as to who was the stronger, but most people thought it was Gisli. They played ball games at Seftjorn pond and there was always a large crowd.

One day, when the gathering was even larger than usual, Gisli suggested that the game be evenly matched.

'That's exactly what we want,' said Thorkel. 'What's more, we don't want you to hold back against Thorgrim. Word is going around that you are not giving your all. I'd be pleased to see you honoured if you are the stronger.'

'We have not been fully proven against each other yet,' said Gisli, 'but perhaps it's leading up to that.'

They started the game and Thorgrim was outmatched. Gisli brought him down and the ball went out of play. Then Gisli went for the ball, but Thorgrim held him back and stopped him from getting it. Then Gisli tackled

Thorgrim so hard that he could do nothing to stop falling. His knuckles were grazed, blood rushed from his nose and the flesh was scraped from his knees. Thorgrim rose very slowly, looked towards Vestein's burial mound, and said:

7.   Spear screeched in his wound
     sorely – I cannot be sorry.

Running, Gisli took the ball and pitched it between Thorgrim's shoulder-blades. The blow pushed him flat on his face. Then Gisli said:

8.   Ball smashed his shoulders
     broadly – I cannot be sorry.

Thorgrim sprang to his feet and said, 'It's clear who is the strongest and the most highly accomplished. Now, let's put an end to this.'

And so they did. The games drew to a close, summer wore on, and there was a growing coldness between Thorgrim and Gisli.

Thorgrim decided to hold a feast at the end of autumn to celebrate the coming of the Winter Nights. There was to be a sacrifice to Frey, and he invited his brother, Bork, Eyjolf Thordarson and many other men of distinction. Gisli also prepared a feast and invited his relatives from Arnarfjord, as well as the two Thorkels, Thorkel the Wealthy and Thorkel Eiriksson. No fewer than sixty people were expected to arrive. There was to be drinking at both places, and the floor at Saebol was strewn with rushes from Seftjorn pond.

Thorgrim and Thorkel were getting their preparations under way and were about to hang up some tapestries in the house because the guests were expected that evening.

Thorgrim said to Thorkel, 'It would be a fine thing now to have those tapestries that Vestein wanted to give to you. It seems to me there's quite a difference between owning them outright and never having them at all. I wish you'd have them sent for.'

Thorkel answered, 'A wise man does all things in moderation. I will not have them sent for.'

'Then I will do it,' said Thorgrim, and he asked Geirmund to go.

Geirmund answered him, 'I don't mind working, but I have no desire to go over there.'

Then Thorgrim went up to him, slapped his face hard and said, 'Go now then, if that makes you feel any better about it.'

'I'll go,' said Geirmund, 'though it seems worse. But you may be certain that I will give a mare for this foal, and you will not be underpaid.'*

Then he left. When he reached Gisli's house, Gisli and Aud were about to hang up the tapestries. Geirmund told them why he was sent and all that had been said.

'Do you want to lend the tapestries, Aud?' asked Gisli.

'You know that I would have neither this nor any other good befall them, nor indeed anything that would add to their honour. That is not why you asked me.'

'Was this my brother Thorkel's wish?' asked Gisli.

'He approved of my coming for them.'

'That is reason enough,' said Gisli, and he went with Geirmund part of the way and then handed over the tapestries.

Gisli walked as far as the hayfield wall with him and said, 'Now this is how things stand – I believe that I have made your journey worthwhile, and I want your help in a matter that concerns me. A gift always looks to be repaid. I want you to unbolt three of the doors tonight. Remember how you came to be sent on this errand.'

Geirmund answered, 'Will your brother Thorkel be in any danger?'

'None at all,' said Gisli.

'Then it will be done,' said Geirmund.

When he returned home he threw down the tapestries, and Thorkel said, 'There is no one like Gisli when it comes to forebearance. He has outdone us here.'

'This is what we needed,' said Thorgrim, and he put up the tapestries.

Later that evening the guests arrived and the sky began to thicken. In the still of the night the snow drifted down and covered all the paths.

16   That evening Bork and Eyjolf arrived with sixty men, so that there were one hundred and twenty all told at Saebol and half as many at Gisli's. Later they began to drink and after that they all went to bed and slept.

Gisli said to his wife, 'I have not fed Thorkel the Wealthy's horse. Walk

---

* The word for such a blow to the face is *buffeit* or *kinnhestur*, the latter literally meaning 'cheek-horse'. Thus Geirmund's pun suggests that he intends to pay back Thorgrim in kind for the blow.

with me and bolt the door, but stay awake while I am gone. When I come back, unbolt the door again.'

He took the spear, Grasida, from the trunk and, wearing a black cloak, a shirt and linen underbreeches, he walked down to the stream that ran between the two farms and that was the water source for both. He took the path to the stream, then waded through it until he reached the path that led to Saebol. Gisli knew the layout of the farmstead at Saebol because he had built it. There was a door that led into the house from the byre, and that is where he entered. Thirty head of cattle stood on each side. He tied the bulls' tails together and closed the byre door, then made sure that the door could not be opened from the inside. After that he went to the farmhouse. Geirmund had done his work – the doors were unbolted. Gisli walked in and closed them again, just as they had been that evening. He took his time doing this, then stood still and listened to see whether anyone was awake. He discovered that they were all asleep.

Lights were burning in three places in the house. He picked up some rushes from the floor, twisted them together, then threw them at one of the lights. It went out. He waited to see whether this had wakened anyone and found that it had not. Then he picked up another bundle of rushes and threw it at the next light, putting that out too. Then he noticed that not everyone was asleep. He saw the hand of a young man reach for the third light, take down the lamp-holder and snuff the flame.

He walked farther into the house and up to the bed closet where his sister, Thordis, and Thorgrim slept. The door was pulled to, and they were both in bed. He went to the bed, felt about inside it and touched his sister's breast. She was sleeping on the near side.

Then Thordis said, 'Why is your hand so cold, Thorgrim?' – and thereby woke him up.

Thorgrim replied, 'Do you want me to turn towards you?'

She thought it had been his hand that touched her. Gisli waited a little longer, warming his hand inside his tunic, while the couple fell asleep again. Then he touched Thorgrim lightly, waking him. Thorgrim thought that Thordis had roused him and he turned towards her. Gisli then pulled the bedclothes off them with one hand, and with the other he plunged Grasida through Thorgrim so that it stuck fast in the bed.

Then Thordis cried out, 'Everyone wake up. Thorgrim, my husband, has been killed!'

Gisli turned quickly towards the byre, leaving the way he had planned,

and then locked up securely after himself. He headed home the same way
he had come, leaving no sign of his tracks. Aud unbolted the door as he
arrived, and Gisli went to his bed as if nothing were amiss and as though
he had done nothing.

All the men at Saebol were exceedingly drunk and no one knew what to
do. They had been caught off guard, and therefore did nothing that was
either useful or appropriate in the situation.

17 Eyjolf spoke, 'An evil and serious thing has happened here and no one
has his wits about him. I think we had better light the lamps and man
the doors quickly to prevent the killer from getting out.'

That was done, but when there was no trace of the killer, everyone
thought it must have been one of their own number who did the deed.

It was not long until dawn came. Then Thorgrim's body was taken and
the spear removed, and he was made ready for burial. Sixty men set out to
Gisli's farm at Hol. Thord the Coward stood outside and when he saw the
band of men he ran inside and said that an army was approaching the farm.
He was jabbering wildly.

'This is good,' said Gisli, and he spoke a verse:

9.   Words could not fell me,
      by the fullest of means.
      I, battle-oak, have brought   *battle-oak*: warrior
      death's end to many a man,
      making my sword's mouth speak.
      Let us go our ways silently;
      though the cove-stallion's rider   *cove-stallion's rider*: seafarer, i.e. warrior
      be fallen, trouble is astir.

Thorkel and Eyjolf came to the farmhouse and walked over to the bed closet
where Gisli and his wife lay. Thorkel, Gisli's brother, went right up to the
closet and saw that Gisli's shoes were lying there, covered in ice and snow. He
pushed them under the footboard so that no one else would see them.

Gisli greeted them and asked what news they brought. Thorkel told him
that there were ill tidings and of great magnitude, then asked Gisli what
lay behind all this and what they should do.

'Great deeds and ill deeds often fall within each other's shadow,' said
Gisli. 'We will take it upon ourselves to make a burial mound for Thorgrim.
This we owe you, and it is our duty to carry it out with honour.'

They accepted his offer and all returned to Saebol together to build a mound. They laid Thorgrim out in a boat and raised the mound in accordance with the old ways.

When the mound had been sealed, Gisli walked to the mouth of the river and lifted a stone so heavy it was more like a boulder. He dropped it into the boat with such a resounding crash that almost every plank of wood gave way.

'If the weather shifts this,' he said, 'then I don't know how to fasten a boat.'

Some people remarked that this was not unlike what Thorgrim had done with Vestein when he spoke of the Hel-shoes.

Everyone then prepared to go home from the funeral.

Gisli said to his brother, Thorkel, 'I believe you owe it to me that we be as friendly as we have ever been in the past – and now let's begin the games.'

Thorkel agreed to this readily, and they both returned home. Gisli had a good many men at his house, and when the feast was over, he bestowed good gifts on all his guests.

18 They drank at Thorgrim's wake and Bork gave good gifts of friendship to many of the company.

The next matter of account was that Bork paid Thorgrim Nef to perform a magic rite, and to this effect – that however willing people might be to help the man who slew Thorgrim, their assistance should be of no avail. A nine-year-old gelding ox was given to Thorgrim for the magic rite, which he then performed. He prepared what he needed to carry it out, building a scaffold on which he practised his obscene and black art in devilish perversity.

Another thing happened that was accounted strange – the snow never settled on the south-west of Thorgrim's burial mound, nor showed any sign of frost. People suggested that Frey had found the sacrifices Thorgrim made to him so endearing that the god had not wanted the ground between them to freeze.

Such was the situation throughout the winter while the brothers jointly held their games. Bork moved in with Thordis and married her. She was with child at the time, and soon gave birth to a boy. He was sprinkled with water and at first named Thorgrim after his father. However, when he grew up he was thought to be so bad-tempered and restless that his name was changed to Snorri* the Godi. Bork lived there for a while and took part in the games.

There was a woman named Audbjorg who lived farther up the valley at Annmarkastadir. She was Thorgrim Nef's sister and once had a husband whose name was Thorkel, but who was nicknamed Annmarki (Flaw). Her son, Thorstein, was one of the strongest at the games, aside from Gisli. Gisli and Thorstein were always on the same side in the games, pitched against Bork and Thorkel.

One day, a great crowd of people came to see the game because they wanted to find out who was the strongest and the best player. And it was the same here as anywhere else – the more people arrived to watch, the greater the eagerness to compete. It is reported that Bork made no headway against Thorstein all day, and finally he became so angry that he broke Thorstein's bat in two. In response to this, Thorstein tackled him and laid him out flat on the ice.

When Gisli saw this he told Thorstein that he must put his all into playing against Bork, and then he said, 'I'll exchange bats with you.'

This they did, then Gisli sat down and fixed the bat. He looked towards Thorgrim's burial mound; there was snow on the ground and the women sat on the slope. His sister Thordis was there and many others. Gisli then spoke a verse which should not have been spoken:

10. I saw the shoots reach
      up through the thawed ground   *Thor*: i.e. man; word-play on
      on the grim Thor's mound;   Thorgrim's name
      I slew that sword of Gaut.   *sword of Gaut* (Odin): warrior
      Thrott's helmet has slain   *Thrott's* (Odin's) *helmet*: warrior
      that tree of gold, and given   *tree of gold*: man
      one, greedy for new land,
      a plot of his own forever.

Thordis remembered the verse, went home and interpreted what it meant. The game then came to a close and Thorstein went home.

There was a man named Thorgeir, and known as Orri (Grouse), who lived at Orrastadir. There was another man, named Berg, and known as Skammfot (Short-leg), who lived at Skammfotarmyri (Short-leg's marsh) on the east side of the river.

---

* The name *Snorri* is a twin form of the name *Snerrir* which means 'unruly', 'argumentative'.

As the men made their way home from the game, Thorstein and Berg began to talk about how it was played, and eventually they began to argue. Berg supported Bork, while Thorstein spoke out against him. Berg hit Thorstein with the back of his axe, but Thorgeir came between them and prevented Thorstein from responding. Thorstein went home to his mother, Audbjorg, and she bound up his wound. She was displeased about what had befallen him.

Old Audbjorg was so uneasy that she had no sleep that night. It was cold outside, but the air was still and the sky cloudless. She walked several times withershins around the outside of the house, sniffing in all directions. As she did this, the weather broke and a heavy, blustering snowstorm started up. This was followed by a thaw in which a flood of water gushed down the hillside and sent an avalanche of snow crashing into Berg's farmhouse. It killed twelve men. The traces of the landslide can be seen to this day.

19   Thorstein went to meet Gisli, who gave him shelter. From there, he went south to Borgarfjord and then abroad. When Bork received news of the disaster at Berg's house, he went to Annmarkastadir and had Audbjorg seized. From there she was taken out to Saltnes and stoned to death.

After this, Gisli left his home and went to Nefsstadir, seized Thorgrim Nef and took him to Saltnes where a sack was placed over his head before he was stoned to death. He was covered over with mud and stones, beside his sister, on the ridge between Haukadal and Medaldal.

All was quiet now, and the spring wore on. Bork went south to Thorsnes and was going to settle down there. He felt that his journey west had brought him no honour – he had lost a man of Thorgrim's calibre and matters had not been put right. He now prepared to go, leaving plans and instructions for what he wanted done at the farm in his absence, since he intended to return to fetch his possessions and his wife. Thorkel Sursson also decided to settle at Thorsnes, and made preparations to accompany Bork, his brother-in-law.

The story has it that Thordis Sursdottir, who was Gisli's sister and Bork's wife, went part of the way with Bork.

Bork spoke: 'Now, tell me why you were so upset when we broke up the games in the autumn. You promised to tell me before I left here.'

They had arrived at Thorgrim's burial mound while they spoke. Suddenly, Thordis stopped and said she would venture no farther. Then she recited the verse that Gisli had composed when he looked at Thorgrim's burial place.

'And I suspect,' she said, 'that you need not look elsewhere concerning Thorgrim's slaying. He will rightly be brought to justice.'

Bork became enraged at this, and said, 'I want to turn back right now and kill Gisli. On the other hand, I can't be sure,' he said, 'how much truth there is in what Thordis says. It's just as likely that there's none. Women's counsel is often cold.'

Thorkel persuaded them to ride on until they reached Sandar estuary, where they stopped and rested their horses. Bork spoke very little. Thorkel said he wanted to meet his friend, Onund, and rode off so fast that he was soon out of sight.

Then, he changed direction and rode to Hol, where he told Gisli what had happened, how Thordis had discovered the truth and solved the meaning of the verse: 'You'll have to regard the matter as out in the open now.'

Gisli fell silent. Then he spoke a verse:

11. My sister, too taken
     with her fine clothes,
     lacks the firm-rooted spirit   *Gudrun, Gjuki's daughter*: tragic heroine
     of Gudrun, Gjuki's daughter,   of *The Saga of the Volsungs*
     that sea-fire's goddess,   *sea-fire*: gold; its *goddess*: woman
     adorned with pearls, who killed
     her husband with undaunted courage
     to avenge her brave brothers.

'I don't think I deserved this from her,' said Gisli. 'I thought I made it clear several times that her honour meant no less to me than my own. There were even times when I put my life in danger for her sake, and she has pronounced my death sentence. But what I need to know now, brother, is what I can expect from you, considering what I have done.'

'I can give you warning if there is an attempt on your life,' said Thorkel, 'but I can afford you no help that might lead to my being accused. I feel I have been greatly wronged by the slaying of Thorgrim, my brother-in-law, my partner and my close friend.'

Gisli answered him, 'It was unthinkable that a man such as Vestein should not be avenged. I would not have answered you as you now answer me, nor would I do what you propose to do.'

Then they parted. Thorkel went to meet Bork and from there they went south to Thorsnes, where Bork put his house in order. Thorkel bought some land at Hvamm on Bardastrond.

Then the Summons Days came round, and Bork travelled west with forty men to summon Gisli to the Thorsnes Assembly. Thorkel Sursson was in his party, as were Thorodd and Outlaw-Stein, Bork's nephews. There was also a Norwegian with them, named Thorgrim. They rode out to the Sandar estuary.

Then Thorkel said, 'I have a debt to collect at a small farm down here, a little farther on', and he named the farm. 'So I'll ride out there and pick up what's due to me. Follow me at your own pace.'

Thorkel then rode on ahead and when he reached the farmstead he had mentioned, he asked the farmer's wife if he might take one of the horses there and let his own stand by the front door.

'And throw some homespun cloth over the saddle of my horse,' he said, 'and when my companions arrive, tell them I'm sitting in the main room counting the silver.'

She lent him a horse and he rode with great haste to the woods at Haukadal, where he met Gisli and told him what was happening – that Bork had come from the west.

20 Now, to return to Bork. He prepared a case against Gisli for the slaying of Thorgrim to be presented at the Thorsnes Assembly. At the same time, Gisli had sold his land to Thorkel Eiriksson and received payment in cash, which was especially convenient for him.

He asked his brother Thorkel for advice. In other words, he wanted to know what Thorkel was prepared to do for him and whether he would assist him. Thorkel's answer was the same as before – he would keep Gisli informed of any planned assault, but stay clear himself of any possible accusations.

Then Thorkel rode off and took a route that brought him up behind Bork and the others, thereby slowing down their pace a little.

Gisli took two cart-horses and headed for the woods with his valuables. His slave, Thord the Coward, went with him.

Gisli said, 'You have often shown obedience to me and done what I wanted, and I owe you some reward.'

As usual, Gisli was wearing his black cloak and was well dressed.

He removed his cape and said, 'I want to give you this cloak, my friend, and I want you to enjoy its use right away. Put it on and sit behind on the sled, and I'll lead the horses and wear your cloak.'

And that is what they did. Then Gisli said, 'Should some men call out to you, make sure you do not answer. If they intend to do you harm, make for the woods.'

Thord had as much wits as he had courage, for he had none of either. Gisli led the oxen and Thord, who was a big man, sat high up on the sled thinking he was very finely dressed and showing off. Now Bork and his men saw them as they made their way towards the woods, and they quickly pursued them. When Thord saw what was happening, he jumped down off the sled and made for the woods as fast as he could. They thought he was Gisli and chased him, calling out to him loudly as they ran. Thord made no reply. Instead, he ran as fast as his feet could carry him. The Norwegian, Thorgrim, threw his spear at Thord, catching him so hard between the shoulder blades that he fell face forward to the ground. That was his death blow.

Then Bork said, 'That was a perfect throw.'

The brothers, Outlaw-Stein and Thorodd, agreed that they would pursue the slave and see whether he had any fight in him, and they turned off into the woods.

To return to Bork and the others – they came up to the man in the black cloak and pulled back his hood to discover that they had been rather less lucky than they imagined. They had killed Thord the Coward when they had meant to kill Gisli.

The story has it that the brothers, Outlaw-Stein and Thorodd, reached the woods and that Gisli was already there. He saw them and they saw him. Then one of them threw a spear at Gisli, which he caught in mid-flight and threw back at Thorodd. It struck the middle of his body and flew right through him. Outlaw-Stein returned to his companions and told them it was difficult to move around in the woods, but Bork wanted to go there anyway, so that is where they went. When they came to the woods, Thorgrim the Norwegian saw a branch move in one place and threw his spear directly at it, hitting Gisli in the calf of his leg. Gisli threw the spear back and it pierced right through Thorgrim and killed him.

The rest of them searched the woods, but they could not find Gisli so they returned to Gisli's farm and initiated a case against him for killing Thorgrim. They rode home, having taken no valuables from the house.

Gisli went up the mountainside behind the farm and bound up his wound while Bork and the others were down at his farmstead. When they left, Gisli returned home. Gisli now prepared to leave. He got a boat and loaded it up with his valuables. His wife, Aud, and his foster-daughter, Gudrid, accompanied him to Husanes, where they all went ashore. Gisli went to the farm at Husanes and met a man there who asked him who he was. Gisli told the man as much as he thought he ought to know, but not the truth. Then he picked up a stone and threw it out to a small islet that lay offshore and asked the farmer to have his son do the same thing when he came home – then they would know who he was. But there was no man who could manage it, and thus it was proven once again that Gisli was more accomplished than most other men. After this, Gisli returned to the boat and rowed out around the headland and across to Arnarfjord, and from there across a smaller fjord that lies within it, known as Geirthjofsfjord. Here he prepared to settle down, and built himself a homestead where he stayed for the whole winter.

21 The next thing that happened was that Gisli sent word to Vestein's uncles, Helgi, Sigurd and Vestgeir, the sons of Bjartmar, asking them to go to the assembly and offer a settlement for him so that he would not be outlawed.

They went to the assembly, but they made no headway with a settlement. Indeed, it was said that they handled matters so badly that they were close to tears before it was over. They related the outcome to Thorkel the Wealthy, saying that they dared not face Gisli to tell him he had been outlawed. Aside from Gisli's sentence nothing else of note took place at the assembly. Thorkel the Wealthy went to meet Gisli to tell him that he had been outlawed.

Then Gisli spoke these verses:

12. The trial at Thorsnes
would not thus
have gone against me
if Vestein's heart
had beat
in the breasts
of the sons
of Bjartmar.

13.   My wife's uncles
       were downcast
       when they ought
       to have been glad.
       Gold-spenders!   *gold-spenders*: generous men
       They behaved
       as if they had been
       pelted with rotten eggs.

14.   News comes from the north:
       the assembly is over,
       harsh sentence passed
       on me – no honour there.
       Giver of pure gold,   *giver of pure gold*: generous man
       this blue-armoured warrior
       shall cruelly repay
       both Bork and Stein.

Then Gisli asked the two Thorkels what he might expect of them, and they both replied that they would give him shelter provided it meant no material loss on their parts. Then Thorkel the Wealthy rode home. It is said that Gisli spent three winters at Geirthjofsfjord, staying some of the time with Thorkel Eiriksson. Then he spent another three winters journeying around Iceland, meeting with various chieftains and trying to elicit their support. As a result of Thorgrim Nef's evil arts, and the magic rite and spells he had performed, Gisli had no success in persuading these chieftains to ally themselves with him; although their support sometimes seemed almost forthcoming, something always obstructed its course. Nevertheless, he spent lengthy periods with Thorkel Eiriksson. By this time he had been outlawed for six years.

At the end of this period, he dwelt partly in Geirthjofsfjord, at Aud's farm, and partly in a hut that he had built north of the river. He had another hideout by a ridge just south of the farm – and he also stayed there from time to time.

22 Now when Bork heard of this, he left home and went to meet Eyjolf the Grey, who at that time was living at Otradal in Arnarfjord. Bork asked him to go and search for the outlaw Gisli and kill him, offering him sixty pieces of silver to do all in his power to find the man. Eyjolf took the money and promised to take care of the matter.

There was a man with Eyjolf named Helgi, who was known as Helgi the Spy. He was sharp-sighted, a fast runner, and he knew all the fjords. He was sent to Geirthjofsfjord to find out whether Gisli was there and discovered that there was indeed a man there, but he did not know whether it was Gisli or someone else. He went back and told Eyjolf the situation. Eyjolf said he was sure it was Gisli, and he reacted quickly by going to Geirthjofsfjord with six men. But he did not find Gisli, so he returned home.

Gisli was a wise man who dreamed a great deal and whose dreams were prophetic. All knowledgeable men agree that Gisli survived as an outlaw longer than any other man, except Grettir Asmundarson.

It is said that one night, when Gisli was staying at Aud's farm, he slept badly and when he awoke she asked him what he had dreamed.

He answered her, 'There are two women I dream of. One is good to me. The other always tells me something that makes matters worse than ever, and she only prophesies ill for me. Just now I dreamed that I appeared to be walking towards a certain house or hall, and it seemed that I walked into the house and recognized there many of my kinsmen and friends. They sat by fires and drank. And there were seven fires, some of them almost burned out and some burning very bright. Then my good dream-woman came in and said that this signified how many years I had left to live, and she advised me to stop following the old faith for the rest of my life, and to refrain from studying any charms or ancient lore. And she told me to be kind to the deaf and the lame and the poor and the helpless, and that is where my dream ended.'

Then Gisli spoke some verses:

15. Bright land of wave's flame,   *wave's flame*: gold; its *land*: woman
     goddess of gold, I came   *goddess of gold*: woman
     to a hall where seven fires,
     to my anguish, were burning.
     On both sides, men on benches
     greeted me kindly, while I,
     wringer of verses, wished each
     and every man there good health.

16.   'Consider, noble Norseman,'
      said the banded goddess,   *banded goddess*: woman
      'how many fires burn
      brightly here in the hall –
      thus many winters are left
      unlived for him who bears
      the shield in battle's storm.
      Better things soon await you.'

17.   'Bringer of death in battle,
      from words spoken by poets,
      take and learn only what is good,'
      said Nauma's gold to me.   *Nauma's* (goddess's) *gold*: woman
      'Almost nothing is worse,
      for the burner of shields,   *burner of shields*: warrior
      the spender of sea-fire,   *sea-fire*: gold; its *spender*: generous man
      than to be versed in evil.'

18.   'Do not be the first to kill,
      nor provoke into fight
      the gods who answer in battle.   *gods* (Njord) *who answer in battle*:
      Give me your word on this.   warriors
      Help the blind and handless,
      ring-giver, shield of Balder.   *shield of Balder*: warrior
      Beware, evil resides in scorn
      shown to the lame and needy.'

23   To return to Bork, he began to put considerable pressure on Eyjolf.
      He felt that Eyjolf had not done what was expected of him and that
he had got less than he expected for his money. Bork said he knew for
certain that Gisli was in Geirthjofsfjord, and he told Eyjolf's men, who were
acting as messengers between them, that either Eyjolf must go and search
for Gisli or he would go and do it himself. Eyjolf responded quickly and
sent Helgi the Spy back to Geirthjofsfjord. This time he had enough food
with him and was away for a week, waiting for Gisli to appear. One day, he
saw a man emerge from a hiding place and recognized him as Gisli. Helgi
made off without delay and told Eyjolf what he had discovered.

      Eyjolf got ready to leave with eight men, and went off to Aud's farm in

Geirthjofsfjord. They did not find Gisli there, so they went and searched the woods, but they could not find him there either. They returned to the farm and Eyjolf offered Aud a large sum of money to disclose Gisli's whereabouts. But that was the last thing she wanted to do. Then they threatened to hurt her, but that produced no result, and they were forced to return home. The whole expedition was considered humiliating, and Eyjolf stayed at home that autumn.

Although he had eluded them this time, Gisli knew they would catch him eventually because the distance between them was so short.* So he left home and rode out to meet his brother, Thorkel, at Hvamm on Bardastrond. He knocked on the door of the chamber where his brother lay and Thorkel came out to greet him.

'I need to know,' said Gisli, 'whether you will help me. I expect it of you. I'm in a tight spot and I have long refrained from asking your assistance.'

Thorkel answered as before, and said that he would offer him no help that might lead to a case being brought against him. He was willing, however, to give him silver and some horses if Gisli needed them, or anything else he had mentioned earlier.

'I can see now,' said Gisli, 'that you don't want to give me any real help. Then let me have three hundreds of homespun cloth, and be comforted with the thought that from this time on I will ask very little of you.'

Thorkel did as he was asked. He gave Gisli the cloth and, in addition, some silver. Gisli said he would accept these but that he would not have acted so ignobly if he had been in his brother's position. Gisli was much affected when they parted. He headed out for Vadil, to Gest Oddleifsson's mother, Thorgerd. He arrived there before dawn and knocked on the door. Thorgerd came to answer. She often used to take in outlaws, and had an underground passage. One end of this passage was by the river, and the other led into the fire-room of her farmhouse. Traces of this can still be seen.

Thorgerd welcomed Gisli warmly: 'I suggest you stay here for a while,' she said, 'but I don't know that I can give you much more than a woman's help.'

Gisli accepted her offer, and added that, considering the kind of help he had had from men, he did not expect to be done any worse by women. He stayed there for the winter and was nowhere treated as well during his days as an outlaw.

---

* The 'short' distance is that between Gisli's hideout (Geirthjofsfjord) and Otradal where Eyjolf lived.

24 When spring came round again, Gisli went to Geirthjofsfjord because he could no longer be away from his wife, Aud – for they loved each other greatly. He stayed there in hiding until autumn and, as the nights lengthened, he dreamed the same dreams over and over again. The bad dream-woman appeared to him and his dreams grew ever more troubled. One time, when Aud asked him what he had dreamed, he told her. Then he spoke a verse:

19.   If old age awaits this battle-spear   *battle-spear*: warrior
      then my dreams lead me astray.
      Sjofn's seamstress, mead-goddess,   *Sjofn's seamstress*: woman; *mead-goddess*:
      comes to me in my sleep,   woman
      and gives this maker of verses
      no cause to believe otherwise.
      Wearer of brooches,   *wearer of brooches*: lady
      this keeps me not from sleep.

Then Gisli told her that the evil dream-woman also came to him often, and always wanted to smear him with gore, bathe him in sacrificial blood and act in a foul manner.

20.   Not all my dreams bode well,
      yet each of them must I tell.
      That woman in my dreams
      takes all my joy, it seems.
      As I fall asleep, she appears,
      and comes to me besmeared
      hideously in human blood,
      and washes me in gory flood.

And again he spoke:

21.   Once more have I told my dream
      to the makers of arrow-floods.   *arrow-floods*: battle
      And words did not fail me.
      Eir's gold, battle-thirsty men   *Eir's* (goddess's) *gold*: woman
      had me made an outlaw.
      They will surely feel
      my weapons bite their armour
      if rage comes upon me now.

Things were quiet for a while. Gisli went back to Thorgerd and stayed with her for another winter, returning to Geirthjofsfjord the following summer where he stayed until autumn. Then he went once again to his brother, Thorkel, and knocked on his door. Thorkel did not want to come out, so Gisli took a piece of wood, scored runes on it and threw it into the house. Thorkel saw the piece of wood, picked it up, looked at it and then stood up and went outside. He greeted Gisli and asked him what news he brought.

Gisli said he had none to tell: 'I've come to meet you, brother, for the last time. Assist me worthily now and I will repay you by never asking anything of you again.'

Thorkel gave him the same answer as before. He offered Gisli horses or a boat, but refused any further help. Gisli accepted the offer of a boat and asked Thorkel to help him get it afloat – which he did. Then he gave Gisli six weights of food and one hundred of homespun cloth. After Gisli had gone aboard, Thorkel stood there on the shore.

Then Gisli said, 'You think you're safe and sound and living in plenty, a friend of many chieftains, who has no need to be on his guard – and I am an outlaw and have many enemies. But I can tell you this, that even so you will be killed before me. We take our leave of each other now on worse terms than we ought and will never see each other again. But know this. I would never have treated you as you have treated me.'

'Your prophecies don't frighten me,' said Thorkel, and after that they parted.

Gisli went out to the island of Hergilsey in Breidafjord. There he removed from his boat the decking, thwarts, oars and all else that was not fastened down, turned the boat over and let it drift ashore in the Nesjar. When people saw the boat, wrecked and washed ashore, they assumed that Gisli had taken it from his brother Thorkel, then capsized and drowned.

Gisli walked to the farmhouse on the island of Hergilsey, where a man named Ingjald lived with his wife, Thorgerd. Ingjald was Gisli's cousin, the son of his mother's sister, and had come to Iceland with Gisli. When they met, he put himself at Gisli's complete disposal, offering to do for him whatever was in his power. Gisli accepted his offer and stayed there for a while.

25   There were both a male slave and a female slave at Ingjald's house. The man was named Svart and the woman Bothild. Ingjald had a son named Helgi, as great and simple-minded an oaf as ever there was. He was tethered by the neck to a heavy stone with a hole in it and left outside to graze like an animal. He was known as Ingjald's Fool and was a very large man, almost a troll.

Gisli stayed there for that winter and built a boat and many other things for Ingjald, and everything he made was easily recognizable because he was a superior craftsman. People showed surprise at the number of well-crafted items that Ingjald owned since it was known that he was no carpenter.

Gisli always spent the summers in Geirthjofsfjord, and by now three years had passed since he had his dreams. Ingjald had proven himself a faithful friend, but suspicions arose and people began to believe that Gisli was alive and living with Ingjald, and that he had not drowned as they had once thought. People started to remark on the fact that Ingjald had three boats and all were skilfully crafted. This gossip reached Eyjolf the Grey, and he sent Helgi out again, this time to the island of Hergilsey. Gisli always stayed in an underground passage when people came to the island. Ingjald was a good host and he invited Helgi to rest there, so he remained for the night.

Ingjald was a hard-working man and rowed out to fish whenever the weather permitted. The following morning, when he was ready to go to sea, he asked Helgi whether he was not eager to be on his way and why he was still in bed. Helgi said that he was not feeling very well, let out a long sigh and rubbed his head. Ingjald told him to lie still, and then went off to sea. Helgi began to groan heavily.

It is said that Thorgerd then went to the underground hiding place, intending to give Gisli some breakfast. There was a partition between the pantry and where Helgi lay in bed. Thorgerd left the pantry and Helgi climbed up the partition and saw that someone's food had been served up. At that very moment, Thorgerd returned and Helgi turned round quickly and fell off the partition. Thorgerd asked him what he was doing climbing up the rafters instead of lying still. He said he was so racked with pains in his joints that he could not lie still.

'Could you help me back to bed?' he said.

She did as he asked and went out with the food. Then Helgi got up and followed her and saw what was going on. After that he went back to bed, lay down and stayed there for the rest of the day.

Ingjald returned that evening, went to Helgi's bed and asked him if he felt any better. Helgi said he was improving and asked if he might be ferried from the island the following morning. He was rowed out to the island of Flatey, and from there he went south to Thorsnes, reporting that he had news that Gisli was staying at Ingjald's house. Bork set out with a party of fourteen men, boarded a ship and sailed south across Breidafjord. That day, Ingjald went fishing and took Gisli with him. The male and female slaves, Svart and Bothild, were in a separate boat, close to the islands known as Skutileyjar.

26 Ingjald saw a ship sailing from the south, and said, 'There's a ship out there and I think it's Bork the Stout.'

'What do you suggest we do now?' asked Gisli. 'Let's see whether your wits match your integrity.'

'I'm not a clever man,' said Ingjald, 'but we have to decide something quickly. Let's row as fast as we can to Hergilsey, get up on top of Vadsteinaberg and fight them off as long as we can keep standing.'

'Just as I anticipated,' said Gisli. 'You hit on the very plan that best shows your integrity. But I would be paying you poorly indeed for all the help you have given me if you lose your life for my sake – and that will never happen. We'll use a different plan. You and your slave, Svart, row out to the island and make ready to defend yourselves there. They will think that it is I who am with you when they sail up past the ness. I'll exchange clothes with the slave, as I did once before, then I'll get into the boat with Bothild.'

Ingjald did as he was advised, but he was clearly very angry.

When they parted company, Bothild said, 'What can be done now?'

Gisli spoke a verse:

22.	The shield-holder seeks	*shield-holder*: warrior
	a plan to part with Ingjald.	
	Let us pour Sudri's mead,	*Sudri's* (dwarf's) *mead*: poetry
	slave-woman, though I	
	accept my fate, whatever it be.	
	Noble woman of low means,	
	lit by the blue wave's lands:	*lit by the blue wave's lands*: adorned with
	I fear nothing for myself.	sea-fire (gold)

Then they rowed south towards Bork and his men, and behaved as if nothing were amiss.

Gisli told them how they should act. 'You will say,' he told her, 'that this is the fool on board, and I'll sit in the prow and mimic him. I'll wrap myself up in the tackle and hang overboard a few times and act as stupidly as I can. If they go past us a little, I'll scull as hard as I can and try to put some more distance between us.'

Bothild rowed towards them, but not close, and pretended to be moving from one fishing ground to another. Bork called out to her and asked her if Gisli was on the island.

'I don't know,' she answered. 'But I do know there's a man out there who surpasses all others in size and skill.'

'I see,' said Bork. 'Is Ingjald the farmer at home?'

'He rowed back to the island quite some time ago,' she said, 'and his slave was with him, as far as I know.'

'That is not what's happened,' said Bork. 'It must be Gisli who is with him. Let's row after them as fast as we can.'

The men answered, 'We're having fun with the idiot', and looked towards him. 'Look at how madly he's behaving.'

Then they said what a terrible thing it was for her to have to look after this fool.

'I agree,' said Bothild, 'but I think it's just idle amusement for you. You don't feel sorry for me at all.'

'Let's indulge no further in this nonsense,' said Bork. 'We must be on our way.'

They left, and Bork and his crew rowed out to Hergilsey and went ashore. Then they saw the men up on Vadsteinaberg and headed that way, thinking they were really in luck. But it was Ingjald and his slave up on the crag.

Bork soon recognized the men and said to Ingjald, 'The best thing you can do is hand over Gisli – or else tell me where he is. You're an unspeakable wretch, hiding my brother's murderer like this when you're my tenant. Don't expect any mercy from me. You deserve to die for this.'

Ingjald replied, 'My clothes are so poor that it would be no great grief if I stopped wearing them out. I'd rather die than not do all I can to keep Gisli from harm.'

It is said that Ingjald served Gisli best, and that his help was the most useful to him. When Thorgrim Nef performed his magic rite, he ordained that no assistance Gisli might receive from men on the mainland would come to anything. However, it never occurred to him to say anything about the islands, and thus Ingjald helped him for longer than most. But this could not last indefinitely.

GISLI SURSSON'S SAGA 539

27 Bork thought it was unwise to attack his tenant, Ingjald, so he and his
men turned instead towards the farmhouse to search for Gisli. As was
to be expected, they did not find him there, so they went about the island
and came to a place where the fool lay eating in a small, grassy hollow,
haltered by the neck to a stone.

Bork spoke: 'Not only is there a great deal of talk about this fool, but he
seems to move around a lot more than I thought. There's nothing here. We
have gone about this task so badly that it doesn't bear thinking about, and
I have no idea when we'll be able to make matters right. That was Gisli in
the boat alongside us, impersonating the fool. He's got a whole bag of tricks,
as well as being a skilled mimic. But think how much it would shame us to
let him slip through our fingers. Let's get after him quickly and make sure
he doesn't escape our clutches.'

They jumped aboard their ship and rowed after Gisli and Bothild, pulling
long strokes with their oars. They saw that the two of them had gone quite
some distance into the sound, and now both vessels rowed at full pace. The
one with the larger crew sped along faster, and finally it came so close that
Bork was within spear-throwing range as Gisli pulled ashore.

Gisli said to the slave-woman, 'Here we part ways. Take these two gold
rings – one you must take to Ingjald and the other to his wife. Tell them to
give you your freedom and accept these as tokens. I also want Svart to be
freed. You have truly saved my life and I want you to reap your reward.'

They parted and Gisli jumped ashore and ran to a ravine in Hjardarnes.
The slave-woman rowed off so hard that the sweat rose from her like steam.

Bork and his men rowed ashore and Outlaw-Stein was the first off the
boat. He ran off to look for Gisli and when he reached the ravine, Gisli
was standing there with his sword drawn. He drove it at once through
Outlaw-Stein's head, split him down to the shoulders, and he fell to the
ground, dead. Bork and the others then came on to the island and Gisli ran
down to the water, intending to swim for the mainland. Bork threw a spear
at him and it struck him in the calf of his leg, wounding him badly. Gisli
removed the spear, but lost his sword, too weary to keep hold of it any
longer. By then, the darkness of night had fallen.

When Gisli reached land he ran into the woods – at that time much of
the country was covered with trees – and Bork and the others ran ashore
to look for him, hoping to restrict him to the woodland. Gisli was so worn
out and stiff that he could hardly walk, and he was also aware that he was
surrounded on all sides by Bork's party of men.

Trying to think of a plan, he went down to the sea, and in the darkness he made his way along the shoreline under the shelter of the over-hanging cliffs until he came to Haug. There he met a farmer named Ref,* a very sly man. Ref greeted him and asked him what was going on. Gisli told him all that had taken place between him and Bork and his men. Ref had a wife named Alfdis, a good-looking woman, but fierce tempered and thoroughly shrewish. She and Ref were more than a match for each other. When Gisli had given his account, he urged Ref to give him all the help he could.

'They will be here soon,' said Gisli. 'I'm in a very tight spot and there aren't too many people around to whom I can turn.'

'I will help you, but on one condition,' said Ref, 'that I alone decide how I go about matters, and you must not interfere.'

'I accept,' said Gisli. 'I will not venture any farther on my way.'

'Come inside then,' said Ref. And so they went in.

Then Ref said to Alfdis, 'Now, I'm going to give you a new bed-fellow.'

And he took off all the bed covering and told Gisli to lie down on the straw. Then he put the covers back over him and now Alfdis lay on top of him.

'And now you stay put,' said Ref, 'whatever happens.'

Then he asked Alfdis to be as difficult to deal with as possible and to act as madly as she could.

'And don't hold yourself back,' said Ref. 'Say whatever comes into your mind. Swear and curse as much as you like. I'll go off to talk with them and say whatever occurs to me.'

When he went out again he saw some men coming – eight of Bork's companions. Bork himself had stayed behind at the Fossa river. These men had come to search for Gisli and to capture him if they found him. Ref was outside and asked them what they were doing.

'We can only tell you what you must already know. Have you any idea where Gisli has gone? Has he come by here by any chance?'

'First,' said Ref, 'he has not been here. If he had chanced it he would have met with a very swift end. And second, do you really think I am any less eager to kill him than you? I have sense enough to know that it would

---

* 'Ref' literally means 'fox', which might suggest links with Reynard in European beast fables and a possible allegorical interpretation of this episode. See *The Saga of Ref the Sly*.

mean no small gain to be trusted by a man such as Bork and be counted his friend.'

They asked, 'Do you mind if we search you and the farm?'

'Of course not,' said Ref, 'please do. Once you're certain he's not here, you'll be able to concentrate on searching elsewhere. Come in and search the place thoroughly.'

They went in, and when Alfdis heard the noise they were making she asked what gang of thugs was out there and what kind of idiots barged in on people in the middle of the night. Ref told her to calm down, and she responded with a flurry of foul language that they were unlikely to forget. They continued to search the place even so, but not as carefully as they might have done if they had not had to suffer such a torrent of abuse from the farmer's wife. Having found nothing, they left and wished the farmer well. He, in return, wished them a good journey. Then they went back to meet Bork and were highly displeased with the whole trip. They felt they had lost a good man, been put to shame and achieved nothing.

News of this spread all over the country and people considered that the men had derived nothing from their futile search for Gisli. Bork went home and told Eyjolf how matters stood. Gisli stayed with Ref for two weeks and then left. They parted good friends and Gisli gave him a knife and a belt – both valuable possessions. Gisli had nothing else with him.

After that Gisli returned to his wife in Geirthjofsfjord. His reputation had increased considerably as a result of what had happened, and it is truly said that there has never been a more accomplished and courageous man than Gisli, and yet fortune did not follow him.

But now to other matters.

28 To return to Bork. That spring, he went with a large group of men to the Thorskafjord Assembly, intending to meet with his friends. Gest travelled east from Bardastrond, as did Thorkel Sursson. They arrived in separate ships.

When Gest was ready to embark, two poorly dressed young men with staffs approached him, and it was noticed that Gest spoke to them in secret. They asked if they might go with him on his ship and he granted them that favour. They journeyed with him to Hallsteinsnes, then went ashore and walked on until they came to the Thorskafjord Assembly.

There was a man named Hallbjorn, a wanderer who travelled around the country, though always with a group of ten or twelve others. He raised a booth for himself at the assembly, and this is where the two young men went. They asked him for a place in the booth, saying that they, too, were wanderers, and he said he would give shelter to anyone who asked for it.

'I've come here many a springtime,' he said, 'and I know all the chieftains and godis.'

The lads said they would be pleased to be in his care and learn from him: 'We're very curious to see all the grand and mighty men we have heard so many stories about.'

Hallbjorn said he would go down to the shore and identify every ship as soon as it came in, and tell them which it was. They thanked him for his kindness, and then they all went down to the shore to watch the ships as they sailed in.

Then the elder lad spoke: 'Who owns the ship that is sailing in now?'

Hallbjorn told him it belonged to Bork the Stout.

'And who is that, sailing in next?'

'Gest the Wise,' he said.

'And that ship, coming in behind him, and putting up at the horn of the fjord?'

'That is Thorkel Sursson,' said Hallbjorn.

They watched as Thorkel came ashore and sat down somewhere while the crew carried their goods and provisions on to to dry ground, out of reach of the tides, and Bork set up their booth. Thorkel was wearing a Russian hat and a grey fur cloak that was pinned at the shoulder with a gold clasp. He carried a sword in his hand. Then Hallbjorn went over to where Thorkel was sitting, and the young men went with him.

One of the lads spoke – it was the elder. He said, 'Who is this noble-looking man sitting here? Never have I seen such a fine and handsome man.'

The man answered, 'Well spoken. My name is Thorkel.'

Then the lad said, 'That must be a very good sword you have there in your hand. Would you allow me to look at it?'

Thorkel answered him, 'Your behaviour is rather unusual, but all right, I'll allow you to,' and he handed him the sword.

The young man took it, turned to one side, unfastened the peace straps and drew the sword.

When Thorkel saw that he said, 'I did not give you permission to draw the sword.'

'I did not ask your permission,' said the lad.

Then he raised the sword in the air and struck Thorkel on the neck with such a fearsome blow that it took off his head.

When this had happened, Hallbjorn leapt up and the lad threw down the blood-stained sword. He grabbed his staff and he ran off with Hallbjorn and the others in his band, who were almost out of their wits with fear, and they all ran past the booth that Bork had set up. People thronged around Thorkel, but no one seemed to know who had done this deed. Bork asked why there was so much noise and commotion around Thorkel just as Hallbjorn and about fifteen of his band ran past the booth. The younger lad was named Helgi, while his older companion, who had done the killing, was named Berg.

It was Helgi who answered: 'I'm not sure what they are discussing, but I think they're arguing about whether Vestein left only daughters behind him, or whether he had a son.'

Hallbjorn ran to his booth, and the lads hurried to some nearby woods and could not be found.

29 People ran into Hallbjorn's booth and asked what had happened. The road-farers told them that two young men, about whom they knew nothing, had come into their group and that they had no idea this would happen. Then they gave descriptions of them and repeated what the young men had said. From what Helgi said Bork surmised that they were Vestein's sons.

Then Bork went to meet Gest and discuss with him what should be done.

Bork said, 'I bear a greater responsibility than anyone else to bring a suit in the wake of my brother-in-law Thorkel's slaying. We think it not unlikely that Vestein's sons did this deed. No one else could have had anything against Thorkel. And it looks as if they've escaped for the moment. Tell me how I should proceed with the case.'

Gest answered him, 'I know what I'd do if I had done the killing. I'd get out of it by changing my name, so that any case brought against me would come to nothing.'

And he discouraged Bork from pursuing the accusation. People were reasonably sure that Gest had conspired with the lads because he was a blood-relation of theirs.

They broke off their talk and the case was dropped. Thorkel was buried according to the old customs, and then everyone went home. Nothing else of note took place at the assembly. Bork was as displeased with this trip as he had often been with the others, and this matter brought much disgrace and dishonour to him.

The young men travelled until they reached Geirthjofsfjord, where they spent five days and five nights out in the open. By night they went to Aud's farm – where Gisli was staying – and knocked on the door. Aud went to the door to greet them and asked their business. Gisli lay in bed in the underground hideout, and she would have raised her voice if he had needed to be on his guard. They told her of Thorkel's slaying and what the situation was, and also how long they had gone without food.

'I'm going to send you,' said Aud, 'across the ridge to Mosdal, to Bjartmar's sons. I'll give you some food and some tokens so that they will give you shelter for a while, and I'm doing this because I'm in no mind to ask Gisli to help you.'

The young men went into the woods, where they could not be traced and, having gone without food for a long time, they ate. When they had satisfied their hunger, they lay down to sleep because by then they were very tired.

30　At this point, the story turns to Aud. She went to Gisli and said, 'Now, it means a great deal to me how you will act and whether you choose to honour me more than I deserve.'

He answered her quickly, 'I know you are going to tell me of my brother Thorkel's death.'

'It is so,' said Aud, 'and the lads have come and want to join you. They feel they have no one else to rely on.'

Gisli answered, 'I could not bear to see my brother's killers or to be with them', and he jumped up and went to draw his sword as he spoke this verse:

23.　Who knows, but Gisli may
　　　again draw cold sword
　　　from sheath when warriors
　　　from the assembly report
　　　the slaying of Thorkel
　　　to the polishers of rings.　　　*polishers of rings*: men
　　　We will dare great deeds,
　　　even to the very death.

Aud told him they had already left – 'for I had sense enough not to risk their tarrying here'.

Gisli said it was better that they did not meet. Then he soon calmed down and things were quiet for a while.

It is said that at this time, according to the prophecy of the dream-woman, Gisli had only two years of life remaining to him. As time passed, Gisli stayed in Geirthjofsfjord and all his dreams and restless nights began again. Now it was mainly the bad dream-woman who came to him, although the good one also appeared sometimes.

One night, Gisli dreamed again that the good dream-woman came to him. She was riding a grey horse, and she invited him to come home with her, to which he agreed. They arrived at a house, which was more like a great hall, and she led him inside. He saw cushions on the raised benches and the whole place was beautifully decorated.

She told him they would stay there and take their pleasure – 'and this is where you will come when you die,' she said, 'and enjoy wealth and great happiness'.

Then Gisli awoke and spoke several verses concerning what he had dreamed:

24.   The thread-goddess invited   *thread-goddess*: woman
      the praise-maker to ride   *praise-maker*: poet
      on a grey steed to her home.
      And as we rode along
      she was gentle to me,
      that bearer of the ale-horn   *bearer of the ale-horn*: woman
      swore she would heal me.
      I remember her words.

25.   The good dream-woman
      led me, the poet, to sleep
      there, where soft beds lay.
      From my mind this will not fade.
      The thread-goddess led me
      to her soft resting place,
      so perfectly arranged,
      and there I lay me down.

26. 'Here will you lie down
      and breathe your last with me,'
      said the Hild of the rings.   *Hild of the rings*: the dream-woman
      'And here, my warrior,
      you will rule over all this wealth
      and have dominion over me,
      and we will have riches
      beyond gold's measure.'

31 It is said that on one occasion when Helgi was sent again to spy in
    Geirthjofsfjord – where everyone believed Gisli to be staying – a man
named Havard went with him. He had come to Iceland earlier that summer
and was a kinsman of Gest Oddleifsson. They were sent into the woods to
cut timber for building, and although that was the apparent purpose of their
journey, it was really a ploy for them to look for Gisli and to see whether
they could locate his hideout. One evening they saw a fire on the ridge,
south of the river. This was at dusk, but it was very dark.

Then Havard asked Helgi what they should do – 'For you are more used
to all this than I am,' he said.

'There is only one thing to do,' said Helgi, 'and that is to build a cairn
here on this hillock, where we are now, so that it can be found tomorrow
when it grows light enough to see.'

This is what they decided to do. When they had built the cairn, Havard
said that he was so drowsy that he could do nothing else than go to sleep –
which he then did. Helgi stayed awake and finished off building the cairn, and
when he was done, Havard awoke and told him to sleep for a while, saying
that he would keep watch. Then Helgi slept for a spell, and while he was
sleeping, Havard began carrying away every single stone of the cairn under
the cover of darkness. When he had done that, he took a great boulder and
hurtled it down on the rock-face near Helgi's head so hard that the ground
shook. Helgi sprang to his feet, shaking with fear, and asked what had happened.

Havard said, 'There's a man in the woods. Many such boulders have been
cast down here tonight.'

'That must have been Gisli,' said Helgi, 'and he must know we're here.
You must surely realize, my friend, that every bone in our bodies would
have been smashed to pieces if that rock had hit us. There's nothing else to
do but get out of here as quickly as possible.'

Then Helgi ran as fast as he could, and Havard went after him and asked him not to run so far ahead. But Helgi took no notice and ran as fast as his feet would carry him. Finally, they both reached the boat, jumped into it and rowed hard without pause until they came to Otradal. Helgi said that he now knew of Gisli's whereabouts.

Eyjolf acted quickly. He left immediately with eleven men – Helgi and Havard among them – and journeyed until they came to Geirthjofsfjord. They scanned the whole wood for the cairn and Gisli's hideout, but found neither. Then Eyjolf asked Havard where they had built the cairn.

He answered, 'I couldn't tell you. Not only was I so tired that I hardly knew what was going on around me, but it was Helgi who finished building the cairn while I slept. I think Gisli must have been aware of us being there, then taken the cairn apart when it was light and we were gone.'

Then Eyjolf said, 'Fortune is not with us in this matter, so we will turn back.'

And they did just that. But first Eyjolf wanted to go and see Aud. They reached the farmhouse and went in, where Eyjolf sat down to talk to Aud, and these were his words – 'I want to make a deal with you, Aud,' he said. 'You tell me where Gisli is and I will give you three hundred pieces of silver, which I have received as the price on his head, and you will not be present when we take his life. In addition, I will arrange a marriage for you that will be superior in every way to this one. And you must consider,' he said, 'how impractical it would be for you to linger in this deserted fjord and suffer from Gisli's ill fortune, never seeing your family and kinfolk again.'

This was her reply: 'I don't expect,' she said, 'that we'll reach agreement on your ability to find me as good a match as this one. Yet, it's true what they say, "death's best consolation is wealth", so let me see whether this silver is as plentiful or as fine as you say.'

So he poured the silver into her lap, and she held it there while he counted it and showed her its value.

Gudrid, her foster-daughter, began to cry.

32 Then Gudrid went to meet Gisli and told him, 'My foster-mother has lost her senses and means to betray you.'

Gisli said, 'Think only good thoughts, for my death will never be the result of Aud's treachery.'

Then he spoke a verse:

27.   The fjord-riders claim   *fjord-riders*: seafarers, strangers
       the mead-goddess has sold   *mead-goddess*: Gisli's wife
       her man, with a mind
       deep and treacherous as the sea.
       But I know the land
       of gold sits and weeps.   *land of gold*: woman
       I do not think this true
       of the proud sea-flame's wearer.   *sea-flame*: gold; its *wearer*: woman

After that the girl went home, but did not say where she had been. By that time Eyjolf had counted all the silver.

Aud spoke: 'By no means is this silver any less or worse than you have said. And now you must agree that I may do with it whatever I choose.'

Eyjolf gladly agreed, and told her that, of course, she might do as she wished with it. Aud took the silver and put it in a large purse, then she stood up and struck Eyjolf on the nose, and blood spurted all over him.

'Take that for your gullibility,' she said, 'and all the harm that ensues from it. There was never any hope that I would render my husband into your hands, you evil man. Take this now for your cowardice and your shame, and remember, you wretch, for as long as you live, that a woman has struck you. And you will not get what you desire, either.'

Then Eyjolf said, 'Seize the cur and kill it, though it be a bitch.'

Then Havard spoke. 'Our expedition has gone badly enough without this disgraceful deed. Stand up to him, men. Don't let him do this.'

Eyjolf said, 'The old saying is true, "the treachery of a friend is worse than that of a foe".'

Havard was a popular man, and many of the party were ready to show him their support, as well as to prevent Eyjolf from carrying out this disgraceful act. So Eyjolf conceded to them and having done that he left.

But before Havard left, Aud spoke to him: 'It would be wrong to hold back the debt that Gisli owes you. Here is a gold ring I want you to have.'

'But it is not a debt I was looking to recover,' said Havard.

'Even so,' said Aud, 'I want to pay you back.'

Actually, she gave him the gold ring for his help.

Havard got himself a horse and rode south to Gest Oddleifsson at Bardastrond, for he had no desire to remain any longer with Eyjolf. Eyjolf went back home to Otradal, and was thoroughly displeased with the outcome of his journey, especially since most people regarded it as disgraceful.

33 As the summer wore on, Gisli stayed in his underground hideout and was very much on his guard. He had no intention of leaving and, besides, he felt that no other refuge was left him since the tally of years in his dreams had now passed away.

It happened that one summer night Gisli once again had a very fitful and restless sleep, and when he awoke Aud asked him what he had dreamed.

He told her that the bad dream-woman had come to him and said, 'Now I will destroy everything that the good dream-woman has said to you, and I will make certain that nothing comes of what she has promised.' Then Gisli spoke a verse:

28.   'Never shall the two of you
         abide together. Your great love
         will slowly turn to poison
         and become sorrow,'
         said the dread woman.
         'He who rules all has sent you
         alone from your house
         to explore the other world.'

'Then in a second dream,' he said, 'this woman came to me and tied a blood-stained cap on my head, and before that she bathed my head in blood and poured it all over me, covering me in gore.'

And he spoke a verse:

29.   I dreamed a dream of her,
         woman of the serpent's lair.
         She washed my hair in Odin's fire   *Odin's fire*: blood
         spilled from the well of swords.   *well of swords*: wound
         And it seemed to me
         those hands of the ring-goddess,   *ring-goddess*: woman
         blood-red, were bathed
         and drenched in gold-breaker's gore. *gold-breaker*: man

Then he spoke another verse:

30.   I thought I felt how
        the valkyrie's hands,
        dripping with sword-rain,   *sword-rain*: blood
        placed a bloody cap
        upon my thickly grown,
        straight-cut locks of hair.
        That is how the thread-goddess   *thread-goddess*: woman
        woke me from my dream.

Gisli began to have so many dreams that he became very frightened of
the dark and dared not be alone any longer. Whenever he closed his eyes,
he saw the same woman. On yet another night, Gisli slept badly and Aud
asked him what happened to him in his dream.

'I dreamed,' said Gisli, 'that some men came upon us. Eyjolf was among
them and many others. We confronted each other, and I know there was an
exchange of blows between us. One of them came first, really howling, and
I think I must have cut him in two at the waist. I thought he had the head
of a wolf. Then many others attacked me. I felt I had my shield in my hand
and that I fought them off for a long while.'

Then Gisli spoke a verse:

31.   My foes sought me out,
        swinging their swords,
        but I did not fall then.
        I was outnumbered,
        yet I fed the raven's maw.   *fed the raven's maw*: killed men
        But your white bosom
        was reddened and steeped
        in my crimson blood.

Then he spoke another:

32.   They could not mar my shield
        with their resounding blows.
        It protected the poet well.
        I had courage enough,
        but they were too many
        and I was overcome,
        swords singing loud
        in the air around me.

And then another:

33.   I brought down one of them
before warriors wounded me,
I fed his corpse to the blood-hawk.   *blood-hawk*: raven
My sword's edge swung and cut
its way through his thighs
slicing his legs in twain.
His sudden fall beneath me
added to my greater glory.

Now autumn drew near, but Gisli's dreams did not ease; indeed, they grew more frequent. One night, after he had slept badly, Aud asked him again what had appeared to him. Gisli spoke a verse:

34.   I felt my life's blood run
down both my sides.
I had to bear that bravely.
Goddess decked in gold,
these are the dreams
that trouble my sleep.
I am an outlaw to most men;
only arrow-storms await me.   *arrow-storms*: battle

And then he spoke another:

35.   I felt my blood spilled
over my arched shoulders
by a corpse-net's wielder
with his sharp sword.
Bearer of golden rings,   *bearer of golden rings*: woman, Gisli's
my hopes of life were meagre   wife
from that raven-feeder's fury;   *raven-feeder*: warrior
herb-goddess, such was my solace.   *herb-goddess*: woman

And then another:

36.   I felt the troll-guard's shakers   *troll-guard*: shield; its *shakers*: warriors
shear off both my hands
with their armour-piercers.
I was mortally wounded.

Then I felt the edge slice
my helmet-stump and split it.   *helmet-stump*: head
Thread-goddess, weapons wielded
gaped above my head.

And yet again:

37.   I felt, as I slept, that above me
      stood a woman with silver headband.
      Her brow was wet, the eyes
      of that bonnet-goddess were weeping.   *bonnet-goddess*: woman
      And that wave of gold-fire   *wave of gold-fire*: woman
      soon bound up my wounds.
      What message, think you,
      has this dream for me?

34 Gisli stayed home that summer, and all was quiet. Then, on the last
       night of summer, Gisli could not sleep and neither could the other
two, Aud and Gudrid.

It was the kind of weather where the air is very still, but there was also
a heavy frost. Then Gisli said he wanted to leave the house and head south
to his hideout under the ridge, to see if he could get some sleep there. All
three of them went. The women were wearing tunics and they trailed along
in the frozen dew. Gisli had a piece of wood, on which he scored runes, and
as he did so the shavings fell to the ground.

They arrived at the hideout and Gisli lay down to see if he could sleep,
while the women stayed awake. A heavy drowsiness came upon him and
he dreamed that some loon birds, larger than cock ptarmigans, came to the
house. They screamed horribly and had been wallowing in blood and gore.

Then Aud asked what he dreamed.

'Yet again, my dreams were not good,' said Gisli, and he spoke a verse:

38.   When we parted, flaxen goddess,   *flaxen goddess*: woman (Gisli's wife)
      my ears rang with a sound
      from my blood-hall's realm   *blood-hall*: heart; its *realm*: the mind
      – and I poured the dwarf's brew.   *poured the dwarf's brew*: made a verse
      I, maker of the sword's voice,   *maker of the sword's voice*: warrior
      heard two loon birds fighting
      and I knew that soon the dew
      of bows would be descending.   *dew of bows*: showers of arrows, battle

At the same moment, they heard men's voices – Eyjolf had arrived with fourteen others. They had been to the farmhouse and seen the trail in the frozen dew, as if it was pointing the way. When Gisli and the two women became aware of the intruders, they climbed up on to the ridge where their vantage point was the best. Each of the women held a large club. Eyjolf and the others had come to the bottom of the ridge.

Then Eyjolf said to Gisli, 'I advise you to retreat no farther. Don't have yourself chased like a coward. You are said to have great courage. We have not met too often, but I'd prefer this encounter to be our last.'

Gisli answered him, 'Then attack like a man, and you may be sure I will retreat no farther. And you should lead the attack, since you bear a greater grudge than the men who come with you.'

'I won't have you decide,' said Eyjolf, 'how I deploy my men.'

'It comes as no surprise,' said Gisli, 'that a coward such as you would not dare to cross weapons with me.'

Then Eyjolf said to Helgi the Spy, 'You would win great acclaim if you were the first to climb the ridge and attack Gisli – a deed of heroism that would long be remembered.'

'I've often noticed,' said Helgi, 'that you usually want other people in front of you when there's any danger. Since you urge me so profoundly, I'll attempt it, but you must show enough courage to come with me and keep close behind – that is, if you're not a completely toothless bitch.'

Helgi found what seemed the best way up, and he carried a large axe in his hand. Gisli was also armed with an axe, and had a sword and shield at his side. He wore a grey cloak, which he had tied with a cord. Helgi made a sudden dash and ran up the slope at Gisli. Gisli turned and swung his sword, striking Helgi in the loins and cutting him asunder so that both halves of his body fell back off the edge of the ridge. Eyjolf made his way up in a different place, where he was confronted by Aud, and she struck him with her club so hard on the arm that it took away all his strength, and he staggered back down.

Then Gisli said, 'I knew long ago that I had married well, but never realized till now that the match was as good as this. Yet the help you gave me now was less than you wished or than you intended, even though the blow was good, for I might have dispatched them both in the same way.'

35   Then two men went to grab hold of Aud and Gudrid, but found the task was not so easy. Twelve men went for Gisli, and made their way up on to the ridge. He fought them off with rocks and weapons so well that his stand became famous.

Then one of Eyjolf's companions ran up to Gisli and said, 'Lay down your fine weapons and give them all to me – and give me your wife, Aud, too.'

Gisli answered him, 'Then show your courage, because neither befits you – neither my weapons nor my wife.'

The man thrust out at Gisli with a spear, and Gisli struck back, shearing the head from the shaft. But the blow was so fierce that his axe smashed against the rocky ground and the blade broke off. He threw it down and took up his sword instead, fighting on and guarding himself with his shield.

Then they launched a spirited attack, but Gisli defended himself well and with great courage. It was a hard and closely fought fight in which Gisli slew two more men, bringing the tally now to four.

Eyjolf ordered them to attack as boldly as they could.

'We're having a hard time of it,' he said, 'but that will not matter if we are rewarded for our efforts.'

Then, when it was least expected, Gisli turned around and ran from the ridge up on to the crag known as Einhamar. There, he faced them and defended himself. This caught them completely off-guard, and they felt their position had worsened considerably. Four of them were dead, and the rest were wounded and weary, so they held off their attack for a while. Then Eyjolf urged them on harder than ever, promising them substantial reward if they defeated Gisli. Eyjolf had with him a group of men of outstanding strength and hardiness.

36   A man named Svein was the first to attack Gisli, but Gisli struck at him, cleft him through the shoulder blades and threw him off the edge of the crag. The others began to wonder where this man's capacity for slaughter was going to end.

Then Gisli said to Eyjolf, 'May the three hundred pieces of silver that you have received for my life be dearly earned, and may you wish that you had added another three hundred for us never to have met. On your head will fall the shame for this great slaughter.'

They looked for a plan – none among them would flee to save his own life. So they went at him in two flanks, and heading the attack with Eyjolf were two of his kinsmen, Thorir and Thord. Both were excellent fighters. The battle was fierce and they succeeded in wounding Gisli in several places with their spears, but he defended himself with great courage and strength, and they faced such an onslaught of rocks and powerful blows that none escaped being wounded. When Gisli struck out he never missed. Now Eyjolf and his kinsmen saw that their names and their honour were at stake, and they attacked harder than ever, thrusting at him with their spears until his guts spilled out. Gisli gathered them up together in his shirt and bound them underneath with the cord.

Then he told them to hold off a while. 'The end you wanted will come,' he said.

Then he spoke a verse:

39.   Goddess of golden rain,
       who gives me great joy,
       may boldly hear report
       of her friend's brave stand.
       I greet the sword's honed edge
       that bites into my flesh,
       knowing that this courage
       was given me by my father.

This was Gisli's last verse. As soon as he had spoken it, he jumped off the crag and drove his sword into the head of Eyjolf's kinsman, Thord, and split him down to the waist. In doing so, Gisli fell down on top of him and breathed his last.

Everyone in Eyjolf's party was badly wounded, and Gisli had died with so many and such great wounds that it was an amazement to all. They say that he never once retreated, and as far as anyone could see his last blow was no weaker than his first.

Thus Gisli's life came to an end, and although he was deemed a man of great prowess, fortune was not always with him.

The men dragged his body down and took his sword from him. Then they covered him over with stones and went down to the sea. Then a sixth man died on the shore. Eyjolf invited Aud to accompany him, but she did not want to go. After that, Eyjolf and the remaining men returned to Otradal, and that same night a seventh man died. An eighth died after being bedridden with his wounds for a year, and although the other wounded men recovered they gained nothing but dishonour.

And it is said everywhere that no man in this land had ever been known to put up a greater stand than Gisli.

37 Eyjolf set out from his home with eleven men and went south to meet Bork the Stout. He told him the news and gave a full account of what had happened. Bork was greatly pleased by this, and he asked Thordis to give Eyjolf a warm welcome.

'Remember,' he said, 'the great love you bore my brother Thorgrim and treat Eyjolf well.'

'I weep for my brother Gisli,' said Thordis. 'Would not a good bowl of porridge be warm enough a welcome for Eyjolf?'

And later in the evening, when she brought in the food, she deliberately dropped a tray of spoons. Eyjolf had laid Gisli's sword between the bench and his feet, and Thordis recognized it. When she bent down to pick up the spoons, she grabbed the sword by the hilt and thrust out at Eyjolf, meaning to strike him in the guts. But she had not noticed that the end of the hilt was turned upwards, and it caught against the table. She had struck him lower than she intended, hit him in the thigh and wounded him sorely.

Bork grabbed hold of Thordis and wrenched the sword away from her, and the others all jumped to their feet and overturned the tables and the food. Bork left it in Eyjolf's hands to decide the penalty for this deed, and he claimed full compensation – the same as was imposed for slaying a man – and said he would have demanded more if Bork had handled this matter less fittingly.

Then Thordis named witnesses and declared herself divorced from Bork, saying that she would never again share his bed – and she stood by her word. She left and went to live at Thordisarstadir, out at Eyri. Bork, however, remained at Helgafell until Snorri the Godi drove him out. After that he went to live at Glerarskogar. Eyjolf went home and was greatly displeased with his visit.

38 Vestein's sons went to Gest Oddleifsson, their kinsman, and urged him to use his power to get them out of the country along with their mother Gunnhild, Gisli's wife Aud, Ingjald's daughter Gudrid and Geirmund her brother. They all went to the Hvita river and Gest paid for their passage abroad.

They were only at sea for a short time before they reached Norway. Berg and the other two men walked around town and tried to find a place to lodge. They met two men, one of whom was a young, well-built lad, dressed in fine red clothes. He asked Berg his name, and Berg told him his true identity and kin since he expected to gain more by using his father's name. The man in red pulled out his sword and dealt Berg a death-blow on the spot. He was Ari Sursson, brother to Gisli and Thorkel.

Berg's companions went back to the ship and told what had happened, and the skipper helped them escape, finding a place for Helgi* on board a ship bound for Greenland. Helgi arrived in that country, became prosperous and was held in great esteem there. Some men were sent out to kill him, but nothing came of it. He eventually died on a hunting expedition, and this was considered a great loss.

Aud and Gunnhild went to Hedeby in Denmark, took the Christian faith and then went on a pilgrimage to Rome. They never returned.

Geirmund remained in Norway, married and prospered there. Gudrid, his sister, also married and was thought to be a woman of wisdom. Many can be counted as her descendants.

Ari Sursson went to Iceland and came ashore at Hvita river. He sold his ship and bought himself some land at Hamar, where he lived for several years. After that he lived in several other places in Myrar, and had many descendants.

And here ends the saga of Gisli Sursson.

Translated by MARTIN S. REGAL

---

* Vestein's son.

THE SAGA OF GUNNLAUG
SERPENT-TONGUE

Gunnlaugs saga ormstungu

Time of action: 990–1010
Time of writing: 1270–1300

The Saga of Gunnlaug Serpent-tongue tells of two poets, Gunnlaug and Hrafn, who compete for the love of Helga the Fair, Egil Skallagrimsson's granddaughter. This love-triangle, a well-known theme from medieval European romances such as the Tristan story, is firmly set in familiar saga terms in west Iceland and at the courts of kings, not only in mainland Scandinavia but also in the Viking realms of the British Isles and in England, from the end of the tenth to the early eleventh centuries.

The saga opens with a prophetic dream about a two eagles who fight to the death over a beautiful swan (the still unborn Helga), prefiguring the plot. Prophetic devices are not uncommon in other sagas (for example, Gudrun's dream in *The Saga of the People of Laxardal*) and show that it is not the events in themselves which are important, but rather characters' reactions to the inevitable situations in which they find themselves. In the same way that events appear first in prophecy and later in reality, the poets do battle twice, first in verse and later with cold steel. In its central section, the saga sends Gunnlaug on a grand tour of royal courts (see map) and establishes a tension between the formality of the court poet's high position and Gunnlaug's own restless temperament and ambiguous motivations. He has a gift for enshrining immortal praise in verse, but can also be malicious and provocative in his dealings with others. Significantly, he begins his journey by insulting Earl Eirik in Norway, and ends it in reconciliation with him, as if he has achieved a degree of mature self-control, but in the meantime he has brought personal tragedy upon himself, when he reluctantly accepts honour with King Ethelred instead of returning to Iceland to claim Helga as his bride.

Fate is a strong presence throughout the saga. There always seems to be a noble motive which sets the course towards tragedy at the points in the plot where events could have taken a different turn. Helga's mother Jofrid refuses to leave the new-born girl to die of exposure at birth; King Ethelred shows his poet great honour by making him stay longer, even though this delay costs Gunnlaug Helga's hand; and Gunnlaug has already fatally wounded Hrafn when he succumbs to trickery, removes his helmet to fetch water and allows himself to be struck a mortal blow. The characterization is straightforward and clear-cut, and in places it approaches heroic and tragic stereotypes, but the fast pace of the plot and the intensity with which the action is recounted keep the reader engaged.

Written around 1300 and preserved complete in a manuscript dated shortly afterwards (Holm perg. 18 4to, 1300–1350), the saga gives an interesting insight into ideas then about the profession of the court poet in the 'golden age'. It is translated by Katrina C. Attwood from *Íslendinga sögur II* (Reykjavík 1987).

THE CAREER OF A COURT POET

Gunnlaug Serpent-tongue travels to the courts of kings and earls, praising them in verse and earning personal renown and fortune as a poet (see map overleaf). From the sagas we know that Icelanders enjoyed special status throughout the Viking world (and among English kings) for their poetic skills; in effect they were the nation's first professional authors. The tradition continued well beyond the Saga Age, even though the Norwegian kings had increasing trouble in understanding the ancient idiom in which their praises were sung. Both Snorri Sturluson and his nephew Sturla Thordarson went to Norway and delivered poetic eulogies there in the thirteenth century.

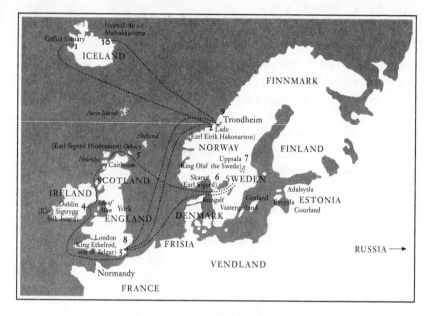

Travels of Gunnlaug Serpent-tongue

1. Gunnlaug lived with his father and grandfather in west Iceland until the age of eighteen. Before going abroad, he was promised the hand of Helga the Fair. (Ch. 4)

2. Gunnlaug visits Earl Eirik at Lade (the earl ruled Norway with his brother Svein 1000–14). When Gunnlaug says he is eighteen years old, the earl comments that he'll not survive another eighteen. Gunnlaug replies with an insult, and is banished. (Ch. 6)

3. In London, King Ethelred (978–1016) gives Gunnlaug a cloak of scarlet in reward for his poem of praise, and a gold ring when he promises to revisit the king. (Ch. 7)

4. King Sigtrygg Silk-beard (996–1042) in Dublin has never had a poem of praise recited to him before, and does not know how to reward Gunnlaug; eventually he gives him his own suit of new clothes, a tunic, cloak and gold bracelet. (Ch. 8)

5. Earl Sigurd in Orkney (980–1014) rewards him for his poem, with the gift of an axe. (Ch. 8)

6. In the town of Skarar in Sweden, Gunnlaug recites a poem for Earl Sigurd, who asks him to stay for the winter. At a Yule feast there, Gunnlaug delivers a verse that reconciles him with Earl Eirik of Lade, who lifts the order of banishment on him. (Ch. 8)

7. Gunnlaug arrives at the court of King Olaf the Swede (995–1022), to find another poet already there: Hrafn Onundarson. Both poets recite eulogies to the king, but refuse to praise the other's accomplishments. Their enmity and rivalry is transferred from the courtly setting to the personal level of a love triangle, when Hrafn goes to Iceland and woos Gunnlaug's prospective bride Helga. (Ch. 9)

8. Gunnlaug revisits King Ethelred in London. Fearing invasion by King Canute of the Danes (1016–35), the king orders Gunnlaug to stay for another fateful year, during which time his rival Hrafn wins Helga's hand. (Ch. 10)

9. Gunnlaug's journey earning renown as a poet comes full circle when he returns to Lade and is fully reconciled with Earl Eirik. Gunnlaug refuses an offer to stay and, sailing with the great singer of King Olaf Tryggvason's praise, Hallfred the Troublesome Poet, he sets off for Iceland to find his beloved. (Ch. 10)

10. By the time Gunnlaug finally makes land in north-east Iceland, it is too late. He hurries south and arrives just as the wedding feast is taking place. The rivalry between Gunnlaug and Hrafn is only resolved when they both die in a duel in Sweden. (Ch. 10 onwards)

This is the saga of Hrafn and of Gunnlaug Serpent-tongue, as told by the priest Ari Thorgilsson the Learned, who was the most knowledgeable of stories of the settlement and other ancient lore of anyone who has lived in Iceland.[*]

I There was a man named Thorstein. He was the son of Egil, the son of Skallagrim, the son of the hersir Kveldulf from Norway. Thorstein's mother was named Asgerd. She was Bjorn's daughter. Thorstein lived at Borg in Borgarfjord. He was rich and a powerful chieftain, wise, tolerant and just in all things. He was no great prodigy of either size or strength, as his father, Egil, had been. Learned men say that Egil was the greatest champion and duellist Iceland has ever known and the most promising of all the farmers' sons, as well as a great scholar and the wisest of men. Thorstein, too, was a great man and was popular with everyone. He was a handsome man with white-blond hair and fine, piercing eyes.

Scholars say that the Myrar folk – the family descended from Egil – were rather a mixed lot. Some of them were exceptionally good-looking men, whereas others are said to have been very ugly. Many members of the family, such as Kjartan Olafsson, Killer-Bardi and Skuli Thorsteinsson were particularly talented in various ways. Some of them were also great poets, like Bjorn, the Champion of the Hitardal people, the priest Einar Skulason, Snorri Sturluson and many others.

Thorstein married Jofrid, the daughter of Gunnar Hlifarson. Gunnar was the best fighter and athlete among the farmers in Iceland at that time. The second best was Gunnar of Hlidarendi, and Steinthor from Eyri was the third. Jofrid was eighteen years old when Thorstein married her. She was a widow, having previously been married to Thorodd, the son of Tunga-Odd. It was their daughter, Hungerd, who was being brought up at Borg by Thorstein. Jofrid was an independent woman. She and Thorstein had several children, although only a few of them appear in this saga. Their eldest son was named Skuli, the next Kollsvein and the third Egil.

2 It is said that, one summer, a ship came ashore in the Gufua estuary. The skipper was a Norwegian named Bergfinn, who was rich and getting on in years. He was a wise man. Farmer Thorstein rode down to the ship. He usually had the greatest say in fixing the prices at the market,

---

[*] This attribution to Ari (in one manuscript) must be fanciful.

and that was the case this time. The Norwegians found themselves lodgings, and Thorstein himself took the skipper in, since Bergfinn asked him if he could stay at his house. Bergfinn was rather withdrawn all winter, but Thorstein was very hospitable to him. The Norwegian was very interested in dreams.

One spring day, Thorstein asked Bergfinn if he wanted to ride with him up to Valfell. The Borgarfjord people held their local assembly there in those days, and Thorstein had been told that the walls of his booth had fallen in. The Norwegian replied that he would indeed like to go, and they set out later that day, taking a servant of Thorstein's with them. They rode until they arrived at Grenjar farm, which was near Valfell. A poor man named Atli, a tenant of Thorstein's, lived there. Thorstein asked him to come and help them with their work, and to bring with him a turf-cutting spade and a shovel. He did so, and when they arrived at the place where the booths were they all set to work digging out the walls.

It was a hot, sunny day, and when they had finished digging out the walls, Thorstein and the Norwegian sat down inside the booth. Thorstein dozed off, but his sleep was rather fitful. The Norwegian was sitting beside him and let him finish his dream undisturbed. When Thorstein woke up, he was in considerable distress. The Norwegian asked him what he had been dreaming about, since he slept so badly.

'Dreams don't mean anything,' Thorstein answered.

Now when they were riding home that evening, the Norwegian again asked what Thorstein had been dreaming about.

'If I tell you the dream,' Thorstein replied, 'you must explain it as it really is.' The Norwegian said that he would take that risk.

Then Thorstein said, 'I seemed to be back home at Borg, standing outside the main doorway, and I looked up at the buildings, and saw a fine, beautiful swan up on the roof-ridge. I thought that I owned her, and I was very pleased with her. Then I saw a huge eagle fly down from the mountains. He flew towards Borg and perched next to the swan and chattered to her happily. She seemed to be well pleased with that. Then I noticed that the eagle had black eyes and claws of iron; he looked like a gallant fellow.

'Next, I saw another bird fly from the south. He flew here to Borg, settled on the house next to the swan and tried to court her. It was a huge eagle too. As soon as the second eagle arrived, the first one seemed to become rather ruffled, and they fought fiercely for a long time, and I saw that they were both bleeding. The fight ended with each of them falling off the roof-ridge, one on each side. They were both dead. The swan remained sitting there, grief-stricken and dejected.

'And then I saw another bird fly from the west. It was a hawk. It perched next to the swan and was gentle with her, and later they flew off in the same direction. Then I woke up. Now this dream is nothing much,' he concluded, 'and must be to do with the winds, which will meet in the sky, blowing from the directions that the birds appeared to be flying from.'

'I don't think that's what it's about,' said the Norwegian.

'Interpret the dream as seems most likely to you,' Thorstein told him, 'and let me hear that.'

'These birds must be the fetches of important people,' said the Norwegian. 'Now, your wife is pregnant and will give birth to a pretty baby girl, and you will love her dearly. Noble men will come from the directions that the eagles in your dream seemed to fly from, and will ask for your daughter's hand. They will love her more strongly than is reasonable and will fight over her, and both of them will die as a result. And then a third man, coming from the direction from which the hawk flew, will ask for her hand, and she will marry him. Now I have interpreted your dream for you. I think things will turn out like that.'

'Your explanation is wicked and unfriendly,' Thorstein replied. 'You can't possibly know how to interpret dreams.'

'You'll see how it turns out,' the Norwegian retorted.

After this, Thorstein began to dislike the Norwegian, who went away that summer. He is now out of the saga.

3   Later in the summer, Thorstein got ready to go to the Althing. Before he left, he said to his wife, Jofrid, 'As matters stand, you are soon going to have a baby. Now if you have a girl, it must be left out to die, but if it is a boy, it will be brought up.'

When the country was completely heathen, it was something of a custom for poor men with many dependants in their families to have their children exposed. Even so, it was always considered a bad thing to do.

When Thorstein had said this, Jofrid replied, 'It is most unworthy for a man of your calibre to talk like that, and it cannot seem right to you to have such a thing done.'

'You know what my temper is like,' Thorstein replied. 'It will not do for anyone to go against my command.'

Then he rode off to the Althing, and Jofrid gave birth to an extremely pretty baby girl. The women wanted to take the child to Jofrid, but she said that there was little point in that, and had her shepherd, whose name was Thorvard, brought to her.

'You are to take my horse and saddle it,' Jofrid told him, 'and take this child west to Egil's daughter Thorgerd at Hjardarholt. Ask her to bring the child up in secret, so that Thorstein never finds out about it. For I look upon the child with such love that I really have no heart to have it left out to die. Now, here are three marks of silver which you are to keep as your reward. Thorgerd will procure a passage abroad for you out there in the west, and will give you whatever you need for your voyage overseas.'

Thorvard did as she said. He rode west to Hjardarholt with the child and gave it to Thorgerd. She had it brought up by some of her tenants who lived at Leysingjastadir on Hvammsfjord. She also secured a passage for Thorvard on a ship berthed at Skeljavik in Steingrimsfjord in the north, and made provision for his voyage. Thorvard sailed abroad from there, and is now out of this saga.

Now when Thorstein came back from the Althing, Jofrid told him that the child had been exposed – just as he said it should be – and that the shepherd had run away, taking her horse with him. Thorstein said she had done well, and found himself another shepherd.

Six years passed without this coming out. Then one day Thorstein rode west to Hjardarholt, to a feast given by his brother-in-law Olaf Peacock, who was then the most respected of all the chieftains in the west country. Thorstein was warmly welcomed at Hjardarholt, as might be expected.

Now it is said that, one day during the feast, Thorgerd was sitting in the high seat talking to her brother Thorstein, while Olaf was making conversation with other men. Three girls were sitting on the bench opposite them.

Then Thorgerd said, 'Brother, how do you like the look of those girls sitting opposite us?'

'Very well,' he replied, 'though one of them is by far the prettiest, and she has Olaf's good looks, as well as the fair complexion and features we men of Myrar have.'

'You are certainly right, brother, when you say that she has the complexion and features of the Myrar men,' Thorgerd said, 'but she has none of Olaf Peacock's looks, since she is not his daughter.'

'How can that be,' Thorstein asked, 'since she's your daughter?'

'Kinsman,' she answered, 'to tell you the truth, this beautiful girl is your daughter, not mine.' Then she told him everything that had happened, and begged him to forgive both her and his wife for this wrong.

'I cannot blame you for this,' Thorstein said. 'In most cases, what will be will be, and you two have smoothed over my own stupidity well enough. I'm so pleased with this girl that I count myself very lucky to have such a beautiful child. But what's her name?'

'She's named Helga,' Thorgerd replied.

'Helga the Fair,' mused Thorstein. 'Now you must get her ready to come home with me.'

And so she did. When he left, Thorstein was given splendid gifts, and Helga rode home to Borg with him and was brought up there, loved and cherished by her father and mother and all her relatives.

4 In those days, Illugi the Black, the son of Hallkel Hrosskelsson, lived at Gilsbakki in Hvitarsida. Illugi's mother was Thurid Dylla, the daughter of Gunnlaug Serpent-tongue. Illugi was the second greatest chieftain in Borgarfjord, after Thorstein Egilsson. He was a great landowner, very strong-willed, and he stood by his friends. He was married to Ingibjorg, the daughter of Asbjorn Hardarson from Ornolfsdal. Ingibjorg's mother was Thorgerd, the daughter of Skeggi from Midfjord. Ingibjorg and Illugi had many children, but only a few of them appear in this saga. One of their sons was named Hermund and another Gunnlaug. They were both promising fellows, and were then in their prime.

It is said that Gunnlaug was somewhat precocious, big and strong, with light chestnut hair, which suited him, dark eyes and a rather ugly nose. He had a pleasant face, a slender waist and broad shoulders. He was very manly, an impetuous fellow by nature, ambitious even in his youth, stubborn in all situations and ruthless. He was a gifted poet, albeit a somewhat abusive one, and was also called Gunnlaug Serpent-tongue. Hermund was the more popular of the two brothers and had the stamp of a chieftain about him.

When Gunnlaug was twelve years old, he asked his father for some wares to cover his travelling expenses, saying that he wanted to go abroad and see how other people lived. Illugi was reluctant to agree to this. He said that people in other countries would not think highly of Gunnlaug when he himself found that he could scarcely manage him as he would wish to at home.

Soon after this, Illugi went out early one morning and saw that his outhouse was open and that half a dozen sacks of wares had been laid out in the yard, with some saddle-pads. He was very surprised at this. Then someone came along leading four horses; it was his son Gunnlaug.

'I put the sacks there,' he said. Illugi asked why he had done so. He said they would do to help cover his travelling expenses.

'You will not undermine my authority,' said Illugi, 'nor are you going anywhere until I see fit.' And he dragged the sacks back inside.

Then Gunnlaug rode off and arrived down at Borg that evening. Farmer Thorstein invited him to stay and he accepted. Gunnlaug told Thorstein what had happened between him and his father. Thorstein said he could stay as long as he liked, and he was there for a year. He studied law with Thorstein and everyone there thought well of him.

Gunnlaug and Helga often amused themselves by playing board games with each other. They quickly took a liking to each other, as events later bore out. They were pretty much the same age. Helga was so beautiful that learned men say that she was the most beautiful woman there has ever been in Iceland. She had such long hair that it could cover her completely, and it was radiant as beaten gold. It was thought that there was no equal to Helga the Fair throughout Borgarfjord or in places further afield.

Now one day, when people were sitting around in the main room at Borg, Gunnlaug said to Thorstein, 'There is still one point of law that you haven't taught me – how to betroth myself to a woman.'

'That's a small matter,' Thorstein replied, and he taught Gunnlaug the procedure.

Then Gunnlaug said, 'Now you should check whether I've understood properly. I'll take you by the hand and act as though I'm betrothing myself to your daughter Helga.'

'I don't see any need for that,' Thorstein said.

Then Gunnlaug grabbed his hand. 'Do this for me,' he said.

'Do what you like,' Thorstein said, 'but let those present here know that it will be as if this had not been said, and there must be no hidden meaning to it.'

Then Gunnlaug named his witnesses and betrothed himself to Helga. Afterwards, he asked whether that would do. Thorstein said that it would, and everyone there thought it was great fun.

5   There was a man named Onund who lived to the south at Mosfell. He was a very wealthy man, and held the godord for the headlands to the south. He was married, and his wife was named Geirny. She was the daughter of Gnup, the son of Molda-Gnup who settled at Grindavik in the south. Their sons were Hrafn, Thorarin and Eindridi. They were all promising men, but Hrafn was the most accomplished of them in everything. He was a big, strong man, well worth looking at, and a good poet. When he

was more or less grown up, he travelled about from country to country and was well respected wherever he went.

Thorodd Eyvindarson the Wise and his son Skafti lived at Hjalli in Olfus in those days. Skafti was Lawspeaker in Iceland at that time. His mother was Rannveig, the daughter of Gnup Molda-Gnupsson, and so Skafti and the sons of Onund were cousins. There was great friendship between them, as well as this blood tie.

Thorfinn Seal-Thorisson was then living out at Raudamel. He had seven sons, and they were all promising men. Their names were Thorgils, Eyjolf and Thorir, and they were the leading men in that district.*

All the men who have been mentioned were living at the same time, and it was about this time that the best thing ever to have happened in Iceland occurred: the whole country became Christian and the entire population abandoned the old faith.

For six years now, Gunnlaug Serpent-tongue, who was mentioned earlier, had been living partly at Borg with Thorstein and partly at Gilsbakki with his father Illugi. By now, he was eighteen years old, and he and his father were getting on much better.

There was a man named Thorkel the Black. He was a member of Illugi's household and a close relative of his, and had grown up at Gilsbakki. He came into an inheritance at As in Vatnsdal up in the north, and asked Gunnlaug to go with him to collect it, which he did. They rode north to As together and, thanks to Gunnlaug's assistance, the men who had Thorkel's money handed it over to them.

On their way home from the north, they stayed overnight at Grimstungur with a wealthy farmer who was living there. In the morning, a shepherd took Gunnlaug's horse, which was covered in sweat when they got it back. Gunnlaug knocked the shepherd senseless. The farmer would not leave it at that, and demanded compensation for the blow. Gunnlaug offered to pay him a mark, but the farmer thought that was too little.† Then Gunnlaug spoke a verse:

---

* The copyist has presumably skipped a section in his exemplar, where the names of Thorfinn's four remaining sons were recorded.

† The farmer's objection appears to be justified, since according to the law code the legal penalty for knocking someone unconscious was lesser outlawry. By contrast, the shepherd was liable for a fine of three marks for stealing the horse.

I.   A mark to the middle-strong man,
         lodgings-lord, I held out in my hand;   *lodgings-lord*: man
         you'll receive a fine silver-grey wire   *silver-grey wire*: piece of silver
         for the one who spits flame from his gums.   *flame*: blood
         It will cause you regret
         if you knowingly let
         the sea-serpent's couch   *sea-serpent's couch*: gold
         slip out of your pouch.

They arranged that Gunnlaug's offer should be accepted, and when the matter was settled Gunnlaug and Thorkel rode home.

A little while later, Gunnlaug asked his father a second time for wares, so that he could travel abroad.

'Now you may have your own way,' Illugi replied, 'since you are better behaved than you used to be.'

Illugi rode off at once and bought Gunnlaug a half-share in a ship from Audun Halter-dog. The ship was beached in the Gufua estuary. This was the same Audun who, according to *The Saga of the People of Laxardal*, would not take the sons of Osvif the Wise abroad after the killing of Kjartan Olafsson, though that happened later than this.

When Illugi came home, Gunnlaug thanked him profusely. Thorkel the Black went along with Gunnlaug, and their wares were loaded on to the ship. While the others were getting ready, Gunnlaug was at Borg, and he thought it was nicer to talk to Helga than to work with the traders.

One day, Thorstein asked Gunnlaug if he would like to ride up to his horses in Langavatnsdal with him. Gunnlaug said that he would, and they rode together until they arrived at Thorstein's shielings, which were at a place called Thorgilsstadir. Thorstein had a stud of four chestnut horses there. The stallion was a splendid creature, but was not an experienced fighter. Thorstein offered to give the horses to Gunnlaug, but he said that he did not need them, since he intended to go abroad. Then they rode over to another stud of horses. There was a grey stallion there with four mares; he was the best horse in Borgarfjord. Thorstein offered to give him to Gunnlaug.

'I don't want this horse any more than I wanted the others,' Gunnlaug answered. 'But why don't you offer me something I will accept?'

'What's that?' Thorstein asked.

'Your daughter, Helga the Fair,' Gunnlaug replied.

'That will not be arranged so swiftly,' he said, and changed the subject.

They rode home, down along the Langa river.

Then Gunnlaug spoke: 'I want to know how you will respond to my proposal.'

'I'm not taking any notice of your nonsense,' Thorstein replied.

'This is quite serious, and not nonsense,' Gunnlaug said.

'You should have worked out what you wanted in the first place,' Thorstein countered. 'Haven't you decided to go abroad? And yet you're carrying on as if you want to get married. It wouldn't be suitable for you and Helga to marry while you are so undecided. I'm not prepared to consider it.'

'Where do you expect to find a match for your daughter if you won't marry her to Illugi the Black's son?' Gunnlaug asked. 'Where in Borgarfjord are there more important people than my father?'

'I don't go in for drawing comparisons between men,' Thorstein parried, 'but if you were such a man as he is you wouldn't be turned away.'

'To whom would you rather marry your daughter than me?' Gunnlaug asked.

'There's a lot of good men around here to choose from,' Thorstein replied. 'Thorfinn at Raudamel has seven sons, all of them very manly.'

'Neither Onund nor Thorfinn can compare with my father,' Gunnlaug answered, 'considering that even you clearly fall short of his mark. What have you done to compare with the time when he took on Thorgrim Kjallaksson the Godi and his sons at the Thorsnes Assembly by himself and came away with everything there was to be had?'*

'I drove away Steinar, the son of Ogmund Sjoni† – and that was considered quite an achievement,' Thorstein replied.

'You had your father, Egil, to help you then,' Gunnlaug retorted. 'Even so, there aren't many farmers who would be safe if they turned down a marriage bond with me.'

'You save your bullying for the people up in the hills,' Thorstein replied. 'It won't count for much down here in the marshes.'

They arrived home later that evening, and the following morning Gunnlaug rode up to Gilsbakki and asked his father to ride back to Borg with him to make a marriage proposal.

'You are an unsettled fellow,' Illugi replied. 'You've already planned to

---

* Illugi's dispute with Thorgrim and his sons, which centred on Illugi's claim for his wife's dowry, is described in *The Saga of the People of Eyri*, Chapter 17.

† Thorstein's feud with Steinar, who had trespassed on land belonging to Thorstein, is described in *Egil's Saga*, Chapters 80–84.

go abroad, yet now you claim that you have to occupy yourself chasing after women. I know that Thorstein doesn't approve of such behaviour.'

'Nevertheless,' Gunnlaug replied, 'while I still intend to go abroad, nothing will please me unless you support me in this.'

Then Illugi rode down from Gilsbakki to Borg, taking eleven men with him. Thorstein gave them a warm welcome.

Early the next morning, Illugi said to Thorstein: 'I want to talk to you.'

'Let's go up on to the Borg* and talk there,' Thorstein suggested.

They did so, and Gunnlaug went along too.

Illugi spoke first: 'My kinsman Gunnlaug says that he has already spoken of this matter on his own behalf; he wants to ask for the hand of your daughter Helga. Now I want to know what is going to come of this. You know all about his breeding and our family's wealth. For our part, we will not neglect to provide either a farm or a godord, if that will help bring it about.'

'The only problem I have with Gunnlaug is that he seems so unsettled,' Thorstein replied. 'But if he were more like you, I shouldn't put it off.'

'If you deny that this would be an equal match for both our families, it will bring an end to our friendship,' Illugi warned.

'For our friendship's sake and because of what you've been saying, Helga will be promised to Gunnlaug, but not formally betrothed to him, and she will wait three years for him. And Gunnlaug must go abroad and follow the example of good men, and I will be free of any obligation if he doesn't come back as required, or if I don't like the way he turns out.'

With that, they parted. Illugi rode home and Gunnlaug rode off to his ship, and the merchants put to sea as soon as they got a fair wind. They sailed to the north of Norway, and then sailed in past Trondheim to Nidaros, where they berthed the ship and unloaded.

6   Earl Eirik Hakonarson and his brother Svein were ruling Norway in those days. Earl Eirik was staying on his family's estate at Lade, and was a powerful chieftain. Skuli Thorsteinsson was there with him: he was one of the earl's followers and was well thought of.

It is said that Gunnlaug and Audun Halter-dog went to Lade with ten other men. Gunnlaug was dressed in a grey tunic and white breeches. He had a boil on his foot, right on the instep, and blood and pus oozed out of

---

* The *Borg* is a high rocky outcrop immediately behind the site of Borg farm from which the farm takes its name.

it when he walked. In this state, he went before the earl with Audun and the others and greeted him politely. The earl recognized Audun, and asked him for news from Iceland, and Audun told him all there was. Then the earl asked Gunnlaug who he was, and Gunnlaug told him his name and what family he came from.

'Skuli Thorsteinsson,' the earl asked, 'what family does this fellow come from in Iceland?'

'My lord,' he replied, 'give him a good welcome. He is the son of the best man in Iceland, Illugi the Black from Gilsbakki, and, what's more, he's my foster-brother.'

'What's the matter with your foot, Icelander?' the earl asked.

'I've got a boil on it, my lord,' he replied.

'But you weren't limping?'

'One mustn't limp while both legs are the same length,' Gunnlaug replied.

Then a man named Thorir, who was one of the earl's followers, spoke: 'The Icelander is rather cocky. We should test him a bit.'

Gunnlaug looked at him, and spoke:

2. A certain follower's
    especially horrible;
    be wary of trusting him:
    he's evil and black.

Then Thorir made as if to grab his axe.

'Leave it be,' said the earl. 'Real men don't pay any attention to things like that. How old are you, Icelander?'

'Just turned eighteen,' Gunnlaug replied.

'I swear that you'll not survive another eighteen,' the earl declared.

'Don't you call curses down on me,' Gunnlaug muttered quite softly, 'but rather pray for yourself.'

'What did you just say, Icelander?' the earl asked.

'I said what I thought fit,' Gunnlaug replied, 'that you should not call curses down on me, but should pray more effective prayers for yourself.'

'What should I pray for then?' asked the earl.

'That you don't meet your death in the same way as your father Earl Hakon did.'*

---

* Earl Hakon Sigurdsson was murdered by his servant Kark, while hiding from his enemy Olaf Tryggvason in a pigsty.

The earl turned as red as blood, and ordered that the fool be arrested at once.

Then Skuli went to the earl and said, 'My lord, do as I ask: pardon the man and let him get out of here as quickly as he can.'

'Let him clear off as fast as he can if he wants quarter,' the earl commanded, 'and never set foot in my kingdom again.'

Then Skuli took Gunnlaug outside and down to the quay, where there was a ship all ready for its voyage to England. Skuli procured a passage in it for Gunnlaug and his kinsman Thorkel, and Gunnlaug entrusted his ship and the other belongings he did not need to keep with him to Audun for safe-keeping. Gunnlaug and Thorkel sailed off into the North Sea, and arrived in the autumn at the port of London, where they drew the ship up on to its rollers.

7   King Ethelred, the son of Edgar, was ruling England at that time. He was a good ruler, and was spending that winter in London. In those days, the language in England was the same as that spoken in Norway and Denmark, but there was a change of language when William the Bastard conquered England. Since William was of French descent, the French language was used in England from then on.

As soon as he arrived in London, Gunnlaug went before the king and greeted him politely and respectfully. The king asked what country he was from. Gunnlaug told him – 'and I have come to you, my lord, because I have composed a poem about you, and I should like you to hear it'.

The king said that he would. Gunnlaug recited the poem expressively and confidently. The refrain goes like this:

3.   All the army's in awe and agog
       at England's good prince, as at God:
       everyone lauds Ethelred the King,
       both the warlike king's race and men's kin.

The king thanked him for the poem and, as a reward, gave him a cloak of scarlet* lined with the finest furs and with an embroidered band stretching down to the hem. He also made him one of his followers. Gunnlaug stayed with the king all winter and was well thought of.

Early one morning, Gunnlaug met three men in a street. Their leader was named Thororm. He was big and strong, and rather obstreperous.

---

* See footnote on p. 311.

'Northerner,' he said, 'lend me some money.'

'It's not a good idea to lend money to strangers,' Gunnlaug replied.

'I'll pay you back on the date we agree between us,' he promised.

'I'll risk it then,' said Gunnlaug, giving Thororm the money.

A little while later, Gunnlaug met the king and told him about the loan.

'Now things have taken a turn for the worse,' the king replied. 'That fellow is the most notorious robber and thug. Have nothing more to do with him, and I will give you the same amount of money.'

'Then your followers are a pretty pathetic lot,' Gunnlaug answered. 'We trample all over innocent men, but let thugs like him walk all over us! That will never happen.'

Shortly afterwards, Gunnlaug met Thororm and demanded his money back, but Thororm said that he would not pay up. Then Gunnlaug spoke this verse:

4.	O god of the sword-spell,	*sword-spell*: battle; its *god*: warrior
	you're unwise to withhold your wealth	
	from me; you've deceived	
	the sword-point's reddener.	*sword-point's reddener*: warrior, who
	I've something else to explain –	reddens the sword's point with blood
	'Serpent-tongue' as a child	
	was my name. Now again	
	here's my chance to prove why.	

'Now I'll give you the choice the law provides for,' said Gunnlaug. 'Either you pay me my money or fight a duel with me in three days' time.'

The thug laughed and said, 'Many people have suffered badly at my hands, and no one has ever challenged me to a duel before. I'm quite ready for it!'

With that, Gunnlaug and Thororm parted for the time being. Gunnlaug told the king how things stood.

'Now we really are in a fix,' he said. 'This man can blunt any weapon just by looking at it. You must do exactly as I tell you. I am going to give you this sword, and you are to fight him with it, but make sure that you show him a different one.'

Gunnlaug thanked the king warmly.

When they were ready for the duel, Thororm asked Gunnlaug what kind of sword he happened to have. Gunnlaug showed him and drew the sword, but he had fastened a loop of rope around the hilt of King's Gift and he slipped it over his wrist.

As soon as he saw the sword, the berserk said, 'I'm not afraid of that sword.'

He struck at Gunnlaug with his sword, and chopped off most of his shield. Then Gunnlaug struck back with his sword King's Gift. The berserk left himself exposed, because he thought Gunnlaug was using the same weapon as he had shown him. Gunnlaug dealt him his death-blow there and then. The king thanked him for this service, and Gunnlaug won great fame for it in England and beyond.

In the spring, when ships were sailing from country to country, Gunnlaug asked Ethelred for permission to do some travelling. The king asked him what he wanted to do.

'I should like to fulfil a vow I have made,' Gunnlaug answered, and spoke this verse:

5. I will most surely visit
    three shapers of war   *shapers of war*: kings
    and two earls of lands,
    as I promised worthy men.
    I will not be back
    before the point-goddess's son   *point-goddess*: valkyrie; her *son*:
    summons me; he gives me   Ethelred
    a red serpent's bed to wear.   *serpent's bed*: gold

'And so it will be, poet,' said the king, giving him a gold arm ring weighing six ounces. 'But,' he continued, 'you must promise to come back to me next autumn, because I don't want to lose such an accomplished man as you.'

8   Then Gunnlaug sailed north to Dublin with some merchants. At that time, Ireland was ruled by King Sigtrygg Silk-beard, the son of Olaf Kvaran and Queen Kormlod. He had only been king for a short while.* Straight away, Gunnlaug went before the king and greeted him politely and respectfully. The king gave him an honourable welcome.

'I have composed a poem about you,' Gunnlaug said, 'and I should like it to have a hearing.'

'No one has ever deigned to bring me a poem before,' the king replied. 'Of course I will listen to it.'

Gunnlaug recited the drapa, and the refrain goes like this:

---

* Sigtrygg appears to have ruled in Dublin from *c.* 996–1042. The chronology of the saga suggests that Gunnlaug visited him in 1003.

6.   To the sorceress's steed   *sorceress's steed*: wolf
        Sigtrygg corpses feeds.

And it contains these lines as well:

7.   I know which offspring,
        descendant of kings,
        I want to proclaim
        – Kvaran's son is his name;
        it is his habit
        to be quite lavish:
        the poet's ring of gold
        he surely won't withhold.

8.   The flinger of Frodi's flame   *Frodi's* (sea-king's) *flame*: gold; its
        should eloquently explain   *flinger*: generous man (Sigtrygg)
        if he's found phrasing neater
        than mine, in drapa metre.

The king thanked Gunnlaug for the poem, and summoned his treasurer. 'How should I reward the poem?' he asked.

'How would you like to, my lord?' the treasurer said.

'What kind of reward would it be if I gave him a pair of knorrs?' the king asked.

'That is too much, my lord,' he replied. 'Other kings give fine treasures – good swords or splendid gold bracelets – as rewards for poems.'

The king gave Gunnlaug his own new suit of scarlet clothes, an embroidered tunic, a cloak lined with exquisite furs and a gold bracelet which weighed a mark. Gunnlaug thanked him profusely and stayed there for a short while. He went on from there to the Orkney Islands.

In those days, the Orkney Islands were ruled by Earl Sigurd Hlodvesson. He thought highly of Icelanders. Gunnlaug greeted the earl politely and said that he had a poem to present to him. The earl said that he would indeed listen to Gunnlaug's poem, since he was from such an important family in Iceland. Gunnlaug recited the poem, which was a well-constructed flokk. As a reward, the earl gave him a broad axe, decorated all over with silver inlay, and invited Gunnlaug to stay with him.

Gunnlaug thanked him for the gift, and for the invitation, too, but said that he had to travel east to Sweden. Then he took passage with some merchants who were sailing to Norway, and that autumn they arrived at

Kungalf in the east. As always, Gunnlaug's kinsman, Thorkel, was still with him. They took a guide from Kungalf up into Vastergotland and so arrived at the market town named Skarar. An earl named Sigurd, who was rather old, was ruling there. Gunnlaug went before him and greeted him politely, saying that he had composed a poem about him. The earl listened carefully as Gunnlaug recited the poem, which was a flokk. Afterwards, the earl thanked Gunnlaug, rewarded him generously and asked him to stay with him over the winter.

Earl Sigurd held a great Yule feast during the winter. Messengers from Earl Eirik arrived on Yule eve. They had travelled down from Norway. There were twelve of them in all, and they were bearing gifts for Earl Sigurd. The earl gave them a warm welcome and seated them next to Gunnlaug for the Yule festival. There was a great deal of merriment. The people of Vastergotland declared that there was no better or more famous earl than Sigurd; the Norwegians thought that Earl Eirik was much better. They argued about this and, in the end, both sides called upon Gunnlaug to settle the matter. It was then that Gunnlaug spoke this verse:

9. Staves of the spear-sister, *spear-sister*: valkyrie; her *staves*:
   you speak of the earl: warriors
   this old man is hoary-haired,
   but has looked on tall waves.
   Before his billow-steed *billow-steed*: ship
   battle-bush Eirik, tossed *battle-bush*: warrior
   by the tempest, has seen
   more blue breakers back in the east.

Both sides, but particularly the Norwegians, were pleased with this assessment. After Yule, the messengers left with splendid gifts from Earl Sigurd to Earl Eirik. They told Earl Eirik about Gunnlaug's assessment. The earl thought that Gunnlaug had shown him both fairness and friendliness, and spread the word that Gunnlaug would find a safe haven in his domain. Gunnlaug later heard what the earl had had to say about the matter. Gunnlaug had asked Earl Sigurd for a guide to take him east into Tiundaland in Sweden, and the earl found him one.

9   In those days, Sweden was ruled by King Olaf the Swede, the son of
     King Eirik the Victorious and Sigrid the Ambitious, daughter of Tosti
the Warlike. He was a powerful and illustrious king, and was very keen to
make his mark.

Gunnlaug arrived in Uppsala around the time of the Swedes' Spring
Assembly. When he managed to get an audience, he greeted the king, who
welcomed him warmly and asked him who he was. He said that he was an
Icelander. Now Hrafn Onundarson was with the king at the time.

'Hrafn,' the king said, 'what family does this fellow come from in Iceland?'

A big, dashing man stood up from the lower bench, came before the king
and said, 'My lord, he comes from the finest of families and is the noblest
of men in his own right.'

'Then let him go and sit next to you,' the king said.

'I have a poem to present to you,' Gunnlaug said, 'and I should like you
to listen to it properly.'

'First go and sit yourselves down,' the king commanded. 'There is no
time now to sit and listen to poems.'

And so they did. Gunnlaug and Hrafn started to chat, telling one another
about their travels. Hrafn said that he had left Iceland for Norway the
previous summer, and had come east to Sweden early that winter. They
were soon good friends.

One day when the assembly was over, Hrafn and Gunnlaug were both
there with the king.

'Now, my lord,' Gunnlaug said, 'I should like you to hear my poem.'

'I could do that now,' the king replied.

'I want to recite my poem now, my lord,' Hrafn said.

'I could listen to that, too,' he replied.

'I want to recite my poem first,' Gunnlaug said, 'if you please.'

'I should go first, my lord,' Hrafn said, 'since I came to your court first.'

'Where did our ancestors ever go with mine trailing in the wake of yours?'
Gunnlaug asked. 'Nowhere, that's where! And that's how it's going to be
with us, too!'

'Let's be polite enough not to fight over this,' Hrafn replied. 'Let's ask
the king to decide.'

'Gunnlaug had better recite his poem first,' the king declared, 'since he
takes it badly if he doesn't get his own way.'

Then Gunnlaug recited the drapa he had composed about King Olaf, and when he had finished, the king said, 'How well is the poem composed, Hrafn?'

'Quite well, my lord,' he answered. 'It is an ostentatious poem, but is ungainly and rather stilted, just like Gunnlaug himself is in temperament.'

'Now you must recite your poem, Hrafn,' the king said.

He did so, and when he had finished, the king asked: 'How well is the poem put together, Gunnlaug?'

'Quite well, my lord,' he replied. 'It is a handsome poem, just like Hrafn himself is, but there's not much to either of them. And,' he continued, 'why did you compose only a flokk for the king, Hrafn? Did you not think he merited a drapa?'

'Let's not talk about this any farther,' Hrafn said. 'It might well crop up again later.' And with that they parted.

A little while later, Hrafn was made one of King Olaf's followers. He asked for permission to leave, which the king granted.

Now when Hrafn was ready to leave, he said to Gunnlaug, 'From now on, our friendship is over, since you tried to do me down in front of the court. Sometime soon, I will cause you no less shame than you tried to heap on me here.'

'Your threats don't scare me,' Gunnlaug replied, 'and I won't be thought a lesser man than you anywhere.'

King Olaf gave Hrafn valuable gifts when they parted, and then Hrafn went away.

Hrafn left the east that spring and went to Trondheim, where he fitted out his ship. He sailed to Iceland during the summer, and brought his ship into Leiruvog, south of Mosfell heath. His family and friends were glad to see him, and he stayed at home with his father over the winter.

Now at the Althing that summer, Hrafn the Poet met his kinsman Skafti the Lawspeaker.

'I should like you to help me ask Thorstein Egilsson for permission to marry his daughter Helga,' Hrafn said.

'Hasn't she already been promised to Gunnlaug Serpent-tongue?' Skafti answered.

'Hasn't the time they agreed passed by now?' Hrafn countered. 'Besides, Gunnlaug's so proud these days that he won't take any notice of this or care about it at all.'

'We'll do as you please,' Skafti replied.

Then they went over to Thorstein Egilsson's booth with several other men. Thorstein gave them a warm welcome.

'My kinsman Hrafn wants to ask for the hand of your daughter Helga,' Skafti explained. 'You know about his family background, his wealth and good breeding, and that he has numerous relatives and friends.'

'She is already promised to Gunnlaug,' Thorstein answered, 'and I want to stick to every detail of the agreement I made with him.'

'Haven't the three winters you agreed between yourselves passed by now?' Skafti asked.

'Yes,' said Thorstein, 'but the summer isn't gone, and he might yet come back during the summer.'

'But if he hasn't come back at the end of the summer, then what hope will we have in the matter?' Skafti asked.

'We'll all come back here next summer,' Thorstein replied, 'and then we'll be able to see what seems to be the best way forward, but there's no point in talking about it any more at the moment.'

With that they parted, and people rode home from the Althing. It was no secret that Hrafn had asked for Helga's hand.

Gunnlaug did not return that summer. At the Althing the next summer, Skafti and Hrafn argued their case vehemently, saying that Thorstein was now free of all his obligations to Gunnlaug.

'I don't have many daughters to look after,' Thorstein said, 'and I'm anxious that no one be provoked to violence on their account. Now I want to see Illugi the Black first.'

And so he did.

When Illugi and Thorstein met, Thorstein asked, 'Do you consider me to be free of all obligation to your son Gunnlaug?'

'Certainly,' Illugi replied, 'if that's how you want it. I cannot add much to this now, because I don't altogether know what Gunnlaug's circumstances are.'

Then Thorstein went back to Skafti. They settled matters by deciding that, if Gunnlaug did not come back that summer, Hrafn and Helga's marriage should take place at Borg at the Winter Nights, but that Thorstein should be without obligation to Hrafn if Gunnlaug were to come back and go through with the wedding. After that, people rode home from the Althing. Gunnlaug's return was still delayed, and Helga did not like the arrangement at all.

10   Now we return to Gunnlaug, who left Sweden for England in the same summer as Hrafn went back to Iceland. He received valuable gifts from King Olaf when he left. King Ethelred gave Gunnlaug a very warm welcome. He stayed with the king all winter, and was thought well of.

In those days, the ruler of Denmark was Canute the Great, the son of Svein. He had recently come into his inheritance, and was continually threatening to lead an army against England, since his father, Svein, had gained considerable power in England before his death there in the west. Furthermore, there was a huge army of Danes in Britain at that time. Its leader was Heming, the son of Earl Strut-Harald and the brother of Earl Sigvaldi. Under King Canute, Heming was in charge of the territory which King Svein had previously won.

During the spring, Gunnlaug asked King Ethelred for permission to leave.

'Since you are my follower,' he replied, 'it is not appropriate for you to leave me when such a war threatens England.'

'That is for you to decide, my lord,' Gunnlaug replied. 'But give me permission to leave next summer, if the Danes don't come.'

'We'll see about it then,' the king answered.

Now that summer and the following winter passed, and the Danes did not come. After midsummer, Gunnlaug obtained the king's permission to leave, went east to Norway and visited Earl Eirik at Lade in Trondheim. The earl gave him a warm welcome this time, and invited him to stay with him. Gunnlaug thanked him for the offer, but said that he wanted to go back to Iceland first, to visit his intended.

'All the ships prepared for Iceland are gone now,' said the earl.

Then a follower said, 'Hallfred the Troublesome Poet was still anchored out under Agdenes yesterday.'

'That might still be the case,' the earl replied. 'He sailed from here five nights ago.'

Then Earl Eirik had Gunnlaug taken out to Hallfred, who was glad to see him. An offshore breeze began to blow, and they were very cheerful. It was late summer.

'Have you heard about Hrafn Onundarson's asking for permission to marry Helga the Fair?' Hallfred asked Gunnlaug.

Gunnlaug said that he had heard about it, but that he did not know the full story. Hallfred told him everything he knew about it, and added that many people said that Hrafn might well prove to be no less brave than Gunnlaug was. Then Gunnlaug spoke this verse:

10.   Though the east wind has toyed
      with the shore-ski this week   *shore-ski*: ship
      I weigh that but little –
      the weather's weaker now.
      I fear more being felt
      to fall short of Hrafn in courage
      than living on to become
      a grey-haired gold-breaker.   *gold-breaker*: man

Then Hallfred said, 'You will need to have better dealings with Hrafn than I did. A few years ago, I brought my ship into Leiruvog, south of Mosfell heath. I ought to have paid Hrafn's farmhand half a mark of silver, but I didn't give it to him. Hrafn rode over to us with sixty men and cut our mooring ropes, and the ship drifted up on to the mud flats and looked as if it would be wrecked. I ended up granting Hrafn self-judgement, and paid him a mark. That is all I have to say about him.'

From then on, they talked only about Helga. Hallfred heaped much praise on her beauty. Then Gunnlaug spoke:

11.   The slander-wary god
      of the sword-storm's spark   *sword-storm*: battle; *its spark*: sword; *god*
      mustn't court the cape of the earth   *of the sword*: warrior (Hrafn)
      with her cover of linen like snow.
      For when I was a lad,   *forearm's fire*: ring; its *headlands*: fingers;
      I played on the headlands   *played* on the fingers: was her favourite
      of the forearm's fire   (*or* caressed her)
      with that land-fishes' bed-land.   *land-fishes*: snakes; their *beds*: gold;
                                    gold-*land*: woman

'That is well composed,' Hallfred said.

They came ashore at Hraunhofn on Melrakkasletta a fortnight before winter, and unloaded the ship.

There was a man named Thord, who was the son of the farmer on Melrakkasletta. He was always challenging the merchants at wrestling, and they generally came off worse against him. Then a bout was arranged between him and Gunnlaug, and the night before, Thord called upon Thor to bring him victory. When they met the next day, they began to wrestle.

Gunnlaug swept both Thord's legs out from under him, and his opponent fell down hard, but Gunnlaug twisted his own ankle out of joint when he put his weight on that leg, and he fell down with Thord.

'Maybe your next fight won't go any better,' Thord said.

'What do you mean?' Gunnlaug asked.

'I'm talking about the quarrel you'll be having with Hrafn when he marries Helga the Fair at the Winter Nights. I was there when it was arranged at the Althing this summer.'

Gunnlaug did not reply. Then his foot was bandaged and the joint reset. It was badly swollen.

Hallfred and Gunnlaug rode south with ten other men, and arrived at Gilsbakki in Borgarfjord on the same Saturday evening that the others were sitting down to the wedding feast at Borg. Illugi was glad to see his son Gunnlaug and his companions. Gunnlaug said that he wanted to ride down to Borg there and then, but Illugi said that this was not wise. Everyone else thought so too, except Gunnlaug, but he was incapacitated by his foot – although he did not let it show – and so the journey did not take place. In the morning, Hallfred rode home to Hreduvatn in Nordurardal. His brother Galti, who was a splendid fellow, was looking after their property there.

II   Now we turn to Hrafn, who was sitting down to his wedding feast at Borg. Most people say that the bride was rather gloomy. It is true that, as the saying goes, 'things learned young last longest', and that was certainly the case with her just then.

It so happened that a man named Sverting, who was the son of Goat-Bjorn, the son of Molda-Gnup, asked for the hand of Hungerd, the daughter of Thorodd and Jofrid. The wedding was to take place up at Skaney later in the winter, after Yule. A relative of Hungerd's, Thorkel the son of Torfi Valbrandsson, lived at Skaney. Torfi's mother was Thorodda, the sister of Tunga-Odd.

Hrafn went home to Mosfell with his wife Helga. One morning, when they had been living there for a little while, Helga was lying awake before they got up, but Hrafn was still sleeping. His sleep was rather fitful, and when he woke up, Helga asked him what he had been dreaming about. Then Hrafn spoke this verse:

12.   I thought I'd been stabbed
       by a yew of serpent's dew   *serpent's dew*: blood; its *yew* (twig):
       and with my blood, O my bride,   sword
       your bed was stained red.
       Beer-bowl's goddess, you weren't   *beer-bowl's goddess*: woman (Helga)
       able to bind up the damage
       that the drubbing-thorn dealt to Hrafn: *drubbing-thorn*: sword
       linden of herbs, that might please you.   *linden* (tree) *of herbs*: woman

'I will never weep over that,' Helga said. 'You have all tricked me wickedly. Gunnlaug must have come back.' And then Helga wept bitterly.

Indeed, a little while later news came of Gunnlaug's return. After this, Helga grew so intractable towards Hrafn that he could not keep her at home, and so they went back to Borg. Hrafn did not enjoy much intimacy with her.

Now people were making plans for the winter's other wedding. Thorkel from Skaney invited Illugi the Black and his sons. But while Illugi was getting ready, Gunnlaug sat in the main room and did not make any move towards getting ready himself.

Illugi went up to him and said, 'Why aren't you getting ready, son?'

'I don't intend to go,' Gunnlaug replied.

'Of course you will go, son,' Illugi said. 'And don't set so much store by yearning for just one woman. Behave as though you haven't noticed, and you'll never be short of women.'

Gunnlaug did as his father said, and they went to the feast. Illugi and his sons were given one high seat, and Thorstein Egilsson, his son-in-law Hrafn and the bridegroom's group had the other one, opposite Illugi. The women were sitting on the cross-bench, and Helga the Fair was next to the bride. She often cast her eyes in Gunnlaug's direction, and so it was proved that, as the saying goes, 'if a woman loves a man, her eyes won't hide it'. Gunnlaug was well turned out, and had on the splendid clothes which King Sigtrygg had given him. He seemed far superior to other men for many reasons, what with his strength, his looks and his figure.

People did not particularly enjoy the wedding feast. On the same day as the men were getting ready to leave, the women started to break up their party, too, and began getting themselves ready for the journey home. Gunnlaug went to talk to Helga, and they chatted for a long time. Then Gunnlaug spoke this verse:

13. For Serpent-tongue no full day
     under mountains' hall was easy   *mountains' hall*: sky
     since Helga the Fair
     took the name of Hrafn's Wife.
     But her father, white-faced
     wielder of whizzing spears,
     took no heed of my tongue.
     – the goddess was married for money.

And he spoke another one, too:

14. Fair wine-goddess, I must reward   *wine-goddess*: woman (Helga)
     your father for the worst wound –
     the land of the flood-flame steals joy   *flood-flame*: gold; its *land*: woman
     from this poet – and also your mother.
     For beneath bedclothes they both
     made a band-goddess so beautiful: *band-goddess*: woman wearing
     the devil take the handiwork   garments of woven bands (Helga)
     of that bold man and woman!

And then Gunnlaug gave Helga the cloak Ethelred had given him, which was very splendid. She thanked him sincerely for the gift.

Then Gunnlaug went outside. By now, mares and stallions – many of them fine animals – had been led into the yard, saddled up and tethered there. Gunnlaug leapt on to one of the stallions and rode at a gallop across the hayfield to where Hrafn was standing. Hrafn had to duck out of his way.

'There's no need to duck, Hrafn,' Gunnlaug said, 'because I don't mean to do you any harm at the moment, though you know what you deserve.'

Hrafn answered with this verse:

15. Glorifier of battle-goddess,   *battle-goddess*: valkyrie; her *glorifier*:
     god of the quick-flying weapon,   warrior; *god of the . . . weapon*: warrior
     it's not fitting for us to fight
     over one fair tunic-goddess.   *tunic-goddess*: woman
     Slaughter-tree, south over sea   *Slaughter-tree*: warrior
     there are many such women,
     you will rest assured of that.
     I set my wave-steed to sail.   *wave-steed*: ship

'There may well be a lot of women,' Gunnlaug replied, 'but it doesn't look that way to me.'

Then Illugi and Thorstein ran over to them, and would not let them fight each other. Gunnlaug spoke a verse:

16.	The fresh-faced goddess	
	of the serpent's day	*serpent's day* (i.e. brightness): gold;
	was handed to Hrafn for pay –	its *goddess*: woman
	he's equal to me, people say –	
	while in the pounding of steel	*pounding of steel*: battle
	peerless Ethelred delayed	
	my journey from the east – that's why	
	the jewel-foe's less greedy for words.	*jewel-foe*: generous man (Gunnlaug)

After that, both parties went home, and nothing worth mentioning happened all winter. Hrafn never again enjoyed intimacy with Helga after she and Gunnlaug had met once more.

That summer, people made their way to the Althing in large groups: Illugi the Black took his sons Gunnlaug and Hermund with him; Thorstein Egilsson took his son Kollsvein; Onund from Mosfell took all his sons; and Sverting the son of Goat-Bjorn also went. Skafti was still Lawspeaker then.

One day during the Althing, when people were thronging to the Law Rock and the legal business was done, Gunnlaug demanded a hearing and said, 'Is Hrafn Onundarson here?'

Hrafn said that he was.

Then Gunnlaug Serpent-tongue said, 'You know that you have married my intended and have drawn yourself into enmity with me because of it. Now I challenge you to a duel to take place here at the Althing in three days' time on Oxararholm (Axe River Island).'

'That's a fine-sounding challenge,' Hrafn replied, 'as might be expected from you. Whenever you like – I'm quite ready for it!'

Both sets of relatives were upset by this, but, in those days, the law said that anyone who felt he'd received underhand treatment from someone else could challenge him to a duel.

Now when the three days were up, they got themselves ready for the duel. Illugi the Black went to the island with his son, along with a large body of men; and Skafti the Lawspeaker went with Hrafn, as did his father and other relatives. Before Gunnlaug went out on to the island, he spoke this verse:

17. I'm ready to tread the isle
     where combat is tried
     – God grant the poet victory –
     a drawn sword in my hand;
     into two I'll slice the hair-seat   *hair-seat*: head
     of Helga's kiss-gulper;   *Helga's kiss-gulper*: her lover,
     finally, with my bright sword,   Hrafn
     I'll unscrew his head from his neck.

   Hrafn replied with this one:

18. The poet doesn't know
     which poet will rejoice –
     wound-sickles are drawn,   *wound-sickles*: swords
     the edge fit to bite leg.
     Both single and a widow,
     from the Thing the thorn-tray will hear   *thorns*: brooch-pins, its *tray*:
     – though bloodied I might be –   woman
     tales of her man's bravery.

Hermund held his brother Gunnlaug's shield for him; and Sverting, Goat-Bjorn's son, held Hrafn's. Whoever was wounded was to pay three marks of silver to release himself from the duel. Hrafn was to strike the first blow, since he had been challenged. He hacked at the top of Gunnlaug's shield, and the blow was so mightily struck that the sword promptly broke off below the hilt. The point of the sword glanced up and caught Gunnlaug on the cheek, scratching him slightly. Straight away, their fathers, along with several other people, ran between them.

Then Gunnlaug said, 'I submit that Hrafn is defeated, because he is weaponless.'

'And I submit that you are defeated,' Hrafn replied, 'because you have been wounded.'

Gunnlaug got very angry and said, all in a rage, that the matter had not been resolved. Then his father, Illugi, said that there should not be any more resolving for the moment.

'Next time Hrafn and I meet, Father,' Gunnlaug said, 'I should like you to be too far away to separate us.'

With that they parted for the time being, and everyone went back to their booths.

Now the following day, it was laid down as law by the Law Council that all duelling should be permanently abolished. This was done on the advice of all the wisest men at the Althing, and all the wisest men in Iceland were there. Thus the duel which Hrafn and Gunnlaug fought was the last one ever to take place in Iceland. This was one of the three most-crowded Althings of all time, the others being the one after the burning of Njal and the one following the Slayings on the Heath.

One morning, when the brothers Hermund and Gunnlaug were on their way to the Oxara river to wash themselves, several women were going to its opposite bank. Helga the Fair was one of them.

Then Hermund asked Gunnlaug, 'Can you see your girlfriend Helga on the other side of the river?'

'Of course I can see her,' Gunnlaug replied. And then he spoke this verse:

19.   The woman was born to bring war
between men – the tree of the valkyrie   *tree of the valkyrie*: warrior
started it all; I wanted her   (perhaps Hrafn, but more
sorely, that log of rare silver.   probably Thorstein) *log of silver*:
Henceforward, my black eyes   woman
are scarcely of use to glance
at the ring-land's light-goddess,   *ring-land*: hand; its *light*: ring;
splendid as a swan.   *goddess* of the ring: woman

Then they went across the river, and Helga and Gunnlaug chatted for a while. When they went back eastwards across the river, Helga stood and stared at Gunnlaug for a long time. Then Gunnlaug looked back across the river and spoke this verse:

20.* The moon of her eyelash – that valkyrie   *moon*: eye
adorned with linen, server of herb-surf,   *herb-surf*: ale; its *server*: woman
shone hawk-sharp upon me
beneath her brow's bright sky;   *brow's sky*: forehead
but that beam from the eyelid-moon   *beam*: gaze
of the goddess of the golden torque   *goddess of the golden torque*: woman
will later bring trouble to me
and to the ring-goddess herself.   *ring-goddess*: woman

After this had happened, everyone rode home from the Althing, and Gunnlaug settled down at home at Gilsbakki. One morning, when he woke up, everyone was up and about except him. He slept in a bed closet further into the hall than were the benches. Then twelve men, all armed to the teeth, came into the hall: Hrafn Onundarson had arrived. Gunnlaug leapt up with a start, and managed to grab his weapons.

'You're not in any danger,' Hrafn said, 'and you'll hear what brings me here right now. You challenged me to a duel at the Althing last summer, and you thought that the matter was not fully resolved. Now I want to suggest that we both leave Iceland this summer and travel to Norway and fight a duel over there. Our relatives won't be able to stand between us there.'

'Well spoken, man!' Gunnlaug replied. 'I accept your proposal with pleasure. And now, Hrafn, you may have whatever hospitality you would like here.'

'That is a kind offer,' Hrafn replied, 'but, for the moment, we must ride on our way.'

And with that they parted. Both sets of relatives were very upset about this, but, because of their own anger, they could do nothing about it. But what fate decreed must come to pass.

---

* This verse is also found in *Kormak's Saga*, and should probably be attributed to him, not to Gunnlaug.

12 Now we return to Hrafn. He fitted out his ship in Leiruvog. The names of two men who travelled with him are known: they were the sons of his father Onund's sister, one named Grim and the other Olaf. They were both worthy men. All Hrafn's relatives thought it was a great blow when he went away, but he explained that he had challenged Gunnlaug to a duel because he was not getting anywhere with Helga; one of them, he said, would have to perish at the hands of the other.

Hrafn set sail when he got a fair breeze, and they brought the ship to Trondheim, where he spent the winter. He received no news of Gunnlaug that winter, and so he waited there for him all summer, and then spent yet another winter in Trondheim at a place named Levanger.

Gunnlaug Serpent-tongue sailed from Melrakkasletta in the north with Hallfred the Troublesome Poet. They left their preparations very late, and put to sea as soon as they got a fair breeze, arriving in the Orkney Islands shortly before winter.

The islands were ruled by Earl Sigurd Hlodvesson at that time, and Gunnlaug went to him and spent the winter there. He was well respected. During the spring, the earl got ready to go plundering. Gunnlaug made preparations to go with him, and they spent the summer plundering over a large part of the Hebrides and the Scottish firths and fought many battles. Wherever they went, Gunnlaug proved himself to be a very brave and valiant fellow, and very manly. Earl Sigurd turned back in the early part of the summer, and then Gunnlaug took passage with some merchants who were sailing to Norway. Gunnlaug and Earl Sigurd parted on very friendly terms.

Gunnlaug went north to Lade in Trondheim to visit Earl Eirik, arriving at the beginning of winter. The earl gave him a warm welcome, and invited him to stay with him. Gunnlaug accepted the invitation. The earl had already heard about the goings-on between Gunnlaug and Hrafn, and he told Gunnlaug that he would not allow them to fight in his realm. Gunnlaug said that such matters were for the earl to decide. He stayed there that winter, and was always rather withdrawn.

Now one day that spring, Gunnlaug and his kinsman Thorkel went out for a walk. They headed away from the town, and in the fields in front of them was a ring of men. Inside the ring, two armed men were fencing. One had been given the name Gunnlaug, and the other one Hrafn. The bystanders said that Icelanders struck out with mincing blows and were slow to remember their promises. Gunnlaug realized that there was a great deal of contempt in this, that it was a focus for mockery, and he went away in silence.

A little while after this, Gunnlaug told the earl that he did not feel inclined to put up with his followers' contempt and mockery concerning the goings-on between himself and Hrafn any longer. He asked the earl to provide him with guides to Levanger. The earl had already been told that Hrafn had left Levanger and gone across into Sweden, and he therefore gave Gunnlaug permission to go, and found him two guides for the journey.

Then Gunnlaug left Lade with six other men, and went to Levanger. He arrived during the evening, but Hrafn had departed from there with four men the same morning. Gunnlaug went from there into Veradal, always arriving in the evening at the place where Hrafn had been the night before. Gunnlaug pressed on until he reached the innermost farm in the valley, which was named Sula, but Hrafn had left there that morning. Gunnlaug did not break his journey there, however, but pressed on through the night, and they caught sight of each other at sunrise the next day. Hrafn had reached a place where there were two lakes, with a stretch of flat land between them. This area was named Gleipnisvellir (Gleipnir's Plains). A small headland called Dingenes jutted out into one of the lakes. Hrafn's party, which was five strong, took up position on the headland. His kinsmen, Grim and Olaf, were with him.

When they met, Gunnlaug said, 'It's good that we have met now.'

Hrafn said that he had no problem with it himself – 'and now you must choose which you prefer,' he said. 'Either we will all fight, or just the two of us, but both sides must be equal.'

Gunnlaug said that he would be quite happy with either arrangement. Then Hrafn's kinsmen, Grim and Olaf, said that they would not stand by while Gunnlaug and Hrafn fought. Thorkel the Black, Gunnlaug's kinsman, said the same.

Then Gunnlaug told the earl's guides: 'You must sit by and help neither side, and be there to tell the story of our encounter.' And so they did.

Then they fell to, and everyone fought bravely. Grim and Olaf together attacked Gunnlaug alone, and the business between them ended in his killing them both, though he was not himself hurt. Thord Kolbeinsson confirms this in the poem he composed about Gunnlaug Serpent-tongue:

21.   Before reaching Hrafn,
        Gunnlaug hacked down Grim
        and Olaf, men pleased
        with the valkyrie's warm wind;   *valkyrie's warm wind*: battle
        blood-bespattered, the brave one
        was the bane of three bold men;
        the god of the wave-charger   *wave-charger*: ship; its *god*: seafarer,
        dealt death out to men.   man

Meanwhile, Hrafn and Thorkel the Black, Gunnlaug's kinsman, were fighting. Thorkel succumbed to Hrafn, and lost his life. In the end, all their companions fell. Then the two of them, Hrafn and Gunnlaug, fought on, setting about each other remorselessly with heavy blows and fearless counterattacks. Gunnlaug was using the sword which Ethelred had given him, and it was a formidable weapon. In the end, he hacked at Hrafn with a mighty blow, and chopped off his leg. Yet Hrafn did not collapse completely, but dropped back to a tree stump and rested the stump of his leg on it.

'Now you're past fighting,' Gunnlaug said, 'and I will not fight with you, a wounded man, any longer.'

'It is true that things have turned against me, rather,' Hrafn replied, 'but I should be able to hold out all right if I could get something to drink.'

'Don't trick me then,' Gunnlaug replied, 'if I bring you water in my helmet.'

'I won't trick you,' Hrafn said.

Then Gunnlaug went to a brook, fetched some water in his helmet and took it to Hrafn. But as Hrafn reached out his left hand for it, he hacked at Gunnlaug's head with the sword in his right hand, causing a hideous wound.

'Now you have cruelly deceived me,' Gunnlaug said, 'and you have behaved in an unmanly way, since I trusted you.'

'That is true,' Hrafn replied, 'and I did it because I would not have you receive the embrace of Helga the Fair.'

Then they fought fiercely again, and it finished in Gunnlaug's overpowering Hrafn, and Hrafn lost his life right there. Then the earl's guides went over and bound Gunnlaug's head wound. He sat still throughout and spoke this verse:

22.   Hrafn, that bold sword-swinger,
      splendid sword-meeting's tree,   *sword-meeting*: battle; its *tree*: warrior
      in the harsh storm of stingers   *stingers*: spears; *spears' storm*: battle
      advanced bravely against me.
      This morning, many metal-flights   *metal-flights*: thrown weapons
      howled round Gunnlaug's head
      on Dingenes, O ring-birch   *ring-birch*: man
      and protector of ranks.   *protector of ranks*: leader of an army,
                                             warrior

Then they saw to the dead men, and afterwards they put Gunnlaug on his horse and brought him down into Levanger. There he lay for three nights, and received the full rites from a priest before he died. He was buried in the church there. Everyone thought the deaths of both Gunnlaug and Hrafn in such circumstances were a great loss.

13   That summer, before this news had been heard out here in Iceland, Illugi the Black had a dream. He was at home at Gilsbakki at the time. He dreamed that Gunnlaug appeared to him, covered in blood, and spoke this verse to him. Illugi remembered the poem when he woke up, and later recited it to other people:

23.   I know that Hrafn hit me
      with the hilt-finned fish   *fish*: sword (with a hilt for fins)
      that hammers on mail,
      but my sharp edge bit his leg   *corpse-scorer*: eagle, which carves up
      when the eagle, corpse-scorer,   corpses with its beak
      drank the mead of warm wounds.   *mead of wounds*: blood
      The war-twig of valkyrie's thorns   *valkyrie's thorns*: warriors; their
      split Gunnlaug's skull.   *war-twig*: sword

On the same night, at Mosfell in the south, it happened that Onund dreamed that Hrafn came to him. He was all covered in blood, and spoke this verse:

24. My sword was stained with gore,
     but the Odin of swords   *Odin* (god) *of swords*: warrior
     sword-swiped me too; on shields   (Gunnlaug)
     shield-giants were tried overseas.   *shield-giants*: enemies of shields,
     I think there stood blood-stained   i.e. swords
     blood-goslings in blood round my brain.   *blood-goslings*: ravens
     Once more the wound-eager wound-raven
     wound-river is fated to wade.   *wound-river*: blood

At the Althing the following summer, Illugi the Black spoke to Onund at the Law Rock.

'How are you going to compensate me for my son,' he asked, 'since your son Hrafn tricked him when they had declared a truce?'

'I don't think there's any onus on me to pay compensation for him,' Onund replied, 'since I've been so sorely wounded by their encounter myself. But I won't ask you for any compensation for my son, either.'

'Then some of your family and friends will suffer for it,' Illugi answered. And all summer, after the Althing, Illugi was very depressed.

People say that during the autumn, Illugi rode off from Gilsbakki with about thirty men, and arrived at Mosfell early in the morning. Onund and his sons rushed into the church, but Illugi captured two of Onund's kinsmen. One of them was named Bjorn and the other Thorgrim. Illugi had Bjorn killed and Thorgrim's foot cut off. After that, Illugi rode home, and Onund sought no reprisals for this act. Hermund Illugason was very upset about his brother's death, and thought that, even though this had been done, Gunnlaug had not been properly avenged.

There was a man named Hrafn, who was a nephew of Onund of Mosfell's. He was an important merchant, and owned a ship which was moored in Hrutafjord.

That spring, Hermund Illugason rode out from home on his own. He went north over Holtavarda heath, across to Hrutafjord and then over to the merchants' ship at Bordeyri. The merchants were almost ready to leave. Skipper Hrafn was ashore, with several other people. Hermund rode up to him, drove his spear through him and then rode away. Hrafn's colleagues were all caught off-guard by Hermund. No compensation was forthcoming for this killing, and with it the feuding between Illugi the Black and Onund was at an end.

Some time later, Thorstein Egilsson married his daughter Helga to a man named Thorkel, the son of Hallkel. He lived out in Hraunsdal, and Helga went back home with him, although she did not really love him. She could never get Gunnlaug out of her mind, even though he was dead. Still, Thorkel was a decent man, rich and a good poet. They had a fair number of children. One of their sons was named Thorarin, another Thorstein, and they had more children besides.

Helga's greatest pleasure was to unfold the cloak which Gunnlaug had given her and stare at it for a long time. Now there was a time when Thorkel and Helga's household was afflicted with a terrible illness, and many people suffered a long time with it. Helga, too, became ill but did not take to her bed. One Saturday evening, Helga sat in the fire-room, resting her head in her husband Thorkel's lap. She sent for the cloak Gunnlaug's Gift, and when it arrived, she sat up and spread it out in front of her. She stared at it for a while. Then she fell back into her husband's arms, dead. Thorkel spoke this verse:

25.   My Helga, good arm-serpent's staff, *arm-serpent*: gold bracelet; its *staff*:
       dead in my arms I did clasp.   woman
       God carried off the life
       of the linen-Lofn, my wife.   *linen-Lofn* (goddess): woman
       But for me, the river-flash's poor craver, *river-flash*: gold; its *craver*: man
       it is heavier to be yet living.

Helga was taken to the church, but Thorkel carried on living in Hraunsdal. As one might expect, he found Helga's death extremely hard to bear.

And this is the end of the saga.

Translated by KATRINA C. ATTWOOD

THE SAGA OF REF THE SLY

Króka-Refs saga

Time of action: 950–1050
Time of writing: 1350–1400

The Saga of Ref the Sly is a fantastical and often picaresque story, in which themes and motifs from continental European literature are smoothly incorporated into the saga tradition. Ref Steinsson, the hero, emerges from a slothful childhood to become as accomplished a warrior as any classical saga champion; he resorts to weapons in order to avenge obvious injustice or personal insults, but shows as much resourcefulness in avoiding direct confrontation as he does in engaging in it.

Only the opening chapters of the saga are set in Iceland; the main action is in Greenland, Norway and Denmark, before Ref's life ends on a pilgrimage to Rome. The Greenland of *The Saga of Ref the Sly* is not the historical settlement familiar from some sagas, nor the realm of trolls and the supernatural that we know from others, but rather a vague and timeless romance backdrop where the hero's ingenuity and inventiveness are given free rein. History, too, is a secondary consideration, since Ref Steinsson is born while Hakon is king in Norway during the mid-tenth century, but is probably only in his thirties when he visits King Harald the Stern, who died at Stamford Bridge in 1066. The saga has no genealogical underpinning and the list of Ref's noble descendants seems fanciful. Above all, this is a saga of pure entertainment, like the continental romances, yet firmly rooted in the practical realities of the Viking Age world.

Ref is a 'coal-biter' or 'male Cinderella' figure: lazy, unpromising and even considered a simpleton in his youth before suddenly developing into a hero with both brawn and brains – Grettir the Strong is another example of the type, although his life takes a completely different course in manhood. Ref also reveals exceptional skills as a craftsman, first with the boat that he builds and sails from Iceland to escape his pursuers, and later in Greenland with the bizarre fortification and conduit system that he builds in the wilderness. From there he flees to Norway with his wife Helga and three children, after killing Bard and thereby incurring the wrath of King Harald, and again saves his skin with an equally strange work of craftsmanship, this time in words: his kenning-laden riddle confessing that he killed Grani in order to rescue Helga from his clutches.

The hero's name Ref ('Fox') may give an important clue to the saga's provenance, suggesting links with Reynard from continental beast epics. In medieval Europe, this genre served as a powerful tool for expressing criticism of power structures and social injustice, but it is difficult to find any explicit message in *The Saga of Ref the Sly*. The continental beast fable also provided an outlet which could entertain without the shackles of religious dogma, and the world of Ref with its relish for the funny and the peculiar seems closer to the licence which was often granted to animals but denied to men. Certainly, Ref has many qualities in common with his animal namesake: he is sly, wary of fighting until he is sure he can win, motivated above all by his own survival, and devotedly protective towards his family.

The saga is dated towards the end of the fourteenth century and preserved complete in only one manuscript, from the second half of the fifteenth century (AM 471 4to). It is translated here by George Clark, from the text printed in *Íslendinga sögur III* (Reykjavík 1987).

I   In the days of King Hakon, the foster-son of King Athelstan, a man named Stein was living in Breidafjord, at the farm at Kvennabrekka. Thorgerd, his wife, was Oddleif's daughter, and Gest of Bardastrond's sister. Stein was rich and an outstanding farmer. He was very old when the story begins.

They had a son, Ref. He was big for his age, good-looking and hard to manage. No one realized how strong he was. He stuck close to the fire and did no useful work but lolled underfoot where people had to walk. The couple felt that it was a great misfortune that their son was so unwilling to behave like other people. Most people said that he was a fool.

There was a man named Thorbjorn who was rich, overbearing, a great fighter and a trouble-maker. He had lived in every quarter of the country, but the chieftains and the public had expelled him from each district in turn because of his unfairness and his manslaughters. He had not paid compensation for any man he had killed. His wife was named Rannveig; she was stupid and domineering. It was generally felt that Thorbjorn would have committed fewer outrages if she had not driven him on. Now Thorbjorn bought land at Saudafell mountain. Many of those who knew his reputation beforehand were apprehensive about his coming.

Stein's and Thorbjorn's farmsteads were not far apart; the river which ran between their farms was the boundary separating their lands. When Thorbjorn had lived there a while, his livestock began straying into Stein's land because Thorbjorn had many grazing animals.

In due course, Stein conferred with his neighbour, Thorbjorn, and said, 'The situation is this: you've lived in the neighbourhood with me for two years, and our relationship has been good rather than bad, though it's generally said that you are not a popular man. Up until now I've suffered no harm because of you or yours, but now your livestock are straying into my fields and grazing on them. Now I wish that you would improve matters in response to my request and have your livestock watched more closely than has been the case up till now. It could fall out, since I am no liar, that people who may have a quarrel with you will believe what I say. And in a case like that, I'll be able to testify that you have not dealt unfairly with me or wrongly desired what is mine.'

Thorbjorn said that no one had ever spoken so moderately and reasonably with him and that he thought that, if more people had spoken to him about matters that seemed out of order, he would have committed fewer impulsive killings: 'This matter will certainly improve as you ask.'

After this they parted. Thorbjorn had changes made for the better so that his livestock caused Stein no further damage, as he had requested.

2   Sometime later Stein fell ill. He declared that he would not have any more illnesses, saying that this one would single-handedly be his death.

He said to his wife, Thorgerd, 'I want you to sell the land after my death and move west to Bardastrond where your brother Gest lives. I have an inkling that Thorbjorn won't be a quiet neighbour for you, even though the two of us have got on well. I expect that your land will seem more convenient to him for grazing now.'

Then Stein died.

Now Thorgerd did not have the heart to let the land go because it seemed beautiful and good in every respect. And before very long, Thorbjorn's watch over his livestock worsened. Now his animals went into Thorgerd's pastures night and day. The result of this overgrazing was that Thorbjorn's stock devastated Thorgerd's hayfields, and for two winters she had to slaughter livestock for want of hay. Thorgerd often spoke of this with Thorbjorn, requesting that he should watch his livestock better, but it did no good. Then she looked to see if people were interested in buying her land, but no one was keen on living close to Thorbjorn. So the land was not sold.

It is said that there was a man named Bardi in the district, a very small man. He was called Bardi the Short. He was very swift-footed and could run as fast as the best horses. He was sharp-sighted and observant. He herded livestock in summer and was reliable and honest in everything. Thorgerd sought this man out at the Spring Assembly and asked if he would work for her watching over livestock and said that he would have what wages he pleased. She made it clear to him that more often than not he could have to watch out for Thorbjorn's straying livestock and told him the long and the short of the conflict between the two farms.

Bardi answered, 'I would not choose any job other than the one with you, given the way you tell it. It doesn't seem too much for me to protect your land against grazing by other people's livestock.'

So Bardi went home with Thorgerd and began tending the livestock. He built himself two sheds, one at the foot of the mountain and the other in the meadows along the river which ran between the houses. He quartered in that one every night and kept Thorbjorn's livestock from Thorgerd's land so that they never got over the river. He stayed on the bank and from there he kept the livestock off. He never crossed the river.

3   Thorgerd's livestock now gave lots of milk which they had not done the previous summers.

On her part, Rannveig, mistress of the other house, felt that her summer's production was poor. One day she spoke with Thorbjorn and asked where the livestock were put to pasture. He said that they grazed along the river every day.

'Is it at all fitting,' she said, 'that that man should be with Thorgerd to bar our livestock from the pasture they have had in past summers? You've done the wrong thing and left the right undone, Thorbjorn, since you've attacked and killed wholly inoffensive men but allow this nitwit to carry on to our shame by barring our livestock from the pasture they want.'

'Who is this man?' said Thorbjorn.

'His name is Bardi,' said Rannveig. 'He's a miserable, tiny wretch, and he sleeps outside every night and prevents our livestock from crossing the river.'

After that Thorbjorn took his horse and rode across the river and came to the shed where Bardi was.

Then Thorbjorn said, 'Is it true that you keep our livestock from this pasture and beat them so that they don't dare graze near the river? That way we're not getting any milk.'

Bardi answered, 'It's no lie that I never let your livestock come on to our land. But it is not true that I beat them or that I prevent them from grazing on your own land. I think that you won't have any less production than you had your first summer here. And you're getting it more honestly.'

Thorbjorn said, 'It seems to me more likely that you are acting unlawfully than I, because you can be declared an outlaw if our autumn round-up goes short. Now I want you to leave off this work or it just won't do.'

Bardi answered, 'I have often undertaken tending livestock so that I do my job, and so it's always been and will be.'

Then Thorbjorn struck Bardi his death-blow and dragged him into the shed and rode home afterwards and reported what had happened. It seemed to Rannveig that the matter was nicely settled, and immediately she had the livestock driven on to Thorgerd's land. The herd went right into the hayfield, pulled down Thorgerd's haystack and did a lot of damage. She came out and saw the cattle standing around the farmyard. It seemed to her that this meant something terrible had happened, and she sent people to drive the cattle off; they found Bardi lying slain in the shed and reported this news to Thorgerd. Then she went into the fire-room and saw Ref, her son.

Then she said, 'I shudder in my heart whenever I see you before my eyes, you disgrace of a son, and how luckless I was when I bore you, you cretin. It would have been better if my child had been a daughter. I might have married her to a man we could rely on. Even if our land is eaten up or haystacks broken down or our people killed, you, you coward, lie about and act as if we had nothing to attend to.'

Ref got up and said, 'The rest will make hard hearing, mother, if your scolding begins like that.'

Then he took down a big halberd. Stein had kept a good supply of weapons. Then he walked from the farmyard and went along the road, throwing the spear ahead of him and running after it. Thorbjorn's men were at work and saw Ref on his way, knew who he was and jeered loudly. Ref went straight to Thorbjorn's farmhouse, and when he got to the door he saw no one outside. He heard the women in their main room and they were asking if Thorbjorn had awakened. He had lain down to sleep. Ref broke off the lower part of his spear-shaft, then walked in quickly and went along the hall. Thorbjorn heard someone coming and asked who was moving there.

Ref said, 'I'm coming here now.'

'Who are you?' said Thorbjorn.

'Someone from another farm,' said Ref.

'But you've got to have a name,' said Thorbjorn.

'My name is Ref.'

And in that instant, Ref slipped into the bed closet.

Thorbjorn had thrown off the bedclothes and said, 'Age is really getting to me when I don't recognize you. You're very welcome, Ref, but what is your business here?'

Ref said, 'What that will be depends entirely on you.'

'How so?' asked Thorbjorn.

Ref answered, 'I have come to ask compensation for the killing of Bardi, my farmhand. I'll be modest about it and accept what is very little for you to pay and yet honourable for me to receive. It will be to my honour that you value my request since you have killed a humble man.'

Thorbjorn got dressed quickly and said, 'Your request is good and it might be that I will pay some compensation, but it's no less likely that I will neither pay damages for him nor for anyone else.'

Ref said, 'It's more appropriate that you pay something.'

Thorbjorn said, 'You speak so well that something has to be forthcoming.'

He was all dressed then, and reached down beneath the bed-frame and brought up a large, single-edged knife with a whetstone.

Then Thorbjorn took a sword in one hand and offered the knife and whetstone to Ref saying, 'One should offer an untempered blade to a softy.'

At the instant, Ref thrust his spear through Thorbjorn's mid-section. Thorbjorn fell backwards. He had not been able to draw the sword because the safety band was still fastened and it all happened quickly. Ref closed the door to the bed closet and headed for the front door. At that moment, the door to the main room opened. There was a large pile of driftwood in front of the main door. Ref decided to jump into the woodpile because he knew Thorbjorn's men were near the road and would notice him at once if he headed for home. The women had heard men talking and were curious. Then they saw blood running along the floor. They called for the farmhands and when they arrived, they saw Thorbjorn had been killed. They searched for Ref and did not find him. No one thought they had seen him going home. The search was given up that evening.

Then Ref got out of the woodpile and went home. He awakened his mother and asked her to come outside. When they were out of the house, she asked if Thorbjorn had paid any compensation for Bardi's killing.

Ref spoke in verse:

1. The squanderer of the sea's fire   *sea's fire*: gold; its *squanderer*:
   today offered me a broad untempered   generous man
   blade and a whetstone with it that was
   too little to take as compensation.
   So, with the wounding serpent   *wounding serpent*: spear
   in my hand, I probed the path
   to his heart and killed
   that free-spending man.

'Well said and bravely done,' she replied. 'Now take the two horses beside the farmyard and bring them to me.'

One horse was saddled and the other fitted with packs full of valuable goods. Then Ref took good clothes. Now he seemed like a very valiant man.

Then Thorgerd said, 'There's a man named Grim who lives near here in a valley on our land. He'll be your guide. I will send you west to Bardastrond to my brother. I want you to stay there until this killing has been settled.'

4   Ref set out and did not stop until he reached Hagi where he got a hearty welcome. When the two kinsmen began talking, Gest asked if he had any news to report. Ref said he had not.

'But do you know any?' Gest asked.

Ref said it was not unlikely that he did and told what he was involved in. Gest said that he would certainly shelter him and asked if he were a master in some skill. Ref said that was not the case at all.

Gest said, 'I can see that you are potentially a master of something and I'll soon see what it is.'

Ref stayed there for some time.

In due course, Gest came to Ref and said, 'Now I know what your gift is. You will be a master craftsman if you wish. I've noticed when you started cutting a bobbin for yarn that it was always cut true, neither twisted nor rough. And of the things you've put your hand to, that carving was the most adroitly done.'

'That could be,' said Ref, 'but I've never built anything.'

Gest said, 'I'd like to put this to the test. I want you to make me a boat for sealing.'

Ref said, 'Get enough and more of tools and material because lots of people, when a project doesn't turn out well, blame the outcome on inadequate supplies. Moreover, I don't want anyone to know about this project because if it turns out well people will probably say that somebody came and taught me how to do it.'

Then Gest had a big boat-shed built and a great deal of timber brought up. A knorr had wrecked on Gest's beach and he had bought all the ship's timbers. Gest had all this timber brought to Ref's shed along with the ship nails. Gest also had a supply of unwrought iron, and Ref said he wanted that brought and said he would forge ship nails for himself. Gest had all kinds of tools brought there as well as a forge and charcoal.

Then Gest said, 'Now I have had everything brought to your shed so that nothing more would be needed, even if you built a cargo vessel capable of sailing to other lands.'

Ref said that Gest could do no more however the project turned out.

Then Ref started work. He rose early and came home late and this went on for three months.

One morning, Gest sent his most trusted man to the shed telling him to find out how the sealing-boat was going – he said that it was probably ready though he knew little about it. The man who was sent got there without Ref's noticing and looked the work over thoroughly. Then he went home and told Gest that a sealing-boat like that would seldom be seen – 'because a bigger ship than that has never come here to Iceland'.

Gest told him to say nothing about it. Two more months passed.

5   One morning when Gest had got up, he saw that Ref was lying in bed. Gest reached out and nudged him, and said, 'You're sleeping late, nephew. Is the sealing-boat ready?'

'You could say,' said Ref, 'that she'll float and I won't do any more until you've seen her.'

'We'll go there today,' said Gest, 'and look at this job.'

Gest went to the shed with only a few people because he did not want it generally known if the project was bungled. When he arrived, there stood a thoroughly seaworthy cargo vessel. Gest inspected the ship very carefully, and Ref's skill seemed all the more remarkable to him since he had never built a ship before.

Gest thanked Ref for the ship-building then and said, 'Now I want to pay you for the ship by giving it to you.'

Ref said that he would gladly accept it.

Word that Ref Steinsson had built an ocean-going cargo vessel went round. This seemed extraordinary news since Ref was generally regarded as a simpleton. It had happened that a Norwegian and his son had once lodged with Ref's father. Ref and the visitor's son were of the same age. The boy had, as a plaything, a Norwegian toy ship made exactly like an ocean-going vessel. When the Norwegian's son went away, he gave Ref this ship which he had for amusement in the fire-room and as a model for his ship-building.

Then the winter passed and the games began.

There was a man named Gellir. He was very much a traveller and spent alternate years in Norway and in Iceland. He was very boisterous and much given to good times. His mother lived nearby at a farm named Hlid. Her name was Sigrid and she was very rich. Her husband was dead, hence Gellir was named Sigridarson. Gellir was very active in sports and was the most competitive of those involved. One day, Gellir went to play with some men at Hagi. Gellir asked if Ref would like to go with him. Ref said he was not suited for sports and would not go. Gellir asked if Ref wanted to excuse himself from going by wrestling with him. Ref said that he would not do that.

Gellir leapt from the saddle and attacked Ref saying, 'For shame! You say you won't wrestle when I want to. Now you'll have to wrestle even though you don't want to.'

He tried every way to throw Ref and could not get him down. Ref fended him off while Gellir pressed his attack with all his strength. But when Gellir went at him less strongly, Ref grasped Gellir with one hand on his belt and the other between his shoulder-blades and threw him on to the frozen ground a short distance away. Gellir came down on his elbows and skinned them both; his face went livid. He sprang up at once, jumped into the saddle, grasped his spear, raised the shaft and struck at Ref. The blow landed on his shoulders and bounced off and hit him on the head. He was not injured. Gellir and his companions galloped off and bragged a lot about it. Gellir claimed that he had struck Ref two great blows and went around with the story saying that Ref would not avenge it. Ref acted as if he did not know. Gest was not home when this happened.

6   After the Yule celebrations, Ref tarred his ship and readied it. Gest brought him all the rigging. It is said that Gellir was on the way from home and his road lay next to the shed and he looked at the ship. One man was travelling with him. Ref heard that Gellir had come by and ran out from under the ship with his adze and went for Gellir.

Ref said, 'Now I'll repay you for two blows with one.'

The blow caught him in the side and went into the body cavity. Gellir fell dead to the ground and his companion rode away.

Ref went home and met Gest who said, 'You look like fortune's favourite, nephew, what's the news?'

Ref spoke in verse:

2.   The goddess of shields was reddened   *goddess of shields:* ogress, i.e. axe
      in Gellir's gore.
      The stroke this day was struck,
      I felled the famous man.   ◆
      I reckon two blows revenged
      and hot blood won for the raven.
      Such deeds are told in stories,
      related by wise men.

'Very well done,' said Gest. 'When I heard it widely reported that Gellir had struck you two blows, I would have preferred that you respond like this. And what are your plans now?'

Ref said, 'I intend to steer my ship to Greenland.'

Gest said, 'You've chosen to do as I would wish because there would be no peace for you in Norway when this killing becomes known. Now I'll supply you with a crew for your ship and give you the goods you'll need to have. And later your mother and I will divide things up as seems good to us.'

Then Ref got his ship ready and manly farmers' sons came forward to follow him. Gest sent him on his way with generous gifts at their parting.

When they parted, Gest said, 'If it turns out you are not destined to come back to Iceland, I wish that you would have a story written about your journey, because it will seem noteworthy to some people since I think you are the second wise man to appear in our family. And surely you are destined for great achievements. And I call on the One Who Made the Sun to strengthen you for good ends now and in the future.'

Ref thanked Gest for his words.

Then they parted and Ref put out to sea. The voyage went well until they caught sight of Greenland, but then they were tossed about and driven north along the coast. In time they came to a fjord in the uninhabited north. On both sides of the fjord, glaciers reached south and out into the sea. Because they had been tossed about at sea, they were keen for land. They cast anchor. Ref rowed ashore and went up the highest mountain to look around. He saw that the fjord reached far into the land and two headlands ran into the fjord from the opposite shores. He went back to his ship. In the morning, he commanded the crew to take the ship in as far as the fjord reached. They did so and when they reached the headlands they saw a big, long fjord started there. When they reached the end of it, there was a good harbour. The hillsides were covered with forests and the shores were green. Glaciers girded it on both sides. There was plenty of game, driftwood on every shore and good fishing. At that time, they could not continue to the settlement. They built a large hall and settled comfortably into it. Ref built a large ferry and got it ready for the voyage to the settlement in the spring, and then they housed the trading vessel.

Afterwards they sailed to the settlement and came into a little bay. Not far from there was a farm. A man named Bjorn lived there. He was married and had one daughter who was named Helga. She was attractive and intelligent and was accounted the most desirable match in that settlement. Ref did not sell his goods but took up building. Bjorn met Ref and asked if he would contract to put up buildings on Bjorn's farm. Ref agreed to that and they fixed the terms. Then Ref set to work and built a splendid farmhouse. That farm is named Hlid.

On the other side of the headland stood the farm named Vik. A man named Thorgils lived there. He was nicknamed Vikarskalli (Baldy from Vik). He was malicious, slanderous and cunning. He was a very difficult person, and people thought it was bad to have dealings with him. He was in his old age and married. His oldest son was named Thengil, the second Orm, the third Thorstein, the fourth Geir. His daughter was named Olof. She was married to a man named Gunnar. Thengil had asked for the hand of Helga, but she did not want to marry him.

At this time, Ref was with Bjorn constructing buildings for his farm, and he asked for the hand of Helga. Bjorn was agreeable. Thormod was one of Bjorn's workers and Helga's foster-father. He was eager to see the match made, and so it came about that the woman was engaged to Ref and the date for the wedding feast was set. The match was made with the condition that Ref and Helga would take over the farm and Bjorn would live with them but without control of the property.

The next spring, Ref took over the farm and acquired many possessions very quickly. He made a great deal of money by building. Helga was a woman with a mind of her own. When Ref and Helga had been together a short time, Bjorn died. Soon afterwards Ref and Helga were granted children. They had a son named Stein. Two years later they had a second named Bjorn. The brothers were very promising.

Ref lived in Greenland for eight years at the same homestead. During those years, he had a ship, a large ferry, under construction: the boat-shed was out on the headland separating Vik and Hlid. He went out to the boat early and came home late. Each night he locked up his adze in the boat-shed and went home unarmed.

7   One evening he went home like that as usual. Ref was able to see a polar bear was up ahead on the headland. The bear quickened his pace when he saw a single man. Then it seemed to Ref that he had acted imprudently. There was new-fallen snow on the ground and it was easy to follow tracks wherever they led. Ref did not see that he had the means to take the bear on unarmed. He turned back to the boat-shed and took his

adze, locked the boat-shed up and then went to the place where the bear had been and it was dead. The brothers, Thorgils's sons, had defeated the bear when they came in from fishing. Ref went on home then.

At this point in the story, the Thorgilssons came home. Their father asked them how the fishing had gone. They said they had got no fish – 'but we got a polar bear'.

Thorgils said, 'You made a wonderful contribution to the support of our household – few would have made a catch like that.'

Thengil said, 'We probably wouldn't have got anything at all if Ref the Timorous hadn't revealed his manliness. I don't think that a fainter heart has come to Greenland than the one in his breast, because a man's tracks run from the boat-shed to the headland and then turn back, and there was piss splattered in the footprints.'

Thengil then said many slanderous things about Ref. Thorgils, his father, was silent.

Thengil then asked why he did not reply: 'Father, don't you know who Ref the Effeminate is?'

Thorgils said, 'It's bad even to speak of such things, and Greenland will always have to blush when it hears Ref named; when he first came here, I saw that Greenland had already been affected by a great scandal. I've had little to do with him because when I was in Iceland he was not like other men in his nature. On the contrary, he was a woman every ninth day and needed a man, and for that reason he was called Ref the Gay and stories of his unspeakable perversions went around constantly. Now I'd like for you to have nothing to do with him.'

And then they left off this talk and went to butcher the bear. But Thorgils's sons repeated this slander everywhere they went and also invented a story that Ref had been sent away from Iceland because of his homosexuality and had been paid a sum of money to go away. They talked this slander so much that it became a commonplace and Ref heard of it. He acted as if he did not know, but he got the ship that he had under construction ready and in the best order possible. He had much of his livestock slaughtered and sold some for Greenland wares. He held a great autumn feast and invited his friends and quietly sold his land for cash. He agreed that he would vacate the land within six months and would give the buyers notice. He had many strong followers, twelve at least. Ref had become very rich. All this happened at hay-time.

8 One day Thormod came to talk with Ref and said, 'Nearly everyone credits a vicious story about you, and Thorgils and his sons started it. And when I urged that the match between you and Helga be made it seemed to us that we were marrying her to a capable man, and so I think you are. But it seems to me that you almost confirm the story spread by bad men when you leave them in peace. And now I ask that you make them blame themselves for their slander.'

Ref answered, 'A man should have his plans worked out before he enters into great undertakings or incites others to them.'

Then they broke off this talk, and Ref set to work and forged himself a huge spear. One could cut or thrust with it. He fitted it with a short shaft which he covered with iron. Then he sharpened it to an edge that would cut whiskers.

When much of the day had passed, Ref left home alone. He had no weapon other than the spear. He went to Vik and arrived there late in the day. Thorgils was in the kitchen cooking. Ref went there and Thorgils asked who it was. Ref announced himself.

Thorgils said, 'There's a lot of smoke in my eyes so I don't recognize you, but you are welcome.'

Ref said, 'Thanks for that.'

Thorgils said, 'What's your business here?'

Ref said, 'I've come to ask compensation for the slanders you've uttered about me.'

Thorgils said, 'When have we spoken ill of you and what is the slander you blame on us?'

Ref repeated the words.

Then Thorgils said, 'I won't deny that we say many things as jokes, but in any case this isn't lying because I believe that every word of this is true.'

Then Ref struck at him with the spear and split him open down to the shoulders. Then he yanked the spear out and walked down to the shore and sat in the boat-house belonging to the brothers, Thorgils's sons. It had got quite dark. Then he heard the sound of oars. When the brothers reached the shore, Thengil leapt from the boat, walked ashore and was about to look for rollers in the boat-house. But when he got there, Ref struck off his head. Thorstein leapt from the boat knowing nothing of this because it was so dark that he could not see to the boat-house. Thorstein took the oars and carried them ashore. When he got to the boat-house, Ref thrust the spear through him.

At that moment Thorstein called out: 'Save yourselves, boys! Our brother Thengil has been killed and I'm run through.'

Orm grasped the oars from the other boat and pushed their ship out. They rowed off and around the headland to Ref's boat-shed, went ashore and thought that Ref would not look for them there. But when they had dragged the ship ashore, Ref came and killed them both.

After that, Ref went home and ordered his men to carry goods and provisions to his ship. Then he had his ferry loaded. It was broad daylight by the time all the goods Ref wanted to take with him were loaded into the ship. Then he chose gifts for the young men who had been with him and asked them to be ready to accompany him when he called on them, whenever that should be. They agreed wholeheartedly to that. Ref then sent word to those who had bought his land that they should take possession of it.

Then Ref, his wife and his sons went aboard the ferry. Stein was nine at the time and Bjorn was seven. The third was named Thormod, and he was three then. Helga's foster-father Thormod was to go also. When the wind stood from the land, Ref ran up the sail, so they put out to sea that day.

For a time, they are out of the story.

9   And now the story turns back to the point where the people of Thorgils' household grieved long and loudly over him when he was killed. In the evening, they went to the shore and found Thengil and Thorstein slain there, and in the morning they found the other two slain. This news went all around and few grieved for Thorgils or his sons. It was regarded as quite a job to be done by one man in one evening, and Ref was thought to have avenged the slander sharply.

Gunnar, Thorgils' son-in-law, heard this news and had watches set at every headland around both settlements in case anyone should catch sight of Ref in the autumn. The property could not be seized because it had all been sold. Gunnar was the leading man in the Western Settlement. There was no news of Ref anywhere. In the spring, Gunnar sent men north into the wilderness to search for Ref, but he was not found and nobody heard anything of him. Gunnar began to think that Ref had perished, since he had taken a ship with only six people, none of them able-bodied. Now four years passed without any word of Ref, and the search for him was abandoned. People thought that surely he had been lost at sea or had driven his ship into the wilderness.

And now we will leave this matter for a while.

10   While these events – and Ref's upbringing – were going on, many
changes took place in the rule of Norway. King Harald Sigurdarson
had succeeded to the kingdom.

In the king's retinue was a man named Bard. He was a follower of the
king's. In summers he made trading voyages to various lands, Iceland or the
British Isles, and so he did the summer we are speaking of now. He got his
ship ready and intended to go out to Iceland. The king had Bard summoned
to him and asked where he intended to steer his ship.

'To Iceland,' said Bard.

The king said, 'I want you to proceed otherwise. You are to sail out to
Greenland and bring us walrus ivory and ship ropes.'

Bard said that the king would decide.

After that, Bard put out to sea and his voyage went extremely well. He
reached Greenland and arranged to winter with Gunnar. And when he had
been there a while, Bard brought the matter up and asked Gunnar how
much truth there was in the story he had heard that an Icelander had
single-handedly killed a father and four sons in one evening and so avenged
the slander regarding him they had made up. Gunnar said something like
that had happened. Bard asked what had become of this man.

'We think,' said Gunnar, 'that he was lost because he was so frightened
that with six others he sailed into the open sea at the onset of winter.'

Bard asked what had gone on among those involved. Gunnar then told
what he knew.

Bard said, 'I would be astonished if that man who escaped your clutches
by the power of his good luck would have sunk. It seems to me that his luck
left him sooner than was to be expected if that happened. Now, have you
searched the wildernesses?'

Gunnar said that they had searched wherever it seemed possible for
people to stay and still further.

Bard said, 'How could he go out on the open sea at the beginning of
winter with only a few people in a ferry? I suppose it seems better to you
to say something like that when Thorgils and his sons are unavenged. I
want you to get a ship ready for us in early spring and we'll travel the
wildernesses, and I surely believe that if I don't find him, it'll confirm that
he was lost.'

Gunnar said that so it should be. Now winter passed. As soon as the ice
broke up, Gunnar got ready for his expedition. They had a ferry and seven
men. They steered for the wildernesses and searched in every hidden bay

and found nothing that seemed to have been a human habitation. Bard was a very sharp-sighted man.

One evening, they came to a large fjord which wound its way inland with many turns. Then it ended. They anchored for the night in a bay. Bard rowed ashore in a boat. He walked up the headland at the mouth of the fjord and looked all around. It was a bright clear night. A breeze was blowing from the sea down the fjord. He saw a raft of kelp driven down the fjord to its head, but then it completely disappeared. Bard wondered about that, and he walked all the way down the lip of the headland, and there he saw another fjord, which was wide and long, begin there. And he saw a large and beautiful valley running up to the mountains. Then he went back to the ship and lay down.

That morning, Bard asked Gunnar if they had explored the whole fjord. Gunnar said they had. Bard said that he wanted to go all the way to where it ended. And so they did, and then they came to the place where the two headlands jutted out from the opposite sides of the fjord. A sound ran between the headlands. It was quite narrow but very deep. Then the fjord opened up again and that inner fjord was very long. They came into a bay late in the evening. The crew didn't want to explore the land, and they all lay down except for Bard. He quickly launched a boat and made for shore and then walked along the water's edge alone until he came to a great pile of shavings. He picked up a shaving and took it with him and then went back to the ship.

In the morning, Bard showed Gunnar the shaving and said, 'I've never in my life seen a shaving cut so skilfully. Was Ref something of a craftsman?'

Gunnar answered, 'He was a master craftsman.'

Bard said, 'I would think, in that case, that we must look for Ref as if he were alive.'

Now they and some others went from the ship. Soon they were able to see where a fortification stood near the edge of the shore. They went up to it and around it and considered it carefully, and they thought that they had never seen such a beautiful building. It was large and strongly built, untarred, and with four corners. They did not see one board overlapping another anywhere; it seemed to be made all of one plank.

And while they were surveying the fortification, a man appeared on the wall. He was of large stature. He greeted Gunnar, who acknowledged the welcome. They recognized him as Ref. He asked where they intended to go.

Bard answered, 'No farther this way.'

Ref asked the news. Bard said that no one would tell him. Then Ref said that one should not ask more than would be thought fitting.

Bard ordered them to drag wood up to the fortification. When the wood was piled all around it, they set it on fire. The wood kindled quickly. But they saw that it promptly went out. They dragged up wood to the fortification anew. Then they saw that a great stream of water came from the fortification and put the fire out. They searched all around the fortification and found no source of water. They built a fire up to the top of the fortification, but as much water came from the top as from the bottom.

Ref appeared on the wall and spoke: 'Is the assault on the fortification going badly?'

Bard spoke: 'You can certainly boast about your witchcraft because we will go back for now. But I promise that if you dare to stay here for another spring, Gunnar and I will have your head at our feet.'

Ref spoke: 'It isn't your destiny nor the destiny of the men of Greenland to guard my corpse, even if I stay here as many years as I have already unless you have the help of wiser men than yourselves.'

11   After that, Bard and Gunnar went to their ship with their men and made for the settlement. In the autumn, they reached the Western Settlement, and Bard spent a second winter with Gunnar.

The next summer, Bard fitted out his ship for Norway and Gunnar gave him gifts. Gunnar sent three valuable possessions to King Harald. The first was a full-grown and very well-trained polar bear. The second was a board game skilfully made of walrus ivory. The third was a walrus skull with all its teeth. It was engraved all over and was extensively inlaid with gold. All the teeth were fast in the skull. That was a splendid treasure.

12   Bard put out to sea and his voyage went well. He came to the ports he would have chosen to visit. He brought many excellent Greenland wares to King Harald.

One day, Bard came before the king and said, 'Here is a board game which the most honourable man in Greenland sent you. His name is Gunnar and he wants no money for it; rather he wants your friendship. I spent two years with him and he was a good fellow to me. He is very eager to be your friend.'

The board game was both for the old game with one king and the new with two.*

The king examined the set for a time and ordered him to thank the one who sent him such a gift: 'We certainly must reciprocate with our friendship.'

Not long after this, Bard had the polar bear led into the hall and before the king. The king's followers were delighted with the bear.

Bard spoke: 'My lord,' he said, 'this animal has been sent to you by Gunnar of Greenland.'

The king spoke: 'This man's gifts are splendid, but what does he want from us in return?'

'Quite simply, my lord, your friendship and wise counsel.'

'Why would that not be appropriate?' said the king.

One day in the course of that winter, Bard requested that the king go to his meeting room. The king did so.

When they were there, Bard brought the head with all its splendour before the king and spoke: 'That very noble man, Gunnar of Greenland, sends this treasure to you.'

The king inspected the head carefully and said that the gift seemed excellent to him and ordered Bard to take care of it.

Then the king spoke: 'Now, Bard, tell me what is behind these gifts – now I know that there is more to it than a matter of friendship only.'

Bard spoke: 'It's just as I said to you, my lord. He wishes to have your friendship and your wise counsel on taking a fox who has done the people of Greenland great harm.'

The king asked what sort of a fox that might be.

Bard said, 'There's an Icelander who killed a father and four sons in a single evening and then sailed into the wilderness with six others, and there he built a fortification out of large timbers. We found him and fired his fortification, but water gushed from all parts of the fortification and put out the fire. There was as much water at the top and the middle as at the bottom. But we found no source of water.'

The king spoke: 'Is this the Ref – or Fox – who built a trading vessel out in Iceland though he had never seen one and in that ship sailed to Greenland,

---

* The 'new' game with two kings is a version of chess. In the old game with one king, the attacking pieces attempt to surround the king so that he cannot move. If that happens, the attacking player wins. The king, with the help of his pieces, attempts to reach one of the four castles in the corners of the board. If the king does so, the defending player wins.

643

and when he had been living there for some years, a great slander regarding him was made up and he avenged it so boldly that he killed five men in a single evening?'

Bard answered, 'We're talking about the same man.'

The king asked what the lie of the land was there, and Bard described it in exact detail.

'Whatever else, such are real men,' the king said.

Bard spoke: 'At our parting, he said that no one would be able to drive him away from there.'

'That could be,' said the king, 'but it could be that he said something quite different. But I will advise you,' said the king, 'not to go there again, because if you do, you won't be coming back.'

Bard answered, 'I have promised Gunnar I would and I can't break my promise.'

Then they ended this talk. The winter wore on.

13 In the spring, Bard fitted out his ship and when it was ready, he went to meet with the king and spoke: 'My lord,' he said, 'have you considered Gunnar's necessity?'

The king spoke: 'I have considered the necessity that you not go to Greenland because you are under no obligation to anger a man who has done you no evil which you should avenge. I have a premonition that the outcome will be bad for you if you go.'

Bard answered, 'You will prophesy more accurately in other matters, my lord.'

The king spoke: 'On the contrary, I think that if this one fails, I will seldom prophesy rightly. But if you really intend to go, then I will give you two some advice, if you and Gunnar think it is really important.'

'I am not the one to decide that,' said Bard.

'Then,' said the king, 'I will suppose that in the little valley that runs up to the glacier there is a lake. Ref probably made a conduit by laying down timber pipes, one after another, until the water reached the lowest-lying corner of the fortification. There, I suppose, are two timber pipes and the water will flow from the one into both, which then fill both sections of the fortification with water. The whole fortification is made of hollow timbers, and every timber connects with the one below and with the one above, so that they fill the whole wall, from top to bottom, with water. In this way, I believe, the system supplies the water. And it seemed to you that there were

no joins in the wood of the wall where the water gushed out everywhere around the fortification because, I believe, he has drilled holes in the timbers, and these are so small that only the wood that can be shaved thinnest can close them, and I surmise that he has used this wood for all the timbers of the wall. And I suppose that all of these twig-like plugs are connected to and withdrawn by a mechanism that he moved only a little when he wanted water to flow from the wall. All these plugs have been skilfully made, and one kind of wood will have been used in making the plugs and timbers.

'Now my advice for Gunnar is that you should go north in two ships, twelve in each. One crew should dig a ditch as long as the fortification is wide, north of it, and quite deep enough to reach up to a man's armpits, and then they will probably find the arrangement for the stream of water. And if it is like that, they can cut off the flow so that it does not supply water to the fortification. The other twelve men should carry wood to the fortification. After that it would seem likely to me that you can burn the fortification because of the water. And now I have given such advice that I promise Gunnar that either Ref will flee the fortification and Greenland or Gunnar will be able to capture him. I am unable to see how he can get away if all this is done, unless he has great cunning in his heart. But I would not wish that you go, Bard, because I don't know what you will bring back from Ref's place.'

Bard said that it could not be otherwise and thanked the king for his advice and cast off from his moorings.

14 To go back to him, Ref was living in the wilderness. His sons became very capable men. This same spring, Ref sent them south to the settlement to meet with those men who had promised him their support as was told before. The brothers went secretly and Gunnar got no intelligence of their movements. When his friends received Ref's messages, they were glad and went at once to meet with him. Then Ref proceeded to have the ship he had sailed from Iceland launched. The boat-shed and tar had protected it so well that it was as tight as a bucket. Then, Ref had the ship loaded with Greenland goods, walrus-hide ropes, walrus ivory and furs. As soon as the ship was ready, they sailed it north into the next fjord and anchored it in a hidden bay. On board were Helga, Ref's wife, Thormod their son and her foster-father Thormod, and the twelve men who came from the settlement. Ref said that he and his older sons would stay in the fortification for a while.

It should be reported that Bard's voyage went extremely well. He made his landfall in Greenland exactly where he would have chosen. Gunnar welcomed Bard joyfully. They immediately assigned men to attend to Bard's cargo, and set off at once for the wilderness with the number of men the king had specified. Now they were familiar with the territory and quickly found their way to the fjord where Ref's fortification stood. Gunnar landed his ship in the outer reach of the fjord because it was loaded with their provisions and awkward to row. It seemed to them easier to walk on in along the fjord. Bard and his crew rowed hard all the way to the fortification. Then Gunnar and his crew arrived. They all walked up to the fortification. As far as they could see, nothing was changed except that a ditch had been dug as wide as the part of the fortification facing the water. The ditch reached to the edge of the shore. The water was very deep at the shore even at low tide. The ditch was no deeper than up to a man's belt.

Just then, a man came walking on the wall. They recognized this man; it was Ref. He greeted them and asked the news.

Bard said he would tell him no news – 'other than that the legs you're standing on in the fortification are doomed'.

'That is,' he said, 'hardly news.'

Bard proceeded at once to have a ditch dug, and they soon found timbers which were wrapped with birch bark. They chopped into the timbers and a great stream of water gushed out. Gunnar and his crew dragged wood up to the fortification and set it alight. At first a great flow of water gushed from the fortification, but it soon dried up. Ref went out on the wall and asked who had given them this advice. Bard said that did not matter.

Ref spoke: 'I know,' he said, 'that none of you would have hit on this plan unless you profited from the counsel of wiser men than yourselves.'

Bard answered, 'Whoever taught us this plan, we will master you and your possessions today and hang you up where you can overlook this homestead of yours – otherwise you'll have to burn.'

Then Ref spoke in a verse:

3.   He who makes blades bound,
      the warrior wont to rule, supposes
      our fate's in his two strong fists;
      that's to be expected.
      But I guess that before he gets me,
      the ring-giver, craver of sword-crashing,   ring-giver: man; *craver of*
      will meet with tricks – there'll be   *sword-crashing*: warrior
      a victory ode for me.

Ref went back into the fortification. They built up the fire and at this point there was a great bed of coals and only a little steam. In that instant, they heard a great crash in the fortification, and quite unexpectedly the part of the wall facing the water fell into the ditch. It was aimed so straight that the wall fell into the ditch running to the shore. The wall was as smooth as a single plank. And just when the wall fell, a ship on wheels ran along it and down to the water. Ref and his sons hoisted the sail. There was a bit of wind blowing along the mountains from the north. Four of Bard's men were under the part of the fortification that fell and they were killed instantly.

15 Then Bard called to his men. The eight of them ran to the ship. They raised their sail at once and rowed as hard as they could under sail. Bard gained quickly on Ref and his sons.

Gunnar explored the fortification but what was left, no one cared to have. Then, with his men he headed out along the inner reach of the fjord to the ship.

Ref saw that Bard would quickly overtake them.

Then he spoke: 'Now, first, we'll run our sail down. I'm sure, because that ship goes quickly, that they can't slow it down easily and that they don't expect that we'll wait for them, so their ship will run on past us on the other side. Then, Stein,' said Ref, 'you must cut their stays, and, Bjorn, you must splash with the oars so that it seems to them that we are rowing away smartly, but do it so that the ship moves as little as possible.'

Then Ref cut the wheels off his ship and thereupon took up a small spear and sharpened it vigorously.

Now it should be reported that Bard and his men both sailed and rowed; they had no inkling that Ref would wait for them. Their ship ran on past Ref's. At that moment, Ref threw his spear at Bard. It flew through him and nailed him to the ship's freeboard. Stein cut through all their stays, the sail went overboard with all its rigging and at that moment the ship seemed likely to capsize. Ref and his sons raised their sail and were quickly far ahead, and they held their course until they sailed out of the fjord. Bard's crew managed to save their rigging and landed beneath a headland.

Gunnar and his men saw that Ref was sailing seaward down the fjord. Then he thought that the outcome of the encounter between Ref and Bard was certainly one that Bard could not report. He ordered his men to hasten to the ship and get before the mouth of the fjord. They did so. At this point, the day was drawing towards its close.

When Ref and his sons came out of the sound and the fjord opened up again, they saw that Gunnar and his men were rowing away from the land as hard as they could. As night fell it grew dark and there was little moonlight.

Then Ref spoke: 'We must row as hard as we can, but, Bjorn, you must lower our sail little by little and after a while drop it.'

And so they did.

Then Gunnar addressed his men: 'You're rowing like weaklings. Just now we were so close to them that I thought we'd overtake them quickly and now they've got so far away from us their ship looks like a tuft of marsh grass. There's probably more wind there so they'll escape us. Now we'll head back for land; we don't want to be driven on the open sea at night chasing Ref.'

And so they did.

In the morning, Bard's men came to Gunnar and said their course had not been smooth. They had Bard's body with them. Gunnar went back to the settlement and was displeased with his expedition. Everyone said the same thing: that seldom would revenge attempted on just one man turn out so badly.

The sailors who had been with Bard exchanged their goods quickly, and in the autumn they sailed to Norway – and there's no report of Gunnar's sending any treasures to King Harald. His crew told the king about Bard's death and his encounter with Ref. It seemed to the king that the outcome was not very unlike his surmise.

16 Then Ref and his sons went to their ship, and both parties were glad to see the other. They prepared for a sea voyage and, as soon as they were ready, they sailed into the open sea. They had a long, easy voyage. They reached Norway in the autumn and landed first at the island of Edoy. The people there asked who commanded the ship. He gave his name as Narfi and said he was an Icelander. Narfi asked where the king was in the country and the Norwegians said that he was in Trondheim. Edoy is six knots from Trondheim. Narfi sailed in to the mainland and anchored his ship in a hidden bay; he left his companions there and rented a six-oared boat and hired a guide. His sons and wife went with him; his men were to watch over the ship there.

Nothing is reported about Narfi's trip before he reached the market town of Nidaros and rented a hut. They stayed there for some days. Narfi very strictly commanded them never to leave Helga alone there. Narfi had a black hooded cape made for himself. He always had a walrus-skin rope around his waist. He had a white beard tied on and said that he was a merchant; then he went around the town dressed in this way. He carried a spear with a short iron-bound shaft in his hand.

The king was in the town with a great company. One of the king's men was named Grani, who was called Sheath-Grani, a handsome man who loved fine weapons and clothing. He liked women and love-making. In this way he grieved many, but people put up with it because he enjoyed the king's favour.

It happened that one day the king held a large assembly and the public was summoned by a blowing of horns. Narfi went to the assembly, with his sons Stein and Thormod. Bjorn stayed behind with his mother. He was no less curious than the others about what was being talked about at the assembly and so he went. Narfi noticed Bjorn and asked him who was with Helga. He said no one. Then Narfi started back towards the hut.

Shortly after Bjorn set out, a man came into the hut. He was dressed in black clothing and acted very grandly. Helga greeted him and asked his name. He said his name was Grani and that he was one of the king's men.

'I've come here,' he said, 'to buy a woman.'

She told him to go elsewhere for that. Grani said that it was a shame that an old man had a young woman so fair and beautiful. She said that, for all of him, she would decide that herself. He said he was not going to be fastidious and reached for her. She sprang up and defended herself. It turned into a wrestling match, and at that moment Narfi came to the window and looked in. When Grani saw a shadow falling on the window, he tore himself free of Helga and went for the door. Narfi wanted to get in front of the door, but Grani got there first and ran for it.

Helga ran to the door and wanted to lay hold of Narfi.

'Let Grani go,' she said, 'he hasn't harmed anything of yours.'

Narfi tore himself away from Helga and ran after Grani and called to him to stop running. Nonetheless, Grani ran until he came to a wooden fence. There was not much distance between them, and Grani saw that he was going to be caught.

He turned around and spoke, 'Consider what you can do. Even if you kill me, it will be the death of you. But as long as you are in the town, I will never do you any harm.'

He tried to talk his way out of it as well as he could.

Narfi spoke, 'It's true that you are ill-disposed in every way. You're an extravagant fop, you think you're a man of great ability and power, you bring shame on many people – and now you are so frightened you don't know what to do or how to conduct yourself. Now prepare yourself because asking for peace will do no good.'

Narfi thrust at him with the spear. Grani had an axe in his hand and parried the thrust. So it went several times. Narfi was too tough for him, and it ended with his driving the spear right through Grani. Narfi dragged him up under the fence while he was in his death throes and then covered up his corpse.

It occurred to Narfi that it was not a good idea to keep the killing secret and so be guilty of murdering the man, and it seemed best to announce the manslaughter to the king himself. First, Narfi went home to the hut and asked Helga to take their things and get them to the ship along with their guide.

Then Narfi went to the assembly. There was a great crowd of people there. Narfi pressed his way between people until he came before the king. At that moment, the king was talking about urgent public matters.

For all that, Narfi spoke up like this:

'My lord king,' he said, 'the two of us, Sword-house Grani and I, had a soup-understanding today when he told my wife he wanted to buy a swamp. I lady-pigged him through the wall's eye. Then he searched it thoroughly and then I searched it thoroughly. Then I nest-balled him and he many-horsed at that. Then I cloak-stuffed him, my lord, and at that he tarred like a ship, and then I wild-swined him, my lord, to a wooden fence not far off and at the end I counterpaned him.'

Narfi immediately left and went to his boat and made his trip as quickly as he could. They kept going through the evening and the night until they reached Narfi's merchantman. Then they put out to sea at once.

17 To return to King Harald, he was at the assembly, as was reported earlier. While Narfi made his announcement, the king did not interrupt his own speech, and no one noticed that he paid any attention to what Narfi was saying.

When he finished his speech, the king had a signal blown for silence and afterwards he spoke: 'Who was this man, unknown to us, who stood before us for a time dressed in his black hooded cloak and belted with a great walrus-hide rope and with his spear in his hand and whence did he come?'

People said that they never knew where he was from; they said he had been in town for a few days and had rented a hut and given his name as Narfi.

The king spoke: 'What did it seem to you he was saying?'

They said that they never knew that was anything other than silliness and folly.

'So it might be,' said the king, 'but he did not seem an insignificant man to me, and where is our follower, Sheath-Grani? Call him into my presence.'

They did so, but did not find him.

Then the king spoke, 'This matter has taken a turn for the worse. This man said "we two, sword-house Grani and I, had a soup-understanding today. He told my wife he wanted to buy a swamp." I guess,' said the king, 'that he encountered my follower, Sheath-Grani, because a sheath is the house of a sword. He probably went around the inns looking for women. It may be that he encountered this Narfi's wife. There's a drink in Iceland called "mysa", but "mysa", or soup, is much the same. So, they had a "mys"-understanding. He said that Sheath-Grani told Narfi's wife he wanted to buy a swamp, but a swamp is a moor and an amour is intercourse, which Grani wanted with her. Then, Narfi said that he "lady-pigged him through the wall's eye", and that's an apt expression since a "lady-pig" is a sow. And you know that a window in a house can be called an eye in its wall, so Narfi "saw" him through the "window" of the room the couple shared. "Then I searched all round, king," he said, "and he searched all round." But when you search something thoroughly, you ransack it, so both of them ran. Narfi must have run along the outside wall of the hut when he saw what was going on between Grani and his wife. Grani probably heard that and broke off the work he had in hand. He tried to save himself by running. "Then I nest-balled him," Narfi said. He must have egged Grani on to take a stand because an egg is a nest-ball. "And he many-horsed at that." But if many horses are always together, they are called a stud of horses, so Grani stood. Then Narfi said he "cloak-stuffed him" and Grani "tarred like a ship". The stuff for making cloaks is wool, so Narfi woolled or walloped him – ran him through with his spear. "And at that he tarred like a ship", but tar is pitch, so Grani pitched like a ship in a storm in his death-throes. "Then I wild-swined him to a wooden fence," said he, "not far off." A wild swine is called a boar, thus Narfi bore Grani's body to a wooden fence. Then he said that he counterpaned him afterwards. A "counterpane" is a quilt or bedcover, thus Narfi covered Grani's body at the end. Now I wish,' said the king, 'that you search for these men, both him who has been slain and the slayer.'

Men did as the king commanded. Then they found Grani dead and Narfi nowhere.

The next morning, the king had the signal blown for an assembly and said this: 'Events that should not be repeated took place here yesterday and therein our follower was slain. I did not expect that any Icelander would dare to do that within our domain. But now I will guess at this man's identity: that same Ref who caused the people of Greenland so much woe has been here.'

And after that the king appointed men to search for this man both by land and by sea. They proceeded according to the king's orders.

18   To turn to Ref's voyage, they sailed directly to Denmark without stopping. Ref immediately sought an audience with the king and told him all the circumstances of his coming and asked to be taken in.

The king said that it seemed to him that necessity had often driven Ref to act harshly: 'You and your sons impress me as persons in whom I would find good service. Now because you have sought to meet with us, and because you have brought those goods – like walrus-hide ropes for our ships – to our country which for some time have not been easy to obtain because of our enemies, we will take you in. I will obtain a farmstead and estates for you as seems good to us, but your sons, Stein and Bjorn, are to stay here with us. Their advancement will depend on my judgement of their qualities when they are put to the test. And your son Thormod is to stay with you.'

Ref said that it was good that the king should make these provisions by himself: 'But, my lord, we will first take care of our business dealings and then prepare the brothers for your service.'

The king said that so it should be.

Ref and his sons went to their ship. It became known that they had great wealth in walrus-hide ropes, walrus ivory and furs, and that they had many kinds of Greenland wares which were seldom seen in Denmark. They had five polar bears and fifty falcons, including fifteen white ones.

19   To go back to the ship which Bard had commanded, it came to Norway that autumn. Then the king learned of the death of Bard and its circumstances.

Then the king had the signal blown for an assembly and announced publicly the death of Bard, his follower from Greenland.

'From this and the events,' said the king, 'surrounding the killing of Grani,

I now know with certainty that this Narfi was Ref Steinsson. I will grant him an addition to his name and call him Ref the Sly. Even though he is a powerful and strong man, we must preserve our dignity and make others fear to slay our followers, and therefore we here today make this man an outlaw the length and breadth of Norway and as far as our realm extends.'

After that, the king appointed Eirik, Grani's brother, and with him sixty men, to go south to Denmark and assassinate Ref.

20   Eirik and the men who were to accompany him got ready for their expedition. They sailed directly to Denmark without stopping and lay at anchor for some days at a good harbour in Jutland.

As soon as they arrived, an old man wearing a tattered cape and hood with two walking sticks and a hoary white beard came down from the country-side. They greeted him warmly and asked the old man's name. He said that he was Sigtrygg. They asked where his family roots were. He said that he was Norwegian by ancestry, but had then been for some time in Denmark where he had become very poor. They said that he must be a good old fellow who could tell them many things. He asked what they wanted to learn. They said that they wanted to enquire about a man who was called Ref, and who, with some others, would have come there that summer in a ship.

Sigtrygg asked, 'Is there something in it for me if I tell you what you want to know?'

They said he would not be short of food for days.

Sigtrygg spoke: 'I won't tell you where to find Ref just for food, because I know from the people's talk that you will make an attempt on his life. These are my terms for leading you to where you will see Ref and his sons and the twelve men who accompanied him this summer: from each of you I will have an ounce of silver, and in addition a valuable item from your ship, and you, moreover, will be obligated to take me to Norway at your expense if I choose. And you must let me direct our expedition until we find Ref.'

They struck this bargain.

Sigtrygg spoke: 'Now we must take down the ship's tent and row out around the headland.'

They did so and anchored offshore.

'Now I'll go ashore,' said the old man, 'and two of you with me, and we'll see what we can find out.'

Then they did so. There was a forest nearby. When they had gone a short distance into the forest, armed men ran up to them. These were Ref's sons and the twelve followers all together. Both of the Norwegians were captured. Sigtrygg threw off his rags and his beard as well. They walked to the sea by another way. There before them were two longships at anchor with two hundred men. King Svein had sent this force to Ref as soon as he heard that spies had been sent against him. Ref and his men armed themselves and attacked Eirik and his men at sea. When they met, the outcome was quick: all but ten of Eirik's men were killed and those were captured.

Then Ref spoke, 'It has turned out, Eirik, that Sigtrygg, your partner and companion whom you met yesterday evening, has come. Now I have done what I promised you, so that you can see Ref and his sons here. Because I killed your brother, I will grant you your life if you swear that you will never make an attempt on my life or the lives of my sons. And you must tell King Harald the whole truth about our encounter. And tell him that now I have repaid him a little for plotting against me when he advised those who wished to take my life. But King Harald is probably not destined to have me killed. And in Denmark only he who has more power than I will be more dangerous to him than I.'

After that, Eirik swore to do all this. Then Ref gave him a twelve-oared boat and those things he needed to have. Ref took the longship they had brought with them and sent it to King Svein.

The king praised Ref's actions highly, saying they were both valiant and magnanimous: 'And now you will have this name,' said King Svein, 'here in our realm, and be called Sigtrygg, because the other name isn't common in this country. And at your name-giving, we wish to give you this gold ring which is worth one mark. And therewith you will have twelve farms out west in Vendil, and those you will choose yourself because I see that you are a very wise man.'

Ref thanked the king eloquently for his princely gifts and the honour which he gave him. Ref and Helga his wife and Thormod, his son, now went to his farms which the king had given Ref. Sigtrygg became a great man.

And, when he had been there for some years, he went on a trip to Rome and visited the holy apostle Peter. And on that journey, Sigtrygg contracted the illness which caused his death, and he was buried in a rich monastery out there in France.

Stein and Bjorn were with King Svein a long time, and he valued them so greatly that he arranged fine marriages for them in Denmark and both of them stayed there and were considered excellent men. From Stein was descended Bishop Absalon who lived in the days of King Valdimar Knutsson. Ref's son Thormod returned to Iceland after the death of King Harald and took over the land at Kvennabrekka and married in Iceland, and many excellent men are descended from him.

And with that we close the saga of Ref the Sly.

Translated by GEORGE CLARK

THE VINLAND SAGAS

THE SAGA OF THE GREENLANDERS
EIRIK THE RED'S SAGA

Grænlendinga saga
Eiríks saga rauða

Time of action: 970–1030
Time of writing: 1220–80

The Vinland Sagas are two separate works that were written down indepen-
dently in Iceland in the early thirteenth century. They contain the oldest
descriptions of the North American continent and tell the story of several
voyages undertaken by people from Iceland and Greenland to North America
around the year 1000 – the first documented voyages across the Atlantic in
which the peoples of Europe and America met for the first time. The
pioneering voyage was led by Leif Eiriksson to a land he named Vinland
('Wineland'). Leif, nicknamed 'the Lucky' after rescuing shipwrecked seamen
on his way back from Vinland, was born on the west coast of Iceland between
975 and 980 and emigrated to Greenland as a young boy in 985 with his
family and the band of explorers led by Eirik the Red, his father.

There is no doubt that *The Vinland Sagas*, like almost all other Sagas of
Icelanders, contain memories of real characters and events, recounted in a
literary medium. However, the roots in the oral memory of people in Iceland
are more transparent in *The Vinland Sagas* than is the case with more stylized
and consciously literary creations. Their episodes show little sign of having
been reshaped into a literary form; they ask to be taken at face value, as
true accounts presented with all the spontaneity of discovery and exploration.
Of course, their oral background also means that *The Vinland Sagas* cannot
be taken as trustworthy contemporary historical documents: They disagree
with each other on certain details and contain material which we would
now classify as fanciful and supernatural, however palpable a part of the

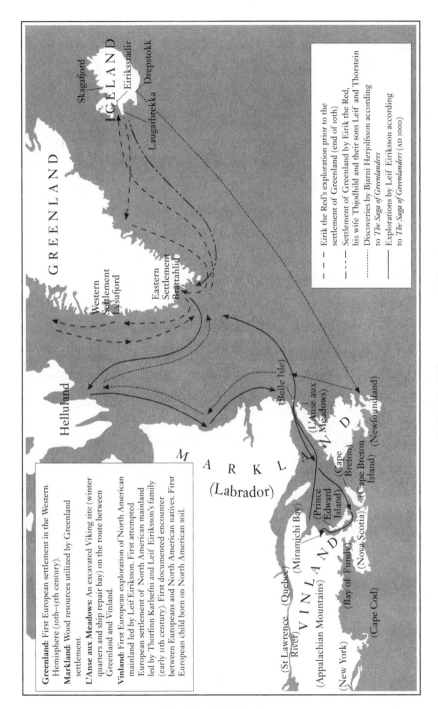

Travels of Leif Eiriksson

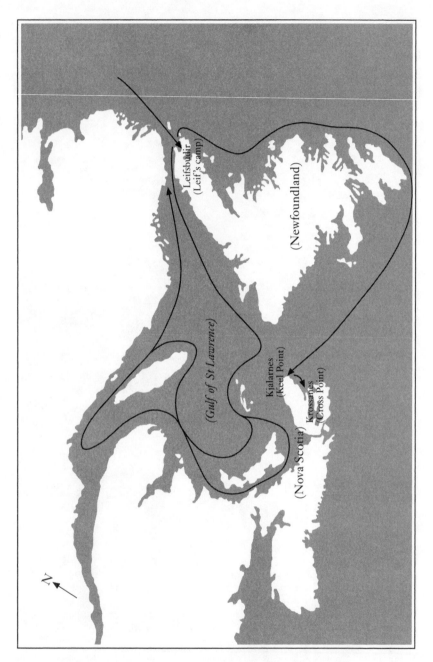

Travels of Thorvald Eiriksson (The Saga of the Greenlanders, *ch.4*)

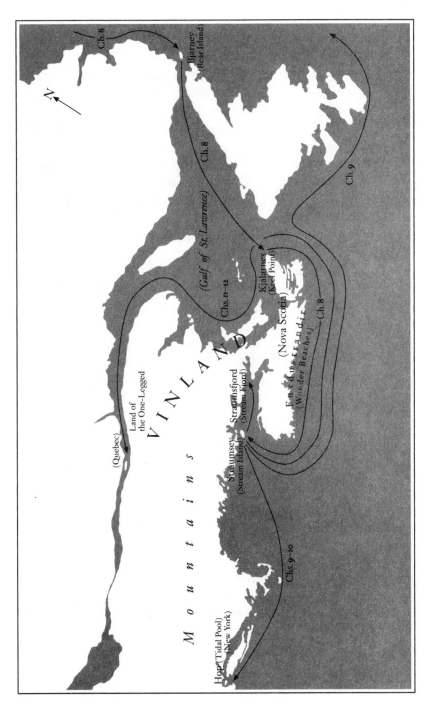

Travels of Gudrid Thorbjarnardottir and Thorfinn Karlsefni (Eirik the Red's Saga)

real world this may have been to people then. That said, the sagas are still our best proof that such voyages to the North American continent took place around the time the sagas tell us. Coincidence or wishful thinking simply could not have produced descriptions of topography, natural resources and native lifestyles which are from a world unknown to people in Europe, but can be corroborated in North America.

A welcome addition to the evidence of the sagas was provided when Helge and Anne Ingstad found remains of buildings in Newfoundland in the early 1960s, which were of the same character as Viking Age buildings in Iceland and Greenland. This eliminated any remaining scepticism about what we also know from the sagas: that the explorers built a camp referred to as Leif's Camp, on the northern tip of Newfoundland, at a site now known as L'Anse aux Meadows, as a stopping place for their voyages farther south to Vinland.

Eirik the Red's Saga is preserved in two Icelandic vellum manuscripts, *Hauksbók* (early fourteenth century) and *Skálholtsbók* (early fifteenth century), which was published in *Íslensk fornrit IV* (supplement, Reykjavík, 1985) and is translated by Keneva Kunz. Both manuscripts were based on an original written after 1263 – which in turn was based on an older text from the early thirteenth century. It hardly tells anything about Eirik, but exalts the memory of the first European couple to have a child in North America: Thorfinn Karlsefni (descended from Aud the Deep-minded, a Viking queen in Dublin and settler in west Iceland in the opening of *The Saga of the People of Laxardal*, and from Kjarval, King of Ireland); and Gudrid Thorbjarnardottir (descended from a Gaelic slave brought to Iceland by the same Aud), who was born and raised in Iceland, then emigrated to Greenland and later went to North America before she finally settled in Iceland again, becoming a nun after a subsequent pilgrimage to Rome.

The conflict between the old pagan culture and Christianity is prominent in the saga; Leif Eiriksson is commissioned by King Olaf Tryggvason to convert the heathen settlers of Greenland to Christianity. More than once, conflicting beliefs struggle to gain the upper hand: in the figure of the Christian Gudrid, who agrees to take part in sorcery to help people in need, for instance, and in the prayers of the voyagers to North America for God's help after rejecting succour from Thor.

The abrupt beginning of *The Saga of the Greenlanders* is explained by its preservation as a part of a larger work about King Olaf Tryggvason, from around 1387. For prefatory details of Eirik the Red's settlement in Iceland

and Greenland can be found in the second chapter of *Eirik the Red's Saga*. The original *Saga of the Greenlanders* was written much earlier, very likely in the beginning of the thirteenth century. The saga focuses on Leif the Lucky's leading role in the Vinland voyages and includes a striking and memorable account of his vicious half-sister Freydis. It is translated by Keneva Kunz from Ólafur Halldórsson's *Grœland í miðaldaritum* (Reykjavík, 1978).

Both *The Vinland Sagas* reflect a genuine family tradition and mention that three bishops in the twelfth and thirteenth centuries could trace their family back to Gudrid and Thorfinn Karlsefni through their son Snorri, the first 'Vinlander'.

Eirik the Red fled from Norway with his father and settled in Iceland where he married a local woman, Thjodhild, in Breidafjord (west Iceland). He seems to have had a nose for trouble, was soon driven out of his district and eventually outlawed. During his exile he explored a land which he had heard of to the west of Iceland, and returned with news about 'Greenland', as he named it to attract others to join him in settling there. This is said to have happened fifteen years before Christianity was adopted by law in Iceland, i.e. in 985.

When it comes to the Vinland voyages themselves, the sagas have two versions to tell – which can nevertheless be matched in many instances (highlighted in bold face in the columns on pp. 632–5). A comparison between the two *Vinland Sagas* shows that their similarities are more striking than their contradictions, most of which can be explained by the oral tradition behind them. By collating them a reasonable sequence of events can be established (see also maps on pp. 627–9 with suggested routes for the respective voyages):

1. Bjarni Herjolfsson sights unknown land west of Greenland.
2. Leif the Lucky, son of Eirik the Red, becomes the first European to explore this land and give names to it, from north to south.
3. Thorvald, son of Eirik the Red, leads an expedition to Vinland.
4. Thorstein, son of Eirik the Red, tries to find Vinland but fails and ends his life in Lysufjord, leaving Gudrid Thorbjarnardottir a widow.
5. Thorfinn Karlsefni and Gudrid Thorbjarnardottir lead the first attempt to settle in the New World, during which they have the first European child born in America, their son Snorri.
6. Freydis, daughter of Eirik the Red, leads a disastrous expedition.
7. Thorfinn Karlsefni and Gudrid Thorbjarnardottir settle for the rest of their lives in Skagafjord, north Iceland.

EIRIK THE RED'S SAGA

Gudrid arrives in Greenland

Gudrid arrives in Greenland with her father in a group of 30 people who leave Iceland. Half of them fall sick and die on the way, but the rest are rescued. A seeress tells Gudrid's fortune, and she goes to Eirik the Red's residence. Leif is instructed by King Olaf of Norway to convert Greenland to Christianity.

Leif finds new lands

Leif is blown off course and finds unknown land west from Greenland where self-sown wheat, grapes and maple trees grow. He rescues some people who have been shipwrecked and is given the nickname 'Lucky'.

Thorstein goes astray in the Atlantic

Thorstein, Eirik's son, gets a ship from Gudrid's father and talks Eirik into coming along. Eirik hides his gold before he leaves, then falls off his horse on the way to the ship and refuses to go. The others sail around in the Atlantic for the whole summer.

Thorstein and Gudrid are married

Thorstein marries Gudrid and they settle down in Lysufjord in the western settlement of Greenland. Thorstein falls ill and dies, but rises briefly from the dead to tell Gudrid's fortune. His remains are taken to consecrated ground in Brattahlid. Gudrid's father dies and she lives as a widow at Brattahlid.

THE SAGA OF THE GREENLANDERS

Bjarni finds new lands

Bjarni Herjolfsson is blown off course and sees unknown, forested land west of Greenland.

Leif explores new lands

Leif buys Bjarni's ship and asks **Eirik to come along, but Eirik claims he is too old and not fit for sailing any more. Eventually, he gives in but falls off a horse on the way to the ship and returns to his farm without going anywhere.**

Leif finds **Helluland, Markland** and **Vinland,** and on his way back he rescues Thorir and his crew, who are shipwrecked on a skerry, 15 people in all. They all get **sick** the following winter and Thorir and many others die, leaving Thorir's wife Gudrid a widow. **Leif is nicknamed 'the Lucky' after rescuing these people.**

Thorvald explores lands and dies on Krossanes

Thorvald, Leif's brother, explores west and east from Leif's camp and eventually **his ship is driven ashore and damaged on a peninsula, Kjalarnes.**

He says he wants to settle nearby, but then they see nine men under three hide-covered boats and kill all but one, who escapes. They are attacked by a huge number of natives who eventually withdraw. **Thorvald is fatally wounded by an arrow** and is buried on a point of land called Krossanes.

Thorstein and Gudrid marry, they go astray at sea

Thorstein Eiriksson marries Gudrid, Thorir's widow, and they set out for Vinland **but go astray at sea and end up in Lysufjord, where Thorstein dies, only to rise briefly from the dead to tell Gudrid's fortune. His remains are taken to consecrated ground in Brattahlid. Gudrid goes to Brattahlid.**

634 THE SAGAS OF ICELANDERS

Karlsefni and Gudrid's voyage

Thorfinn Karlsefni arrives in Greenland and marries Gudrid. There is much talk about going to Vinland and Karlsefni and Gudrid decide to set off, with Eirik's daughter, Freydis, and her husband, Thorvard, and Eirik's son Thorvald. They find **Helluland, Markland** and Bjarney as well as **a keel from a ship at Kjalarnes.**

Stay in Straumsfjord

They pass Furdustrandir (Wonder Beaches) and stay in Straumsfjord where **they find a beached whale**. One ship goes north around Kjalarnes in search of **Vinland** but is blown off course. Karlsefni continues south to Hop, taking his own **livestock** with him.

Meeting and fighting with natives in Hop

Here they meet the natives (Skraelings) and **Karlsefni and his men trade with them**, selling them red cloth **for pieces of skin. Karlsefni prevents his men from selling their own weapons. A bull eventually scares the natives away.**

The natives fight Karlsefni and his men – the men flee, but the pregnant Freydis scares the natives away by baring her breasts and slapping them with a sword.

The natives find a dead man with an iron axe in his head, pick up the axe and try it successfully on wood, but when it breaks on stone they throw it away.

On his way back, Karlsefni kills five natives who are sleeping in skin sacks.

Thorvald dies in the Land of the One-Legged

Karlsefni sails around Kjalarnes and reaches a river where a uniped appears and **shoots Thorvald, Eirik the Red's son, with an arrow. He draws it out and before dying, jests about how fat the paunch was that it struck.**

Snorri in Straumsfjord

Back in Straumsfjord, they begin to **quarrel about women. Snorri, son of Gudrid and Karlsefni,** is three years old. They take hostages on the way back and lose still another ship.

Karlsefni and Gudrid in Skagafjord

Back in Iceland, Karlsefni and Gudrid settle on Reynines in Skagafjord. His mother dislikes Gudrid (because she feels Gudrid's family is not a match for Karlsefni's) but accepts her in the end. **Three bishops are counted among the descendants of Snorri, son of Karlsefni and Gudrid.**

Karlsefni and Gudrid's voyage

Thorfinn Karlsefni arrives in Greenland and marries Gudrid. There is much talk about going to Vinland and **Karlsefni and Gudrid decide to go, intending to settle since they take livestock over with them.**

Stay in Leif's camp

They reach Leif's camp where there is plenty of fresh **beached whale**, and they also live off the land, collect grapes and hunt.

Meeting and fighting with natives

After one winter they become aware of **natives, who turn out to be afraid of Karlsefni's bull. They trade with the natives** who offer **furs** and want **weapons** in exchange, which **Karlsefni forbids. Gudrid gives birth to Snorri** and sees a phantom. Karlsefni plans to use their bull to scare off the natives. They attack, many natives die and one of them **tries an iron axe on one of his companions, killing him. Their chief picks it up and throws it into the sea**.

The following spring Karlsefni decides to return to Greenland, taking plenty of wood, berries and skins with him.

Freydis leads a Voyage

Freydis Eiriksdottir leads a voyage with her husband, **Thorvard** from Gardar. The members of the expedition end up fighting among themselves in Leif's camp, incited by Freydis. She kills the women herself and the survivors all go back to Greenland, where she is condemned by Leif.

Karlsefni and Gudrid in Skagafjord

Karlsefni goes to Norway and sells his goods before returning to Glaumbaer in **Skagafjord** where he and Gudrid settle down with their son **Snorri**. She goes on a pilgrimage to Rome, builds a church and becomes a nun. **Three bishops are counted among their descendants.**

THE SAGA OF THE GREENLANDERS

I   Herjolf was the son of Bard Herjolfsson and a kinsman of Ingolf, the settler of Iceland. Ingolf gave to Herjolf the land between Vog and Reykjanes.

At first, Herjolf farmed at Drepstokk. His wife was named Thorgerd and their son was Bjarni; he was a promising young man. While still a youthful age he longed to sail abroad. He soon earned himself both a good deal of wealth and a good name, and spent his winters alternately abroad and with his father. Soon Bjarni had his own ship making trading voyages. During the last winter Bjarni spent in Norway, Herjolf decided to accompany Eirik the Red to Greenland and left his farm. One of the men on Herjolf's ship was from the Hebrides, a Christian, who composed the drapa of the Sea Fences (Breakers). It has this refrain:

I ask you, unblemished monks' tester,	*monk's tester:* Christ
to be the ward of my travels;	
may the lord of the peaks' pane	*peaks' pane:* heavens
shade my path with his hawk's perch.	*hawk's perch:* hand

Herjolf farmed at Herjolfsnes. He was the most respected of men.

Eirik the Red farmed at Brattahlid. There he was held in the highest esteem, and everyone deferred to his authority. Eirik's children were Leif, Thorvald, Thorstein and a daughter, Freydis. She was married to a man named Thorvard, and they farmed at Gardar, where the bishop's seat is now. She was a domineering woman, but Thorvard was a man of no consequence. She had been married to him mainly for his money.

Heathen were the people of Greenland at that time.

Bjarni steered his ship into Eyrar in the summer of the year that his father had sailed from Iceland. Bjarni was greatly moved by the news and would not have his cargo unloaded. His crew then asked what he was waiting for, and he answered that he intended to follow his custom of spending the winter with his father – 'and I want to set sail for Greenland, if you will join me'.

All of them said they would follow his counsel.

Bjarni then spoke: 'Our journey will be thought an ill-considered one, since none of us has sailed the Greenland Sea.'

Despite this they set sail once they had made ready and sailed for three days, until the land had disappeared below the horizon. Then the wind dropped and they were beset by winds from the north and fog; for many days they did not know where they were sailing.

After that they saw the sun and could take their bearings. Hoisting the sail, they sailed for the rest of the day before sighting land. They speculated among themselves as to what land this would be, for Bjarni said he suspected this was not Greenland.

They asked whether he wished to sail up close into the shore of this country or not. 'My advice is that we sail in close to the land.'

They did so, and soon saw that the land was not mountainous but did have small hills, and was covered with forests. Keeping it on their port side, they turned their sail-end landwards and angled away from the shore.

They sailed for another two days before sighting land once again.

They asked Bjarni whether he now thought this to be Greenland.

He said he thought this no more likely to be Greenland than the previous land – 'since there are said to be very large glaciers in Greenland'.

They soon approached the land and saw that it was flat and wooded. The wind died and the crew members said they thought it advisable to put ashore, but Bjarni was against it. They claimed they needed both timber and water.

'You've no shortage of those provisions,' Bjarni said, but he was criticized somewhat by his crew for this.

He told them to hoist the sail and they did so, turning the stern towards shore and sailing seawards. For three days they sailed with the wind from the south-west until they saw a third land. This land had high mountains, capped by a glacier.

They asked whether Bjarni wished to make land here, but he said he did not wish to do so – 'as this land seems to me to offer nothing of use'.

This time they did not lower the sail, but followed the shoreline until they saw that the land was an island. Once more they turned their stern landwards and sailed out to sea with the same breeze. But the wind soon grew and Bjarni told them to lower the sail and not to proceed faster than both their ship and rigging could safely withstand. They sailed for four days.

Upon seeing a fourth land they asked Bjarni whether he thought this was Greenland or not.

Bjarni answered, 'This land is most like what I have been told of Greenland, and we'll head for shore here.'

This they did and made land along a headland in the evening of the day, finding a boat there. On this point Herjolf, Bjarni's father, lived, and it was named for him and has since been called Herjolfsnes (Herjolf's point). Bjarni now joined his father and ceased his merchant voyages. He remained on his father's farm as long as Herjolf lived and took over the farm after his death.

2   Following this, Bjarni Herjolfsson sailed from Greenland to Earl Eirik, who received him well. Bjarni told of his voyage, during which he had sighted various lands, and many people thought him short on curiosity, since he had nothing to tell of these lands, and he was criticized somewhat for this.

Bjarni became one of the earl's followers and sailed to Greenland the following summer. There was now much talk of looking for new lands.

Leif, the son of Eirik the Red of Brattahlid, sought out Bjarni and purchased his ship. He hired himself a crew numbering thirty-five men altogether. Leif asked his father Eirik to head the expedition.

Eirik was reluctant to agree, saying he was getting on in years and not as good at bearing the cold and wet as before. Leif said he still commanded the greatest good fortune of all his kinsmen. Eirik gave in to Leif's urgings and, when they were almost ready, set out from his farm on horseback. When he had but a short distance left to the ship, the horse he was riding stumbled and threw Eirik, injuring his foot. Eirik then spoke: 'I am not intended to find any other land than this one where we now live. This will be the end of our travelling together.'

Eirik returned home to Brattahlid, and Leif boarded his ship, along with his companions, thirty-five men altogether. One of the crew was a man named Tyrkir, from a more southerly country.

Once they had made the ship ready, they put to sea and found first the land which Bjarni and his companions had seen last. They sailed up to the shore and cast anchor, put out a boat and rowed ashore. There they found no grass, but large glaciers covered the highlands, and the land was like a single flat slab of rock from the glaciers to the sea. This land seemed to them of little use.

Leif then spoke: 'As far as this land is concerned it can't be said of us as of Bjarni, that we did not set foot on shore. I am now going to name this land and call it Helluland (Stone-slab land).'

They then returned to their ship, put out to sea and found a second land. Once more they sailed close to the shore and cast anchor, put out a boat and went ashore. This land was flat and forested, sloping gently seaward, and they came across many beaches of white sand.

Leif then spoke: 'This land will be named for what it has to offer and called Markland (Forest Land).' They then returned to the ship without delay.

After this they sailed out to sea and spent two days at sea with a north-easterly wind before they saw land. They sailed towards it and came to an island, which lay to the north of the land, where they went ashore. In the fine weather they found dew on the grass, that they collected in their hands and drank, and thought they had never tasted anything as sweet.

Afterwards they returned to their ship and sailed into the sound which lay between the island and the headland that stretched out northwards from the land. They rounded the headland and steered westward. Here there were extensive shallows at low tide and their ship was soon stranded, and the sea looked far away to those aboard ship.

Their curiosity to see the land was so great that they could not be bothered to wait for the tide to come in and float their stranded ship, and they ran aground where a river flowed into the sea from a lake. When the incoming tide floated the ship again, they took the boat and rowed to the ship and moved it up into the river and from there into the lake, where they cast anchor. They carried their sleeping-sacks ashore and built booths. Later they decided to spend the winter there and built large houses.

There was no lack of salmon both in the lake and in the river, and this salmon was larger than they had ever seen before.

It seemed to them the land was so good that livestock would need no fodder during the winter. The temperature never dropped below freezing, and the grass only withered very slightly. The days and nights were much more equal in length than in Greenland or Iceland. In the depth of winter the sun was aloft by mid-morning and still visible at mid-afternoon.*

When they had finished building their houses, Leif spoke to his companions: 'I want to divide our company into two groups, as I wish to explore

---

* This sentence has been the subject of no small amount of speculation, for instance, by equating *eyktarstaður* with the point of Nones and *dagmálastaður* as the point of late morning, in an attempt to fix a location for Vinland, which has been to little real avail as the meaning of these obsolete terms of reference is impossible to interpret with any certainty. Interesting discussions on this and many other aspects of the Vinland voyages are raised by Gwyn Jones in *The North Atlantic Saga*, Páll Bergþórsson in *The Wineland Millennium* and Anna Yates in *Leifur Eiríksson and Vinland the Good.*

the land. One half is to remain at home by the longhouses while the other half explores the land. They are never to go any farther than will enable them to return that same evening and no one is to separate from the group.'

This they did for some time. Leif accompanied them sometimes, and at other times remained at home by the houses. Leif was a large, strong man, of very striking appearance and wise, as well as being a man of moderation in all things.

3   One evening it happened that one man, the southerner Tyrkir, was missing from their company. Leif was very upset by this, as Tyrkir had spent many years with him and his father and had treated Leif as a child very affectionately. Leif criticized his companions harshly and prepared to search for Tyrkir, taking twelve men with him.

When they had gone only a short way from the houses, however, Tyrkir came towards him and they welcomed him gladly.

Leif soon realized that the companion of his childhood was pleased about something. Tyrkir had a protruding forehead and darting eyes, with dark wrinkles in his face; he was short in stature and frail-looking, but a master of all types of crafts.

Leif then asked him, 'Why were you so late returning, foster-father, and how did you become separated from the rest?'

For a long time Tyrkir only spoke in German, with his eyes darting in all directions and his face contorted. The others understood nothing of what he was saying.

After a while he spoke in Norse: 'I had gone only a bit farther than the rest of you. But I have news to tell you: I found grapevines and grapes.'

'Are you really sure of this, foster-father?' Leif said.

'I'm absolutely sure,' he replied, 'because where I was born there was no lack of grapevines and grapes.'

They went to sleep after that, and the following morning Leif spoke to his crew: 'We'll divide our time between two tasks, taking one day for one task and one day for the other, picking grapes or cutting vines* and felling the trees to make a load for my ship.' They agreed on this course.

---

* As philologist Ólafur Halldórsson points out, it is conceivable that references here and elsewhere to 'cutting [grape] vines' (*vínviður*) could result from a copying error or misunderstanding, and that instead of *vínber* and *vínviður* (grapes and grapevines) the text should read *vínber* and *viður* (grapes, literally wine berries, and wood). The latter would be much more understandable as a valuable product worth transporting home to treeless Greenland. It could also be 'original', reflecting the general unfamiliarity of Northerners with grapes and vines and supporting suggestions that the 'wine berries' of Vinland grew on trees.

It is said that the boat which was drawn behind the ship was filled with grapes.

Then they cut a load for the ship.

When spring came they made the ship ready and set sail. Leif named the land for its natural features and called it Vinland (Wineland). They headed out to sea and had favourable winds, until they came in sight of Greenland and the mountains under its glaciers.

Then one of the crew spoke up, asking, 'Why do you steer a course so close to the wind?'

Leif answered, 'I'm watching my course, but there's more to it than that: do you see anything of note?'

The crew said they saw nothing worthy of note.

'I'm not sure,' Leif said, 'whether it's a ship or a skerry that I see.'

They then saw it and said it was a skerry. Leif saw so much better than they did, that he could make out men on the skerry.

'I want to steer us close into the wind,' Leif said, 'so that we can reach them; if these men should be in need of our help, we have to try to give it to them. If they should prove to be hostile, we have all the advantages on our side and they have none.'

They managed to sail close to the skerry and lowered their sail, cast anchor and put out one of the two extra boats they had taken with them.

Leif then asked who was in charge of the company.

The man who replied said his name was Thorir and that he was of Norwegian origin. 'And what is your name?'

Leif told him his name.

'Are you the son of Eirik the Red of Brattahlid?' he asked.

Leif said he was. 'Now I want to invite all of you,' Leif said, 'to come on board my ship, bringing as much of your valuables as the ship can carry.'

After they had accepted his offer, the ship sailed to Eiriksfjord with all this cargo until they reached Brattahlid, where they unloaded the ship. Leif then invited Thorir to spend the winter with him there, along with Thorir's wife Gudrid and three other men, and found places for the other members of both his own and Thorir's crew. Leif rescued fifteen men from the skerry. After this he was called Leif the Lucky.

Leif had now become very wealthy and was held in much respect.

That winter Thorir's crew were stricken by illness and he himself died, along with most of his company. Eirik the Red also died that winter.

There was great discussion of Leif's Vinland voyage and his brother

Thorvald felt they had not explored enough of the land. Leif then said to Thorvald, 'You go to Vinland, brother, and take my ship if you wish, but before you do so I want the ship to make a trip to the skerry to fetch the wood that Thorir had there.'

And so this was done.

4   In consultation with his brother Leif, Thorvald now prepared for this journey with thirty companions. They made their ship ready and put to sea, and nothing is told of their journey until they came to Vinland, to Leif's camp, where they laid up their ship and settled in for the winter, fishing for their food.

That spring Thorvald said they should make their ship ready and several men were to take the ship's boat and go to the west of the land and explore there during the summer. They thought the land fine and well forested, with white beaches and only a short distance between the forest and the sea. There were many islands and wide stretches of shallow sea.

Nowhere did they see signs of men or animals. On one of the westerly islands they did find a wooden grain cover, but discovered no other work by human hands and headed back, returning to Leif's camp in the autumn.

The second summer Thorvald explored the country to the east on the large ship, going north around the land. They ran into stormy weather around one headland, and they were driven ashore, smashing the keel of the ship. They stayed there a long time, repairing their ship. Thorvald then said to his companions, 'I want us to raise the broken keel up on this point and call it Kjalarnes (Keel point).' This they did.

They then left to sail to the east of the country and entered the mouths of the next fjords until they reached a cape stretching out seawards. It was covered with forest. After they secured their ship in a sheltered cove and put out gangways to the land, Thorvald and all his companions went ashore.

He then spoke: 'This is an attractive spot, and here I would like to build my farm.' As they headed back to the ship they saw three hillocks on the beach inland from the cape. Upon coming closer they saw they were three hide-covered boats, with three men under each of them. They divided their forces and managed to capture all of them except one, who escaped with his boat. They killed the other eight and went back to the cape. On surveying the area they saw a number of hillocks further up the fjord, and assumed them to be settlements.

Following this they were stricken by sleep, so that they could no longer keep their eyes open, and all of them fell asleep. Then a voice was heard calling, and they all woke up. 'Wake up, Thorvald, and all your companions,' the voice warned, 'if you wish to save your lives. Get to the ship with all your men and leave this land as quickly as you can.'

A vast number of hide-covered boats came down the fjord, heading towards them.

Thorvald then spoke: 'We will set up breastworks along the sides of the ship and defend ourselves as well as possible, but fight back as little as we can.'

They did as he said, and after the natives had shot at them for a while, they fled as rapidly as they could.

Thorvald then asked his men if they had been wounded, and they replied that they were unhurt.

'I have been wounded under my arm,' he said. 'An arrow flew between the edge of the ship and the shield into my armpit. Here is the arrow, and this wound will cause my death. I now advise you to prepare for your return journey as quickly as possible, but take me to that cape I thought was such a good farm site. Perhaps the words I spoke will prove true enough and I will dwell there awhile. You will bury me there and mark my grave with crosses at the head and foot, and call the spot Krossanes (Cross point) after that.'

Greenland had been converted to Christianity by that time, although Eirik the Red had died before the conversion.

Thorvald then died, and they did everything as he had advised, then left to meet up with their companions. Each group told its news to the other and they spent the winter there loading the ships with grapes and grapevines.

In the spring they made ready for the voyage back to Greenland. They steered the ship into Eiriksfjord and had plenty of news to tell Leif.

5   Among the events taking place meanwhile in Greenland was the marriage of Thorstein Eiriksson to Gudrid Thorbjarnardottir, who had previously been married to Thorir the Norwegian who was spoken of earlier.

Thorstein Eiriksson now wished to sail to Vinland to retrieve his brother Thorvald's body and made the same ship ready once more. He selected his companions for their strength and size, taking with him twenty-five men and his wife, Gudrid. Once they had made ready, they set sail and were out of sight of land. They were tossed about at sea all summer and did not know where they were.

The first week of winter had passed when they made land in Lysufjord, in the western settlement in Greenland. Thorstein managed to find places for all his crew members. But he and his wife had no accommodation and remained alone on the ship for several nights. In those days Christianity was still in its infancy in Greenland.

One day some men came to their tent early in the day. The leader of the group asked what men were in the tent.

Thorstein answered, 'There are two of us,' he said, 'and who is asking?'

'Thorstein is my name, and I am called Thorstein the Black. My reason for coming is to invite you and your wife to stay the winter with me.'

Thorstein Eiriksson said he wished to seek his wife's guidance, and when she told him to decide he agreed to the offer.

'Then I'll return with a team of oxen to fetch you tomorrow, as I do not lack the means to put you up. But it will be an unexciting stay, as there are only the two of us, my wife and myself, and I prefer my own company. Also I have another faith than you, although I expect yours is the better of the two.'

He then came with a team of oxen to fetch them the next day, and so they went to stay with Thorstein the Black, and he provided for them generously.

Gudrid was a woman of striking appearance and wise as well, who knew how to behave among strangers.

It was early in the winter when the first of Thorstein Eiriksson's companions were stricken by illness and many of them died there.

Thorstein asked that coffins be made for the bodies of those who had died, and that they be taken to the ship and secured away there – 'as when summer comes I intend to take all the bodies back to Eiriksfjord'.

It was not long until the sickness came to Thorstein's house, and his wife, Grimhild, was the first to fall ill. She was a very large woman, with the strength of a man, yet she bowed to the illness. Soon after that Thorstein Eiriksson was stricken, and both of them lay ill until Grimhild, the wife of Thorstein the Black, died.

After she had died, Thorstein the Black left the main room to seek a plank to place her body on.

Gudrid then spoke: 'Don't be away long, dear Thorstein,' she said.

He promised to do as she asked.

Thorstein Eiriksson then spoke: 'Strange are the actions of the mistress of the house now; she's struggling to raise herself up on her elbow, stretching her feet out from the bedboards and feeling for her shoes.'

At this Thorstein the Black returned and Grimhild collapsed that same instant, with a cracking sound coming from every timber in the room.

Thorstein then made a coffin for Grimhild's body and took it away and secured it. He was a large, strong man, and needed to call upon all his strength before he managed to remove his wife from the farm.

Thorstein Eiriksson's condition worsened and he died. His wife, Gudrid, was overtaken by grief. All of them were in the main room. Gudrid had been sitting on a stool in front of the bench where her husband, Thorstein, had lain.

Thorstein the farmer then took Gudrid from her stool into his arms and sat with her on the bench across from her husband Thorstein's corpse and said many encouraging things, consoling her and promising her that he would take her to Eiriksfjord with her husband Thorstein's body and those of his companions. 'And we'll invite other people to stay here,' he said 'to provide you with solace and companionship.'

She thanked him.

Thorstein Eiriksson then sat up and spoke: 'Where is Gudrid?'

Three times he spoke these words, but she remained silent.

Then she spoke to Thorstein the farmer: 'Shall I answer his question or not?'

He told her not to answer. Thorstein the farmer then crossed the floor and sat on the chair and Gudrid on his knee.

Then Thorstein the farmer spoke: 'What is it you want, namesake?' he said.

He answered after a short pause: 'I want to tell Gudrid her fate, to make it easier for her to resign herself to my death, for I have gone to a good resting place. I can tell you, Gudrid, that you will be married to an Icelander, and you will live a long life together, and have many descendants, promising, bright and fine, sweet and well-scented. You will leave Greenland to go to Norway and from there to Iceland and set up house in Iceland. There you will live a long time, outliving your husband. You will travel abroad, go south on a pilgrimage and return to Iceland to your farm, where a church will be built. There you will remain and take holy orders and there you will die.'

At that Thorstein Eiriksson fell back, and his corpse was made ready and taken to the ship.

Thorstein the farmer kept all his promises to Gudrid faithfully. In the spring he sold his farm and livestock and loaded all his possessions aboard the ship with Gudrid. He made the ship ready and hired a crew and sailed to Eiriksfjord. The bodies were then buried in the churchyard.

Gudrid went to stay with Leif at Brattahlid, and Thorstein the Black built a farm in Eiriksfjord where he stayed as long as he lived, and was regarded as a most capable man.

6   That same summer a ship from Norway arrived in Greenland. The skipper of the ship was named Thorfinn Karlsefni. He was the son of Thord Horse-head, the son of Snorri Thordarson of Hofdi.

Thorfinn Karlsefni was a very wealthy man. He spent the winter with Leif Eiriksson in Brattahlid. He was soon attracted by Gudrid and asked her to marry him, but she referred him to Leif for an answer. She was then engaged to him and their wedding took place that winter.

The discussion of a voyage to Vinland continued as before, and people strongly urged Karlsefni to make the journey, Gudrid among them. Once he had decided to make the journey he hired himself a crew of sixty men and five women.

Karlsefni and his crew made an agreement that anything of value they obtained would be divided equally among them. They took all sorts of livestock with them, for they intended to settle in the country if they could.

Karlsefni asked Leif for his houses in Vinland, and Leif said he would lend but not give them to him.

They then put out to sea in their ship and arrived without mishap at Leif's booths, where they unloaded their sleeping-sacks. They soon had plenty of good provisions, since a fine, large rorqual had stranded on the beach. After they had gone and carved up the whale they had no lack of food. The livestock made its way inland, but the male animals soon became irritable and hard to handle. They had brought one bull with them.

Karlsefni had trees felled and hewn to load aboard his ship and had the timber piled on a large rock to dry. They had plenty of supplies from the natural bounty there, including grapes, all sorts of fish and game, and other good things.

After the first winter passed and summer came, they became aware of natives. A large group of men came out of the woods close to where the cattle were pastured. The bull began bellowing and snorting very loudly. This frightened the natives, who ran off with their burdens, which included fur pelts and sables and all kinds of skins. They headed for Karlsefni's farm and tried to get into the house, but Karlsefni had the door defended. Neither group understood the language of the other.

The natives then set down their packs and opened them, offering their goods, preferably in exchange for weapons, but Karlsefni forbade the men to trade weapons.

He sought a solution by having the women bring out milk and milk products. Once they saw these products the natives wished to purchase them and nothing else. The trading with the natives resulted in them bearing off their purchases in their stomachs, leaving their packs and skins with Karlsefni and his companions. This done, they departed.

Karlsefni next had a sturdy palisade built around his farm, where they prepared to defend themselves. At this time Gudrid, Karlsefni's wife, gave birth to a boy, who was named Snorri. Near the beginning of their second winter the natives visited them again, in much greater numbers than before and with the same goods as before.

Karlsefni then spoke to the women: 'Bring out whatever food was most in demand last time, and nothing else.'

When the natives saw this they threw their packs in over the palisade. Gudrid sat inside in the doorway, with the cradle of her son, Snorri. A shadow fell across the doorway and a woman entered, rather short in stature, wearing a close-fitting tunic, with a shawl over her head and light red-brown hair. She was pale and had eyes so large that eyes of such size had never been seen in a human head.

She came to where Gudrid was sitting and spoke: 'What is your name?' she said.

'My name is Gudrid, and what is yours?'

'My name is Gudrid,' the other woman said.

Gudrid, Karlsefni's wife, then motioned to her with her hand to sit down beside her, but just as she did so a great crash was heard and the woman disappeared. At that moment one of the natives had been killed by one of Karlsefni's servants for trying to take weapons from them, and they quickly ran off, leaving their clothes and trade goods lying behind. No one but Gudrid had seen the woman.

'We have to decide on a plan,' said Karlsefni, 'since I expect they will return for a third time, hostile and in greater numbers. We'll follow this plan: ten men will go out on this headland and let themselves be seen there, while the rest of us go into the forest and cut a clearing for our cattle. When approaching from the forest we will take our bull and let him head our group into battle.'

In the place where they planned to take them on there was water on one side and a forest on the other. They followed the proposal Karlsefni had made.

The natives soon came to the place Karlsefni had intended for the battle. They fought and a large number of the natives were killed.

One of the men in the natives' group was tall and handsome, and Karlsefni thought him likely to be their leader.

One of the natives then picked up an axe, peered at it awhile and then aimed at one of his companions and struck him. The other fellow was killed outright. The tall man then picked up the axe, examined it awhile and then threw it as far out into the sea as he could. After that the natives fled into the woods at top speed, and they had no more dealings with them.

Karlsefni and his companions spent the entire winter there, but in the spring he declared that he wished to remain no longer and wanted to return to Greenland. They made ready for their journey, taking with them plenty of the land's products – grapevines, berries and skins. They set sail and arrived safely in Eiriksfjord where they stayed over the winter.

7   Discussion soon began again of a Vinland voyage, since the trip seemed to bring men both wealth and renown.

The same summer that Karlsefni returned from Vinland a ship arrived in Greenland from Norway. The skippers were two brothers, Helgi and Finnbogi, who spent the winter in Greenland. They were Icelanders, from the East Fjords.

We now turn to Freydis Eiriksdottir, who set out on a journey from Gardar to meet with the two brothers, Helgi and Finnbogi, and to propose that they all make the journey to Vinland on their ship and have a half-share of any profits from it. They agreed to this.

From there she went to her brother Leif and asked him to give her the houses he had built in Vinland. He replied as he had before, that he would lend the houses but not give them to anyone.

According to the agreement between Freydis and the two brothers, each was to have thirty fighting men aboard his ship and women in addition. Freydis broke the agreement straight away, however, and took five extra men, concealing them so that the brothers were not aware of them until they had reached Vinland.

They put to sea, having agreed beforehand to try to stick together if possible on the way, and they almost managed this. The brothers arrived slightly earlier, however, and had unloaded their ship and carried their belongings to Leif's houses when Freydis arrived. Her group unloaded their ship and carried its belongings up to the houses.

Freydis then said, 'Why did you put your belongings here?'

'We thought,' they answered, 'that you intended to keep your word to us.'

'Leif lent me the houses,' she said, 'not you.'

Helgi then spoke: 'We brothers will never be a match for your ill-will.' They removed their things and built themselves a longhouse farther from the sea, on the bank of a lake, and settled in well. Freydis had wood cut to make a load for her ship.

When winter came the brothers suggested that they hold games and arrange entertainment. This went on for a while, until disagreements arose. The ill-feelings split the party so that the games ceased and each group kept to its own houses. This continued for much of the winter.

Early one morning Freydis got up and dressed, but did not put on any footwear. The weather had left a thick dew on the grass. She took her husband's cape and placed it over her shoulders and went to the brothers' longhouse and came to the doorway. A man had gone out a short while earlier and left the door half-open. She opened the door and stood silently in the doorway awhile. Finnbogi lay awake at the inner end of the house.

He spoke: 'What do you want here, Freydis?'

She answered, 'I want you to get up and come outside. I have to speak to you.'

He did as she said. They went over to a tree trunk lying near the wall of the house and sat down there.

'How do you like it here?' she asked.

'I think the land has much to offer, but I don't like the ill-feeling between us, as I don't think there is reason for it.'

'What you say is true,' she said, 'and I agree. But my purpose in coming to see you was that I want to exchange ships with the two of you, as you have a larger ship than I do and I want to leave this place.'

'I suppose I can agree to that,' he said, 'if that will please you.'

After this they parted. She returned home and Finnbogi went back to his bed. When she climbed back into bed her cold feet woke Thorvard, who asked why she was so cold and wet.

She answered vehemently, 'I went to the brothers, to ask to purchase their ship, as I wanted a larger ship. They reacted so angrily; they struck me and treated me very badly, but you're such a coward that you will repay neither dishonour done to me nor to yourself. I am now paying the price of being so far from my home in Greenland, and unless you avenge this, I will divorce you!'

Not being able to ignore her upbraiding any longer, he told the men to get up as quickly as they could and arm themselves. Having done so, they went at once to the longhouse of the brothers, entered while those inside were still asleep and took them, tied them up and, once bound, led them outside. Freydis, however, had each one of the men who was brought out killed.

Soon all the men had been killed and only the women were left, as no one would kill them.

Freydis then spoke: 'Hand me an axe.'

This was done, and she then attacked the five women there and killed them all.

They returned to their house after this wicked deed, and it was clear that Freydis was highly pleased with what she had accomplished. She spoke to her companions: 'If we are fortunate enough to make it back to Greenland,' she said, 'I will have anyone who tells of these events killed. We will say that they remained behind here when we took our leave.'

Early in the spring they loaded the ship, which the brothers had owned, with all the produce they could gather and the ship would hold. They then set sail and had a good voyage, sailing their ship into Eiriksfjord in early summer. Karlsefni was there already, with his ship all set to sail and only waiting for a favourable wind. It was said that no ship sailing from Greenland had been loaded with a more valuable cargo than the one he commanded.

8 Freydis returned to her farm and livestock, which had not suffered from her absence. She made sure all her companions were well rewarded, since she wished to have her misdeeds concealed. She stayed on her farm after that.

Not everyone was so close-mouthed that they could keep silent about these misdeeds or wickedness, and eventually word got out. In time it reached the ears of Leif, her brother, who thought the story a terrible one.

Leif then took three men from Freydis's company and forced them all under torture to tell the truth about the events, and their accounts agreed in every detail.

'I am not the one to deal my sister, Freydis, the punishment she deserves,' Leif said, 'but I predict that their descendants will not get on well in this world.'

As things turned out, after that no one expected anything but evil from them.

To return to Karlsefni, he made his ship ready and set sail. They had a good passage and made land in Norway safely. He remained there over the winter, sold his goods, and both he and his wife were treated lavishly by the leading men in Norway. The following spring he made his ship ready to sail to Iceland.

When he was ready to sail and the ship lay at the landing stage awaiting a favourable wind, he was approached by a southerner, from Bremen in Saxony. He asked Karlsefni to sell him the carved decoration on the prow.*

'I don't care to sell it,' he replied.

'I'll give you half a mark of gold for it,' the southerner said.

Karlsefni thought this a good offer and the purchase was concluded. The southerner then took the decoration and departed. Karlsefni did not know of what wood it was made, but it was of maple† which had been brought from Vinland.

Karlsefni then put to sea and made land in north Iceland, in Skagafjord, where he had his ship drawn ashore for the winter. In the spring he purchased the land at Glaumbaer and established his farm there, where he lived for the remainder of his days. He was the most respected of men. He and his wife, Gudrid, had a great number of descendants, and a fine clan they were.

After Karlsefni's death Gudrid took over the running of the household, together with her son Snorri who had been born in Vinland.

When Snorri married, Gudrid travelled abroad, made a pilgrimage south and returned to her son Snorri's farm. By then he had had a church built at Glaumbaer. Later Gudrid became a nun and anchoress, staying there for the remainder of her life.

Snorri had a son named Thorgeir, who was the father of Yngveld, the mother of Bishop Brand. Snorri Karlsefnisson's daughter Hallfrid was the wife of Runolf, the father of Bishop Thorlak. Bjorn, another son of

---

* The Icelandic word *húsasnotra* could refer not to a decoration but to a kind of astrolabe.
† The Icelandic word *mösur* could also refer to burl or burly wood.

Karlsefni and Gudrid, was the father of Thorunn, the mother of Bishop Bjorn.

There are a great number of people descended from Karlsefni, who founded a prosperous clan. It was Karlsefni who gave the most extensive reports of anyone of all of these voyages, some of which have now been set down in writing.

Translated by KENEVA KUNZ

EIRIK THE RED'S SAGA

I   There was a warrior king named Oleif who was called Oleif the White. He was the son of King Ingjald, who was the son of Helgi, who was son of Olaf, who was son of Gudrod, who was son of Halfdan White-leg, king of the people of Oppland.

Oleif went on Viking expeditions around Britain, conquering the shire of Dublin, over which he declared himself king. As his wife he took Aud the Deep-minded, the daughter of Ketil Flat-nose, son of Bjorn Buna, an excellent man from Norway. Their son was named Thorstein the Red.

After Oleif was killed in battle in Ireland, Aud and Thorstein went to the Hebrides. There Thorstein married Thurid, the daughter of Eyvind the Easterner and sister of Helgi the Lean. They had a large number of children.

Thorstein became a warrior king, throwing in his lot with Earl Sigurd the Powerful, the son of Eystein Glumra. They conquered Caithness and Sutherland, Ross and Moray, and more than half of Scotland. Thorstein became king there until the Scots betrayed him and he was killed in battle.

Aud was at Caithness when she learned of the death of Thorstein. She had a knorr built secretly in the forest and, when it was finished, set out for the Orkneys. There she arranged the marriage of Groa, Thorstein the Red's daughter. Groa was the mother of Grelod, who was married to Earl Thorfinn the Skull-splitter.

After this Aud set out for Iceland. On her ship she had a crew of twenty free-born men. Aud reached Iceland and spent the first winter in Bjarnarhofn with her brother Bjorn. Afterwards Aud claimed all the land in the Dales between the Dagverdara and Skraumuhlaupsa rivers and settled at Hvamm. She used to pray on the Krossholar hill, where she had crosses erected, for she was baptized and a devout Christian. Accompanying her on her journey to Iceland were many men of good family who had been taken prisoner by Vikings raiding around Britain and were called bondsmen.

One of them was named Vifil. He was a man of very good family who had been taken prisoner in Britain and was called a bondsman until Aud gave him his freedom. When Aud gave her crew farm sites, Vifil asked her why she had not given him one like the others. Aud replied that it made no difference [whether he owned land or not], he would be considered just as fine a man wherever he was. Aud gave him Vifilsdal and he settled there. He had a wife and two sons, Thorgeir and Thorbjorn. They were promising men and grew up with their father.

2   There was a man named Thorvald, the son of Asvald Ulfsson, son of Ox-Thorir. His son was named Eirik the Red. Father and son left Jaeren and sailed to Iceland because [they had been involved in] slayings. They claimed land on the coast of Hornstrandir and settled at Drangar. There Thorvald died.

As his wife Eirik took Thjodhild, the daughter of Jorund Atlason. Her mother, Thorbjorg Ship-breast, was married to Thorbjorn of Haukadal then. Eirik then moved south, cleared land in Haukadal and built a farm at Eiriksstadir by Vatnshorn.

Eirik's slaves then caused a landslide to fall on the farm of Valthjof at Valthjofsstadir. His kinsman Filth-Eyjolf killed the slaves near Skeidsbrekkur above Vatnshorn. For this, Eirik slew Filth-Eyjolf. He also killed Hrafn the Dueller at Leikskalar. Geirstein and Odd of Jorvi, Eyjolf's kinsmen, sought redress for his killing.

After this Eirik was outlawed from Haukadal. He claimed the islands Brokey and Oxney and farmed at Tradir on Sudurey island the first winter. It was then Eirik lent Thorgest bedstead boards. Later he moved to Oxney where he farmed at Eiriksstadir. He then asked for the bedstead boards back without success. Eirik went to Breidabolstad and took the boards, and Thorgest came after him. They fought not far from the farm at Drangar, where two of Thorgest's sons were killed, along with several other men.

After that both of them kept a large following. Eirik had the support of Styr and Eyjolf of Sviney, Thorbjorn Vifilsson and the sons of Thorbrand of Alftafjord, while Thord Bellower and Thorgeir of Hitardal, Aslak of Langadal and his son Illugi gave their support to Thorgest. Eirik and his companions were sentenced to outlawry at the Thorsnes Assembly. He made his ship ready in Eiriksvog and Eyjolf hid him in Dimunarvog while Thorgest and his men searched the islands for him. Thorbjorn, Eyjolf and Styr accompanied Eirik through the islands. Eirik said he intended to seek out the land that Gunnbjorn, the son of Ulf Crow, had seen when he was driven off course westward and discovered Gunnbjarnarsker (Gunnbjorn's skerry). If he found the land he promised to return to his friends and they parted with great warmth. Eirik promised to support them in any way he could if they should need his help.

Eirik sailed seaward from Snaefellsnes and approached land [in Greenland] under the glacier called Hvitserk (White shift). From there he sailed southwards, seeking suitable land for settlement.

He spent the first winter on Eiriksey island, near the middle of the eastern settlement.* The following spring he travelled to Eiriksfjord where he settled. That summer he travelled around the [then] uninhabited western settlement, giving names to a number of sites. The second winter he spent in Eiriksholmar near Hvarfsgnipa, and the third summer he sailed as far north as Snaefell and into Hrafnsfjord. There he thought he had reached the head of Eiriksfjord. He then returned to spend the third winter in Eiriksey, at the mouth of Eiriksfjord.

The following summer he sailed to Iceland and made land in Breidafjord. He spent the winter with Ingolf at Holmlatur. The following spring he fought with Thorgest and lost, after which they made their peace.

In the summer Eirik left to settle in the country he had found, which he called Greenland, as he said people would be attracted there if it had a favourable name.

3   Thorgeir Vifilsson took as his wife Arnora, the daughter of Einar of Laugarbrekka, the son of Sigmund, son of Ketil Thistle who had claimed land in Thistilfjord.

Einar had another daughter named Hallveig. She was married to Thorbjorn Vifilsson and was given land at Laugarbrekka, at Hellisvellir. Thorbjorn moved his household there and became a man of great worth. He ran a prosperous farm and lived in grand style. Gudrid was the name of Thorbjorn's daughter. She was the most attractive of women and one to be reckoned with in all her dealings.

A man named Orm farmed at Arnarstapi. His wife was named Halldis. Orm was a good farmer and a great friend of Thorbjorn's. The couple fostered Gudrid, who spent long periods of time there.

A man named Thorgeir farmed at Thorgeirsfell. He was very rich in livestock and was a freed slave. He had a son named Einar, a handsome and capable man, with a liking for fine dress. Einar went on trading voyages

---

* This was in the south-west of Greenland.

abroad, at which he was quite successful, and he usually spent the winters in Iceland and Norway by turn.

It is said that one autumn, when Einar was in Iceland, he travelled with his goods out to the Snaefellsnes peninsula, intending to sell them. He came to Arnarstapi and Orm invited him to stay with them, which Einar accepted, as friendship was included in the bargain. Einar's goods were placed in a shed. He took them out to show to Orm and his household, and asked Orm to choose as much as he wished for himself. Orm accepted and praised Einar as both a merchant of good repute and man of great fortune. While they were occupied with the goods a woman passed in front of the shed doorway.

Einar asked Orm who this beautiful woman was who had passed in front of the doorway – 'I haven't seen her here before.'

Orm said, 'That is Gudrid, my foster-daughter, the daughter of the farmer Thorbjorn of Laugarbrekka.'

Einar spoke: 'She'd make a fine match. Or has anyone already turned up to ask for her hand?'

Orm answered, 'She's been asked for right enough, my friend, but is no easy prize. As it turns out, she is choosy about her husband, as is her father as well.'

'Be that as it may,' Einar spoke, 'she's the woman I intend to propose to, and I would like you to put my proposal to her father, and if you do your best to support my suit I'll repay you with the truest of friendship. Farmer Thorbjorn should see that we'd be well connected, as he's a man of high repute and has a good farm, but I'm told his means have been much depleted. My father and I lack neither land nor means, so we'd be a considerable support to Thorbjorn if the match were concluded.'

Orm answered, 'Though I think of myself as your friend, I'm not eager to breach the question with him, for Thorbjorn is prone to take offence, and a man with no small sense of his own worth.'

Einar replied he would not be satisfied unless the proposal was made, and Orm said he would have his way. Einar headed south once more until he arrived back home.

Some time later Thorbjorn held an autumn feast, as was his custom, for he lived in high style. Orm from Arnarstapi attended and many other friends of Thorbjorn's.

Orm managed to speak privately to Thorbjorn and told him of the recent visit by Einar of Thorgeirsfell, who was becoming a man of promise. Orm then put Einar's proposal to Thorbjorn and said it would be suitable on a number of accounts – 'it would be a considerable support to you as far as money is concerned'.

Thorbjorn answered, 'I never expected to hear such words from you, telling me to marry my daughter to the son of a slave, as you suggest now, since you think I'm running short of money. She'll not go back with you, since you think her worthy of such a lowly match.'

Orm then returned home and all the other guests went to their homes. Gudrid stayed behind with her father and spent that winter at home. When spring came Thorbjorn invited some friends to a feast. The provisions were plentiful, and it was attended by many people who enjoyed the finest of feasts.

During the feasting Thorbjorn called for silence, then spoke: 'Here I have lived a life of some length. I have enjoyed the kindness and warmth of others, and to my mind our dealings have gone well. My financial situation, however, which has not up to now been considered an unworthy one, is on the decline. So I would rather leave my farm than live with this loss of honour, and rather leave the country than shame my family. I intend to take up the offer made to me by my friend Eirik the Red, when he took his leave of me in Breidafjord. I intend to head for Greenland this summer if things go as I wish.'

These plans caused a great stir, as Thorbjorn had long been popular, but it was generally felt that once he had spoken in this way there would be little point in trying to dissuade him. Thorbjorn gave people gifts and the feast came to an end after this, with everyone returning to their homes.

Thorbjorn sold his lands and bought a ship which had been beached at the Hraunhafnaros estuary. Thirty men accompanied him on his voyage. Among them were Orm of Arnarstapi and his wife, and other friends of Thorbjorn's who did not want to part with him.

After this they set sail but the weather, which had been favourable when they set out, changed. The favourable wind dropped and they were beset by storms, so that they made little progress during the summer. Following this, illness plagued their company, and Orm and his wife and half the company died. The sea swelled and their boat took on much water but, despite many other hardships, they made land in Greenland at Herjolfsnes during the Winter Nights.

At Herjolfsnes lived a man named Thorkel. He was a capable man and the best of farmers. He gave Thorbjorn and all his companions shelter for the winter, treating them generously. Thorbjorn and all his companions were highly pleased.

4   This was a very lean time in Greenland. Those who had gone hunting had had poor catches, and some of them had failed to return.

In the district there lived a woman named Thorbjorg, a seeress who was called the 'Little Prophetess'. She was one of ten sisters, all of whom had the gift of prophecy, and was the only one of them still alive.

It was Thorbjorg's custom to spend the winter visiting, one after another, farms to which she had been invited, mostly by people curious to learn of their own future or what was in store for the coming year. Since Thorkel was the leading farmer there, people felt it was up to him to try to find out when the hard times which had been oppressing them would let up. Thorkel invited the seeress to visit and preparations were made to entertain her well, as was the custom of the time when a woman of this type was received. A high seat was set for her, complete with cushion. This was to be stuffed with chicken feathers.

When she arrived one evening, along with the man who had been sent to fetch her, she was wearing a black mantle with a strap, which was adorned with precious stones right down to the hem. About her neck she wore a string of glass beads and on her head a hood of black lambskin lined with white catskin. She bore a staff with a knob at the top, adorned with brass set with stones on top. About her waist she had a linked charm belt with a large purse. In it she kept the charms which she needed for her predictions. She wore calfskin boots lined with fur, with long, sturdy laces and large pewter knobs on the ends. On her hands she wore gloves of catskin, white and lined with fur.

When she entered, everyone was supposed to offer her respectful greetings, and she responded according to how the person appealed to her. Farmer Thorkel took the wise woman by the hand and led her to the seat which had been prepared for her. He then asked her to survey his flock, servants and buildings. She had little to say about all of it.

That evening tables were set up and food prepared for the seeress. A porridge of kid's milk was made for her and as meat she was given the hearts of all the animals available there. She had a spoon of brass and a knife with an ivory shaft, its two halves clasped with bronze bands, and the point of which had broken off.

Once the tables had been cleared away, Thorkel approached Thorbjorg and asked what she thought of the house there and the conduct of the household, and how soon he could expect an answer to what he had asked and everyone wished to know. She answered that she would not reveal this until the next day after having spent the night there.

Late the following day she was provided with things she required to carry out her magic rites. She asked for women who knew the chants required for carrying out magic rites, which are called ward songs.* But such women were not to be found. Then the people of the household were asked if there was anyone with such knowledge.

Gudrid answered, 'I have neither magical powers nor the gift of prophecy, but in Iceland my foster-mother, Halldis, taught me chants she called ward songs.'

Thorbjorg answered, 'Then you know more than I expected.'

Gudrid said, 'These are the sort of actions in which I intend to take no part, because I am a Christian woman.'

Thorbjorg answered: 'It could be that you could help the people here by so doing, and you'd be no worse a woman for that. But I expect Thorkel to provide me with what I need.'

Thorkel then urged Gudrid, who said she would do as he wished. The women formed a warding ring around the platform raised for sorcery, with Thorbjorg perched atop it. Gudrid spoke the chant so well and so beautifully that people there said they had never heard anyone recite in a fairer voice.

The seeress thanked her for her chant. She said many spirits had been attracted who thought the chant fair to hear – 'though earlier they wished to turn their backs on us and refused to do our bidding. Many things are now clear to me which were earlier concealed from both me and others. And I can tell you that this spell of hardship will last no longer, and times will improve as the spring advances. The bout of illness which has long plagued you will also improve sooner than you expect. And you, Gudrid, I will reward on the spot for the help we have received, since your fate is now very clear to me. You will make the most honourable of matches here in Greenland, though you won't be putting down roots here, as your path leads to Iceland and from you will be descended a long and worthy line. Over all the branches of that family a bright ray will shine. May you fare well, now, my child.'

After that people approached the wise woman to learn what each of them was most curious to know. She made them good answer, and little that she predicted did not occur.

Following this an escort arrived from another farm and the seeress

---

* Literally, 'ward enticers' (*varðlokkur*), chants likely to have been intended to attract the spirits to the sorceress, who was enclosed in a ring of wards as described below.

departed. Thorbjorn was also sent for, as he had refused to remain at home on the farm while such heathen practices were going on.

With the arrival of spring the weather soon improved, as Thorbjorg had predicted. Thorbjorn made his ship ready and sailed until he reached Brattahlid. Eirik received him with open arms and declared how good it was that he had come. Thorbjorn and his family spent the winter with him.

The following spring Eirik gave Thorbjorn land at Stokkanes, where he built an impressive farmhouse and lived from then on.

5   Eirik had a wife named Thjodhild, and two sons, Thorstein and Leif. Both of them were promising young men. Thorstein lived at home with his father, and there was no man in Greenland who was considered as handsome as he.

Leif had sailed to Norway where he was one of King Olaf Tryggvason's men.

But when Leif sailed from Greenland that summer the ship was driven off course to land in the Hebrides. From there they failed to get a favourable wind and had to stay in the islands for much of the summer.

Leif fell in love with a woman named Thorgunna. She was of very good family, and Leif realized that she knew a thing or two.

When Leif was leaving Thorgunna asked to go with him. Leif asked whether her kinsmen were of any mind to agree to this, and she declared she did not care. Leif said he was reluctant to abduct a woman of such high birth from a foreign country – 'there are so few of us'.

Thorgunna spoke: 'I'm not sure you'll like the alternative better.'

'I'll take my chances on that,' Leif said.

'Then I will tell you,' Thorgunna said, 'that I am with child, and that this child is yours. It's my guess that I will give birth to a boy, in due course. And even though you ignore him, I will raise the boy and send him to you in Greenland as soon as he is of an age to travel with others. But it's my guess that he will serve you as well as you have served me now with your departure. I intend to come to Greenland myself before it's all over.'

He gave her a gold ring, a Greenland cape and a belt of ivory.

The boy, who was named Thorgils, did come to Greenland and Leif recognized him as his son. – Some men say that this Thorgils came to Iceland before the hauntings at Froda* in the summer. – Thorgils stayed in

---

* The story is told in *The Saga of the People of Eyri*.

Greenland after that, and before it was all over he was also thought to have something preternatural about him.

Leif and his men left the Hebrides and made land in Norway in the autumn. Leif became one of the king's men, and King Olaf Tryggvason showed him much honour, as Leif appeared to him to be a man of good breeding.

On one occasion the king spoke to Leif privately and asked, 'Do you intend to sail to Greenland this summer?'

Leif answered, 'I would like to do so, if it is your wish.'

The king answered, 'It could well be so; you will go as my envoy and convert Greenland to Christianity.'

Leif said the king should decide that, but added that he feared this message would meet with a harsh reception in Greenland. The king said he saw no man more suitable for the job than Leif – 'and you'll have the good fortune that's needed'.

'If that's so,' Leif declared, 'then only because I enjoy yours as well.'

Once he had made ready, Leif set sail. After being tossed about at sea for a long time he chanced upon land where he had not expected any to be found. Fields of self-sown wheat and vines were growing there; also, there were trees known as maple, and they took specimens of all of them.

Leif also chanced upon men clinging to a ship's wreck, whom he brought home and found shelter for over the winter. In so doing he showed his strong character and kindness. He converted the country to Christianity.* Afterwards he became known as Leif the Lucky.

Leif made land in Eiriksfjord and went home to the farm at Brattahlid. There he was received warmly. He soon began to advocate Christianity and the true catholic faith throughout the country, revealing the messages of King Olaf Tryggvason to the people, and telling them how excellent and glorious this faith was.

Eirik was reluctant to give up his faith, but Thjodhild was quick to convert and had a church built a fair distance from the house. It was called Thjodhild's church and there she prayed, along with those other people who converted to Christianity, of whom there were many. After her conversion, Thjodhild refused to sleep with Eirik, much to his displeasure.

The suggestion that men go to seek out the land which Leif had found soon gained wide support. The leading proponent was Eirik's son, Thorstein,

---

* This sentence, or even the whole paragraph, appears to be misplaced. Presumably 'the country' refers to Greenland.

a good, wise and popular man. Eirik was also urged to go, as people valued most his good fortune and leadership. For a long time he was against going, but when his friends urged him he did not refuse.

They made ready the ship on which Thorbjorn had sailed to Greenland, with twenty men to go on the journey. They took few trading goods, but all the more weapons and provisions.

The morning that he left, Eirik took a small chest containing gold and silver. He hid the money and then went on his way. After going only a short way he fell from his horse, breaking several ribs and injuring his shoulder, so that he cried out, 'Ow, ow!' Because of his mishap he sent word to his wife to retrieve the money he had hidden, saying he had been punished for having hidden it.

They then sailed out of Eiriksfjord in fine spirits, pleased with their prospects.

They were tossed about at sea for a long time and failed to reach their intended destination. They came in sight of Iceland and noticed birds from Ireland. Their ship was driven to and fro across the sea until they returned to Greenland in the autumn, worn out and in poor shape, and made land when it was almost winter in Eiriksfjord.

Eirik then spoke: 'More cheerful we were in the summer to leave this fjord than now to return to it, though we have much to welcome us.'

Thorstein spoke: 'We'd be doing the generous thing by seeing to those men who have no house to go to and providing for them over the winter.'

Eirik answered, 'It's usually true, as they say, that you can't know a good question until you have the answer, and so it'll turn out here. We'll do as you say.'

All those men who had no other house to go to were taken in by father and son for the winter. They went home to Brattahlid then and spent the winter there.

6   The next thing to be told of is the proposal made by Thorstein Eiriksson to Gudrid Thorbjarnardottir. He was given a favourable answer by both Gudrid and her father, and so Thorstein married Gudrid and their wedding was held at Brattahlid that autumn. The wedding feast was a grand one and the guests were many.

Thorstein had a farm and livestock in the western settlement at a place called Lysufjord. A man there named Thorstein owned a half-share in this farm; his wife was named Sigrid. Thorstein and Gudrid went to his namesake in Lysufjord that autumn where they were received warmly. They spent the winter there.

It then happened that sickness struck the farm shortly after the beginning of winter. The foreman, named Gardi, was an unpopular man. He was the first to fall ill and die. It was not long until the inhabitants caught the sickness, one after the other and died, until Thorstein Eiriksson and Sigrid, the farmer's wife, fell ill, too.

One evening Sigrid wanted to go to the outhouse which stood opposite the door of the farmhouse. Gudrid went with her and as they looked at the doorway Sigrid cried, 'Oh!'

Gudrid spoke: 'We have acted carelessly, you shouldn't be exposed to the cold at all; we must get back inside as quickly as we can!'

Sigrid answered, 'I won't go out with things as they are! All of those who are dead are standing there before the door; among them I recognize your husband Thorstein and myself as well. How horrible to see it!'

When it had passed, she spoke: 'I don't see them now.'

Thorstein, whom she had seen with a whip in his hand, ready to strike the dead, had also disappeared. They then entered the house.

Before morning came she was dead and a coffin was made for her body. That same day men were going fishing and Thorstein accompanied them down to where the boats were beached. Towards dusk he went again to check on their catch. Then Thorstein Eiriksson sent him word to come to him, saying there was no peace at home as the farmer's wife was trying to rise up and get into the bed with him. When he entered she had reached the sideboards of the bed. He took hold of her and drove an axe into her breast.

Thorstein Eiriksson died near sundown. Thorstein told Gudrid to lie down and sleep; he would keep watch over the bodies that night, he said. Gudrid did so and soon fell asleep.

Only a little of the night had passed when Thorstein rose up, saying that he wished Gudrid to be summoned and wanted to speak to her: 'It is God's will that I be granted an exception for this brief time to improve my prospects.'

Thorstein went to Gudrid, woke her and told her to cross herself and ask the Lord for help – 'Thorstein Eiriksson has spoken to me and said he wanted to see you. It is your decision; I will not advise you either way.'

She answered, 'It may be that there is a purpose for this strange occurrence, and it will have consequences long to be remembered. I expect that God will grant me his protection. I will take the chance, with God's mercy, of speaking to him, as I cannot escape any threat to myself. I would rather he need not look farther, and I suspect that would be the alternative.'

Gudrid then went to see Thorstein, and he seemed to her to shed tears. He spoke several words in her ear in a low voice, so that she alone heard, and said that those men rejoiced who kept their faith well and it brought mercy and salvation. Yet he said many kept their faith poorly.

'These practices will not do which have been followed here in Greenland after the coming of Christianity: burying people in unconsecrated ground with little if any service said over them. I want to have my corpse taken to a church, along with those of the other people who have died here. But Gardi should be burned on a pyre straight away, as he has caused all the hauntings which have occurred here this winter.'

He also spoke of his situation and declared that her future held great things in store, but he warned her against marrying a Greenlander. He also asked her to donate their money to a church or to poor people, and then he sank down for the second time.

It had been common practice in Greenland, since Christianity had been adopted, to bury people in unconsecrated ground on the farms where they died. A pole was set up on the breast of each corpse until a priest came, then the pole was pulled out and consecrated water poured into the hole and a burial service performed, even though this was only done much later.

The bodies were taken to the church in Eiriksfjord, and priests held burial services for them.

After this Thorbjorn died. All of his money went to Gudrid. Eirik invited her to live with them and saw that she was well provided for.

7   There was a man named Thorfinn Karlsefni, the son of Thord Horse-head who lived in north Iceland, at the place now called Reynines in Skagafjord. Karlsefni was a man of good family and good means. His mother was named Thorunn. He went on trading voyages and was a merchant of good repute.

One summer Karlsefni made his ship ready for a voyage to Greenland. Snorri Thorbrandsson of Alftafjord was to accompany him and they took a party of forty men with them.

A man named Bjarni Grimolfsson, from Breidafjord, and another named Thorhall Gamlason, from the East Fjords, made their ship ready the same summer as Karlsefni and were also heading for Greenland. There were forty men on their ship. The two ships set sail once they had made ready.

There is no mention of how long they were at sea. But it is said that both these ships sailed into Eiriksfjord that autumn.

Eirik rode to the ships, along with other Greenlanders, and busy trading commenced. The skippers of the vessels invited Eirik to take his pick of their wares, and Eirik repaid them generously, as he invited both crews home to stay the winter with him in Brattahlid. This the merchants accepted and went home with him. Their goods were later transported to Brattahlid, where there was no lack of good and ample outbuildings to store them in. The merchants were highly pleased with their winter stay with Eirik.

But as Yule approached, Eirik grew sadder than was his wont. On one occasion Karlsefni spoke to him privately and asked, 'Is something troubling you, Eirik? You seem to me to be more silent than before. You have treated us very generously, and we owe it to you to repay you by any means we can. Tell me what is causing your sadness.'

Eirik answered, 'You have also accepted with gratitude and respect, and I don't feel that your contribution to our exchange has been lacking in any way. But I'll regret it if word gets round that you've spent here a Yuletide as lean as the one now approaching.'

Karlsefni answered, 'It won't be that at all. We've malt and flour and grain aboard our ships, and you may help yourself to them as you will, to prepare a feast worthy of your generous hospitality.'

Eirik accepted this. Preparations for a Yule feast began, which proved to be so bountiful that men could scarcely recall having seen its like.

After Yule Karlsefni approached Eirik to ask for Gudrid's hand, as it seemed to him that she was under Eirik's protection, and both an attractive and knowledgeable woman. Eirik answered that he would support his suit, and that she was a fine match – 'and it's likely that her fate will turn out as prophesied,' he added, even if she did marry Karlsefni, whom he knew to be a worthy man. The subject was broached with Gudrid and she allowed herself to be guided by Eirik's advice. No more needs to be said on that point, except that the match was agreed and the celebrations extended to include the wedding which took place.

That winter there was much merrymaking in Brattahlid; many board games were played, there was storytelling and plenty of other entertainment to brighten the life of the household.

8   There were great discussions that winter in Brattahlid of Snorri and Karlsefni setting sail for Vinland, and people talked at length about it. In the end Snorri and Karlsefni made their vessel ready, intending to sail in search of Vinland that summer. Bjarni and Thorhall decided to accompany them on the voyage, taking their own ship and their companions who had sailed with them on the voyage out.

A man named Thorvard was married to Freydis, who was an illegitimate daughter of Eirik the Red. He went with them, along with Thorvald, Eirik's son, and Thorhall who was called the Huntsman. For years he had accompanied Eirik on hunting trips in the summers, and was entrusted with many tasks. Thorhall was a large man, dark and coarse-featured; he was getting on in years and difficult to handle. He was a silent man, who was not generally given to conversation, devious and yet insulting in his speech, and who usually did his best to make trouble. He had paid scant heed to the faith since it had come to Greenland. Thorhall was not popular with most people but he had long been in Eirik's confidence. He was among those on the ship with Thorvald and Thorvard, as he had a wide knowledge of the uninhabited regions. They had the ship which Thorbjorn had brought to Greenland and set sail with Karlsefni and his group. Most of the men aboard were from Greenland. The crews of the three ships made a hundred plus forty men.

They sailed along the coast to the western settlement, then to the Bear islands and from there with a northerly wind. After two days at sea they sighted land and rowed over in boats to explore it. There they found many flat slabs of stone, so large that two men could lie foot-to-foot across them. There were many foxes there. They gave the land the name Helluland (Stone-slab land).

After that they sailed with a northerly wind for two days, and again sighted land, with large forests and many animals. An island lay to the south-east, off the coast, where they discovered a bear, and they called it Bjarney (Bear Island), and the forested land itself Markland.

After another two days passed they again sighted land and approached the shore where a peninsula jutted out. They sailed upwind along the coast, keeping the land on the starboard. The country was wild with a long shoreline and sand flats. They rowed ashore in boats and, discovering the keel of a ship there, named this point Kjalarnes (Keel point). They also gave the beaches the name Furdustrandir (Wonder beaches) for their surprising length. After this the coastline was indented with numerous inlets which they skirted in their ships.

When Leif had served King Olaf Tryggvason and was told by him to convert Greenland to Christianity, the king had given him two Scots, a man named Haki and a woman called Hekja. The king told him to call upon them whenever he needed someone with speed, as they were fleeter of foot than any deer. Leif and Eirik had sent them to accompany Karlsefni.

After sailing the length of the Furdustrandir, they put the two Scots ashore and told them to run southwards to explore the country and return before three days' time had elapsed. They were dressed in a garment known as a *kjafal*, which had a hood at the top but no arms, and was open at the sides and fastened between the legs with a button and loop; they wore nothing else.

The ships cast anchor and lay to during this time.

After three days had passed the two returned to the shore, one of them with grapes in hand and the other with self-sown wheat. Karlsefni said that they had found good land. After taking them on board once more, they sailed onwards, until they reached a fjord cutting into the coast. They steered the ships into the fjord with an island near its mouth, where there were strong currents, and called the island Straumsey (Stream island). There were so many birds there that they could hardly walk without stepping on eggs. They sailed up into the fjord, which they called Straumsfjord, unloaded the cargo from the ships and began settling in.

They had brought all sorts of livestock with them and explored the land and its resources. There were mountains there, and a pleasant landscape. They paid little attention to things other than exploring the land. The grass there grew tall.

They spent the winter there, and it was a harsh winter, for which they had made little preparation, and they grew short of food and caught nothing when hunting or fishing. They went out to the island, expecting to find some prey to hunt or food on the beaches. They found little food, but their livestock improved there. After this they entreated God to send them something to eat, but the response was not as quick in coming as their need was urgent. Thorhall disappeared and men went to look for him. They searched for three days, and on the fourth Karlsefni and Bjarni found him at the edge of a cliff. He was staring skywards, with his mouth, nostrils and eyes wide open, scratching and pinching himself and mumbling something.

They asked what he was doing there, and he replied that it made no difference. He said they need not look so surprised and said for most of his life he had got along without their advice. They told him to come back with them and he did so.

Shortly afterwards they found a beached whale and flocked to the site to carve it up, although they failed to recognize what type it was. Karlsefni had a wide knowledge of whales, but even he did not recognize it. The cooks boiled the meat and they ate it, but it made everyone ill.

Thorhall then came up and spoke: 'Didn't Old Redbeard prove to be more help than your Christ? This was my payment for the poem I composed about Thor, my guardian, who's seldom disappointed me.'

Once they heard this no one wanted to eat the whale meat, they cast it off a cliff and threw themselves on God's mercy. The weather improved so they could go fishing, and from then on they had supplies in plenty.

In the spring they moved further into Straumsfjord and lived on the produce of both shores of the fjord: hunting game inland, gathering eggs on the island and fishing at sea.

9   They then began to discuss and plan the continuation of their journey. Thorhall wanted to head north, past Furdustrandir and around Kjalarnes to seek Vinland. Karlsefni wished to sail south along the east shore, feeling the land would be more substantial the farther south it was, and he felt it was advisable to explore both.

Thorhall then made his ship ready close to the island, with no more than nine men to accompany him. The rest of their company went with Karlsefni.

One day as Thorhall was carrying water aboard his ship he drank of it and spoke this verse:

1.	With promises of fine drinks	
	the war-trees wheedled,	*war-trees:* warriors
	spurring me to journey	
	to these scanty shores.	
	War-oak of the helmet god,	*war-oak:* warrior, *helmet god:* Odin
	I now wield but a bucket,	
	no sweet wine do I sup	
	stooping at the spring.	

After that they set out, and Karlsefni followed them as far as the island. Before hoisting the sail Thorhall spoke this verse:

2.   We'll return to where
     our countrymen await us,
     head our sand-heaven's horse   *sand-heaven:* sea, its *horse:* ship
     to scout the ship's wide plains.   *ship's . . . plains:* seas
     Let the wielders of sword storms   *wielders of sword storms:* warriors
     laud the land, unwearied,
     settle Wonder Beaches
     and serve up their whale.

They then separated and Thorhall and his crew sailed north past Furdu-strandir and Kjalarnes, and from there attempted to sail to the west of it. But they ran into storms and were driven ashore in Ireland, where they were beaten and enslaved. There Thorhall died.

10   Karlsefni headed south around the coast, with Snorri and Bjarni and the rest of their company. They sailed a long time, until they came to a river which flowed into a lake and from there into the sea. There were wide sandbars beyond the mouth of the river, and they could only sail into the river at high tide. Karlsefni and his company sailed into the lagoon and called the land Hop (Tidal pool). There they found fields of self-sown wheat in the low-lying areas and vines growing on the hills. Every stream was teeming with fish. They dug trenches along the high-water mark and when the tide ebbed there were halibut* in them. There were a great number of deer of all kinds in the forest.

They stayed there for a fortnight, enjoying themselves and finding nothing unusual. They had taken their livestock with them.

Early one morning they noticed nine hide-covered boats, and the people in them waved wooden poles that made a swishing sound as they turned them around sunwise.

Karlsefni then spoke: 'What can this mean?'

Snorri replied: 'It may be a sign of peace; we should take a white shield and lift it up in return.'

This they did.

The others then rowed towards them and were astonished at the sight of them as they landed on the shore. They were short in height with threatening

---

* Although the Icelandic term *helgir fiskar* (literally 'holy fishes') means 'halibut' in English, these could be any type of flatfish.

features and tangled hair on their heads. Their eyes were large and their cheeks broad. They stayed there awhile, marvelling, then rowed away again to the south around the point.

The group had built their booths up above the lake, with some of the huts farther inland, and others close to the shore.

They remained there that winter. There was no snow at all and the livestock could fend for themselves out of doors.

II One morning, as spring advanced, they noticed a large number of hide-covered boats rowing up from the south around the point. There were so many of them that it looked as if bits of coal had been tossed over the water, and there was a pole waving from each boat. They signalled with their shields and began trading with the visitors, who mostly wished to trade for red cloth. They also wanted to purchase swords and spears, but Karlsefni and Snorri forbade this. They traded dark pelts for the cloth, and for each pelt they took cloth a hand in length, which they bound about their heads.

This went on for some time, until there was little cloth left. They then cut the cloth into smaller pieces, each no wider than a finger's width, but the natives gave just as much for it or more.

At this point a bull, owned by Karlsefni and his companions, ran out of the forest and bellowed loudly. The natives took fright at this, ran to their boats and rowed off to the south. Three weeks passed and there was no sign of them.

After that they saw a large group of native boats approach from the south, as thick as a steady stream. They were waving poles counter-sunwise now and all of them were shrieking loudly. The men took up their red shields and went towards them. They met and began fighting. A hard barrage rained down and the natives also had catapults. Karlsefni and Snorri then saw the natives lift up on poles a large round object, about the size of a sheep's gut and black in colour, which came flying up on the land and made a threatening noise when it landed. It struck great fear into Karlsefni and his men, who decided their best course was to flee upriver, since the native party seemed to be attacking from all sides, until they reached a cliff wall where they could put up a good fight.

Freydis came out of the camp as they were fleeing. She called, 'Why do you flee such miserable opponents, men like you who look to me to be capable of killing them off like sheep? Had I a weapon I'm sure I would fight better than any of you.' They paid no attention to what she said. Freydis wanted to go with them, but moved somewhat slowly, as she was with child. She followed them into the forest, but the natives reached her. She came across a slain man, Thorbrand Snorrason, who had been struck in the head by a slab of stone. His sword lay beside him, and this she snatched up and prepared to defend herself with it as the natives approached her. Freeing one of her breasts from her shift, she smacked the sword with it. This frightened the natives, who turned and ran back to their boats and rowed away.

Karlsefni and his men came back to her and praised her luck.

Two of Karlsefni's men were killed and many of the natives were slain, yet Karlsefni and his men were outnumbered. They returned to the booths wondering who these numerous people were who had attacked them on land. But it now looked to them as if the company in the boats had been the sole attackers, and any other attackers had only been an illusion.

The natives also found one of the dead men, whose axe lay beside him. One of them picked up the axe and chopped at a tree, and then each took his turn at it. They thought this thing which cut so well a real treasure. One of them struck a stone and the axe broke. He thought a thing which could not withstand stone to be of little worth, and tossed it away.

The party then realized that, despite everything the land had to offer there, they would be under constant threat of attack from its prior inhabitants. They made ready to depart for their own country. Sailing north along the shore, they discovered five natives sleeping in skin sacks near the shore. Beside them they had vessels filled with deer marrow blended with blood. They assumed these men to be outlaws and killed them.

They then came to a headland thick with deer. The point looked like a huge dunghill, as the deer gathered there at night to sleep. They then entered Straumsfjord, where they found food in plenty. Some people say that Bjarni and Gudrid had remained behind there with a hundred others and gone no farther, and that it was Karlsefni and Snorri who went further south with some forty men, stayed no more than two months at Hop and returned the same summer.

The group stayed there while Karlsefni went on one ship to look for Thorhall. They sailed north around Kjalarnes Point and then westwards of it, keeping the land on their port side. They saw nothing but wild forest. When they had sailed for a long time they reached a river flowing from east to west. They sailed into the mouth of the river and lay to near the south bank.

12   One morning Karlsefni's men saw something shiny above a clearing in the trees, and they called out. It moved and proved to be a one-legged creature which darted down to where the ship lay tied. Thorvald, Eirik the Red's son, was at the helm, and the one-legged man shot an arrow into his intestine. Thorvald drew the arrow out and spoke: 'Fat paunch that was. We've found a land of fine resources, though we'll hardly enjoy much of them.' Thorvald died from the wound shortly after. The one-legged man then ran off back north. They pursued him and caught glimpses of him now and again. He then fled into a cove and they turned back.

One of the men then spoke this verse:

3.   True it was
      that our men tracked
      a one-legged creature
      down to the shore.
      The uncanny fellow
      fled in a flash,
      though rough was his way,
      hear us, Karlsefni!

They soon left to head northwards where they thought they sighted the Land of the One-Legged, but did not want to put their lives in further danger. They saw mountains which they felt to be the same as those near Hop, and both these places seemed to be equally far away from Straumsfjord.

They returned to spend their third winter in Straumsfjord. Many quarrels arose, as the men who had no wives sought to take those of the married men. Karlsefni's son Snorri was born there the first autumn and was three years old when they left.

They had southerly winds and reached Markland, where they met five natives. One was bearded, two were women and two of them children. Karlsefni and his men caught the boys but the others escaped and disappeared into the earth. They took the boys with them and taught them their language and had them baptized. They called their mother Vethild and their father Ovaegi. They said that kings ruled the land of the natives; one of them was called Avaldamon and the other Valdidida. No houses were there, they said, but people slept in caves or holes. They spoke of another land, across from their own. There people dressed in white clothing, shouted loudly and bore poles and waved banners. This people assumed to be the land of the white men.*

They then came to Greenland and spent the winter with Eirik the Red.

13 Bjarni Grimolfsson and his group were borne into the Greenland Straits and entered Madkasjo (Sea of Worms), although they failed to realize it until the ship under them had become infested with shipworms. They then discussed what to do. They had a ship's boat in tow which had been smeared with tar made of seal blubber. It is said that shell maggots cannot infest wood smeared with such tar. The majority proposed to set as many men into the boat as it could carry. When this was tried, it turned out to have room for no more than half of them.

Bjarni then said they should decide by lot who should go in the boat, and not decide by status. Although all of the people there wanted to go into the boat, it couldn't take them all. So they decided to draw lots to decide who would board the boat and who would remain aboard the trading vessel. The outcome was that it fell to Bjarni and almost half of those on board to go in the boat.

Those who had been selected left the ship and boarded the boat.

Once they were aboard the boat one young Icelander, who had sailed with Bjarni, called out to him, 'Are you going to desert me now, Bjarni?'

'So it must be,' Bjarni answered.

He said, 'That's not what you promised me when I left my father's house in Iceland to follow you.'

Bjarni answered, 'I don't see we've much other choice now. What would you advise?'

He said, 'I see the solution – that we change places, you come up here and I'll take your place there.'

'So be it,' Bjarni answered, 'as I see you put a high price on life and are very upset about dying.'

They then changed places. The man climbed into the boat and Bjarni aboard the ship. People say that Bjarni died there in the Sea of Worms, along with the others on board his ship. The ship's boat and those on it went on their way and made land, after which they told this tale.

---

* Some scholars have suggested this refers to Native Americans, others to a Christian ceremony, as the term 'white men' was used for Christians. One manuscript supplies the explanation that it refers to 'Ireland the Great'.

14 The following summer Karlsefni sailed for Iceland and Gudrid with him. He came home to his farm at Reynines.

His mother thought his match hardly worthy, and Gudrid did not stay on the farm the first winter. But when she learned what an outstanding woman Gudrid was, Gudrid moved to the farm and the two women got along well.

Karlsefni's son Snorri had a daughter, Hallfrid, who was the mother of Bishop Thorlak Runolfsson.

Karlsefni and Gudrid had a son named Thorbjorn, whose daughter Thorunn was the mother of Bishop Bjorn.

Thorgeir, Snorri Karlsefni's son, was the father of Yngvild, the mother of the first Bishop Brand.

And here ends this saga.

Translated by KENEVA KUNZ

TALES

THE TALE OF THORSTEIN STAFF-STRUCK

*Þorsteins þáttur stangarhöggs**

There was a man named Thorarin living in Sunnudal. He was old and saw poorly. He had been a great Viking in his youth. He was not an easy man to get along with, even though he was old. He had one son named Thorstein. Thorstein was a large, strong, even-tempered man, and he worked so hard on his father's farm that he was just as productive as three other men together. Thorarin was not a very wealthy man, but he owned plenty of weapons. The father and son also owned some stud-horses, and they earned most of the money they had by selling stallions, for all of them were good riding-horses and spirited.

There was a man named Thord. He was a farmhand of Bjarni's at Hof. He took care of Bjarni's riding-horses because he was regarded as being good with horses. Thord was very overbearing, and he made people feel that he worked for a powerful man, though he himself became no more valuable or popular for that.

Two men named Thorhall and Thorvald were working for Bjarni at that time. They were always gossiping about everything they heard in the district.

Thorstein and Thord arranged a horse-fight for young stallions. At the fight, Thord's horse was getting the worst of it. Now when Thord found that his horse was being beaten, he dealt Thorstein's horse a heavy blow in the jaw. Thorstein saw this and dealt Thord's horse an even greater blow. Thord's horse ran off, and people really started shouting. Thord then struck Thorstein on the brow with his horse-prod, causing the skin to tear and slip down over his eye. Thorstein then cut off part of his shirt, and bandaged his brow, acting as if nothing had happened, and he asked people not to tell his father about it. The matter was dropped then and there.

---

* From *AM 162 C fol.*, *AM 156 fol.* and *AM 496 4to*. Translated from *Íslendinga sögur III*.

Thorvald and Thorhall taunted him about this and nicknamed him Thorstein Staff-struck.

Shortly before Yule that winter, the women at Sunnudal got up for work. Thorstein got up too and carried in the hay but then lay back down on the bench. Then old Thorarin, his father, came into the room and asked who was lying there. Thorstein said he was.

'Why were you on your feet so early, son?' asked old Thorarin.

Thorstein answered, 'I don't think there are many others to do the work that must be done around here.'

'Don't you have a headache, son?' asked old Thorarin.

'Not that I am aware of,' said Thorstein.

'What can you tell me, son, about the horse-fight that took place last summer? Weren't you knocked unconscious, kinsman, like a dog?'

'I do not see any honour,' said Thorstein, 'in calling it an attack rather than an accident.'

Thorarin said, 'I would not have thought that I had a coward for a son.'

'Do not say anything now, Father,' said Thorstein, 'that you will later learn is an exaggeration.'

'I will not say as much now,' said Thorarin, 'as I have a mind to.'

Thorstein then got up and grabbed his weapons. He then set off and walked over to the barn where Thord was taking care of Bjarni's horses. Thord was there.

Thorstein found Thord and said to him, 'I want to know, Thord my friend, whether that blow I took from you at the horse-fight last summer was an accident or dealt intentionally, and whether you are willing to compensate me for it.'

Thord answered, 'If you have two mouths, then put your tongue in each of them and say with one that it was an accident, if you like, and with the other that it was dealt in earnest. And that is all the compensation you're going to get from me.'

'Then prepare yourself,' said Thorstein, 'for the possibility that I won't come seeking again.'

Thorstein then ran up to Thord and dealt him his death-blow.

Afterwards he went to the farmhouse at Hof and found a woman outside and said to her, 'Tell Bjarni that a bull has gored his stable-boy Thord, and that Thord will be waiting there until he goes to the barn.'

'You go home,' she replied, 'and I will tell him when I please.'

Thorstein then went home, and the woman to her work.

Bjarni got up that morning, and when he had sat down at the table, he asked where Thord was. The others replied that he must have gone to the horses.

'I would have expected him back by now,' said Bjarni, 'if he were well.'

Then the woman Thorstein had met spoke up and said, 'It's true, as we're often reminded, that we women aren't very smart. Thorstein Staff-struck was here this morning and said that a bull had gored Thord and that he needed help. But I didn't want to wake you then, and afterwards I forgot all about it.'

Bjarni got up from the table, and then went to the barn and found Thord there, dead. He was then buried.

Afterwards, Bjarni prepared an action and had Thorstein outlawed for the killing. But Thorstein remained at home in Sunnudal working for his father, and Bjarni did nothing about it.

That autumn at Hof, the men were sitting by the fire preparing sheep-heads, and Bjarni was lying outside on top of the fire-room wall listening to what they were saying.

Then the brothers Thorhall and Thorvald spoke up and said, 'We never expected, when we were hired at Killer-Bjarni's, that we'd be preparing sheep-heads here, while this outlaw Thorstein is preparing the heads of geldings. It would have been better of him to yield more to his kinsmen in Bodvarsdal than to have his outlaw living like his equal in Sunnudal. But those who are laid down will be done with once they are wounded, and we don't know when he will wipe this stain off his honour.'

A man answered, 'That kind of thing is worse said than unsaid, and anyone would think that trolls had been moving your tongues. We feel that he does not want to deprive the blind father and the other dependants there in Sunnudal of their bread and butter. But it will surprise me if you roast lamb-heads here much longer or praise what happened in Bodvarsdal.'

Then everyone went to eat and to sleep, and Bjarni did not show that he had heard what had been said.

The next morning, Bjarni woke Thorhall and Thorvald and told them to ride to Sunnudal and bring him back Thorstein's severed head by breakfast time.

'You two seem to me,' he said, 'the most likely to wipe the stain from my honour, if I don't have the strength to do it myself.'

Now they knew that they had said too much but went, nevertheless, over to Sunnudal. Thorstein was standing in the doorway whetting a short sword.

When they arrived, he asked them where they were going, and they claimed they were supposed to look for some horses. Thorstein said that they would not have to look far for those 'right here by the hayfield wall'.

'We might not find the horses if you don't show us exactly where they are.'

Then Thorstein stepped outside. And when they had walked out into the hayfield, Thorvald brandished his axe and ran towards him, but Thorstein blocked him with his arm, and he fell down, and Thorstein thrust his short sword through him. Thorhall then wanted to attack, but he went the same way as Thorvald. Thorstein then tied both of them on to their horses and laid the reins over the horses' manes, and drove them homeward. The horses then went home to Hof.

Some farmhands were outside at Hof, and they went in and told Bjarni that Thorvald and Thorhall were home and that their journey had not been made in vain. Bjarni then went outside and saw what the situation was. He did not say any more about it, but had them buried. Then all remained quiet until Yule.

Rannveig spoke up one evening when she and Bjarni had gone to bed: 'What do you think is being discussed most often these days around the district?' she said.

'I don't know,' said Bjarni. 'Many people's words sound like nonsense to me.'

'These days, people say most often that they don't know what Thorstein Staff-struck will have to do before you find it necessary to take revenge on him. He has now slain three of your farmhands. Your thingmen do not think they can count on you for support as long as this goes unavenged. You both do wrong and leave right undone.'

Bjarni answered, 'Now the saying applies that no one learns from another's mistakes. But I will heed what you are telling me, even though Thorstein has killed few innocent men.'

They ended their discussion and slept through the night.

In the morning, Rannveig awoke as Bjarni was taking down his shield. She asked where he was going.

He answered, 'Now Thorstein from Sunnudal and I are going to settle this matter of honour.'

'How many of you are going?' she asked.

'I am not going to lead an army against Thorstein,' he said. 'I will go alone.'

'Don't risk your life alone,' she said, 'against the weapons of that horrible man.'

Bjarni said, 'Now, aren't you being like those women who urge one moment what they regret the next? Well I have listened to enough taunting, both from you and from others, and it won't do any good to try to stop me when I want to go.'

Bjarni then went to Sunnudal. Thorstein was standing in the doorway, and they exchanged a few words.

Bjarni said, 'You are to fight me in single combat today, Thorstein, on the hill here in the hayfield.'

'I am not at all prepared,' said Thorstein, 'to fight with you, but I will leave Iceland on the first ship, for I know that you will have the decency to provide my father with farm help if I go.'

'You aren't going to talk yourself out of this,' said Bjarni.

'You will permit me to see my father first?' asked Thorstein.

'Of course,' said Bjarni.

Thorstein went inside and told his father that Bjarni had come and challenged him to single combat.

Old Thorarin answered, 'Anybody who tangles with a more powerful man in his own district and has dishonoured him cannot expect to wear out too many shirts. I don't feel sorry for you because I think you've brought this on yourself. Now take your weapons and defend yourself bravely, for I would never have stooped before a man like Bjarni in my day, even though he is a great champion. Still, I would rather lose you than have a coward for a son.'

Thorstein then went outside, and they went up on the hill and began to fight hard, badly damaging each other's protective gear.

And when they had fought for a very long time, Bjarni said to Thorstein, 'I'm thirsty now, for I am less used to hard work than you are.'

'Then go to the brook,' said Thorstein, 'and drink.'

Bjarni did so, laying his sword down beside him.

Thorstein picked it up, looked at it and said, 'You could not have had this sword with you in Bodvarsdal.'

Bjarni did not answer. They then went back up the hill and fought for a while. Bjarni found the man a skilled fighter, and the going seemed more difficult than he thought it would be.

'A lot is going wrong for me today,' said Bjarni; 'Now my shoelace has come untied.'

'Tie it then,' said Thorstein.

Bjarni then bent over.

Thorstein went inside, took two shields and a sword, went back up the hill to Bjarni and said to him, 'Here is a shield and sword from my father, and this one will not be blunted any more than the one you already have. I do not want to suffer your blows without a shield any more, but I would gladly have us end this game, for I am afraid that your good fortune will accomplish more than my bad luck, and everyone is eager to live through a struggle if he has the power to do so.'

'It won't do you any good to try and talk your way out of this,' said Bjarni. 'The fight's not over.'

'I will not strike eagerly,' said Thorstein.

Then Bjarni chopped Thorstein's entire shield away from him, and Thorstein chopped Bjarni's away from him.

'Now you're swinging,' said Bjarni.

Thorstein answered, 'You did not deal a lighter blow.'

Bjarni said, 'The same weapon you had earlier today is biting harder for you now.'

Thorstein said, 'I would save myself from a mishap if I could, and I fight in fear of you. I am still willing to submit entirely to your judgement.'

It was then Bjarni's turn to swing, and both of them were now shield-less.

Then Bjarni said, 'It would be a poor bargain to choose a crime over good luck. I will consider myself fully compensated for my three farmhands if you will promise me your loyalty.'

Thorstein said, 'I have had opportunities today to betray you, had my misfortune been stronger than your luck. I will not betray you.'

'I see that you are an excellent man,' said Bjarni. 'You must allow me to go in and see your father,' he said, 'and tell him what I want to.'

'Go as you like for my part,' said Thorstein, 'but be careful.'

Then Bjarni went up to the bed closet where old Thorarin was lying. Thorarin asked who was there, and Bjarni said it was he.

'What's the news, Bjarni my friend?' asked Thorarin.

'Your son Thorstein's death,' answered Bjarni.

'Did he put up any defence?' asked Thorarin.

'I don't think any man has been as keen in battle as your son Thorstein.'

'It doesn't seem strange to me,' said the old man, 'given that you've now defeated my son, that you were a tough opponent in Bodvarsdal.'

Then Bjarni said, 'I want to invite you to Hof. You will hold one of the two seats of honour as long as you live, and I will be as a son to you.'

'I'm in the position,' said the old man, 'of someone who has no power, and only a fool rejoices in promises. Besides, the promises of you chieftains are such, when you want to comfort a man after you've done something like this, that your relief lasts only a month; then we are treated like other paupers, and with that our injuries are not soon forgotten. Yet whoever makes a bargain with a man like you may nevertheless be pleased with his lot, no matter what people say, and I will accept your offer, so come here into the bed closet. You'll have to come close, because this old man is shaky on his feet from age and poor health, and I'm not quite free from being affected by my son's death.'

Bjarni stepped into the bed closet and took old Thorarin's hand. Then he realized that Thorarin was groping for a short sword and wanted to stab him.

Bjarni pulled back his hand and said, 'You miserable old fart! Now you'll get what you deserve! Your son Thorstein is alive and he is going to live with me at Hof. You will be given slaves to do your farm work, and you will not lack anything as long as you live.'

Thorstein then went home to Hof with Bjarni and remained with him until the day he died, and no man was thought to be his equal in integrity and bravery.

Bjarni maintained his honour, and he became more popular and more even-keeled the older he grew. He dealt with difficulties better than anyone, and he turned strongly towards religion during the latter part of his life. Bjarni travelled abroad and made a pilgrimage to Rome. He died on that journey. He now rests in a city called Vateri, a great city not far this side of Rome.

Bjarni was blessed with many descendants. His son was Beard-Broddi, who appears frequently in sagas and was the most excellent man of his day. Bjarni's daughter was named Halla, the mother of Gudrid, whom Kolbein the Lawspeaker married. Another of Bjarni's daughters was Yngvild, whom Thorstein Sidu-Hallsson married. Their son was Magnus, the father of Einar, the father of Bishop Magnus. Amundi was another of Thorstein and Yngvild's sons. He married Sigrid, the daughter of Thorgrim the Blind. Amundi's daughter was Hallfrid, the mother of Amundi, the father of Gudmund, the father of Magnus the Godi and of Thora, whom Thorvald Gizurarson married, and of another Thora, the mother of Orm of Svinafell. Another of Amundi's daughters was Gudrun, the mother of Thordis, the mother of Helga, the mother of Gudny Bodvarsdottir, the mother of Thord, Sighvat and Snorri Sturluson. Another of Amundi's daughters was Rannveig, the mother of Stein, the father of Gudrun, the mother of Arnfrid, whom Stout-Helgi married. Another daughter of Amundi's was Thorkatla, the mother of Arnbjorg, the mother of Finn the Priest, Thorgeir and Thurid. And many leading men are descended from them.

There ends the story of Thorstein Staff-struck.

Translated by ANTHONY MAXWELL

THE TALE OF HALLDOR SNORRASON II

Halldórs þáttur Snorrasonar hinn síðari[*]

I   As has been told earlier, Halldor Snorrason had been in Constantinople with Harald, and had come west with him, from Russia to Norway. He had received much honour and respect from King Harald. He was with the king that winter while he was staying in Kaupang.

But as the winter passed and spring approached, people began preparing their trading voyages early because there had been little or no passage of ships from Norway recently, owing to the hostilities and unrest that had existed between Norway and Denmark. As the spring passed, King Harald became aware that Halldor Snorrason was growing ever more unhappy. One day, the king asked him what was on his mind.

Halldor answered, 'I long to go to Iceland, my lord.'

The king said, 'Many others would have shown greater longing to go home. What means of travel have you got? How are you spending your money?'

He answered, 'I'm spending it quickly, because I have nothing but the clothes I am wearing.'

'A long service and many perils have received little reward then. I will give you a ship and a crew. Your father will be able to see that you haven't served me for nothing.'

Halldor thanked the king for the gift. Several days later, Halldor met the king and the king asked him how many crew members he had taken on.

He answered, 'All those men available for service have already got themselves positions, so I can get no one. Therefore I expect that the ship that you gave me will have to be left behind.'

The king said, 'Then the gift was not an act of friendship. We will wait and see what happens about oarsmen.'

---

[*] *Morkinskinna* version. Translated from *Íslendinga sögur III.*

The following day, horns announced a meeting in the town, and it was said that the king wished to talk with the townspeople and the merchants. The king arrived late at the meeting and looked troubled when he arrived.

He said, 'We have heard it said that war has begun in the east of our kingdom, in Vik. Svein, the king of the Danes, is in charge of the Danish army, and means to do us harm, but we do not mean to give up our land in any way. For this reason, we are banning all ships from leaving the country until I have taken such things as I want from each ship, both men and provisions. Only one knorr of no great size, which Halldor Snorrason owns, will go to Iceland. Those of you who have already prepared your trips might find this a little hard, but we have found it necessary to make such an imposition. We would think it better if there were peace, so that everyone who wished could go.'

After that the meeting broke up. Shortly afterwards, Halldor came to an audience with the king. The king asked how things were going with the preparations, and whether he had enough oarsmen.

Halldor answered, 'I have probably taken on far too many now, because many more came to me asking for passage than I could offer places to. People are always pestering me. They are breaking my house down trying to reach me. I have no peace from begging men around here, day or night.'

The king answered, 'Keep those oarsmen that you have taken on, and we will see what happens.'

The next day, another meeting was called, and it was said that the king wished to talk to the merchants again. This time the king did not arrive late, because he got there first. He now looked calm.

He stood up and said, 'There is some good news to announce. What you heard said about war the day before yesterday was nothing but false rumours and lies. We will now permit each ship to leave the country and go wherever its owner wishes his ship to go. Come back in the autumn, and bring us treasures, and you, in return, will receive gifts of quality and friendship.'

All the merchants who were there were pleased about this, and wished the king good health.

Halldor went to Iceland in the summer and spent that winter with his father. He went abroad again in the summer and then, once again, joined Harald's followers. However, it is said that Halldor was not as attached to the king as he had been before, and he stayed up in the evenings when the king went to sleep.

2   There was a man named Thorir the England-trader, who had been a
     great merchant. He had spent much time sailing to various countries,
and had brought the king treasures. Thorir was one of King Harald's
followers, and was now very old.

Thorir came to speak to the king, saying, 'As you know, I am an old man,
and get tired quickly. I do not think I am capable of following the customs
of the king's men, such as drinking toasts and such related things. I am now
going to look elsewhere, even though being with you is best and most
agreeable to me.'

The king answered, 'It is possible for us to find a solution, my friend.
Stay here with my followers. You have my permission to drink no more
than you wish.'

Bard was a man from Oppland, a good comrade, and not very old. He
was an intimate friend of King Harald's. These three men, Bard, Thorir and
Halldor, shared a bench, and one evening, just as the king walked by where
they were sitting and drinking, Halldor was passing over the horn. It was a
great animal horn, and nearly transparent. It was possible to see quite well
through it that he had drunk half as much as Thorir, who was a slow drinker.

Then the king spoke: 'It takes a while before you see people in their true
colours, Halldor,' he said. 'So you break faith in drinking with old men, and
rush off to whores in the late evening instead of following your king.'

Halldor made no answer, but Bard could sense that he disliked the king's
comments. Bard went to meet the king early in the morning.

'You are an early riser, Bard,' said the king.

'I have come to reproach you, my lord,' said Bard. 'You spoke badly and
unjustly to your friend Halldor yesterday evening, when you accused him
of not drinking his share. It was Thorir's horn and he had already given up
and would have returned it to the tray if Halldor had not drunk it for him.
It was also a great lie when you said that he paid visits to loose women.
People might wish that he followed you more closely, though.'

The king answered, and said that when he and Halldor met, they would
settle the matter between themselves.

Bard met Halldor and told him of the king's good words to him, and said
it was obvious that he should take no notice of the king's outburst. Bard had
the main role in bringing them together again.

Yule was approaching, and there was little warmth between the king and
Halldor. When Yule came, as is the custom there, forfeits were listed for
breaches in etiquette. One morning at Yule, the bell-ringing was altered.

The candle-bearers paid the bell-ringers to ring much earlier than usual. Halldor was ordered to pay the forfeit along with many other men. They had to sit in the straw all day long, and were supposed to drink the forfeit-cup. Halldor remained in his seat. In spite of this, they brought him the forfeit-cup, but he refused to drink it. They then told the king.

'That cannot be true,' said the king. 'He will take it if I bring it to him.'

He then took the forfeit-horn and went to Halldor. Halldor stood up for him, and the king asked him to drink the forfeit-cup.

Halldor answered, 'I don't see why I should have to pay a forfeit when you played a trick with the ringing in order to make people break the rules.'

The king answered, 'But you will drink the forfeit-cup no less than other men.'

'It may well be that you will bring it about that I drink, King,' said Halldor. 'But I can tell you that Sigurd Sow wouldn't have managed to force Snorri the Godi to do so.'*

He reached out for the horn, and took it and drank it up, but the king was infuriated and went back to his seat.

When the eighth day of Yule arrived, men were given payment for their service. It was termed Harald's Coinage. The main part of it was copper; at best it was only half silver. When Halldor received the payment, he put the silver in the skirt of his tunic and looked at it, and did not consider that the silver was pure. He hit the silver from below with one hand and it all went down into the straw.

Bard spoke, saying that he was mistreating it: 'The king will feel insulted, and that his payment is being questioned.'

'That doesn't bother me,' said Halldor. 'I've got little to lose.'

3   It is now said that they were getting their ships ready after Yule because the king meant to go to the south. But when the king was more than prepared, Halldor still had not got ready.

Bard said, 'Why aren't you getting prepared, Halldor?'

'I don't want to,' he said, 'and I don't mean to go. I can now see that the king doesn't approve of me.'

Bard said, 'He will still want you to go, though.'

Later on, Bard went to meet the king and told him that Halldor was not

---

* Sigurd Sow was Harald's father. Snorri was Halldor's father.

getting ready – 'You can expect it to be difficult to find anyone to put in the prow in place of him.'

The king said, 'Tell him that I expect him to accompany me. This present coldness that exists between us isn't serious.'

Bard met Halldor and said that the king by no means wanted to lose his services. It ended up with Halldor going, and he and the king went southwards down the coast.

One night, when they were sailing, Halldor said to the man at the helm, 'Change course.'

The king spoke to the helmsman: 'Go right ahead,' he said.

Halldor spoke a second time: 'Change course.'

The king said the same thing again.

Halldor said, 'You're heading straight for the skerry.'

And they landed on it. The bottom of the ship then gave way, and they had to be carried ashore in other ships. A tent was then pitched on land and the ship repaired.

Bard was woken up by Halldor tying up his leather sleeping sack. Bard asked him what he was planning.

Halldor said he intended to join a cargo vessel which was lying a short distance away from them – 'It may well be that from now on the dust-clouds from our horses will head in separate directions, but things have been tested to the limit. I don't want the king to ruin any more of his ships, or other valuables, just for the sake of ridiculing me so that I have less respect than before.'

'Wait a little,' said Bard, 'I want to meet the king again.'

When he arrived, the king said, 'You are up early, Bard.'

'There is need for it, my lord. Halldor is preparing to leave, and feels that you have treated him in an unfriendly fashion. It is a little difficult taking care of you two. He now means to leave, and join up with a ship, and go off to Iceland in anger. Such a parting will be rather undeserved. I don't think that you will find another man as trustworthy as he is.'

The king said that they would make things up, and that he would not take any offence at this.

Bard met Halldor and told him of the king's friendly words.

Halldor answered, 'Why should I serve him any longer? I don't even get paid honestly.'

Bard said, 'Don't mention that. You can well accept what landholders' sons get. You didn't show much consideration last time when you threw the silver into the straw and ruined everything. And you must know that the king took that as a personal insult.'

Halldor answered, 'I do not know that my service has ever been as great a swindle as the king's payment was.'

'That's true,' said Bard. 'Wait a bit. I want to see the king again.'

And that is what he did.

When Bard met the king, he said, 'Give Halldor his payment in pure silver. He is worth it.'

The king answered, 'Don't you think it a little impudent to demand that Halldor should have a different payment than that which landholders' sons have received, especially after the disrespect he showed the last payment?'

Bard answered, 'On the other hand, my lord, there is greater importance in his loyalty and in the good friendship that existed between the two of you for a long time, and, then, in addition to that, there is your magnanimity. You know Halldor's temperament and stubbornness, and it will be to your credit to do him honour.'

The king answered, 'Give him the silver.'

This was done.

Bard came to Halldor and gave him twelve ounces of refined silver and said, 'Can't you see that whatever you nag the king about you get? He wants you to have from him what you say you need.'

Halldor said, 'Nonetheless, I won't go on the king's ship again. If he wants my company any longer, then I want a ship of my own to command.'

Bard answered, 'It is not fitting that landholders should give up their ships for you. You are being too demanding.'

Halldor said that he would not go otherwise.

Bard told the king what had been demanded on Halldor's part – 'And if the oarsmen of the ship are as trustworthy as the skipper, then that is as it should be.'

The king said, 'Even though this might be thought somewhat forward, something will be done about it.'

Svein of Lyrgja, a landholder, commanded a ship. The king had him called to a meeting.

'It's like this,' said the king. 'As you know, you come from a great family. For that reason, I want you to be on my ship, but that means I will need another man to take command of your ship. You are a clever man, and I especially want you to give me advice.'

He said, 'You have more often gone to other men for advice before now, and I have little skill at that. Who is meant to have the ship?'

'Halldor Snorrason will have it,' said the king.

Svein said, 'I didn't expect you to choose an Icelander for this, and that you would remove me from the command of a ship.'

The king said, 'His family in Iceland is no worse than yours here in Norway. It is not so long ago that those now living in Iceland were Norwegian.'

It went as the king wished. Halldor took over the ship, and they then went east to Oslo and held feasts there.

4   It is told that one day when the king and his men were sitting and drinking in the king's chamber, Halldor was there too, and his men who were supposed to be looking after the ship arrived. All of them were wet, and they said that Svein and his men had taken the ship and thrown them overboard. Halldor stood up and went before the king and asked whether he was supposed to own the ship, and whether the king's word would be kept. The king answered and stated that of course he was supposed to own it, then told the king's men that they should take six ships with a triple crew on each and go with Halldor.

They now went after Svein, and had him chased to land, and when Svein ran ashore, Halldor took the ship and went back to the king.

When the feasts were over, the king went north up the coast, and then to Trondheim towards the end of the summer.

Svein of Lyrgja sent the king word that he wanted to place the whole matter in the king's hands, and that the king should settle things between Svein and Halldor as he wished, but that he would prefer to buy the ship if the king was agreeable to that. When the king saw that Svein had placed the whole matter under his judgement, he wanted to act in such a way that both parties would be satisfied. He told Halldor to sell him the ship, but wanted him to get a respectable price for it. Svein should then have the ship. After this, the king came to a deal with Halldor, and bought the ship. He paid Halldor everything except for half a mark of gold, which was left over. Halldor made few demands for it, and it was not paid, and that is how it went that winter.

When the spring was approaching, Halldor told the king that he wanted to go to Iceland in the summer, and stated that it would suit him if he were now paid what remained of the money for the ship. But the king was evasive about the payment, and did not think much of Halldor's demand, but did not ban him from going home.

During the spring, Halldor prepared his ship on the river Nid, and then moved it up to Brattaeyri. And when they were all prepared and there was a fair wind, Halldor went into the town with several men late in the evening. He had his weapons with him. They went to where the king and queen were sleeping. Halldor's travelling companions waited outside beneath the overhang of the upper floor while he walked in with his weapons. He made some noise and commotion, and this woke the king and the queen up. The king asked who was breaking in on them in the night.

'Halldor is here, and ready to sail with a fair wind, and it would be advisable for you to pay me the money now.'

'That cannot be done so quickly,' said the king. 'We will pay you the money tomorrow.'

'I want it right now,' said Halldor, 'and I'm not leaving until my errand has been completed. I know your temperament, and, however you may act at this moment, I'm well aware what you must be thinking about my visit and my demands for money. I'll have little belief in what you say from now on; indeed it's unlikely that we'll be meeting each other so very often. I have the advantage, and mean to make use of it. I see that the queen has a ring on her arm that is the perfect equivalent. Let me have that.'

The king answered, 'We'll have to go and fetch some scales and weigh the ring then.'

'No need,' said Halldor. 'I'll take it for my debt. You're not going to do any cheating this time. Hand it over immediately.'

The queen spoke: 'Can't you see,' she said, 'that he is standing over you, ready to kill you?'

Then she removed the ring and gave it to Halldor.

He took it, thanked them both for the payment and wished them a good life, 'and we will now part'.

He then went out and spoke to his travelling companions, and told them to run to the ship as fast as possible, 'because I've got little desire to hang about much longer in this town'.

They did so, and boarded the ship, and immediately some of them hoisted up the sail, while others got the rowing-boat ready, and others pulled up the anchor. Everyone did what they could. As they were sailing out, there was no lack of horn-blowing in the town. The last thing they saw was that three longships were afloat, and were setting off after them. They pulled ahead, though, and reached the sea. There they got separated, and Halldor made a good start for Iceland. The king's men turned back when they saw that Halldor was pulling ahead and had reached the open sea.

5   Halldor Snorrason was a large, handsome man, the strongest and most courageous of men in battle. King Harald bore witness to the fact that of all the men who had been with him, Halldor was the one who was least affected by shocks; whether faced with mortal danger or joyful news, he was never more or less happy than usual. He never ate food or drank or slept more or less than he was accustomed to, whether the times were good or bad. Halldor was a man of few words. He spoke abruptly and frankly, was sharp-tempered and rough, and highly competitive in all things with anyone he had dealings with. This caused trouble with King Harald when he had enough other men to serve him. That is why they got on so badly together after Harald became King of Norway.

When Halldor reached Iceland, he set up a farm at Hjardarholt. A few summers later, King Harald sent a message to Halldor Snorrason saying he should enter his service again, and that his respect had never been as great as it would be if he agreed to go; and that he would place him higher than any other man of low birth if he accepted this invitation.

When the message reached him, Halldor replied with these words: 'I will never go to meet King Harald from this time forth. Each of us now can keep what he has got. I am aware of his character. I know perfectly well that he would carry out his promise to place no man in Norway higher than me if I went to meet him, because he would place me on the highest of gallows if he had any say in the matter.'

And when King Harald was growing older, it is said that he sent Halldor word that he should send him some fox-skins. The king wanted to have them made into a blanket to go over his bed, because he felt he needed more warmth.

When this message of the king's reached Halldor, it is said that at first he uttered the following words: 'The early rooster is getting old,' he said, but he sent him the skins.

They never met again after they parted in Trondheim, even though that time things had been a little abrupt. He lived in Hjardarholt until the end of his life, and became an old man.

Translated by TERRY GUNNELL

THE TALE OF SARCASTIC HALLI
*Sneglu-Halla þáttur**

1   The beginning of this story is when King Harald Sigurdarson was ruling over Norway. That was in the period after the death of his kinsman, King Magnus. It is said that King Harald was a very wise and very shrewd man. Almost everything that he counselled turned out well. He was a good poet and always mocked whomever he pleased. And when he was in a good mood, he was extremely patient even if abusive obscenities were directed at him. At this time, he was married to Thora Thorbergsdottir. Thorberg was Arni's son. Harald took great pleasure in poetry and always had people about him who knew how to compose poems.

There was a man named Thjodolf. He was an Icelander whose family came from Svarfadardal. He was a well-mannered man and a great poet. He was on very warm terms with King Harald. The king called him his chief poet and honoured him above all his other poets. Thjodolf was of humble origins, well brought up and envious of newcomers.

King Harald loved Icelanders very much. He gave Iceland many valuable goods including the good bell for Thingvellir. And when the great famine came to Iceland – and such another has not come – he sent four knorrs loaded with flour, one to each quarter, and he had a great many poor people transported from Iceland.

2   There was a man named Bard who was one of King Harald's followers. He sailed out to Iceland, landed at Gasir and took lodgings there for the winter.

A man named Halli, nicknamed Sarcastic Halli, took passage to Norway with Bard. Halli was a good poet and a very impudent person. He was a tall

* From *Flateyjarbók*. Translated from *Íslendinga sögur III*.

man, long-necked, with narrow shoulders and long arms, and was rather ill-proportioned. His family was from Fljot.

They sailed as soon as they were ready and had a long passage. That autumn they reached Norway north of Trondheim at the islands called Hitra, and then sailed in towards Agdenes and lay up there that night. And the next morning they sailed into the fjord with a light breeze. And when they reached Reine, they saw three longships rowing out down the fjord. The third was a dragon-ship. And as the ships were rowing past the trading vessel, a man dressed in scarlet and with a golden band around his forehead came out on the poop deck of the dragon-ship; he was tall and of noble bearing.

This man spoke: 'Who commands your ship, and where did you stay this winter, and where did you first make land, and where did you lie up last night?'

The merchants were nearly struck dumb when so much was asked all at once, but then Halli answered, 'We were in Iceland for the winter, and sailed from Gasir, and made land at Hitra, last night we lay up at Agdenes (Agdi's Ness), and our skipper is called Bard.'

This man, who in fact was King Harald Sigurdarson, then asked, 'Didn't Agdi fuck you?'

'Not yet,' said Halli.

The king grinned and spoke: 'Is there some agreement that he will do you this service sometime later?'

'No,' said Halli, 'and one particular consideration was crucial to our suffering no disgrace at his hands.'

'What was that?' asked the king.

Halli knew perfectly well whom he was talking to – 'It was this, my lord,' he said, 'if you're so curious to know this: in this matter Agdi was waiting for nobler men than ourselves, and he expected your arrival there tonight, and he will pay you this debt fully.'

'You are being extremely impudent,' said the king.

What more they said at that time is not known. The merchants sailed on in to Kaupang, unloaded their cargo and rented a house in the town.

A few days later the king returned to the town; he had gone out to the islands on a pleasure trip. Halli asked Bard to take him to the king and said he wanted to request winter quarters, but Bard invited Halli to stay with him. Halli thanked him but said that he wanted to be with the king if that option were open.

3   One day Bard went to meet the king and Halli went with him. Bard greeted the king. The king acknowledged his greeting warmly and made many enquiries about Iceland and also asked if Bard had brought any Icelanders to Norway.

Bard said he had brought one Icelander – 'and his name is Halli and he is here now, my lord, and wishes to ask to stay for the winter with you'.

Then Halli went before the king and greeted him.

The king received him warmly and asked if he had been the one who answered him in the fjord 'when we met you and your companions'.

'I'm the very man,' said Halli.

The king said that he would not withhold food from Halli and asked him to stay at one of his estates. Halli said that he wanted to be at court or look for a place elsewhere.

The king said that it always turned out – 'that I get blamed if our friendship with you doesn't go well, even though that seems hardly likely to me this time. You Icelanders are stubborn and unsociable. Now stay if you wish, but you are responsible for yourself whatever happens.'

Halli said that it would be so and thanked the king. And then he was with the king's followers and everyone liked him. An old and agreeable follower named Sigurd was Halli's bench-companion.

King Harald's custom was to eat one meal a day. The food was served first to him, as would be expected, and he was always very well satisfied by the time the food was served to the others. But when he was satisfied, he rapped on the table with the handle of his knife, and then the tables were to be cleared at once. Many were still hungry.

It happened on one occasion that the king was walking in the street attended by his followers, and many of them were not nearly satisfied. And then they heard a noisy quarrel at an inn. It was a tanner and a blacksmith, and they were almost attacking one another. The king stopped and watched for a while.

Then he said, 'Let's go. I don't want to get involved in this, but, Thjodolf, compose a verse about them.'

'My lord,' said Thjodolf, 'that's hardly suitable considering that I am called your chief poet.'

The king answered, 'It's more difficult than you think. You are to make them into altogether different people than they really are. Make one of them into Sigurd Fafnisbani (Killer of the Serpent Fafnir) and the other into Fafnir, but nevertheless identify each one's trade.'

Then Thjodolf spoke a verse:

1. Sigurd of the sledge-hammer goaded   *Sigurd* (legendary hero) *of the*
    the snake of the scary skin-scraper,   *hammer*: the blacksmith; *snake of*
    but the scrape-dragon of skins   *the skin-scraper*: the tanner
    slithered away from the moor of socks.   *scrape-dragon of skins*: the tanner
    Folk feared the serpent, fitted out   moor of socks: floor
    with footwear, before the long-nosed king
    of tongs set about him,   *king of tongs*: the blacksmith
    the serpent of ox-skin.   *serpent of ox-skin*: the tanner

'That is well composed,' said the king, 'and now compose another verse and make one into Thor and the other into the giant Geirrod, and nevertheless identify each one's trade.'

Then Thjodolf spoke a verse:

2. Thor of the great bellows threw   *Thor of the bellows*: the blacksmith
    from the malicious town   *town of taunts*: mouth; *jaw-*
    of taunts jaw-lightning   *lightning*: abusive words; *giant*
    at the giant of goat-flesh.   (i.e. enemy) *of goat-flesh*: the
    Gladsome Geirrod of the worn   tanner; *Geirrod of the . . . skin-*
    skin-scraper from Thor's forge took   *scraper*: the tanner; *forge*: mouth
    with sound-grippers sparks   *sound-grippers*: ears
    from that smithy of spells.   *smithy of spells*: mouth; its *sparks*:
         abusive words

'You're not over-praised,' said the king, 'when you're called a master-poet.'

And they all applauded the verses as well composed. Halli was not present. And that evening when people sat drinking they recited the verses for Halli, and said that he could not compose like that even though he thought himself a very good poet.

Halli said that he knew he made worse poetry than Thjodolf did – 'I'll fall especially short, if I don't try to compose a verse, and even more so if I am not present.'

This was reported to the king and represented that Halli thought himself to be no less a poet than Thjodolf.

The king said that Halli would probably not be that – 'but it may be that we can put him to the test soon'.

4   One day when people were sitting at table, a dwarf named Tuta came
     into the hall. He was Frisian by descent. He had been with King
Harald for a very long time. He was no taller than a three-year-old child,
but was very thick-set and broad-shouldered; he had a large, elderly-looking
head, his back was not noticeably short, but below, where his legs were, he
was cropped.

King Harald had a coat of mail which he called Emma. He had had it
made in Byzantium. It was so long that it reached down to King Harald's
shoes when he stood upright. It was all of double thickness and so strong
that no weapon ever pierced it. The king ordered the dwarf to be dressed
in the coat of mail and had a helmet placed on his head, and he girded a
sword on him. After that Tuta walked into the hall as was written above
and the man seemed a wonder.

The king called for silence and then announced: 'The man who composes
a poem about the dwarf which to me seems well composed will receive this
knife and belt from me' – and he laid them on the table before him – 'but
understand clearly that if I think the poem is not well composed, he will
have my displeasure as well as lose both possessions.'

And as soon as the king had made his announcement, a man on the
outermost bench composed a poem, and he was Sarcastic Halli.

3.   A kinsman of the Frisians' clan
      appears to me in chain-mail clothed.
      Decked out with a helmet, the dwarf
      goes round the court in ring-mail.
      At dawn he never flees the fire,
      our Tuta, veteran of many kitchen raids.
      I see swinging by the side
      of the rye-bread's waster a sword.

The king ordered the prizes to be given to Halli – 'and you are to have
them by right because the verse is well composed'.

One day when the king was finished eating, he struck the table with the
handle of his knife and ordered the tables to be cleared. The servers did so.
Halli was far from being satisfied, so he took a chop from the dish, kept it
and spoke this verse:

4.   I don't give a damn
     for Harald's hammering.
     I keep my moustache munching on
     and full-fed I go to bed.

In the morning, when the king and his followers had taken their seats,
Halli came into the hall and to the king. He had his sword and shield slung
over his back.

He spoke a verse:

5.   For butter I'll have to barter,
     oh king, my sword and,
     speeder of the clash of shields,   *clash of shields*: battle; its *speeder*: king
     my red buckler for bread.
     The helmsman's warriors hunger.   *helmsman*: ruler, king
     We walk around really wanting food.
     For sure my belt draws ever nearer
     my backbone – Harald's starving me!

The king did not answer at all and acted as if he had not heard, although
everyone knew he was displeased.

Another day, the king was out walking in the street with his followers.
Halli was in the procession. He rushed on past the king.

The king spoke this:

6.   'Where are you heading, Halli?'

Halli answered:

     'I'm briskly running to buy a cow.'
     'You've probably ordered some porridge,'

said the king.

     'When buttered, it's the best of food,'

said Halli.

And then Halli ran into a house and thence to a kitchen. He had ordered
himself a stone-kettle of porridge there, and sat down and ate his porridge.

The king saw that Halli had gone into the house. He summoned Thjodolf and two other men to look for Halli. The king went into the house. They found him where he was eating his porridge. The king came to him and saw how Halli was occupied. The king was very angry and asked Halli if he had come from Iceland and visited chieftains in order to create scandal and gossip.

'Don't talk like that, my lord,' said Halli. 'Constantly I see that you do not reject good food.'

Then Halli stood up and threw down the kettle, and the handle rattled against it. Then Thjodolf recited this:

7. The handle rattled and Halli
    has pigged out on porridge.
    A cow's-horn spoon better suits him,
    I say, than something fine.

Then the king went away and was very angry.

And that evening food was not served to Halli as it was to the others. And when people had been eating for a while, two men came in carrying a large trough of porridge with a spoon and set it before Halli. He set to and ate as much as he wanted and then stopped.

The king ordered Halli to eat more. He said he would not eat more at that time. Then King Harald drew his sword and ordered Halli to eat the porridge until he burst. Halli said that he would not burst himself on porridge, but the king could take his life if he had made up his mind to do that. Then the king sat down and sheathed his sword.

5 One day somewhat later, the king took a dish containing a roasted piglet from his table and ordered the dwarf Tuta to take it to Halli – 'and tell him that if he wants to preserve his life he must compose a verse and deliver it before you reach him, but do not tell him this until you get to the middle of the room'.

'I'm not keen on doing this,' said Tuta, 'because I like Halli.'

'I see,' the king said, 'that you think the verse he composed about you was good and you certainly know how to listen carefully. Now go at once and do as I command.'

Tuta took the dish and walked to the middle of the floor, and said, 'Halli, compose a verse at the king's command, and have it finished before I reach you if you want to preserve your life.'

Halli stood up and reached his hand out for the dish and recited a verse:

8.   The poet received a dead piglet
      from a ruler well-regarded.
      The god of the ring-land sees a swine   *ring-land*: shield; its *god*: warrior
      standing before him on the board.   *board*: table
      The swine's red sides I see.
      I recite a poem rapidly made.
      A warrior has burnt the swine's snout off, *warrior*: i.e. the cook
      may you give in good health, king.

Then the king said, 'Now I will give up my anger, Halli, because the verse is as well performed as it was quickly undertaken.'

6   It is said that one day Halli went before the king when he was cheerful and happy. Thjodolf and many other people were there. Halli said that he had composed a drapa about the king and asked for a hearing. The king asked if Halli had ever composed such a poem before. Halli said that he had not.

'Some people would say,' said the king, 'that you're taking on quite a job considering the calibre of poets who have previously composed poems about me for various reasons. But what seems advisable to you, Thjodolf?'

'My lord, I cannot give you advice,' said Thjodolf, 'but on the other hand I might be able to give Halli some sound advice.'

'What is that?' asked the king.

'First of all, my lord, that he should not deceive you.'

'What deception did he practise just now?' asked the king.

'He was being deceptive when he said that he had not composed a long poem before,' said Thjodolf, 'but I say that he has.'

'What long poem is that,' asked the king, 'and what is it about?'

Thjodolf answered, 'We call it Polled-Cow Verses, which he composed about cows he tended out in Iceland.'

'Is that true, Halli?' asked the king.

'That's right,' said Halli.

'Why did you say that you had not composed a long poem?' asked the king.

'Because,' said Halli, 'it would not seem to be much of a poem if it were to be heard, and would hardly be praised.'

'We want to hear that first,' said the king.

'Then there will have to be more than one amusement,' said Halli.

'What's the second?' asked the king.

'Thjodolf must perform Food Trough Verses which he composed out in Iceland,' said Halli, 'and it's all right that Thjodolf should attack me or denigrate me because my eye-teeth and molars have come in so that I am quite able to answer him word for word.'

The king grinned at that and thought it was fun to set them against each other.

'What is that long poem like and what is it about?' asked the king.

Halli answered, 'It's about his carrying out ashes with his siblings, and he was thought to be capable of nothing more because of his lack of intelligence, and moreover it was necessary to make sure there were no live coals in the ashes because he had no more brains than he needed at that time.'

The king asked if that was true.

'It's true, my lord,' said Thjodolf.

'Why did you have such contemptible work?' asked the king.

'Because, my lord,' said Thjodolf, 'I wanted to get all of us out to play quickly, and no other work was assigned to me.'

'The cause of that,' said Halli, 'was that it was believed that you didn't have the brains to be a workman.'

'You two mustn't quarrel,' said the king, 'but we wish to hear both these poems.' And so it had to be and each of them performed his poem.

And when the poems were finished, the king said, 'Both poems are minor and moreover the subjects are trivial, but yours, Thjodolf, was the slighter.'

'That's so,' said Thjodolf, 'and, my lord, Halli is very sarcastic. But it seems to me he's more obligated to avenge his father than engage in verbal duels with me here in Norway.'

'Is that true, Halli?' asked the king.

'It's true,' said Halli.

'Why did you leave Iceland to meet with chieftains given that you had not avenged your father?' asked the king.

'Because, my lord,' said Halli, 'I was a child when my father was killed, and my relatives took over the case and settled it on my behalf. And in our country it's thought bad to be called a truce-breaker.'

The king answered, 'It's a duty not to violate truces or settlements. You've answered this very well.'

'So I thought, my lord,' said Halli, 'but Thjodolf may very well speak arrogantly in such matters since I know no one who has avenged his father as grimly as he.'

'Certainly Thjodolf is likely to have done that boldly,' said the king, 'but what is the proof that he did more in this than other men?'

'Most of all, my lord,' said Halli, 'that he ate his father's killer.'

At this people set up an uproar, and it seemed to them they had never heard of such a monstrosity. The king grinned at this and ordered silence.

'Show that what you've said is true, Halli,' said the king.

Halli said, 'I think that Thorljot was Thjodolf's father. He lived in Svarfadardal in Iceland, and he was very poor and had many children. It's the custom in Iceland that in the autumn the farmers assemble to discuss the poor people, and at that time no one was named sooner than Thorljot, Thjodolf's father. One farmer was so generous that he gave him a calf which was one summer old. Then Thorljot fetched the calf and had a lead on it with a noose in the end of the lead. When he got to his hayfield wall, he lifted the calf up on to the wall and it was extremely high and even higher on the inner side because the turves for the wall had been dug there. Then he went over the wall and the calf rolled off the wall on the outside. The noose at the end of the lead tightened around Thorljot's neck, and he couldn't reach the ground with his feet. So each was hanging on his own side of the wall, and both were dead when people came up. The children dragged the calf home and prepared it for food, and I think that Thjodolf ate his full share of it.'

'That would be very close to reasonable,' said the king.

Thjodolf drew his sword and wanted to strike Halli. Men ran between them.

The king said that neither should dare do the other harm – 'Thjodolf, you went for Halli first.'

Then it was as the king would have it. Halli performed his drapa and it was highly regarded. The king rewarded him with a generous sum in cash.

Then the winter wore on and all was quiet.

7   There was a man named Einar who was nicknamed Fly. He was the son of Harek from Thjotta. He was a landholder and the king's envoy to Halogaland; he had the sole right to collect the king's tribute from the Lapps. At this time he was on very good terms with the king, though their relationship had its ups and downs – Einar was not completely reliable. He killed men if they did not do everything he wanted, and paid compensation for no man. Einar was expected by the king to attend Yule.

Halli and his bench-companion Sigurd fell into talk about Einar. Sigurd informed Halli that no one dared to oppose Einar or behave other than he wished and that he paid no compensation for his killings or robberies.

'Men like that would be called bad chieftains in my country,' said Halli.

'Do speak carefully, companion,' said Sigurd, 'because he is quick to take offence at what is said if it displeases him.'

'Even though all of you are so afraid of him that you don't dare to say a word against him,' said Halli, 'I tell you that I would surely accuse him if he did me wrong and I believe he would compensate me.'

'Why you more than others?' asked Sigurd.

'That will be clear to him,' said Halli

They argued about the matter until Halli offered to make a bet with Sigurd on it. Sigurd put up a gold arm ring which weighed half a mark, and Halli put up his head.

Einar came that Yule. He sat next to the king and his men sat closer to the door. He was given all the service which the king had himself.

And one day, when all had eaten, the king spoke: 'Now we want to have more amusement than just drinking. Einar, tell us what news you have from your travels.'

Einar answered, 'I can't make up any sagas about it, my lord, even though we treated some Lapp farmers or fishermen roughly.'

The king answered, 'Tell the whole story because we are easily satisfied, and it all seems entertaining to us even though it seems trivial to you who are constantly engaged in battles.'

'At any rate, the main thing to report, my lord,' said Einar, 'is that last summer when we went north to Finnmark we encountered a ship and crew from Iceland which had been driven off course and had lain up there for the winter. I charged them with having traded with the Lapps without your permission or mine. They denied it and would not admit it, but we thought they were not being truthful and asked them to allow a search, but they flatly refused. I told them then that they would have what was worse for them but appropriate, and ordered my men to arm and attack them. I had five longships and we attacked them from both sides and didn't leave off until we had cleared the ship. One Icelander whom they called Einar defended himself so well that I have never encountered his equal. Surely that man was a loss and we would never have overcome that ship if everyone on board had been like him.'

'You did badly,' said the king, 'when you killed men who were innocent even though they didn't do everything as you wished.'

'I won't run that risk,' said Einar. 'And, my lord, some people say you don't always act righteously. But they turned out to be guilty because we found many Lapp goods in the ship.'

Halli heard what they were saying and threw his knife down on the table and stopped eating. Sigurd asked if he were ill.

He said not but this was worse than sickness – 'Einar Fly announced the death of Einar, my brother, whom he said he killed on the trading vessel last summer, and now it is appropriate to seek compensation from this Einar.'

'Don't say anything about it, companion,' said Sigurd, 'that's the most promising course.'

'No,' said Halli, 'my brother would not act like that in my case if he had to bring a suit following my killing.'

Then he jumped over his table and went up before the high seat and spoke: 'You announced news which concerns me greatly, Einar, in the matter of the killing of Einar my brother whom you said you struck down on the trading vessel last summer. Now I want to know whether you will pay me some compensation for my brother.'

'Haven't you heard that I don't pay compensation for anyone?' asked Einar.

'I was not obliged to believe,' said Halli, 'that you were utterly wicked even though I have heard that said.'

'Take a walk,' said Einar, 'or be the worse for it.'

Halli went to sit down. Sigurd asked him how it had gone. Halli replied that he had got a threat instead of monetary compensation. Sigurd told him not to raise the matter again and the bet would be off.

Halli said that Sigurd was behaving well, 'but I will raise the matter again'.

And the next day, Halli went before Einar and said, 'I want to bring up the matter, Einar, and see if you are willing to compensate me in some way for my brother.'

Einar answered, 'You're persistent about this and if you don't get out of here you'll fare as your brother did, or worse.'

The king told him not to answer like that: 'It's extremely painful for the kinsmen, and one can't know what is in other people's minds. But, Halli, don't raise this matter again because bigger men than you have had to endure such harm from him.'

Halli said, 'So it will probably have to be.'

Then he went to his place. Sigurd welcomed him warmly and asked how it had gone. Halli said that he had got a threat from Einar instead of compensation.

'So I thought it would be,' said Sigurd. 'The bet is off.'

'You are behaving well,' said Halli, 'but I will raise the matter a third time.'

'I'll give you the ring now,' said Sigurd, 'on condition that you let this lie quietly, because I am partly responsible for this in the first place.'

'You make clear what kind of man you are,' said Halli, 'and you are not to blame no matter how this turns out. But I will try one more time.'

And early the next day when the king and Einar Fly were washing their hands, Halli came up and greeted the king. The king asked what he wanted.

'My lord,' Halli answered, 'I want to tell you my dream. It seemed to me that I was quite another man than I am.'

'What man did you think yourself to be?' said the king.

'I thought myself to be the poet Thorleif, and Einar Fly seemed to me to be Earl Hakon Sigurdarson. I thought I had composed a slanderous poem about him, and I remembered some of the slander when I awakened.'

Then Halli went down the hall towards the door and mumbled something but people were not able to catch any of the words.

The king said, 'This was not a dream, rather he compared these two cases. And it will go with the two of you as it did with Hakon the Earl of Lade and the poet Thorleif. Halli is doing the same thing. He shrinks from nothing. We can both see how a slanderous poem has damaged more powerful men than you, Einar. Earl Hakon was one, and that will be remembered as long as the northern countries are inhabited. One short verse composed about a highly esteemed man, if it is remembered afterwards, is worse than paying a small bribe. Do please satisfy him in some way.'

'You will decide, my lord,' said Einar, 'and tell him he may take from my treasurer the three marks of silver in the purse I just gave him.'

This was reported to Halli. He went to meet the treasurer and told him. He said that there were four marks of silver in the purse. Halli said that he was to have three. Then Halli went to Einar and told him.

'You will have taken what was in the purse,' said Einar.

'No,' said Halli, 'you'll have to take my life in some other way than by my turning thief for your money. I saw that was what you had intended for me.'

And so it was. Einar had thought that Halli would take what was in the purse and that seemed to Einar an offence quite worthy of death.

Then Halli went to his seat and showed the money to Sigurd. Sigurd took the ring and told Halli that he had won it fairly.

Halli said, 'We are not equally good men then – keep and enjoy the ring, best of men. And to tell you the truth, I was not related to this man whom Einar killed, but I wanted to see if I could get money out of him.'

'You have no equal in trickery,' said Sigurd.

After Yule, Einar went off north to Halogaland.

8   In the spring, Halli asked the king for permission to go to Denmark on a trading expedition.

The king said that he could go as he wished – 'and come back soon because we find good entertainment in your company, but go warily on account of Einar Fly. He will be ill-disposed toward you, and I hardly know of any other time when he slipped up so badly.'

Halli took passage south to Denmark with some merchants and then went to Jutland. A man named Raud had the stewardship there, and Halli got food and lodging with him.

At some point it happened that Raud was to hold a large assembly, and when people were to plead their cases, there was so much uproar and noise that no one could bring his case forward. With that people went home that evening.

And that evening when people came to drink, Raud said, 'It would be a cunning man who could find a plan so that all these people would be quiet.'

Halli said, 'I can manage it, whenever I wish, so that every mother's son here will be quiet.'

'You can't manage that, Icelander,' said Raud.

The next day people came to the assembly, and then there was as much shouting and noise as the day before and no settlement was reached in any case. At that, people went home.

Then Raud asked, 'Halli, do you want to bet that you can manage to bring silence to the assembly?'

Halli said he was ready to do this.

Raud responded, 'You bet your head and I will bet a gold arm ring which weighs one mark.'

'So it will be,' said Halli.

In the morning, Halli asked Raud if the bet was on. Raud said it was. Then people came to the assembly, and there was as much shouting as on the preceding days, or more.

And when people least expected anything, Halli jumped up and shouted as loudly as he could, 'Listen everybody! I need to speak. I've lost my hone and honing grease and my bag with all its tackle which is better for a male to have than to lose.'

Everyone fell silent. Some men thought he had gone mad, others thought that he would announce some message from the king. And when all was silent, Halli sat down and took the ring. But when people realized that this was nothing but mockery, there was as much uproar as before, and Halli ran away because Raud wanted to take his life and thought this had been an enormous cheat. Halli did not stop until he got to England.

9 Then Harold Godwin's son was ruling England. Halli went straight to the king and said he had composed a drapa about him and asked for a hearing. The king gave him a hearing. Halli sat down at the king's knee and delivered his poem. When the poem was finished, the king asked his poet, who was with him, how the poem was. He said he thought that it was good. The king asked Halli to stay there with him, but Halli said that he was already prepared to go to Norway.

The king said then that it would go the same way, 'in rewarding you for the poem as it goes in our benefiting from it because no fame accrues to us from a poem no one knows. Now sit on the floor and I will have silver poured over your head. Keep what sticks to your hair. It seems to me the prospects look the same on both sides because we will not get to learn the poem.'

Halli responded, 'It's true both that only small rewards are due and that the rewards will be small. But, my lord, you will surely allow me to go out and answer nature's call.'

'Go just as you wish,' said the king.

Halli went out to where the shipwrights were and put tar on his head and shaped his hair so that it would be like a dish and then went inside and asked them to pour the silver over him. The king said that he was crafty. And it was poured over him and he got a lot of silver.

Then he went where the ships were that were sailing for Norway, but they had all gone except for one which was taken by many people with very heavy cargo. Halli had plenty of money and wanted very much to get away because he had not composed a poem about the king but had just recited rubbish, and on that account he could not teach it. The skipper told him to find a scheme so that the people from southern lands would leave the ship and then he would gladly take him. At that time winter was at hand. Halli was there with them in common sleeping quarters for a while.

One night Halli was much troubled in his sleep, and it was a very long time before they could awaken him. They asked what he had dreamed.

He said that he was finished with asking for passage away from there – 'It seemed to me as if a terrible-looking man came up and recited this:

9.   There's roaring where I've grasped the tall
      sea-weed since giving up my life.
      It's very clear I'm residing with Ran.   *Ran*: sea-goddess
      Some have lodgings with lobsters.
      It's bright staying with the whitings.
      I have lands beyond the sea-shore.
      So now I sit, pale, in heaps of sea-weed.
      Pale sea-weed undulates about my neck,
      pale sea-weed undulates about my neck.'*

And when the men from the southern lands heard about this dream, they left the ship and thought it would be their death if they sailed in it. Then Halli immediately took passage on the ship and said it was a trick and no dream.

They put out to sea as soon as they were ready and reached Norway in the autumn, and Halli immediately went to King Harald. He welcomed Halli warmly and asked if he had composed poems about other rulers.

Then Halli spoke this verse:

10.   I composed a thula   *thula*: a mnemonic list in verse form
      about an earl.†
      Not among the Danes   *Danes*: regarded as unpoetic people

---

* In the other version of the poem, presented in the Morkinskinna manuscript, line 3 reads 'A revolution took place! I'm residing with Ran'; line 6, 'I landed out beyond the beach'; and line 9 'Pale seaweed undulates about me where your neck will be.'
† Harold Godwinson who was Earl of Wessex and for nine months in 1066 King of England; his tenure of the throne was unsuccessfully challenged by Halli's patron, Harald Sigurdarson, and successfully by William the Conqueror.

has a poorer drapa appeared.
Fourteen mistakes in metre
and ten terrible rhymes.
It's obvious to anyone,
it goes upside-down.
So he has to compose
who knows how to – badly.

The king grinned at this and it seemed to him that Halli was always
entertaining.

10   In the spring, King Harald went to the Gulathing Assembly. And one
day the king asked Halli how he was doing for women at the assembly.
Halli answered:

11.   This Gulathing's great
we fuck whatever we fancy.

From there the king went north to Trondheim. When they sailed past
Stad, Thjodolf and Halli were assigned the cooking and serving. Halli was
very seasick and lay under the ship's boat and Thjodolf had to serve alone.
And when he was carrying the food, he fell over Halli's leg which was
sticking out from under the boat.
Thjodolf spoke this verse:

12.   Sticking out from under the boat
is a sole-bucket. You're fucking now?   *sole-bucket*: shoe

Halli answered:

I made this servant into a waiter
and caused Thjodolf to cook the food.

And then the king continued on his way until he reached Kaupang.
Thora the queen was on the expedition, and she disliked Halli, but the
king liked him and thought that Halli was always entertaining.
It is said that one day the king was walking in the street and his followers
were with him. Halli was in the procession. The king had an axe in his hand;
its blade was inlaid with gold and the shaft was wound round with silver
and it had a large silver band on the upper part of the shaft and a precious
stone was set into it. It was an excellent possession. Halli kept looking at

the axe. The king noticed that at once and asked Halli if he liked it. Halli said he liked it very much.

'Have you seen a better axe?'

'I don't think so,' said Halli.

'Will you allow yourself to be fucked for the axe?' said the king.

'I will not,' said Halli, 'but it seems understandable to me that you should want to sell the axe for the same price that you paid for it.'

'So it will be, Halli,' said the king. 'Take it and use it for the best – it was given to me and so will I give it to you.'

Halli thanked the king.

That evening when people came to drink, the queen spoke to the king and said it was scandalous – 'and it's not a reasonable exchange to give Halli goods which are hardly meant for commoners to reward him for his obscene language when some men receive little in return for good service'.

The king said that he would decide to whom he would give his possessions – 'I don't wish to take those words of Halli's which are ambiguous in a bad sense.'

The king had Halli summoned and it was done. Halli bowed to him.

The king ordered Halli to make an ambiguous statement about Queen Thora – 'and I'll see how she endures it'.

Then Halli bowed to Thora and spoke this verse:

13.   You're the most fitting by far,
       by a long mark, Thora,
       to roll down from a rising crag
       all the foreskin on Harald's prick.

'Seize him and kill him,' said the queen. 'I won't put up with his abusive obscenities.'

The king ordered that no one be so bold as to lay hold of Halli for all of this, 'but it can be changed, if you think that another woman is more suitable to lie beside me and be my queen – you hardly know how to hear your praise'.

The poet Thjodolf had gone to Iceland while Halli was absent from the king. Thjodolf had shipped a good stallion from Iceland and intended to give him to the king, and Thjodolf had the stallion led into the king's courtyard and shown to the king. The king went to see the stallion, and it was big and fat. Halli was there when the horse stuck out his prick.

Halli spoke this verse:

14.   Always a young she-pig –
       Thjodolf's horse has
       wholly befouled his prick;
       he's a master fucker.

'Tut tut,' said the king, 'he will never come into my possession at this rate.'

Halli became one of the king's followers and asked permission to go to Iceland. The king told him to go warily because of Einar Fly.

Halli travelled out to Iceland and settled down. His money ran out and he took up fishing, and one time he and his crew had such great difficulty rowing back that they just reached land. That evening the porridge was brought to Halli, and when he had eaten a few bites, he fell backward, dead.

Harald learned of the deaths of two of his men from Iceland, Bolli the Elegant and Sarcastic Halli.

He said of Bolli, 'The warrior must have fallen victim to spears.'

But of Halli he said, 'The poor devil must have burst eating porridge.'

And so I conclude the story of Sarcastic Halli.

Translated by GEORGE CLARK

THE TALE OF THORSTEIN SHIVER

Þorsteins þáttur skelks*

I   It is said that the following summer King Olaf attended feasts in the east around Vik and elsewhere. He feasted at a farm called Reim with a large company of men. There was a man accompanying the king at that time named Thorstein Thorkelsson. His father Thorkel was the son of Asgeir Scatter-brain, who was the son of Audun Shaft. Thorstein was an Icelandic man, who had come to the king the previous winter.

In the evening while people were sitting at the drinking tables, King Olaf made a speech. He said that none of his men should go alone to the privy during the night, and that anyone who had to go must have his bed-fellow accompany him, or else be guilty of disobeying him. Everyone drank heartily that night, and when the tables were taken down they all went to bed.

Now in the middle of the night, Thorstein the Icelander woke up and had to go to the toilet. The man lying next to him was sleeping soundly, and Thorstein certainly did not want to wake him. So he got up, slipped into his shoes, threw on a heavy cloak and went out to the privy. The outhouse was big enough for eleven people to sit on each side of it. Thorstein sat on the seat nearest the door. When he had been sitting there a few moments, he saw a demon climb up on to the seat farthest in and sit down.

Thorstein asked, 'Who's there?'

The fiend answered, 'It's Thorkel the Thin who fell upon corpses with King Harald War-tooth.'

'And where did you come from?' asked Thorstein.

The demon answered that he had just arrived from Hell.

'What can you tell me about that place?' asked Thorstein.

* From *Flateyjarbók*. Translated from *Íslendinga sögur III*.

He replied, 'What do you want to know?'

'Who endures the torments of Hell best?'

'No one endures them better,' replied the demon, 'than Sigurd Fafnisbani (Killer of the Serpent Fafnir).'

'What kind of torment does he suffer?'

'He kindles the oven,' answered the ghost.

'That doesn't strike me as much of a torment,' said Thorstein.

'Oh yes it is,' replied the demon, 'for he is also the kindling!'

'There is something in that then,' Thorstein said. 'Now who has the hardest time enduring Hell's torments?'

The ghost answered, 'Starkad the Old takes it worst, for he cries out so terribly that his screaming is a greater torment to the rest of us fiends than almost anything else, and we never get any reprieve from it.'

'What torment is it,' asked Thorstein, 'that he takes so badly, as brave a man as he is said to have been?'

'He stands up to his ankles in fire.'

'Why, that doesn't seem like much to me,' replied Thorstein, 'as great a hero as he was.'

'Then you don't see it,' said the ghost. 'Only the soles of his feet are sticking up out of the flames!'

'That is something,' said Thorstein. 'Now let me hear you scream once the way that he does.'

'All right,' said the demon.

He then threw open his jaws and let fly a great howl, while Thorstein pulled the fur trimming of his cloak up around his head.

He was not very impressed and asked, 'Is that the best he can scream?'

'Far from it,' replied the ghost, 'for that is the cry of us petty devils.'

'Scream like Starkad does once,' said Thorstein.

'All right,' said the demon.

He then began to scream a second time so terribly that Thorstein thought it monstrous that such a little fiend could howl so loudly. Again Thorstein wrapped his cloak around his head, but the crying paralysed him, and he fainted.

Then the demon asked, 'Why are you so quiet now?'

When he had recovered, Thorstein replied, 'I'm silent because I'm amazed at what a horrible voice you have, as little a demon as you appear to be. Was that Starkad's loudest cry?'

'Not even close,' he answered, 'rather his quietest.'

'Stop beating about the bush,' said Thorstein, 'and let me hear the loudest cry.'

The demon agreed to it. Thorstein then prepared himself by folding the cloak, winding it around his head and then holding it there with both hands. The ghost had moved closer to Thorstein by three seats with each cry, so that there were now only three seats left between them. The demon then inflated his cheeks in a terrible manner, rolled his eyes and began to howl so loudly that it exceeded all measure for Thorstein.

At that very moment, the church bell rang out, and Thorstein fell unconscious to the floor. The demon reacted to the bell by tumbling to the floor. The sound could be heard for a long time down in the ground. Thorstein recovered quickly. He stood up and went to his bed and lay down.

2   Now in the morning everyone got up. The king went to the chapel and heard Mass. After that they sat down to eat. The king was not terribly cheerful.

He addressed his men, 'Did anybody go alone to the privy last night?'

Thorstein came forth and fell down before the king, admitting that he had disobeyed his order.

The king replied, 'It was not such a serious offence against me, but you prove what is said about you Icelanders – that you are very stubborn. But did anything happen?'

Thorstein then told the whole story.

The king asked, 'What good did you think his crying would do you?'

'I want to tell you that, my lord. I thought that since you had warned all of us not to go out there alone, and since the devil showed up, that we would not leave the place unharmed. But I reckoned that you would wake up when he cried out, my lord, and I knew I would be helped if you found out about it.'

'Indeed it happened,' said the king, 'that I woke up to the sound, and I knew what was going on. I had the bell rung because I knew that nothing else could help you. But weren't you frightened when the demon began to scream?'

Thorstein answered, 'I don't know what it means to be frightened, my lord.'

'Was there no fear in your heart?' asked the king.

'I wouldn't say so,' Thorstein replied, 'because when I heard the last cry a shiver nearly ran down my spine.'

The king replied, 'You will now receive your nickname and be called Thorstein Shiver from now on. Here is a sword I'd like to give you in honour of the occasion.'

Thorstein thanked him.

It is said that Thorstein was made one of King Olaf's men and stayed with him thereafter until he fell on Olaf's longship The Serpent alongside the king's other champions.

Translated by ANTHONY MAXWELL

THE TALE OF AUDUN FROM
THE WEST FJORDS

*Auðunar þáttur vestfirska**

I   There was a man named Audun. His family came from the West Fjords, and he had little money. He sailed abroad from the fjords under the supervision of a good farmer named Thorstein and the skipper Thorir, who had been staying with Thorstein that winter. Audun had been living there too, working for Thorstein in exchange for provisions and passage abroad. Audun put most of what money he had away for his mother before he boarded the ship. It was intended to pay for three years' food and lodging.

They set sail, their journey went well and Audun spent the following winter with Thorir, who owned a farm in More.

The next summer they travelled to Greenland and spent the winter there.

It is mentioned that Audun bought a bear there, a great treasure for which he traded everything he owned.

The following summer they sailed back to Norway. They had a good voyage, and Audun had his bear with him. He planned to travel south to Denmark to meet King Svein and give him the animal.

Now when he arrived in the south of the country where the king was staying, he left the ship, leading the bear behind him, and rented a room. King Harald was soon told that a bear, a great treasure owned by an Icelandic man, had arrived there. The king immediately sent men to summon him, and when Audun appeared before the king he greeted him.

The king returned his greeting and asked, 'Do you have a great treasure of a bear?'

He answered that he did have a bear.

The king asked, 'Would you sell me the animal for the same price you paid for it?'

* Translated from *Íslendinga sögur III*.

He answered, 'I do not want to do that, my lord.'

'Would you then,' the king asked, 'let me give you double what you paid? That would be fairer, if you have traded everything you own for it.'

'I do not want to do that, my lord,' he answered.

The king asked, 'Will you give it to me, then?'

He answered, 'No, my lord.'

The king asked, 'What will you do with it, then?'

'Go,' he answered, 'to Denmark and give it to King Svein.'

King Harald said, 'Are you so ignorant that you have not heard about the enmity between our countries, or do you reckon your luck so great that you can go with treasures where others cannot travel safely, even though they do so of necessity?'

Audun answered, 'My lord, that is in your power. But I will not agree to do anything other than what I have intended.'

The king then said, 'Why not go ahead, then, and go your way as you please? But come to see me when you return and tell me how King Svein has rewarded you for the bear. It may well be that you are a fortunate man.'

'I promise to do that,' said Audun.

He then travelled south along the coast and east into Vik, and from there on to Denmark. But by then all of his travel money was spent, and he was forced to beg for food, both for himself and for the bear.

He met a steward of the king named Aki and asked him for provisions for himself and the bear.

'I plan,' he said, 'to give the bear to King Svein.'

Aki told him that he would sell him provisions if he wanted, but Audun replied that he had no money to pay for them.

'I want, nevertheless,' he said, 'to find a way to take the bear to the king.'

'I will give you the provisions you need to reach the king, but in exchange I want to own half of the bear. You should consider the fact that the bear will die if you do not have the money for all the food you need. Then you will not have any bear at all.'

And when Audun had thought about what the steward had proposed, he found it reasonable. So they agreed that he would sell Aki half of the bear, and that the king should be the judge of the whole arrangement later.

Now both of them were to go to see the king together. So they went to see the king and stood there before his table. The king pondered over who this man, whom he did not know, might be.

He asked Audun, 'Who are you?'

He answered, 'I am an Icelandic man, my lord, and I have just come from Greenland and Norway. I wanted to give you this bear. I gave everything I owned for it, but I have made a blunder, for I now own only half of the bear.'

He then told the king what had taken place between the steward Aki and himself.

The king asked, 'Is what he says true, Aki?'

'It is true,' Aki replied.

The king asked, 'Did you think it appropriate, given the fact that I have made you a powerful man, to impede and hinder a man from bringing me a treasure that he has given all his possessions to buy, when King Harald thought it advisable to give him safe conduct, even though he is our enemy? Now consider how fair this was on your part. Why, you deserve to be killed! I am not going to go that far, but you will leave the country immediately and never be caught in my eyesight again. But you, Audun, I will thank as if you had given me the entire bear. And please do stay.'

He accepted that and remained with King Svein for a while.

2   After some time had passed, Audun said to the king, 'I am now eager to leave here, my lord.'

The king answered, hesitatingly somewhat, 'Where do you plan to go, if you do not care to remain here with us?'

He replied, 'I want to make a pilgrimage to Rome.'

'If your plan had not been so noble,' the king replied, 'your eagerness to leave here would have displeased me.'

The king then gave him a very great deal of silver, and he travelled south with a group of pilgrims. The king made all the arrangements for his journey and asked him to come to see him when he returned.

Audun then went his way until he arrived in Rome. When he had stayed there as long as he wished, he headed back. But on the way he fell terribly ill and lost a great deal of weight. All of the money the king had given him for the journey was used up, so he was reduced to vagrancy and had to beg for food. He grew bald and was quite miserable.

He arrived back in Denmark at Easter and went to where the king was staying, yet he did not dare show himself in public. He waited in a wing of the church and planned to meet the king as he walked to church that evening.

But when he saw the king and his men all dressed up, he could not bring himself to appear before them.

When the king went to feast in the hall, Audun was fed outside as is the custom with pilgrims while they still bear their staff and scrip.

Now that evening when the king went to Vespers, Audun planned to talk with him. But as much as he had hesitated before, he did so even more now when the king's men were drunk.

As they walked back inside, the king noticed a man who seemed not to have the courage to approach him.

So when his men had gone inside, the king turned and said, 'Let him come forward now, he who wishes to speak with me. I have a suspicion that you must be the man.'

Then Audun came forward and fell down at the king's feet, but the king scarcely recognized him. As soon as the king realized who he was, though, he took Audun's hand and welcomed him.

'You have changed much,' he said, 'since we last met', and he led him inside.

Now when the king's men saw him, they laughed at him.

But the king said, 'You have no cause to laugh, for he has better provided for his soul than you have.'

The king then had a bath prepared for him and gave him clothing, and Audun remained there with him.

3　　It is told that sometime during the spring, the king invited Audun to remain with him permanently and told him he would make him his cup-bearer and honour him highly.

Audun said, 'God reward you, my lord, for all the honour you would bestow upon me, but as a matter of fact I am thinking of sailing to Iceland.'

The king replied, 'That seems an odd choice.'

Audun said, 'I cannot live with the fact, my lord, that I am held in honour here with you, while my mother is a vagrant in Iceland. For the provisions I left for her before I sailed from Iceland will now be exhausted.'

The king replied, 'That was well and nobly put, and you will turn out to be a fortunate man. That reason alone could make your leaving here acceptable to me. Stay with me now until a ship is prepared.'

And so he did.

One late spring day King Svein walked down to the docks where men were preparing ships to sail to various countries: to the Baltic and Saxony, to Sweden and Norway. He and Audun came upon a beautiful ship that was being outfitted.

The king asked, 'How do you like this ship, Audun?'

He answered, 'Very well, my lord.'

The king said, 'I want to give you this ship as repayment for the bear.'

He thanked him for the gift as best he could.

After a while, when the ship was ready, King Svein said to Audun, 'Now you wish to leave, and I am not going to hinder you. But I have heard that your country is poorly provided with harbours, and that in many places there is only open coastline, which is dangerous for ships. Now, say you are shipwrecked, and you lose your ship and goods. Then you will have little to show that you have met King Svein and given him a treasure.'

The king then gave him a leather pouch full of silver, 'so that you won't be left entirely penniless if you are shipwrecked, if you manage to hold on to this.

'It could still happen,' the king continued, 'that you lose this too. Little good it would do you then that you have met King Svein and given him a treasure.'

The king then drew a ring off his arm, gave it to Audun and said, 'Even if things turn out so badly that you are shipwrecked and you lose this money, you will not be penniless if you make it ashore, for many survive shipwrecks wearing gold. And it will still be evident that you have met King Svein, if you hold on to the arm-ring.

'I would advise you, though,' he said, 'not to give the arm-ring away unless you feel you must repay a very great favour done you by a noble man. Then give that man the arm-ring, for it would befit men of high standing to accept it. Now farewell!'

4   Audun then set sail and arrived in Norway, where he had his cargo carried ashore. This was a greater chore than it had been the last time he was in Norway. He then went to see King Harald to keep the promise he had made him before he sailed to Denmark.

He greeted the king warmly.

King Harald returned his greeting and said, 'Sit down and drink with us.' And so he did.

King Harald then asked, 'How did King Svein reward you for the bear?'

Audun replied, 'By accepting the gift from me.'

The king said, 'Why, I would have done that! What else did he give you for it?'

Audun replied, 'He gave me silver so that I could make a pilgrimage.'

Then King Harald said, 'King Svein gives many men silver for pilgrimages and for other things, even when they do not bring him treasures. Now what else did he give you?'

'He offered,' Audun replied, 'to make me his cup-bearer and to bestow high honours upon me.'

'A nice gesture,' said the king, 'but surely he gave you something more?'

Audun replied, 'He gave me a knorr with goods most highly desired here in Norway.'

'Graciously done,' said the king, 'and I would have rewarded you likewise. Did he give you anything else?'

Audun replied, 'He gave me a leather pouch full of silver and said that I would not be penniless even if my ship were wrecked off the coast of Iceland.'

The king said, 'Splendid! Even I would not have done that. I'd have considered myself free from obligation after giving you the ship. Did he give you anything else?'

'He did indeed give me more, my lord,' Audun said. 'He gave me the arm-ring that I wear on my arm and told me that all my money could be lost, but that I still would not be penniless if I had the ring. He told me not to give it to anyone unless I felt obliged to repay a noble man so dearly that I would be willing to part with it. And I have now found that man, for you had the power to deprive me of both the bear and my life, yet you let me travel in peace to a place where others could not go.'

The king warmly accepted the gift and gave Audun fine gifts in return before they parted.

Audun set aside his money for the journey to Iceland and travelled there early that summer. He was considered an exceedingly fortunate man.

Thorstein Gyduson is descended from this man Audun.

Translated by ANTHONY MAXWELL

THE TALE OF THE STORY-WISE ICELANDER

Íslendings þáttur sögufróða*

It so happened one summer that a bright young Icelandic man came to the king and asked to be taken into his care. The king asked if he knew any lore, and he claimed that he could tell stories. The king then said that he would keep him, but that he would be obligated always to entertain anyone who asked him. He did so and grew popular among the king's men. They gave him clothes, and the king gave him weapons. And so it went until Yule.

Then the Icelander grew sad. The king asked why, and he answered that he was just in a bad mood.

'That can't be it,' the king said, 'so let me guess. I would guess that you have run out of stories to tell. This winter you have always entertained anyone who has asked you. Now you are upset that you're out of stories at Yule.'

'It is just as you say,' he replied. 'I have only one story left, and that one I dare not tell here, for it is the story of your travels.'

The king said, 'And that is exactly the story I most desire to hear. Now don't tell any stories until Yule, since people are busy now. But on the first day of Yule begin the story, and tell a little bit of it. I will arrange it with you so that the story lasts as long as Yule. Now a lot of drinking takes place at Yuletide, and there is little time for sitting around and hearing stories. Nor will you be able to see, while you are telling, whether I am pleased or not.'

So it happened, and the Icelander told his story. He began on the first day of Yule and spoke for a while. But the king soon told him to stop.

Then people started drinking, and many of them discussed how bold it was of the Icelander to tell that story, or how they thought the king would

* From *Morkinskinna*. Translated from *Íslendinga sögur III*.

like it. Some thought that he told the story well, but some were less patient. And so it went on during Yule.

The king made sure that people listened carefully, and under his direction the story and Yule ended at the same time.

On Twelfth Night, after the story had ended earlier in the day, the king said, 'Aren't you curious, Icelander, to know how I liked the story?'

'I am afraid to know, my lord,' he answered.

The king said, 'I liked it very much, and it was no worse than the matter permitted. But who taught you the story?'

He answered, 'It was my habit out in my country to travel each summer to the Thing, and I learned part of the story each summer from Halldor Snorrason.'

'In that case it is no wonder,' the king said, 'that you know it well. Your luck will now be with you. Be welcome here with me, and I will grant you whatever you want.'

The king secured him good wares, and he grew into vigorous manhood.

Translated by ANTHONY MAXWELL

REFERENCE SECTION

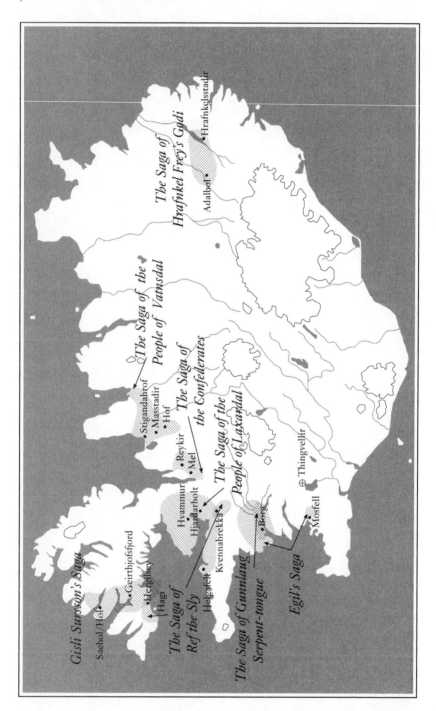

Saga Sites in Iceland

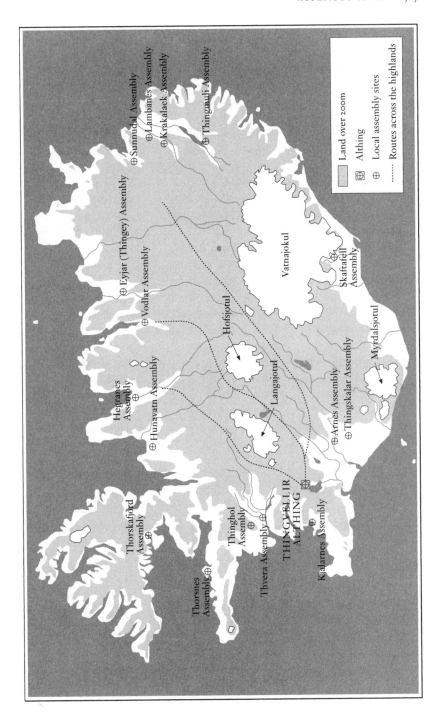

Assembly Sites

Kings of Norway	Kings of Demark	Kings of England
Harald Fair-hair –932	Gorm the Old –940	Ethelred I, King of
Erik Blood-axe 930–34	Harald Black-tooth	Wessex 866–71
Hakon Haraldsson, King	Gormsson –c. 986	Alfred the Great, King
Athelstan's foster-son	Sveinn Fork-beard	of Wessex 871–99
934–60	Haraldsson 986–1014	Edward the Elder, King
Harald Grey-cloak 960–75	Harald Sveinsson 1014–18	of Wessex 899–924
Hakon Sigurdarson the	Knut (Canute) Sveinsson	Athelstan the Faithful
Powerful 975–95	the Great 1018–35	925–39
Olaf Tryggvason 995–1000	Hardicanute 1035–42	Edmund I 939–46
Eirik (d. 1013) and Svein	Magnus Olafsson the	Eadred 946–55
Hakonarson 1000–1015	Good 1042–7	Eadwig 955–9
Olaf Haraldsson the Saint	Svein Ulfsson 1047–74	Edgar 959–75
1014–30	Harald Hein Sveinsson	Edward the Martyr 975–8
Svein Knutsson (son of	1074–80	Ethelred II, the Unready
Canute the Great)	Knut the Saint 1080–86	978–1013; 1014–16
1030–35	Olaf Hunger 1086–95	Svein Fork-beard 1013–14
Magnus Olafsson the	Eirik the Good 1095–1103	Edmund II, Ironside 1016
Good 1035–47	Nikulas 1103–34	Knut (Canute) Sveinsson
Harald Sigurdarson the	Eirik Eimuni 1134–7	the Great 1016–35
Stern 1046–66	Eirik Lamb 1137–46	Harold I 1035–40
Magnus Haraldsson	Svein Svidandi 1146–57	Hardicanute 1040–42
1066–9	Knut Magnusson 1166–7	Edward the Confessor
Olaf the Quiet 1067–93	Valdemar Knutsson the	1042–66
Magnus Bare-leg 1093–1103	Old 1157–82	Harold Godwinson (II)
Olaf (d. 1116), Eystein		1066
(d. 1122) and Sigurd		William I, the
Jerusalem-farer, sons of		Conqueror 1066–87
Magnus 1103–30		William II 1087–1100
Magnus Sigurdarson the		Henry I 1100–1135
Blind 1130–35		Stephen 1135–54
Harald Magnusson Gilli		
1130–36		
Sigurd (d. 1155), Eystein		
(d. 1157) and Ingi		
Haraldsson 1136–61		
Hakon Broad-shoulder		
Sigurdarson 1157–62		
Magnus Erlingsson 1161–84		

Historical Events linked to the Sagas
(Scandinavian history is given in italics)

Lawspeakers in Iceland

Settlement of Iceland begins *c.* 870
Battle of Havsfjord (Harald Fair-hair takes control of Norway) c. 885–900
Establishment of the *Althing c.* 930
Beginning of the Commonwealth 930
Battle of Brunanburh/Wen Heath in England c. 937
Division of Iceland into Quarters *c.* 965
Discovery of Greenland 985–6
Christianity accepted in Iceland 1000
Battle of Svold (the death of King Olaf Tryggvason of Norway) c. 1000
First trips to Vinland *c.* 1000–1011
Agreement between the Icelanders and Olaf Haraldsson the Saint, King of Norway 1020–30
Battle of Stiklestad in Norway (the death of King Olaf Haraldsson the Saint) 1030
Isleif Gizurarson becomes the first bishop of Iceland (at Skalholt) 1056
Battle of Stamford Bridge (the death of King Harald Sigurdarson in England) 1066
Ari Thorgilsson the Learned born *c.* 1068
Jon Ogmundarson becomes the first bishop of Holar (in the north of Iceland) 1106
Íslendingabók (The Book of Icelanders) written by Ari the Learned *c.* 1122–33
First Kings' Sagas compiled *c.* 1150
Snorri Sturluson born 1179 (d. 1241)
First Sagas of Icelanders compiled *c.* 1220
First Legendary Sagas (*fornaldarsögur*) compiled *c.* 1220
Heimskringla compiled by Snorri Sturluson *c.* 1220–30
Codex Regius of the Eddic poems compiled *c.* 1260
End of the Commonwealth 1262
Möðruvallabók codex of the sagas compiled mid-fourteenth century

Ulfljot –930
Hrafn Haengsson (son of Ketil Haeng) 930–49
Thorarin Ragi's Brother Oleifsson 950–69
Thorkel Moon Thorsteinsson 970–84
Thorgeir Thorkelsson the Godi, from Ljosavatn 985–1001
Grim Svertingsson 1002–3
Skafti Thoroddsson 1004–30
Stein Thorgestsson 1031–3
Thorkel Tjorvason 1034–53
Gellir Bolverksson 1054–62
Gunnar Thorgrimsson the Wise 1063–5
Kolbein Flosason 1066–71
Gellir Bolverksson 1072–4
Gunnar Thorgrimsson the Wise 1075
Sighvat Surtsson 1076–83
Markus Skeggjason 1084–1107
Ulfhedin Gunnarsson 1108–16
Bergthor Hrafnsson 1117–22

Illustrations and Diagrams

SHIPS

No full-sized ships have been found in excavations in Iceland, only small boats which have been placed in graves. Several types of ships are mentioned in the sagas, however, and it is obvious that they had a variety of purposes, ranging from the local ferrying of travellers to foreign warfare, trade and the transportation of cargo across the open sea.

It is worth noting that, unlike today's ocean-going vessels, the ships of this time were open to the elements and had no decks in the modern sense of the word. Navigation was largely carried out by means of the sun, stars, landmarks, and knowledge of birds and whales. The ships were propelled by the wind (with the use of large sails) and human strength (through the use of oars). They were steered by a single rudder which was attached to the starboard side of the vessel, near the stern.

There seems to have been a distinction, though not a firm one, between a 'ship' and a 'boat', in that a ship (*skip*) was seen as being a vessel that usually had more than twelve oars, while a boat (*bátur*) had fewer than twelve. There was no sharp difference between warships and trading ships, since trading ships were sometimes used for warfare. Nonetheless, warships tended to be large, long and slender, and designed for both sailing and rowing. They were usually divided laterally into spaces for pairs of rowers, known as *rúm* (literally 'rooms'). The warships of kings, such as the famous Long Serpent and Bison belonging to Olaf Tryggvason and Olaf Haraldsson of Norway, often had more than thirty 'rooms', that is more than sixty oars. Trading vessels tended to be somewhat different.

All trading ships were broader in proportion to their length than warships. They had a rounder form, a bigger freeboard and a deeper draught than the longships. As they were designed almost exclusively for sailing, in most cases the mast was fixed. On the permanent deck fore and aft it was possible to stand or sit in a row if necessary, for here (but not amidships) there were oar-holes in the ship's side. All the middle part of the ships was occupied by the cargo.

(Brøgger and Shetelig, p. 179)

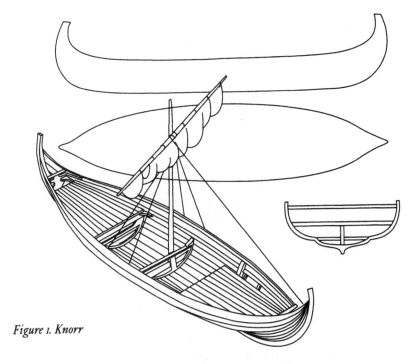

Figure 1. Knorr

It is unlikely that warships ever sailed to Iceland, but the saga heroes are often said to have gone raiding on their trips abroad. The most important ship for the Icelanders was the knorr (*knörr*). Smaller, broad boats of a similar kind were used for centuries in Iceland, especially in the area around Breidafjord. Such boats might well be similar to the smaller cargo vessels (*byrðingar*) mentioned in the sagas.

The most common ships:
The cargo vessel was short and broad, smaller than the knorr, and mainly intended for coastal trade, although on occasion such vessels seem to have been ocean-going. They tended to have crews of between twelve and twenty men. The vessel known as Skuldelev 3, like the other Skuldelev ships now on display in Roskilde, is probably an example of a cargo vessel. It is *c.* 13.8m long and 3.3m in the beam.

The knorr was a large, wide-bodied, sturdy, ocean-going cargo ship, the biggest of the trading ships. The settlers of Iceland and Greenland, and the Vinland explorers, seem to have most commonly used the knorr, which was capable of carrying not only people but also livestock, cargo and large amounts of supplies. An example of the knorr (referred to as Skuldelev 1) was found in Roskilde fjord in Denmark and is on display in Roskilde. This is *c.* 16.3m long and *c.* 4.5m in the beam. (See Figure 1.)

The expression longship (*langskip*) was a collective, general term used for large warships, more than thirty-two oars. Some of these were of great size, like King Olaf Tryggvason's Long Serpent, which is said to have had thirty-four 'rooms',

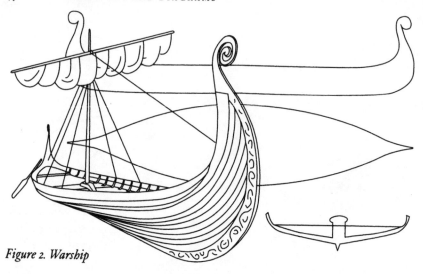

Figure 2. Warship

making a total of sixty-eight oarsmen, and probably also had space for additional warriors. As in the case of the warship (*karfi*) (see below), the size was usually indicated by the number of places for rowers. The ship known as Skuldelev 2, now on display in Roskilde, is thought to be a longship. This vessel, which probably was 28–9m long and *c.* 4.5m in the beam, might have carried between fifty and sixty men. Nonetheless, it is somewhat smaller than many of the Norwegian longships described in the sagas.

The warship was generally smaller than the longships owned by kings and great chieftains. The size clearly varied: they range from a warship with sixteen oars on each side, mentioned in the *Saga of Grettir the Strong*, to the warship with six oars on each side which is said to have been owned by a child in *Egil's Saga*. The Gokstad and Oseberg ships, on display in Oslo, have been identified as being this type of vessel. The Gokstad ship has sixteen oars on each side, and was 23.3m long and 5.25m in the beam. (See Figure 2.)

The famous dragon (*dreki*) was also a warship. The term is mainly used in later, more fictive sagas, but makes an early appearance in *Egil's Saga*. The dragon, however, was not a specific type of ship, rather a form of description. It originates in the occasional use of apparently removable dragon heads (and sometimes even tails) which were attached to the prows (and sterns) of vessels. According to an old Icelandic law, dragon heads had to be removed from ships which were heading towards land, so as not to frighten the local nature spirits that guarded Iceland.

Various other expressions for ships that appear in the sagas:

The ferry (*ferja*) was used for cargo and local transport, but we have no description of its size or what it looked like.

The general term trading vessel (*kaupskip*) simply refers to any vessel engaged in trade (*kaup*). The term was probably usually synonymous with the word knorr.

The expressions large warship (*skeið*), light ship/boat/smack (*skúta*) and swift warship (*snekkja*) are, as Brøgger and Shetelig have pointed out (p. 169), hardly classifications by size or equipment, but rather tend to be 'used merely in a transferred sense as indistinct imagery'.

See further: Brøgger, A. W. and Shetelig, H., *The Viking Ships.* Oslo, 1951.

Foote, Peter and Wilson, D. M., *The Viking Achievement.* London, 1979.

Campbell, James Graham, *The Viking World.* London, 1980.

THE FARM

The farm (bær) was a basic social and economic unit in Iceland. Although farms varied in size, there was presumably only one building on a 'farm' at the time of settlement, an all-purpose building known as a hall or farmhouse (*skáli*) or longhouse (*langhús*), constructed on the model of the farmhouses the settlers had inhabited in Norway. Over time, additional rooms and/or wings were often added to the original construction.

The Icelandic farmhouse shown in the illustrations is based on information provided by the excavations at Stong (Stöng) in the Thjorsardal valley in the south of Iceland. Stong is regarded as having been an average-sized farm by Icelandic standards. The settlement was abandoned as a result of the devastating ash-fall from the great eruption of Hekla in 1104.

The illustrations are intended to help readers visualize the farm, and understand the specialized vocabulary used to describe it. Many of these terms can be found in the Glossary.

The plan of the farmstead (Figure 3) shows an overall layout of a typical farm. It is based on measurements carried out by the archaeologist Daniel Bruun, but it should be stressed that the layout of these farms was far from fixed. Nonetheless, the plan indicates the common positioning of the haystack wall/yard (*stakkgarður*) in the often-mentioned hayfield (*tún*). The hayfield wall (*túngarður*) surrounds the farm and its hayfield.

Also placed outside the main farm are the animal sheds. With the exception of a cow shed, no barns or other animal sheds came to light at Stong, but these must have existed as they did on most farms. Sometimes they were attached to the farmhouse, but more often were independent constructions some distance away from the building. Sheep sheds, in particular, tended to be built farther away from the hall, and closer to the meadows used for grazing.

The smithy is also separate (for safety reasons), and the same often appears to have applied to the fire room/fire hall (*eldhús/eldaskáli*). The latter was essentially a form of specialized kitchen. It was not only used for cooking, but was also the site of other daily household activities carried out around the fire. Indeed, sometimes the term

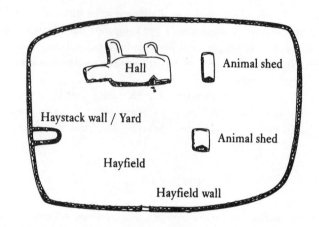

Figure 3. Icelandic Farm

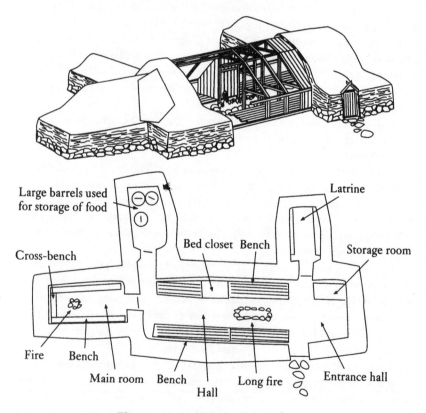

Figures 4 and 5. The Farmhouse at Stong

eldhús seems to refer not to a separate building, but to the farmhouse, instead of the word hall, stressing the presence of the fire and warmth in the living quarters.

Figure 4 is a cross-section of the hall at Stong, giving an idea of the way the buildings were constructed. The framework was timber. The main weight of the roof rested on beams, which, in turn, were supported by pillars on either side of the hall. The high-seat pillars (*öndvegissúlur*) that some settlers brought with them from Norway might have been related to the pillars placed on either side of the high seat (*hásæti*). The outer walls of most farms in Iceland were constructed of a thick layer of turf and stone, which served to insulate the building. The smoke from the main fire was usually let out through a vent in the roof, but the living quarters would still have been rather smoke-ridden.

Figure 5 depicts the layout of the farmhouse excavated at Stong. The purpose of the area, here marked 'latrine', is uncertain, but this role makes sense on the basis of the layout of the room, and the description given in *The Tale of Thorstein Shiver*, for example. For information about the bed closet, see the Glossary.

See further: Foote and Wilson, *The Viking Achievement.*

Campbell, *The Viking World.*

SOCIAL AND POLITICAL STRUCTURE

The notion of kinship is central to the sense of honour and duty in the sagas, and thereby to their action. Kinship essentially involves a sense of belonging, not unlike that underlying the Celtic clan systems. The Icelandic word for kin or clan (*ætt*) is cognate with other words meaning 'to own' and 'direction' – the notion could be described as a 'social compass'.

Establishing kinship is one justification for the long genealogies, which tend to strike non-Icelandic readers as idiosyncratic detours, and also for the preludes in Norway before the main saga action begins. Members of the modern nuclear family or close relatives are only part of the picture, since kinsmen are all those who are linked through a common ancestor – preferably one of high birth and high repute – as far back as five or six generations or even more.

Marriage ties, sworn brotherhood and other bonds could create conflicting loyalties with respect to the duty of revenge, of course, as seen in so many sagas, but by the same token they could serve as instruments for resolving such vendettas. A strict pecking order laid down the successive incumbents for the duty of revenge within the fairly immediate family, with a 'multiplier effect' if those seeking vengeance were killed in the process. The obligation to take revenge was inherited, just like wealth, property and claims.

Patriarchy was the order of the day, although notable exceptions are found. Likewise, the physical duty of revenge devolved only upon males, but women were often responsible for instigating it, either by urging a husband or brother to action with slurs

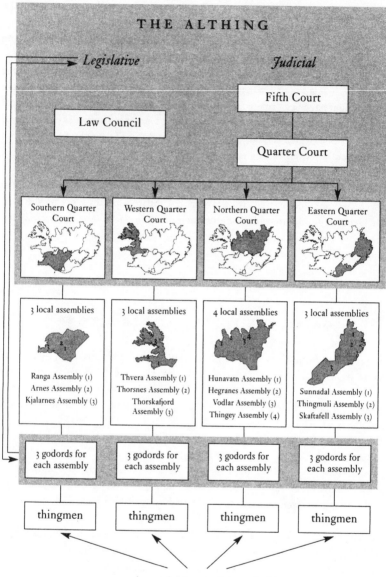

THE ALTHING

Legislative   *Judicial*

Fifth Court

Law Council

Quarter Court

Southern Quarter Court	Western Quarter Court	Northern Quarter Court	Eastern Quarter Court

3 local assemblies	3 local assemblies	4 local assemblies	3 local assemblies
Ranga Assembly (1)	Thvera Assembly (1)	Hunavatn Assembly (1)	Sunnadal Assembly (1)
Arnes Assembly (2)	Thorsnes Assembly (2)	Hegranes Assembly (2)	Thingmuli Assembly (2)
Kjalarnes Assembly (3)	Thorskafjord Assembly (3)	Vodlar Assembly (3)	Skaftafell Assembly (3)
		Thingey Assembly (4)	

3 godords for each assembly	3 godords for each assembly	3 godords for each assembly	3 godords for each assembly

thingmen	thingmen	thingmen	thingmen

members of thingmen's households

about their cowardice, or by bringing up their sons with a vengeful sense of purpose and even supplying them with old weapons that had become family heirlooms.

Iceland was unique among European societies in the tenth to thirteenth centuries in two respects in particular: it had no king and no executive power to follow through the pronouncements of its highly sophisticated legislative and judicial institutions. The lack of executive power meant that there was no means for preventing men from taking the law into their own hands, which gave rise to many memorable conflicts recorded in the sagas, but also led to the gradual disintegration of the Commonwealth in the thirteenth century.

The Althing served not only as a general or national assembly (which is what its name means), but also as the main festival and social gathering of the year, where people exchanged stories and news, renewed acquaintance with old friends and relatives, and the like. Originally it was inaugurated (with a pagan ceremony) by the leading godi (*allsherjargoði*) who was a descendant of the first settler Ingolf Arnarson, in the tenth week of summer. Early in the eleventh century the opening day was changed to the Thursday of the eleventh week of summer (18–24 June). Legislative authority at the Althing was in the hands of the Law Council, while there were two levels of judiciary, the Quarter Courts and the Fifth Court.

The Law Council was originally comprised of the thirty-six godis, along with two thingmen for each, and the Lawspeaker, who was the highest authority in the Commonwealth, elected by the Law Council for a term of three years. It was the duty of the Lawspeaker to recite the entire procedures of the assembly and one-third of the laws of the country every year. He presided over the meetings of the Law Council and ruled on points of legal interpretation.

Quarter Courts, established at the Althing around 965, evolved from earlier regional Spring Assemblies, probably panels of nine men, which had dealt with cases involving people from the same quarter. Three new godords were created in the north when the Quarter Courts were set up. The godis appointed thirty-six men to the Quarter Court and their decisions had to be unanimous.

Around 1005, the Fifth Court was established as a kind of court of appeal to hear cases which were unresolved by the Quarter Courts. The godis appointed forty-eight members to the Fifth Court, and the two sides in each case were allowed to reject six each. A simple majority among the remaining thirty-six decided the outcome, and lots were drawn in the event of a tie. With the creation of the Fifth Court, the number of godis was increased correspondingly, and with their two thingmen each and the Lawspeaker, the Law Council was then comprised of 145 people in all.

The Althing was inaugurated or consecrated by the leading godi and dissolved by Weapon Taking. 'Weapon Taking is when a Thing is dismissed and the people all ride home again', *The Saga of Hrafnkel Frey's Godi* states, referring to the idea that the persons attending the assembly were supposed to be unarmed and settle their affairs peacefully; presumably the shedding of blood would have violated not only the authority of the law but also, originally at least, the sanctity of the site.

A confiscation court was appointed by a godi to seize and share out the property of a man who had been found guilty. It was supposed to meet within an arrow-shot (a specific distance, perhaps 200 fathoms) from the limits of the guilty man's farm. The procedure is described in *The Saga of Hrafnkel Frey's Godi*. 'No man is a full outlaw as long as the confiscation court has not been held, and that has to take place at his home. It must be done fourteen days after Weapon Taking,' says Thorgeir Thjostarsson to Sam when they prepare to ride away from the Althing after Hrafnkel has been sentenced to full outlawry. They go to Hrafnkel's farm, capture him and his men, and tie them up. Then Sam goes 'to a safe place an arrow-shot away from the farm' to carry out the confiscation court, 'on some rocky knoll where there is neither a ploughed field nor a meadow'. Not all confiscation courts succeeded in their task, because force sometimes had to be shown if not exerted. Some men who had been sentenced to outlawry remained on their property with a band of followers to defend it, and others made a quick getaway, taking everything with them that they could.

Legal disputes feature prominently in *The Sagas of Icelanders*, and the prosecution and defence of a case followed clearly defined procedures. Cases were prepared locally some time before the Thing, and could be dismissed there if they were technically flawed. Preparation generally took one of two forms: a panel of neighbours could be called, comprised of five or nine people who lived near the scene of the incident or the home of the accused, to testify to what had happened; or a party could go to the home of the accused to summons him during the Summons Days, two weeks before the Spring Assembly but three or four weeks before the Althing.

The accused generally did not attend the assembly, but was defended by someone, who called witnesses and was entitled to disqualify members of the panel. Panels did not adjudicate the details and facts of the case in the modern sense, but only determined whether the incident had taken place. The case was then summed up and a ruling passed on it by the court.

Penalties depended upon the seriousness of the case and took the form of either monetary compensation or outlawry. Lesser outlawry lasted for three years, while full outlawry meant that a man must not be fed or helped and was tantamount to a death sentence. A confiscation court would seize the belongings of a man outlawed for three years or life.

Cases were often settled without going through this complex court procedure: by arbitration, a ruling from a third party who was accepted by both sides, or by self-judgement by either of the parties involved in the case. Duels were another method. They originally took place on small islands and proceeded according to strict rules. The duel features in a number of sagas but was formally banned in Iceland in 1006. Mainland Scandinavian Vikings, berserks and troublemakers are often depicted in the sagas as terrorizing peaceful farmers by challenging them to duels for their wives or daughters.

OLD ICELANDIC YEAR AND DAY

Months of the Year and Important Dates

In medieval Scandinavia, 'summer' lasted approximately from April to October, 'winter' approximately from October to April. In some cases, there were several different names for the old lunar months, and only one of the names has been chosen for this table. The original Icelandic names are given in italics.

Important Dates	Old Icelandic Lunar Months	Western Calendar
Early days of summer (*Sumarmál*)		April
	Harpa-month (*Harpa*)	
Spring Assemblies take place		May
at the end of the fourth week	Lamb-fold-time (*Stekktíð*)	
of summer		June
	Sun-month (*Sólmánuður*)	
Moving Days (*Fardagar*)		July
	Midsummer (*Miðsumar*)	
Althing is held when ten weeks		August
of summer have passed	Hay-time (*Heyannir*)	
		September
Autumn Meeting takes place	Harvest-month (*Haustmánuður*)	
no later than eight weeks		October
before the end of summer	Slaughtering-month (*Gormánuður*)	
		November
Winter Nights (*Veturnætur*)	Ylir (*Ýlir*)	
		December
Yule (*Jól*)	Ram-month (*Hrútmánuður*)	
		January
	Thorri-month (*Þorri*)	
		February
	Goa-month (*Góa*)	
		March
	Last month of winter (*Einmánuður*)	

Hours of the Day		
6 a.m.	*rismál/miður morgunn*	hour of rising/mid-morning
9 a.m.	*dagmál*	breakfast time
12 (noon)	*hádegi/miðdegi*	midday/noon
3 p.m.	*undorn/nón*	mid-afternoon
6 p.m.	*miður aftann*	mid-evening
9 p.m.	*náttmál*	night-meal
12 (midnight)	*elding/ótta*	last part of the night

Glossary

The Icelandic term is printed in italics after the head-word, with modern spelling. See also tables on dates and times in Old Icelandic Year and Day.

Althing	*alþingi*: General assembly. See Introduction, pp. xlvi–xlvii and 'Social and Political Structure'.
arch of raised turf	*jarðarmen*: In order to confirm sworn brotherhood, the participants had to mix their blood and walk under an arch of raised turf: 'A long piece of sod was cut from a grassy field but the ends left uncut. It was raised up into an arch, under which the person carrying out the ordeal had to pass' (*The Saga of the People of Laxardal*, ch. 18).
Autumn Meeting	*leið, leiðarþing*: Held after the Althing and generally lasting one or two days at the end of July or beginning of August. Proceedings and decisions from the Althing were announced at the Autumn Meeting, which had no judicial role.
ball game	*knattleikur*: A game played with a hard ball and a bat, possibly similar to the Gaelic game known as hurling, which is still played in Scotland and Ireland. The exact rules, however, are uncertain. See, for example, the description of the game in *Gisli Sursson's Saga*, chs. 15 and 18.
bat	*knattdrepa, knatttré*: See ball game.
bed closet	*hvílugólf, lokrekkja, lokhvíla, lokrekkjugólf*: A private sleeping area used by the heads of better-off households. The closet was partitioned off from the rest of the house, and had a door that was secured from the inside. (See illustration in 'The Farm'.)
berserk	*berserkur*: (Literally 'bear-shirt'). A man who slipped or

deliberately worked himself into an animal-like frenzy, which hugely increased his strength and made him apparently immune to the effect of blows from weapons. The berserks are paradoxical figures, prized as warriors and evidently regarded as having supernatural powers (perhaps bestowed on them by Odin, the god of warriors), but in the sagas, this mysticism is beginning to wear off. They are often presented as stock figures, generally bullies who are none too bright, and when heroes do away with them, there is usually little regret, and a great deal of local relief. Closely related to the original concept of the berserk (implied by its literal meaning) are the shape-shifters.

black Often used here to translate *blár*, which in modern Icelandic means only 'blue'.

bloody wound *áverki*: Almost always used in a legal sense, that is with regard to a visible, most likely bloody wound, which could result in legal actions for compensation, or some more drastic proceedings like the taking of revenge.

board game *tafl*: *Tafl* probably often refers to chess which had plainly reached Scandinavia before the twelfth century. However, in certain cases it might also refer to another board game known as *hnefatafl*. The rules of the latter game are uncertain, even though we know what the boards looked like.

booth *búð*: A temporary dwelling used by those who attended the various assemblies. Structurally, it seems to have involved permanent walls which were covered by a tent-like roof, probably made of cloth.

bride-price *mundur*: In formal terms, this was the amount that the prospective husband's family gave to the prospective wife's family at the wedding. According to Icelandic law this was the personal property of the wife. See also dowry.

compensation *manngjöld, bætur*: Penalties imposed by the courts were of three main kinds: awards of compensation in cash; sentences of lesser outlawry, which could be lessened or dropped by the payment of compensation; and sentences of full outlawry with no chance of being compounded. In certain cases, a man's right to immediate vengeance was recognized, but for many offences compensation was the fixed legal penalty and the injured party had little choice but to accept the settlement offered by the court, an arbitrator or a man who had been given the right to self-judgement (*sjálfdæmi*). It was certainly legal to put pressure on the guilty party to pay. Neither court verdicts nor legislation, nor even the constitutional arrangements, had any coercive power behind them other than the free initiative of individual chieftains with their armed following.

confiscation court
cross-bench

féránsdómur: See 'Social and Political Structure'.

pallur, þverpallur: A raised platform, or bench at the inner end of the main room, where women were usually seated.

directions

austur/vestur/norður/suður (east/west/north/south): These directional terms are used in a very wide sense in the sagas; they are largely dependent on context, and they cannot always be trusted to reflect compass directions. Internationally, 'the east' generally refers to the countries to the east and south-east of Iceland, and although 'eastern' usually refers to a Norwegian, it can also apply to a Swede (especially since the concept of nationality was still not entirely clear when the sagas were being written), and might even be used for a person who has picked up Russian habits. 'The west', or to 'go west', tends to refer to Ireland and what are now the British Isles, but might even refer to lands even farther afield; the point of orientation is west of Norway. When confined to Iceland, directional terms sometimes refer to the quarter to which a person is travelling, e.g. a man going to the Althing from the east of the country might be said to be going 'south' rather than the geographically more accurate 'west', and a person going home to the West Fjords from the Althing is said to be going 'west' rather than 'north'.

dis

dís, pl. *dísir*: These appear to have been high-ranking female guardian spirits that watched over farms, families and, occasionally, individuals. They have certain traits in common with fetches and valkyries, but were seen as being much more powerful, almost like minor local deities, since a sacrifice was made to them during the Winter Nights every year.

dowry	*heimanfylgja*: Literally 'that which accompanies the bride from her home'. This was the amount of money (or land) that a bride's father contributed at her wedding. Like the bride-price, it remained legally her property. However, the husband controlled the couple's financial affairs and was responsible for the use to which both these assets were put.
drapa	*drápa*: A heroic, laudatory poem, usually in the complicated metre preferred by the Icelandic poets. Such poems were in fashion between the tenth and thirteenth centuries. They were usually composed in honour of kings, earls and other prominent men; or they might be directed towards a loved one, composed in memory of the deceased or in relation to some religious matter. A drapa usually consisted of three parts: an introduction, a middle section including one or more refrains, and a conclusion. It was usually clearly distinguished from the flokk, which tended to be shorter, less laudatory and without refrains (see *The Saga of Gunnlaug Serpent-tongue*, ch. 9). For an example of a drapa, see *Egil's Saga*, ch. 61.
duel	*hólmganga*: Used for a formally organized duel, literally meaning 'going to the island'. This is probably because the area prescribed for the fight formed a small 'island' with clearly defined boundaries which separated the action from the outside world; it might also refer to the fact that small islands were originally favoured sites for duels. The rules included that the two duellists slashed at each other alternately, the seconds protecting the principal fighters with shields. Shields hacked to pieces could be replaced by up to three shields on either side. If blood was shed, the fight could be ended and the wounded man could buy himself off with a compensation payment of three marks of silver, either on the spot or later. The rules are stated in detail in *Kormak's Saga*.

The duelling laws had it that the cloak was to be five ells square, with loops at the corners, and pegs had to be put down there of the kind that had a head at one end. They were called tarses, and he who made the preparations was to approach the tarses in such a way that he could see the sky between his legs while grasping his ear lobes with the invocation that has since been used again in the sacrifice known as the tarse-sacrifice. There were to be three spaces marked out all round the cloak, each a foot in breadth, and outside the marked spaces there should be four strings, named hazel poles; what you had was a hazel-poled stretch of ground, when that was done. You were supposed to have three shields, but when they were used up, you were to go on to the cloak, even if you had withdrawn from it before, and from then on you were supposed to protect yourself with weapons. He who was challenged had to strike. If one of the two was wounded in such a way that blood fell on to the cloak, there was no obligation to continue fighting. If someone stepped with just one foot outside the hazel poles, he was said to be retreating, or to be running if he did so with both. There would be a man to hold the shield for each one of the two fighting. He who was the more wounded of the two was to release himself by paying duel ransom, to the tune of three marks of silver. (Ch. 10).

The duel was formally banned by law in Iceland in 1006, six years after the Icelanders had accepted Christianity: see *The Saga of Gunnlaug Serpent-tongue*, ch. 11.

earl   *jarl*: Title generally restricted to men of high rank in northern countries (though not in Iceland), who could be independent rulers or subordinate to a king. The title could be inherited, or it could be conferred by a king on a prominent supporter or leader of military forces. The earls of Lade who appear in a number of sagas and tales ruled large sections of northern Norway (and often many southerly areas as well) for several centuries. Another prominent, almost independent, earldom was that of Orkney and Shetland.

east   *austur*. See directions.

fetch   *fylgja*: Literally 'someone that accompanies', a fetch was a personal spirit which was closely attached to families and individuals, and often symbolized the fate that people were born with. If it appeared to an individual or others close to him or her, it would often signal the impending doom of that person. Fetches could take various forms, sometimes appearing in the shape of an animal. For an example, see *The Saga of the*

People of Vatnsdal, ch. 36. As with most ghosts mentioned in the sagas, Icelandic fetches tended to be corporeal.

fire hall, fire room   *eldaskáli, eldhús*: In literal terms, the fire room or fire hall was a room or special building (as perhaps at Jarlshof in Shetland) containing a fire, and its primary function was that of a kitchen. Such a definition, however, would be too limited, since the fire hall/fire room was also used for eating, working and sleeping. Indeed, in many cases the words *eldhús* and *eldaskáli* seem to have been synonymous with the word *skáli* meaning the hall of a farm. See Figure 4 in 'The Farm'.

flokk   *flokkur*: A short poem, distinguished from a drapa. See also drapa.

follower   *hirðmaður*: A member of the inner circle of followers that surrounded the Scandinavian kings, a sworn king's man.

foster-   *fóstur-, fóstri, fóstra*: Childen during the saga period were often brought up by foster-parents, who received either payment or support in return from the real parents. Being fostered was therefore somewhat different from being adopted: it was essentially a legal agreement and, more importantly, a form of alliance. Nonetheless, fostered children were seen as being part of the family circle emotionally, and in some cases legally. Relationships and loyalties between foster-kindred could become very strong. See also Introduction, p. xl. It should be noted that the expressions *fóstri/fóstra* were also used for people who had the function of looking after, bringing up and teaching the children on the farm.

freed slave   *lausingi, leysingi*: A slave could be set or bought free, and thus acquired the general status of a free man, although this status was low, since if he/she died with no heir, his/her inheritance would return to the original owner. The children of freed slaves, however, were completely free.

full outlawry   *skóggangur*: Outlawry for life. One of the terms applied to a man sentenced to full outlawry was *skógarmaður*, which literally means 'forest man', even though in Iceland there was scant possibility of his taking refuge in a forest. Full outlawry simply meant banishment from civilized society, whether the local land district, the province or the whole country. It also meant the confiscation of the outlaw's property to pay the prosecutor, cover debts and sometimes provide an allowance for the dependants he had left behind. A full outlaw was to be neither fed nor offered shelter. According to one legal codex from Norway, it was 'as if he were dead'. He had lost all goods, and all rights. Wherever he went he could be killed without any legal redress. His children became illegitimate and his body was to be buried in unconsecrated ground.

games   *leikar*: *Leikur* (sing.) in Icelandic contained the same breadth of meaning as 'game' in English. The games meetings described in the sagas would probably have included a whole range of 'play' activities. Essentially, they involved men's sports, such as wrestling, ball games, 'skin-throwing games', 'scraper games' and horse-fights. Games of this kind took place whenever people came together, and seem to have formed a regular feature of assemblies and other gatherings (including the Althing) and religious festivals such as the Winter Nights. Sometimes prominent men invited people together specifically to take part in games.

games meeting   *leikmót*: Special gatherings where various games took place. These might last for several days, visitors staying in temporary *leikskálar* (literally 'games halls', also occuring as a place-name in, for example, *The Saga of Hrafnkel Frey's Godi*, ch. 3).

ghosts/spirits   *draugar, afturgöngur, haugbúar*: Ghosts in medieval Scandinavia were seen as being corporeal, and thus capable of wrestling or fighting with opponents. This idea is naturally associated with the ancient pagan belief in Scandinavia and elsewhere that the dead should be buried with the possessions that they were going to need in the next life, such as ships, horses and weapons: in some way, the body was going to live again and need these items. There are many examples in the sagas of people encountering or seeing 'living ghosts' inside grave mounds. These spirits were called *haugbúar* (literally 'mound-dwellers'). Because of the fear of spirits walking again and disturbing the living, there were various measures that could be taken to ensure some degree of peace and quiet for the living: see, for example, *Egil's Saga*, ch. 59, and *Gisli Sursson's Saga*, chs. 14 and 17.

giant   *jötunn*, *risi*: According to Nordic mythology, the giants (*jötnar*) had existed from the dawn of time. In many ways, they can be seen as the personification of the more powerful natural elements and the enemies of the gods and mankind. The original belief was that they lived in the distant north and east in Jotunheim ('the world of the giants'), where they were eternally planning the eventual overthrow of the gods. The final battle between them, Ragnarok ('the fate of the gods'), would mark the end of the world. The original giants were clever and devious, and had an even greater knowledge of the world and the future than that which was available to Odin. *Risi* is a later coinage, when old beliefs were fading and the ancient giants were merging into the troll figure, which was also losing its original characteristics; it refers primarily to the physical size of these beings, which live in the mountains on the borders of civilization.

godi   *goði*: This word was little known outside Iceland in early Christian times, and seems to refer to a particularly Icelandic concept. A godi was a local chieftain who had legal and administrative responsibilities in Iceland. The name seems to have originally meant 'priest', or at least a person having a special relationship with gods or supernatural powers, and thus shows an early connection between religious and secular power. As time went on, however, the chief function of a godi came to be secular. The first godis were chosen from the leading families who settled Iceland in *c.* 870–930. See Introduction, pp. xlvi–xlvii and 'Social and Political Structure'.

godord   *goðorð*: The authority and rank of a godi, including his social and legal responsibilities towards his thingmen.

halberd   *atgeir*: *Atgeir* is translated as halberd, which it seems to have resembled even though no specimens of this combination of spear and axe have been found in archaeological excavations in Iceland.

hall   *skáli*: *Skáli* was used both for large halls such as those used by kings, and for the main farmhouse on the typical Icelandic farm. (See illustrations in 'The Farm'.)

hand   *spönn*: A measurement, originally the width of a man's hand (approximately 16–17 cm).

hayfield   *tún*: An enclosed field for hay cultivation close to or surrounding a farm house. This was the only 'cultivated' part of a farm and produced the best hay. Other hay, generally of lesser quality, came from the meadows which could be a good distance from the farm itself. (See Figure 3 in 'The Farm'.)

hayfield wall   *túngarður*: A wall of stones surrounding the hayfield in order to protect the haystacks from the livestock.

haystack wall/yard   *stakkgarður*: A small enclosed yard to protect the haystacks from the livestock.

hersir   *hersir*: A local leader in western and northern Norway; his rank was hereditary. Originally the hersirs were probably those who took command when the men of the district were called to arms.

high seat   *öndvegi*: The central section of one bench in the hall (at the inner end, or in the middle of the 'senior' side, to the right as one entered) was the rightful high seat of the owner of the farm. Even though it is usually referred to in English as the 'high seat', this position was not necessarily higher in elevation, only in honour. Opposite the owner sat the guest of honour.

high-seat pillars   *öndvegissúlur*: The high seat was often adorned with decorated high-seat pillars, which had a religious significance. There are several accounts of how those emigrating from Norway to Iceland took their high-seat pillars with them. As they approached land they threw the carved wood posts overboard. It was believed that the pillars would be guided by divine forces to the place where the travellers were destined to live. See, for example, *The Saga of the People of Laxardal*, ch. 3.

homespun (cloth)   *vaðmál*: For centuries wool and woollen products were Iceland's chief exports, especially in the form of strong and durable homespun cloth. It could be bought and sold in bolts or made up into items such as homespun cloaks. There were strict regulations on homespun, as it was used as a standard exchange product and often referred to in ounces, meaning its equivalent value expressed as a weight in silver. One ounce could equal three to six ells of homespun, one ell being roughly 50 cm.

homespun cloak   *vararfeldur*: A cloak made of homespun, woven from wool with a shaggy exterior like sheepskin.

horse-fight   *hestaat/hestavíg*: A popular sport among the Icelanders, which seems to have taken place especially in the autumn, particularly at Autumn Meetings. Two horses were goaded to fight against each other, until one was killed or ran away. Understandably, emotions ran high, and horse-fights commonly led to feuds.

hundred   *hundrað*: A 'long hundred' or one hundred and twenty. The expression, however, rarely refers to an accurate number, rather a generalized 'round' figure.

judgement circle   *dómhringur*: The courts of heathen times appear to have been surrounded by a judgement circle, marked out with hazel poles and ropes, where judgements were made or announced: see the description of the Gula Assembly in *Egil's Saga*, ch. 57. The circle was sacrosanct, and weapons were not allowed inside it – nor was violence.

knorr   *knörr*: An ocean-going cargo vessel: see also 'Ships'.

lampoon   *níð*: In the sagas *níð* refers to two forms of slander that need to be distinguished. The verbal form lampoon commonly was slanderous verse containing hints of lack of masculinity or deviant sexual practices. Such verses obviously spread like wildfire, and were capable of doing great damage to a person's honour and respect. Insults of this kind were not only illegal; they also tended to start or escalate serious feuds because of the element of dishonour. As the eddic poem *Hávamál* (The Sayings of the High One) states, 'the tongue is the slayer of the head' (tunga er höfuðs bani'): *Hávamál*, st. 73. For the other form of *níð*, see scorn-pole.

Law Council   *Lögrétta*: The legislative assembly at the Althing. See also Introduction, pp. xlvi–xlvii and 'Social and Political Structure'.

Law Rock   *Lögberg*: The raised spot at the *Althing* at Thingvellir, where the Lawspeaker may have recited the law code, and where public announcements and speeches were made. See also Introduction, pp. xlvi–xlvii and 'Social and Political Structure'.

Lawspeaker	*lögsögumaður, lögmaður*: means literally 'the man who recites the law', referring to the time before the advent of writing when the Lawspeaker had to learn the law by heart and recite one-third of it every year, perhaps at the Law Rock. If he was unsure about the text, he had to consult a team of five or more 'lawmen' (*lögmenn*) who knew the law well. The Lawspeaker presided over the assembly at the Althing and was responsible for the preservation and clarification of legal tradition. He could exert influence, as in the case about whether the Icelanders should accept Christianity, but should not be regarded as having ruled the country. See also Introduction, pp. xlvi–xlvii and 'Social and Political Structure'.
leather (sleeping) sack	*húðfat*: A large leather bag used by travellers for sleeping.
lesser outlawry	*fjörbaugsgarður*: Differed from full or greater outlawry in that the lesser outlaw was only banished from society for three years. Furthermore, his land was not confiscated, and money was put aside to support his family. This made it possible for him to return later and continue a normal life. *Fjörbaugsgarður* means literally 'life-ring enclosure'. 'Life-ring' refers to the silver ring that the outlaw originally had to pay the godi in order to spare his life. (This was later fixed at a value of one mark.) 'Enclosure' refers to three sacrosanct homes no more than one day's journey from each other where the outlaw was permitted to stay while he arranged passage out of Iceland. He was allowed limited movement along the tracks directly joining these farms, and en route to the ship which would take him abroad. Anywhere else the outlaw was fair game and could be killed without redress. He had to leave the country and begin his sentence within the space of three summers after the verdict, but once abroad retained normal rights.
longhouse	*skáli*: See hall.
longship	*langskip*: The largest warship. See also 'Ships'.
magic rite	*seiður*: The exact nature of magic ritual, or *seiður*, is somewhat obscure. It appears that it was originally only practised by women. Although there are several

accounts of males who performed this rite (including the god Odin), they are almost always looked down on as having engaged in an 'effeminate' activity. The magic rite seems to have had two main purposes: a spell to influence people or the elements (as in *The Saga of the People of Laxardal*, chs. 35–7, and *Gisli Sursson's Saga*, ch. 18), and a means of finding out about the future (as in *Eirik the Red's Saga*, ch. 4). There are evidently parallels between *seiður* and shamanistic rituals such as those carried out by the Lapps and Native Americans. See also *seeress*.

magician
: *seiðmaður*: Literally means 'a man who practises *seiður*'. See also magic rite.

main room
: *stofa*: A room off the hall of a farmhouse. See also 'The Farm'.

mark
: *mörk*: A measurement of weight, eight ounces, approximately 214 grams.

Moving Days
: *fardagar*: Four successive days in the seventh week of 'summer' (in May) during which householders in Iceland could change their abode.

nature spirit
: *vættur*: There were various kinds of nature spirits that the Icelanders (and other Scandinavians) believed in, and sometimes gave sacrifices to. There are early references to elves (*álfar*) in mainland Scandinavia. Like their modern-day equivalents, the 'hidden people' (a generic expression used in both Norway and Iceland), were of human size. Even closer to nature were the guardian spirits (*landvættir*), which inhabited the landscape. The well-being of the inhabitants of the country depended on their welfare and support, as can be seen in *Egil's Saga*, ch. 58, when Egil raises a scorn-pole facing the guardian spirits of Norway. According to the earliest Icelandic law, Ulfljot's Law, people approaching Iceland by sea had to remove the dragon heads from the prows of their ships to avoid frightening the guardian spirits.

neighbour
: *búi*: In a legal context, neighbour often has a formal meaning: people who were called on to 'witness' the testimony of princapl figures in a case, and form a panel.

north
: *norður*. See directions.

ounce, ounces
: *eyrir*, pl. *aurar*: A unit of weight, varying slightly through

time, but roughly 27 grams. Eight ounces were equal
to one mark.

outlawry   *útlegð, skóggangur, fjörbaugsgarður*: Two of the Icelandic
words, *útlegð*, literally meaning 'lying, or sleeping, outside', and *skóggangur*, 'forest-walking', stress the idea of
the outlaw having been ejected from the safe boundaries
of civilized society and being forced to live in the wild,
alongside the animals and nature spirits, little better
than an animal himself. The word *útlagi* ('outlaw') is
closely related to *útlegð*, but has also taken on the
additional meaning of 'outside the law', which for early
Scandinavians was synonymous with 'lying outside
society'. Law was what made society. See also full
outlawry and lesser outlawry.

panel   *kviður*: The panel was a form of 'jury' that delivered a
verdict on the facts, motives and/or circumstances
behind a case. They were not as important as witnesses,
but could still carry a great deal of weight, especially
if there were no witnesses to a particular action. The
panels were composed of neighbours. Nine-man panels
were called for more serious cases; five-man for less
important ones. The verdict was based on the majority's
decision.

quarter   *fjórðungur*: Administratively, Iceland was divided into
four quarters based on the four cardinal directions. See
Introduction, p. xlvi and 'Social and Political Structure'.

Quarter Court   *fjórðungsdómur*: Four Quarter Courts were established
at the Althing in *c.* 965. See Introduction, pp. xlvi and
'Social and Political Structure'.

Russia   *Garðaríki*: Literally means 'the realm of towns', and
refers very generally to the area running between the
Baltic Sea and the White Sea in the north and the Black
Sea and the Caspian Sea in the south. The name 'Russia'
was originally drawn from the word 'Rus', the local
name for the Scandinavian traders, mercenaries and
adventurers who regularly travelled the rivers between
the coast of the Baltic and Constantinople (then known
as *Mikligarður*, 'the great city'). *Garðaríki* contained,
among others, the towns and cities of Kiev, Novgorod,
Staraja Ladoga, Izborsk, Bjeloozero, Rostov and Cher-
nigov, all of which were controlled by the Scandinavians

for some time between the ninth and eleventh centuries. It was argued in the past that the Scandinavians had a large role in establishing some of these towns, if not the original Russian state.

sacrifice   *blót*: There is great uncertainty about the nature of pagan worship and cult-activities in Scandinavia, and just as the theology and mythology of the Nordic peoples seem to have varied according to area, it is highly questionable whether any standardized rules of ritual practice ever existed there. It should also be remembered that the population of Iceland came from all over Scandinavia, as well as from Ireland and the islands off Scotland. Religion was very much an individual matter, and practices varied. The few references to sacrifices in the sagas are somewhat vague, but these sometimes seem to have involved the ritual slaughter of animals. Human sacrifices are only specifically described in sources describing very early times, long before the time span of the sagas, for example in the *Saga of the Ynglings*, the first part of Snorri Sturluson's *Heimskringla*.

scorn-pole   *níð*: In the sagas *níð* refers to two forms of slander that need to be distinguished. The physical form scorn-pole generally refers to figures made of wood that were understood by all to represent one or more persons in local society. These figures were sometimes depicted in some compromising sexual position. Such a public insult attracted attention and seriously damaged the honour of the person or persons in question. The figures were strictly illegal, and a common reason for killings and/or local feuds. See, for example, *Gisli Sursson's Saga*, ch. 2. In *Egil's Saga*, a scorn-pole with a horse's head on it is used to place a curse on the king. For the verbal form of *níð*, see lampoon.

seeress   *völva*: The magic rites (*seiður*) performed by male magicians were essentially, and originally, a female activity. For a detailed account of a seeress using such a rite to gain knowledge of the future, see *Eirik the Red's Saga*, ch. 4. Seeresses could also gain such knowledge by 'sitting outside' (*útiseta*) at night on graves, at crossroads or at other powerful natural sites. The most famous

examples of prophecies in Old Icelandic literature are
the eddic poems *Völuspá* (The Prophecy of the Seeress)
and *Baldurs draumar* (The Dreams of Balder), both of
which deal with the coming of Ragnarok ('the fate of
the gods'). See also magic rite and magician.

shape-shifter *hamrammur*, adj.: Closely associated with the berserks,
those who were *hamrammir* (pl.) were believed to change
their shape at night or in times of stress, or leave their
bodies (which appeared asleep) and take the physical
form of animals such as bears or wolves. There are
again faint associations with shamanistic activities and
figures known in folklore throughout the world, such
as the werewolf. The transformation was not necessarily
intentional. Three of the best examples in Icelandic
literature are the figures of Kveldulf (literally 'Night
wolf') in *Egil's Saga*, ch. 1, and Sigmund and Sinfjotli in
the legendary *Völsunga saga* (*The Saga of the Volsungs*),
ed. Jesse L. Byock (London: Penguin, 1999), ch. 8.

shieling *sel*: A roughly constructed hut in the highland grazing
pastures away from the farm, where shepherds and
cowherders lived during the summer. Milking and the
preparation of various dairy products took place here,
as did other important farm activities like the collection
of peat and charcoal burning (depending on the sur-
roundings). This arrangement was well known throughout the Scandinavian countries from the earliest times.

single combat *einvígi*: The less formal fight between two men. This
is differentiated from the formally organized duel which
was fought according to defined rules and rituals.

slander *níð*: See lampoon.

slave *þræll*: Slavery was quite an important aspect of Viking
Age trade. A large number of slaves were taken from
the Baltic nations and the western European countries
that were raided and invaded by Scandinavians between
the eighth and eleventh centuries. In addition, the
Scandinavians had few scruples against taking slaves
from the other Nordic countries. Judging from their
names and appearance, a large number of the slaves
mentioned in the sagas seem to have come from Ireland
and Scotland. Stereotypically they are presented in the
sagas as being stupid and lazy. The eddic poem *Rígsþula*

(The Chant of Rig) describes the mythical origins and the characteristics of the four main Scandinavian classes: the slaves, the farmers, the aristocracy and the kings. By law, slaves had hardly any rights at all, and they and their families could only be freed if their owners chose to do so, or somebody else bought their freedom: see freed slave. In the Icelandic Commonwealth, a slave who was wounded was entitled to one-third of the compensation money; the rest went to his owner.

south   *suður*: See directions.

spirits   See ghosts.

Spring Assembly   *vorþing*: The local assembly, held each spring. They were thirteen in all and were the first regular assemblies to be held in Iceland. Lasting four to seven days between 7 and 27 May, they were jointly supervised by three godis. The Spring Assembly had a dual legal and economic function. It included a court of thirty-six men, twelve appointed by each of the godis, where local actions were heard, while major cases and those which could not be resolved locally were sent on to the Althing. In its other function it was a forum for settling debts, deciding prices and the like. Godis probably used the Spring Assembly to urge their followers to ride to the Althing; those who remained behind paid the costs of those who went.

sprinkled with water   *vatni ausinn*: Even before the arrival of Christianity, the Scandinavians practised a naming ceremony clearly similar to that involved in the modern-day 'christening'. It is mentioned in eddic poems such as *Rígsþula* (The Chant of Rig), st. 21, and *Hávamál* (The Sayings of the High One), st. 158. The action of sprinkling a child with water and naming it meant that the child was initiated into society. After this ceremony, a child could not be taken out to die of exposure (a common practice in pagan times).

steward   *stallari*: A high-ranking follower of the king, empowered to act as his representative at important meetings. The stewards were also responsible for preparations for war, and for overseeing other king's men.

Summons Days   *stefnudagar*: The days during which someone could be summoned to appear at a given Spring Assembly or Althing for a legal case.

sworn brotherhood
fóstbræðralag: This was seen as another form of foster-brotherhood, but instead of being arranged by the parents (see foster-), it was a relationship that was decided by the individuals themselves. Sworn brothers literally were 'blood-brothers': they swore unending loyalty to each other, sealing this pact by going though a religious ceremony involving a form of symbolic rebirth, in which they joined blood and passed beneath an arch of raised turf. See also *Gisli Surrson's Saga*, ch. 6.

tale
þáttur: A short narrative, often included as an episode in a larger whole, in many cases in a saga based on the life of a king.

temple
hof: In spite of the description of the 'temple' at Hofstadir ('Temple Place', see Introduction, p. xlv) and other temples mentioned in the sagas, there is no certainty that buildings erected for the sole purpose of pagan worship ever existed in Iceland or the other Scandinavian countries. To date, no such building has been found in archaeological excavations. In all likelihood, pagan rituals and sacrifices took place outdoors or in a specified area in certain large farmhouses belonging to priests, where the idols of the gods would also have been kept.

Thing
alþingi: See Althing.

thingman/men
þingmaður/þingmenn: Every free man and landowner was required to serve as a thingman ('assembly man') by aligning himself with a godi. He would either accompany the godi to assemblies and other functions or pay a tax supposed to cover the godi's costs of attending them. See Introduction, pp. xlvi–xlvii and 'Social and Political Structure'.

troll
tröll: Trolls in the minds of the Icelanders were not the huge, stupid figures that we read about in later Scandinavian wonder-tales and legends. At the time of the sagas, they were essentially evil nature spirits, a little like large dark elves. It is only in later times that they come to blend with the image of the Scandinavian giants.

unmanly behaviour

ergi, regi: The worst of all insults in the Scandinavian vocabulary was that of 'unmanly behaviour'. The suggestion that a man was behaving like a woman could imply homosexuality or cowardice, or both.

Weapon Taking

vopnatak: The time when people were allowed to take up their weapons again at the end of a meeting of the Althing. Weapons were not permitted in the sanctified area of the courts (see Althing). The term Weapon Taking came to signify the ending of the assembly and the moment that a sentence of outlawry came into effect (thus giving the outlaw some time to get away).

weight

vætt: The equivalent of 160 marks, or about 40 kilos.

west

vestur: See directions.

Winter Nights

veturnætur: The period of two days when the winter began, around the middle of October. This was a particularly holy time of the year, when sacrifices were made to the disir, and other social activities such as games meetings and weddings often took place. See, for example, *Gisli Sursson's Saga*, ch. 15. It was also the time when animals were slaughtered so that their meat could be stored over the winter.

Index of Characters

This index lists all the characters in the sagas and tales in this edition, apart from the gods. It follows the Icelandic naming convention of the patronymic (occasionally the matronymic), as well as giving nicknames. For most characters there is also an identifier in parentheses, stating main family-tie, place of residence or the like. Nicknames in parentheses refer to the father in the patronymic, not the character him- or herself. For example, the entry *Aldis Ljotsdottir (the Dueller)* refers to Aldis, daughter of Ljot the Dueller; he is found under the entry *Ljot Thjodreksson the Dueller of Ingjaldssand*.

Some details of family ties have been incorporated from sources not included in the present edition.